AF269761

DUMBARTON OAKS
MEDIEVAL LIBRARY

Daniel Donoghue, General Editor

ANIMAL FABLES OF THE COURTLY MEDITERRANEAN

DOML 73

Animal Fables of the Courtly Mediterranean

The Eugenian Recension of *Stephanites and Ichnelates*

Edited and Translated by

ALISON NOBLE

with ALEXANDER ALEXAKIS

and RICHARD P. H. GREENFIELD

DUMBARTON OAKS
MEDIEVAL LIBRARY

HARVARD UNIVERSITY PRESS

CAMBRIDGE, MASSACHUSETTS

LONDON, ENGLAND

2022

Printed in the United States of America

First Printing

Library of Congress Cataloging-in-Publication Data

Names: Eugenius, Admiral of Sicily, approximately 1130–approximately 1203. | Noble, Alison (Alison Elizabeth), editor, translator. | Alexakis, Alexander, editor, translator. | Greenfield, Richard P. H., editor, translator.

Title: Animal fables of the courtly Mediterranean : the Eugenian recension of Stephanites and Ichnelates / edited and translated by Alison Noble with Alexander Alexakis and Richard P. H. Greenfield.

Other titles: Kalīlah wa-Dimnah. Greek. | Dumbarton Oaks medieval library ; 73.

Description: Cambridge, Massachusetts : Harvard University Press, 2022. | Series: Dumbarton Oaks medieval library; DOML 73 | The present volume represents an expanded twelfth-century Sicilian version of Symeon Seth's eleventh-century Greek translation of the Arabic work Kalīla wa-Dimnah, itself a version of the Middle Persian work known as the Fables of Bidpai. This Greek version includes additional material translated from Arabic that brings it closer to the Arabic Kalīla wa-Dimnah in both form and content from Seth's version, and a unique preface that associates this Sicilian recension with a known historical figure of the time, the admiral, or emir, Eugenios of Palermo. | Includes bibliographical references and index.

Identifiers: LCCN 2021041914 | ISBN 9780674271272 (cloth)

Subjects: LCSH: Fables, Arabic—Translations into Greek—Early works to 1800. | Animals in literature—Early works to 1800.

Classification: LCC PA5303.B5 A55 2022 | DDC 398.24/5—dc23/eng/20211221

LC record available at https://lccn.loc.gov/2021041914

Contents

CONTENTS

Introduction

Stephanites and Ichnelates, the two jackals who give their name to this work and who are principal characters in the main fable, were introduced to readers in Constantinople in the late eleventh century via a translation from the Arabic work *Kalīla wa-Dimna.*[1] The translator, Symeon Seth, gave the work its Greek title and dedicated it to Alexios I Komnenos, crowned emperor in 1081. The present volume, however, represents a later, expanded version of the work, one originating in twelfth-century Sicily and associated with Eugenios of Palermo.

The Development and Transmission of *Stephanites and Ichnelates*

The Arabic text, *Kalīla wa-Dimna,* is itself a version and translation of a Middle Persian work, probably called *Karirak ud Damanak,* whose origins are in the Sanskrit *Panchatantra* and *Mahabharata* and at whose core are five chapters that correspond to the five books of the *Panchatantra.*[2] This latter has a frame story in its introduction concerning a king who is in despair over the stupidity of his sons and their inability to learn the art of government. He asks a wise Brahmin for help, who promises to teach them, by means of fables,

all they need to know. The structure of a frame story was adopted and maintained over the course of the many adaptations and translations that followed, although the growing number of fables and substories came to dominate this fluid work.

According to one of the prologues, the books that make up the work were brought from India and translated from Sanskrit into Middle Persian in the sixth century CE by Borzuya or Burzoy (rendered Περζουέ or Περζωέ [Perzoué] in the later Greek version), a physician at the court of the Sassanian king Chosroes I.[3] During Chosroes's reign (531–579 CE) the Sassanian Empire was influenced by both Greek and Indian culture and works were translated into Middle Persian from Greek, Sanskrit, and Syriac.[4] Borzuya evidently added five more fables to the original five of the *Panchatantra:* three from the *Mahabharata,* one of Buddhist origin, and another of either Indian or Persian origin (see below, for the content of *Stephanites and Ichnelates*). Two prologues were also added at this time: Borzuya's autobiography, and an account of his mission to India.

The Middle Persian version is lost, but a translation was made into Old Syriac in the Sassanian Empire, probably in the sixth century.[5] Some two hundred years later, it was also translated into Arabic, by Ibn al-Muqaffaʿ, a writer and translator of Persian origin employed first by the Umayyad and then, from 750, by the ʿAbbasid court.[6] Through his writings he contributed to the creation of a new literary Arabic, the genre of *adab*—the presentation of knowledge in an aesthetically pleasing literary style—which was linked to the court and used to introduce works translated into Arabic from the older, more established cultures of Greek, Syr-

iac, and Persian as part of the ʿAbbasids' program of cultural integration.[7] He named his version *Kalīla wa-Dimna,* and a comparison with the Syriac translation shows that he made many changes to the text, adding his own prologue and probably five more chapters: two of Indian origin, two of unknown origin, and one likely of his own creation.[8] There are more than 140 known manuscripts of the Arabic version, indicating the work's popularity, though none (so far discovered) is earlier than the thirteenth century—a gap of some five hundred years from its composition. There are many differences between these manuscripts, as fables were rewritten and material was added or omitted.[9]

Direct translations and versions were made from Arabic into Syriac, Hebrew, medieval Spanish, Persian, and Greek, but only the Greek will be further discussed here.[10] Two independent Greek translations were evidently made in the eleventh century. One is possibly from southern Italy or Sicily and did not become widely known; it is found in one thirteenth-century manuscript containing three episodes from the end of the work.[11] In contrast, the other, by the abovementioned Symeon Seth, did become popular. This Greek version later expanded, as more stories were translated and added from the Arabic version. It came to be represented by many manuscripts, with much variation between them, and the history of the text has not yet been fully resolved.[12] The work's popularity is attested by the early translations made from it into Church Slavonic, Medieval Latin, Italian, and German.[13] There is also an early Modern Greek paraphrase.[14]

Biographical information on Seth is scant and inconclusive, but it is likely that he came from Antioch and that

his mother tongue was a local dialect of Arabic.[15] Besides *Stephanites and Ichnelates,* he is the author of works in the fields of medicine, natural philosophy, and, possibly, astronomy and astrology: he may have practiced medicine, and he may have been an astrologer. He wrote a *Refutation of Galen,* demonstrating the problems caused by an overreliance on Galen's theories, and a dietary treatise—a "lexicon on the properties of foodstuffs"—in which he is the first in Byzantine medical writings to refer to substances of eastern origin, such as camphor, musk, amber, and hashish.[16] In his introduction to this latter work, he claims that he has selected the best accounts of different foodstuffs from Greek, Persian, Arab, and Indian medical traditions. In both these works he is, however, reticent about his Arabic sources, perhaps for reasons of cultural sensitivity, as Arabs were considered to be enemies on both military and religious grounds.[17] Seth's works can be seen in the context of the increasing engagement with Arab learning in the late eleventh century, which was favorable to translating activity, and there is evidence of translations being made from Arabic and Syriac on subjects such as astronomy, astrology, medicine, and literature.[18]

One group of manuscripts of *Stephanites and Ichnelates,* also from Constantinople and representing a version believed to date from the first half of the twelfth century, contains Seth's translation largely unchanged, with additional material translated from Arabic—the remainder of his last, unfinished chapter and two additional chapters. The focus of the present volume, however, is another group of manuscripts representing a version originating in twelfth century Sicily. This too is based on Seth's translation, and also has

additional material translated from Arabic—in this case the three prologues, additional stories within some of the chapters, and additional chapters.[19] The changes found in this Sicilian, or Eugenian, version demonstrate the fluid nature of the work, and bring it closer to the Arabic *Kalīla wa-Dimna* in both form and content than Seth's version: the reinstatement of substories increases the length of the chapters and also adds a narrative level, thereby increasing the complexity of the structure. In addition to material translated from Arabic, this version also contains material found only here: prefaces mentioning a known historical figure of the time, the admiral, or emir, Eugenios of Palermo.[20]

Eugenios of Palermo and Twelfth-Century Sicily

Eugenios came from an Italo-Greek family from Troina, Sicily, a center for the Greek-speaking Orthodox Christians of the island during the Islamic period and therefore a contact zone with the surrounding Muslim population. The family had become established in Palermo by the first half of the twelfth century and had close ties to the ruling regime.[21]

Eugenios is thought to have been born around 1130, the same year that Roger II, count of Sicily and duke of Apulia, was crowned king of Sicily, and he thus grew up during the period of relative political stability that existed under Roger's rule.[22] Although nothing is known of his education and early life, he appears very much as a product of the Sicilian milieu in the second quarter of the twelfth century, in which both Greek and Arab influences were strong at the Norman court. Eugenios is first mentioned in the sources in connection with a manuscript of Ptolemy's *Almagest,* being de-

scribed by a scholar who had traveled to Sicily to consult it as "a man most learned in Greek and Arabic, and not unskilled in Latin."[23] This manuscript had been brought to Sicily by Henry Aristippus, a member of the inner council of William I (r. 1154–1166) and a prolific and skilled translator from Greek into Latin, who had returned from an embassy to Constantinople between 1158 and 1160 with gifts of manuscripts from the Byzantine emperor Manuel Komnenos.[24] As a multilingual kingdom, Sicily was a favorable milieu for translations from Greek and Arabic into Latin, facilitated by the presence on the island of Greek- and Arabic-speaking scholars, and was particularly well placed for translations from Greek, owing to uninterrupted contact with the Byzantine Empire and access to Greek manuscripts held in the libraries of Constantinople.[25]

Eugenios translated both Greek and Arabic into Latin. He is best known for his translation of Ptolemy's *Optics* from Arabic into Latin, a work he prefaced with an introduction commenting on the difficulty of translating from Arabic into Latin or Greek, owing to their great lexical and syntactical differences. The introduction also shows his mastery of Latin prose style and his understanding of mathematics. He is the likely translator, now from Greek into Latin, of a book of Byzantine prophecies, the *Prophecies of the Eritraean Sibyl,* also obtained from the library of Manuel I Komnenos. Furthermore, Eugenios is the author of twenty-four poems in Greek (whose subjects include the vices and virtues, religious themes, natural phenomena, political theory, and moral and political philosophy) and of some panegyric verses to a King William (probably William I) extolling the military virtues of the Norman kings. While

in prison in Germany (see below), he composed a long poem on the wheel of fortune.[26]

Aside from his literary activities, Eugenios was employed by the Norman administration and is first mentioned in his official capacity as *magister duane baronum* in 1174.[27] In August 1190, Tancred, the last of the Norman dynasty in Sicily, awarded him the title of emir. He was implicated in the supposed conspiracy discovered shortly after the coronation of Henry VI in 1194 and was taken to the fortress of Trifels in Germany as a prisoner, along with members of Tancred's family and supporters. However, he was soon freed, presumably because his skills and experience were needed by the new administration. Between 1196 and 1202, his last mention in the sources, he is recorded as being active in Puglia, Bari, and Campania, fulfilling such roles as advising Henry VI's chancellor and ruling on legal cases.[28]

Eugenios, who probably died around 1202 or 1203, thus spent his formative years under Roger II and his working life under William I, William II, Tancred, Henry VI, and Frederick II—six rulers and a change of dynasty. This period witnessed a steep decline in the use of the Greek language and the influence of Greek culture in the kingdom of Sicily. By the time of Frederick II, trilingual figures such as Eugenios, who embodied the multiculturalism of Roger II's reign, would have been rare. Eugenios's connection to *Stephanites and Ichnelates* is discussed below, but it is clear from his already mentioned translating activity that he would have been capable of carrying out himself, or at least overseeing, the translation of additional sections of *Kalīla wa-Dimna* from Arabic into Greek. It is also not unlikely that a work of Arab literature such as this was circulating in Sicily:

Arab poets, writers, and scholars are known to have been present at Roger's court, including the geographer al-Idrisi, who stayed on into the reign of William I.[29] It is unusual at this time, however, for a work to have been translated into Greek rather than into the prestige language of Latin, when a Greek education had come to be of little practical value.[30] As suggested above, Latin had come to be used increasingly in the kingdom from the end of Roger II's reign, and this trend continued under William I and subsequent rulers, to the detriment of Greek and Arab culture.[31] However, in contrast to the fate of much of Sicilian and southern Italian translation activity during this period, which appears to have been limited to the court and to have had little effect outside it, the Sicilian—or Eugenian—version of *Stephanites and Ichnelates* survived and flourished.[32]

The Content of *Stephanites and Ichnelates*

The evidence connecting Eugenios to the recension of *Stephanites and Ichnelates* that forms the subject of the present volume is established by mention of his name in the prefatory material found in one group of manuscripts. This reference appears at the end of some lines of verse that trace the history of this work of "Indian wisdom" through Persian and Arabic into Greek. The presence of Eugenios's name in this material has been interpreted as indicating that he himself was the translator, but the statement a little later that "we" translated it with the help of men who had a good knowledge of Arabic suggests that Eugenios may have been the commissioner and donor, but not the translator. Whatever his exact role, the nature of the work and its history suggest

the possibility that it might have been prepared for a ruler, either as a result of a royal commission (following the example of Alexios I Komnenos's commission of Symeon Seth and King Chosroes's alleged tasking of Borzuya) or as a gift. In addition, the advice contained within—the benefit of which is emphasized repeatedly in this prefatory material—would have accorded well with the interest in Arab learning and culture apparent at the courts of Roger II and William I. Against this theory, however, is the fact that it was translated into Greek, rather than into Latin, and therefore the intended audience may have been well-educated Greek speakers in Sicily and southern Italy, possibly a group of like-minded friends who met to read and discuss literature for pleasure.[33]

The work begins with a collection of diverse prefatory material, including the epigram, discussed above, naming Eugenios of Panormos (Palermo) in connection with the work, and Eugenios's own introduction, in which he defends the contents, saying that one should be willing to acquire knowledge no matter what its source and practice an allegorical interpretation of the work.

In the Eugenian recension three prologues follow, translated from Arabic, which have originated during the long course of the work's transmission and development from its Indian sources. The reader encounters the prologues in the following order: the account of Perzoué's (Borzuya's) journey to India (Prologue A), the introduction to the work by Ibn al-Muqaffaʿ (Prologue B), and Perzoué's autobiography (Prologue C). The current Prologue A may have started out as an independent work, written by someone who had read either Perzoué's autobiography (Prologue C) or perhaps the

shorter version of his journey that is found in a small number of Arabic manuscripts, and it later became attached to the book itself; the reason it is placed first would be because it was the most recently added.[34] The second prologue (Prologue B), that by Ibn al-Muqaffaʿ, urges the reader by means of stories to pay proper attention to the book and to take note of the lessons it provides. He explains that these lessons should be applied in practice, not just understood theoretically. He also stresses the value of friendship. The use of stories to illustrate the points he wants to make finds its parallel in the work itself.[35] In the third prologue (Prologue C), the figure of Perzoué recounts his family origins, upbringing, and choice of medicine as a profession. He then describes his quest for religious and philosophical enlightenment, allowing for an exposition on the transitory nature of existence and the hope for eternal reward through the performance of good deeds. The prologue recounts how he becomes disenchanted with medicine because of its imperfections, seeks enlightenment from different religions, but is ultimately dissatisfied and rejects them all. He is attracted to asceticism but, after much internal debate and indecision, appears to choose good works as his path to salvation.[36]

The main text of the Eugenian recension of *Stephanites and Ichnelates,* as it is published here, is divided into fifteen chapters of unequal length and bears the hallmarks of the fluid transmission of the work. Chapter 1 and chapters 3 to 6 correspond to the original five books of the *Panchatantra;* chapter 7 (a tale of Buddhist origin), chapters 8, 9, and 10 (tales from the *Mahabharata*), and chapter 14 (of either Indian or Persian origin) are believed to have been added at the time of the composition of the Middle Persian version.

Chapter 2, which continues the story of chapter 1, is believed to have been added by Ibn al-Muqaffaʿ.[37] Chapters 11 to 13 and chapter 15 are also thought to have been added at that time.[38]

The *Panchatantra* is a work of practical knowledge, showing how to succeed and do well in life: it is the clever who succeed, not the morally good. This, then, is the message given by the chapters taken from this work, by the stories taken from book 12 of the *Mahabharata* (chapters 8, 9, and 10), by the Buddhist tale of the king and his dreams (chapter 7), and by the Indian or Persian tale about the mice (chapter 14). Chapter 2, which is found in the Arabic version and translations from it (but not in the Old Syriac version, translated from Middle Persian), has a very different message. Here, in the story of Ichnelates's trial, good triumphs over evil, and it is likely that this chapter, with its very different ethos, was not part of the Middle Persian version.[39] The same is true for chapters 11, 12, 13, and 15, which are likewise found in the Arabic version and its translations, but not in the Old Syriac.

Chapter 1, by far the longest, tells the story of a bull, a lion king, and his two jackal courtiers, Stephanites and Ichnelates, who give their names to the whole work. Ichnelates, jealous of the friendship between the bull and the lion, which he helped bring about, causes distrust and hostility between them, resulting in the lion killing the bull. Chapter 2 continues this story: the lion, filled with regret over his action, and on the advice of his mother, brings Ichnelates to trial over his role in the affair. The jackal is, ultimately, found guilty. Chapter 3 is a tale about a dove, a crow, a mouse, a turtle, and a gazelle, who, thanks to their steadfast friend-

ship, manage to outwit the hunters who are their enemies. Chapter 4 is a tale of war between owls and crows, in which the crows are victorious thanks to cleverness and trickery. Chapter 5 tells the story of an ape and a turtle who are friends, but when the turtle discovers he needs to kill the ape, he fails to act decisively and thus permits the ape to save himself. Chapter 6 is a short tale demonstrating the dangers of acting too hastily. Chapter 7 tells of a king who is saved from disaster by his sensible wife and intelligent counselor. Chapter 8 tells how a mouse and a weasel become friends temporarily, so each can save the other from immediate danger. Chapter 9 features a king and his pet bird, and tells how one should keep away from one's enemy, regardless of the promises he may make. In chapter 10, the trusted jackal advisor to a lion king is reinstated after the plots of his jealous courtiers are revealed. Chapter 11 tells the story of how, thanks to his kindness, a hermit triumphs over an ungrateful goldsmith. Chapter 12 shows how hard work, intelligence, and beauty are less important than luck or fate in determining success. In chapter 13, a lioness stops eating meat after being made aware of the harm she has been doing to others. Chapter 14 is about the importance of a king having good counselors, and chapter 15 tells of the perils of not being satisfied with what one has.

Language

Unfortunately, one cannot be absolutely certain concerning the stylistic level of the Eugenian version, due to the fact that all four manuscripts that form the basis for our current text (see the Note on the Text for details) adhere to a con-

taminated line of transmission; as Marc Lauxtermann points out, we do not know how the text we have now differs from the original translation as commissioned by Eugenios.[40] In places where manuscript P preserves Homeric words, manuscripts BL and O use vocabulary of a lower register, but all four use elements of lower style in different sections, such as, for example, the articular infinitive in the genitive to indicate purpose.[41] One of the newly translated substories (1.21) is a ribald tale of a prostitute who attempts to murder her maid's lover: both its subject matter and its language could indicate a change of genre and intended audience from Seth's work, which had been dedicated to the Byzantine emperor and was thus meant for the court.[42] It is therefore possible, but far from certain, that using a different literary style was a deliberate choice by Eugenios or his translators as being more appropriate to the subject matter; there are instances of the use of the vernacular juxtaposed with passages in formal style in other Byzantine literature of the twelfth century.[43] This "lowering" of the register and subject matter, if it is indeed original, may have contributed to the popularity of the Eugenian recension: it is sometimes found in manuscripts alongside Aesop's *Fables* and *Syntipas,*[44] indicating the genre to which it was held to belong, one which could be described as fiction or storytelling.

I would like to thank all those who with their encouragement, advice, and expertise have provided assistance with this volume, and all at the Dumbarton Oaks Medieval Library for their immense patience during the long course of its preparation. Margaret Mullett and Alice-Mary Tal-

bot initially encouraged me to undertake the project; Alice-Mary expertly edited the early part of the translation, and John Duffy did likewise for the early part of the text. Alice-Mary's successors as Byzantine Greek co-editors of the series, Richard Greenfield and Alexander Alexakis, were very closely involved in the production of the final text, translation, and notes, particularly for the later chapters. The extent of their involvement is reflected in the "with" of the credits: both I and the volume have benefited enormously from their experience and expertise. Tyler fellow Hannelore Segers acted as my pre-editor, offering many helpful corrections and suggestions, and assisted with various sections of the book, including the index. Louis-Patrick St-Pierre, a research fellow at Queen's University, helped review the proofs. Without the meticulous technical care, consistent help, and wide-ranging knowledge of Nicole Eddy, the managing editor for the Dumbarton Oaks Medieval Library, this volume would fall short in very many ways. Last, but certainly not least, Robert Jordan has for many years been the person I turned to first for help with Greek translation problems; he has always taken a keen interest in the activities of the jackals and the other animal protagonists of these tales. Any remaining errors are, of course, my own.

Notes

1 The meaning of the root of *Kalīla* in Arabic relates to a "crown," and so became *Stephanites,* "crown wearing" in Greek; likewise, *Dimna* in Arabic, meaning "traces" or "remnants," became *Ichnelates,* "a tracker."

2 For an introduction to the Persian and Arabic versions, see François de Blois, *Burzoy's Voyage to India and the Origin of the Book of "Kalīlah wa Dimnah"* (London, 1990), and especially p. 12 for the evolution of the names, from Karataka and Damanaka in the *Panchatantra,* to Karirak and Damanak in Middle Persian, to Kalīla and Dimna in Arabic. For the *Pan-*

chatantra see Franklin Edgerton, *The "Panchatantra" Reconstructed,* 2 vols. (New Haven, CT, 1924); for a more recent English translation, see Patrick Olivelle, *The Five Discourses on Worldly Wisdom by Viṣṇuśarman* (New York, 2006). For the *Mahabharata,* see *Mahabhárata,* ed. and trans. Adam Bowles, Alex Cherniak, Kate Crosby, Kathleen Garbutt, William J. Johnson, Justin Meiland, Vaughan Pilikian, Paul Wilmot, and Alexander Wynne, Clay Sanskrit Library (New York, 2005–).

3 See the entry for Borzūya in *Encyclopaedia Iranica* (London, 1982–2019), vol. 4, fasc. 4, pp. 381–82.

4 For Greek see Dimitri Gutas, Anthony Kaldellis, and Brian Long, "Intellectual Exchanges with the Arab World," in *The Cambridge Intellectual History of Byzantium,* ed. Anthony Kaldellis and Niketas Siniossoglou (Cambridge, 2017), 79–98, at 81. See also de Blois, *Burzoy's Voyage,* 32, and Richard Frye, *The History of Ancient Iran* (Munich, 1984), 330. For Sanskrit see Farrokh Kaveh, *Shadows in the Desert: Ancient Persia at War* (Oxford, 2007), 241–42. For translations from Syriac, see Manfred Ullmann, *Islamic Medicine* (Edinburgh, 1978), 16–20.

5 See Friedrich Schulthess, *Kalila und Dimna: Die altsyrische Version des indischen Fürstenspiegels ("Pantchatantra") oder Bidpai's Fabeln* (Berlin, 1911). See also de Blois, *Burzoy's Voyage,* 2.

6 For an overview of the life and works of Ibn al-Muqaffaʿ, see "Ebn al-Moqaffaʿ," *Encyclopaedia Iranica,* vol. 8, fasc. 1, pp. 39–43, and Francesco Gabrieli, "Ibn al-Muḳaffaʿ," *EI2,* vol. 3, pp. 883–85. See also István Kristó-Nagy, *La pensée d'Ibn al-Muqaffaʿ: Un "agent double" dans le monde persan et arabe* (Paris, 2013). For the cultural context to his translation and how he adapted the work in line with the ethos of the ʿAbbasid rulers, and for further bibliography, see Bettina Krönung, "The Wisdom of the Beasts: The Arabic *Book of Kalīla and Dimna* and the Byzantine *Book of Stephanites and Ichnelates,*" in *Fictional Storytelling in the Medieval Eastern Mediterranean and Beyond,* ed. Carolina Cupane and Bettina Krönung (Leiden, 2016), 427–60, at 438–45.

7 On the difficult-to-translate concept of *adab,* see Catherine Mayeur-Jaouen, "Introduction" in *Adab and Modernity: A "Civilising Process"? (Sixteenth–Twenty-First Century),* ed. Catherine Mayeur-Jaouen (Leiden, 2020), 1–46.

8 For an introduction and overview, see "Kalila wa-Dimna," in *EI2,* vol. 4, pp. 503–6.

9 See Beatrice Gruendler, Jan J. van Ginkel, Rima Redwan, Khouloud Khalfallah, Isabel Toral, Johannes Stephan, Matthew L. Keegan, Theodore S. Beers, Mahmoud Kozae, and Marwa M. Ahmed, "An Interim Report on the Editorial and Analytical Work of the AnonymClassic Project," *Medieval Worlds* 11 (2020): 241–79, https://medievalworlds.net/0xc1aa5576%200x003ba1d6.pdf. The Project's goal is to document the changes in the text, not to try to find an "original," and to create a synoptic digital edition. See also Martin Sprengling, "Kalila Studies I," *American Journal of Semitic Languages and Literatures* 40 (1924): 81–97. Sprengling found about eighty manuscripts, versions, and lists of chapters. For a printed Arabic edition, faithful to the manuscript on which it is based, see Louis Cheikho, *La version arabe de Kalilah et Dimnah ou les fables de Bidpai, traduit du persan par Abdallah Ibn al-Muqaffaʿ* (Beirut, 1905; repr., Amsterdam, 1981).

10 For the history of the text and its versions and translations, see Johannes Niehoff-Panagiotidis, *Übersetzung und Rezeption: Die byzantinischen-neugriechischen und spanischen Adaptionen von "Kalila wa-Dimna"* (Wiesbaden, 2003), 9–60. For the Greek and Spanish versions, see also David Hernández de la Fuente, "Greek and Spanish Versions of *Kalila and Dimna,* with an Example of Fantastic Ornithology," *Literatura* 21, no. 1 (2019): 35–60. See also the Bibliography for some editions and translations of these other versions.

11 See Elinor Husselmann, *A Fragment of "Kalilah and Dimnah" from Ms. 397 in the Pierpoint Morgan Library* (London, 1938).

12 For the edition of Seth's version, see Lars-Olof Sjöberg, *Stephanites und Ichnelates: Überlieferungsgeschichte und Text* (Uppsala, 1962). On pages 62–63 he lists forty-four manuscripts. A more detailed study by Alexander Alexakis of the manuscript tradition of this text is intended for the Dumbarton Oaks Medieval Library Supplement series. For an examination of Seth's translation technique by means of a comparison with the Arabic published editions, see Hélène Condylis-Bassoukos, *"Stéphanitès kai Ichnélatès," traduction grecque (XIe siècle) du livre "Kalīla wa-Dimna" d'Ibn al-Muqaffaʿ (VIIIe siècle): Étude lexicologique et litteraire* (Louvain, 1997).

13 For Church Slavonic, see Niehoff-Panagiotidis, *Übersetzung und Rezeption,* 43, and Sjöberg, *Stephanites,* 112–14. For the Medieval Latin edition, see Alfons Hilka, "Eine lateinische Übersetzung der griechischen Version des Kalilabuchs," in *Beiträge zur lateinischen Erzählungsliteratur des Mittellal-*

ters II, special issue, *Abhandlungen der Gesellschaft der Wissenschaften zu Göttingen philologisch-historische Klasse, neue Folge* 21, no. 3 (1928): 59–155. See also Sjöberg, *Stephanites,* 114–16, and Marc Lauxtermann, "The Eugenian Recension of *Stephanites and Ichnelates:* Prologue and Paratexts," *Νέα Ῥώμη* 15 (2018): 63–65, for its dating to the thirteenth century, its connection with Sicily and southern Italy, and for further bibliography. The Italian translation is *Del governo de' regni: Sotto morali esempi di animali ragionanti tra loro* (Ferrara, 1583). See also Sjöberg, *Stephanites,* 116–20, and John-Theophanes Papademetriou, "The Sources and the Character of *Del governo de' regni,*" *Transactions and Proceedings of the American Philological Association,* 92 (1961): 422–39. The German translation is Christian B. Lehmus, *Abuschalem und sein Hofphilosoph oder die Weisheit Indiens in einer Reihe von Fabeln* (Leipzig, 1778); and see Sjöberg, *Stephanites,* 120–21.

14 Completed by Theodosios Zygomalas in 1584; see Sjöberg, *Stephanites,* 122–32, and Loukia Stefou, *Die neugriechische metaphrase von "Stephanites und Ichnelates" durch Theodosios Zygomalas* (Madrid, 2011).

15 For an examination of Seth's life and works, and further bibliography, see Gutas, Kaldellis, and Long, "Intellectual Exchanges," 92–98; also Sjöberg, *Stephanites,* 87–99.

16 For the edition, translation, and introduction to the *Refutation of Galen,* see Petros Bouras-Vallianatos, "Galen's Reception in Byzantium: Symeon Seth and His Refutation of Galenic Theories on Human Physiology," *Greek, Roman, and Byzantine Studies* 55, no.2 (2015): 431–69. Seth's dietary treatise has been edited by Bernhard Langkavel, *Syntagma de alimentorum facultatibus* (Leipzig, 1868). See also Alison Noble, "Foodstuffs in Symeon Seth's *Syntagma de alimentorum facultatibus,*" accessed June 29, 2021, https://www.doaks.org/research/byzantine/scholarly-activities/knowing-bodies-passionate-souls-sense-perceptions-in-byzantium/seths-alimentary-treatise.

17 Gutas, Kaldellis, and Long, "Intellectual Exchanges," 96.

18 See Gutas, Kaldellis, and Long, "Intellectual Exchanges," 89, for the possibility that the context for the increased openness to Eastern learning in the late eleventh century was the imperial crisis faced by Emperor Alexios I Komnenos and his dealings with the enemies of the empire—the acquisition of knowledge as a source of power. For a list of translations into Byzantine Greek, see Anthony Kaldellis, "Catalogue of Translations

into Byzantine Greek from Texts in Any Other Language, 300–1453 AD," accessed May 3, 2021, https://www.academia.edu/36711128/Kaldellis_Catalogue_of_Translations_into_Byzantine_Greek_version_III.

19 The earliest surviving manuscript containing the Eugenian prologues has the additional chapters, and some of the additional stories, added by a later hand. See the Note on the Text for details.

20 See Vera von Falkenhausen, "Eugenio da Palermo," in *Dizionario biografico degli Italiani* (Rome, 1993), vol. 43, pp. 502–5, and Evelyn Jamison, *Admiral Eugenius of Sicily* (London, 1957).

21 For the rank and title of emir, or *amiratus,* see Jeremy Johns, *Arabic Administration in Norman Sicily: The Royal Diwan* (Cambridge, 2002), 68–74. On such elite Italo-Greek families, see Eleni Tounta, "The Italo-Greek Courtiers and Their Saint: Constructing the Italo-Greek Elite's Collective Identity in the Twelfth-Century Norman Kingdom of Sicily," *Mediterranean Studies* 28, no. 1 (2020): 88–129.

22 For the history of Norman Sicily in this period, see especially Hubert Houben, *Roger II of Sicily: A Ruler between East and West* (Cambridge, 2002); compare also Donald Matthew, *The Norman Kingdom of Sicily* (Cambridge, 1992).

23 Houben, *Roger II,* 99, and von Falkenhausen, "Eugenio," 503.

24 In a dedicatory letter to his translation of Plato's *Phaedo,* Aristippus describes Sicily as a center for the study of philosophy and natural science and mentions some of the works held in its libraries. See Houben, *Roger II,* 98–99.

25 Works by Euclid, Proclus, Aristotle, Ptolemy, and Plato were translated into Latin: see Marie-Thérèse d'Alverny, "Translations and Translators," in *Renaissance and Renewal in the Twelfth Century,* ed. R. L. Benson, G. Constable, and C. D. Lanham (Oxford, 1982), 421–62, at 427 and 433–37.

26 Von Falkenhausen, "Eugenio," 503, provides a full bibliography for his poetical works.

27 See Hiroshi Takayama, *The Administration of the Norman Kingdom of Sicily* (Leiden, 1993), 145–62, for a detailed account of this administrative office, which was responsible for royal property and legal, judicial, and financial affairs in areas other than Sicily and Calabria. Takayama lists the functions as granting royal lands and properties, communicating and promulgating royal ordinances, granting permission for the sale of lands, lend-

ing money, buying property, paying sums owed, holding trials, controlling officials, and receiving indictments. According to Takayama, Eugenios is mentioned in the sources in this capacity in 1174, 1175, 1178, 1187, 1189, and 1190.

28 Von Falkenhausen, "Eugenio," 502–3. It appears that he spent most of his career in Puglia and Campania, areas of the kingdom where Latin was used. His signature, however, is always in Greek.

29 Houben, *Roger II,* 107.

30 See Lauxtermann, "The Eugenian Recension," 87–88, 97, and Alex Metcalfe, *Muslims and Christians in Norman Sicily: Arabic-Speakers and the End of Islam* (London and New York, 2003), 106. See also Tounta, "The Italo-Greek Courtiers," 96, 109.

31 See Vera von Falkenhausen, "I grupi etnici nel regno di Ruggero II e la loro participazione al potere," in *Società, potere e popolo nell'età di Ruggero II* (Bari, 1977), 133–56, at 152. Metcalfe, *Muslims and Christians,* 100, 104, and 182, describes the decline of Greek as a prestige language of the ruling elite following Roger II's death.

32 See Houben, *Roger II,* 112, for more on the court and for the contrast with that of Spain, and p. 100 for the contrast with Salerno; see also Antonino De Stefano, *La cultura in Sicilia nel periodo normanno* (Bologna, 1954), 85–86, for the lack of further dissemination or impact for translations carried out in Sicily during this period.

33 Lauxtermann, "The Eugenian Recension," 95–97, points out that the rubrics seem to address an audience and emphasize the value of friendship. See also Tounta, "The Italo-Greek Courtiers," 95, for the possibility that literary texts were read aloud at the social gatherings of this group, and Margaret Mullett, "Performing Court Literature in Medieval Byzantium: Tales Told in Tents," in *In the Presence of Power: Court and Performance in the Pre-Modern Middle East,* ed. Maurice Pomerantz and Evelyn Birge Vitz (New York, 2017), 121–41, especially 125–27 for Seth's *Stephanites* as a possible source of oral storytelling at the court of Alexios I Komnenos.

34 For a detailed discussion of the long and short versions of Burzoy's voyage, and the possible origins of the long version, see de Blois, *Burzoy's Voyage,* 40–43 and 51–57; and for his theory of how the two Middle Persian prologues may have become separated from each other by that of Ibn al-Muqaffaʿ, see pp. 63–65.

35 Lauxtermann, "The Eugenian Recension," 96–97, notes how the Greek translation of this prologue differs from the Arabic original, which recommends the work as an example of free intellectual inquiry in which the reader can engage and explore different cultures and belief systems, an idea not retained in the Greek translation.

36 De Blois, *Burzoy's Voyage,* 32–33, proposes that his attraction to asceticism was probably influenced by his time in India.

37 Some of the manuscripts on which this volume is based (BLO, see the Note on the Text) have no division between chapters 1 and 2—the end of 1 and the beginning of 2 are in the same paragraph. It is likely that this feature corresponds to the Arabic manuscript(s) being used by the translators. Manuscript P divides the first chapter of BLO into two and employs the term τμῆμα (section) for each one of the fifteen chapters instead of the expected κεφάλαιον or λόγος (as used in BLO).

38 For a discussion of the possible origins of these later chapters, see de Blois, *Burzoy's Voyage,* 14–15.

39 For more on this, see de Blois, *Burzoy's Voyage,* 15–17.

40 Lauxtermann, "The Eugenian Recension," 65.

41 For examples of the lower register in BLO compared to P, see 1.8 μινυνθάδιος P: ὀλιγοχρόνιος BLO; 1.17 ὑψιπέτηλα P: ὑψίκομα BLO; 2.3 ἀλλ' ἐξαύδα P: εἰπὲ οὖν ἡμῖν BLO; 3.2 ὑψιπέτηλον P: ὑψηλὸν BLO; and especially 6.3 ῥυδὸν ἀφνειὸς P: ῥοιζηδὸν ἀφνειὸς BLO and all other manuscripts.

42 For further examples of words belonging to a "lower" language register, see Niehoff-Panagiotidis, *Übersetzung und Rezeption,* 75.

43 For example, the "Ptochoprodromic poems" attributed to Theodore Prodromos, and Michael Glykas's appeal to the emperor from prison. For the rise in the use of the vernacular in this period, see Margaret Alexiou, *After Antiquity: Greek Language, Myth and Metaphor* (Ithaca and London, 2002), 23–27, and 127–29, for a discussion of the poems.

44 A collection of stories with human and animal protagonists translated from Syriac into Greek in the eleventh century; see Michael Andreopoulos, *The Book of Syntipas the Philosopher,* in *The Byzantine Sinbad,* ed. Jeffrey Beneker and Craig A. Gibson, Dumbarton Oaks Medieval Library 67 (Cambridge, MA, 2021).

ANIMAL FABLES OF THE COURTLY MEDITERRANEAN

Φυσιολογικὸν βιβλίον ἔχον λόγους εἰς τμήματα ιεʹ τὸ καλούμενον *Στεφανίτης καὶ Ἰχνηλάτης*

[Preface]

Τὴν βίβλον ταύτην Περζουὲ πόνος ἔσχεν.
Ἡδονῆς ἀνάπλεα τὰ τῆδε σκόπει.
Λόγοι σοφιστῶν μετασχηματισθέντες.

2 Μυθικὴ βίβλος ἐξ Ἰνδικῆς σοφίας
προσενεχθεῖσα πρὸς Περσικὴν παιδείαν,
αἰνιγματωδῶς συντείνουσα τὰς πράξεις,
πρὸς βιωτικοὺς καὶ βαρβαρώδεις ὕθλους
μεταβληθεῖσα πρὸς γλῶτταν τῶν Ἑλλήνων,
παρὰ τοῦ σοφοῦ, ἐνδόξου καὶ μεγάλου,
τοῦ καὶ ἀμηρᾶ τοῦ ῥηγὸς Σικελίας,
Καλαβρίας τε, πρίγκιπος Ἰταλίας·
οὕσπερ εὑρηκὼς ὡς γνωστικοὺς τοῖς πᾶσιν,
τοῦτο δέδωκε πρὸς ἡμᾶς τὸ βιβλίον,
ὥσπερ δώρημα διδασκαλίας πλέον,
εὐγενὴς Εὐγένιος, ὁ τῆς Πανόρμου.

A Book of Inquiry into Nature Containing Discourses in Fifteen Chapters Called *Stephanites and Ichnelates*

Preface

This book is the progeny of Perzoué's toil,
so consider its content filled with much pleasure,
for the words of wise men are now translated here.

It's a fabulous book of Indian wisdom 2
produced for the sake of Persian education,
by means of dark riddles relating the actions
of men to popular and foreign drivel,
which has here been translated into Greek language
by that wise man, that great man, held in high repute,
the admiral of the king of Sicily
and of Calabria and prince of Italy.
As he found them enlightening for everyone,
he has now donated the present book to us
as a gift that is full of very much teaching,
that noble man Eugenios of Panormos.

3 *"Χρήσασθε ἐξ Αἰγυπτίων σκεύη χρυσᾶ καὶ ἀργυρᾶ,"* λέγει τις τῶν θείων ἀνδρῶν, ὅτι τὸν ἐν προσοχῇ ὄντα δυνατὸν καὶ ἐκ τῶν ἐναντίων κτήσασθαι τὸ ὠφέλιμον, ὥσπερ δὴ καὶ τοὐναντίον συμβαίνειν εἴωθε τῷ μὴ ζῶντι προσεκτικῶς· ἀλλὰ καὶ τὸν μακάριον Ἰακώβ, φασί, τὰ ἐξ Ἀσσυρίων αὐτῷ κτηθέντα ἐν τῇ Γῇ τῆς Ἐπαγγελίας μετενέγκαι. Καὶ Ῥαχήλ, τὴν πατριαρχικὴν ψυχήν, καὶ τὰ πατρικὰ εἴδωλα κλέψασαν ὑπὸ τῆς ἱστορίας ἐκδιδασκόμεθα. Καὶ ὁ Παροιμιαστὴς ἐκπέμπει πρὸς μέλιτταν καὶ ἐκ παντὸς ἄνθους τὸ χρήσιμον κτᾶσθαι μιμουμένοις αὐτὴν διὰ τῆς παραινέσεως ἐγκελεύεται.

Οὕτω δὴ καὶ ἡμεῖς, τὰ ἐξ Ἰνδικῆς λεγέντα μυθοπλαστίας εὑρηκότες τῇ τῶν Ἀράβων γλώσσῃ ἐγκείμενα, σκοτεινὸν δὲ καὶ παρηλλαγμένον λόγον ἐπέχοντα καὶ <δι'> αἰνιγμάτων τε καὶ παραβολῶν ἱστορικῶς ἡμᾶς ἐκπαιδεύοντα, οὐκ ᾠήθημεν τοῖς τῆς λήθης ἐνθάψαι βυθοῖς, ἀλλ' εἰς τὸ φανερὸν τῇ τῶν Ἑλλήνων γλώττῃ ἀναγαγεῖν. Ἐπὶ τούτων καί τισιν ἀνδράσι χρησάμενοι ἀντιλαμβανομένοις τῇ ἡμῶν προθυμίᾳ εὖ εἰδόσι τῆς τῶν Ἀράβων γλώσσης, ἐξ αὐτῆς πρὸς τὴν Ἑλλάδα γλῶσσαν διεπορθμεύσαμεν.

4 Οὕτω γάρ τοι καὶ τὴν Ἑλληνικὴν σοφίαν ἐκ μυθικῶν πλασμάτων τὴν ἀρχὴν λαβεῖν ἐπαιδεύθημεν, εἴπερ πιστευτέον τῷ λέγοντι οὕτως· "Ὁ μῦθος ἐκ ποιητῶν προῆλθεν, γέγονέ τε καὶ ῥητόρων, Αἰσωπειόν τε προσαγορευόμενον καὶ Συβαριτικόν, Κιλίκιόν τε καὶ Κύπριον, διὰ τὸ ἀρχῆθεν ἐκ τῶν τοιούτων συστῆναι τὰ μυθικά." Καὶ ἡμεῖς τοίνυν εἰδότες <ὅτι> πρὸς ἠθικὴν ἀρετὴν καὶ προσοχὴν τῶν ἐν βίῳ συμπιπτόντων πραγμάτων ὀνησιφόρα φανήσονται τὰ

"*You should make use of gold and silver vessels* which derive 3
from the Egyptians," says one of the holy men, because someone who is attentive is able to acquire what is beneficial even from his enemies, just as the opposite usually happens with someone who does not live attentively. Even the blessed Jacob, so they say, took along with him to the Promised Land what he had acquired from the Assyrians, and Rachel, the patriarch's soul, even stole her father's idols, as we are taught by history. The author of Proverbs refers us to the bee, and enjoins us with this advice, by imitating her, to make use of what is valuable from every flower.

In this way we too, having discovered what is told in fabulous stories from India wrapped up in the language of the Arabs, stories which contain an obscure and devious sense and teach us literally through riddles and parables, did not think it right to bury them in the depths of oblivion, but to raise them up into the light in the language of the Greeks. We thus translated them from Arabic into the Greek language, using for this purpose some men who had a good knowledge of the language of the Arabs to help us with our desire.

For we have thus, indeed, been taught that even Hellenic 4
wisdom had its beginning in fabulous tales, if the person who says the following is to be believed: "The fable originated with poets, but also came to be used by orators. It is called Aesopic and Sybaritic, Cilician and Cyprian on account of the origin from which these people composed the books of myths." And so, since we knew that these fables would clearly be profitable regarding moral virtue and attention to things that occur in life, we have collected them with

μυθεύματα, πολλῷ πόνῳ ταῦτα συναγηοχότες, τῇ Ἑλληνικῇ μετηνέγκαμεν γλώττῃ. Καὶ γάρ τοι καὶ τὴν τοῦ Ἄισματος τῶν Ἀισμάτων πραγματείαν, ἐξ αἰσθητῶν, μᾶλλον δὲ ἐρωτικῶν, πραγμάτων ὁ θειότατος Σολομὼν συνεστήσατο. Ἣν οἱ θεοφόροι πατέρες, ἀνάξιον ἡγούμενοι τὰς φωνὰς τοῦ Ἁγίου Πνεύματος ἱστορικῶς οὕτω καὶ χαμερπῶς ἐκλαμβάνεσθαι, πρὸς τὴν κατὰ σάρκα τοῦ Λόγου νύμφευσιν ἑτεροτροπολογικῶς ἀλληγόρευσαν. Οὕτω μέντοι καὶ τοῖς ἐντυγχάνουσι τοῖς ποιήμασι τοῖσδε <δεῖ> μὴ μέμψιν ἐπάγειν πρὸς ἡμᾶς διὰ τὸ ἀνάξιον ἡγεῖσθαι τὴν Ἑλληνικοῖς καὶ θεολογικοῖς ποιήμασιν ἐπιβαίνουσαν γλῶτταν ἡμῶν, καὶ ταῖς μυθικαῖς καταχραίνειν καὶ βαρβαρώδεσιν ἀγροικίαις, καὶ τὸ πιστοὺς ὄντας ἀνωφελέσιν ἐκπονεῖσθαι τοῖς ἀναγνώσμασιν, ἀλλὰ τὸ ἐκ μυθεύσεως καρπούμενοι ὄφελος, τὸ βλαβερὸν εἰς κόρακας εἰκότως ἀπορρίψωμεν, ἐπεὶ καὶ τὴν ἡμετέραν φύσιν ἐκ νοερᾶς καὶ αἰσθητῆς οὐσίας ὁ Τεχνίτης καὶ Λόγος συνεστήσατο. Ἀλλ' ὁ μὲν τὴν σάρκα προθέμενος ἀποτυγχάνει τοῦ Πνεύματος, ὁ δὲ οἰκειούμενος τῷ Πνεύματι καὶ αὐτὴν πᾶσαν τὴν λυομένην σάρκα πρὸς ἀθανασίαν μείζονα οὐσιοποιεῖ, ὥσπερ παρὰ τοῦ Σωτῆρος ἐκδιδασκόμεθα.

5 Οὕτω δὲ ἀναγνοὺς καὶ σὺ τούσδε τοὺς λόγους,
ἐπεὶ καὶ ἐν βάτῳ ῥόδα ἐκφύονται,
ἀλλ' ἡ μέλιττα τοῖς ῥόδοις ἐφιζάνει,
τὸ χρήσιμον ζήτησον ὡς τερπνὸν ῥόδον,
τὰ δ' ἐναντία ὡς ἀκάνθας ἐκτρέπου.

6 Ἀνακεφαλαίωσις τῆς παρούσης πραγματείας αὕτη·

great labor and have translated them into the Greek language. For, indeed, even the most holy Solomon composed the subject matter of the Song of Songs from sensual material, or, rather, from erotic material, but the divinely inspired fathers, who thought it was improper that the words of the Holy Spirit should be thus taken in a literal and unspiritual sense, understood it figuratively and allegorized it as referring to the marriage in the flesh of the Word. Thus also, those who read these compositions should not find fault with us because they think it unworthy to defile our language, which is employed for secular and theological writings, with mythical and barbarous rusticities and to have the faithful practice unprofitable reading. But, in order to reap the benefit from recounting mythical tales, let us reasonably throw to the crows what is harmful, since the Architect and the Word formed our nature from a rational and sentient essence. But, while someone who prefers the flesh fails to attain the Spirit, someone who identifies themself with the Spirit makes all this perishable flesh assume an essence that leads to greater immortality, as we are taught by the Savior.

So, as you now yourself peruse these discourses, 5
since even when roses grow in a bramble bush
it is upon the roses that the bee alights,
look for what is useful like a most pleasant rose,
but make sure you avoid the opposite like thorns.

This is a summary of the present work: first, Perzoué's 6

πρῶτον μὲν ἡ περὶ τοῦ Περζουὲ ἀποστολὴ πρὸς Ἰνδίαν καὶ διάγνωσις τῶν ἐκεῖσε, ἔπειτα ἡ Ἰνδικὴ βίβλος ἣν ἐκόμισεν ἐξ Ἰνδίας, δύο μὲν ἔχουσαν πραγματείας—μίαν μὲν τὴν τοῦ *Στεφανίτου καὶ Ἰχνηλάτου,* ἑτέραν δὲ τὴν *Περιτραχήλιον Περιστεράν*—καὶ ὅσα περιέχουσι ἀμφότεραι τροπικὰ μυθεύματα.

mission to India and a discussion of what was there; then, the Indian book which he brought back from India. It comprises two works—one is the book of *Stephanites and Ichnelates,* the other is *The Collared Dove*—and whatever allegorical fables both contain.

[Prologue A]

Χοσρόης ὁ τῶν Περσῶν βασιλεύς, ὁ καὶ Ἀνασουράνος ὀνομαζόμενος ὁ τοῦ Καϊδὰδ υἱός, μαθὼν περί τινος βιβλίου ἐν τῇ χώρᾳ τῶν Ἰνδῶν συγγραφέντος παρὰ τῶν ἐν τῇ τοιαύτῃ χώρᾳ γνωστικῶν καὶ σοφῶν, ἔχοντος μύθους ὠφελίμους πᾶσιν ἀνθρώποις τοῖς ἐν βίῳ διατρίβουσι, μικροῖς τε καὶ μεγάλοις, ἄρχουσι καὶ ἀρχομένοις, ὄνομα δὲ αὐτῷ *Κηλίλαι καὶ Δίμναι,* ὅπερ ἐστὶ *Στεφανίτης καὶ Ἰχνηλάτης,* ὃ καὶ ἀπέκειτο ἐν τοῖς βασιλικοῖς ταμείοις ἐγκεκρυμμένον, περὶ οὗ πληροφορίαν ὁ βασιλεὺς Χοσρόης λαβὼν καὶ περὶ τῶν ἐγκειμένων ἐν αὐτῷ ὠφελίμων μύθων, προσέταξεν εὑρεθῆναί τινα γνωστικὸν ἄνδρα, εἰδήμονα τῆς τῶν Ἰνδῶν γλώττης. Καὶ δὴ προσήγαγον αὐτῷ ἄνδρα ἐχέφρονα καὶ πλήρη πάσης παιδεύσεως, ἰατρὸν τῇ ἐνούσῃ αὐτῷ ἐπιστήμῃ, Περζουὲ καλούμενον· ὃς καὶ παραγενόμενος τοῦ βασιλέως ἐνώπιον, προσεκύνησεν αὐτόν, καὶ ἀναστάς, ἵστατο διαλογιζόμενος.

2 Ἔφη αὐτῷ ὁ βασιλεύς· "Ἤκουσταί μοι περὶ τῆς σῆς γνώσεως καὶ νουνεχείας καὶ ἀρετῆς· ἀκήκοα δὲ καὶ περὶ βιβλίου τινὸς ἐν τῇ Ἰνδίᾳ ὄντος καὶ ἀξιολογωτάτου τυγχάνοντος. Καὶ ὅτι μοι πολλὴ ἐπιθυμία ἐστὶ πρὸς τὸ κτήσασθαι τὴν τοιαύτην βίβλον, νῦν οὖν μοι πρὸς τοῦτο ἐξυπηρέτησον, ἐνδειξάμενός μοι πᾶσαν σπουδὴν καὶ ἀκρίβειαν

Prologue A

Chosroes, the king of the Persians, who was also called Anasouranos the son of Kaïdad, learned of a book written in the land of the Indians by the learned and wise men of that country that had beneficial stories for everyone who passes through life, both small and great, the rulers and the ruled. The name of this book was *Kelilai and Dimnai,* also known in Greek as *Stephanites and Ichnelates,* and it lay hidden in the royal treasury. When King Chosroes received information about this book and about the beneficial nature of the stories contained in it, he ordered a knowledgeable man to be found who was fluent in the Indian language. And so they brought him a clever man called Perzoué, who was well educated in all subjects, but a physician in his particular discipline. When he came into the presence of the king, he prostrated himself and, once he had arisen, stood deep in thought.

The king said to him: "I have been told about your knowl- 2
edge, good sense and virtue. I have also heard about a book in India which is most remarkable. As I have really set my heart on getting hold of this book, help me now in this, and show me your great enthusiasm and care in searching for

εἰς τὴν τούτου ζήτησιν καὶ ἀνεύρεσιν, ἀλλὰ καὶ ἑτέρων βιβλίων τῶν μὴ ὄντων ἡμῖν." Καὶ προσέταξε δοθῆναι αὐτῷ χρήματα ἱκανὰ πρός τε χρῆσιν τῆς ὁδοιπορίας αὐτοῦ καὶ πρὸς ἄλλο ὅπερ βουλητὸν αὐτῷ ἦν, καὶ λέγει αὐτῷ· "Εἰ ταῦτα τὰ χρήματα προσαναλώσῃς καὶ ἑτέρας ἐξόδου δεηθῇς, γράψον ἡμῖν· μόνον τὴν ἐπιθυμίαν πλήρωσον."

3 Ἀπελθὼν τοίνυν ὁ Περζουὲ καὶ καταλαβὼν τὴν Ἰνδικὴν χώραν, διέτριβεν ἔν τε τοῖς βασιλικοῖς πυλῶσι καὶ προαυλίοις, ἔν τε τοῖς μεγιστᾶσιν αὐτοῦ καὶ τοῖς σοφοῖς καὶ γνωστικοῖς ἅπασι. Καὶ ἀπήρχετο καθεκάστην χαιρετίζων αὐτούς, καὶ γνώριμον ἑαυτὸν αὐτοῖς διὰ τῆς συνεχοῦς ὁμιλίας ἀποκαθιστῶν, ὑποδεικνύων αὐτοῖς ὅπως τε χάριν παιδεύσεως καὶ ὠφελείας ἀφίκετο, καὶ τῆς διδαχῆς καὶ βοηθείας αὐτῶν ἀπεδέετο. Τὴν δὲ ἐνοικοῦσαν αὐτῷ σοφίαν ἀπέκρυβε, καὶ ὡς μαθητὴς παρ' αὐτῶν ἐδιδάσκετο. Τὰ δὲ περὶ τῆς βίβλου καὶ τῆς ταύτης ζητήσεως, μυστικῶς καὶ κρυφίως ἐξηρεύνα. Διατρίψας δ' ἐκεῖσε χρόνον ἱκανὸν ἐκτήσατο φίλους πολλοὺς ἐκ τῶν μεγιστάνων καὶ τῶν ἰδιωτῶν καὶ ἀπὸ πάσης παιδεύσεως. Εὑρὼν δὲ τῶν τοιούτων τινὰ νουνεχῆ καὶ πλήρη ὄντα σοφίας καὶ γνώσεως, καὶ ἀκριβῶς τὰ κατ' αὐτὸν γνούς, καὶ τὴν αὐτοῦ προαίρεσιν ἔν τε μυστηρίοις οὖσαν ἱκανήν, καὶ ἄλλως ἐπιτήδειον ὄντα εἰς ἐκπλήρωσιν τῆς δουλείας καὶ ἐπιθυμίας αὐτοῦ, ἐξήγγειλεν αὐτῷ καὶ δι' ὧν παραγέγονε. Καὶ ἤρξατο συνεσθίειν καὶ πίνειν μετ' αὐτοῦ καὶ ἐξόδους ἱκανὰς καταβάλλειν· ἐν μιᾷ οὖν τῶν ἡμερῶν λέγει αὐτῷ καταμόνας.

4 "Ἀδελφέ, βούλομαί σοι φανερῶσαι μυστήριον ἕτερον· καὶ γὰρ ἐλήλυθα περὶ πράγματος οὗπερ οὐκ ἐφανέρωσά

this and finding it, as well as other books we don't have." And he ordered that Perzoué should be given enough money to use during his journey and for anything else he wanted, and he said to him: "If you spend this money and incur other expenses, write to me. Just carry out my wishes."

So Perzoué departed and, when he reached India, he 3
spent time in the royal portals and courtyards, among the king's nobles and all the wise men and intellectuals. He went and greeted them every day, making himself known to them through his constant conversation, and he let them know that he had come for education and assistance, and that he needed their teaching and help. But he hid the wisdom he possessed and was taught as a pupil by them. And as far as the book went and his search for it, that he pursued secretly and covertly. After he had spent quite some time there, he made many friends among both nobles and ordinary people who were also well educated. When he found one man among them who was smart, full of wisdom and knowledge, and, after he had learned all about him and that he was sufficiently committed to keeping secrets, and was useful in other ways for fulfilling his service and desire, he told him why he had come. He began to eat and drink with him and to spend a lot of money. And one day he speaks to him alone.

"My brother, I want to reveal another secret to you, for I 4
have come for something that I haven't told you about. For a

σοι. Ὁ γὰρ ἐχέφρων ἀνὴρ καὶ συνετὸς ἐκ σημείων καὶ αἰνιγμάτων ὁμιλῶν γνωρίζει πρὸς τὸν ὁμιλοῦντα τὰ αὐτοῦ κρύφια." Ἀκούσας δὲ ὁ Ἰνδὺς ταῦτα λέγει πρὸς αὐτόν· "Εἰ τάχα καὶ οὐκ ἐφανέρωσάς μοι περὶ οὗ πράγματος ἐνταῦθα ἐλήλυθας, ἀλλὰ δῆλον ἐξ ὧν χλεύης ἕνεκα τὰ τῆς φιλίας ὑπέπλασας. Ἐγὼ δὲ οὐκ ἠβουλήθην περὶ τούτων ἐλέγξαι σε, ὥστε πειραθῆναί με μᾶλλον τὰ τῆς φιλίας σου καὶ τῆς σῆς γνώσεως καὶ παιδεύσεως τὰ τελέσματα. Ἀλλ' ἐπειδὴ σὺ πρῶτος ἤρξω περὶ τούτων, ἔχω σοὶ φανερὰ ποιῆσαι πάντα τὰ ἐν σοὶ κρύφια, καὶ δι' ὧν ἐνταῦθα ἐλήλυθας. Καὶ γὰρ διὰ τοῦτο ἐλήλυθας, εἰς τὸ συλῆσαι τοὺς τιμίους θησαυροὺς τῆς ἡμῶν χώρας καὶ ἀπαγαγεῖν πρὸς τὸν βασιλέα σου. Ἐγὼ δὲ τήν τε προθυμίαν καὶ τὴν ὑπομονήν σου θεασάμενος, καὶ πῶς καλῶς ἔκρυψας τὰ ἐν σοί, ἔτι πλέον ἐπόθησα τὴν φιλίαν σου, καὶ ὅτι οὐκ εἶδόν τινα ὅμοιον τῆς σῆς γνώσεως καὶ παιδεύσεως καὶ ὑπομονῆς καὶ γνώμης, τὸν δυνάμενον τὰ ἑαυτοῦ μυστήρια καλῶς κρύπτειν, ὅταν ἐν ἀλλοτρίῳ τόπῳ καὶ βασιλεῖ ᾗ καὶ ἐν λαῷ ἀγνοοῦντι τὴν ἑαυτοῦ γνώμην. Ὁ γὰρ νουνεχὴς ἀνὴρ ἐν ὀκτὼ εἴδεσιν ἀρετῶν γνωρίζεται."

5 *Περὶ τῶν ὀκτὼ ἀρετῶν,*
ἃς ὀφείλει διατηρεῖν ὁ καλὸς ἄνθρωπος.

"Πρῶτον μέν, ἀπὸ τῆς πραότητος καὶ ἐπιεικίας· δεύτερον, ἐκ τοῦ γινώσκειν τὴν ἑαυτοῦ ὑπόληψιν καὶ φυλάττειν αὐτήν· τρίτον, τὸ ὑποτάσσεσθαι τοῖς βασιλεῦσι καὶ ἀκολουθεῖν τοῖς αὐτῶν θελήμασι· τέταρτον, ἐκ τοῦ καλῶς

sensible and intelligent man makes his secrets known to his companion by speaking through signs and riddles." When the Indian heard this, he said to him: "Although you perhaps didn't reveal to me the reason you came here, it was still clear from what you pretended to do out of friendship that you were dissimulating. But I didn't want to question you over this, so that I might get to know your friendship and the results of your knowledge and education. But since you broached the subject first, I can reveal all your secrets to you, and what you came here for. You came for this reason: to steal the precious treasures of our country and take them back to your king. But, when I saw your eagerness and patience, and how well you kept your secrets to yourself, I desired your friendship even more, because I had not seen your equal in knowledge, education, patience, and judgment, or in his ability to keep his own secrets well hidden when in a foreign place, under a foreign king, and among a people ignorant of his intention. For the intelligent man is known by eight kinds of virtues."

About the eight virtues which the 5
good man ought to maintain.

"First, he is known from his gentleness and reasonableness; second, from knowing his own reputation and defending it. Third, from submitting to rulers and following their wishes; fourth, from revealing his secrets in a proper manner to his

φανεροῦν τὰ ἑαυτοῦ μυστήρια τοῖς φίλοις αὐτοῦ τοῖς πιστοῖς· πέμπτον, ἐκ τοῦ διατρίβειν τοῖς βασιλικοῖς πυλῶσι φρονίμως, καὶ μετὰ κολακείας καὶ καλολογίας ἀπαντᾶν πᾶσι τοῖς τοῦ βασιλέως. Ἕκτον δέ, ἐκ τοῦ κρύπτειν τὰ ἑαυτοῦ μυστήρια καὶ μὴ κοινωνεῖν αὐτὰ κακοήθεσιν ἀνδράσι καὶ πονηροῖς· ἕβδομον, ἐκ τοῦ προσέχειν τὴν ἑαυτοῦ γλῶτταν πρὸς τὸ μὴ φθέγγεσθαι ἀφελεῖς καὶ βλαβεροὺς λόγους· ὄγδοον δέ, ἐκ τοῦ μὴ ἀποκρίνεσθαι περὶ ὧν οὐκ ἐρωτᾶται ἐν ἀγωγῇ. Καὶ ὁ ἔχων ταύτας τὰς ὀκτὼ ἀρετὰς προξενεῖ ἑαυτῷ τὰ ἀγαθὰ καὶ ἔσεται ἀπὸ πάσης βλάβης ἀνώτερος, καὶ δεῖ τὸν τοιοῦτον ἀντιλαμβάνεσθαι καὶ βοηθεῖν εἰς πάντα τὰ ἑαυτοῦ θελήματα. Αὗται τοίνυν αἱ ὀκτὼ ἀρεταὶ εἰς σὲ πεπλήρωνται. Καὶ τῷ Θεῷ εὔχομαι, ὅπως σε βοηθήσῃ ἐπιτυχεῖν ὧν ζητεῖς. Ὃ δέ μοι ἀνήγγειλας, εἰς μέγιστόν σοι φθόνον ἐνέβαλε, καὶ ἐπικίνδυνόν ἐστι τοῦ τοιούτου ἐπιτυχεῖν. Ἀλλ' ὅμως ἡ τοῦ Θεοῦ ἐπικουρία βοηθήσει ἡμῖν."

6 Ἰδὼν δὲ ὁ Περζουὲ ὅτι ἀπεκαλύφθησαν πάντα τὰ ἐν τῇ καρδίᾳ αὐτοῦ τῷ Ἰνδεῖ, καὶ ὅτι οὐ δολερά ἐστιν ἡ φιλία αὐτοῦ πρὸς αὐτόν, διὰ τὸ μηδενὸς ῥήματος σκωπτικοῦ ἢ ἀκαίρου φθεγξαμένου τὸ παράπαν αὐτοῦ, ἀλλ' ὥσπερ τινὶ τῶν γνησιωτάτων ἀδελφῶν μετ' ἐπιεικίας ἀποκρινομένου, ἔλαβε θάρρος εὔδρομον τὸ πέρας ἀναφανῆναι τῆς ἐπιθυμίας αὐτοῦ.

7 Λέγει οὖν πάλιν πρὸς αὐτὸν ὁ Ἰνδύς· "Ἰδοὺ πολλάς σοι ἐνεστησάμην παγίδας πρὸς τὸ συλῆσαι λόγον ἐκ τοῦ σοῦ στόματος, κατέλαβον δέ σου ἐκ τῶν μικρῶν ῥημάτων τὰ μέγιστα, καὶ ἐκ τῶν φανερῶν τὰ κρυπτά. Καὶ μεγάλως

trusty friends; fifth, from prudently spending his days in the king's portals, and meeting all the king's people with flattery and elegant speech. Sixth, from concealing his own secrets and not sharing them with malicious and wicked men; seventh, from guarding his own tongue against saying foolish or hurtful words; eighth, from not responding to things he has not been asked about concerning his conduct. The man who possesses these eight virtues secures for himself what is good, and will be beyond all harm, and one should help and assist such a man in all his wishes. So, these eight virtues are realized in you. And I pray to God that he will help you get what you are seeking. But what you have told me makes you the object of the greatest ill will, and getting hold of something like this is dangerous. However, God's help will assist us."

Perzoué saw that everything in his heart was plainly re- 6
vealed to the Indian, and that the latter's friendship toward him was not feigned, since he said nothing at all that was in any way mocking or inappropriate, but was answering fairly, as if to one of his truest brothers. So he swiftly took courage to reveal the object of his desire.

Then the Indian spoke to him again, saying: "Look, I set 7
many traps for you to steal the words out of your mouth, and I understood your big secrets from little words, and what was hidden from what you revealed. And I was delighted by

ἠδύνθην τῆς σῆς γνώσεως καὶ παιδεύσεως ἕνεκα, ἥν σοι ὁ Θεὸς ἐδωρήσατο. Καὶ γὰρ ὁ σοφός, ὅταν τι μυστήριον προτεθήσεται αὐτῷ, καὶ λάβῃ τὴν αὐτοῦ ζήτησιν ἐκ τοῦ παραθέντος, ὡμοίωται ἀνθρώπῳ οἰκοδομήσαντι τὴν αὐτοῦ οἰκίαν ἐπὶ στερεὰν πέτραν, ἥτις πλεονάσαντος ὑετοῦ οὐ σαλεύεται, ἢ ἐν ὄρει, ἥτις παρὰ τῶν ἐμπνεόντων ἀνέμων ἐκεῖσε οὐ πίπτει. Καὶ οὐχ ὑπάρχει τι κρεῖττον φιλίας καθαρᾶς καὶ ἀγάπης, καὶ ὁ ἔχων ταύτην ἄξιός ἐστι κοινωνεῖν τῷ ἑαυτοῦ φίλῳ ἄχρι καὶ θανάτου αὐτοῦ, καὶ μὴ κρύπτειν αὐτῷ τι. Καὶ πρῶτον μὲν ἀρετὴ παιδεύσεως ὑπάρχει τὸ φυλάττειν μυστήρια, εἰ τάχα δὲ καὶ οὐ κρύπτονται. Καὶ γὰρ ὁπόταν ἐν δυσὶν ἀνθρώποις ῥηθῇ μυστήριον, ἴσως καὶ ἐν τρισίν, καὶ ὅταν ἐν τοῖς τρισὶ γένηται, φανεροῦται τοῖς πᾶσι, καὶ οὐ δύναταί τις κρύψαι αὐτό, καὶ ὥσπερ νέφος ἐσκορπισμένον ἐστί. Πλὴν ἐγὼ χαίρω δὴ καὶ εὐφραίνομαι ἐπὶ τῇ σῇ φιλίᾳ· καὶ τὸ πρᾶγμα τοῦτο ὅπερ ζητεῖς ἀπ' ἐμοῦ μυστικῶς, ἀναγκαῖόν ἐστι μὴ φανῆναι πᾶσιν ἀνθρώποις. Ὁπόταν γὰρ ἀποκαλυφθήσεται, τότε ἀπώλειά μοι γενήσεται τελεία, καὶ οὔτε πλοῦτος οὔτε φιλία δύναταί με σῶσαι· ὁ γὰρ ἡμέτερος βασιλεὺς θρασὺς καὶ θηριώδης ἐστί, καὶ κολάζει περὶ μικροῦ πράγματος."

8 Λέγει οὖν αὐτῷ ὁ Περζουέ· "Οἱ τῆς φιλίας διδάσκαλοι μεγάλως ἐπαινοῦσι καὶ δοξάζουσι τοὺς τὰ μυστήρια τῶν φίλων αὐτῶν κρύπτοντας καὶ παραφυλάσσοντας, εἰ καὶ ἐπώδυνά εἰσι καὶ ἐπικίνδυνα. Οὕτω κἀγὼ θαρρήσας, πεποιθώς εἰμι τοῦ πέρας λαβεῖν ὅπερ σοι μυστήριον ἐνεθέμην. Καὶ γὰρ μέγα καὶ ἔνδοξόν ἐστι τὸ τοιοῦτον, κἂν μετὰ φόβου ἐκπληροῖς μοι τοῦτο. Πλὴν ἐγὼ γινώσκω, ὅτι

the knowledge and education that God had given you. For the wise man, when some secret is put in front of him and he takes up the investigation of it from the one who suggested it to him, is like a man who has built his house on a solid rock, for this is not shaken after excessive rain or, if it is on a mountain, does not fall down because of the winds that blow there. For there is nothing better than pure friendship and love, and whoever possesses this should share with his friend even until death itself, and not hide anything from him. For the prime virtue of education is keeping secrets, even if, eventually, nothing remains hidden. For whenever a secret is spoken of between two people, and equally so among three, when this happens among three it becomes known to all and no one is able to keep it hidden, and it resembles a scattered cloud. However, I am glad of your friendship and happy with it, but this thing that you are trying to obtain secretly from me must not be revealed to anyone. For as soon as it were to be revealed, then my ruin would be complete and neither riches nor friendship could save me, for our king is rash and savage and punishes the least thing."

So Perzoué said to him: "The teachers of friendship glo- 8
rify and are full of praise for those who keep their friends' secrets hidden and closely guarded, even if these are painful and dangerous. So I too have become bold, and I am confident that the secret which I have entrusted to you will achieve its end. For this is something that is great and important, even if you do it for me with fear. Anyway, I

ἀβλαβὴς ἔσῃ ἕνεκεν ἐμοῦ. Μόνον βλέπε τοὺς συμπολίτας σου, μὴ δι' αὐτῶν τι φανερωθῇ. Ἀλλ' ἰδοὺ ἐλπίζω εἰς ὃν ἤδη τὴν ἀρχὴν ἀνεθέμεθα, ὅτι ἐμοῦ ἀπερχομένου, σοῦ δὲ ἐνταῦθα προσμένοντος, οὐ γνωσθήσεται. Μεταξὺ γὰρ ἐμοῦ καὶ σοῦ ἄλλος οὐ κεκοινώνηται, εἰ μὴ Θεός, καὶ ἐμοῦ ἀποδημοῦντος, ἄφοβος ἔσῃ."

9 Ἀκούσας δὲ ὁ Ἰνδὺς ταῦτα παρέσχεν αὐτῷ τὰ ζητούμενα βιβλία. Καὶ ποιήσας ἐκεῖσε χρόνον ἱκανόν, καὶ δαπανήσας πάνθ' ὅσα ἐπεφέρετο, καὶ κατατήξας τὸ σῶμα αὐτοῦ ἐν πολλῷ κόπῳ καὶ μόχθῳ καὶ ἐγρηγόρσει, μάλιστα διὰ τὸν τοῦ βασιλέως φόβον, ἀπεπλήρωσε τὸ βιβλίον καὶ ἄλλα τινὰ βιβλία βιωφελῆ. Γράφει οὖν ἔκτοτε πρὸς τὸν αὐτοῦ βασιλέα Ἀνασουράνον, ὅσον τε ὑπέστη κόπον καὶ ὅπως ἀπεπλήρωσε τὴν αὐτοῦ πρόσταξιν, περαιώσας τὸ αὐτοῦ καταθύμιον. Μαθὼν δὲ ταῦτα ὁ βασιλεὺς καὶ περιχαρὴς γενόμενος λίαν, αὐτίκα γράφει πρὸς τὸν Περζουέ, ἀποστείλας αὐτῷ καὶ χρήματα τοῦ ταχέως παραγενέσθαι πρὸς αὐτόν, μήπως διὰ τῆς μακροημερίας συμβήσεται αὐτῷ τι καὶ στερηθήσεται τοῦ ζητουμένου. Ηὐχαρίστησε δὲ τῷ Θεῷ τῷ χορηγήσαντι καὶ δωρησαμένῳ αὐτῷ τὴν τῶν Ἰνδικῶν βιβλίων ἀπόλαυσιν· ὑπέσχετο δὲ αὐτῷ καὶ ἀνταμείψεσι πολλῶν καὶ μεγίστων χαρίτων τὴν τούτου προθυμίαν ἀφοσιώσασθαι, τούς τε κόπους ἐν διπλῷ ἀπολαβεῖν περὶ ὧν ὑπέμεινε κακοπαθειῶν.

10 Ἀναγνοὺς δὲ ὁ Περζουὲ τὰ τοῦ βασιλέως αὐτοῦ γράμματα, εὐθὺς πρὸς τὴν Περσικὴν ἤρξατο ὁδεύειν ὁδόν. Καταλαβὼν δὲ τὴν Περσίαν, ὑπεμνήσθη τῷ βασιλεῖ περὶ αὐτοῦ· καὶ προσκαλεσάμενος αὐτόν, ὑπεδέξατο αὐτὸν

know that you will not be harmed because of me. Just watch your fellow citizens, in case anything is revealed by them. And look, I hope that what we have already set in motion will not be made known, because I'm going away but you are remaining here. For in the meantime no one else but me and you is in on this, except God; and when I'm gone, you won't be afraid."

When the Indian heard this, he provided Perzoué with 9 the books he sought. And after Perzoué had passed a long time there, had spent all that he had brought with him, and had worn himself out physically with a lot of hard work, toil, and vigilance, especially out of fear of the king, he finished copying the book, along with some other books that were helpful in life. He then wrote to his own king, Anasouranos, telling him how much hard work he had undertaken and how he had fulfilled his mission by carrying out what the king had intended. When the king learned this, he was very happy and immediately wrote back to Perzoué. He also sent Perzoué money so that he could quickly return to him, in case, through delay, something might happen to him and he would be robbed of what he sought. The king also thanked God, who had provided him with the Indian books and given him the pleasure of them. And he promised Perzoué that he would formally recognize his enthusiastic engagement in this enterprise with many great favors, and that he would be compensated for his labors twice over, in light of the suffering he had endured for them.

When Perzoué read the letter from his king, he at once 10 began the journey back to Persia. After he had arrived there, he reminded the king about himself, and the king summoned him and received him with joy, saying: "Wel-

χαρμοσύνως, καὶ λέγει αὐτῷ· "Χαίροις, δοῦλε πιστέ· καὶ γὰρ πάντα τὰ παρ' ἐμοῦ ὑποσχεθέντα σοι ἔχεις, δωρούμενός σοι πρὸς τούτοις καὶ πλείονα ὑπὲρ ὧν ὑπέστης κόπων τε καὶ κινδύνων." Κελεύει δὲ αὐτὸν ἡμέρας ἑπτὰ οἴκοι καταμένειν καὶ ἀνάπαυλαν γενέσθαι τῶν κόπων αὐτοῦ. Μετὰ δὲ τὴν τούτων παρέλευσιν, προσκαλεσάμενος αὐτὸν καὶ πᾶσαν τὴν σύγκλητον καὶ τὸν ὑπ' αὐτῷ σύμπαντα λαόν, καὶ ἀνοίξας τὰ βιβλία ἅπερ ἐκόμισεν, ἀνεγνώσθησαν ἔμπροσθεν αὐτοῦ καὶ πάντων ἐνώπιον. Καὶ ἀκούσαντες πάντες καὶ θαυμάσαντες τήν τε σοφίαν καὶ τὴν παίδευσιν, ἥνπερ διὰ γλώττης τῶν ἀλόγων ζῴων καὶ πετεινῶν ἐλάλησεν, καὶ τῷ Θεῷ προσηκόντως εὐχαριστήσαντες τῷ δωρησαμένῳ τῷ τε βασιλεῖ καὶ αὐτοῖς τοιαύτην σοφίαν καὶ παίδευσιν, ἀπονείμαντες καὶ τῷ Περζουὲ χάριν ὑπὲρ ὧν ἐπόνησε καὶ ἐμόχθησε, τότε κελεύει ὁ βασιλεὺς ἀνεῳχθῆναι πάντα τὰ αὐτοῦ βεστιάρια τῶν τε μαργάρων καὶ λίθων καὶ χρυσίου αὐτοῦ καὶ πάντων τῶν ὑφασμάτων καὶ τῶν λοιπῶν, καὶ μεθ' ὅρκων προστάσσει αὐτὸν πάνθ' ὅσα καὶ βούλεται ἀπολαβεῖν.

11 Ὁ δὲ Περζουέ, καίπερ νουνεχὴς ὢν καὶ σωφρόνως διάγων, προσκυνήσας αὐτὸν καὶ εὐχαριστήσας δι' ὧν παρ' αὐτοῦ εὐηργέτητο, ἔφη· "Ὁ Θεὸς ὁ χαρισάμενός σοι, ἐνδοξότατε βασιλεῦ, τὴν ἐνταῦθα μεγίστην δόξαν, αὐτός σοι καὶ τὴν αἰωνίζουσαν καὶ ἀεὶ διαμένουσαν βασιλείαν καὶ δόξαν χαρίσοιτο. Ἐγὼ δὲ ὁ δοῦλός σου, οὐ χρεία μοί ἐστί τις περὶ τῶν τοῦ κόσμου τούτου πραγμάτων, ἀλλ' ἀρκεῖ μοι πρὸς δῶρα ἡ χορηγηθεῖσά μοι παρὰ τῆς σῆς βασιλείας τιμή. Ἀλλὰ διὰ τὸ ἀρέσαι, αἰτοῦμαι μίαν πῆχυν ἐκ τῶν

come, *faithful servant,* for although you have everything that I promised you, I am also giving you more, in addition to those things, for the labors and the dangers you have undertaken." He ordered Perzoué to stay at home for seven days to rest from his labors. After this time had passed, he summoned him, together with the whole senate and all his subjects and, after opening the books that Perzoué had brought, they were read aloud in front of him and in the presence of everyone. All who heard were amazed at the wisdom and instruction that this man spoke through the tongue of irrational animals and birds, and they duly thanked God who had given such wisdom and instruction both to the king and themselves; and they also thanked Perzoué for what he had labored at and toiled to achieve. Then the king ordered that all his vaults of pearls, of precious stones, of his gold, of all his robes, and of everything else should be opened, and he commanded Perzoué with oaths to take everything he wanted.

So Perzoué, although he was sensible and lived modestly, 11
prostrated himself before the king and thanked him for the kindness that had been shown by him, and said, "May God, who has himself bestowed on you, most glorious king, the greatest earthly glory, also bestow on you an everlasting and eternal kingdom and glory. I am your servant and have no need of any of the things of this world; rather, the honor bestowed upon me by your royal highness is gift enough for me. But, to please you, I ask to take one cubit of the cloth

ὑφασμάτων τῆς χώρας Φουϊστὰν λαβεῖν, ὅπως δι' αὐτῆς δοξασθήσομαι ὑπὸ πάσης τῆς συγγενείας μου." Καὶ λαβὼν ταύτην καὶ εὐχαριστήσας τῷ βασιλεῖ εἶπεν· "*Εἰς τὸν αἰῶνα ζήσεται* ἡ βασιλεία σου, ὅτι ἀπέλαβον τὰς παρ' αὐτῆς δωρηθείσας μοι χάριτας. Δεῖ γὰρ τὸν νουνεχῆ ἄνθρωπον εὐχαριστεῖν, ὁπόταν δωρηθήσηται αὐτῷ τι, κἂν ὡς ἄξιος λάβῃ αὐτό. Ἐγὼ δὲ εὐχαριστῶ τῇ μεγίστῃ βασιλείᾳ σου, καὶ δέομαι τῷ μεγαλοδώρῳ Θεῷ τοῦ ἐν ὑγείᾳ καὶ εὐσταθείᾳ διάγειν αὐτήν. Πλὴν μικρᾶς αἰτήσεως χάριν αἰτῶ παρὰ τῆς βασιλείας σου δωρηθῆναί μοι· καὶ αὕτη πρός με μεγάλη ἐστὶ καὶ ἔνδοξος."

12 Λέγει αὐτῷ ὁ βασιλεύς· "Αἴτησον ὅπερ βούλει· καὶ γάρ μοι δεκτέον ἐστὶ τὸ παρά σου αἴτημα, ὁποῖον τυγχάνει, καὶ οὐκ ἀποπεμφθῇς, εἰ τῶν ἡμίσεων αὐτῆς μοι τῆς βασιλείας αἰτήσεις. Ἄξια γάρ σοι καὶ ταῦτα τυγχάνει, δι' οὕσπερ ὑπέστης κόπους διὰ τὸ πληρωτὴν ἀποδειχθῆναί σε τῆς ἡμετέρας ἐφέσεως." Καὶ ὁ Περζουὲ πρὸς αὐτόν· "Ὁ Θεός, βασιλεῦ, ἀξίους ἐπιδώσει σοι τοὺς μισθούς, ὅτι καὶ ἀνάξιον ὄντα με τοιαύτας ἐπαμείβεις μοι δωρεάς τε καὶ χάριτας. Νῦν οὖν μοι καὶ εἰς ἔργον ἀφοσίου τὴν αἴτησιν· προστάξεις καὶ γάρ μου τὸ ὄνομα ἐν τοῖς πίναξι γραφῆναι τοῖς σοῖς παρὰ τοῦ Παρζετζεμχὰρ τοῦ υἱοῦ Πακτακίου καὶ Πασχητικῆς, ὅπως τὰ συμβάντα μοι καὶ ἅπερ ὑπέστην μὴ λήθῃ τῷ χρόνῳ παραδοθήσεται, ἀλλ' ἐν τοῖς πίναξι τοῦ βιβλίου τούτου τεθήσεσθαι τοῦ *Κιλίλε καὶ Δίμνε,* ὅπως ἀναφέρωμαι ἐν αὐτοῖς πάντοτε, καὶ μετὰ θάνατόν μου εἰς δόξαν ἔσται ἐμὴν καὶ παντὸς τοῦ γένους μου."

13 Ἀκούσας δὲ ταῦτα ὁ βασιλεὺς καὶ οἱ ἄρχοντες αὐτοῦ,

from the land of Phouistan, so that through it I will be honored by all my family." Taking it, he thanked the king and said, "May your majesty *live forever,* since I received the gifts given to me by you. For a sensible person should give thanks whenever he is given something, even if he receives it deservedly. I also thank your very great majesty, and beseech the munificent God that you may live in strength and vigor. But I do request that the favor of a request be granted to me by your majesty, one that is small but that to me is great and splendid."

The king said to him, "Ask for whatever you wish, for I 12
must accept your request whatever it may be, and you will not be sent away, even if you ask for half of my kingdom itself. For you deserve that too, because of the labors you undertook to demonstrate that you were the person who could fulfill our desire." Perzoué replied to him, "My king, God will give you your just rewards, since, though I am unworthy, you are giving me such gifts and favors. So now fulfill my request by an act: order that my name be inscribed in the prologue by Parzetzemchar, the son of Paktakios and Paschetike, so that what happened to me and what I undertook will not be forgotten over time, but will be recorded in the prologue of this book of *Kelilai and Dimnai,* so that I may be recorded in it forever and that, after my death, it will be to my glory and that of all my family."

When they heard this, the king and his nobles were 13

ἐθαύμασαν τὴν τοῦ Περζουὲ νουνεχῆ καὶ ὑψηλὴν θεωρίαν καὶ πῶς ᾐτήσατο δόξαν ἐν τῷ σύμπαντι διαμένουσαν. Λέγει οὖν αὐτῷ ὁ βασιλεύς· "Ἡ αἴτησίς σου πληρωθήσεται ἀκωλύτως, καὶ γὰρ ἄξιος εἶ τοῦ τοιούτου δωρήματος." Καὶ εὐθέως ἀποστείλας ὁ βασιλεὺς προσεκαλέσατο τὸν Παρζετζεμχάρ. Καὶ παραγενόμενος, λέγει αὐτῷ ὁ βασιλεύς· "Σὺ γινώσκεις τὴν τοῦ Περζουὲ πρὸς ἡμᾶς εὐγνωμοσύνην, καὶ ὅσους κόπους καὶ μόχθους ὑπέστη διὰ τὴν τοῦ τοιούτου βιβλίου ἀνάρρυσιν καὶ ἡμετέραν θεραπείαν. Ἠβουλήθην δὲ καὶ αὐτὸς ἀμείψασθαι αὐτὸν ἐκ τῶν οἰκείων χρημάτων, καὶ οὐκ ἠθέλησεν, ἀλλ' ᾐτήσατο εὔκολον ἀντάμειψιν τοῦ κόπου αὐτοῦ, τοῦ ἀπογραφῆναι αὐτὸν ἐν τοῖς πίναξι καὶ ἀναφέρεσθαι διὰ παντὸς ἐν αὐτοῖς. Ὅθεν καὶ γραφήτω παρὰ σοῦ ἐν ἀρχῇ τοῦ βιβλίου καὶ πάνθ' ὅσα πέπραχεν, ἐπαίνεσαί τε αὐτὸν κατὰ τὴν ἐνοῦσάν σοι δύναμιν. Ἐν γὰρ τῷ ἐγκωμίῳ αὐτοῦ καὶ σὺ οὐκ ἄμοιρος τῇ γραφῇ ἀναφανήσῃ, ἀλλὰ καὶ κοινωνὸς εἰς τὴν τοιαύτην ἀνάμνησιν ἔσῃ. Καὶ τελέσας τοῦτο ὑπόμνησον πρὸς ἡμᾶς, ὅπως ἐκκλησιάσαντες τήν τε σύγκλητον καὶ πάντα τὸν λαόν, ἀναγνωσθήσεται εἰς ἐπήκοον πάντων, καὶ γνώσονται τήν τε σοφίαν καὶ σύνεσιν καὶ τὴν παρὰ τῆς βασιλείας μου πρὸς αὐτὸν γεγενημένην εὐεργεσίαν." Ἀκούσας δὲ ταῦτα ὁ Περζουέ, καὶ ὅτι γε τοιαύτης δόξης τε καὶ τιμῆς τετύχηκε παρὰ τοῦ βασιλέως, προσεκύνησεν ἐνώπιον αὐτοῦ, καὶ μεγάλως εὐχαριστήσας ἐξῆλθεν.

14 Ὁ δέ γε Παρζετζεμχὰρ ἤρξατο γράφειν ἐν τοῖς πίναξι καὶ ἀναγράφειν πάντα τὰ τοῦ Περζουέ, ἀπό τε τῆς γεννήσεως αὐτοῦ καὶ τῆς μαθήσεως καὶ παιδεύσεως, καὶ

amazed at Perzoué's good sense and lofty reasoning, and at how he asked for everlasting glory. So the king said to him, "Your request will be fulfilled without delay, for you are worthy of such a gift." And the king immediately sent and summoned Parzetzemchar. When he arrived, the king said to him, "You are aware of Perzoué's loyalty to us, and what great labors and efforts he undertook for us in the recovery of this book and in our service. I myself wanted to compensate him from my own wealth, but he did not want this. He asked instead for this simple reward for his labor, that he be written into the preface and be remembered in it forever. So, let all that he has done be written down by you at the beginning of the book, and praise him to the best of your ability. For, you too will not be absent from what is written in his eulogy, but will also have a share in this commemoration. Let us know when you have finished, so that when the senate and all the people have been assembled, it will be read out in the hearing of all, so that they will know his wisdom and good sense, as well as the benefit that has come to him from my majesty." When Perzoué heard this, and that he had received such glory and honor from the king, he prostrated himself before him and, after thanking him profusely, departed.

So, indeed, Parzetzemchar started to write in the preface 14
and to record everything about Perzoué, of his birth and learning and education, and of when he was sent to India by

ἀφ' οὗπερ ἐστάλη παρὰ τοῦ βασιλέως εἰς τὴν Ἰνδίαν, καὶ πάντα τὰ συμβησόμενα αὐτῷ διὰ τὴν τῆς εὑρεθείσης βίβλου ἐξεύρεσιν. Ἐπαίνων τε ἀξίων ὡς ἐνὸν παρ' αὐτοῦ συγγραφέντων, ὅπως τε τῶν προσκαίρων πάντων καταφρονητὴν ἀναδειχθέντα, τῶν δὲ μελλόντων ἐπιποθήσαντα καὶ πάντα πληρώσαντα ὡς τῷ βασιλεῖ προώριστο, ὑπεμνήσθη αὐτῷ δὴ τῷ βασιλεῖ.

Καὶ προσκαλεσάμενος ὁ βασιλεὺς τούς τε ἄρχοντας αὐτοῦ καὶ τοὺς τῶν ἐνδόξων σοφοὺς σὺν τῷ Παρζετζεμχάρ, παραγενομένου δὲ καὶ τοῦ Περζουέ, καὶ ἀναγνωσθέντων τῶν γραφέντων ἐπὶ πάντων ἐνώπιον, καὶ περιχαρὴς ὁ βασιλεὺς γενόμενος, καὶ πάντες οἱ παρατυχόντες ἐπὶ τοῖς γραφεῖσι θαυμάσαντες τήν τε γνῶσιν τοῦ Παρζετζεμχάρ, καὶ ὅπως κατὰ τάξιν ἀψευδῆ τὰ τῶν ἐγκωμίων ἐγγέγραπται, καὶ μεγάλως αὐτόν τε ὁ βασιλεὺς καὶ πάντες εὐχαριστήσαντες, προσέταξε δοθῆναι αὐτῷ καὶ χάριτας ἀπό τε χρυσίου καὶ λίθων καὶ ὑφασμάτων. Ὁ δέ γε Περζουὲ εὐχαριστήσας τὸν Παρζετζεμχὰρ καὶ ἀσπασάμενος τὴν χεῖρα καὶ τὴν κεφαλὴν αὐτοῦ, καὶ τὸν βασιλέα δοξάσας, ἔφη· "Εἰς τοὺς αἰῶνας ζῆθι, πλουσιόδωρε βασιλεῦ, ὑπὲρ ὧν ἄρτι τετίμηκας καὶ ἐδόξασάς με καὶ ἠξίωσας ἀναφέρεσθαί μου τὸ ὄνομα ἐν τῇ βίβλῳ ταύτῃ μέχρι τῆς στάσεως τοῦδε τοῦ κόσμου· ὅθεν καὶ ἀξιωθείης τυχεῖν τῶν ἀνταμοιβῶν ἔν τε τῷ παρόντι αἰῶνι καὶ ἐν τῷ μέλλοντι. Καὶ ζῆθι ἐν πολλοῖς ἔτεσι μετὰ γαλήνης καὶ εὐφροσύνης καὶ χαρᾶς καὶ ἀγαλλιάσεως· ἡ γὰρ γλῶττά μου ἀδυνατεῖ πρὸς πλείονα εὐχαριστίαν καὶ ἔπαινον τῆς βασιλείας σου. Ὁ δὲ Θεὸς τῆς εἰρήνης ἔσται μετ' αὐτῆς εἰς τοὺς αἰῶνας. Ἀμήν."

the king, and everything that happened to him on account of the search for the book that had been found. This was composed by him with as much appropriate praise as possible, and how Perzoué had displayed disdain for all that is transitory but longed for what is in the future. Once he had accomplished everything as had been stipulated by the king, he informed the king himself.

The king then summoned his nobles and the wise among those of high repute, together with Parzetzemchar and, with Perzoué also present, what had been written was read out in the presence of all. The king was very pleased, and all present were amazed by what had been written, both at the knowledge of Parzetzemchar and at how the details of the eulogies had been correctly written in order. The king and everyone else thanked him profusely, and the king ordered that he should be given gifts of thanks of gold, precious stones, and cloth. Perzoué also thanked Parzetzemchar, kissing his hand and his head, and when he had praised the king, he said, "May you live forever, munificent king, for the way in which you have now honored and praised me, and for having judged my name worthy to be remembered in this book until the end of the world; for this reason may you be judged worthy to obtain the same in the present age and in that to come. May you live for many years in peace, joy, pleasure, and happiness, for my tongue is unable to thank and praise your majesty any more. The God of peace will be with your majesty forever. Amen."

[Prologue B]

Βίβλος μυθικὴ μεταβληθεῖσα ἀπὸ γλώττης Ἰνδικῆς εἰς τὴν Περσικήν, ἀπὸ δὲ ταύτης εἰς τὴν Ἑλλάδα.

Ἡ παροῦσα βίβλος συνεγράφη παρὰ Ἰνδῶν ἀπό τε μύθων καὶ παραβολῶν καὶ λόγων ἀνθρώπων γνωστικῶν καὶ σοφῶν καὶ τὰ αὐτῶν τεχνουργήματα, καὶ πῶς ἐλάλησαν διὰ στόματος τῶν ἀλόγων ζῴων καὶ τῶν πετεινῶν, ἐκθέμενοι τὰ τοιαῦτα καλῶς, ὅπως γένωνται τοῖς μὲν σοφοῖς γνῶσις καὶ σύνεσις, τοῖς δὲ ἄφροσιν, ὡς κἀγώ, γέλοιά τε καὶ παίγνια, τοῖς δὲ νεομαθέσι καὶ νέοις καὶ τοῖς ἄλλοις πᾶσι τοῖς βουλομένοις ἐν προθυμίᾳ μανθάνειν καὶ εὐκόλως ταῦτα ἀποστοματίζειν ὠφέλειά τε καὶ παίδευσις, ἵν' ὅταν τέλειοι γένωνται, ἐκ τῶν τοιούτων παραδειγμάτων κυβερνήσωσιν ἑαυτούς, ὡς οἱ εὑρίσκοντες θησαυρούς, πολὺ τιμιώτερα ἢ ὥσπερ ὁ παρὰ γονέων καταλειφθεὶς θησαυρὸς τοῖς παισὶν αὐτῶν, ἵνα μὴ ἐνδεεῖς ἔσονται τοῦ λοιποῦ, ἀλλὰ καὶ ἄμοχθοι.

2 Ἡ γὰρ ὁδὸς καὶ ῥίζα τῆς διδαχῆς πολυειδής ἐστι καὶ πολύτροπος, καθώσπερ παρὰ τῶν ἐν δυνάμει λόγου τε καὶ σοφίας τῇ γραφῇ παρεδόθη πρὸς ὠφέλειαν πάντων τῶν ἐντυγχανόντων αὐτοῖς. Ὅθεν καὶ δέον ἐστὶ τοῖς ἀναγινώ-

Prologue B

A book of fables, translated from the Indian language into Persian, and from that into Greek.

The present book was compiled by Indians from fables, parables, and the words of enlightened and wise men, to judge by their works, and how they spoke through the mouths of dumb beasts and birds. These things they set out well, so that there might be knowledge and good sense in them for the wise, laughter and amusement for the foolish like me, and profit and education for the recently educated, the young, and anyone else wishing eagerly to learn and readily commit these things to memory. Thus, when they are grown up, such people, like those who find treasure, may conduct themselves in a manner more worthy than that afforded by a treasure left by parents to their children so that they will not be in need in the future, but will even be comfortably off.

For the path and foundation of education is diverse and 2
varied, as it was committed to writing by those who had authority in words and wisdom for the benefit of all those who read it. For this reason, the readers of this book must

σκουσι τήνδε τὴν βίβλον ἐπιγνῶναι καὶ τὴν ἐγκειμένην δύναμιν τῶν ῥημάτων τῶν λόγων αὐτῆς, καὶ δι' ἣν αἰτίαν ἐγράφη καθ' ἓν κεφάλαιον καὶ μὴ παρέργως καὶ ὡς μυθικὰ παρατρέχειν αὐτά, ἀλλὰ μᾶλλον γινώσκειν, ἃ ἀναγινώσκει· ὁ γὰρ μὴ γινώσκων ἅπερ διὰ χειλέων ἐκφέρεται ῥήματα, καταγινώσκειν ἑαυτὸν δεῖ, ὅτι ζημιοῦται τὸν ἐγκείμενον ἐν τοῖς τοιούτοις νοῦν, καὶ ματαία καὶ ἀνωφελὴς γενήσεται ἡ τοῦ τοιούτου ἀνάγνωσις καὶ διάγνωσις.

3 *Περὶ ἄφρονος ἀνδρὸς τοῦ εὑρόντος θησαυρόν.*

Καὶ ὁμοιωθήσεται ἀνθρώπῳ, ὃς ἀνελθὼν ἐν μιᾷ τῶν ἡμερῶν ἔν τινι ὄρει, καὶ εὑρὼν ἐκεῖσε μέγιστον σκεῦος χρυσίου πλῆρες καὶ λίθων τιμίων, εἶπεν ἐν ἑαυτῷ· "Πορεύσομαι καὶ ἐρωτήσω τινὶ τῶν σοφῶν ἀνθρώπων, πῶς τὸν τοιοῦτον θησαυρὸν καὶ ἐν τίνι τρόπῳ πρὸς τὸν ἐμὸν οἶκον ἀγαγεῖν δυνήσομαι." Στραφεὶς δὲ πάλιν εἰς τὴν ἑαυτοῦ ἀφροσύνην καὶ ματαιότητα, ἀναλογισάμενος εἶπεν ἐν ἑαυτῷ· "Οἵαν ματαιότητα ἐγὼ ὁ ἄνους ἐλογισάμην ποιῆσαι· καὶ γὰρ εἰ οὕτως εἶχον διαπράξασθαι ὁ ἄθλιος, μερίδα εἶχον εἰσπράττεσθαι παρὰ τοῦ ὁδηγήσαντός μοι. Οὐχὶ κρεῖττόν ἐστιν ἐμοὶ μόνῳ ταῦτα φυλάξαι ἢ μετ' ἄλλου τινὸς μερίσαι;" Πορευθεὶς τοίνυν ὁ τοιοῦτος μωρὸς καὶ ἄπληστος πλεονέκτης, καὶ τῷ ἰδίῳ καὶ ἀναισθήτῳ λογισμῷ μελετήσας, εὗρε τοὺς ἐπὶ τοῖς ὤμοις ἐξ ἔθους βαστάζοντας, καὶ λέγει αὐτοῖς· "Δεῦτε, ἀγαπητοί, μετ' ἐμοῦ πρὸς ὃν ἐπιφέρω ὑμᾶς τόπον, καὶ λάβετε τὸν μισθὸν τοῦ κόπου ὑμῶν." Οἱ δὲ ὠμοφόροι εἶπον αὐτῷ· "Ὅπου βούλει

recognize the inherent power in the phrasing of its words, and why it was written chapter by chapter, and not just carelessly rush through them because they are fables; but rather you must try to understand what you read. For someone who does not understand the phrases produced by his lips in speech should censure himself because he is missing the sense inherent in the words, and the reading and analysis of such a person will be of no benefit and a waste of time.

About a foolish man who found a treasure. 3

He will be like a man who climbed a mountain one day and, when he found a large vessel full of gold and precious stones there, said to himself, "I'll go and ask one of the wise men how and in what way I can transport such a treasure to my house." But, relapsing into his foolishness and stupidity, he reconsidered the matter and said to himself, "Silly me, what sort of stupidity did I think of doing? For if I had done that, I, poor wretch, would have had to pay a share to the person who gave me guidance. Isn't it better to keep these things for myself alone than share them with someone else?" So, as he was such a stupid, insatiable, and greedy fellow, he went on his way and, after he had turned it over in his own witless mind, he found porters who were used to carrying loads on their shoulders, and said to them, "Come with me, dear friends, to the place I'm taking you to, and receive the wages for your labor." The porters replied to him, "We'll go

πορευσόμεθα.” Τότε παραλαβὼν ἐκ τῶν τοιούτων ὡσεὶ δέκα ἄνδρας, ἐπορεύθη μετ’ αὐτῶν ἐν τῷ τόπῳ, ἐν ᾧ ἦν ὁ θησαυρὸς ἐκεῖνος, ὃν ὁ προρρηθεὶς ἀνούστατος ἐκεῖνος ἀνὴρ εὗρεν.

4 Ἀνοίξας αὐτὸν ἔφη αὐτοῖς· “Δεῦτε, φίλοι, πληρώσατε τοὺς σάκκους ὑμῶν ἐκ τοῦδε τοῦ χρυσίου καὶ τῶν τιμίων λίθων, καὶ βαστάσαντες ἅπαντες κομίσατε ταῦτα πάντα ἐν τῇ τοῦ οἴκου μου εὐρυχωρίᾳ.” Ταῦτα οἱ ὠμοφόροι παρὰ τοῦ ἀνοήτου ἐκείνου καὶ πλεονέκτου ἀκούσαντες ἐχάρησαν χαρὰν μεγάλην καὶ εἶπον ἐν ἑαυτοῖς· “Ὦ ἄνδρες σοφώτατοι, εὖ ἂν ἔχοι, καὶ ἡδέως τὸ προσταχθὲν ποιήσωμεν.” Καὶ εὐθέως ἐμπλήσαντες τοὺς σάκκους αὐτῶν ἔκ τε τοῦ χρυσίου καὶ τῶν τιμίων λίθων ἔφησαν τῷ ἀνοήτῳ ἐκείνῳ ἀνδρὶ καὶ πλεονέκτῃ· “Κύριε, πάνσοφε ἀνήρ, εἰ κελεύεις, ἄκουσον τῆς σοφῆς ἡμῶν συμβουλῆς, <ἵνα μὴ ἀπολέσωμεν τὸν παρόντα θησαυρόν>.” Ὁ δὲ πρὸς αὐτοὺς ἀπεκρίνατο· “Ἵνα τί μοι τὰ τοιαῦτα οὐ λέγετε; Διὰ τοῦτο καὶ γὰρ ὑμᾶς ἐνταῦθα ἤνεγκα, ἵνα μηδεὶς ἐξ αὐτῶν τῶν θησαυρῶν ὄληται.” Καὶ λέγουσιν αὐτῷ ἐκεῖνοι· “Κύριε, μὴ πορευθῶμεν ὁμοῦ πάντες, ἵνα μή τις ἐκ τῶν ὑπερεχόντων ἡμᾶς θεωρήσας κατανοήσῃ ὅτι ταῦτα ἐν τῷ οἴκῳ σου ἐπιφέρομεν, καὶ ἀπολοῦνται ταῦτα τὰ ἀγαθὰ ἐκ τῆς ὑμετέρας σοφίας· ἀλλὰ μᾶλλον εἷς καθεὶς πορευθῶμεν ἐν τῷ οἴκῳ σου, σὺ δὲ περιφύλαξον τὸν τόπον, ὅθεν ἐξῆλθεν ὁ θησαυρὸς μέχρις ἂν πορευθέντες αὖθις πρὸς σὲ μετὰ σπουδῆς ὑποστρέψωμεν.” Ἤρεσε δὲ αὕτη ἡ βουλὴ τῷ ἀπλήστῳ ἐκείνῳ καὶ πλεονέκτῃ, καὶ εἶπεν αὐτοῖς· “Καλῶς εἴπατε, καὶ οὕτω γενέσθω.” Τότε ἄραντες ἕκαστος τὸν σάκκον

wherever you want." Then, taking about ten men from among them, he went with them to the place where that treasure was, which this previously mentioned most silly man had found.

After he had opened it up, he said to them, "Come, 4
friends, and fill your sacks with this gold and these precious stones; lift everything up and take it all to the empty room in my house." When the porters heard these words from that witless and greedy man, they were overjoyed and said to themselves, "May it go well for us, the wisest of men, and let us gladly do what we've been asked." They immediately filled their sacks with the gold and precious stones, and said to that witless and greedy man, "Sir, most wise man, please, listen to our wise advice so that we don't lose the treasure that is here." He replied to them, "Why don't you tell me this? For this was why I brought you here, so none of these treasures would get lost." They said to him, "Sir, we shouldn't all travel together in case someone in authority should see us and realize that we're taking these things to your house, and these good things be lost by your wise self. But instead, let us go one by one to your house while you keep watch over the place where the treasure came from until we come back again and quickly return to you." That insatiable and greedy man liked this advice, and he said to them, "Well said, let's do that." Then each one carried away his sack filled

αὐτοῦ πεπληρωμένον χρυσίου καὶ λίθων τιμίων, ἐπορεύθη ἔνθα ἂν ἠβουλήθη.

Ἑσπέρας δὲ ἤδη γενομένης, καὶ ὁ μωρὸς ἐκεῖνος ἀνὴρ στραφεὶς ἐν τῷ οἴκῳ αὐτοῦ μετὰ χαρᾶς καὶ εὐφροσύνης λέγει τῇ γυναικὶ αὐτοῦ· "Δεῖξόν μοι, ὦ γύναι, ποῦ κατέθηκας τὸ χρυσίον καὶ τοὺς τιμίους λίθους, οὓς οἱ ὠμοφόροι ἐνθάδε προσήνεγκαν, ὅπως ἴδωμεν μή τι ἐξ αὐτῶν ἐνοσφίσαντο." Ἡ δὲ γυνὴ ἐν ἐκστάσει γενομένη ἔφη αὐτῷ· "Καὶ τί ἐστι, κύριε, ὅπερ μοι λαλεῖς;" Ὁ δὲ ἔφη· "Ἅπερ ἤκουσας." Ἡ δέ· "Οὔτε ἤκουσα, κύριε, οὔτε τοῖς ὀφθαλμοῖς μου εἶδον, οὔτε ταῖς χερσί μου ἡψάμην." Ὁ δὲ ἀνὴρ αὐτῆς ἔκθαμβος γενόμενος εἶπε πρὸς αὐτήν· "Μὴ οὐκ ἔστειλά σοι σήμερον μετὰ τῶν ὠμοφόρων πλεῖον ἢ χίλια καὶ μυρία νομίσματα καὶ λίθους πολυτελεῖς;" Καὶ ἡ γυνή· "Οὐδαμῶς, κύριέ μου, ἀλλ' ὅσα μοι ἐρεῖς, ἀγνοῶ." Ἐκεῖνος δὲ ἐκπλαγεὶς ἐπὶ τῷ γεγονότι, ἔγνω ἑαυτὸν ἀπατηθέντα. Καὶ οὕτως ὁ τοῦ ἀνοήτου ἐκείνου καὶ πλεονέκτου οἶκος ὑπελείφθη κενός, μηδὲν ὠφεληθείς, εἰ μὴ κόπους καὶ πόνους καὶ ἀγῶνας. Οὕτω δεῖ λοιπὸν καὶ τὸν ἀναγινώσκοντα τὸ βιβλίον τοῦτο γνῶναι καὶ τὴν ἐν κρυπτῷ ἑρμηνείαν αὐτοῦ, καὶ τὴν τοῦ ἑτέρου λόγου· εἰ γὰρ μὴ γνῷ τὴν δύναμιν, οὐδεμίαν ὠφέλειαν καὶ ἐκ τοῦ φανεροῦ λόγου ὀνηθήσεται, ὥσπερ δὴ καὶ ὁ ἔχων κάρυα, ἐὰν μὴ κλάσῃ ταῦτα, οὐδέν τι ὀνηθήσεται παρ' αὐτῶν.

with gold and precious stones, and went wherever he wanted.

When evening had already fallen, that stupid man returned home happily and cheerfully and said to his wife, "Woman, show me where you have stored the gold and precious stones that the porters brought here, so that we may see that they didn't steal any of it." His wife said to him in astonishment, "Sir, what's this that you're telling me?" And he said, "What you heard!" And she said, "Sir, I didn't hear anything, nor did I see anything with my eyes, nor touch anything with my hands." Her husband was astounded, and said to her, "Didn't I send more than eleven thousand *nomismata* and very valuable stones to you today by way of the porters?" And his wife: "Not at all, sir, and I don't understand any of what you're saying to me." He was aghast at what had occurred and realized he had been deceived. In this way the home of that witless and greedy man was left empty, and nothing was gained except trouble, toil, and anguish. So, then, someone who understands this book should also understand its hidden meaning, and that of the other story. For if he does not understand its significance, he will gain no benefit even from an obvious story, just as the person who has some nuts will get no benefit from them unless he cracks them open.

6 *Περὶ ἀνδρὸς ἀμαθοῦς.*

Ἔσται δὲ πάλιν, ὡς ἄνθρωπός τις ἐζήτει μαθεῖν λέξιν τινά, καὶ ἀπελθὼν πρός τινα τῶν ἑαυτοῦ φίλων ἔχων καὶ κίτρινον χαρτίον, ᾐτήσατο αὐτὸν ὅπως γράψῃ αὐτῷ λέξιν Ἀραβικήν. Καὶ γράψας δέδωκεν αὐτῷ ταύτην. Καὶ λαβὼν ἐκεῖνος τὸ χαρτίον ἀπῆλθεν εἰς τὸν οἶκον αὐτοῦ, καὶ ἀνεγίνωσκεν αὐτὴν ἀνερμηνεύτως, καὶ ἤρξατο μετὰ τῶν ἀνθρώπων ὁμιλεῖν, οἰόμενος μεμαθηκέναι τὴν λέξιν, καὶ λαλήσας μετ᾽ αὐτῶν ἔσφαλεν. Λέγουσιν αὐτῷ· "Ἔσφαλες, ὦ φίλε." Λέγει αὐτοῖς· "Ἔσφαλε καὶ ὁ κίτρινος χάρτης ὁ ἐν τῷ οἴκῳ μου." Διὰ τοῦτο δεῖ τὸν ἀναγινώσκοντα ἵνα γινώσκῃ τὸ ἀναγινωσκόμενον ἀκριβῶς, ὅπως διὰ τῆς γνώσεως αὐτοῦ παιδευθήσεται καὶ συνετὸς γενήσεται. Καὶ γὰρ δεῖ τὸν ἄνθρωπον μὴ παραδραμεῖν δύο πράγματα, ἀλλ᾽ ἐξ αὐτῶν πλεονάσαι, τὴν λέξιν καὶ τὴν τῶν μελλόντων ζήτησιν.

7 Ἐρρέθη δὲ ὅτι ἄνθρωπος δέεται ἐν τῇ ζωῇ αὐτοῦ δύο πραγμάτων, τήν τε γνῶσιν καὶ τὴν παίδευσιν· αὗται γὰρ καθαρίζουσι τὸν νοῦν· καὶ ὥσπερ τὸ ἔλαιον φωτίζει τὸν λύχνον, οὕτω καὶ ἡ παιδεία φωτίζει τὸν ἄνθρωπον καὶ ἡ γνῶσις σῴζει αὐτόν· καὶ ὃς ἔχει γνῶσιν καὶ μὴ κατ᾽ αὐτὴν πράξει, ζημιωθήσεται.

Περὶ ἀνδρὸς ἀμερίμνου.

Λέγεται γὰρ ὡς ἐρρέθη περί τινος ἀνθρώπου, ὅτι ἐν μιᾷ νυκτὶ εἰσῆλθε κλέπτης ἐν τῷ οἴκῳ αὐτοῦ· καὶ ἐξυπνισθεὶς

About an uneducated man. 6

Again, he will be like the man who wanted to learn a certain phrase, and who, taking a piece of yellow paper to one of his friends, asked his friend to write an Arabic phrase for him. The friend wrote it and gave it to him. The man took the piece of paper home with him and read it, but without understanding it. He began to talk to people, thinking that he had learned the phrase, and when he spoke with them, he made a mistake. They said to him, "You made a mistake, my friend," and he replied to them, "Then the yellow piece of paper in my house was also mistaken." For this reason the reader must understand exactly what he is reading, so that through its knowledge he will educate himself and become smart. For there are two things a person should not overlook, but rather develop: knowledge of language and inquiry about the future.

It has been said that a man needs two things in his life: 7
knowledge and education, for these purify the mind. And just as the oil illuminates a lamp, so education illuminates a man and knowledge saves him; and someone who has knowledge but does not act in accordance with it will suffer harm.

About a careless man.

For it is said that a story was told about a man, that one night a burglar got into his house. The man woke up, noticed

καὶ κατανοήσας αὐτὸν εἶπεν ἐν ἑαυτῷ· "Ἐάσω τοῦτον, ὅπως συνάξῃ πάντα ἅπερ κέκτημαι, καὶ εὐθέως εἰσπηδήσας κρατήσω αὐτόν, καὶ ἄχρηστον τοῦτον ποιήσω." Χρονίσας δὲ ἐν τῷ κοιτῶνι αὐτοῦ, ὕπνωσεν· ὁ δὲ κλέπτης συνάξας ἅπαντα τὸν αὐτοῦ βίον, ἀπέδρασεν. Ἀναστὰς δὲ ἀπὸ τοῦ ὕπνου κατεδίκαζεν ἑαυτόν, καὶ ὑπέλαβεν ὅτι ἡ αὐτοῦ γνῶσις εἰς οὐδὲν ἐγένετο διὰ τὸ μὴ προαρπάσαι αὐτὸν τὸν καιρὸν καὶ πρᾶξαι ὅπερ ἠβούλετο πρὸς τὸν κλέπτην· καὶ γὰρ ἡ γνῶσίς ἐστι δένδρον, ἡ δὲ πρᾶξις ὁ καρπὸς αὐτῆς. Οὕτω καὶ ὁ ζητῶν τὴν γνῶσιν ἕνεκα τῆς ἐξ αὐτῆς ὠφελείας μανθάνει ταύτην· εἰ δὲ μὴ ὠφεληθῇ ἐξ αὐτῆς, μάτην ἐπιζητεῖ αὐτήν.

8 Ὥσπερ γὰρ ἄνθρωπός τις ἰδὼν ἐπίφοβον ὁδόν, καὶ πορευθεὶς ἐν αὐτῇ ἐκινδύνευσεν, οὐχὶ γελασθήσεται καὶ καταμέμψονται πάντες τὴν μωρίαν αὐτοῦ; Ὁμοιοῦται δὲ ἀνθρώπῳ ἀκολουθοῦντι τὸ θέλημα αὐτοῦ καὶ μὴ προσέχοντι τὰ τῆς γνώσεως, ἢ ἀρρώστῳ θεωροῦντι βρώματα τὰ μὲν βλαβερὰ τὰ δὲ ἀβλαβῆ, <ὃς> καὶ νικώμενος ὑπὸ τῆς ἐπιθυμίας ἐσθίει τὰ βλαβερά, καὶ καταγελᾶται ὑπὸ τῶν εὖ φρονούντων. Ὡσαύτως καὶ ὁ γνωστικὸς ἄνθρωπος, ὁ γινώσκων τό τε ἀγαθὸν καὶ τὸ πονηρόν, καὶ καταλείψας τὸ ἀγαθόν, ποιήσας τὸ πονηρόν, καὶ ὑπὸ τῶν εὖ φρονούντων καταγελασθήσεται. Καθώσπερ δύο τινὲς περιπατοῦντες, ὁ εἷς τυφλός, ὁ δὲ ἕτερος ὑγιᾶ τὰ ὄμματα κεκτημένος, ἐὰν *ἀμφότεροι εἰς βόθυνον ἐμπεσοῦνται,* οὐχὶ μεμφθήσεται ὁ θεωρῶν πλεῖον; Καὶ πάλιν ὁ μανθάνων γνῶσιν δι' ἑτέρου ὠφέλειαν ὁμοιοῦται πηγῇ, ἥτις ὠφελεῖ ἑτέρους,

the burglar and said to himself: "I'll leave him to collect up all my possessions, then I'll immediately rush in, overpower him, and make him helpless." But while he was lingering in his bedroom, he fell asleep, and the burglar gathered up all the man's possessions and made his escape. When the man woke up from his sleep, he blamed himself and realized that his knowledge was of no use, because he had not seized the moment to do what he had wanted to the burglar. For knowledge is a tree, and action is its fruit. And so, a person who searches for knowledge for the sake of the benefit it brings gains knowledge, but unless he derives benefit from it, he seeks it in vain.

Just the same, will a man who saw a frightening road and 8
put himself in danger by traveling along it, not be laughed at, and will everyone not blame him for his stupidity? He is like a man who follows his desire and does not take heed of what he knows; or a sick person contemplating food, some of which is harmful and some not, who is overcome by his desire and eats what is harmful and thus is ridiculed by those who have good sense. In the same way, even the knowledgeable man, who understands both good and evil, but abandons what is good and does evil, will also be ridiculed by people of good sense. Just as if two people, one of whom is blind and the other has healthy eyes, *should both fall into a ditch* while walking around, would the one who can see not be blamed more? Again, someone who acquires knowledge in order to help someone else is like a well, which is of

ἑαυτὴν δὲ οὔ. Καὶ δέον τὸν ζητοῦντα γνῶσιν, πρῶτον μὲν παραινέσαι ἑαυτόν, εἶθ' οὕτως ἑτέρους διδάξαι· ὁ δὲ φιλόκοσμος, δέον αὐτῷ ἐπικτήσασθαι τρία τινὰ πράγματα, γνῶσιν, πλοῦτον, καὶ προαίρεσιν.

9 Ἐρρέθη δὲ ὅτι ὁ ζητῶν πράγματα καὶ μὴ γινώσκων τὴν ὠφέλειαν αὐτῶν, μάτην κοπιᾷ καὶ ἄφρων καλεῖται· ὅστις δὲ ἀναγινώσκει τὸ βιβλίον τοῦτο καὶ ἀγωνίζεται εἰς τὴν τούτου διδαχὴν καὶ μὴ πράττει κατὰ τὴν γνῶσιν αὐτοῦ, τυφλὸς καλεῖται. Καὶ δέον ἐστὶ τὸν νουνεχῆ ἄνθρωπον μὴ ζητεῖν βλάβην ἑτέρου πρὸς τὴν ἑαυτοῦ ὠφέλειαν· ὁ γὰρ ἀθετῶν τὸν ἑαυτοῦ φίλον ζημιωθήσεται καὶ πάθει καὶ αὐτὸς ὅπερ ἔπαθεν ἄνθρωπός τις.

10 *Περὶ τῶν δύο σησαμοπρατῶν.*

Ἐρρέθη γὰρ ὅτι δύο σησαμοπρᾶται εἶχον ἀποθήκην μίαν, πλὴν τὸ τοῦ ἑνὸς σησάμιον κεχωρισμένον ἦν ἀπὸ τοῦ ἑτέρου. Καὶ βουληθεὶς ὁ εἷς κλέψαι τὸ τοῦ ἑτέρου σησάμιον, ἔλαβε σινδόνα καὶ ἐσκέπασεν αὐτό· ἀπῆλθεν δὲ πρὸς ἕτερον φίλον αὐτοῦ καὶ εἶπεν· "Βούλομαι συλῆσαι τὸ τοῦ κοινωνοῦ μου σησάμιον καὶ ἔσται ἡμῖν κοινόν." Ἑσπέρας δὲ φθασάσης, ἐλθὼν ὁ κοινωνὸς καὶ ἰδὼν τὸν ἴδιον σήσαμον ἐσκεπασμένον τῇ σινδόνι τοῦ κοινωνοῦ αὐτοῦ, εἶπεν ἐν ἑαυτῷ ἀγαθῶς· "Ἴδε πόσον ἀγαθὸν ὁ συγκοινωνός μου καλῶς διατεθεὶς τὴν σήμερον ἐποιήσατό μοι σκεπάσας τὸν ἡμέτερον σήσαμον, τὸν δὲ ἴδιον ἀμελήσας· ἀλλ' ἄξιόν ἐστι κἀμὲ ἆραι τὴν σινδόνα αὐτοῦ καὶ σκεπάσαι τὸν αὐτοῦ σήσαμον." Καὶ λαβὼν τὴν σινδόνα ἐσκέπασεν αὐτόν. Ὁ δὲ

benefit to others but not to itself. He who seeks knowledge must first advise himself, then in that way teach others. Someone who is fond of the world must also gain three particular things: knowledge, wealth, and a sense of purpose.

For it has been said that someone who seeks after things 9
without understanding their benefit, labors in vain and is called foolish. And whoever reads this book and strives to gain the instruction within it, but does not then act in accordance with his knowledge, will be called blind. And the sensible man must not seek to harm another for his own benefit. For the person who breaks faith with his own friend will be punished, and will suffer the very things that a certain man suffered.

About the two sesame merchants. 10

For it has been said that two sesame merchants had one storehouse, except that the sesame seeds of the one were kept separate from those of the other. One of the merchants wanted to steal the other's sesame seeds, so he took a cloth and covered them. He then went off to another man, who was a friend of his, and said, "I want to steal my partner's sesame seeds, and we will share them." When evening fell, however, his partner went and saw his own seeds covered with the cloth belonging to his partner. Being a good man, he said to himself, "See what a good turn my partner has kindly done for me today, by covering up my seeds and neglecting his own. I really should take his cloth and cover his seeds with it." So, he took the cloth and covered them. The

τὸν δόλον μέλλων ποιῆσαι, ἐλθὼν μετὰ τοῦ φίλου αὐτοῦ νυκτός, καὶ εἰσελθὼν εἰς τὴν ἀποθήκην, ἤρξατο καταψηλαφᾶν, ὅπως εὕρῃ τὸν ἴδιον σήσαμον ἐσκεπασμένον τῇ σινδόνι, ὡς ἐδόκει ταύτην καταλιπεῖν. Καὶ κλέψας τὸν ἴδιον σήσαμον, ἔδωκε τὸν μὲν ἥμισυ πρὸς τὸν φίλον αὐτοῦ, τὸν δὲ ἕτερον ἥμισυ αὐτὸς ἐπεβάστασε. Πρωΐας δὲ ἤδη γενομένης, ἐλθὼν μετὰ τοῦ συντρόφου αὐτοῦ εἰς τὴν ἀποθήκην, καὶ ἰδὼν ὅτι τὸν ἴδιον σήσαμον ἔκλεψε, καὶ πενθήσας, ἐν θλίψει πολλῇ περιέπεσε, γνοὺς ὅτι ὅπερ ἔλαβεν ὁ φίλος αὐτοῦ οὐκ ἀντιστρέφεται παρ’ αὐτοῦ· καὶ γὰρ οὐκ ἠδυνήθη φανερῶσαι αὐτό, ἵνα μὴ γένηται χεῖρον.

11 Καὶ δέον τὸν ζητοῦντα καὶ ἐπιχειροῦντα περί τινος πράγματος μὴ πρότερον τούτου ἐφάπτεσθαι, πρὶν ἂν τὸ τέλος τοῦδε ὁρᾶν ὁποῖόν ἐστιν· ὁ δὲ μὴ ἐπιστάμενος, ἀλλ’ ἀπερισκέπτως ἐμπίπτων τοῖς πράγμασι, πολλὰ μὲν κοπιάσει, εἰς οὐδὲν δὲ ὠφεληθήσεται. Καὶ οὐδεὶς δύναται πλουτῆσαι, εἰ μὴ μετὰ μόχθου πολλοῦ, οὐδὲ πάλιν ἀπελπίσαι ἀπὸ πραγμάτων εὑρισκομένων καὶ δυναμένων γενέσθαι· καὶ πρὸ πάντων δέον αὐτῷ τοῦ φροντίζειν τὰ τῶν αἰωνίων καὶ μὴ τῶν προσκαίρων. Ἐρρέθη γὰρ ὅτι δύο πράγματα κοσμοῦσι τὸν ἄνθρωπον, ὁ πλοῦτος καὶ ἡ παιδεία· ἐὰν δέ τι τῶν τοιούτων ἐκπεσεῖται, ἔοικεν ἄνευ ξύλου πῦρ ἅπτειν. Καὶ γὰρ πολλοί εἰσιν οἱ ἀπροσδοκήτως πλούτου ἐπιτυγχάνοντες.

partner who was going to carry out the deception came at night with his friend and entered the storehouse. He began to feel around in order to find his own sesame seeds, which were now covered by the cloth. As he thought this was where he had left it, he stole his own sesame seeds, gave half to his friend and took the other half away himself. When morning came, he went with his partner to the storehouse and saw that he had stolen his own sesame seeds. He lamented and fell into deep distress because he knew that what his friend had taken would not be returned by him, for he was unable to reveal it so as not to make matters worse.

The person who plans and attempts some action must 11
not apply himself to it too soon, before he sees what its outcome is going to be: someone who does not understand things, but thoughtlessly gets involved in them will toil much, but get no benefit. No one can get rich without a lot of hard work, but nor again should he lose hope also of becoming wealthy by means of things which are found. Above all else, he must think about eternal, not ephemeral things. For it has been said that two things adorn a man: wealth and education; and if he should lose one of these, it would be like lighting a fire without wood. For there are many people who come into wealth unexpectedly.

12 *Περὶ τοῦ πένητος τοῦ εὐτυχήσαντος ὑπὸ κλέπτου.*

Καὶ γὰρ ἐρρέθη περί τινος ἀνθρώπου πένητος λίαν ὥστε μὴ ἔχοντος κἂν σκέπην ἐν τῷ σώματι αὐτοῦ. Ἀπελθὼν οὖν πρὸς τοὺς φίλους αὐτοῦ ᾐτήσατο αὐτοῖς ἔνδυμα, καὶ οὐδεὶς ἐδίδου αὐτῷ· καὶ ὑποστρέψας ἐν τῇ οἰκίᾳ, ἐν τῷ κοιτῶνι αὐτοῦ γυμνὸς πεσὼν ἐκοιμήθη. Εἶχε δὲ ὑποκάτω τοῦ κοιτῶνος αὐτοῦ πίθον ἔχοντα σῖτον οὐκ ὀλίγον. Ἐν δὲ τῇ νυκτὶ εἰσῆλθε κλέπτης τις, καὶ μὴ εὑρὼν ἆραί τι, λέγει ἐν ἑαυτῷ· "Πῶς ἐξέλθω κενός; Κἂν τὸν σῖτον ἐκ τοῦ πίθου λαβεῖν ἔχω." Καὶ ἐκδυσάμενος τὸν χιτῶνα αὐτοῦ βαλεῖν σῖτον, εἰσεπήδησεν ὁ κύριος τοῦ οἴκου, καὶ διώξας αὐτὸν γυμνὸν ὄντα καὶ τύψας αὐτόν, ἔλαβε τὸν χιτῶνα αὐτοῦ καὶ ἐνεδύσατο αὐτόν, τὸν δὲ σῖτον ὑπέστρεψεν ἐν τῷ πίθῳ αὐτοῦ.

13 *Περὶ περιστερᾶς.*

Οὕτω δεῖ τὸν ἄνθρωπον μὴ <ἀπ>ελπίζειν ἀπὸ πραγμάτων εὑρισκομένων, μηδὲ διώκειν πρᾶγμα ἀκατάληπτον· καὶ πάλιν μὴ ἐλπίζειν ἐπὶ τοῦτον τὸν μῦθον καὶ καταλείψει τὸν ἀγῶνα· *καὶ γὰρ ὁ ζητῶν εὑρίσκει*, εἰ τάχα καὶ ἴδῃ τινὰ εὑρίσκοντα ἄνευ ζητήσεως, μὴ ἀκολουθήσῃ αὐτῷ· καὶ γὰρ πολλοὶ τῶν ἀνθρώπων διὰ τῆς ζητήσεως εὑρίσκουσι· καὶ δεῖ αὐτοὺς ἐρευνᾶν τὰ πράγματα, καὶ δοκιμάζειν τὴν τούτων διαφοράν. Καὶ εἰ δεῖ ἅπερ ὠφελεῖ καταδιώκειν, ὁμοίως καὶ ἀποδρᾶν ἀπὸ τῶν κακῶν, ὥσπερ ἔπαθε καὶ ἄλλος, μήπως καὶ αὐτὸς πάθῃ τὰ ὅμοια, καὶ ἔστιν ὥσπερ ἡ

About the poor man who benefited from a thief. 12

It has thus been said about a very poor man, that he did not even have a covering for his body. So, he went to his friends and asked for some clothing, but no one gave him anything. He returned home, lay on his bed naked, and fell asleep. But he did have a storage jar beneath his bed which contained a lot of grain. During the night a thief came in, and not finding anything to take, said to himself: "How can I leave empty-handed? At least let me take the grain from the jar." When he had taken off his tunic to put the grain in, the owner of the house leaped up, chased the naked thief, and beat him. Then he took the man's tunic and put it on, and returned the grain to his jar.

About a dove. 13

So, someone should not lose hope of finding things, but neither should he pursue the impossible. And again, he should not put his hopes in that plan and abandon the struggle; for *he who seeks, finds,* and if he may perhaps see someone find things without seeking them, he should not follow him. For many people find things by looking for them, and they need to search for things and investigate their value. And if one should pursue whatever is beneficial, so one should avoid bad things, just as one should avoid what someone else suffered, so that one may not suffer the same, and be

περιστερά. Ἐκείνη γὰρ θεωροῦσα τὰ νοσσία αὐτῆς θυόμενα ἔμπροσθεν αὐτῆς, οὐ ξενίζεται τοῦ τόπου ἐκείνου, ἀλλ' ἐπιμένει ἕως οὗ καὶ αὕτη σφαγῇ.

14 Καὶ ὀφείλει ἄνθρωπος τιθέναι ὅρον καὶ μὴ παραδραμεῖν αὐτόν, μηδὲ ἀμελῆσαι πρᾶγμα· καὶ ἵνα γινώσκῃ ὅτι πᾶς ἄνθρωπος ἀγωνίζεται καὶ ὅστις ἔχει τὸν ἀγῶνα αὐτοῦ, περὶ τῶν μελλόντων ζήσεται, ὁ δὲ περὶ τῶν προσκαίρων ζημιωθήσεται. Ὁ δὲ ἀγωνιζόμενος περὶ τῶν ἀμφοτέρων, καὶ ζήσεται καὶ δοξασθήσεται ὁ τοιοῦτος ἄνθρωπος.

15 Ἐρρέθη δὲ ὅτι δέον τὸν κοσμικὸν ἄνθρωπον ἐπικτήσασθαι τρία πράγματα· τὸ φυλάξασθαι τὴν ἑαυτοῦ πίστιν, τὸ ζητεῖν τὴν ἀναγκαίαν τροφήν, καὶ τὸ ὀρθῶς μετὰ τῶν ἀνθρώπων διάγειν. Ἐλέχθη δὲ καὶ ὅστις ἐστὶν ῥάθυμος καὶ ἄμελος, καὶ πιστεύων λόγοις ἀσυστάτοις, τοῖς μὴ δεχομένοις παρὰ τοῦ νοὸς αὐτοῦ, ὁμοιοῦται ἀνθρώπῳ ἀκολουθοῦντι τῷ αὐτοῦ θελήματι καὶ πιστεύοντι τὰ μὴ ἀληθῆ, καὶ δεῖ τὸν νουνεχῆ μὴ ἀκολουθεῖν τῷ θελήματι αὐτοῦ, μάλιστα τῷ ὑπὸ σκάνδαλον. Καὶ πάλιν δεῖ αὐτὸν [τοῦ] μὴ δέχεσθαι λόγον ἀνθρώπου, εἴπερ καὶ ἀψευδής ἐστιν ὁ λέγων αὐτόν, καὶ μὴ ἀκολουθεῖν τοῖς σφάλμασι καὶ ῥαθυμεῖν εἰς τὴν τῶν πραγμάτων γνῶσιν. Καὶ δεῖ πάλιν τοῦτον μὴ πολυπραγμονεῖν εἰς πρᾶγμα ἀδύνατον, μηδὲ ὁρμῆσαι κατ' αὐτοῦ ἄνευ προμελέτης καὶ ὁμοιωθῆναι ἀνθρώπῳ ἐκστρατεύσαντι ἀπὸ τῆς ὁδοῦ· ὅσον γὰρ βιάζῃ, τοσοῦτον μακρύνεται τῆς ὁδοῦ ἐκείνης καὶ ἀπόλλυται, καὶ ἑτέρῳ ἀνδρί, οὗπερ ἐν τῷ ὀφθαλμῷ εἰσῆλθέ τι, καὶ τρίψας αὐτὸν πολλὰ ἐτυφλώθη.

like the dove. For when she sees her nestlings being killed in front of her, she does not abandon that place, but stays until she herself may be killed.

And it is necessary for someone to have a goal and not 14
turn aside from it, nor be careless about the matter. And know this, that everyone is striving, and whoever is striving for what is in the future will live, but the person who is striving for things in the present will fail. But whoever strives for both, that person will both live and be glorified.

It is said that a man of the world should work, in addi- 15
tion, on three things: maintaining his faith, seeking what he needs to eat, and living correctly with people. But it is also said that someone who is frivolous and careless, and who believes words that are not verified, those that are not authenticated by his mind, is like a man who follows his own will and believes what is not true, and the smart man should not follow his own will, especially when it leads to a sinful act. Again, he should not take a man at his word, even though the person speaking is truthful, and he should not be guided by errors or be negligent in his knowledge of things. And again, this person should not concern himself with something that is impossible, nor set out after this without preparation or he will be like someone who leaves the road; for as much as he may try, he gets farther from that road and is lost. He will also be like someone else, who got something in his eye and, by rubbing it a lot, went blind.

16 Καὶ δεῖ τὸν νουνεχῆ ἄνθρωπον [τοῦ] γινώσκειν ὅτι ἡ ἀντάμειψις ἀληθής ἐστι καὶ προσέχειν ἑαυτόν· καὶ γὰρ ὁ προφέρων τῷ φίλῳ αὐτοῦ ἅπερ μισεῖ, ἀδικεῖ τὴν ἑαυτοῦ ψυχήν. Καὶ οἱ ἀναγινώσκοντες τὸ βιβλίον τοῦτο, δέον αὐτοῖς μὴ παραδραμεῖν λόγον τινὰ χάριν ὠφελείας αὐτῶν· καὶ γὰρ μελετῶντες τοῦτο ἐν ἐπιγνώσει ὠφεληθήσονται. Ἡμεῖς δὲ ἰδόντες τοὺς Πέρσας ἑρμηνεύσαντας τὸ βιβλίον τοῦτο ἀπὸ τῆς Περσικῆς γλώττης εἰς τὴν Ἀραβικήν, Ῥωμαϊκῶς τεθείκαμεν ταῦτα ἐν τῇ ἀρχῇ τοῦ βιβλίου, ἵνα οἱ ἀναγινώσκοντες αὐτὰ πλείονα γνῶσιν λάβωσιν.

And the sensible person should understand that his reward is true and watch himself. For someone who offers his friend things that he hates, wrongs his own soul. And the readers of this book should not skip a word, given how beneficial it is to them; for, by studying it conscientiously, they will receive benefit. But, since we saw how the Persians had translated this book from the Persian language into Arabic, we have placed these things at the start of the book in Greek, so that those reading them may receive even more knowledge. 16

[Prologue C]

Βιβλίον πρῶτον περὶ τῶν προσρημάτων τῶν λεχθέντων τῷ Περζουέ, ἔχον μύθους αὐτοῦ ὠφελίμους καὶ μεταγλωττισθὲν παρὰ Συμεὼν μαγίστρου καὶ φιλοσόφου τοῦ Σήθ.

Εἶπεν ὁ Περζουέ, ὁ πρῶτος ἰατρὸς τῆς Περσίας, ὁ μεταβαλὼν τὴν ἑρμηνείαν τῆς βίβλου ταύτης ἀπὸ τῆς Ἰνδικῆς γλώττης εἰς τὴν Περσικὴν διάλεκτον, ὅτι·

Ὁ πατήρ μου ἐκ τῶν ἐπισήμων ἀνθρώπων ἦν καὶ πολεμιστῶν, ἡ δὲ μήτηρ μου ἐκ τῶν θυγατέρων τῶν μεγάλων σατραπῶν· καὶ διὰ τῆς χάριτος τοῦ Θεοῦ ἤμην παρ' αὐτοῖς ἀγαπώμενος, καὶ προεῖχον ἐπὶ πᾶσι τοῖς ἀδελφοῖς μου. Παρεδόθην δὲ παρ' αὐτῶν τοῦ μανθάνειν τὴν ἰατρικὴν ἐπιστήμην· ταύτην δὲ διελθὼν καὶ κατωρθωκὼς ἐν ἑπτὰ ἔτεσι, καὶ θαρρήσας ὅτι μεμάθηκα, εἶπον πρὸς ἑαυτόν· "Τέσσαρα πράγματα διώκουσι πάντες ἄνθρωποι, τὸν πλοῦτον, τὴν ἡδονήν, τὴν ἐξουσίαν, καὶ ἔσχατον τὸν μισθόν, καὶ δεῖ με διακρίνειν ταῦτα καὶ ζητῆσαι τὸ κρεῖττον." Καὶ ταῦτα συνθέμενος τῷ ἰδίῳ λογισμῷ, ἐνενόησα εἶναι τὸν μισθόν, ὅστις διὰ τῆς ἰατρικῆς ἐπιστήμης καταλαμβάνεται, ἣν δή τινα τῶν ἄλλων προέκρινα, διὸ καὶ ἐπαινετή

Prologue C

The first book concerning the prologue to the things recounted by Perzoué, containing his useful tales and translated by the teacher and philosopher, Symeon Seth.

Perzoué, the foremost physician in Persia, who translated this book from the Indian tongue into the Persian language, said:

My father was descended from distinguished people and from warriors, my mother from the daughters of powerful provincial governors. By God's grace I was loved by them, and I was preferred to all my brothers. I was sent by them to study medical science, and I completed this successfully in seven years. Confident in what I had learned, I said to myself, "All men seek four things: wealth, pleasure, power and, lastly, their reward; and I must distinguish between them so that I may seek the one that is better." Considering these with my own reasoning, I decided this was the reward which is gained through medical science. So, I chose this over the

ἐστι παρὰ τοῖς ἐχέφροσι καὶ τετιμημένη παρὰ πάσης θρησκείας.

2 Εὗρον δὲ ἐν τοῖς ἰατρικοῖς βιβλίοις, ὅτι ἀξιέπαινός ἐστιν ὁ ζητῶν ταύτην τὴν ἐπιστήμην, διὰ τὸν τῆς ἐσχάτης ἡμέρας μισθόν. Ἕνεκεν τούτου προέκρινα ταύτην, οὐχὶ διὰ τὸν πρόσκαιρον μισθόν, ἀλλὰ διὰ τὸν αἰώνιον, μήπως ἔσομαι ὥσπερ ὁ ἔμπορος ὁ ζημιωθείς, ὃς ἔδωκεν ὑάκινθον δι' οὗ ἠδύνατο πλουτῆσαι καὶ ἔλαβεν ἀντ' αὐτοῦ χάντρον μηδὲν ἀξιούμενον αὐτοῦ. Εὗρον δὲ πάλιν, ὅτι ὁ ζητῶν διὰ ταύτης τῆς ἐπιστήμης τὸν αἰώνιον μισθόν, οὐκ ἐκλείψει αὐτῷ τι, οὔτε ἐν τῷ νῦν αἰῶνι δηλονότι, οὔτε ἐν τῷ μέλλοντι, ἀλλ' ἔσται ὡς ὁ γεωργὸς ὁ καθαίρων τὴν ἑαυτοῦ γῆν, οὐχὶ διὰ τὸν χόρτον, ἀλλὰ διὰ τὸν καρπόν. Καὶ εὐθέως ἠρξάμην εἰς τὴν τῶν ἀσθενούντων ἐπιμέλειαν ἕνεκεν τοῦ αἰωνίου μισθοῦ, καὶ τοὺς μὲν ἰάτρευον δι' οἰκείων χειρῶν, τοὺς δὲ διὰ λόγων καὶ ἐπιτάξεων, παρέχων αὐτοῖς τὰ δέοντα καὶ μὴ ζητῶν ἐν τούτῳ παρά τινος μισθόν, εἰ μὴ ἔπαινον παρὰ τοῖς ὁμοίοις μου ἢ τοῖς ἐνδοξοτέροις καὶ πλουσιωτέροις, καὶ τοῦ εἶναι ἀγαθὸς ἐν ἔργῳ καὶ λόγῳ.

3 Ἐπεθύμησε δὲ ἡ ψυχή μου τὰ πρόσκαιρα, ἐγὼ δὲ φιλονεικῶν παρῄνεσα λέγων αὐτῇ· "Οὐκ οἶδας, ὦ ψυχή, τὰ βλάπτοντα καὶ ὠφελοῦντα; Οὐκ ἀποδιδράσκεις ἀπὸ πραγμάτων, ὧν οἱ ἔχοντες οὐ χαίρουσιν ἐν αὐτοῖς, ἀλλὰ μόνον κόπους ἔχουσι καὶ θλίψεις μεγάλας εἰς τὴν τούτων ὑποχώρησιν καί, τὸ τελευταῖον, κόλασιν αἰώνιον; Ψυχή, οὐ μέμνησαι τῶν αἰωνίων; Οὐκ αἰσχύνῃ συγκοινωνεῖν τοῖς μωροῖς καὶ ἄφροσιν ἐν τῇ ἀγάπῃ τοῦ φθειρομένου βίου τούτου; Ὁ γὰρ ἔχων ἐκ τοῦ κόσμου τοῦ ματαίου τούτου

others, as it is something that is praised by sensible people and respected by every religion.

I discovered in medical books that the person who seeks this knowledge is praiseworthy, because of its reward on the day of judgment. That is the reason I chose it, not because of its transitory reward, but because of its eternal one, so that I will not be like the merchant who made a loss when he gave away a sapphire which could have made him rich and received in exchange a bead worth nothing to him. On the contrary, I discovered that the person who seeks an eternal reward through this knowledge will not want for anything, that is to say, neither in this present age nor in the one to come, but he will be like the farmer who clears his land not for grass but for crops. And I immediately began to care for the sick for the sake of eternal reward, treating some with my own hands, and others with words and instructions. I supplied them with what they needed and did not seek payment for this from anyone, apart from the respect of my peers or those who were richer and more famous, and to be a good man, in word and deed. 2

When my soul desired what was transitory, I challenged it and exhorted it by saying to it: "My soul, do you not know what is harmful and what is beneficial? Do you not flee from things which do not make people happy when they have them but only cause them to experience troubles and great afflictions when they lose them and, finally, eternal punishment? My soul, have you forgotten the eternal things? Are you not ashamed to associate with the stupid and the foolish in your love of this transitory life? For if someone possesses something from this vain world, it is not his nor does 3

τι, οὐκ ἔστιν αὐτοῦ, οὔτε μένει ἐν αὐτῷ· καὶ γὰρ οἱ μωροί, ὡς κἀγώ, διώκουσι ταῦτα καὶ φιλοῦσι. Ψυχή, φεῦγε τὰ πρόσκαιρα καὶ ζήτει τὰ αἰώνια, καὶ αὐτάρκως ἔχου τῇ ἀναγκαίᾳ τροφῇ, καὶ βασίλευε ἐπ' ἔργων ἀγαθῶν ὅσον δύνασαι, καὶ μὴ φιλήσῃς τὰ πρόσκαιρα. Μνήσθητι δὲ τὴν τοῦ σώματός σου σύστασιν καὶ τὰ αὐτῷ συμβαίνοντα πάντα, καὶ ὅτι ἐκ τεσσάρων στοιχείων ἤτοι χυμῶν ἐναντίως ἐχομένων συνίσταται τὸ πήλινον τοῦτο σῶμα· τῶν χυμῶν δὲ ἡ σύστασίς ἐστιν ἡ ζωή· ἡ δὲ ζωὴ παρατρέχουσα, καὶ ὥσπερ ξόανον πολυόρμητόν ἐστι κρατούμενον ὑπὸ ἥλων· ἀνασπασθέντων δὲ τῶν ἥλων καταλύεται τὸ ξόανον.

4 "Ψυχή, μὴ πλανηθῇς ἐν τῇ τῶν φίλων συνοδίᾳ, μήτε ἀγωνισθῇς ἐν ὅλῳ σου τῷ βίῳ ἐν τῇ τῶν νέων συναυλίᾳ μετ' αὐτῶν· ἡ γὰρ τούτων συνοδία μικρὸν μὲν εὐφραίνει, πολὺ δὲ λυπεῖ· τὸ δὲ τέλος αὐτῶν, ἔχθρας χωρισμός. Καὶ ἔσῃ ὥσπερ κοχλιάριον, δι' οὗ γνωρίζεται τῶν βρωμάτων ἡ πιότης, ὅταν δὲ θλασθῇ, καίουσιν αὐτό. Ψυχή, μὴ ἀπολέσῃς σαυτὴν εἰς τὸ συνάξαι χρήματα διὰ τὴν τῶν συγγενῶν καὶ ἀδελφῶν θεραπείαν· καὶ ἔσῃ ὥσπερ τὸ θυμίαμα τὸ εὐωδιάζον ἑτέρους ἑαυτὸ δὲ καῖον. Ψυχὴ μή σε πλανήσει ὁ πλοῦτος καὶ ἡ δόξα ἡ ἐπαίρουσα τὸν ἄνθρωπον, καὶ σκοτιζόμενος οὐ γινώσκει τὴν αὐτοῦ ἀτιμίαν, εἰ μὴ ὅταν ἀποχωρισθῇ ἀπ' αὐτῆς—καθὼς καὶ αἱ τῆς κεφαλῆς τρίχαι, ὅταν μέν εἰσιν ἐν αὐτῇ, τιμῶνται, ὅταν δὲ ἀποχωρισθῶσι ταύτης, βδελύσσονται. Ψυχή, ἐπιμελοῦ εἰς τὰς τῶν ἀσθενῶν ἰατρείας, καὶ μὴ εἴπῃς ὅτι πολλὴ ἔξοδός ἐστι, καὶ οἱ πλείονες τῶν ἀνθρώπων ἀγνοοῦσι τὴν ταύτης ὠφέλειαν· ἀλλ' ὁμοιώθητι ἀνθρώπῳ σῴζοντι ἕτερον ἐξ ἀνάγκης καὶ

it remain with him. For foolish people, like myself, pursue these things and love them. My soul, flee the temporal and seek the eternal; be satisfied only with what you need to eat, make yourself the master of good deeds as much as you are able, and do not love the temporal. Remember the composition of your body and all that happens to it, and that this bodily clay is composed of four elements, or humors, opposed to each other. The disposition of the humors is life; but life is fleeting, and, just as with an easily moveable wooden image that is held together by nails, when the nails are pulled out, the image falls to pieces.

"My soul, do not wander about in the company of friends, 4
and do not spend your whole life contending with them in the congregation of youths, for their company brings little joy but much distress, and their end, a separation in enmity. For you will be like a spoon, which is used to taste the richness of food, but which people burn when it is broken. My soul, do not destroy yourself by collecting money to treat relatives and brothers; for then you will be like incense which makes others fragrant but is itself burned. My soul, wealth and glory will lead you astray, that glory which puffs someone up so that, being blinded, he does not then recognize his own dishonor except when he is parted from it—just as hairs are valued when they are attached to the head but, when they fall out, are viewed with disgust. My soul, see to the healing of the sick, and do not say that it costs a lot and the majority of people do not understand its benefit. Rather, be like the person who saves another from suffering

ἐξαιρουμένῳ αὐτὸν ἐξ αὐτῆς καὶ τρέφοντι αὐτὸν ἐν τῇ αὐτοῦ εὐημερίᾳ καὶ ζωῇ, ἵνα δι' αὐτοῦ ἀπολάβῃ τῶν αἰωνίων ἐκείνων. Καὶ ἐπεὶ οὗτος τοσοῦτον μισθὸν ἐλπίζει δι' ἑνὸς καὶ μόνου εὐεργεσίαν, πόσῳ μᾶλλον ὁ τοὺς ἀναριθμήτους ἀνθρώπους ἰατρεύων, τοὺς ὄντας ἐπ' ἀσθενείας ἐπικινδύνους καὶ δοκοῦντας ἀποχωρισθῆναι τοῦ κόσμου καὶ τῆς αὐτοῦ ἡδονῆς, τῆς τε συζυγίας καὶ τέκνων καὶ τῶν λοιπῶν καὶ στρέφων αὐτοὺς εἰς εὐρωστίαν; Οὐχὶ διὰ τούτων ἐλπίζει πλείονα τὸν μισθὸν ἀπολαβεῖν ἐν τῷ μέλλοντι;

5 "Ψυχή, μὴ προσκολληθῇς τῶν προσκαίρων καὶ μακρυνθῇς τῶν αἰωνίων, μηδὲ προκρίνῃς τὰ μικρὰ ὑπὲρ τῶν μειζόνων, καὶ μὴ διαπιπράσκῃ τὰ πολύτιμα ἐν ὀλίγῃ τιμῇ. Ὥσπερ ἔμπορός τις εἶχεν ἐν ἀποθήκῃ δαμάσκηνα, καὶ εἶπεν ἐν ἑαυτῷ· 'Ἐὰν πράσω αὐτὰ διὰ ζυγίου, κόπον πολὺν παρέξω ἐμαυτῷ.' Καὶ πέπρακεν αὐτὰ ἄνευ ζυγίου εἰς μικρὰν τιμήν, καὶ ἄφρων ἐφάνη."

6 Καὶ παραινέσας τὴν ἐμαυτοῦ ψυχήν, οὐκ εἶχε ἀποδρᾶσαι ἀπ' ἐμοῦ, ἀλλὰ πεισθεῖσα τοῖς λόγοις ἀπηλλοτριώθη τῶν τοιούτων. Καὶ ἠρξάμην ἐπιμελεῖσθαι τῶν ἀσθενούντων, ζητῶν τὸν αἰώνιον μισθόν· καὶ σὺν πᾶσι τούτοις οὐκ ὑστερήθην τὴν πρόσκαιρον δόξαν καὶ τιμὴν παρὰ τοῖς βασιλεῦσι πρὸ τοῦ με ἀπελθεῖν εἰς Ἰνδίαν. Μετὰ δὲ ταῦτα ἐπέτυχον τῶν ἐλπιζομένων ἐπέκεινα καὶ ὧν οὐκ ἤμην ἄξιος.

7 Μαθὼν δὲ τὴν ἰατρικὴν ἐπιστήμην καὶ κατασκοπεύσας αὐτήν, οὐχ εὗρόν τινα ἰατρὸν δυνάμενον ἰατρεῦσαι ἄρρωστον καὶ δοῦναι αὐτῷ τελείαν ῥῶσιν τῷ ἀσθενοῦντι· καὶ κατεφρόνησα τὴν ἰατρικὴν λίαν. Εὑρὼν δὲ τὴν ἐπιμέλειαν τῶν αἰωνίων ῥυομένην τὸν ἄνθρωπον ἀπὸ πάσης νόσου,

and sets him free from it, nursing him back to prosperity and life, so that through him he may receive those eternal things. And since this person hopes for such a great reward because of one single good deed, how much more may the person do so who heals countless people whose lives are endangered by illness, and who expect to be separated from the world and its pleasures, and from their spouse and children and everyone else? By doing this, does he not hope to receive a greater reward in the future?

"My soul, do not cling to transitory things and separate 5
yourself from the eternal, nor choose small matters over greater, and do not sell what is priceless at a low price. Like a merchant who had plums in a storehouse, who said to himself, 'If I charge for the plums using a set of scales, I will make a lot of work for myself.' So he sold them without scales, for little value, and appeared foolish."

After I had advised my own soul, it could not escape me, 6
but, convinced by my words, it was alienated from such things. And I thus began to take care of the sick, seeking eternal reward. And, despite all this, I was not deprived of transitory glory and honor among kings, before going off to India. After that I found more than I had hoped for, and of which I was not worthy.

But, after I had learned medical science, when I exam- 7
ined closely those who practiced it, I did not find any physician capable of treating a sick person and of giving perfect strength back to the invalid, and I deeply despised the practice of medicine. And when I discovered that caring about what is eternal delivers a person from every disease, I sought

ἔτι πλέον ἐζήτησα τὴν ἀκτημοσύνην, καὶ δραξάμενος ταύτης, ἐσκανδαλίσθην περὶ τῶν θρησκειῶν· καὶ γὰρ ἐν τῇ ἰατρικῇ οὐχ εὗρον θρησκείαν μίαν τοῦ ὁδηγηθῆναι δι' αὐτῆς. Καὶ γὰρ αἱ θρησκεῖαι πολλαί εἰσι. Καὶ κρατοῦσι ταύτας οἱ μὲν ἀπὸ γονέων, οἱ δὲ βίᾳ, ἕτεροι διὰ δόξαν ἐπίγειον, καὶ ἑκάστῳ δοκεῖ ἀληθὲς εἶναι τὸ παρ' αὐτοῦ λατρευόμενον, τὸ δὲ τοῦ ἑτέρου μάταιον καὶ ψευδές· ἀμφιβάλλουσι δὲ περὶ τοῦ πλάστου καὶ τοῦ πλάσματος καὶ περὶ πραγμάτων ἑτέρων ἀμφιβολίαν ἰσχυράν, [καὶ] ἕκαστος ἐξ αὐτῶν μεμφόμενος καὶ ψέγων τὸν ἕτερον. Ἰδὼν δὲ ταῦτα ἠβουλήθην διαλέξασθαι μετὰ τῶν πρωτοκρειττοτέρων αὐτῶν, ὅπως μάθω τὴν ἀλήθειαν, καὶ καταλιπὼν καὶ παριδὼν τὸ ψεῦδος ἀκολουθήσω τῇ ἀληθείᾳ, καὶ κρατήσω αὐτὴν ἀσκανδάλιστον, καὶ μὴ πιστεύσω πράγματος, ὅπερ ἀγνοῶ, ἀλλ' ἀκολουθήσω ὑπὲρ ᾧ φρονῶ. Ποιήσας δὲ τοῦτο καὶ ζητήσας αὐτοὺς εὗρον ἕνα ἕκαστον ἐπαινοῦντα τὴν ἑαυτοῦ θρησκείαν καὶ διαβάλλοντα τοῦ ἑτέρου· καὶ ἐκ τούτου ἐφάνη μοι, ὅτι ἕκαστος ἀκολουθεῖ τῷ οἰκείῳ θελήματι, καὶ πάντες ἄνευ δικαιοσύνης λαλοῦσιν. Ἰδὼν δὲ ταῦτα οὐχ ᾑρετισάμην ἀκολουθῆσαί τινι ἐξ αὐτῶν, ὅπως μὴ ἔσομαι ὥσπερ ἐκεῖνος ὁ πεπλανημένος.

8 *Περὶ ἄφρονος κλέπτου πιστεύσαντος τῷ "Σελέμ."*

Ἐρρέθη γὰρ ὅτι κλέπτης τις ἦλθεν ἐπὶ δώματός τινος μετὰ τῶν συντρόφων αὐτοῦ συλῆσαι τὸν οἶκον. Γνοὺς δὲ ὁ οἰκοδεσπότης αὐτοὺς κοιμώμενος μετὰ τῆς γυναικὸς αὐτοῦ, ἐξύπνισεν αὐτὴν λέγων· "Ὡς οἶμαι, κλέπται

poverty even more and, embracing it, I was shocked by the religions, for I did not find a single religion which would guide me in the practice of medicine. For there are many religions, and some people adopt them from their parents, others by force, others for earthly glory, and each person believes that the one worshiped by him is true, but that of the other person is mistaken and false. They quarrel about the creator and the creation and about other things in fierce disagreement, and each of them blames and finds fault with the other. When I saw this, I wanted to discuss with the foremost among them, how I might learn the truth and, leaving behind and disregarding what was false, how I might follow the truth and hold on to it without stumbling, and not believe in something that I did not grasp, but follow what I understood. After I had done this and had questioned them, I found that each one praised his own religion and defamed the other; and from this it seemed to me that each one follows his own inclination, and all of them speak without justification. So, when I saw this, I chose not to follow any of them, so that I would not be like that man who was misled.

About a foolish thief who believed in the "Selem." 8

For it has been said that a thief climbed onto the roof of a house with his accomplices in order to rob the household. The master of the house, who was asleep with his wife, became aware of them and woke her up. He said to her, "I

ἀνῆλθον ἐπὶ τοῦ δώματος ἡμῶν· καὶ ἰδοὺ προσποιοῦμαι κοιμᾶσθαι· σὺ δέ με ἐξύπνισον μεγάλῃ φωνῇ καὶ εἰπέ μοι· 'Ὦ ἄνερ, γνώρισόν μοι πόθεν τὸν πλοῦτον, ὅνπερ ἔχομεν, συνῆξας καὶ τοὺς θησαυρούς;' Ἐμοῦ δὲ μὴ ἀνταποκρινομένου σοι, ἔτι βόησον ἐρωτῶσά με." Ποιήσασα δὲ τοῦτο ἡ γυνή, ἤκουσαν οἱ λησταὶ καὶ ἤρξαντο ἀκροᾶσθαι. Εἶπε δὲ ὁ ἀνὴρ τῇ γυναικὶ αὐτοῦ· "Ὁ Θεὸς ἐδωρήσατο ἡμῖν πλοῦτον πολύν, καὶ δεῖ σε φαγεῖν καὶ πιεῖν καὶ εὐφραίνεσθαι, καὶ μὴ ἐρωτᾶν περὶ πραγμάτων ὧν οὐ δύναμαί σε φανερῶσαι, μήπως ἀκούσωσι ταῦτά τινες—καὶ γὰρ οἱ τοῖχοι ὦτα ἔχουσι—καὶ συμβήσεται ἡμῖν κίνδυνος." Λέγει αὐτῷ ἡ γυνή, ὅτι "οὐκ ἔστι τις πλησίον ἡμῶν τοῦ ἀκοῦσαι." Λέγει αὐτῇ ὁ ἀνήρ· "Ἐπεὶ ἠνάγκασάς με, εἰπεῖν σε ἔχω, ἀλλ' ὅρα μήπως γνῶσί τινες ἢ οἱ σοὶ ἀδελφοί, ἢ συγγενεῖς, καὶ ἀπολέσωμεν τὴν ὠφέλειαν ἡμῶν· ταῦτα γὰρ ἀπὸ κλεψίας ἐσύναξα." Λέγει αὐτῷ ἡ γυνή· "Καὶ πῶς ἐσύναξας ταῦτα πάντα; Ἅπαντες γὰρ ὡς πιστὸν ἔχοντές σε, οὐ σκανδαλίζονται ἐν σοί." Λέγει αὐτῇ· "Ἐπαοιδίαν τινὰ μεμάθηκα ἐπὶ τῇ κλεψίᾳ, καὶ δι' αὐτῆς οὐ γινώσκει μοί τις οὐδὲ σκανδαλίζεται εἰς ἐμέ." Λέγει αὐτῷ· "Καὶ πῶς λέγεις τοῦτο, κύριέ μου;" Ὁ δὲ λέγει αὐτῇ· "Ἐξηρχόμην ἐν νυκτὶ φεγγώδει, καὶ μετ' ἐμοῦ οἱ σύντροφοί μου, καὶ ἀνηρχόμεθα ἐπὶ τῶν θυρίδων τοῦ οἴκου, ὅθεν ἐβουλόμεθα εἰσελθεῖν, καὶ ἔλεγον τὴν ἐπαοιδίαν ταύτην ἐπὶ τῆς θυρίδος, τὸ 'Σελὲμ Σελέμ,' ἕως ἑπτάκις, καὶ ἔδραττον τὰς ἀκτῖνας τῆς σελήνης, καὶ εἰσηρχόμην ἐν τῷ οἴκῳ, καὶ οὐκ ἐγινωσκόμην παρά τινος, καὶ ἐλάμβανον ἐκ τοῦ οἴκου ὅπερ ἤθελον, καὶ πάλιν κρατῶν τὰς τῆς σελήνης ἀκτῖνας, λέγων καὶ ἐπὶ

think thieves have climbed up onto our house. Look, I'm pretending to be asleep. But you wake me up with a loud cry and say to me, 'Husband, tell me how you've amassed the wealth we have and our treasures?' When I don't answer, keep on shouting and asking me." When his wife did this, the thieves heard and began to listen. The husband said to his wife, "God granted us great wealth, and you should eat and drink and be happy, and not ask about things which I can't reveal to you, in case people hear them—for the walls have ears—and we're put in danger." His wife said to him, "There's no one near us to hear it." And her husband replied, "Since you've forced me, I have to tell you, but see that none of your brothers or relatives find out, and we lose what we've gained, for I got these things by theft." His wife said to him, "How did you get all these things? For everyone regards you as trustworthy, and has no problem with you." He replied to her, "I have learned an incantation for theft, and by this means no one notices me or has a problem with me." She said to him, "So how do you say it, sir?" And he said to her, "I would go out on a brightly lit night, together with my companions, and we would climb up to the windows of the house we wanted to enter, and I would recite the incantation at the window, the 'Selem Selem' one, seven times, and, grasping the moonbeams, I would enter the house. I wouldn't be noticed by anyone and would take whatever I wanted from the house, and then, grasping the moonbeams again and re-

στόματος τὴν ἐπαοιδίαν, ἀνηρχόμην ἐπὶ τοῦ δώματος, καὶ οὕτως ποιῶν διεσῳζόμην."

9 Καὶ ἀκούσαντες οἱ κλέπται ἐχάρησαν χαρὰν μεγάλην λέγοντες· "Μεμαθήκαμεν ἐκ τοῦ οἴκου τούτου πρᾶγμα, ὅπερ κρεῖττον ἡμῖν ἐστιν παρὰ πάντων τῶν ὄντων ἐν αὐτῷ. Καὶ ὅπου δ' ἂν πορευθῶμεν, ἄφοβοί ἐσμεν." Δοκήσαντες δὲ ὑπνῶσαι τὸν τοῦ οἴκου κύριον σὺν τῇ γυναικὶ αὐτοῦ, καὶ πιστεύσαντες τοῖς λόγοις αὐτοῦ, προσῆλθεν ὁ πρῶτος αὐτῶν τῇ θυρίδι, ὅθεν τὸ φῶς εἰσήρχετο, καὶ εἶπε "Σελὲμ Σελὲμ" ἑπτάκις· καὶ ἀγκαλισάμενος τὴν ἀκτῖνα τοῦ κατελθεῖν, ἔπεσε κατὰ κεφαλῆς. Καὶ εἰσπηδήσας ὁ τοῦ οἴκου κύριος ἔχων ἐν τῇ χειρὶ αὐτοῦ ξύλον, [καὶ] εἶπε· "Σὺ τίς εἶ;" Λέγει αὐτῷ· "Ἐγώ εἰμι ὁ πεπλανημένος ὁ πιστεύων τὰ μὴ ἀληθῆ."

10 Τοιοῦτο παθεῖν μέλλω εἴπερ ἐκείνοις ἀκολουθήσω, οὗτος δέ ἐστιν ὁ καρπὸς τῶν θρησκειῶν αὐτῶν. Καὶ φυλάξας ἐμαυτὸν ἀπὸ τῶν σκανδάλων, ὅπως μὴ γένηταί μοι ἀπώλεια, στραφεὶς πάλιν, ἐζήτησα περὶ θρησκειῶν, ὅπως κρατήσω ἐξ αὐτῶν τήν τε ὠφέλειαν καὶ ἀλήθειαν· καὶ μὴ εὑρών τινα ἔχοντα πρός με ἀπολογίαν εἰς ὃ ἐζήτουν τοῦ ἱκανῶσαι καὶ στέρξαι τὸν νοῦν μου ἐν αὐτῷ, ἠβουλήθην ἀκολουθῆσαι τοῖς ἐμοῖς γονεῦσιν ἐν οἷς ἐσέβοντο. Καὶ πάλιν στραφεὶς παρῄνεσα τῇ ψυχῇ μου λέγων πρὸς αὐτήν· "Ἀπαραίτητος εἶ ἐν τῷ ζητήματι τούτῳ· καὶ γὰρ εὑρήκαμεν τοὺς μάγους ἀκολουθοῦντας τοῖς ἑαυτῶν γονεῦσιν·" καὶ ἐμνήσθην τοῦ ἀνδρὸς ἐκείνου τοῦ ἐσθίοντος ἀτάκτως, ὃς καὶ μεμφθεὶς ὑπό τινος εἶπεν· "Οὕτως εἶδον τοὺς γονεῖς

citing the incantation aloud, I would go up onto the roof of the house, and by doing this reach safety."

When they heard this, the thieves were very happy and said, "We've learned something from this house which is more valuable to us than all the things inside it. Wherever we go, we won't be afraid." Since they assumed the master of the house and his wife had fallen asleep, and they believed his words, their leader went up to the window where the light was shining in and recited "Selem Selem" seven times. But when he clasped the moonbeam to go down, he fell headlong. The master of the house rushed in with a club in his hand and said, "Who are you?" The thief said to him, "I am someone who has been led astray by believing what is not true." 9

I said to myself, that is what I am going to suffer if I follow them, for this is the fruit of religions. And to protect myself from trouble, so that I should not come to ruin, I returned to the subject again and inquired into religions, in order to obtain the benefit and truth from them. And because I did not find anyone who could offer me an answer to what I was seeking that would satisfy and settle my mind, I wanted to follow my parents in their worship. So I returned to the subject again, and I advised my soul, saying to it, "You are not to be deflected from this pursuit, for I have found magi who follow their parents." But then I remembered that man who was a sloppy eater and who, when he was criticized by someone, said, "This is how I saw my parents eat." 10

μου ἐσθίοντας.” Καὶ διὰ τοῦτο οὐκ ἠδυνήθην μεῖναι ἐν τῇ τῶν γονέων μου θρησκείᾳ. Καὶ πάλιν στραφεὶς εἰς ἀναζήτησιν τῶν θρησκειῶν, καὶ ἐρωτήσας τὰ ἐν αὐταῖς, συνέβη μοι πλησιᾶσαι ἡ τελευτὴ καὶ ἡ τοῦ κόσμου ἀναχώρησις· καὶ ἐγένετό μοι ὡσεὶ σκιὰ ὁ κόσμος οὗτος· τὴν δὲ ἀγαθοεργίαν ἔπραττον ἐλπίζων ἐν ταύτῃ τοῦ συναριθμηθῆναί με τοῖς ἀγαθοῖς ἐργάταις· ἐδειλίων δὲ μήπως ἡ ἀναστροφή μου κωλύσῃ με ἐκ τῆς ἀγαθοεργίας, καὶ καταλάβῃ με ἡ τελευτή μου, καὶ πάθω ὅπερ ἔπαθεν ἄνθρωπός τις.

11 *Περὶ ἄφρονος ἀνδρὸς τοῦ ἐρασθέντος γυναικὸς ὑπάνδρου.*

Ἐράσθη γὰρ μιᾶς τῶν ὑπάνδρων, ἥτις ὀρύξασα πλησίον τοῦ φρέατος εἰσοδοέξοδον τῷ μοιχῷ, καὶ θεῖσα τὸ ἀνοικτήριον πλησίον τούτου, καὶ δεικνῦσα, παρήγγειλεν αὐτῷ τοῦ εἶναι ἕτοιμον εἰς φυγήν, εἴ πως ἐπισυμβήσεται αὐτοῖς φόβος τις. Ἐν μιᾷ οὖν τῶν ἡμερῶν ὄντος τοῦ μοιχοῦ μετ’ αὐτῆς ἐν τῷ οἴκῳ, παρέστη ὁ ἀνὴρ αὐτῆς ἐν τῇ πύλῃ. Ἡ δὲ γυνὴ εἶπε τῷ μοιχῷ· “Δράμε μέχρι τοῦ φρέατος καὶ εὑρήσεις τὴν ἔξοδόν σου.” Ἀπελθὼν δὲ οὗτος εὗρε τὸ φρέαρ μετηρμένον, καὶ στραφεὶς πρὸς τὴν γυναῖκα ἔφη· “Οὐκ οἶδα τὴν ὁδόν.” Ἡ δὲ λέγει πρὸς αὐτόν· “Οὐκ οἶδας, μωρέ, ὅτι διὰ τῆς ἐμβασίας τοῦ λάκκου εὑρεῖν ἔχεις τὴν φυγήν;” Ὁ δὲ εἶπε πρὸς αὐτήν· “Ὁ ἔρως σου ἐχάωσέ μου τὴν ὁδόν.” Εἶπε δὲ αὐτῷ· “Ἄθλιε, σῶσον σεαυτόν, καὶ μὴ ἀντίστρεφε λόγους ὡς οἱ μωροί.” Εἶπε δὲ αὐτῇ· “Καὶ πῶς πορεύσομαι χαώσας τὴν ὁδὸν πλανηθεὶς παρὰ σοῦ;” Σταθεὶς

And for this reason I could not stay in my parents' religion. Yet again I returned to the investigation of religions, and while I was asking about what they offered, my end and departure from the world drew nigh, and this world became like a shadow for me. So I occupied myself with doing good, hoping that in this way I would be counted among those who do good works. But I was afraid that my way of life would prevent me from good deeds and that my death would overtake me, and that I would suffer what a certain man did.

About a foolish man who was the lover 11
of a married woman.

For this man fell passionately in love with a married woman, who excavated a passageway for him near the way in and out of the cistern and placed the key near to it; she showed it to him, telling him to be ready to run away if anything should happen to frighten them. So one day when her lover was with her in the house, her husband appeared at the door. The woman said to her lover, "Run to the cistern, and you'll find your way out." He went off, but found the cistern covered, so he returned to the woman and said, "I don't know the way." She said to him, "Don't you know, you idiot, that you can make your escape through the inlet for the pit?" But he replied to her, "Desire for you made me lose my way." She said to him, "Save yourself, you wretched fool, and don't stand here talking back to me like someone stupid." He said to her, "How can I leave, when I've lost the way because I've been led astray by you?" As the wretched man stood there at

δὲ ὁ ἄθλιος ἐν ἀπορίᾳ, εἰσῆλθεν ὁ ἀνὴρ αὐτῆς, καὶ κρατήσας αὐτὸν ἔτυψεν ἀνηλεῶς, παραδοὺς αὐτὸν τῷ ἡγεμόνι.

12 Ἐγὼ δὲ μετὰ φόβου ταῦτα λογισάμενος καὶ πρὸς ἑαυτὸν συστρεφόμενος, ᾑρετισάμην τὴν ἀγαθοεργίαν ποιεῖν, ἥνπερ μαρτυροῦσι πᾶσαι αἱ θρησκεῖαι. Ἠθέλησα δὲ ἀποδρᾶσαι τὸν φόβον, καὶ μὴ τύπτειν τινά, μήτε αἰσχρολογεῖν, μήτε κλέπτειν, μήτε θυμωθῆναι, μήτε ἐν δολίῳ εἶναι· ἀπέδρασα δὲ καὶ τὴν ἡδονὴν τῶν γυναικῶν, καὶ ἐκτησάμην σωφροσύνην· ἐφύλαξα δὲ καὶ τὴν γλῶσσάν μου ἀπὸ ψεύδους καὶ ἀπὸ παντὸς λόγου ἀργοῦ καὶ βλαβεροῦ· ἠγάπησα δὲ καὶ τοῦ εἶναι πάντοτε ἀγαθός, τὴν δὲ ἀνάστασιν καὶ ἀνταπόδοσιν οὐκ ἠπίστησα. Ἐμακρύνθην δὲ καὶ τῶν πονηρῶν, καὶ πλησιάσας τοῖς ἀγαθοῖς ἔγνων ὅτι οὐκ ἔστιν ἕτερος, οὔτε φίλος, οὔτε σύζυγος ὥσπερ ἡ ἀγαθωσύνη· καὶ γάρ, Θεοῦ θέλοντος, εὐκόλως κτᾶται· καὶ ὅτι αὕτη ἐνδοξοτέρα ἐστὶν ὑπὲρ γονέων καὶ φίλων, διδάσκουσα πάντοτε ἀγαθοποιεῖν· μεταδιδομένη δέ, οὐ πληροῦται, ἀλλὰ περισσεύεται πλέον· οὐ φθείρεται, οὐ συμπαλαιοῦται, οὐκ ἀπαιτεῖται παρὰ ἐξουσίας, οὐ φείδεται πυρός, οὐ δειλιᾷ κλέπταις, οὐ φοβεῖται θηρία, ἀλλὰ πλεῖον κοσμεῖται, καὶ πάντοτε ἄφοβος ὑπάρχει. Εὗρον δὲ τὸν ἀποδράσαντα πάντων τῶν ἀγαθῶν ἔργων καὶ ἀσχοληθέντα εἰς τὴν τοῦ βίου τρυφήν, τὴν πικρὰν γλυκύτητα καὶ ἡδονήν, ὅμοιον ἀνθρώπῳ ἀπολέσαντι χρήματα πολλὰ καὶ τὴν αὐτῶν ὠφέλειαν διὰ μιᾶς ἡμέρας γέλοια.

a loss, the woman's husband came in, grabbed hold of him, beat him mercilessly, and handed him over to the governor.

So, after I had thought fearfully about these matters, I 12
applied them to myself, and chose to do good works, which is something all religions favor. To avoid this fear I wished not to hit anyone, nor use foul language, nor steal, nor get angry, nor be deceitful. I also shunned the pleasure of women, and I acquired self-control. I guarded my tongue against falsehood, and against all idle and harmful speech, and I delighted in always being good, and did not doubt resurrection and requital. I distanced myself from the wicked and drew close to the virtuous, for I knew that there was nothing else, neither a friend nor a partner, like virtue. For, God willing, virtue is easily acquired, and because it is honored above parents and friends, it always teaches us to do good. When it is shared, it is not used up, but becomes more abundant. It does not perish, does not grow old, does not yield to authority, does not draw back from fire, is not cowardly when faced with thieves, does not fear wild beasts, but is honored the more, and is always fearless. I discovered that a person who has run away from all good deeds and occupied himself in a life of luxury, bitter sweetness, and pleasure, is like a man who wastes great wealth and its benefit on one day of fun.

13 *Περὶ ἄφρονος ἐμπόρου.*

Ἐρρέθη γὰρ ὅτι ἔμπορός τις ἐμισθώσατό τινα ἡμέραν μίαν εἰς νομίσματα ἑκατὸν τοῦ τρυπῆσαι αὐτῷ μαργαρίτας. Γενάμενοι δὲ ἐν τῷ οἴκῳ, εἶδε σεῖστρα πάνυ καλὰ κρεμάμενα, καὶ λέγει αὐτῷ· "Λάβε, κροῦσαι αὐτά." Καὶ λαβὼν ἔκρουσε ταῦτα μεθ' ἡδονῆς. Ἀκούσας δὲ ὁ μισθωσάμενος αὐτὸν ὅλην τὴν ἡμέραν ἡδύνετο. Ὀψίας δὲ γεναμένης, ᾐτήσατο ὁ μισθωτὸς τὸν μισθὸν αὐτοῦ, καὶ λέγει αὐτῷ· "Ὡς οὐκ ἐποίησας αὐτά, τί αἰτεῖς;" Ὁ δὲ λέγει αὐτῷ· "Ὡς προσέταξας, οὕτως ἐποίησα." Ἄκων δὲ ἐπλήρωσε τὸν μισθὸν αὐτοῦ· καὶ κατελείφθησαν οἱ μαργαρῖται αὐτοῦ ἀτρύπητοι.

14 *Περὶ σεμνοῦ βίου.*

Οὕτω καὶ ἐγώ, καταμαθὼν εἶναι ἀσυστάτους τὰς τοῦ κόσμου ἡδονὰς ᾑρετισάμην τὴν ἄσκησιν· καὶ γὰρ δι' αὐτῆς εὐθεῖαί εἰσιν αἱ ὁδοὶ τῆς ἀναστάσεως, ὥσπερ οἱ γονεῖς παρέχουσιν εὐθείας ὁδοὺς εἰς τοὺς ἑαυτῶν παῖδας. Καὶ εἶδον αὐτὴν ὡς πύργον ὀχυρὸν φυλάττουσαν τὸν ἄνθρωπον ἀπὸ παντὸς πονηροῦ· καὶ ἡ πύλη αὐτῆς ἀνεῳγμένη ὑπάρχει τοῖς θέλουσιν εἰσελθεῖν εἰς τὴν ἀένναον τρυφὴν τοῦ παραδείσου. Εὗρον δὲ τὸν ἀσκητὴν ἐν ἡσυχίᾳ πρόσχαρον, εὐχάριστον, αὐτάρκη, ἀμέριμνον, ταπεινόν, ἀποφυγόντα πάντα τὰ τοῦ κόσμου, καὶ γεγονότα πάσης βλάβης καὶ θλίψεως ἀνώτερον. Καὶ ἀποφυγὼν τὸν φθόνον ἐκολλήθην τῇ ἀγάπῃ, καὶ καταφρονήσας τῶν ῥεόντων τέλειος

About a foolish merchant. 13

It has thus been said that a merchant hired someone for one day for one hundred *nomismata* to pierce pearls for him. When they were in the house, however, the man saw some very beautiful *sistra* hanging there, and the merchant said to him, "Take them down and play them." So, taking them down, he played them with pleasure. The man who hired him listened and enjoyed himself all day. But, when evening came, the hired man asked for his wage. The merchant said to him, "As you haven't done anything, why are you asking?" But he replied to him, "I did what you told me to." So he paid him his wages unwillingly, and his pearls remained unpierced.

About a proper life. 14

Since I had thus learned that the pleasures of the world are insubstantial, I chose asceticism, for through this the paths to resurrection are straight, just as parents provide straight paths for their children. I saw this as a strong tower which protects a person against all evil; and its gate is open to those who wish to enter the eternal delight of paradise. I found the ascetic, in his spiritual tranquility, agreeable, pleasant, self-sufficient, free from care, and humble, for he had escaped all the things of the world and had risen above all harm and distress. Fleeing envy, I was devoted to love; scorning things that change, I became perfect in under-

γέγονα τῇ συνέσει, καὶ ἰδὼν τὰ μέλλοντα ἄφοβος ἐγενόμην, καὶ μὴ ἁμαρτήσας ἐρρύσθην ἐγώ. Καταμαθὼν δὲ τὴν τῶν ἀσκητῶν ὁδόν, πλεῖον ταύτην ἐπόθησα, ὥστε βουληθεὶς μετ' αὐτῶν εἶναι, πάλιν ἐφοβήθην, μήπως οὐ δυνηθῶ ὑπομεῖναι διὰ τὰ προλαβόμενά μου ἤθη, καὶ βλαβῶ πλεῖον. Καὶ δειλιάσας, μήπως τὸν κόσμον καταλιπὼν ἀκολουθήσω τοῖς ἀσκηταῖς καὶ ἀπολέσω τὴν εὐεργεσίαν δι' ἧς ἤλπιζον τῶν αἰωνίων ἀγαθῶν, καὶ ἔσομαι ὥσπερ ὁ κύων ὁ βαστάζων ἐν τῷ στόματι αὐτοῦ μέρος τι κρέατος, ἐλθὼν δὲ ἔν τινι ποταμῷ καὶ ἰδὼν τὴν σκιὰν τοῦ κρέατος ἐν τῷ ὕδατι, εἰσεπήδησε τοῦ λαβεῖν αὐτό, καὶ ὅπερ κατεῖχεν ἐχάωσε, καὶ κατελείφθη κενός, καὶ δειλιάσας τὴν ἄσκησιν λίαν, καὶ φοβηθεὶς μήπως ἀγανακτήσω καὶ οὐ δυνηθῶ φέρειν τὴν αὐτῆς ὑπομονήν, <οὐκ> ἠβουλήθην μεῖναι εἰς τὴν αὐτῆς τάξιν.

Καὶ πάλιν διακρίνας ἀναμεταξὺ τοῦ ἀσκητοῦ καὶ τοῦ φιλοκόσμου, καὶ τὰ συμβαίνοντα αὐτοῖς πάντα, ἐφάνησάν μοι ἐπίσης, διότι οὐκ ἔστιν ἐν τῷ κόσμῳ ἡδονή τις ἡ μὴ προξενοῦσα βλάβην καὶ θλῖψιν. Καὶ γὰρ ὁ κόσμος ἐστὶν ὡς τὸ ἁλμυρὸν ὕδωρ, ὅ, ὅσον τις πίνει, τοσοῦτον διψᾷ· καὶ ὥσπερ τὸ ὀστοῦν τὸ ἔχον κρέατος ὀσμήν, ὅπερ εὑρὼν ὁ κύων καὶ ζητήσας τὴν τοῦ κρέατος ἡδονήν, ἐπληγώθη τὸ στόμα αὐτοῦ, καὶ ὅσον ζητεῖ τοῦ φαγεῖν αὐτό, τοσοῦτον πληγοῦται καὶ αἱματοῦται· νομίζων γὰρ κρέας μαστίζειν, μειζότερον πλήττεται, καὶ μὴ τιτρώσκων, μᾶλλον τιτρώσκεται· καὶ ὥσπερ ἡ γὺψ ἢ ἡ ἐνίβλα ἁρπάσασα μέρος τι κρέατος, εἶτα ὑπὸ τῶν πετεινῶν τοῦ οὐρανοῦ περικυκλωθεῖσα, καὶ ἄκουσα τούτου στερεῖται, μηδὲν ὠφεληθεῖσα, εἰ

standing; regarding what is to come, I became fearless; and, by not committing sin, I was saved. The more I learned the path of the ascetics, the more I longed for it, with the result that, although I wanted to be with them, I became afraid again that I would not be able to endure it because of my previous way of life, and I would suffer more harm. I was fearful that, by leaving the world behind to follow the ascetics, I would ruin the good work through which I hoped for eternal benefit, and would be like the dog with a piece of meat in its mouth, which came to a river and, seeing the reflection of the meat in the water jumped in to get it, lost the meat it had, and was left with nothing. So, I became very fearful of the ascetic way of life and, because I was afraid that I would be discontented and unable to summon up the patient endurance it requires, I did not wish to remain in its order.

And once again, in choosing between the ascetic and the 15
man who loves the world, and everything that happens to them, it seemed to me that they were evenly balanced, for there is no worldly pleasure that does not bring harm and affliction. For the world is like salty water: however much one drinks, one is just as thirsty. And it is just like the bone smelling of meat that the dog finds and, in trying to get the pleasure of the meat from it, hurts its mouth, and the more it tries to eat it, the more it hurts itself and bleeds. For thinking that it is chewing meat, it wounds itself more seriously, and although it does no damage to the bone, it damages itself instead. It is also like the vulture or the bird of prey, which snatched a piece of meat and was then surrounded by the birds of the sky so that it was forcibly deprived of it and derived no benefit except for getting toil

μὴ κόπους καὶ μόχθους πολλοὺς ἀποκερδήσασα· καὶ ὥσπερ τὸ ἀγγεῖον τὸ ἔχον μέλι, κάτωθεν δὲ τοῦ μέλιτος δηλητήριον· καὶ οἱ ἐσθίοντες αὐτό, πρῶτον μὲν γλυκαίνονται, ὕστερον δὲ ἀπολοῦνται· καὶ ὥσπερ ὁ βλέπων ἐνύπνιον καὶ χαίρων αὐτὸς ἐν ἑαυτῷ, ὅταν δὲ ἔξυπνος γένηται, ἀπόλλυται ἡ χαρὰ αὐτοῦ· καὶ ὥσπερ ἡ ἀστραπὴ ἡ φαίνουσα τῷ ὁδοιπόρῳ ῥιπῇ, παρελθούσης δέ, μένει ἐν τῇ σκοτείᾳ· καὶ ὥσπερ ἡ σκώληξ τῆς μετάξης ἡ νήθουσα καθ' ἑαυτήν· ὅσον γὰρ νήθει, πλέον μακρύνεται ἡ ἔξοδος τῆς ἐργασίας αὐτῆς. Καταμαθὼν δὲ τῶν τοιούτων πραγμάτων, ᾑρετισάμην τὴν ἄσκησιν. Καὶ εἶπον τῇ ψυχῇ μου· "Οὐ δεῖ σε φυγεῖν τὴν ἄσκησιν καὶ μένειν ἐν τοῖς βιωτικοῖς, ὅταν ἐννοήσῃς τὰς πονηρίας τὰς ἐν αὐτοῖς, οὐδὲ τότε δυνήσῃ ἐκφυγεῖν, ἢ ὅταν ἐννοηθῇς τὴν στένωσιν καὶ τοὺς κόπους οὓς ἔχει, οὐδὲ τότε τοῦ βίου μακρυνθῆναι." Ἐμπεσὼν τοίνυν εἰς βυθὸν ἀπορίας καὶ μὴ δυνηθεὶς ἐγνωκέναι πῶς δεῖ με εἶναι, ἐγενόμην ὥσπερ ἀσύνετος κριτὴς ὁ κρίνων καὶ δικαιῶν τὸν ἐνάγοντα, καὶ πάλιν καταδικάζων αὐτὸν ὁ δίκαιος κριτής.

16 Πάλιν δὲ καταμαθὼν τὸν ἀγῶνα τῆς ἀσκήσεως καὶ τὴν ἔνδειαν αὐτῆς τὴν πρόσκαιρον καὶ τὴν μετ' αὐτῆς τρυφὴν καὶ ἄνεσιν τὴν αἰώνιον, ταύτην ᾑρετισάμην· καὶ βλέψας τῆς ψυχῆς τὴν ἀκορεσίαν πρὸς τὴν τοῦ βίου ἡδονήν, εἶπον· "Ὦ πόσην πικρότητα καὶ δριμύτητα ἔχει." Εἶπον δὲ πάλιν· "Ποία τρυφὴ καὶ ἡδονή ἐστιν ἡ <μὴ> παρὰ μικροῦ διερχομένη; Καὶ τίς οὐ προκρίνει μικρὰν πικρότητα δι' ἀένναον γλυκύτητα; Καὶ γὰρ ἐὰν συμφωνηθῇ ἀνθρώπῳ τινὶ ζῆσαι ἑκατὸν ἔτη ἐν λύπῃ καὶ στενοχωρίᾳ καὶ μετὰ

and a lot of trouble. Again, it is like the jar which contains honey, but with poison underneath the honey: those who eat it taste sweetness at first but later are bound to die. It is also like someone who has a dream and is happy in it, but when he wakes up, his happiness is lost. And it is like lightning that is seen in a flash by the traveler but, when it has passed, he remains in the dark. It is also like the silkworm which spins against its own interests, for the more it spins, the more the end of its work is prolonged. So, when I had considered such matters, I chose asceticism, and I said to my soul, "You should not run away from asceticism and remain involved in worldly affairs, for when you consider the evils in the latter, then you will not be able to flee it; on the other hand, when you consider the constriction and the labors which it involves then you will not be able to distance yourself from life." So I fell into the depths of perplexity and, since I was unable to decide how I should live, I became like a stupid judge, who judges and rules in favor of the accuser and then the just judge rules against the same person.

But when I considered the struggle of asceticism once 16
more, and both its poverty in the present but the eternal delight and repose which it brings, I chose it for myself. And when I saw my soul's insatiable desire for the pleasure of life, I said, "What great bitterness and severity it has." But then I said, "What joy and pleasure does not pass away in a short time? Who would not choose a little bitterness in exchange for eternal sweetness? Even if someone were to make an agreement to live in grief and poverty for a hundred years

ταῦτα ἀπελθεῖν εἰς ἄνεσιν καὶ ἀνάπαυσιν αἰώνιον, <οὐκ ἂν> προέκρινεν ἑαυτὸν ζῆσαι ἐν στενοχωρίᾳ μικρὸν διὰ τὸ ἀπολαῦσαι αἰώνια; Ἢ οὐκ ἔστιν ὁ βίος οὗτος πολυώδυνος, καὶ πολυβάσανος, καὶ πολυκίνδυνος, καὶ ἡ ἀναστροφὴ τοῦ ἀνθρώπου ἡ ἐν αὐτῷ θλῖψις, καὶ ἀνάγκη, καὶ βάσανος ἀπὸ τῆς ἀρχῆς αὐτοῦ καὶ μέχρι τέλους;" Καὶ γὰρ ἡ ἀρχὴ τοῦ ἀνθρώπου, ὡς ἐρρέθη παρ' ἰατροῖς, ἐστὶν ὥσπερ ἡ μύξα πεσοῦσα ἐν τῇ μήτρᾳ τῆς γυναικός, καὶ συναφθεῖσα τῷ αἵματι αὐτῆς, καὶ παχυνθεῖσα διαμερίζεται εἰς μέλη. Καὶ ἔστιν ἐν σκοτίᾳ καὶ στενοχωρίᾳ, οὐκ ἐσθίων, οὐ πίνων· ὅταν δὲ ἔλθῃ ἡ ὥρα τῆς γεννήσεως αὐτοῦ, μετὰ βίας πολλῆς καὶ πόνου ἐξέρχεται· ὅταν δὲ ἐξέλθῃ, ὑπομένει τὰς τῆς βρεφουργίας ἀνάγκας, ἀπό τε πείνης, καὶ δίψης, καὶ κρύους. Καὶ ἡ θλῖψις ἡ τελευταία καὶ μεγάλη—ἡ ἀπογαλάκτησις. Καὶ ἡ τῶν μαθημάτων αὖθις παίδευσις, ἥτις διὰ πόνου καὶ πολλοῦ ἀγῶνος ἐκφέρεται, καὶ αἱ ἀσθένειαι, καὶ οἱ πόνοι, καὶ αἱ φαρμακοποσίαι. Ὅταν δὲ νόμου ἡλικίας γένηται, ἀγωνίζεται περὶ πλούτου, καὶ συζυγίας, καὶ τέκνων, καὶ περὶ ἀκορεσίας καὶ μόχθων καὶ πραγμάτων ἐπικινδύνων, καὶ ἀναφέρεται ἐν τούτοις, ἔχων μεθ' ἑαυτοῦ ἐχθροὺς τέσσαρας—τὸ αἷμα, τὸ φλέγμα, τὸν χυμόν, καὶ τὴν χολήν—ἔπειτα τὰ δηλητήρια, τὰ ἰοβόλα θηρία, τὰ ἕρποντα, τοὺς λέοντας, τὸν καύσωνα, τὸ κρύος, τὸν ἀέρα, τὸν ὑετὸν καὶ τὰ πολυποίκιλα βάσανα τοῦ γήρως καὶ ἐὰν συμβῇ πολυετῆσαι, δεινόν· καὶ ἐὰν τὰ προρρηθέντα οὐ φοβηθῇ, κἂν τοῦ θανάτου τὴν ὥραν δεῖ φοβεῖσθαι, καὶ τὴν ἀποχώρησιν τοῦ κόσμου τούτου, τέκνων καὶ συγγενῶν καὶ φίλων καὶ ἀδελφῶν καὶ πάντων τῶν ἐλπιζομένων ἐν τῷ

and afterward go to eternal repose and rest, would he not choose to live in poverty for a short time in order to enjoy himself eternally? Is this life not indeed very painful, with much torment, and much danger, and a man's time in it one of affliction, anguish, and torture from start to finish?" For the beginning of a man, as it is described by physicians, is like mucus falling into a woman's womb and, when this has combined with her blood and become thick, it divides into limbs, and it exists in darkness and confinement, without eating or drinking. When the time for his birth arrives, he emerges with great violence and labor, and, when he has emerged, he endures the anguish of infancy from hunger, thirst, and cold. Then there is the final great affliction—weaning, and the learning of lessons, which is acquired with labor and much struggle, and the sicknesses, the diseases, and the medicines to be taken. When he comes of age he struggles over wealth, and marriage, and children, and with insatiable desire, and hardships, and dangerous matters, and he brings these upon himself, as he has within him four competing enemies—blood, phlegm, black bile, and yellow bile—then there are also the poisons, venomous animals, reptiles, lions, fever, cold, weather, rain, and the manifold torments of old age, and it is worse if he happens to live for a long time. Even if he does not fear the things already mentioned, he must at least fear the hour of his death and his departure from this world, and from his children, relatives, friends, and brothers, and from all for which he hoped in

βίῳ τούτῳ, ἔσχατον δὲ πάντων τὴν τῶν κολάσεων μνείαν. Ὅστις δὲ οὐ φοβεῖται ταῦτα καὶ ἀσχοληθῇ ἐν τῷ βίῳ τούτῳ καὶ ἐν ταῖς αὐτοῦ ἡδοναῖς ταῖς φθειρομέναις καὶ ῥεούσαις, ἄφρων καὶ ἀσύνετος καλεῖται. Καὶ γὰρ ἐὰν καί ἐστι βασιλεὺς καὶ ἐκ Θεοῦ εὐτυχέστατος καὶ πάντων τῶν βλαβερῶν καὶ θλίψεων ἀνώτερος καὶ πάσας τὰς ἀρετὰς κεκτημένος, ὁ βίος αὐτοῦ φθαρτὸς ὀπισθοποδεῖ αὐτὸν πανταχόθεν.

17 Ἐλθὼν δὲ πάλιν εἰς ἔννοιαν τῶν τοῦ βίου πραγμάτων, εἶδον τὸν ἄνθρωπον τιμιώτερον πάντων τῶν κτισμάτων καὶ αὐτὸν ἐπὶ τὰ πονηρὰ βλέποντα καὶ μὴ φροντίζοντα τῆς ἑαυτοῦ σωτηρίας διὰ τῆς τῶν αἰσθητῶν ἡδονῆς· καὶ πλήρης θαύματος εἶπον ἐν ἑαυτῷ· "Ὅμοιός ἐστιν ὁ ἄνθρωπος ἀνδρί τινι, ὅστις ἔφυγεν ἀπὸ φόβου δεινοῦ μονοκέρωτος, καὶ συναντήσας λάκκῳ ἔχοντι ἐν τῷ στόματι αὐτοῦ δένδρον ὑψηλόν, ἀνελθὼν ἐκρεμάσθη ἐν αὐτῷ· καὶ κρατήσας δύο κλάδους τοῦ δένδρου ταῖς χερσίν, τοὺς πόδας αὐτοῦ ἔθηκεν ἐν τόπῳ τινὶ θαρρῶν στερεωθῆναι ἐν αὐτῷ. Ἦσαν δὲ ὄφεις τέσσαρες εἰς τὸ δένδρον ἐκβάλλοντες τὰς κεφαλὰς αὐτῶν ἐκ τῶν τρωγλῶν αὐτῶν καὶ τρυπῶντες τὸ δένδρον. Παρακύψας δὲ κάτωθεν εἶδε δράκοντα ἐν τῇ ῥίζῃ τοῦ δένδρου ἀνεῳγμένον ἔχοντα τὸ στόμα αὐτοῦ ὥστε καταπιεῖν αὐτόν· εἶδε δὲ καὶ δύο μύας, τὸν μὲν ἕνα λευκὸν τὸν δὲ ἕτερον μέλανα, ἐσθίοντας ἀεννάως τὰς ῥίζας τῶν κλάδων ὧν ἐκράτει καὶ ὅσον ἦν ἐκτεμεῖν αὐτάς. Ἐν ἀπορίᾳ δὲ γενόμενος περὶ τούτων, ἐζήτει πῶς δεῖ αὐτὸν ταῦτα ἀποδράσειν. Ἀναβλέψας δὲ εἶδε μέλι ῥέον ἄνωθεν ἐκ τῆς κορυφῆς τοῦ δένδρου, καὶ γευσάμενος

this life, and, last of all, there is the remembrance of the punishments to come. Anyone who does not fear these things and is preoccupied with this life and its perishable and fleeting pleasures is clearly foolish and stupid. For even if he is a king who is most favored by God and is above every oppression and affliction, and he possesses all the virtues, his mortal life stays with him everywhere.

Again, after I had reached an understanding of life's af- 17
fairs, I saw that when a human being, who is more valuable than all created beings, comes face to face with wicked things, he does not take care of his own salvation because of the pleasure he derives from perceptible things. Full of wonder, I said to myself, "A human being is like a man who was fleeing in fear from a terrible unicorn and, when he came to a pit with a tall tree at its edge, he climbed up and hung onto it. He took hold of two of the tree's branches with his hands and put his feet somewhere in order to steady himself on it. But there were four snakes in the tree, poking their heads out from their holes and burrowing into the tree. Looking down, he saw a serpent in the roots of the tree with its mouth open so as to swallow him. And he saw two mice, one white, the other black, constantly gnawing the bases of the branches he was holding on to and about to cut them off. Since he was distressed by what was happening, he started seeking how he might escape all this. But then, looking up, he saw honey running out of the crown of the tree above

αὐτό, ἐγλυκάνθη τῆς ἡδονῆς, καὶ ἐπελάθετο τῆς αὐτοῦ σωτηρίας, καὶ οὐκ ἐμνήσθη τοῦ δεινοῦ μονοκέρωτος, οὔτε τῶν τεσσάρων ὄφεων, οὔτε τοῦ φοβεροῦ δράκοντος, οὔτε τῶν δύο μυῶν τῶν ἐσθιόντων τὰς ῥίζας τῶν κλάδων ὑπὸ τοὺς πόδας αὐτοῦ καὶ ὅτι, ὁπόταν φάγωσιν αὐτὰς καὶ ἐκκοπῶσιν οἱ κλάδοι, πεσεῖται ἐν τῷ φάρυγγι τοῦ δράκοντος· ἀλλ' ἀσχοληθεὶς ἐκεῖνος εἰς τὴν γλυκύτητα τοῦ μέλιτος, ἀπώλετο."

18 Ὡμοίωσα δὲ τὸν μονόκερων τῷ θανάτῳ, τῷ ἀκολουθοῦντι καὶ διώκοντι τὸν ἄνθρωπον ἐν ᾧ τόπῳ ἀπέρχεται καὶ οὐ δύναταί τις ἐξ αὐτοῦ ἀποκρυβῆναι· τὸν δὲ λάκκον, τῷ βίῳ τούτῳ, τῷ πλήρει κακίας καὶ πονηρίας καὶ δεινῆς διατριβῆς καὶ ἀπωλείας· τοὺς δὲ δύο κλάδους τοὺς συγκοπτομένους ὑπὸ τῶν μυῶν, τῇ προσκαίρῳ ταύτῃ ζωῇ· τοὺς δὲ τέσσαρας ὄφεις, τοῖς τέσσαρσι χυμοῖς τοῖς συνιστῶσι τὸν ἄνθρωπον· ὅταν γὰρ εἷς ἐξ αὐτῶν κινηθῇ κατά τινος ἔσται ὥσπερ ὁ ὄφις, ὁ δάκνων καὶ θανατῶν τὸν ἄνθρωπον τῷ φαρμάκῳ αὐτοῦ. Τὸν δὲ δράκοντα τῷ στόματι τοῦ Ἅιδου, ὃν οὐ δύναταί τις παραδραμεῖν· τοὺς δὲ δύο μύας, τὸν μὲν λευκὸν τῇ ἡμέρᾳ, τὸν δὲ μέλανα τῇ νυκτὶ ταῖς ἐσθιούσαις ἀεννάως καὶ φθειρούσαις τὴν ζωὴν τοῦ ἀνθρώπου. Ὅσον γὰρ παρέρχεται ἡ ἡμέρα τῇ ἡμέρᾳ καὶ ἡ νὺξ τῇ νυκτί, τοσοῦτον ἐκλείπεται ἡ ζωὴ τοῦ ἀνθρώπου καὶ οὐ νοεῖ. Τὸ δὲ μέλι, τῇ πικρᾷ γλυκύτητι τοῦ βίου τούτου, τῇ ἡδυνούσῃ τὰς τοῦ ἀνθρώπου αἰσθήσεις, ἀηδῶς δὲ καὶ μετὰ πικρίας χωριζούσῃ αὐτὸν ἀπὸ τῆς αὐτοῦ σωτηρίας.

19 Καταμαθὼν δὲ ταῦτα πάντα ἐγώ, ἠράσθην τῆς ἐμαυτοῦ πολιτείας καὶ μεγάλως ἠγωνίσθην εἰς τὴν ἀγαθοεργίαν,

and, when he tasted it, he was overcome by the pleasure of the sweetness and forgot about saving himself. He did not remember the terrible unicorn, nor the four snakes, nor the fearsome serpent, nor the two mice eating the bases of the branches under his feet, nor that, when they had eaten through them and the branches were severed, he would fall into the serpent's mouth. And so, preoccupied with the sweetness of the honey, he perished."

I likened the unicorn to death, which follows and pursues 18
a man wherever he goes and from which no one can hide. And the pit I likened to this life, full of evil and wickedness and terrible time wasting and depravity; the two branches being cut off by the mice to the present transitory existence; and the four snakes to the four humors which maintain a man, for whenever one of them is roused against someone, it will be like the snake which bites and kills a man through its venom. And the serpent I likened to the mouth of Hades, which no one can avoid. As for the two mice, the white one I likened to the day and the black one to the night, which both constantly eat away at and destroy a man's life. For just as day follows day and night follows night, so the life of a man passes without him realizing it. And the honey I likened to the bitter sweetness of this life, which delights a man's senses, but unpleasantly and bitterly separates him from his salvation.

After I had considered all these things, I loved my own 19
way of life, and struggled mightily in doing good deeds, so

ὅπως δι' αὐτῆς εὕρω καιρὸν ὁδηγίας πρὸς τὴν ἐμαυτοῦ πολιτείαν τῆς σωτηρίας. Καὶ στέρξας ἐν τούτοις, ἀπεστάλθην παρὰ τοῦ ἐμοῦ βασιλέως Χοσρόου εἰς τὴν Ἰνδίαν, εἶτα ὑπέστρεψα εἰς τὴν ἐμὴν χώραν μεταγράψας καὶ βιβλία ἱκανά, ἐξ ὧν δὴ καὶ τουτὶ τὸ βιβλίον ὑπάρχει, τὸ καλούμενον *Κυλίλε καὶ Δίμνε* Ἀραβικῶς, ὅπερ λέγεται *Στεφανίτης καὶ Ἰχνηλάτης* Ἑλληνικῶς.

that in this way I might find an opportune guide to make my way of life that of salvation. And although I was content with them, I was sent by my king, Chosroes, to India; then I returned to my country after translating a lot of books, among which was also this book, called *Kelilai and Dimnai* in Arabic, which in Greek means *Stephanites and Ichnelates.*

Τὰ κατὰ *Στεφανίτην καὶ Ἰχνηλάτην*

Ἀρχὴ σὺν Θεῷ περὶ τῶν ιε΄ τμημάτων τῶν εὑρεθέντων ἐν τῇ Ἰνδικῇ χώρᾳ, καὶ λεχθέντων παρά τινος φιλοσόφου τῷ βασιλεῖ Ἀβεσαλώμ, καὶ μετακομισθέντων ἐκ τῆς Ἰνδίας τῷ βασιλεῖ Χοσρόῃ εἰς Περσίαν, παρὰ τοῦ Περζωὲ τοῦ σοφοῦ ἰατροῦ, καὶ πάλιν μεταγλωττισθέντων ἀραβικῶς καὶ ὕστερον μετενεχθέντων ἐκ τῆς τῶν Ἀράβων διαλέκτου, παρὰ Συμεὼν Μαγίστρου καὶ φιλοσόφου τοῦ Σὴθ εἰς τὴν Ἑλληνικὴν διάλεκτον. Βιβλίον ὡραῖον, ἐν ᾧ ὑπάρχει μυθικὴ διήγησις, τὸ κατὰ τὸν *Στεφανίτην καὶ Ἰχνηλάτην* λεγόμενον, Σαρακηνῇ διαλέκτῳ *Κυλίλε καὶ Δίμνε.*

Ἀρχὴ τοῦδε τοῦ βιβλίου.

Λόγος πρῶτος

Ὁ τῶν Ἰνδῶν βασιλεὺς Ἀβεσαλὼμ ἤρετό τινα τῶν περὶ αὐτὸν φιλοσόφων, λέγων· "Βούλομαί σε ὑποδειγματίσαι μοι, ὅπως ὁ πονηρὸς καὶ δόλιος ἀνὴρ μεσολαβὼν εἰς ἔχθραν μεταβάλλει τὴν μεταξύ τινων συστᾶσαν φιλίαν." Ὁ δὲ φίλοσοφος ὑπολαβὼν οὕτως ἔφη·

CONCERNING *STEPHANITES AND ICHNELATES*

The beginning, with God, of the fifteen chapters which were devised in the Indian country and recounted by a philosopher to the king Abesalom, and transferred from India to the king Chosroes in Persia by the wise physician Perzoué, and again translated into Arabic and later rendered from the Arabs' language by the teacher and philosopher Symeon Seth into the Greek language. It is a wonderful book, in which there is a mythical account called *Stephanites and Ichnelates* and, in the Saracen language, *Kelilai and Dimnai.*

THE BEGINNING OF THE BOOK.

Chapter 1

The king of the Indians, Abesalom, questioned one of his philosophers, and said, "I want you to give me an example of how a wicked and treacherous man turns the friendship that exists between people into hatred by interfering." And the philosopher answered as follows:

2 *Περὶ ἐμπόρου πολυόλβου.*

Λέγεται ὡς ἔμπορός τις πολύολβος ὢν καὶ *βίου ἐπηετανοῦ* κατὰ τὴν ποίησιν εὐπορῶν καὶ παῖδας ἔχων νωχελεῖς καὶ μὴ βουλομένους δι' ὄκνον ἄσκησίν τινα τέχνης μεταχειρίσασθαι, παραινετικοῖς τοιοῖσδε πρὸς αὐτοὺς ἐχρήσατο ῥήμασιν· "Ὦ τέκνα," λέγων, "ὁ ἐν τῷ βίῳ ἀναστρεφόμενος τριῶν δεῖται πραγμάτων· αὐτάρκους περιουσίας, δόξης τῆς παρὰ ἀνθρώπων, καὶ ἐπιτυχίας τῶν ἀποταμιευομένων ἐκεῖσε τοῖς δικαίοις ἀγαθῶν. Ταῦτα δὲ τὰ τρία οὐκ ἄλλως ἐπιγίνεταί τινι, εἰ μή γε διὰ τῶν τεσσάρων τούτων, δηλονότι, τοῦ κτᾶσθαι τὸν πλοῦτον ἐκ πόρου δικαίου καὶ εὐλόγου, καὶ τὰ ἐπικτηθέντα οἰκονομεῖν καλῶς καὶ διεξάγειν, εἶτα καὶ τοῦ μεταδιδόναι τῶν ἐπικτηθέντων τοῖς δεομένοις—ὅπερ μᾶλλον λυσιτελεῖ ἐν τῇ μελλούσῃ βιοτῇ. Πρὸς τούτοις, καὶ ἐκ τοῦ ἐκκλίνειν τὰ ἐπισυμβαίνοντα συμπτώματα ὅσον τὸ κατὰ δύναμιν.

3 "Εἴ τις οὖν ἕν τινι τῶν τεσσάρων τούτων παραδράμῃ τε καὶ παρέλθῃ οὐδὲν ἀνύσει. Εἰ γὰρ μὴ πλοῦτον εὐπορήσῃ, οὐκ ἂν καλῶς περὶ τὸν βίον ἀναστραφῇ οὔτε τινὰς εὐεργετῆσαι δυνηθείη. Εἰ δὲ πλούσιος μέν ἐστιν, οὐ μὴν δὲ καλῶς τὸν βίον οἰκονομεῖ, τάχιστ' ἂν τοῖς πένησι συναρίθμιος γενήσεται. Εἰ γὰρ καὶ τὰς δαπάνας εὐτελεῖς καὶ ἐλαχίστας ποιεῖται καὶ κατὰ μικρὸν μὴ ἐπιγενομένης τούτῳ προσθήκης τινός, ἔστιν ὅτε καὶ ὁ σύμπας αὐτῷ πλοῦτος ἀναλωθήσεται καθάπερ αὐτὸ τὸ στίμμι, ὅπερ κατὰ μικρὸν ὡς χοῦς μεταδιδόμενον δαπανᾶται. Εἰ δὲ ὁ μὲν πλοῦτος ἐπικτηθῇ καὶ τῆς εἰσφορᾶς ἐπιμέλεια γένηται, οὐ μὴν δ' ἐκ

CHAPTER I

About a very rich merchant. 2

It is said that a merchant, who was very rich and enjoyed an *abundant lifestyle,* as the poet says, in keeping with his trade, also had lazy children who, through idleness, did not want to turn their hand to the practice of any craft. He gave the following words of advice to them, saying, "Children, someone who gets on in life needs three things: sufficient resources, a good reputation among men, and success in obtaining the good things that are in store for the righteous in the other world. But these three only come to someone by means of these other four things, namely, making money in an honest and lawful way; good administration and management of what's been gained; then giving away part of what has been gained to the needy—which is of more benefit in the life to come; and in addition to these, the avoidance, as far as possible, of chance mishaps.

"So, if someone omits and disregards any one of these 3
four things, he will accomplish nothing. If he has no means of creating wealth, he won't be able to get on in life, nor do good for anyone. And if he is rich but doesn't manage his life well, then he'll quite quickly be numbered among the poor. For, even if his expenditures are frugal and very small, but no additional income is added, little by little, to what he has, the time will come when all his wealth will be spent, just like eyeliner which, although applied gradually like dust, is used up. And if additional wealth is made and care is taken over further income, but still none of it is given away nor

τούτου μεταδοθῇ τι, οὐδ' ἔνθα δεῖ καταβληθῇ, πένης ὁ τοῦτον ἔχων τῷ ὄντι λογίζεται καὶ αἴτιος ὁ τοιοῦτος παντελοῦς ἀπωλείας γενήσεται καὶ διαρραγήσεται τὰ τῆς εὐπορίας, καθάπερ οἱ σωλῆνες διαρρήγνυνται, ὅτε ἐν αὐτοῖς ὕδωρ προστιθέμενον καὶ αὖξον μὴ πόρον ἀπορροίας εὑρίσκει." Τούτων ἀκούσαντες οἱ παῖδες τῶν παραινέσεων ἐπείσθησαν τῇ τοῦ πατρὸς συμβουλῇ.

4 *Περὶ τοῦ ταύρου.*

Καὶ ὁ πρῶτος αὐτῶν πρὸς ἐμπορίαν ἀπεστάλη ἔχων μεθ' ἑαυτοῦ ἅμαξαν ὑπὸ δύο ταύρων ἑλκομένην, καὶ συνέβη κατὰ τὴν ὁδὸν βαλτώδει τινὶ τόπῳ θάτερον τῶν ταύρων συμποδισθῆναι. Ἐφ' ᾧ ὁρμηθεὶς ὁ ἔμπορος ἅμα τοῖς ὑπ' αὐτὸν ἀνήγαγον τὸν ταῦρον τοῦ πηλοῦ· ὁ δὲ δι' ἥνπερ ὑπέστη βίαν ἑλκόμενός τε καὶ ἀνθέλκων, ἀτονήσας κατελείφθη ἐκεῖσε περαιτέρω προχωρεῖν μὴ δυνάμενος. Καὶ παντελεῖ συσχεθεὶς ἀπορίᾳ ἠρέμα βαδίσας πεδίον εὗρε χλοηφόρον καὶ ὑδατῶδες, ἐν ᾧ καὶ ἔμεινε διαιτώμενος. Οὐ πολὺ δὲ τὸ ἐν μέσῳ καὶ πάνυ ἐλιπάνθη καὶ ἐπαχύνθη, καὶ ἤρξατο τοῖς κέρασι τὴν γῆν κατορύσσειν καὶ μέγα μυκᾶσθαι.

5 *Περὶ λέοντος.*

Διῆγε δὲ πλησίον αὐτοῦ λέων τις βασιλεὺς τῶν θηρίων, παρῴκουν δὲ τούτῳ γένη ζῴων διάφορα· λέοντές τε καὶ ἄρκοι, λύκοι τε καὶ λαγωοί, πάρδοι τε καὶ ἀλώπεκες, θῶές τε καὶ λυκοπάνθηρες καὶ ἕτερα εἴδη. Ὁ δὲ λέων ἐπηρμένος

distributed where it should be, the person who possesses this is, in reality, considered a poor man, and it will be the cause of his complete perdition, and his prosperity will burst apart, just as pipes burst when the water in them is increased and can find no additional outlet for the flow." When the children heard these words of guidance they were persuaded by their father's advice.

About the bull. 4

The first of them set off to trade, taking with him a wagon pulled by two bulls, and it happened along the way that one of the bulls became stuck in a swamp. When this happened, the merchant rushed over with his servants and tried to lead the bull out of the mud. But the bull, which resisted with all his might, dragging and pulling back, became exhausted and was left behind there since he was unable to go any further. Forced by his complete distress, he slowly made his way out and found a grassy and well-watered plain, where he stayed and took up residence. Not long after, he became extremely fat and sleek, and began to dig up the earth with his horns and bellow loudly.

About the lion. 5

Near him there also lived a lion who was king of the beasts, and there were various kinds of animals living with him: lions and bears, wolves and hares, leopards and foxes, jackals, and other kinds. This lion, who was puffed up and

ἦν καὶ οἰηματίας καὶ ἐλλιπὴς τὴν φρόνησιν. Καὶ ἀκούσας τῶν τοῦ ταύρου μυκηθμῶν καὶ ἀνήκοος τοῦ τοιούτου ἤχου ὤν, ἐδειλίασε σφόδρα· καὶ οὐκ ἠθέλησε τὴν δειλίαν αὐτοῦ τοῖς ὑπ' αὐτὸν φανερῶσαι, ἀλλ' ἔστη ἐφ' ἑνὸς τόπου ἀμετακίνητος.

6 *Περὶ Στεφανίτου καὶ Ἰχνηλάτου.*

Παρῆσαν δὲ ἐκεῖσε σὺν τοῖς ὑπ' αὐτὸν θῶες δύο, ὁ μὲν Στεφανίτης, ὁ δὲ Ἰχνηλάτης καλούμενος, πονηροὶ μὲν καὶ ἀμφότεροι καὶ ποικίλοι τὴν φρόνησιν. Πλὴν ὁ Ἰχνηλάτης πονηρότερος τούτου καὶ πλεῖον ἐφιέμενος τῆς τῶν πραγμάτων καταλήψεως· ὃς δὴ καὶ εἶπε τῷ Στεφανίτῃ· "Τί δῆτα, ὦ ἑταῖρε, ὁρῶμεν τὸν λέοντα ἀμετακίνητον ὥσπερ πεπηγότα καὶ κατὰ τὸ εἰωθὸς μὴ καταδυναστεύοντα;" Ὁ δὲ Στεφανίτης ὑπολαβὼν ἔφη· "Τί σοι κοινὸν καὶ ταῖς τοιαύταις ἀνοήτοις ἐρωτήσεσιν; Οὐδὲν γὰρ ἡμῖν πρόσεστιν ἀνιαρόν, ἀλλὰ τῇ πύλῃ προσκαρτεροῦμεν τοῦ ἡμετέρου βασιλέως τὴν ἐφήμερον ἑκάστοτε τροφὴν πορίζόμενοι· ἀλλ' οὐδ' οἷοί ἐσμεν περὶ βασιλέων διαλέγεσθαι καὶ τὰ τούτων περισκοπεῖν. Παῦσον οὖν τῶν τοιούτων, καὶ ἴσθι ὡς ὁ χρώμενος ἀνοικείοις αὐτῷ ἔργοις τε καὶ λόγοις πείσεται ἐκεῖνος κατὰ πάντα τὰ τοῦ πιθήκου."

7 *Περὶ πίθηκος.*

"Λέγεται γάρ, ὡς πίθηξ τις ἰδὼν τέκτονα ξύλα σχίζοντα καὶ πάλοις δυσὶ ταῦτα διαιροῦντα, καὶ τὸν μὲν ἕνα τούτων ἀφαιροῦντα, τὸν δὲ ἕτερον προσπηγνῦντα, καὶ τοῦτον

conceited, also lacked good sense. When he heard the bellowing of the bull he was very frightened, as he had never heard such a sound, but he didn't want to show his fear to his subordinates, so he stood in one place without moving.

About Stephanites and Ichnelates. 6

There were also two jackals there among his subordinates, one called Stephanites and the other Ichnelates; both were wicked and had cunning minds, except that Ichnelates was the wickeder of the two and more adept in his grasp of matters. He said to Stephanites, "Why are we seeing the lion standing still, comrade, as though he has frozen stiff, and not being domineering as he usually is?" But Stephanites replied and said, "What business is it of yours to ask such silly questions? For we have nothing difficult to do except wait faithfully at the gate of our king and get our food there every day; we're in no position to discuss kings or speculate about their affairs. So stop this, and understand that someone who gets involved with actions and words with which he's not familiar will suffer all that the ape did."

About an ape. 7

"For it is said that an ape saw a carpenter splitting logs and breaking them apart with two stakes, by removing one and inserting the other; and he likened him to a man astride a

παρεικάσας ἐφίππῳ ἀνδρί. Διά τινα χρείαν ὁ τέκτων ἀπεδήμησε· ὁ δὲ πίθηξ τοῦ ξύλου ἐπιβὰς ἐπεχείρησε ποιεῖν τὰ ὅμοια. Καὶ τῶν ὄρχεων αὐτοῦ τῷ τοῦ ξύλου ῥήγματι συμπιεσθέντων ἐλιποθύμησε ὁ ἄθλιος· καὶ τοῦ τέκτονος καταλαβόντος ἐτιμωρήθη τὰ μέγιστα.

8 "Οὕτω καὶ σὺ πάθῃς, εἰ τοιούτοις χρᾶσαι." Καὶ ὁ Ἰχνηλάτης ὑπολαβὼν ἔφη· "Ἔγνων, ἅπερ προέτεινας, ἀλλ' ἴσθι, ὡς οὐ πᾶς ὁ προσεγγίζων τοῖς βασιλεῦσι διὰ βίου σπατάλην πρόσεισιν, ἀλλ' ἔστιν ὅτε καὶ δόξης ἐφιέμενος, εὐφραινούσης μὲν τοὺς φίλους, ἀνιώσης δὲ τοὺς ἐχθρούς. Χθαμαλῶν γὰρ καὶ χαμερπῶν ἀνδρῶν ἐστι τὸ ἀρκεῖσθαι τοῖς τυχοῦσι, καὶ στέργειν τούτοις, ἐπεὶ καὶ ὁ κύων πολλάκις ὀστοῦν εὑρίσκων ξηρότατον, ἐφήδεται τούτου. Ὁ δέ γε ὑψίνους ἀνὴρ οὐ μέχρι τῶν οὐδαμινῶν ἵσταται καὶ τῶν εὐτελῶν, ἀλλὰ τὰ ἄνω ἐπιζητεῖ, καὶ τὰ ἄξια τούτων καταδιώκει. Καθάπερ ὁ λέων ὁ τὸν λαγωὸν κατέχων, ἐπειδὰν ἴδῃ τὴν κάμηλον, ἀφεὶς ἐκεῖνον κατατρέχει αὐτῆς. Ἢ οὐκ οἶσθα τὸν κύνα τῷ οὐραίῳ σαίνοντα, ἄχρις ὅτου τὸ τρύφος ἀπολαύσῃ τοῦ ἄρτου· τὸν δὲ μέγαν ἐλέφαντα προσφερομένης αὐτῷ τῆς τροφῆς ἀπαναινόμενον καὶ μὴ προσιέμενον, ἀλλὰ μόλις τῷ κολακεύεσθαι ταύτην ἐσθίοντα; Καὶ γὰρ ὁ μεγαλόθυμος ἀνὴρ καὶ μεγαλεπήβολός τε καὶ εὐμετάδοτος κἂν μὴ ἐπὶ μακρὸν χρόνον τὸν βίον μεταλλάξῃ, ἀλλὰ μακροβιώτατος γνωρίζεται. Ὁ δέ γε βίου στενότητι καὶ ἀπορίᾳ συζῶν καὶ μήτε ἑαυτὸν μήτε ἑτέρους ὠφελῶν, βραχύβιος οὗτός ἐστι καὶ μινυνθάδιος εἰ καὶ εἰς βαθὺ καταντήσει γῆρας."

horse. When the craftsman went away for some reason, the ape mounted the log and tried to do the same thing. And as his testicles got pinched in the split in the log, the poor thing fainted; and when the craftsman found him, he was punished most severely.

"And that's what you'll suffer, if you get involved in such 8
matters." Ichnelates said in reply, "I take your point, but, you know, not everyone who approaches a king does so for the sake of lifelong luxury; there are times when one does this for the sake of glory, which makes one's friends happy but upsets one's enemies. For it is the mark of inferior and groveling men to be content with what fate deals them and to delight in it, since even a dog is often glad of a completely dried-up bone when he finds it. An ambitious man, on the other hand, does not aim at worthless trifles but searches for superior things and pursues things that are worthwhile, just as a lion which has caught a hare lets go of it, if he sees a camel, and chases after that instead. Don't you know that the dog wags its tail until it gets its piece of bread, but the great elephant refuses and won't accept food that is offered to him, and hardly eats it after much coaxing? For an ambitious man who undertakes great enterprises and is generous is known as very long-lived, even if he should die after not living very long; whereas someone who lives his life in straitened and difficult circumstances, and wants neither to help himself nor others, even if he reaches a ripe old age, actually has a short life that is soon over."

9 Ὁ δὲ Στεφανίτης ἔφη· "Ἔγνων, ἃ λέγεις, ἀλλὰ ἀναλόγισαι, ὡς ἕκαστος ἴδιον μέτρον ἔχει, καὶ ὁ ἐχέφρων, ὅτε ἐστὶ παρὰ τοῖς ὁμοτίμοις ἔντιμος, δεῖ τοῦτον ἀρκεῖσθαι τῷ ἰδίῳ βαθμῷ. Τοιοῦτοί ἐσμεν καὶ ἡμεῖς· οὐκοῦν ἀσπαστέον τὸ μέτρον τὸ καθ' ἡμᾶς." Ὁ δὲ Ἰχνηλάτης ἔφη· "Κοιναὶ πᾶσαι αἱ τοῦ βίου ἀξίαι· καὶ ὁ μὲν μεγαλόνους ἀνὴρ ἀεὶ ποιεῖται τὴν ἄνοδον, ὁ δὲ χαμερπὴς ἀεὶ κάτεισιν. Δυσχερὲς γὰρ τὸ κάτωθεν ἄνω ἀποπηδᾶν, εὐχερὲς δὲ τὸ ἀπὸ τῶν ἄνω κατιέναι ἐπὶ τὰ χθαμαλώτερα, ὥσπερ καὶ ὁ λίθος δυσχερῶς μὲν ἄνω αἴρεται, ῥᾳδίως δὲ κάτω φέρεται. Δεῖ οὖν καὶ ἡμᾶς τὰ ἄνω ἐπιζητεῖν ὅσον τὸ κατὰ δύναμιν, καὶ μὴ στέργειν τῷ οἰκείῳ μέτρῳ, ἐξὸν ἀεὶ μεταβαίνειν εἰς ἕτερα. Ὅθεν καὶ βούλομαι τὴν τοῦ λέοντος ἄρτι περίστασιν πρόφασιν λαβεῖν τῆς πρὸς αὐτὸν ὁμιλίας καὶ οἰκειώσεως· ὁρῶ γὰρ αὐτὸν ἀσυλλόγιστον καὶ πάντῃ ἠπορημένον ἅμα τοῖς ὑπ' αὐτὸν στρατιώταις, καὶ ἴσως οἶμαι τυχεῖν παρ' αὐτοῦ ἀξίας τινός."

10 Ὁ δὲ Στεφανίτης ἀποκριθεὶς ἔφη· "Καὶ πόθεν σοι δῆλον, ὡς ὁ λέων ἠπόρηται;" Ὁ δὲ Ἰχνηλάτης· "Οἶδα," φησίν, "τὸν τούτου λογισμόν· ὁ γὰρ ἐχέφρων ἀνὴρ δύναται γνῶναι καὶ διαγνῶναι τὰ τοῦ πλησίον διανοήματα στοχαζόμενος καὶ κατανοῶν τοῦτον ἔκ τε τῆς διαθέσεως καὶ τοῦ σχήματος." Ὁ δὲ Στεφανίτης εἶπεν· "Καὶ πῶς ἐλπίζεις χάριν εὑρεῖν παρὰ τῷ λέοντι, μηδέποτε βασιλεῦσιν ὑπηρετήσας μηδ' ἐπιστήμην ἔχων αὐτὸς τῆς ὁμιλίας αὐτῶν καὶ τῆς παιδείας;" Ὁ δὲ Ἰχνηλάτης ἀπεκρίνατο· "Οἶδεν ὁ ἐχέφρων ἀνὴρ εὐφυῶς ἀναστρέφεσθαι καὶ ἐν οἷς ἀπειρίαν ἔχει. Ὁ δὲ μὴ τοιοῦτος καὶ περὶ τὴν ἰδίαν τύχην σφάλλεται." Ὁ

Stephanites said, “I understand what you’re saying, but 9
you should take into account that each man has his own measure, and that the sensible man, when he’s respected by his peers, should be satisfied with his personal standing. We’re the same too, so we should welcome the measure that’s our due.” But Ichnelates said, “Just deserts in life are there for everyone alike: the ambitious man always takes the way up, but the one who grovels will always go down. For it’s hard to jump up from the bottom, but easy to go down from the superior to the inferior, just as a stone is lifted up with difficulty but is easily dropped. So, we too should seek out what is superior as much as our strength allows, and not be content with our own standards, as it’s always possible to change them for others. And this is why I want to use the lion’s present situation as a pretext for talking to him and making him my friend, for I see that he doesn’t have a clue and, along with his soldiers, doesn’t have any idea what to do, and I think I may perhaps earn some respect from him.”

Stephanites responded and said, “And what makes it clear 10
to you that the lion is at a loss?” And Ichnelates said, “I know what he’s thinking; for a smart man is able to understand and discern his neighbor’s thoughts, guessing and understanding them from his attitude and demeanor.” “And how,” said Stephanites, “do you hope to find favor with the lion, when you’ve never ever served any kings, nor have any knowledge yourself of their conversation and education?” Ichnelates replied, “The smart man knows how to behave properly even in situations in which he has no experience. But someone who is not like that even gets in the way of his

Στεφανίτης ἔφη· "Ὁ ἐξουσιαστὴς οὐκ εἴωθεν προσλαμβάνεσθαι τὸν κρείττονα τῶν παρ᾽ αὐτῷ, ἀλλὰ καὶ τὸν τῶν λοιπῶν πλησιέστερον παρομοιούμενος τῇ ἀμπέλῳ. Αὕτη γὰρ οὐ τοῖς κρείττοσι τῶν δένδρων ἀλλὰ καὶ τοῖς πλησιεστέροις περιπλέκεται. Πῶς οὖν δυνήσῃ οἰκειοῦσθαι τῷ λέοντι τούτου πόρρω ἀπῳκισμένος ὑπάρχων;" Ὁ δὲ Ἰχνηλάτης εἶπεν· "Ἔγνων ὅσα λέγεις, καὶ ἀληθῆ εἰσιν· ἀλλ᾽ οἶδα τοὺς οἰκειοτέρους ἡμῶν μὴ ὄντας πρότερον τοιούτους ἀλλ᾽ ἀναχθέντας τῶν κάτωθεν εἰς ὕψος μέγα· βούλομαι οὖν κἀγὼ τοιούτοις ἐπιχειρῆσαι. Λέγεται γάρ, ὡς πᾶς ὁ προσανέχων τῇ βασιλικῇ πύλῃ καὶ τὴν μὲν ὑπερηφανίαν ἀπορρίψας, τὸν δὲ θυμὸν δαμάσας καὶ χαλινώσας, καὶ τὴν βλάβην ὑπομένων καὶ τοῖς πᾶσιν ὑπείκων, οὗτος οἰκειοῦται τάχιστα τῷ βασιλεῖ."

11 Ὁ δὲ Στεφανίτης ἔφη· "Καὶ ὑπόθου νῦν, ὅτι προσήγγισας τῷ λέοντι· πῶς οὖν δυνήσῃ χάριν εὑρεῖν παρ᾽ αὐτῷ;" Ὁ δὲ Ἰχνηλάτης φησίν· "Ὅτε προσεγγίσω τούτῳ καὶ γνώσομαι τὴν τῶν ἠθῶν αὐτοῦ καὶ τῆς γνώμης ῥοπήν, ἕψομαι ταύτῃ· καὶ βουλόμενον μέν τινι ἐπιχειρῆσαι τῶν λυσιτελῶν διεγείρω μᾶλλον αὐτὸν πρὸς τὴν πρᾶξιν αὐτοῦ καὶ παρασκευάσω τοῦτον πλεῖον τῷ τελεσιουργήματι ἐπιτέρπεσθαι. Μεταχειριζομένῳ δέ τινος τῶν ἀσυμφόρων ἀποκαλύψω αὐτῷ τὴν ἐκ τοῦ τοιούτου ἔργου βλάβην καὶ τὸ ἐν τῇ ἐγκαταλείψει αὐτοῦ λυσιτελές. Καὶ τοῦτο εὐμεθόδως καὶ κολακευτικῶς ἐργάσομαι, καὶ οἶμαι ὡς τοιουτοτρόπως ὁ λέων με ἀγαπήσει καὶ τῶν ἄλλων προκρινεῖ· ὁ γὰρ συνετὸς ἀνὴρ δύναται τὸ ἀληθὲς ἀκυρῶσαι καὶ τὸ ψεῦδος συστῆσαι, ὥσπερ δὴ καὶ ὁ ἄριστος γραφεὺς παραχαράττων

own fortune." And Stephanites said, "Someone in authority doesn't usually seek the help of the best of his associates, but of the one who is closer than the others, just like the vine does. For that too does not twine itself around the better trees, but those which are closer. How will you be able to become friends with the lion, when you are so far removed from him?" And Ichnelates said, "I understand that what you're telling me is true, but I know that those who are more friendly with the lion than we are were not like that before, but have been raised to high status from inferior circumstances. So I too want to attempt this. For it's said that anyone who waits patiently at the king's gate, and has cast away his pride and subdued and curbed his spirit, enduring insults and giving in to all and sundry, quickly becomes a friend of the king."

Stephanites asked, "And so now, assuming that you get 11
close to the lion, how will you possibly be able to find favor with him?" And Ichnelates said, "When I'm close to him, I'll understand his character and I'll align myself with the inclination of his mind; and if he wants to attempt something useful, I'll certainly encourage him in his action and I'll prepare him to be even more pleased with the accomplishment. But if he tries something unprofitable, I'll show him the harm of such an action and the advantage of abandoning it. And I'll do this cunningly and flatteringly, and I think that, in such a way, the lion will like me and prefer me to the others. For a clever man is able to subvert the truth and establish falsehood, just as an excellent painter also has the power

ἰσχύει τὴν ἀλήθειαν, σχηματίζων εἰσελεύσεις τινῶν καὶ ἐξελεύσεις ἐν ἐπιπέδῳ."

12 Ὁ δὲ Στεφανίτης ἔφη· "Εἰ ταῦτα, βούλει, δεῖ σε παραφυλάττεσθαι τὴν παρὰ τῷ βασιλεῖ οἰκειότητα. Γέγραπται γὰρ ὡς οὐδεὶς ἐχέφρων τῶνδε τῶν τριῶν κατατολμᾷ, ἀλλ' οὐδὲ ῥᾳδίως ἐξ αὐτῶν σῴζεται· λέγω δή, τῆς πρὸς τοὺς βασιλεῖς ἐγγύτητος καὶ τῆς τοῦ δηλητηρίου διὰ πεῖραν μεταλήψεως καὶ τοῦ ταῖς γυναιξὶν πιστεύειν μυστήρια. Παρείκασται γὰρ ὁ βασιλεὺς ὄρει κρημνώδει καὶ δυσβάτῳ, παντοίαις ὀπώραις καὶ πόαις κομῶντι, καὶ θηρίων καὶ λεόντων πλήρει, ἐφ' ᾧ καὶ ἡ ἀνέλευσις δυσχερὴς καὶ ἡ διαμονὴ ἐπισφαλής." Ὁ δὲ Ἰχνηλάτης εἶπεν· "Ἀληθῶς εἶπας, ἀλλ' ὁ μὴ κινδύνων κατατολμῶν οὐ τυγχάνει τῶν ἐφετῶν, καὶ ὁ πρὸς πᾶν πρᾶγμα ἐπτοημένος ἄμοιρος ἁπάντων μένει. Λέγεται γάρ, ὡς τὰ τρία ταῦτα οὐδεὶς ὑπεισέρχεται τῶν μικροψύχων· λέγω δὴ τὰς βασιλικὰς ὑπηρεσίας καὶ τὴν διὰ θαλάττης ἐμπορίαν καὶ τὴν ταχεῖαν πρὸς τὸν ἐχθρὸν συμπλοκήν. Δύο γὰρ ἀφωρίσθησαν τόποι τῷ μεγαλόφρονι ἀνδρί, αἵ τε βασίλειαι αὐλαὶ καὶ αἱ ἐν ἐρήμοις παρὰ τοῖς ἀσκηταῖς διατριβαί, ὥσπερ καὶ τῷ ἐλέφαντι ἥ τε ἔρημος καὶ ἡ ἐν τοῖς βασιλείοις διαγωγή." Ὁ δὲ Στεφανίτης ἔφη· "Οὐ συναινῶ σοι περὶ τὰ τοιαῦτα, ἀλλ' ἄπελθε καὶ ποίει, ὃ βούλει."

13 Ὁ δὲ Ἰχνηλάτης εὐθέως ἀπελθὼν πρὸς τὸν λέοντα προσεκύνησεν αὐτόν· ὁ δὲ λέων ἐπηρώτησεν αὐτόν, ἔνθα διῆγε τὸν τοσοῦτον καιρόν. Ὁ δὲ Ἰχνηλάτης εἶπεν· "Οὐ διαλείπω ἀεὶ προσανέχων τῇ βασιλικῇ πύλῃ, ἐλπίζων πάντως ἀξιοῦσθαι συνεργίας τινὸς μεταδοῦναι τῷ βασιλεῖ,

to manipulate the truth, when depicting things on a flat surface as though they are coming nearer and receding."

12 And Stephanites said, "If that's what you want, you should be careful about becoming friends with the king. For it's been written that no sensible person dares to attempt the following three things nor, indeed, easily preserves himself from them: I mean, getting close to kings, taking poison as an experiment, and entrusting secrets to women. For the king is like a precipitous and inaccessible mountain, covered with all sorts of fruit and herbs, and full of wild animals and lions: ascending it is difficult and staying on it treacherous." And Ichnelates said, "You've spoken truly, but someone who doesn't take risks doesn't obtain his desires, and someone who's frightened of doing anything gets left out of everything. For it is said that no one who is faint of heart undertakes the following three things: I mean royal service, trade by sea, and swift engagement with the enemy. For two places have been reserved for the ambitious man, royal halls and the life lived by the ascetics in the desert, just as also both the desert and life in the palace are for the elephant." Stephanites said, "I don't agree with you about this, but go and do what you want."

13 When Ichnelates had gone off to the lion and had bowed down before him, the lion asked him where he spent all his time. Ichnelates said, "I never cease waiting at the royal gate, hoping to be thought worthy in every way by providing some assistance to the king, as I know that some things

εἰδὼς ὥς τινα τῶν πραγμάτων ἐπιδέονταί ποτε καὶ τῆς τῶν χθαμαλῶν καὶ ἀδήλων ἀνδρῶν συμμεταλήψεως. Καὶ πολλοὶ τῶν τῆς κάτω τύχης πολλάκις ἐν μεγίστοις λυσιτελοῦσι πράγμασι· τῷ γὰρ ἐρριμμένῳ καὶ ἐπὶ γῆς κειμένῳ ξύλῳ ἐνίοτε χρώμεθα πρὸς ὠτὸς κνησμονήν." Ὡς οὖν ἤκουσεν ὁ λέων τῶν τοιούτων λόγων, εἶπε πρὸς τοὺς ὑπ' αὐτόν· "Ὁ εὐσυνείδητος καὶ λόγιος ἀνὴρ ἀγνοεῖται πολλάκις ἄχρι τῆς ὁμιλίας, καθάπερ τὸ ὑποκρυπτόμενον πῦρ, ὁπόταν εἰς φῶς ἐξέλθῃ, ἀέριον τὴν φλόγα ἀπεργάζεται." Ὡς οὖν ἔγνω ὁ Ἰχνηλάτης ὅτι ἀρεστὸς κατεφάνη τῷ λέοντι, ἔφη· "Ὦ βασιλεῦ, δεῖ τὴν ποίμνην τοῦ βασιλέως ἀναφέρειν εἰς αὐτὸν ἅπαντα τὰ δέοντα· τηνικαῦτα γὰρ ἑκάστῳ τὴν ἀξίαν ἐκεῖνος ἀπονέμει τιμήν. Καθάπερ γὰρ τὰ διάφορα σπέρματα ὑπὸ τὴν γῆν κείμενα οὐκ ἐμφαίνεται οἷά εἰσιν, εἰ μή γε τῆς γῆς ἀναβλαστήσῃ, οὕτω καὶ ἕκαστος τῶν ἀνθρώπων διὰ τῶν οἰκείων αὐτοῦ ἔργων ὁποῖός ἐστιν δείκνυται. Καὶ δεῖ τὸν βασιλέα μήτε τὸν τῆς κεφαλῆς κόσμον προσάπτειν τοῖς ποσί, μήτε τῶν ποδῶν τῇ κεφαλῇ ἐπισυνάπτειν. Ἐπεὶ καὶ ὁ τὸν ὑάκινθον καὶ τοὺς τιμίους μαργαρίτας τῷ μολύβδῳ συμπλέκων, ἑαυτὸν μᾶλλον ἢ τοὺς μαργαρίτας ἠτίμωσεν. Δεῖ γὰρ τὸν μὲν ἄρχοντα διακρίνειν τοὺς ὑπ' αὐτόν, τὸν δὲ στρατηγὸν τοὺς στρατιώτας, τὸν δ' ἀρχιερέα τοὺς λογικοὺς ἄνδρας καὶ τοὺς σπουδαίους.

14 "Οὐ γὰρ τῷ πλήθει κατορθοῦσιν οἱ ἡγεμόνες τὰ τρόπαια, ἀλλὰ τῇ ἀρίστῃ ἐπιλογῇ, καὶ ὀλίγοι ὑάκινθοι πολλῶν ἑτέρων εὐμεγέθων σωμάτων καὶ πραγμάτων ὀνησιμώτεροι καὶ τιμιώτεροι. Καὶ χρὴ τὸν ἡγεμόνα μὴ καταφρονεῖν

sometimes require the participation of humble and obscure men. Many people of inferior status are often of use in great affairs, since we also sometimes use a stick which has been thrown away and is lying on the ground to scratch our ear." When the lion heard these words, he said to his subordinates, "The quick-witted and eloquent man often seems ignorant until he speaks, just as when a hidden fire emerges into the light, its flame leaps into the air." Since Ichnelates realized that he had appeared pleasing to the lion, he said, "My king, the king's flock must bring to him all that is due; for then he assigns the proper honor to each. For just as the various seeds lying under the earth do not show what kind they are unless they send up shoots from the ground, so also each man shows by his own deeds what sort of person he is. And the king must neither attach an adornment meant for his head to his feet, nor must he fasten that for his feet to his head. For someone who sets an aquamarine and precious pearls in lead has dishonored himself rather than the pearls. For a ruler must distinguish between his subordinates, the general between his soldiers, and the high priest between the spiritual and the zealous.

"For leaders do not set up trophies of victory by force of 14
numbers but by making the best choice, and a few aquamarines are more valuable and profitable than many other large objects and things. A leader should never look down upon

τινός ποτε τῶν ὑπ’ αὐτὸν εὐτελῶν· *τὸ γὰρ μικρὸν οὐ μικρόν, ὅταν ἐκφέρῃ μέγα.* Δεῖ δὲ καὶ τὸν ἐξουσιαστὴν μὴ τοὺς κατὰ γένος περιφανεῖς μόνον προσάγεσθαι, ἀλλὰ τοὺς ἀξιολογωτέρους καὶ λυσιτελεῖν δυναμένους. Μήτε μὴν τοῖς περὶ αὐτὸν μόνοις ἀρκεῖσθαι καὶ τούτοις προσανέχειν, ἀλλὰ καὶ πόρρωθεν τοὺς συνέσει τε καὶ παιδείᾳ κεκοσμημένους μετακαλεῖσθαι. Οὐδὲν γὰρ ἐγγύτερόν τινι παρὰ τὸ ἴδιον σῶμα· ἀλλ’ ὅτε νόσος τούτῳ ἐπισυμβῇ, τὰ πορρωτέρω φάρμακα ὁ νοσῶν ἐπιζητεῖ. Καὶ οἱ μῦες πολλάκις βασιλικοῖς οἰκήμασι παρεδρεύουσιν, ἀλλ’ οὐ προτιμώτεροι τῆς ἐγγύτητος ἕνεκα, καὶ ὁ ἱέραξ ἄγριος ὢν μετακαλεῖται παρὰ βασιλέων καὶ προσλαμβάνεται διὰ τὴν ἐν αὐτῷ λυσιτέλειαν, καὶ ἐπὶ βραχίονος φέρεται.” Τούτων ἀκούσας τῶν ῥημάτων ὁ λέων κατεπλάγη σφόδρα τοῦ Ἰχνηλάτου τὴν σύνεσιν, καί φησι πρὸς τοὺς συνέδρους αὐτοῦ· “Οὐ δεῖ τὸν ἐξουσιαστὴν παρορᾶν τοὺς σπουδαίους ἄνδρας, κἂν ὦσι τῆς κάτω τύχης, ἀλλ’ ἑκάστῳ τὸ κατ’ ἀξίαν ἀπονέμειν, κἂν ἅπαντες ἀπαρέσκωνται.”

Ἰδὼν οὖν ὁ Ἰχνηλάτης εὐμενῆ τὴν τοῦ λέοντος πρὸς αὐτὸν ῥοπήν, ὡμίλησε μετὰ παρρησίας αὐτῷ καταμόνας λέγων· “Τί τοῦτο, ὦ βασιλεῦ, ὅτι οὐ μεθίστασαι τῶν ἐνταῦθα οὐδὲ μεταβαίνεις ἐπὶ τόπον ἕτερον, ἀλλ’ ἔμεινας ἀμετακίνητος ἐπὶ πολὺν καιρὸν ἤδη;” Καὶ ὁ λέων, τὴν ἑαυτοῦ δειλίαν σπεύδων τηνικαῦτα ἀποκαλύψαι, ἤκουσε παραυτίκα μυκηθμῶν ταύρου μεγίστου. Καὶ ἀκούσας ἔτι μᾶλλον περίτρομος γεγονὼς ἔφη· “Δέδοικα μὴ ἀνάλογον εἴη τὸ φώνημα τοῦ τοιούτου ζῴου τῷ ἰδίῳ σώματι· ἔτι δὲ καὶ ἡ δύναμις ἀναλογοῦσα τῷ σώματι· καὶ εἰ οὕτως ἔχει,

one of his less important subordinates, *for a small thing is not small when it produces something great.* Someone in authority must also not associate himself only with those who are notable because of their family, but with those who are worthy of mention and able to be of use. And he should not be satisfied only with those around him and rely on them, but should also bring in those from far away who are endowed with intelligence and education. For nothing is nearer to anyone than his own body, but when he falls sick, the sick man searches for medicine further away. Mice too will often frequent royal buildings, but they are not preferable because of their nearness, whereas the hawk, although wild, is brought in by kings and assists them by its usefulness, and is carried on their arm." When the lion heard these words, he was completely amazed at Ichnelates's intelligence, and said to his counselors, "A person in authority must not overlook excellent men, even if they are of inferior status, but should allot to each according to his worth, even if everyone else is displeased."

So when Ichnelates saw that the lion's attitude toward 15
him was favorable, he spoke freely to him in private, and said, "Why is it, my king, that you haven't moved from here or gone somewhere else, but have remained motionless for a long time now?" The lion, who was anxious to hide his cowardice at that time, suddenly heard the bellowing of the great bull. And, when he heard it, he became even more terrified, and said, "I'm afraid that the voice of this animal may be in proportion to its body, and what's more, that its strength may be in proportion to its body, and if that's the

φευκτέον ἐνθένδε.” Ὁ δὲ Ἰχνηλάτης ὑπολαβὼν εἶπε· “Μὴ φοβοῦ, ὦ βασιλεῦ, τὰς ὑπερόγκους ταύτας καὶ μεγίστας φωνάς· κεναὶ γὰρ πολλάκις εἰσὶν αὗται, καὶ ἀδρανεῖς καὶ ὑπόσαθροι.”

16 *Περὶ ἀλώπεκος.*

“Λέγεται γὰρ ὡς ἀλώπηξ τις πεινῶσα καὶ τροφὴν ἐπιζητοῦσα προστετύχηκεν ἔν τινι ὕλῃ τυμπάνῳ δένδρου ἀπηωρημένῳ καὶ <τῷ> ὑπὸ ἀνέμων κινεῖσθαι ἀλαλαγμὸν ποιουμένῳ διὰ τῆς τῶν κλώνων κινήσεως· οὗπερ ἡ ἀλώπηξ ἀκούσασα ἐδειλίασε προσεγγίσαι. Εἶτα τῇ πείνῃ καὶ τῇ ὀρέξει ἡττηθεῖσα, κατετόλμησε τούτου· καὶ πλησιάσασα, ᾤετο πολλῶν καὶ πιμελῶν κρεάτων ἐντυχεῖν. Τῷ μεγέθει τοῦ τυμπάνου τὴν ὄψιν πλανηθεῖσα καὶ πάντα κάλων κινήσασα διέρρηξεν αὐτό· καὶ κενὸν ἰδοῦσα ἔφη, ‘Βαβαί, πῶς τὰ χείρονα τῶν σωμάτων εὐμεγεθέστερα καὶ μεγαλοφωνότερά εἰσι καὶ τοὺς μεγάλους πτοοῦσι.’

17 “Τοιοῦτόν τι καὶ ἡμεῖς, ὦ βασιλεῦ, τὴν τήμερον πάσχομεν ὑπὸ τῆς τοῦ τοιούτου ζῴου φωνῆς πλανώμενοί τε καὶ δεδιττόμενοι. Καὶ εἰ βούλει, ἀπελεύσομαι πρὸς αὐτὸ καὶ ἴδω, οἷόν ἐστι, καὶ τάχιον ὑποστρέψω πρός σε.” Καὶ τοῦτο ἀρεστὸν ἐφάνη τῷ λέοντι, καὶ ἐξαπέστειλεν αὐτόν· τοῦ δὲ ἀπελθόντος, πολὺς κατέλαβε τὸν λέοντα μετάμελος ἐπὶ τῇ ἀποστολῇ αὐτοῦ καὶ καθ’ ἑαυτὸν ἐλογίζετο· “Τί ἄρα παθὼν τῷ Ἰχνηλάτῃ οὕτω προσερρύην; Οὐ δεῖ γάρ,” φησί, “τὸν ἐξουσιαστὴν πιστεύειν τῷ ἐπὶ πλεῖστον καιρὸν ἀναιτίως παρεωραμένῳ, ἢ τῷ πλεονέκτῃ καὶ ἀπλήστῳ ἀνδρὶ ἢ

case I'll have to run away from here." And Ichnelates replied, "Don't be afraid, my king, of these big and very loud noises, for they are often empty, powerless, and quite feeble."

About a fox. 16

"For it is said that a hungry fox, who was looking for food, came across a wooden drum hanging on a tree in a forest. This was being moved by the wind and was making a loud noise because of the motion of the branches. So when the fox saw it, she was afraid to approach. But then, overcome by hunger and longing, she made an attempt on it, and after she had approached it she thought that she had found a lot of fatty meat. She was misled by the apparent size of the drum, and so, using all the means at her disposal, she broke it. And when she saw that the drum was empty, she said, 'Would you believe it! How can such big and noisy things be worse than their bodies and frighten grown-ups?'

"We are also experiencing something of the kind today, 17
my king, for we are being misled and frightened by the sound of an animal of this sort. If you wish, I shall go to it and see what kind it is and quickly return to you." This seemed good to the lion, and he sent Ichnelates off. But when he had gone, a deep regret came over the lion for sending him, and he thought to himself, "What on earth made me turn to Ichnelates like this? After all," he said, "someone in authority should not trust someone who, without good reason, is ignored most of the time, or a grasping and greedy

τῷ μὴ ἐν καιρῷ περιστάσεως οἰκείως παρ' αὐτοῦ συνεργηθέντι ἢ πλοῦτον καὶ δόξαν ἀφαιρεθέντι καὶ τοῖς τοιούτοις. Ὁ γὰρ Ἰχνηλάτης ἐκ πολλοῦ ἤδη συνετώτατος ὢν πρὸς τῇ ἐμῇ πύλῃ προσέρριπτο· ἴσως γὰρ διὰ τοῦτο οὐ πιστῶς ἐκολάκευέ μοι· καὶ δέδοικα μή, εὑρὼν τὸ μεγαλοφωνότατον τουτὶ ζῷον ἐμοῦ μεῖζον τῇ δυνάμει καὶ εὐσθενέστερον, τούτῳ προσρυῇ καὶ ἀναγγελεῖ τὰ ἐμὰ ἐλαττώματα." Ταῦτα καὶ τὰ τοιαῦτα λογιζομένου τοῦ λέοντος, ἐφάνη μόνος ὁ Ἰχνηλάτης. Ὡς οὖν εἶδε τοῦτον ὁ λέων, ἐθάρσησε καὶ εἶπε πρὸς αὐτόν· "Τί ἔδρασας;" Ὁ δὲ Ἰχνηλάτης εἶπεν· "Εἶδον τὸ μεγαλοφωνότατον ζῷον ἐκεῖνον, καὶ ταῦρός ἐστι, καὶ ἐπλησίασα τούτῳ καὶ ὡμίλησα καὶ διηλέχθην, καὶ οὐδεμία μοι βλάβη ἐπεγένετο ἐξ αὐτοῦ." Ὁ δὲ λέων ἔφη· "Μὴ λάβῃς τὸ μὴ βλαβῆναί σε τεκμήριον τῆς τοῦ ζῴου ἀδυναμίας. Ὁ γὰρ σφοδρὸς ἄνεμος καὶ ἡ πολλὴ λαῖλαψ τὰ μὲν ἀδρανῆ τῶν φυτῶν οὐ καταβλάπτει, τὰ δὲ ὑψιπέτηλα δένδρα πρόρριζα ἐκτίλλει καὶ λίαν κατακλᾷ." Ὁ δὲ Ἰχνηλάτης εἶπε· "Μὴ οἴου, ὦ βασιλεῦ, τὸ τοιοῦτον ζῷον δυνατώτατον εἶναι. Εἰ γὰρ βούλει, παραστήσω σοι τοῦτο καὶ ὑπήκοόν σοι ἔσται καὶ ὑπὸ χεῖρα." Εὐφρανθεὶς οὖν ἐπὶ τούτοις ὁ λέων, προσέταξεν αὐτῷ ποιῆσαι τὸ ὑποσχεθέν.

18 Ὁ δὲ Ἰχνηλάτης ἀπελθὼν πρὸς τὸν ταῦρον θαρσαλέως ἔφη αὐτῷ· "Ὁ λέων πρὸς σέ με ἐξαπέστειλεν ἄξοντά σε πρὸς αὐτόν. Εἰ μὲν οὖν σπεύσεις πρὸς τὴν ἐκείνου πορείαν, συγγνωμονήσει σοι τὴν μέχρι τοῦδε καθυστέρησιν καὶ τὴν περὶ τὴν ὑπάντησιν αὐτοῦ ἀμέλειαν. Εἰ δὲ ἐνδοιάσεις, ἀναφέρω αὐτῷ τὰ κατὰ σέ." Ὁ δὲ ταῦρος εἶπεν· "Καὶ τίς ἐστιν οὗτος ὁ λέων ὁ πρός με ἐξαποστείλας σε; Καὶ ποῦ

man, or one who has not cooperated appropriately with him in a crisis, or one who has been deprived of wealth and glory, and others of this sort. For Ichnelates, for a long time now, although he is very smart, was left at my gate. Perhaps for this reason he was dissatisfied with me, and I'm worried that, if he finds that this animal with the very loud voice is greater and mightier than me in strength, he will turn to him and tell him my weaknesses." But while he was debating these matters with himself, Ichnelates appeared alone. And when the lion saw him, he took courage and said to him, "What did you do?" And Ichnelates said, "I saw the animal with the loud voice; he's a bull, and I approached him and spoke to him and had a conversation with him, and no harm came to me from him." And the lion said, "Do not take the fact that you weren't harmed as proof of the animal's weakness. For the violent wind and the mighty storm don't damage feeble plants, but may uproot and tear down towering trees and snap them right off." But Ichnelates said, "Do not think, my king, that this animal is very powerful. If you want, I'll present him to you, and he'll be obedient and subject to you." The lion was happy at this and ordered him to do what had been suggested.

Ichnelates went off to the bull and said confidently to 18
him, "The lion sent me to you so that I may take you to him. So, if you hurry on your way to him, he'll forgive your delay until now and your negligence about going to meet him. But if you hesitate, I'll report back to him about you." The bull said, "And who is this lion who sent you to me? Where does

διάγει;" Ὁ δὲ Ἰχνηλάτης ἔφη· "Βασιλεύς ἐστι τῶν θηρίων καὶ ἐν τῷδε τῷ τόπῳ διάγει μετὰ καὶ τῆς ὑπ' αὐτὸν στρατιᾶς." Ὁ δὲ ταῦρος δειλιάσας ἠκολούθησεν αὐτῷ ἄχρι τοῦ λέοντος. Καὶ ὁ λέων τοῦτον ἰδών, εὐμενῶς προσεδέξατο καὶ ἐπηρώτησε περὶ τῶν κατ' αὐτόν. Ὁ δὲ ταῦρος ἀνήγγειλεν αὐτῷ ἅπαντα· καὶ ὑπέσχετο τούτῳ ὁ λέων πᾶν ἀγαθὸν καὶ ἀνέθηκεν αὐτῷ τὰ τῆς ἀρχῆς αὐτοῦ καὶ πάντων προέκρινεν τῶν ὑπ' αὐτόν.

19 Ὅπερ ἰδὼν ὁ Ἰχνηλάτης ἐφθόνησε καὶ μὴ ἀνασχόμενος ἀπεκάλυψε τὸν φθόνον τῷ ἑταίρῳ αὐτοῦ Στεφανίτῃ, καὶ ἔφη· "Οὐ θαυμάζεις, ὅπερ ἔδρασα κατ' ἐμαυτοῦ; Τὰ γὰρ λυσιτελοῦντα τῷ λέοντι τελέσας ἔλαθον ἐμαυτὸν βλάψας, προσενεγκὼν ἐκεῖνον τὸν καθυστερήσαντά μου τῇ ἀξίᾳ κατὰ πολὺ ταῦρον." Ὁ δὲ Στεφανίτης εἶπε· "Καὶ τί βούλει ποιεῖν;" Ὁ δὲ Ἰχνηλάτης ἔφη· "Βούλομαι ἀποκατασταθῆναί με εἰς τὴν προτέραν μου τάξιν τε καὶ κατάστασιν· δεῖ γὰρ τὸν νουνεχῆ τὰ τρία ταῦτα μεταχειρίζεσθαι καὶ διαλογίζεσθαι· πρῶτον μέν, ἃ πέπονθεν ἀγαθά τε καὶ ἐναντία, καὶ τὰ μὲν αἴτια τῶν κακῶν ἀποφεύγειν, τὰ δὲ τῶν ἀγαθῶν διώκειν. Εἶτα καὶ τὰ ἐνεστῶτα καλὰ ἢ φαῦλα, καὶ σπεύδειν κατέχειν μὲν τὰ καλά, ἀποφεύγειν δὲ τὰ φαῦλα· καὶ σκοπεῖν μετὰ τοῦτο τὸ μέλλον καὶ ὡσαύτως τί ποιεῖν. Διελογισάμην οὖν κἀγὼ τὴν προτέραν μου κατάστασιν, καὶ οὐχ εὗρον πόρον τῆς ἀποκαταστάσεως, ἀλλ' ἢ τῷ δόλῳ τὸν ταῦρον ἀποκτεῖναι· τοῦτο γάρ μοι λυσιτελές, ἴσως δὲ καὶ τῷ λέοντι." Ὁ δὲ Στεφανίτης εἶπεν· "Οὐχ ὁρῶ βλάβην τῷ λέοντι ἐπιγενομένην ἐκ τῆς τοῦ ταύρου οἰκειώσεως." Ὁ δὲ Ἰχνηλάτης ἔφη· "Ὁ λέων ὅλως αὐτοῦ ἐγεγόνει, τοὺς

he live?" Ichnelates replied, "He is the king of the beasts, and he lives here with the army that serves him." The bull was afraid and followed him to the lion. When the lion saw him, he received him graciously and asked him about himself. The bull told him everything, and the lion promised him everything good and referred all the affairs of his kingdom to him, and favored him above all his subordinates.

When Ichnelates saw this he became jealous and, not be- 19
ing able to bear it, revealed his jealousy to his comrade Stephanites, and said, "Aren't you surprised at what I've done to myself? For while I was doing things that benefitted the lion, I didn't notice that I was harming myself by bringing in the bull who is so much less worthy of respect than me." Stephanites said, "So, what do you want to do?" And Ichnelates said, "I want to get myself restored to my former position and status. For a smart man should deal with and consider these three things: first, the things he has experienced, both good and contrary, and flee those which have been a cause of evil but pursue those which have been a cause of good; then also present circumstances, good and bad, and be eager to grasp the good ones, but flee the bad ones; and after that he must look to the future and thus what he should do. So, I have considered my former situation, and I have found no way of restoring it, other than to kill the bull by cunning. For that will be beneficial for me and perhaps also for the lion." But Stephanites said, "I don't see any harm coming to the lion from his relationship with the bull." But Ichnelates said, "The lion has become

λοιποὺς παραγκωνισάμενος, δι' ἓξ δὲ πραγμάτων ὁ βασιλεὺς περιφρονεῖται καὶ καθαιρεῖται· τῷ μὴ χρῆσθαι τοῖς προσφόροις τῷ καιρῷ, ἀλλ' ἔνθα δεῖ δεινότητος καὶ αὐστηρίας ἐκεῖσε μαλθακίζεσθαι· καὶ ἔνθα δεῖ κολακείας τοὐναντίον θρασύνεσθαι· καὶ τῷ μὴ ἱκανῶν καὶ συνετῶν καὶ πιστῶν εὐπορεῖν ὑπηκόων, ἢ οἰκείων συμβούλων καὶ τῷ στασιάζειν τοὺς ὑπ' αὐτόν· καὶ τῷ ἡττᾶσθαι ταῖς ἀλόγοις ὀρέξεσι· καὶ τῷ ὑπείκειν τῷ θυμῷ· πρὸς τούτοις δὲ πᾶσι, καὶ ταῖς τῶν καιρῶν μεταβολαῖς." Ὁ δὲ Στεφανίτης εἶπε· "Καὶ πῶς δυνήσῃ βλάψαι τὸν ταῦρον, πολύ σου ὄντα δυνατώτερον καὶ πλειόνων φίλων εὐποροῦντα καὶ ὑπηκόων;" Ὁ δὲ Ἰχνηλάτης ἔφη· "Μὴ ἀπίδῃς πρὸς τὴν ἐμὴν εὐτέλειαν καὶ ἀσθένειαν· οὐ γὰρ ἡ νίκη τῇ δυνάμει καὶ τῇ ῥώμῃ τοῦ σώματος ἕπεται· πολλοὶ γὰρ τῶν δυνατωτέρων ὑπὸ τῶν τυχόντων ἡττήθησαν." Εἶτα πρὸς τούτοις εἶπεν ὁ Στεφανίτης· "Ναὶ ἀληθῶς οὕτως ἔχει, ἀλλ' ὅρα μὴ ποιήσας σύ τι βλαφθήσῃ."

20 *Περὶ ἀσκητοῦ καὶ κλέπτου καὶ τῶν ὁραθέντων παρὰ τοῦ ἀσκητοῦ.*

"Λέγεται γὰρ ὥς τινι ἀσκητῇ ἐδόθησαν παρὰ τοῦ βασιλέως ὑφάσματα πολύτιμα. Ἰδὼν δὲ αὐτὰ κλέπτης τις καὶ ἐλθὼν πρὸς αὐτὸν δολερῶς εἶπεν αὐτῷ· 'Βούλομαί σου μαθητὴς γενέσθαι καὶ σὺν σοὶ εἶναι καὶ τὰς ἀρετάς σου ἐκμιμήσασθαι.' Προσδεχθεὶς τοίνυν παρὰ τοῦ μοναχοῦ καὶ μεθ' ἡμέρας εὑρὼν ἄδειαν ὁ κλέπτης, λαβὼν τὰ ὑφάσματα ἀπέδρασεν. Γνοὺς δὲ ὁ ἀσκητὴς τὸν δρασμόν, ἐδίωκεν

completely controlled by him, and has pushed the rest aside, and a king is despised and destroyed through six things: not acting appropriately to the circumstances, but being soft when he should be harsh and severe; and being brash instead of using flattery; and by not having enough wise subjects, or friendly counselors, and by disagreeing with his subjects; and by yielding to his irrational appetites; and giving in to anger; and, besides all these, by changing circumstances." But Stephanites said, "And how will you be able to harm the bull, since he is much more powerful than you and has many more friends and subjects?" But Ichnelates said, "Don't just look at my inferiority and weakness, for victory does not depend on physical power and strength, for many powerful men have been overcome by lesser people." Then Stephanites said in response to this, "Yes, that's true, but watch out that you don't do anything to hurt yourself."

About an ascetic and a thief and 20
what the ascetic saw.

"For it is said that an ascetic was once given valuable robes by the king. When a thief saw them, he came up to him and said deceitfully, 'I want to become your disciple, and to be with you, and to imitate your virtues.' Then, when he had been accepted by the monk, after a few days the thief found an opportunity, took the robes, and ran off. When the ascetic discovered the thief's flight, he chased after him. And

ὀπίσω αὐτοῦ. Καὶ ἐν τῷ ὁδεύειν αὐτόν, εἶδε δύο κριοὺς μαχομένους ἀλλήλοις ὥστε τὰ αἵματα αὐτῶν καταρρέειν ἐπὶ τὴν γῆν. Ἐλθοῦσα δέ τις ἀλώπηξ ἐκεῖσε ἐξέλειχε πάντα τὰ ἕλκη αὐτῶν· καὶ συγκρούσαντες οἱ κριοὶ ἀλλήλοις, ἀπέκτειναν τὴν ἀλώπεκα."

21 *Περὶ γυναικὸς πόρνης.*

"Ὁ δὲ ἀσκητὴς καταλαβὼν τὴν πόλιν νυκτός, καὶ μὴ ἔχων ποῦ καταλῦσαι, εἰσῆλθε μεῖναι ἐν οἰκίᾳ πόρνης τινός. Εἶχε δὲ ἡ πόρνη δούλην τινά, συμπάσχουσαν καὶ συμπορνεύουσαν μετ' αὐτῆς. Ἡ δὲ δούλη ἔσχε τινὰ ἐραστήν, καὶ ἐπόθει αὐτὴν πάνυ ὁ ἐραστής, τὴν δὲ κυρίαν αὐτῆς ἐβδελύσσετο. Ζηλοτυπήσασα δὲ αὐτὴν ἡ κυρία αὐτῆς ἠβουλήθη ἀποκτεῖναι τὸν ἐραστὴν αὐτῆς. Ἐν μιᾷ οὖν νυκτὶ ποτίσασα τοῦτον οἶνον καὶ κοιμήσασα, ἔσχε δηλητήριον κατεσκευασμένον ἐν καλάμῳ, καὶ θήσασα τοῦτο ἐν τῷ ἀφεδρῶνι αὐτοῦ ἐφύσησε τοῦτο εἰς τὰ ἔγκατα αὐτοῦ τοῦ φαρμακῶσαι αὐτόν. Ἐξῆλθε γοῦν ἀπὸ τοῦ ἀφεδρῶνος αὐτοῦ πνοή, καὶ στραφὲν τὸ δηλητήριον εἰς τὸν λαιμὸν αὐτῆς ἀπὸ τοῦ καλάμου, ἀπέκτεινεν ταύτην."

22 *Περὶ τῆς γυναικὸς σκυτοτόμου.*

"Ταῦτα δὲ πάντα ἐθεώρει ὁ ἀσκητής. Ἐγερθεὶς δὲ τῇ ἑξῆς, κατέλυσεν ἐν οἴκῳ τινὸς σκυτοτόμου. Ὁ δὲ σκυτοτόμος κληθεὶς ὑπό τινος φίλου αὐτοῦ, παρήγγειλε τῇ γυναικὶ αὐτοῦ τιμῆσαι τὸν ἀσκητὴν καὶ ἀναπαῦσαι αὐτὸν ἐξ ὧν ἔχει. Ἔσχε δὲ ἡ γυνὴ αὐτοῦ μοιχὸν καὶ μαυλίστριαν

while he was on his way, he saw two rams fighting each other so that their blood was flowing onto the ground. A fox came there and began to lick their wounds; and as the rams butted each other, they killed the fox."

About a prostitute. 21

"The ascetic reached the city at night and, as he had nowhere to spend the night, he went to stay in the house of a prostitute. The prostitute had a servant, who did the same as she did and was also a prostitute. And the servant had a lover, but although the lover was completely besotted with her, he hated her mistress. The servant's mistress was jealous of her and wanted to kill her lover. So that night, after she had given him wine to drink and put him to sleep, she had some poison prepared in a straw; she put this into his anus and blew it into his bowels to poison him. But, in truth, a fart came out of his anus and sent the poison back out of the straw into her throat, and killed her."

About the tanner's wife. 22

"The ascetic observed all this. When he got up the next day, he went to stay in the house of a tanner. But the tanner was called away by one of his friends, so he ordered his wife to respect the ascetic and make him comfortable as best she could. The tanner's wife had a lover and a go-between who

γυναῖκα τινὸς συσκιαστοῦ· ἀπελθόντος δὲ τοῦ σκυτοτόμου, εἶπεν ἡ γυνὴ αὐτοῦ πρὸς τὴν μαυλίστριαν αὐτῆς· 'Ἄπελθε, καὶ ἔνεγκε τὸν φίλον μου· ὁ γὰρ ἀνήρ μου ταύτῃ τῇ νυκτὶ ἔξω μένει.' Ἀπῆλθε δὲ ἡ μαυλίστρια καὶ ἤνεγκε τὸν φίλον αὐτῆς καὶ ἐλθόντος τοῦ μοιχοῦ αὐτῆς ἤδη, καὶ καθίσαντος πρὸς τῷ πυλῶνι, καὶ ταύτην ἡδέως ἀσπαζομένου, κατέλαβεν ὁ ἀνὴρ αὐτῆς ὁ σκυτοτόμος μεμεθυσμένος· καὶ ἀνιὼν ἐθεάσατο ταύτην ταῖς τοῦ μοιχοῦ ἀγκάλαις συνεσφιγμένην. Καὶ λυπηθεὶς ἐπὶ τῷ ἀπροσδοκήτῳ αὐτοῦ θεάματι, ἐσκανδαλίσθη καὶ εἰσελθὼν ἐν τῷ οἴκῳ αὐτοῦ, ἔδησε τὴν γυναῖκα αὐτοῦ ἐν τῷ στύλῳ καὶ ἔτυψεν αὐτὴν ἀφειδῶς· καὶ ἀπελθὼν ἐκοιμήθη ἐν τῷ κοιτῶνι αὐτοῦ.

23 "Ὑπνώττοντος δὲ αὐτοῦ ἦλθεν ἡ μαυλίστρια αὐτῆς καὶ λέγει αὐτῇ· "Ὁ φίλος σου κάθηται ἀγανακτῶν ἐν τῷ πυλῶνι ἔξω.' Καὶ λέγει αὐτῇ ἡ τοῦ σκυτοτόμου γυνή· 'Σὺ βλέπεις, ὦ φίλη μου, τὸ συμβάν μοι· ἀλλ' οὖν δέομαί σου, ὅπως λύσῃς με καὶ δήσῃς σεαυτὴν τῷ στύλῳ, ἕως οὗ ἀπέλθω πρὸς τὸν ἐραστήν μου καὶ συνομιλήσω αὐτῷ· καὶ συντόμως ὑποστρέψω πρὸς σέ, καὶ ἔσται μοι παρὰ σοῦ αὕτη ἡ χάρις ποιηθεῖσα.' Ἡ δὲ ἐποίησεν οὕτως, καὶ λύσασα τὴν γυναῖκα τοῦ σκυτοτόμου, ἔδησεν ἑαυτὴν ἐν τῷ στύλῳ ἐκείνῳ. Ἐξυπνισθεὶς δὲ ὁ σκυτοτόμος, εὐθὺς ἐφώνησε τὴν ἰδίαν γυναῖκα. Ἡ δὲ μαυλίστρια, ἡ γυνὴ τοῦ συσκιαστοῦ, οὐκ ἀπεκρίνατο αὐτῷ παντελῶς φοβουμένη μήπως γνωρίσῃ αὐτήν. Πλησθεὶς δὲ ὁ σκυτοτόμος θυμοῦ καὶ νομίσας περιφρονεῖσθαι παρὰ τῆς ἰδίας γυναικὸς καὶ ὅτι ἡ αὐτοῦ γυνὴ ὑπάρχει δεδεμένη, λαβὼν μάχαιραν ἀπέ-

was the wife of a tentmaker, and when the tanner went away, this woman said to her go-between, ‘Go and get my lover, for my husband is staying out tonight.’ The go-between went off and got her lover, but when the adulterer had already arrived and was sitting by the gate fondly embracing her, her husband, the tanner, came back drunk. As he approached, he saw her squeezed tight in the adulterer’s arms. Upset by this unexpected sight, the tanner was scandalized and, going into the house, tied his wife to the pillar and beat her mercilessly. Then he went to sleep in his bedroom.

“While he was sleeping, the wife’s go-between arrived 23
and said to her, ‘Your lover is sitting outside in the gateway, and he’s angry.’ The tanner’s wife said to her, ‘You see, my friend, what’s happened to me; so, please, release me and tie yourself to the pillar while I go to my lover and consort with him. I’ll return to you soon, and you’ll be doing this as a favor to me.’ She did this, and when she had released the tanner’s wife, she tied herself up to that pillar. But the tanner woke up and right away called to his wife. The go-between, the wife of the tentmaker, didn’t answer him as she was terrified that he would recognize her. The tanner, full of anger and thinking that he was being ignored by his wife, and that it was his wife who was tied up, took a knife and cut off the

τεμε τὴν ῥῖνα αὐτῆς τῆς μαυλιστρίας. Καὶ πάλιν στραφεὶς ἐκοιμήθη ἐν τῷ κοιτῶνι αὐτοῦ.

24 "Ἐλθοῦσα δὲ ἡ γυνὴ τοῦ σκυτοτόμου καὶ ἰδοῦσα τὸ γεγονὸς εἰς τὴν ἑαυτῆς μαυλίστριαν, λύσασα ταύτην ἀπέλυσε καὶ ἀπῆλθεν εἰς τὸν οἶκον αὐτῆς, ἔχουσα τὴν ἰδίαν ῥῖνα ἐκκεκομμένην. Ἀπελθούσης δὲ τῆς μαυλιστρίας, ἔδησεν ἑαυτὴν ἡ γυνὴ τοῦ σκυτοτόμου ἐν τῷ στύλῳ, καὶ ἤρξατο βοᾶν πρὸς τὸν Θεὸν κατὰ τοῦ ἀνδρὸς αὐτῆς καὶ λέγουσα· 'Κύριε, εἰ μὲν ἠδικήθην παρὰ τοῦ ἀνδρός μου ἀδίκως, κολληθήτω ἡ ῥίς μου εἰς τὸν τόπον αὐτῆς καὶ ὑγιὴς γενηθήτω.' Καὶ στραφεῖσα πρὸς τὸν ἄνδρα αὐτῆς εἶπεν· 'Ὦ ἀνόσιε, ἀνάστηθι, καὶ ἴδε τὸ ἔλεος τοῦ Θεοῦ καὶ τὴν αὐτοῦ χάριν τὴν ἐπ' ἐμοὶ γενομένην, πῶς ὑγιᾶ με κατέστησεν.' Ὁ δὲ λέγει αὐτῇ· 'Τίνες εἰσὶν οὗτοι οἱ λόγοι, ὦ μάγισσα;' Καὶ ὑφάψας λύχνον, εἶδεν αὐτὴν ὑγιᾶ. Καὶ μεγάλως μετανοήσας ἐφ' οἷς ἥμαρτεν πρὸς αὐτήν, παρεκάλει αὐτῇ καὶ συγγνώμην ᾔτει τοῦ σφάλματος.

25 "Ἡ δὲ γυνὴ τοῦ συσκιαστοῦ ἐλθοῦσα εἰς τὴν ἑαυτῆς οἰκίαν ἐπανουργεύσατο ὅπως κρύψῃ τὴν ἑαυτῆς αἰσχύνην. Ὀρθρίσας οὖν ὁ ἀνὴρ αὐτῆς λέγει αὐτῇ· 'Ἐπίδος μοι τὰ ἐργαλεῖά μου ἀπελθεῖν ἐν τῷ ἐργαστηρίῳ!' Ἡ δέ, λαβοῦσα τὸ ξυράφιον μόνον ἐπέδωκεν τῷ ἀνδρὶ αὐτῆς ἐκεῖσε. Ὁ δὲ λέγει αὐτῇ· 'Πάντα τὰ ἐργαλεῖά μοι δός· ἄπελθε καὶ ἀλλέως μὴ ποίει!' Καὶ στραφεῖσα πάλιν ἡ γυνὴ δέδωκεν αὐτῷ τὸ ξυράφιον μόνον. Ὁ δὲ ἀνὴρ αὐτῆς ὀργισθεὶς ἔρριψε τὸ ξυράφιον μετὰ θυμοῦ πρὸς αὐτήν. Εὐθὺς δὲ ἐκείνη λαβοῦσα τὴν ῥῖνα αὐτῆς καὶ κράξασα φωνῇ μεγάλῃ εἶπεν· 'Τὴν ῥῖνα μου, τὴν ῥῖνα μου!'

go-between's nose. He then returned to his bedroom and went back to sleep.

"When the tanner's wife came and saw what had hap- 24
pened to her go-between, she released her and sent her away, and the woman went back to her house with her nose cut off. When the go-between had gone, the tanner's wife tied herself to the pillar and began to cry out to God, accusing her husband and saying, 'Lord, if I was unjustly wronged by my husband, let my nose be stuck back in its place and become whole again.' And turning toward her husband she said, 'Get up, you monster, and see God's mercy and his grace which has come upon me, and how he has made me well.' And he said to her, 'What are you saying, you witch?' But when he had lit a lamp, he saw she was well again, and he deeply repented of the wrongs he had done to her, consoled her, and sought her forgiveness for his mistake.

"When the wife of the tentmaker arrived at her own 25
house, she contrived a way by which she might hide her shame. So, when her husband got up, he said to her, 'Give me my tools so I can go to the workshop!' But she took just the razor and gave it to her husband there. He said to her, 'Give me all the tools. Go on, and don't do anything else!' And the wife came back again and gave him only the razor. But her husband got angry and threw the razor at her in a rage. And she again took hold of her nose and cried out in a loud voice, 'My nose, my nose!'

26 “Ἐφώνησε δὲ τοὺς γείτονας καὶ τοὺς ἰδίους· οἱ δὲ συγγενεῖς αὐτῆς εἵλκυσαν αὐτὸν βιαίως πρὸς τὸν κριτήν. Ὁ δὲ δικαστὴς λέγει πρὸς αὐτόν· ‘Τίνος χάριν πεποίηκας τὸ τοιοῦτον;’ Καὶ μὴ ἔχων αὐτὸς πρόφασίν τινα εἰπεῖν, προσέταξε τοῦτον κολασθῆναι. Ὁ δὲ ἀσκητὴς προσελθὼν ἔπεσε παρὰ τοῖς γόνασι τοῦ κριτοῦ, καὶ εἶπεν αὐτῷ· ‘Μὴ δοκῇς, κύριέ μου, ὅτι ὁ κλέπτης ἔλαβε τὰ ὑφάσματα ἅπερ μοι ἔδωσαν, καὶ ζητῶ αὐτά, ἢ οἱ κριοὶ ἀπέκτειναν τὴν ἀλώπεκα, ἢ τὸ δηλητήριον ἀπέκτεινε τὴν πόρνην, ἢ οὗτος ὁ τιμωρούμενος ἔτεμε τὴν ῥῖνα τῆς γυναικὸς αὐτοῦ. Ἀλλ’ ἡμεῖς πεποιήκαμεν πάντα, ἅπερ πεπόνθαμεν·’ καὶ ἀνήγγειλεν αὐτῷ πάντα ἅπερ ἔπαθεν αὐτὸς καὶ εἶδεν, καὶ ἐρρύσατο τὸν ἄνθρωπον ἐκ τῆς τιμωρίας.

27 “Οὕτω καὶ σὺ σεαυτὸν βλάψεις, εἴπερ ποιήσεις εἰς ἕτερόν τι κακόν.” Εἶτα εἶπε πρὸς τούτοις ὁ Ἰχνηλάτης· “Ἀληθῶς ἔφης, ἀλλ’ εἰπόν σοι καὶ πάλιν ἐρῶ· πολλοὶ γὰρ τῶν δυνατωτέρων ὑπὸ τῶν τυχόντων ἡττήθησαν.”

Περὶ τῆς ἀδικίας τοῦ κόρακος.

“Λέγεται γὰρ ὡς κόραξ τις ἐμφωλεύων τινὶ τῶν ὀρεινῶν δένδρων παρά τινος ὄφεως καθ’ ἕκαστον ἠδικεῖτο ἐνιαυτόν, ἐν τούτῳ τοὺς νεοττοὺς αὐτοῦ κατεσθίοντος. Ὡς οὖν πολλάκις τοῦτο εἰς αὐτὸν ἔδρασεν, ἀπελθὼν οὗτος εἴς τινα φίλτατον αὐτῷ θῶα, εἶπεν· ‘Βούλομαί σοι συμβούλῳ χρήσασθαι· οἶδας γάρ, οἵας πάσχω παρὰ τοῦ ὄφεως ἀδικίας. Ἔδοξέ μοι συμφέρον εἶναι προσεγγίσαι τούτῳ ὑπνώττοντι καὶ τοὺς ὀφθαλμοὺς αὐτοῦ ἐξορύξαι.’ Ὁ δὲ θὼς ἔφη· ‘Οὐ

"She called her neighbors and family. Her relatives hauled her husband forcibly in front of the judge. And the magistrate said to him, 'Why did you do such a thing?' And since he had no excuse to give, he sentenced him to be punished. But the ascetic approached and fell at the judge's knees and said to him, 'Don't imagine, my lord, that the thief took the robes which they gave to me and which I'm seeking, or that the rams killed the fox, or that the poison killed the prostitute, or that the man who is being punished cut off his wife's nose, but rather we have caused everything we have experienced.' And he told him everything he had experienced and seen, and released the man from punishment. 26

"And you too will harm yourself like this, if you do anything else bad," continued Stephanites. Then Ichnelates said in response to this, "What you say is true, but I've said to you and I'll say it again, many powerful men have been overcome by lesser people." 27

About the wronged crow.

"For it is said that a crow who nested in one of the trees in the mountains was wronged each year by a snake which ate its chicks there. So, when the snake had done this to it many times, the crow went off to a jackal who was very friendly with him, and said, 'I want to consult you as an adviser, for you know what I suffer from the snake's wrongdoing. I thought it would be helpful to me to get close to it while it was sleeping and tear out its eyes.' But the jackal said,

καλῶς ἐβουλεύσω, ἀλλὰ σκόπησον μηχανὴν ἑτέραν, δι' ἧς ἐκεῖνον μὲν ἀπολέσεις, σὺ δὲ ἀπήμαντος διατηρηθῇς, μήπως ταὐτόν τι πάθῃς τῷ τοῦ κύκνου.'"

28 *Περὶ κύκνου.*

"'Λέγεται γὰρ ὡς κύκνος τις παρά τινι λίμνῃ πλήρει ἰχθύων οἰκῶν κἀκ τούτων τρεφόμενος ἐγήρασε καὶ πρὸς τὴν ἁλιείαν ἠτόνησε. Καὶ πείνῃ κατασχεθεὶς καὶ ἀνίᾳ πολλῇ, ἀνῆλθεν ἐπί τι ὄρος καὶ ἀνερχόμενος συνήντησε καρκίνῳ τινι, κατηφὴς ὢν αὐτὸς καὶ σκυθρωπός. Ὁ δὲ καρκίνος εὐθὺς εἶπε πρὸς αὐτόν· "Τί ξύννους μοι φαίνῃ καὶ ἀθυμῶν;" Ὁ δὲ κύκνος ἔφη· "Καὶ πῶς οὐκ ἀθυμήσω; πρότερον γὰρ παρήδρευον τῇ λίμνῃ ταύτῃ καὶ ἀπὸ τῶν ἰχθύων αὐτῆς, ἱκανῶν ὄντων, δαψιλῶς ἐτρεφόμην. Σήμερον δὲ ἑώρακα δύο ἁλιεῖς παραγενομένους εἰς τοῦτον τὸν τόπον καὶ πρὸς ἀλλήλους διαλεγομένους ὅπως ἂν πάντας τοὺς ἰχθύας σαγηνεύσωσιν." Ὁ δὲ καρκίνος ταῦτα ἀκούσας, παρεγένετο ἐπὶ τοὺς ἰχθύας, καὶ ἀνήγγειλεν αὐτοῖς, ὅσα παρὰ τοῦ κύκνου ἔμαθε. Οἱ δὲ προσῆλθον τῷ κύκνῳ λέγοντες· "Ἄρτι συμβούλῳ σοι χρησόμεθα, ὁ γὰρ συνετὸς ἀνὴρ πολλάκις συμβουλεύεται τῷ ἰδίῳ ἐχθρῷ, νουνεχεῖ ὄντι, ὅτε κοινὴ αὐτοῖς ἡ τοῦ πράγματος ὠφέλεια εἴη." Ὁ δὲ κύκνος ἔφη· "Οὐδεμία μοι ἑτέρα πρόκειται μηχανή, ἢ τὸ μεταθῆναι ὑμᾶς ἀπὸ τοῦδε τοῦ τόπου ἐπί τινα ἕτερον τόπον βαλτώδη καὶ καλαμώδη καὶ ὑδατώδη." Οἱ δὲ εἶπον· "Καὶ λοιπὸν μετάστησον σὺ ἡμᾶς πάντας ἐπὶ τὸν τοιοῦτον τόπον." Ὁ δὲ κύκνος ἔφη· "Δέδοικα, μὴ πρὸ τοῦ μεταστῆσαι πάντας

'You've not planned this well. Think of a different way you may destroy it, but stay safe yourself, so that you don't suffer the same fate as the swan.'"

About a swan. 28

"'For it is said that a swan lived beside a lake full of fish and, feeding himself on these, grew old and became too exhausted to fish. Gripped by hunger and great distress, he went up a mountain, and as he was going up, downcast and looking sad, he met a crab. The crab immediately said to him, "Why do you seem so deep in thought and depressed?" And the swan replied, "How could I not be depressed? I used to live on this lake before, and I was well fed on the fish in it, which are plentiful. But today I saw two fishermen arrive at this place and they were talking to each other about how they might catch all the fish in a net." When the crab heard this, he went to the fish and told them what he had learned from the swan. And they went to the swan and said, "We'll use you as an adviser, for a smart man often uses his enemy as an adviser, if the enemy has good sense, when they both have a common interest in the matter." And the swan said, "I see no other solution, except to move you from this place to another one that's swampy and reedy and full of water." And they said, "All right, move all of us to that place." But the swan said, "I'm afraid that before I can

ὑμᾶς καταλάβωσί με οἱ ἁλιεῖς· ὅμως ὅσον μοι τὸ κατὰ δύναμιν τοῦτο καὶ ἐπιχειρήσω.”

29 “‘Καὶ ἤρξατο ἐπὶ τῇ τοιαύτῃ προφάσει μετακομίζειν ἑκάστῃ ἡμέρᾳ τινὰς ἰχθύας ἐπὶ τὸν τοῦ ὄρους κρημνὸν καὶ ἐσθίειν αὐτούς, τῶν ἄλλων οἰομένων, ὡς ἐπὶ τὸν ὑποσχεθέντα αὐτοῖς τόπον παρ’ αὐτοῦ ἅπαντες μετοικίζονται. Μιᾷ δὲ τῶν ἡμερῶν ἠξίωσε τοῦτον καὶ ὁ καρκίνος ὥστε μετακομίσαι αὐτὸν ὡς ἕνα τῶν ἰχθύων, καὶ λαβὼν τοῦτον ὁ κύκνος, ἀπήγαγε εἰς τὸν κρημνὸν ἔνθα τοὺς ἰχθύας κατήσθιε, βουλόμενος καὶ αὐτὸν καταφαγεῖν. Ἰδὼν οὖν ὁ καρκίνος τὰ τῶν ἰχθύων ὀστᾶ ἐκεῖσε κείμενα ἐφώρασε τὸν δόλον παραυτίκα καὶ καθ’ ἑαυτὸν διελογίζετο, ὡς βιοθανατήσει καὶ ὡς ἵνα εἴτε συμπλακῇ τῷ κύκνῳ εἴτε ὑπείξῃ, καὶ δεῖν ἔγνω μὴ ἄδοξον ὑποστῆναι θάνατον, ἀλλ’ *ἢ καλῶς ζῆν ἢ καλῶς τεθνηκέναι*· καὶ ἐπισχὼν ἀθρόως ταῖς χηλαῖς αὐτοῦ τὸν τοῦ κύκνου τράχηλον βιαίως ἀπέπνιξε.

“‘Διὰ τοῦτο οὖν σοι ταῦτα διεξῆλθον, ὦ κόραξ, ἵνα μάθῃς ἀκριβῶς, ὡς πολλάκις ἐπιβουλεύων τίς τινι, ταῖς οἰκίαις ἄρκυσιν ἁλίσκεται· ἀλλά σε δεῖ οὑτωσὶ τὴν τοῦ ὄφεως ἀπώλειαν μεταχειρίσασθαι· εἰ γὰρ δύνῃ ὑψιπέτησον, καὶ στοχασάμενος κάτωθεν γυναικεῖον κόσμον τὸν τιμιώτερον, ἄφελε τοῦτον καὶ τῷ φωλεῷ ἐγκατάθου τοῦ ὄφεως. Ἕψονται γάρ σοί τινες διὰ τοῦτον, καὶ εὑρόντες οὗτοι τὸν ὄφιν ἀναιροῦσιν.’ Ὃ δὴ καὶ δράσας ὁ κόραξ, ἀπηλλάγη τοῦ ὄφεως.”

30 Εἶτα εἶπεν πρὸς τούτοις ὁ Ἰχνηλάτης τῷ Στεφανίτῃ· “Ταῦτά οὖν σοι διεξῄειν ἐγώ, ὡς ἂν διαγνῷς ὡς ἐπικρατεστέρα ἐστὶν ἡ φρόνησις ἐκ πάντων τῆς δυνάμεως.” Ὁ δὲ

move you the fishermen may catch me. But I'll try and do as much as I can."

29 "'And on this pretext he began to take some fish every day up to the mountain crags and eat them, while the others thought they were all being moved by him to the location they had been promised. But one day the crab also asked him to carry him like one of the fish, so the swan picked him up and took him away to the crags where he used to eat the fish, wishing to eat him as well. So, when the crab saw the fish bones lying there, he immediately saw through the trick and, he argued with himself, since he too was going to die a violent death, whether he got into a fight with the swan or just submitted, he thought that he should not suffer an inglorious death, but should *live well or die well.* So he suddenly grasped the neck of the swan with his pincers, and violently choked him to death.

"'I've gone through these matters in detail for you for this reason, crow,' said the jackal, 'so that you may clearly learn that someone who plots against someone else is often caught in his own nets. But you must contrive the destruction of the snake in this way: if you're able, fly high, take aim at the most valuable piece of a woman's jewelry down below, and take it; then put it in the den of the snake. For some people will follow you because of this, and when they find the snake, they'll kill it.' And when the crow did this, he got rid of the snake."

30 In relation to this, Ichnelates said to Stephanites, "I've been going through all this in detail for you so that you may understand that good sense is in every way superior to

Στεφανίτης εἶπεν· "Εἰ μὴ πρὸς τῇ ἀνδρείᾳ ὁ ταῦρος καὶ ἀγχίνους ἦν, ἐνεχώρει ἂν τοιαῦτά σοι λέγειν, ἀλλ' ἔστι καὶ συνετώτατος· τὰ τοιαῦτα κατάλειψον." Ὁ δὲ Ἰχνηλάτης ἔφη· "Ἀληθῶς εἶπας ὡς τοιοῦτός ἐστιν, ἀλλ' ἐν τούτῳ δύναμαι καταβαλεῖν αὐτόν, τῷ θαρρεῖν μοι καὶ πιστεύειν ἐν πολλοῖς τῶν πραγμάτων, ὥς τε διὰ τοῦ τοιούτου τρόπου ὁ λαγωὸς τὸν λέοντα κατέβαλεν."

31 *Περὶ πανουργίας λαγωοῦ.*

"Λέγεται γὰρ ὡς λέων τις ᾤκει χλοηφόρον καὶ ὑδατῶδες πεδίον, ἐν ᾧ καὶ γένη θηρίων ἐνέμοντο διάφορα, τῶν μὲν ἄλλων ἀφθόνως καὶ δαψιλῶς εὐμοιρούντων, μόνῳ δὲ τῷ φόβῳ τοῦ λέοντος παρενοχλούμενα. Βουλὴν δὲ συστησάμενα προσῆλθον τῷ λέοντι καὶ εἶπον αὐτῷ· 'Συνείδομεν οὖν πάντες ἡμεῖς, ὦ βασιλεῦ, ἵνα σὲ μὲν μόχθων καὶ κόπων ἀπαλλάξωμεν, ἡμῖν δὲ αὐτοῖς ἀμεριμνίαν ποιήσωμεν. Σὺ μὲν γὰρ ἱδρῶτι πολλῷ καὶ μόχθῳ μόλις θηρεύεις ἕνα ἐξ ἡμῶν, ἡμεῖς δὲ πάλιν τῇ ἀοριστίᾳ τοῦ θηρευομένου περίδειλοι ὁσημέραι διατελοῦμεν. Δεῖν οὖν ἔγνωμεν ἑκάστῃ ἡμέρᾳ δεξιοῦσθαί σου τὴν τράπεζαν ἕνα ἐξ ἡμῶν.' Καὶ τοῦτο ἀσπαστὸν ἐφάνη τῷ λέοντι καὶ διετέλεσαν ἡμέρας ἱκανὰς κλῆρον βάλλοντες κατ' ἀλλήλων καὶ τὸν εἰσπεσόντα τῷ κλήρῳ πρὸς τὸν λέοντα ἐξαπέστελλον. Ὡς οὖν ὁ κλῆρος ἦλθέ ποτε καὶ ἐπὶ τὸν λαγωόν, εἶπεν αὐτοῖς· 'Εἰ συνεργήσετέ μοι, ὦ θῆρες, ἀπαλλάξω ὑμᾶς τοῦ βαρυτάτου τούτου ἐπιτιμίου.' Οἱ δὲ εἶπον· '"Ο βούλει, ποιήσομεν.' Ὁ δὲ εἶπεν· 'Παραγγείλατε τῷ ἐφέλκοντί με πρὸς τὸν λέοντα

strength." But Stephanites said, "If, besides his bravery, the bull wasn't also shrewd, it would be appropriate for you to say such things, but he's also very smart. So stop doing this." But Ichnelates said, "What you say is true, as he is like that, but I'll be able to overthrow him in this way, because he has confidence in me and trusts me in many matters, just as the hare also overthrew the lion in such a way."

About a hare's cunning. 31

"For it is said that a lion had his home on a grassy and well-watered plain, in which there were various kinds of wild animals who lived happily in plenty and abundance in other respects, but were troubled only by their fear of the lion. So they came up with a plan, went to the lion, and said to him, 'We've all decided, our king, to set you free from toil and trouble, and free ourselves from care. For it causes you much sweat and labor each time you hunt one of us down, while we, on the other hand, are continuously terrified by the uncertainty of being hunted every day. We've thus concluded that one of us should grace your table each day.' This seemed welcome to the lion, and many days passed with them casting lots against each other and sending off to the lion the one on whom the lot fell. Then, when the lot fell upon the hare, he said to them, 'If you'll work with me, animals, I'll set you free from this very oppressive penalty.' 'We'll do whatever you want,' they said. And he said, 'Tell the one who

μὴ κατεπείγειν με πρὸς τὴν πορείαν, ἀλλ' ὅτε πλησίον αὐτοῦ γενόμεθα, ἀποκρυβῆναι αὐτόν.'

32 "Οἱ δὲ τὸ προσταχθὲν τοῦτο ἐποίησαν, καὶ ὁ λαγωὸς ἀπερχόμενος βραδυτέρᾳ τῇ πορείᾳ ἐχρήσατο ὥστε τὸν λέοντα ὑπὸ τῆς πείνης ἀγριωθῆναι. Ὡς οὖν εἶδε τὸν λαγωόν, εἶπε πρὸς αὐτόν· 'Τί, ὅτι μέχρι τοῦδε ἐβράδυνας, καὶ οὐχ ὡς οἱ λοιποὶ τάχιον ἦλθες;' Ὁ δὲ εἶπε· 'Λαγωὸν εἱλκόμην πρὸς σέ, καί τίς μοι συναντήσας λέων ἥρπασε τοῦτον, πολλὰ αὐτῷ ἐμοῦ ἐπιφωνησαμένου καὶ προδιαμαρτυρουμένου, ὡς δίαιτά σοι ἐπέμφθη, ἀλλ' οὐκ εἰσακουσθέντος. Καὶ εἴπερ βούλει, ἀπάξω σε πρὸς αὐτόν.' Θυμωθεὶς οὖν ὁ λέων, εἶπε τῷ λαγωῷ ὡς· '"Εψομαί σοι, ἔνθα ἐστὶν ἐκεῖνος.' Ὁ δὲ ἀπήγαγε τοῦτον ἐπί τι φρέαρ τῶν βαθυτάτων καὶ παρεσκεύασε αὐτὸν ἐν αὐτῷ προκύψαι ὥστε ἰδεῖν τὸν λέοντα. Καὶ συμπροέκυψεν καὶ οὗτος αὐτῷ καὶ εἶπεν· ''Ιδοὺ ὁ λέων ὁ τὴν ἁρπαγὴν ποιήσας, καὶ ὁ ἁρπαγεὶς λαγωός,' ὑποδείξας αὐτῷ ἐν τῷ ὕδατι τοῦ φρέατος τὸ ἑαυτοῦ καὶ τὸ ἐκείνου ἐκτύπωμα, ὑφ' ὧν ὁ λέων πλανηθεὶς ἔρριψεν ἑαυτὸν ἐν τῷ φρέατι καὶ ἀπεπνίγη.

"Τοιούτως κἀγὼ θαρρῶ ἐν πᾶσί μου προσεμπιστεύειν τὸν ταῦρον." Ὁ δὲ Στεφανίτης εἶπεν· "Εἰ δύνασαι τὸν ταῦρον ἀπολέσαι μὴ καταβλαπτομένου τοῦ λέοντος, τὸ ἔργον ἐπιχείρησον. Καὶ γὰρ σύ τε κἀγὼ καὶ ἕτεροι πλεῖστοι τῶν καθ' ἡμᾶς διὰ τῆς τοῦ ταύρου οἰκειώσεως παρεωράθημεν νῦν. Εἰ δὲ τοῦτο ἀδύνατόν ἐστίν σοι, ἀπόσχου τοῦ ἐγχειρήματος, παράβασις γὰρ τὸ τοιοῦτον πρᾶγμα καὶ παρασπόνδησίς ἐστιν."

is to take me to the lion not to hurry me during the journey, but to hide when we get near to him.'

"They did as they were told, and the hare went off and 32
made the journey very slowly, so that the lion would become wild with hunger. So, when he saw the hare, he said to him, 'What kept you so long? Why didn't you come more quickly like the others?' And he replied, 'I was dragging a hare to you when a lion met me and grabbed it, even though I was calling out and protesting a lot that it had been sent as food for you, but he didn't listen. If you want, I'll take you to him.' The lion grew angry and said to the hare, 'I'll follow you to where he is.' And the hare led him off to a very deep well and convinced him to lean over so as to see the lion. The hare also leaned over it with him and said, 'Look, there's the lion that did the grabbing, and the hare that was grabbed,' showing him both the lion's and his own reflection in the water of the well. The lion was deceived by these, threw himself into the well and drowned.

"In the same way, I too am sure the bull trusts me completely," concluded Ichnelates. And Stephanites said, "If you can destroy the bull without the lion being harmed, then try to do that. For both you and I, and many others along with us, have now been completely overlooked because of the lion's relationship with the bull. But if you can't do that, then give up the attempt, for it's a betrayal and a breach of trust."

33 *Περὶ τῆς κατασκευῆς τοῦ Ἰχνηλάτου πρὸς τὸν λέοντα τοῦ ἀναιρεθῆναι τὸν ταῦρον.*

Εἶτα μιᾷ τῶν ἡμερῶν εἰσῆλθεν ὁ Ἰχνηλάτης πρὸς τὸν λέοντα, σύννους ὢν καὶ κατηφείας μεστός, καὶ ἐπηρώτησε τοῦτον ὁ λέων περὶ τοῦ πάθους καὶ ἔφη· "Μή τι συνέβη καινόν;" Ὁ δὲ Ἰχνηλάτης εἶπε· "Συμβέβηκέ τι πρᾶγμα ἀποτρόπαιόν σοί τε κἀμοί, ἀλλ᾽ ὅταν ὁ λέγων ἐπαίσθηται ὡς τὰ λεχθησόμενα παρ᾽ αὐτοῦ δυσάρεστα τῷ ἀκούοντι φανήσεται, οὐ τοῦ λέγειν κατατολμᾷ—εἴ γε καὶ δι᾽ εὔνοιαν τοῦτο πράττει τοῦ ἀκούοντος—εἰ μή γε πολλάκις καὶ θαρρήσει τῇ συνέσει αὐτοῦ, δόξαντος παραίνεσιν εὐνοϊκὴν εἶναι τὰ ὑποτιθέμενα. Εἰδὼς οὖν σε καὶ αὐτός, ὦ βασιλεῦ, συνέσει καὶ ἀγχινοίᾳ κεκοσμημένον, ἐθάρρησα διαλεχθῆναί σοι, περὶ ὧν ἀκούειν οὐ βούλει. Οἶδα γὰρ ὡς οὐκ ἐνδοιάζεις περὶ τὴν ἀκραιφνῆ καὶ εἰλικρινῆ δούλωσίν μου, καὶ νοῶ μὲν ὡς ἄπιστά σοι φανήσεται τὰ ῥήματά μου, διαλογίζομαι δὲ πάλιν, ὡς καὶ αἱ ἡμέτεραι ψυχαὶ τῆς σῆς ἀνήρτηνται ψυχῆς καὶ γνώμης καὶ ἐξουσίας, καὶ ἀναγκαῖόν μοι φαίνεται τὸ μηδὲν τῶν δεόντων καὶ λυσιτελούντων ἀποκρύπτειν σοι. Οὐ δεῖ γὰρ οὔτε τὸ ὑπήκοον τὴν πρὸς τοὺς δεσπότας εὔνοιαν συγκαλύπτειν, οὔτε τὸν νοσοῦντα μὴ ἀνακοινοῦσθαι τὰ τῆς νόσου τῷ ἰατρῷ, οὔτε τὸν πένητα σπεύδειν λαθεῖν τὴν ἑαυτοῦ πενίαν τοὺς φίλους.

34 "Ἀνέμαθον οὖν παρά τινος ἀξιοπίστου, ὡς ὁ ταῦρος τοῖς ἄρχουσι τοῖς ὑπὸ σὲ συνωμίλησε καταμόνας καὶ εἶπεν αὐτοῖς· 'Ἐπειράθην τοῦ λέοντος καὶ διέγνων ἀκριβῶς τὴν

About Ichnelates's stratagem with the lion for getting rid of the bull. 33

One day, then, Ichnelates, looking gloomy and very dejected, went up to the lion. The lion asked him what was wrong and said, "Something new hasn't happened, has it?" Ichnelates said, "Something has happened that bodes ill both for you and for me. But when the speaker believes that the things he says are going to seem unpleasant to the hearer, he doesn't dare say anything—at least if he is acting out of goodwill toward the listener—unless he has often had proof of the hearer's intelligence, and that he will consider what is being suggested to be friendly advice. So, as I know that you yourself, my king, are adorned with intelligence and sagacity, I've taken courage to discuss with you matters that you don't wish to hear. I know that you don't doubt my pure and absolute devotion, and so, although I'm aware that on the one hand my words will appear unbelievable to you, on the other I reflected that, as our lives are dependent on your life and judgment and authority, I feel I should not keep secret from you anything that is appropriate and profitable. For a subject should not conceal his love for his masters, and a sick man should tell the physician the details of his illness, and a poor man should not seek to conceal his poverty from his friends.

"Well then, I learned from someone trustworthy that the 34
bull spoke in private with your ministers and said to them, 'I have put the lion to the test, and have accurately determined

ἀνδρείαν αὐτοῦ καὶ τὴν φρόνησιν, καὶ εὗρον αὐτὸν παντελῶς ἐν τούτοις ἀφελῆ καὶ ἀνίσχυρον.' Καὶ ἐκ τῶν τοιούτων αὐτοῦ προοιμίων ἐτεκμηράμην τὴν τούτου ἀσέβειαν καὶ παρασπόνδησιν, ὅτι, σοῦ τὸν τοιοῦτον ὑπὲρ πάντας ὑψώσαντος καὶ ὁμότιμον σεαυτῷ καταστήσαντος, διενοήθη τῆς σῆς περιδράξασθαι ἀρχῆς. Καὶ δεῖ τοὺς βασιλεῖς, ὅτε τινῶν ἐπαίσθωνται τῆς οἰκείας ἀρχῆς καὶ βασιλείας ἐφιεμένων, προκαταβάλλειν τούτους καὶ ἀφανίζειν πρὶν ἢ ἐπὶ μέγα τὰ τῆς ἐφέσεως ἀρθῇ καὶ ἐπὶ μεῖζον αὐξηθῇ τὸ κακόν. Τούτου γὰρ γενομένου, ἀνέγκλητα ἴσως γίνεται τὰ συμπτώματα. Οἱ μὲν γὰρ ἱκανώτατοι τῶν ἀνθρώπων παντὶ τρόπῳ σπεύδουσι μὴ ἐμπεσεῖν ἀπευκταίῳ τινὶ καὶ ἐναντίῳ συμπτώματι. Οἱ δὲ ἥττονες τούτων καὶ καταδεέστεροι περιπίπτουσι μὲν ἴσως τισί, μηχανῶνται δ' ὅμως τὴν οἰκείαν ἀνάρρυσιν. Οἱ δὲ ἄλλοι πάντῃ ἀφελεῖς περιπεσόντες οὐκ ἀναφέρουσιν, οὔτε μὴν ἀναρρύονται, καὶ τοῦτό ἐστι παρόμοιον τῷ τῶν τριῶν ἰχθύων."

35 *Περὶ τῶν τριῶν ἰχθύων.*

"Λέγεται γὰρ ὡς ἔν τινι λιμνηδίῳ πρὸς ποταμὸν συνάπτοντι τρεῖς διῃτῶντο ἰχθύες, ὧν ὁ μὲν εἷς συνετώτατος ἦν, ὁ δὲ ἕτερος ἧττον ἐχέφρων, ὁ δὲ ἕτερος πάντῃ ἠλίθιος. Ἔτυχε δὲ μιᾷ τῶν ἡμερῶν διελθεῖν ἁλιεῖς δύο ἐπὶ τὸ τοιοῦτον λιμνήσιον ὕδωρ καὶ συνθεῖναι πρὸς ἀλλήλους, ὁπόταν ὑποστρέψωσι, σαγηνεῦσαι τοὺς τρεῖς ἰχθύας. Καὶ ὁ μὲν οὖν συνετώτατος ἰχθὺς ἅμα τῷ ἀκοῦσαι τῶν τοιούτων ἀπεδήμησε τῆς λίμνης πρὸς ἐκεῖνον τὸν ποταμόν. Οἱ δὲ

his courage and wisdom, and I have found him to be foolish and weak in these respects.' From these initial points concerning the bull," Ichnelates continued, "I've recognized his disloyalty and breach of trust; for, although you exalted him over everyone, and set him in honor equal to your own, he intended to seize your realm. But kings, when they become aware that people are taking aim at their realm and kingdom, must take them down first and eradicate them before their attempt is very well advanced and their evil grows too large. For if this happens, the situation may perhaps be avoided. For the most capable people seek in every way not to be faced with some hopeless and hostile situation. Weaker people and those who are inferior may perhaps get into some trouble, but they still contrive to rescue their affairs. But those others who are completely foolish, do not recover when they fall into misfortune nor do they get themselves out of it; and this is like the story of the three fish."

About the three fish. 35

"For it is said that in a pond adjoining a river there lived three fish, one of whom was most intelligent, another less smart, and the other completely stupid. One day two fishermen happened to pass by that marshy water and they agreed with each other that, when they returned, they would use a net to catch the three fish. So, as soon as he heard this, the very intelligent fish left the pond for the river. But the other

λοιποὶ δύο ἀμελήσαντες τῆς ἑαυτῶν σωτηρίας προσεκαρτέρησαν. Οἱ μὲν οὖν ἁλιεῖς ἐλθόντες φραγμῷ τὸν μεταξὺ τοῦ λιμνηδίου καὶ τοῦ ποταμοῦ πόρον κατωχύρωσαν. Ὅπερ ἰδὼν ὁ ἧττον ἐχέφρων ἰχθὺς μετεμελήθη ἐπὶ τῇ τοῦ δέοντος ἀβλεψίᾳ καὶ εἶπε καθ' ἑαυτόν· 'Τοιαύτη ἐστὶν ἡ τῶν ἀμελούντων ἀπόβασις· ποία οὖν μηχανή ἐστι τῆς ἐμῆς σωτηρίας; Σπανίως γὰρ δρᾷ καὶ καιρίως ἡ μετὰ σπουδῆς ἐπιτηδευομένη μηχανή, ἀλλὰ μηδέν τι τῶν εἰκότων παραλείψω.' Εἶτα ὑπεκρίθη τοῦ θανεῖν καὶ ὕπτιος ἐπὶ τοῦ ὕδατος ἐφέρετο· ὃ δὴ πιστεύσαντες οἱ ἁλιεῖς καὶ ταῖς οἰκείαις χερσὶ συλλαβόντες αὐτὸν καὶ βαστάσαντες ὡς τεθνεῶτα μεταξὺ τοῦ λιμνηδίου καὶ τοῦ ποταμοῦ ἔθηκαν. Καὶ εὐθὺς τῷ ποταμῷ εἰσπηδήσας ἐσώθη. Ὁ δὲ ἠλίθιος ἰχθὺς ἐκεῖνος πολλὰ μογήσας πηδῶν καὶ ἔνθεν κἀκεῖθεν ἀναστραφεὶς καὶ περισκιρτήσας, βιαίως ἐσαγηνεύθη. Οὕτω καὶ πᾶς ἀνόητος πείσεται."

36 Ὁ δὲ λέων ἔφη· "Ἔγνων σου τὸ ὑπόδειγμα, ἀλλ' οὐ δοκῶ τὸν ταῦρον μήποτέ τι παρ' ἐμοῦ παθόντα ἐναντίον δόλιον περὶ ἐμὲ φανῆναι καὶ πονηρόν." Ὁ δὲ Ἰχνηλάτης εἶπεν· "Τὸ μηδὲν παρὰ σοῦ ἐναντίον παθεῖν παρεσκεύασεν αὐτὸν σκαιωρίαν κατὰ σοῦ τηλικαύτην συρράψαι. Τοσοῦτον γὰρ αὐτὸν ἀνύψωσας ὡς πρὸς μηδένα ἕτερον ἀφορᾶν βαθμὸν ἢ τὸν σόν. Ὁ γὰρ ἀσυνείδητος καὶ πονηρὸς ἀνὴρ εὐνοίᾳ κέχρηται τὸ πρότερον ἄχρις ὅτου καταλάβοι βαθμόν, οὗ μή ἐστιν ἄξιος. Καὶ τοῦτον καταλαβών, μηχανᾶται σὺν δόλῳ καὶ κακοεργίᾳ ἔτι περαιτέρω προβῆναι, καὶ δι' οὐδὲν ἕτερον ἐξυπηρετεῖ τοῖς ἡγεμόσιν ἢ τὸ τυχεῖν τινος

two, who didn't care about their safety, stayed there. Then the fishermen came and blocked the passage between the pond and the river with a barrier. When the fish who was less smart saw this, he regretted his lack of proper foresight, and said to himself, 'This is the outcome for those who are careless. But how can I keep myself safe? For although a trick pursued hastily is seldom effective or timely, I won't neglect to do anything within reason.' Then he pretended to be dead and floated on his back up to the water's surface. The fishermen believed this, so they took hold of him with their hands and, lifting him up as if he were dead, put him down between the pond and the river. And he immediately leaped into the river and was saved. But the foolish one, after much effort, and leaping, turning, and jumping about this way and that, was firmly caught in the net. That's what happens to every idiot."

But the lion said, "I understand your illustration, but I 36
don't think that the bull, who has never experienced any hostility from me, appears to be treacherous and wicked toward me." But Ichnelates said, "The fact that he has never experienced any hostility from you has caused him in this case to devise such a plot against you. For you have exalted him so much that he has no other rank in view but yours. Indeed, the foolish and wicked man makes use of goodwill to begin with, until he reaches a rank of which he is not worthy. And once he has reached this, he schemes with deceit and wickedness to advance still further. For he assists the leaders as much as he can for no other reason than to gain

τῶν ἐφετῶν· καὶ ὑποκρίνεται μὲν τὸ σπουδαίως φαίνεσθαι ἄχρι τῆς τῶν ἐλπιζομένων καταλήψεως. Τούτων δὲ τυχών, πρὸς τὴν πονηρὰν αὖθις ἐπανακάμπτει φύσιν, ὥσπερ δὴ καὶ ἡ τοῦ κυνὸς οὐρὰ φύσει λοξὴ οὖσα καὶ διεστραμμένη, ἐπειδὰν μίτῳ δεσμευθῇ καὶ ἐκτανθῇ ἰθυτενὴς φαίνεται, ἀπολυθεῖσα δὲ τοῦ δεσμοῦ, αὖθις καμπύλη γίνεται. Καὶ ἴσθι, ὦ βασιλεῦ, ὡς ὁ μὴ δεχόμενος παρὰ τῶν εὐνοϊκῶς ὁμιλούντων τοὺς ἐπαχθεῖς λόγους ἔοικε τῷ νοσοῦντι καὶ τὴν χρῆσιν τῶν πικρῶν φαρμάκων καὶ τῶν λυσιτελῶν ἀποστρεφομένῳ καὶ τοῦ ἰατροῦ παρακούοντι.

37 "Καὶ ἔσο πρὸς τούτοις εἰδώς, ὡς κρείττων ἐν ὑπηκόοις καὶ φίλοις ἐκεῖνός ἐστιν, ὁ τῆς εὐνοίας ἀντιποιούμενος· καὶ ἐν τοῖς ἔργοις βέλτιον τὸ ἀγαθὴν ἔχειν ἀπόβασιν· ἐν δὲ τοῖς ἐπαίνοις ὁ παρὰ τῶν ἀγαθῶν ἀνδρῶν θρυλλούμενος ἔπαινος· ἐν δὲ τοῖς ἡγεμόσιν ὁ μὴ τῇ οἰήσει καὶ τῇ ὑπερηφανίᾳ ἑαυτὸν ἐκδιδούς· ἐν δὲ τοῖς πλουσίοις ὁ μὴ ὑπὸ τοῦ πολλοῦ μόχθου καὶ πόνου συνεχόμενός τε καὶ περισπώμενος· ἐν δὲ τοῖς φίλοις, ὁ μὴ ἀντερίζων. Λέγεται δὲ καὶ τοῦτο ὡς αἱρετώτερόν ἐστιν ἐπὶ πυρὸς καὶ ὄφεων ἐπιβαίνειν τινὰ ἢ συνοικεῖν τινι τῶν ἐπιβουλευότων τῇ ζωῇ αὐτοῦ." Ὁ δὲ λέων ἔφη· "Εὐνοϊκώτατα λέγεις καὶ ἀπότομα, ἀλλὰ εἰ θῶμεν τὸν ταῦρον οὑτωσὶ ἐχθρωδῶς πρὸς ἡμᾶς διακεῖσθαι, οὐ δυνήσεται βλάψαι τὸ σύνολον, χλοηνόμος ὢν ἐμοῦ αἱμοβόρου ὑπάρχοντος. Μᾶλλον γὰρ ἡ φύσις ἐκεῖνον μοι τροφὴν παρεσκεύασεν." Ὁ δὲ Ἰχνηλάτης εἶπεν· "Μὴ πλανηθῇς τῷ τοιούτου σκοπῷ, εἰ μὴ γὰρ δι' ἑαυτοῦ σε ὁ ταῦρος καταβαλεῖν δυνήσεται, δι' ἑτέρων τοῦτο ποιήσει. Λέγεται γάρ, ὡς εἴ σε ξεναγωγήσει τις, μὴ

some of what he desires, and he pretends to appear zealous until he achieves what he hopes for. And when this happens, he immediately reverts to his wicked nature, just indeed as a dog's tail that is naturally curled and twisted is carried straight when it's bound with thread and stretched, but becomes curved again when it is released from its binding. And know, my king, that he who does not accept troubling words from those who speak to him out of kindness is like the sick man who rejects the use of bitter medicine and other helpful remedies, and takes no notice of his physician.

"And be aware too, that the person who repays kindness 37
is the one who has more subjects and friends; and with actions, that which has a good outcome is better; and, in matters of praise, the praise which is repeated by good men; and among leaders, the one who does not give himself over to conceit and pride; and among rich men, the one who is not hindered and put off by a lot of hard work and toil; and among friends, the one who does not antagonize you. For this, too, is said, that it is preferable for someone to walk into fire and upon snakes than to live with someone who is plotting against his life." The lion said, "You speak very well and succinctly, but if we suppose that the bull has this hostile attitude toward us, he won't be able to do any harm at all, since he's an herbivore while I'm a carnivore. Rather, nature has provided him to me for food." But Ichnelates said, "Don't be mistaken about his aim, for if the bull is unable to overthrow you by himself, he will do so through others. For it's said that even if someone guides you, you should not

πρότερον τούτῳ τὴν ἑαυτοῦ πιστεύσῃς σωτηρίαν πρὶν ἢ τὴν τούτου διάθεσιν διαγνῷς, ἵνα μὴ ταὐτόν τι πάθῃς τῷ τῆς φθειρός."

38 *Περὶ φθειρὸς καὶ ψύλλου.*

"Λέγεται γὰρ ὡς φθείρ τις δεμνίοις τινὸς τῶν μεγιστάνων ἐπὶ μακρῷ ἐνεκρύπτετο χρόνῳ τρεφομένη τῷ αἵματι αὐτοῦ ὑπνώττοντος, καὶ ἠρέμα τουτῳ προσέρπουσα ἀφόρητος ἦν. Μιᾷ δὲ τῶν νυκτῶν κατέλυσέ τις παρ' αὐτῇ ψύλλος, ὅστις ἀνυποστόλως καὶ αὐθαδῶς πλήξας τὸν ἄνδρα ὑπνώττοντα ἐξύπνησε. Καὶ εὐθέως ὁ τοιοῦτος τὴν ἑαυτοῦ στρωμνὴν ψηλαφήσας, καὶ τὴν φθεῖρα εὑρὼν ἀπέκτεινε, τοῦ ψύλλου ταχέως ἐκπηδήσαντος καὶ σωθέντος.

"Εἰ οὖν σὺ τὸν ταῦρον οὐ φοβῇ, τοὺς ὑπὸ σὲ δειλιάσεις ἐπανισταμένους σοι."

39 Ὁ δὲ λέων τοῖς τούτου λόγοις πεισθεὶς ἔφη· "Καὶ τί δεῖ πρὸς ταῦτα ποιεῖν;" Ὁ δὲ Ἰχνηλάτης εἶπεν· "Ὁ σεσημμένος ὀδοὺς οὐκ ἄλλως ἰᾶται, εἰ μὴ ἐκβληθῇ, καὶ τῆς διαφθαρείσης τροφῆς ἡ βλάβη διὰ τοῦ ἐμέτου ἐκδιώκεται." Ὁ δὲ λέων ἔφη· "Δηλώσω λοιπὸν τούτῳ ἀπελθεῖν, ἔνθα βούλεται." Ὁ δὲ Ἰχνηλάτης, εἰδὼς ὡς, εἰ ὁμιλήσει τῷ λέοντι ὁ ταῦρος, ἀποκαλυφθήσεται μεταξὺ αὐτῶν ἡ τούτου σκαιωρία εἶπεν· "Οὐ συνορῶ τοῦτο εἶναι λυσιτελές· εἰ γὰρ διαγνώσεται ὁ ταῦρος, ὡς παρὰ σοῦ ἐφωράθη, ἀναιδείᾳ χρήσεται καὶ πρὸς ἀντιπαράταξιν παρασκευασθήσεται. Οἱ γὰρ συνετώτατοι βασιλεῖς φανερῶς μὲν τιμωροῦσι τὸν προδήλως ἁμαρτήσαντα, κρυφίως δὲ τὸν ἀδήλως." Ὁ δὲ

entrust your safety to him until you understand his disposition, so that you don't suffer the same fate as the louse."

About a louse and a flea. 38

"For it's said that a louse hid itself for a long time in the bedding of one of the nobles, sucking his blood while he slept, and because it crawled quietly onto him it was inescapable. But one night a flea moved in with it, and this bit the sleeping man brazenly and remorselessly and woke him up. The latter immediately examined his mattress and, finding the louse, killed it, while the flea leaped out quickly and was saved.

"So, even if you may not fear the bull," said Ichnelates, "you should be afraid of your subordinates rebelling against you."

The lion was persuaded by his words and said, "So what's 39
to be done about this?" And Ichnelates replied, "The only way to cure a rotten tooth is to pull it out, and the only way to avoid the harm caused by spoiled food is by vomiting." And the lion said, "All right, I'll tell him to go away, wherever he wants." But Ichnelates, realizing that, if the bull spoke with the lion, the mischief he had been making between them would be revealed, said, "I don't think this would be beneficial, for if the bull realizes that he's been discovered by you, he'll behave shamelessly and get ready for confrontation. The most intelligent kings publicly punish someone who has manifestly done wrong, but do so secretly to someone who has acted clandestinely." But the lion said, "When a

λέων ἔφη· "Ὅτε βασιλεὺς ἐξ ὑπολήψεως ἐπενέγκῃ τινὶ τιμωρίαν καὶ ἀτιμίαν, καὶ μὴ ἀληθὴς δειχθῇ ἡ ὑπόληψις, ἑαυτὸν μᾶλλον ἠτίμωσεν." Ὁ δὲ Ἰχνηλάτης εἶπεν· "Ὅτε εἰσέλθῃ πρὸς σὲ ὁ ταῦρος, ἕτοιμος ἔσο· ἐκ γὰρ πρώτης ὀφθαλμῶν ἐπιβολῆς διαγνώσεις τὸ βούλευμα αὐτοῦ. Ὄψει γὰρ ὠχρὸν τὸν τοιοῦτον καὶ ὑπότρομον τὰ μέλη καὶ ἐπ' ἀριστερὰ καὶ ἐπὶ δεξιὰ μετακλινόμενον καὶ κερατίσαι βουλόμενον τὸν παρατυχόντα." Ὁ δὲ λέων ἔφη· "Εἰ τοιαῦτα σημεῖα ἴδω, πληροφορήσομαι ἐπὶ τοῖς εἰρημένοις."

40 *Περὶ τῆς ἐπελεύσεως τοῦ Ἰχνηλάτου πρὸς τὸν ταῦρον.*

Ἠβουλήθη οὖν ὁ Ἰχνηλάτης πρὸς τὸν ταῦρον ἀπελθεῖν καὶ διεγεῖραι τοῦτον κατὰ τοῦ λέοντος· καὶ συνεῖδε μὴ ἄνευ γνώσεως τοῦ λέοντος προσομιλῆσαι αὐτῷ, μήπως ἀκούσας ὁ λέων τὸ τοιοῦτον, διαγνῷ τὸν δόλον, καὶ εἶπεν· "Εἰ προστάξεις μοι, ὦ βασιλεῦ, ἀπελεύσομαι πρὸς αὐτὸν καὶ ἴδω τὴν τούτου διάθεσιν καὶ οὐ λήσεταί μοι ἡ διάνοια αὐτοῦ ἐκ πρώτης ὁμιλίας." Ὁ δὲ λέων προσέταξεν αὐτῷ ἀπελθεῖν· ὁ δὲ Ἰχνηλάτης καταλαβὼν πρὸς τὸν ταῦρον, εἰσῆλθε σκυθρωπὸς καὶ κατηφής. Ὁ δὲ ταῦρος εὐμενῶς προσεδέξατο αὐτὸν καὶ περὶ τῆς βραδυτῆτος ἐπηρώτησε καὶ εἶπε· "Πάντως ἀγαθὸν τὸ ταύτης αἴτιον;" Ὁ δὲ Ἰχνηλάτης εἶπε· "Καὶ ποῖον πάρεστιν ἀγαθὸν τῷ μὴ ἑαυτοῦ κυριεύοντι, ἀλλ' ἑτέρῳ ἀνηρτημένῳ ἀπίστῳ καὶ ἀβεβαίῳ;" Ὁ δὲ ταῦρος ἔφη· "Καὶ τί γέγονεν καινόν;" Ὁ δὲ Ἰχνηλάτης εἶπε· "Καὶ τίς δυνήσεται τὴν εἱμαρμένην διεκφυγεῖν; Ἢ τίς τοῖς ἡγεμόσι παρεδρεύων καὶ ἐξυπηρετῶν αὐτοῖς

king inflicts punishment and disgrace upon someone on suspicion and the charge proves to be untrue, then he has instead disgraced himself." But Ichnelates said, "When the bull comes to you, be ready. You'll know his intention from the first glance. For you'll see that he's pale, his limbs are trembling, he's turning from side to side, and wants to gore with his horns whoever's there." And the lion said, "If I see such signs, I shall be convinced by what you've said."

About Ichnelates's approach to the bull. 40

So Ichnelates wanted to go to the bull and rouse him against the lion. He decided not to speak to him without the lion's knowledge so that the lion would not hear about this and discover his treachery, so he said, "If you order me, my king, I will go to the bull and see what his attitude is, and his intention will be clear to me as soon as we talk." The lion ordered him to go and, when Ichnelates reached the bull, he went up to him, looking very sad and downcast. The bull received him politely and asked about his sluggishness, "Can anything good be the reason for this?" And Ichnelates said, "What's good for someone who's not his own master, but who is led by someone else who's untrustworthy and unreliable?" And the bull asked, "What's happened now?" And Ichnelates said, "Who can escape his fate? Or who, when waiting upon his masters and serving them, may escape

ἀβλαβὴς ἀπαλλαγῇ; Ἐοίκασι γὰρ οὗτοι πόρναις γυναιξίν, αἵτινες πολλοῖς ἀνδράσι συζεύγνυνται, ἢ διδασκαλείῳ εἰς ὃ φοιτῶσιν οἱ παῖδες καὶ ὑποχωροῦσιν ἀεὶ ἑτέρων ἀνθ' ἑτέρων εἰσερχομένων. Οἶδας τὴν μεταξὺ ἡμῶν συστᾶσαν φιλίαν καὶ ὡς αἴτιός σοι γέγονα τῆς πρὸς τὸν λέοντα οἰκειώσεως, καὶ τοῦτό μοι πείθει εὐνοϊκώτατα προσομιλῆσαί σοι νῦν· εἶπε γάρ μοί τις τῶν πιστοτάτων αὐτοῦ καὶ ἀληθῶν, ὡς ὁ λέων εἶπε πρός τινας τοὺς ὑπ' αὐτόν, ὅτι βούλεταί σε φαγεῖν διὰ τὸ λιπανθῆναι καὶ ὀγκωθῆναί σε. Καὶ τοῦτο ἀκούσας ἦλθον δηλῶσαί σοι τὸν σκοπὸν αὐτοῦ, ἵνα περιποιήσῃς σεαυτῷ τὸ ἀσφαλές."

41 Ὡς οὖν ἤκουσεν ὁ ταῦρος τῶν τοιούτων λόγων, ἐφρόντισέ τε καὶ σύννους γέγονε κατὰ πολὺ καὶ ἔφη· "Καὶ τί κακὸν ἔδρασα τῷ λέοντι ἤ τινι τῶν περὶ αὐτόν, ἵνα τοιαῦτα περὶ ἐμοῦ διανοηθῇ; Ἀλλ' ὅμως, οἱ περὶ αὐτὸν πονηροὶ ὄντες, κατεψεύσαντό μου, τῷ φθόνῳ φερόμενοι. Ἡ γὰρ τῶν πονηρῶν ὁμιλία ἐναντίας ἀπογεννᾶν εἴωθεν ὑπολήψεις περὶ τοὺς ἀγαθούς." Ὁ δὲ Ἰχνηλάτης ὑπολαβὼν εἶπεν· "Οὐκ ἔστι τοῦτο αἴτιον ταύτης αὐτοῦ τῆς πρὸς σὲ διαθέσεως· ἀλλ' ἔστιν ἀεὶ ἄστατος καὶ ἀβέβαιος, ἄφιλός τε καὶ ἀγνώμων, καὶ πρῶτον μὲν γλυκύς, εἶτα δὲ πικρὸς ἀναφαινόμενος." Ὁ δὲ ταῦρος ἔφη· "Καλῶς εἶπας. Ἐγευσάμην γὰρ αὐτοῦ τῆς γλυκύτητος πρότερον καὶ κατήντησα μέχρι τοῦ πικροῦ τούτου δηλητηρίου. Καὶ τί δεῖ με διάγειν παρὰ λέοντι αἱμοβόρῳ, χλοηνόμον ὄντα; Ἀλλ' ὅμως ἡ πλεονεκτικὴ γνώμη τοιούτῳ με συμπτώματι περιέπλεξε, παρόμοιόν τι παθόντα ταῖς ἄφροσι μελίσσαις, αἵτινες ἀσπαστὸν ἡγούμεναι τὸ ἐπικαθῆσθαι τοῖς νυμφαίοις ἄνθε-

unscathed? For they are like female prostitutes who have intercourse with many men, or a school that children attend and leave, and where some are always coming in instead of others. You know the friendship that exists between us, and that I'm the reason you've come to have a close relationship with the lion, and it's this that is convincing me to talk with you nicely now. For one of his most trustworthy and faithful people told me that the lion said to some of his subordinates that he wants to eat you because you've grown fat and beefy. When I heard this, I came to make his plan known to you so that you may ensure your safety."

When the bull heard these words, he was concerned and 41
became very anxious. "What harm have I done to the lion," he said, "or to one of his subordinates, that he should think such things about me? But still, those around him are wicked and have told lies about me, as they're driven by jealousy. For it is the speech of wicked men that usually gives birth to hostile suspicions about good people." But Ichnelates replied, "That's not the cause of his attitude toward you. He's always fickle and unreliable, unfriendly and ungrateful, and he appears at first to be sweet, but then bitter." And the bull said, "You've spoken well. For I tasted his sweetness earlier, and then came across his most bitter poison. As I'm an herbivore, what can I do to live alongside the carnivorous lion? But still, it's having a greedy disposition that has got me into this situation, as I have suffered something like the silly bees who think they're welcome to settle on the flowers of

σιν οὐ πρότερον ἀφίστανται πρὶν ἢ συμμυόντων ἐπὶ τὰ ἄνθη τῶν φύλλων ἀποπνιγῶσιν. Ὁ γὰρ μὴ τοῖς ὀλίγοις ἀρκούμενος ἐν τῷ βίῳ ἀλλ' ἐκτείνων τὸν ὀφθαλμὸν ἐπὶ τὰ πόρρω καὶ τὰ πολλὰ καὶ μὴ διαλογιζόμενος ἐπὶ τὰ ἔμπροσθέν τε καὶ ὄπισθεν πείσεται καὶ τὰ τῶν μυιῶν, αἵτινες οὐκ ἀρκοῦνται τοῖς δένδροις καὶ τοῖς ἄνθεσιν, ἀλλ' ἐνίοτε περιπέτονται καὶ προσκάθηνται καὶ τῷ ῥύπῳ τῶν ὤτων τοῦ ἐλέφαντος, καὶ διὰ τοῦτο πολλάκις καὶ θνήσκουσι πληγεῖσαι." Ὁ δὲ Ἰχνηλάτης εἶπε· "Ἄφες τὰ πολλὰ καὶ τὰ καίρια σκόπει βουλὴν ἐφευρών, ἥ σε σώσει τοῦ μόρου." Ὁ δὲ ταῦρος ἔφη· "Ὁ μὲν τοῦ λέοντος σκοπὸς ἀκέραιός ἐστι καὶ ἀγαθός, ἀλλ' οἱ περὶ αὐτὸν πονηροὶ ὄντες οὐκ ἐῶσι αὐτὸν ἀγαθύνεσθαι, καὶ τὸ τοιοῦτον σύστημα πολλάκις, κἂν ἀδύνατον ᾖ, ἀλλ' ἀναιρεῖ τὸν ἀθῷον καὶ ὅσιον ὡς ὁ λύκος καὶ ὁ κόραξ καὶ ὁ θὼς ἔδρασαν κατὰ τῆς καμήλου πρὸς τὸν λέοντα."

42 *Περὶ τῆς ἀναιρέσεως τῆς καμήλου παρὰ τῶν τριῶν ζῴων.*

"Λέγεται γὰρ ὡς λέων τις παρά τινι διῃτᾶτο ὕλῃ, ἧς πλησίον ὁδός τις ἦν· ἦσαν δὲ ἐκεῖσε τρία ζῷα ἀλλήλοις συμφιλιούμενα· λύκος, κόραξ, καὶ θώς. Ἐμπόρων δέ ποτέ τινων διερχομένων ἀπελείφθη ἡ ἐξ αὐτῶν κάμηλος, ἥτις πρὸς τὸν λέοντα ἐλθοῦσα ἀνήγγειλε τὰ κατ' αὐτήν. Ὁ δὲ λέων εἶπεν αὐτῇ· 'Εἰ βούλει τὴν ἐμὴν συναυλίαν ἐφεῖταί σοι τοῦτο καὶ διάξεις ἐν ἀμεριμνίᾳ καὶ βίου εὐθηνίᾳ καὶ ἀνέσει πολλῇ πάντα τὸν τῆς ζωῆς σου χρόνον.' Καὶ διέμεινεν ἐκεῖσε ἡ κάμηλος, ἄχρις ὅτου μιᾷ τῶν ἡμερῶν ἐξελθὼν

the water lily but do not get away before they are suffocated on the flowers when the petals close together. For someone who is not satisfied with the small things in life, but casts his gaze at things that are far away and great, and does not stop to consider what is in front of him and behind him, will also experience what those flies do who, not satisfied with the trees and the flowers, sometimes also fly around and settle on the dirt on the elephant's ears, and so often die when they're struck." And Ichnelates said, "Forget everything else and focus on what's important, which is finding a plan that will save you from death." And the bull said, "The lion's intentions are innocent and good, but those around him are wicked and do not allow him to do good; and that group, even though it is powerless itself, often kills the innocent and pure creature, just as the wolf, the crow and the jackal made happen with regard to the lion against the camel."

About the killing of the camel by the three animals. 42

"For it is said that a lion once lived in a forest which was near a road, and there were also three animals there who were friends with each other: a wolf, a crow, and a jackal. On one occasion, when some merchants were passing through, one of their camels was left behind, and she went to the lion and told her story. The lion said to her, 'If you want my companionship, this place is available to you, and you may live in peace, in good circumstances, and with plenty of rest your whole life long.' And the camel stayed there until one day,

ὁ λέων ἐπὶ θήραν συνήντησεν ἐλέφαντι καὶ συνεπλάκη τούτῳ καὶ τραυματίας βίᾳ ὑπέστρεψε καθῃμαγμένος τὰς σάρκας. Καὶ ἀνεκλίθη τότε τῇ νόσῳ δεδαμασμένος, μήτε θηρεῦσαι δυνάμενος μήθ' ἑτέρωθι μεταβῆναι. Ἀπέλιπον οὖν αἱ τροφαὶ καὶ τοῖς περὶ αὐτόν, καὶ ἔγνω ὁ λέων τὸ τοιοῦτον καὶ εἶπεν αὐτοῖς· 'Ὡς οἶμαι, ἀπειρήκατε τῷ λιμῷ πιεζόμενοι.' Οἱ δὲ εἶπον· 'Ἡμεῖς μὲν ἑαυτῶν φροντίσαι δυνάμεθα, περὶ σοῦ δὲ μόνον ἀλύομεν, καὶ εἴ γε ἠδυνήθημεν ἐφευρεῖν πόρον, δι' οὗ σὺ μὲν αὐτὸς ὠφεληθήσῃ, ἡμεῖς δὲ πάντες βλαβησόμεθα, προθύμως ἂν τὸ τοιοῦτον ἐπράξαμεν.'

43 "Ὁ δὲ λέων εἶπεν· 'Οὐκ ἐνδοιάζω περὶ τῆς ὑμετέρας εὐνοίας, ἀλλὰ διασκέδασθητε πανταχοῦ, ὅπως εὑρήσετε τὰ αὐτάρκη ὑμῖν καὶ μοί.' Οἱ δὲ ἔγγιόν τι ἀναχωρήσαντες συνελογίσαντο πρὸς ἀλλήλους λέγοντες· 'Τί ἡμῖν καὶ τῇ καμήλῳ ταύτῃ τῇ χλοηνόμῳ καὶ ἑτεροφυεῖ οὔσῃ πρὸς ἡμᾶς καὶ ἑτεροβίῳ; Ἀλλ' εἰ δοκεῖ, διερεθίσωμεν τὸν λέοντα ταύτην καταφαγεῖν.' Καὶ ὁ μὲν θὼς εἶπε· 'Τοῦτο ἀδύνατόν ἡμῖν ἐστιν ἀριδηλώτατα διασαφῆσαι τῷ λέοντι, ἤδη αὐτῷ συνθήκας πρὸς αὐτὴν ποιησαμένῳ.' Ὁ δὲ κόραξ εἶπε· 'Μείνατε ὑμεῖς ἐνταῦθα, καὶ ἐάσατε κἀμὲ κἀκεῖνον.' Εἶτα ὁ κόραξ ἀπηλλάγη πρὸς τὸν λέοντα. Ὡς οὖν εἶδεν αὐτὸν ὁ λέων, εἶπεν· 'Ἆραγε ἐπῄσθου τινὸς ἢ διέγνως;' Ὁ δὲ εἶπεν· 'Καὶ πῶς διαγνώσεται τὰ περὶ αὐτὸν ὁ μὴ ὄψεως εὐπορῶν; Ἡμεῖς γὰρ ἀφῃρέθημεν ταύτην, δι' ἣν ὑπέστημεν ἔνδειαν, ἀλλὰ δυνάμεθα ἀνακληθῆναι, εἰ ἐπακούσεις ἡμῖν καὶ πατάξεις τὴν κάμηλον τὴν μέσῳ ἡμῶν ἀναστρεφομένην.' Ὁ δὲ λέων ὀργισθεὶς εἶπε· 'Βαβαὶ τῆς ἀπηνείας

while the lion was out hunting, he encountered an elephant, engaged in a fight with it, and returned seriously wounded with his body all bloody. He lay down then, overwhelmed by his infirmity, unable either to hunt or to move from that place. So, the food also ran out for those around him and the lion, realizing this, said to them, ‘I think you’re done for because you’re starving.’ But they replied, ‘We can take care of ourselves, we’re just worried about you, and if we can find a way for you yourself to get help, even if we all get hurt, we’ll willingly do that.’

“The lion said, ‘I don’t doubt your goodwill, so go off in 43
all directions and you may be able to find enough food for both you and me.’ They went off a little way away and spoke among themselves, saying, ‘What do we care about that herbivorous camel, which is a different kind of animal from us and leads a different life? If you agree, let’s provoke the lion into eating it.’ And the jackal said, ‘We can’t make this at all obvious to the lion, as he has already made an agreement with her.’ And the crow said, ‘You stay here and leave me alone with him.’ Then the crow went off to the lion. When the lion saw him, he said, ‘What’s going on? Did you hear of something, or decide anything?’ The crow said, ‘How can someone who does not have good eyesight make out his surroundings? We’ve lost what we needed for our survival, but we can recover, if you listen to us and kill the camel that has come to live among us.’ But the lion was angry and said,

καὶ τῆς τραχύτητός σου. Οὐκ οἶσθα, ὡς συνθήκας καὶ φιλικὰς συμφωνίας πρὸς αὐτὴν πεποίηκα; Καὶ διὰ τοῦτο οὐκ ἔδει σε τοιούτοις προσομιλεῖν ἡμᾶς ῥήμασιν. Ἀδύνατόν μοι γὰρ τὸ τοιοῦτον καθέστηκεν.'

44 "Ὁ δὲ κόραξ πάλιν εἶπε· 'Καλῶς εἴρηκας, ὦ βασιλεῦ, ἀλλὰ ἡ μία ψυχὴ πολλάκις ὑπὲρ ὅλου οἴκου προδίδοται, καὶ ὁ οἶκος ὅλος ὑπὲρ πόλεως, καὶ ἡ πόλις ὑπὲρ κλίματος, καὶ τὸ κλίμα ὑπὲρ βασιλείας. Καὶ ἡμεῖς σὺν σοὶ κατατρυχόμεθα νῦν τῷ λιμῷ καὶ τῇ τῶν ἀναγκαίων ἐνδείᾳ, ἀλλ' εὑρήσομέν σοι πόρον, δι' οὗ διατηρηθήσῃ πάσης ὑπέρτερος μέμψεως.' Καὶ ταῦτα εἰπὼν ἐπανέζευξε πρὸς τοὺς ἑταίρους αὐτοῦ καὶ ἀνήγγειλεν αὐτοῖς ὅσα τε εἶπε τῷ λέοντι καὶ ὅσα παρ' αὐτοῦ ἤκουσεν. Οἱ δὲ τοιοῦτον δόλον συνέρραψαν ὥστε ὁμοῦ πάντες σὺν τῇ καμήλῳ προσελθεῖν τῷ λέοντι καὶ ἕκαστον δωρήσασθαι ἑαυτὸν πρὸς διατροφὴν αὐτοῦ, καὶ ἀπόλογον τοὺς λοιποὺς ὑπὲρ ἑκάστου ποιήσασθαι, πλὴν τῆς καμήλου. Καὶ τοῦτο σκαιωρήσαντες, προσῆλθον τῷ λέοντι. Καὶ πρῶτος ὁ κόραξ εἶπεν· 'Ὁρῶ σε, ὦ βασιλεῦ, πάνυ τῇ νόσῳ βεβαρημένον καὶ τῇ ἀτροφίᾳ καὶ ἀσιτίᾳ κατεστιγμένον καὶ πολλαί σου αἱ εἰς ἐμὲ πρότερον εὐπραγίαι, ἀλλ' οὐκ ἔχω τι, ὅ γε προσοίσω σοι, εἰ μὴ μόνον ἑαυτόν· λοιπὸν ἀνυποστόλως με κατέσθιε.' Οἱ δὲ εἶπον· 'Παῦσαι τοῦ λήρου, βραχὺς γὰρ εἶ τὸ σῶμα καὶ μηδαμινός.' Ὁ δὲ θὼς εἶπεν· 'Ἀλλ' ἐγώ σοι, ὦ βασιλεῦ, ἱκανὴ τροφὴ ἔσομαι σήμερον.' Ὁ δὲ λύκος ἔφη· 'Παῦσαι καὶ σύ, δυσῶδες γάρ σου τὸ σῶμα καὶ πρὸς τροφὴν ἀνεπιτήδειον· μᾶλλον ἐγὼ πρὸς τοῦτο εὐθετώτερος καὶ ἑτοιμότερος καὶ εὐθυμότερος.' Ὁ δὲ κόραξ καὶ ὁ

'Dear me, how cruel and harsh you are! Don't you know that I've made an agreement and pact of friendship with her? And because of this you should not have said such words to me. It's impossible for me to do such a thing.'

"The crow again said, 'You have spoken well, my king, but 44
one life is often given up for the sake of an entire household, and an entire household for the sake of a city, and a city for the sake of a region, and a region for the sake of a kingdom. We, as well as you, are now being exhausted by hunger and the lack of the bare necessities, but we'll find you a way which will keep you beyond all reproach.' When he had said this, he rejoined his friends and reported to them what he had said to the lion, and what he had heard from him. And they concocted a trick, so that they would all go to the lion, along with the camel, and each one would present himself to the lion as his food, and they would each speak in defense of the others, except of the camel. When they had put this plan together, they went to the lion. The crow spoke first: 'I see you, my king, burdened by illness and showing signs of starvation and malnourishment. You did many good things for me before, and I don't have anything to offer you except just myself. So, please, eat me without any hesitation.' But the others said, 'Stop talking nonsense, your body is small and good for nothing.' And the jackal said, 'But I, my king, will be enough food for you today.' And the wolf said, 'You be quiet, too. Your body smells bad and isn't fit to eat! I'm more willing, ready and happy for this instead.' But the crow

θῶς ἀπεκρίναντο· ‘Εἴ τις βούλεται κυνάγχῃ περιπεσεῖν ὅλως, ἀπογευσάσθω σου τῶν σαρκῶν.’ Ὑπέλαβεν οὖν ἡ κάμηλος, ὡς καὶ ὑπὲρ αὐτῆς τὸν ἀπόλογον ποιήσονται, καὶ εἶπεν· ‘Ἀλλ’ ἐγὼ καὶ σαρκῶν ἱκανῶς εὐπορῶ καὶ ἡδυτάτη τροφὴ τῷ βουλομένῳ ἔσομαι.’ Οἱ δὲ ὁμοῦ μέγα ἐβόησαν· ‘Ἀληθέστατα εἶπας, κάμηλε,’ καὶ εὐθὺς διεσπάραξαν αὐτήν.

45 “Δέδοικα οὖν κἀγώ, μὴ ταὐτὸν πάθω τῇ καμήλῳ παρὰ τῶν ὑπηκόων τοῦ λέοντος καὶ μὴ βουλομένου ἴσως αὐτοῦ τὴν ἐμὴν ἀπώλειαν· *ῥανὶς γὰρ ἐνδελεχοῦσα στερρὰν κοιλαίνει πέτραν,* ἀλλ’ ἑτοιμασθήσομαι λοιπὸν πρὸς ἀντιπαράταξιν τοῦ λέοντος. Οὐ γὰρ τοσοῦτος μισθὸς ἀποταμιεύεται τῷ πολλὰ εὐχομένῳ ἢ τῷ ἱλαρῷ δότῃ ἢ τῷ ἀσκητῇ, ὅσος τῷ ἑαυτὸν θανάτου ῥυσαμένῳ κἂν πρὸς μίαν καιροῦ ῥοπήν.” Ὁ δὲ Ἰχνηλάτης εἶπεν· “Οὐ δεῖ τινα κινδυνώδει πράγματι δι’ ἑαυτοῦ προσπλακῆναι· καὶ γὰρ ὁ ἐχέφρων ἀνὴρ μετὰ πᾶσαν ἄλλην μέθοδον τῷ πολέμῳ ὕστερον ἐπιχειρεῖ. Οὐ δεῖ δὲ καταφρονεῖν τοῦ ἐχθροῦ, καὶ εἰ ἀδύνατός ἐστι, καὶ μάλιστα εἰ συνέσει κατωχύρωται. Ἐπάκουσον οὖν μου εὐνοϊκῶς σοι προσομιλοῦντος· ὁ γὰρ μὴ τοὺς ὀνησιφόρους λόγους παρὰ τῶν φίλων δεχόμενος ταὐτόν τι πείσεται τῷ τοῦ ἀλκυόνος, ὅπερ ἔπαθε παρὰ τῆς νηρηΐδος, ἥτις ἔκλεψε τοὺς νεοσσοὺς αὐτοῦ, καὶ πάλιν φοβηθεῖσα ὑπέστρεψεν αὐτοὺς πρὸς αὐτόν, διὰ τὴν ἀντιπαράταξιν.”

and the jackal replied, 'If anyone wants to give himself a sore throat, he should taste your flesh.' Then the camel assumed that they would also make a speech in her defense, and said, 'But I have both an ample sufficiency of flesh and will be very sweet food for anyone who wishes.' They at once shouted loudly, 'What you say really is true, camel,' and they immediately tore her to pieces.

"So I too," continued the bull, "am afraid of suffering the 45
same fate as the camel at the hands of the lion's subjects, even though he himself probably does not want my destruction, *for a constantly falling drop hollows out solid rock.* But I will be prepared from now on to stand up to the lion. For a reward is not reserved so much for someone who prays a lot, nor for someone who gives cheerfully, nor for the ascetic, as for someone who has delivered himself from death at a critical moment." And Ichnelates said, "One shouldn't involve oneself in dangerous affairs, for the smart man eventually turns to war only after every other means. And one shouldn't look down on one's enemy, even if he's weak, and especially so, if he's made stronger by his intelligence. So, pay attention to me, as I'm giving you good advice; for someone who does not accept helpful words from friends will suffer what the kingfisher suffered from the sea nymph which stole his chicks but returned them to him when she was frightened by his retaliation."

46 *Περὶ ἁλκυόνος.*

“Λέγεται γὰρ ὡς ἔν τινι αἰγιαλῷ κατῴκει ὄρνεον καλούμενον ἁλκυὼν σὺν τῇ συνεύνῳ αὐτοῦ. Ἡ δὲ σύνευνος ἐγγίσασα τοῦ τεκεῖν εἶπε τῷ ἀνδρὶ αὐτῆς· ‘Εἰ εὑρήσεις ἡμῖν τόπον ὀχυρὸν τοῦ φωλεῦσαι καὶ γεννῆσαι ἐν αὐτῷ, κρεῖττον ἡμῖν ἐστι· καὶ γὰρ φοβοῦμαι μήποτε αὐξησάσης τῆς θαλάσσης ἔλθῃ ἡ νηρηίς, καὶ λάβῃ ἡμῶν τὰ νοσσία.’ Ὁ δὲ εἶπεν αὐτῇ· ‘Τέξαι ἐνθάδε· καὶ γὰρ οὗτος ὁ τόπος ἐστὶ χλοηφόρος καὶ ὑδατώδης καὶ πάνυ ἡμῖν ἐπιτήδειος.’ Λέγει δὲ αὐτῷ ἡ ὁμόζυγος· ‘Λοιπόν, εὐνοϊκῶς πρόσεχε· καὶ γὰρ οὐκ ἄφοβος ἔσομαι ἐν τούτῳ τῷ τόπῳ ἀπο τῆς βλάβης τῆς νηρηίδος αὐτῆς.’ Ὁ δὲ εἶπεν αὐτῇ· ‘Ὡς οἶμαι, οὐ μὴ τολμήσῃ ποιῆσαι τοῦτο διὰ τὴν ἀντιπάθειαν.’ Ἡ δὲ εἶπε πρὸς αὐτόν· ‘Οὐκ αἰσχύνει τοιαῦτα λέγων καὶ φοβερίζων τὴν νηρηίδα; Ἢ οὐκ οἶσθα τὴν σὴν δύναμιν; Ἀλλ’ οὖν ἄκουσόν μου καὶ μετάστησον ἡμᾶς ἐκ τοῦ τόπου τούτου. Οἱ γὰρ μὴ ὑπακούοντες τοῖς εὐνοϊκῶς συμβουλεύουσι, πείσονται τὸ τῆς χελώνης.’”

47 *Περὶ νησσῶν καὶ χελώνης.*

“‘Λέγεται γὰρ ὡς ἔν τινι πηγῇ διῃτῶντο δύο νῆσσαι καὶ μία χελώνη ἀλλήλαις αὗται συμφιλιούμεναι. Μιᾷ δὲ τῶν ἡμερῶν ἀπέλειψε τὸ τῆς πηγῆς ὕδωρ καὶ διὰ τοῦτο δεῖν ᾠήθησαν αἱ νῆτται ἐκεῖναι ἐκεῖθεν μεταστῆναι ἐπὶ ὕδωρ ἕτερον. Ὡς οὖν ἔμελλον ἀπᾶραι, εἶπεν αὐταῖς ἡ χελώνη· “Ὑμῖν μὲν οὐδὲν μελήσει περὶ τῆς τοῦ ὕδατος λείψεως,

About a kingfisher. 46

“For it is said that a bird called a kingfisher lived on a seashore with his mate. Since his mate was on the point of laying her eggs, she said to her husband, ‘If you find us a secure place to nest in and to produce our young, that will be better for us, for I’m afraid that, when the sea rises again, the sea nymph will come and take our chicks.’ And he said, ‘Lay your eggs here, as this place has vegetation and water and suits us very well.’ His mate said to him, ‘All right, I asked you nicely. For I’m going to be afraid of harm from the sea nymph in this place.’ But he said to her, ‘I don’t think she’ll try to do this, because of the retribution she’ll face.’ But she said to him, ‘Aren’t you ashamed to say such things, and to threaten the sea nymph? Don’t you understand your own strength? So listen to me, and take us away from this place. Those who don’t pay attention to those who kindly offer good advice will suffer the fate of the turtle.’”

About ducks and a turtle. 47

“‘For it is said that two ducks and a turtle who were friends with each other lived in a spring. One day the water in the spring started to fail, and as a result of this the ducks thought they should move from there to a different stretch of water. As they were about to leave, the turtle said to them, “You don’t have to worry at all about the water failing, but as for

ἀλλ᾽ ἐμοί, τῇ ἀθλίᾳ, μὴ ἐχούσῃ πόρον ζωῆς ἕτερον. Ἀλλ᾽ ἄρατέ με ἀπὸ τῶν ὧδε καὶ μεταναστεύσατε σὺν ὑμῖν." Αἱ δὲ εἶπον· "Εἰ μὴ πρότερον ἐπομόσεις ἡμῖν, ὡς οὐδένα λόγον εἴπῃς παρ᾽ ἡμῶν φερομένη, οὐκ ἄν σε μετακινήσωμεν ἢ μετοικίσωμεν." Ἡ δὲ ἐπωμόσατο. Καὶ λαβοῦσαι αἱ νῆτται ξύλον ἀπευθυσμένον ἐπέτρεψαν ταύτῃ δακεῖν τὸ μέσον αὐτοῦ, καὶ συλλαβοῦσαι ἑκάστη τὸ τοῦ ξύλου ἐκείνου ἄκρον ἦραν εἰς ἀέρα δι᾽ αὐτοῦ τὴν χελώνην ἐκεῖθεν. Ἔτυχον δέ τινες τηνικαῦτα διερχόμενοι κάτωθεν, καὶ ἰδόντες τὴν χελώνην ἀνηρτημένην ἐθαύμαζον λέγοντες· "Ἴδετε τέρας μέγιστον, χελώνην μεταξὺ δύο νηττῶν ἐν ἀέρι φερομένην." Ἡ δὲ τοῦτο ἀκούσασα ἔφη· "Εἰς τὰ ἄνωθεν ἵπταμαι ἄνευ ὑμῶν." Καὶ ἐν τῷ μέλλειν εἰπεῖν τοῦτο ἀνοίξασα τὸ στόμα αὐτῆς, καὶ εἰς γῆν πεσοῦσα συνετρίβη. Τοιαῦτα πείσεται καὶ ὁ μὴ ἀκούων τοῦ εὐνοϊκῶς αὐτῷ ὁμιλοῦντος.'

48 "Ὁ δὲ ἁλκυὼν εἶπεν· 'Ἔγνων ἅ μοι λέγεις, ἀλλ᾽ οὖν σὺ τέξαι καὶ μὴ φοβοῦ τὴν νηρηίδα.' Γεννήσασα δὲ αὕτη ἐκεῖσε, ἦλθεν ἡ νηρηίς, καὶ λαβοῦσα τὰ νοσσία αὐτῆς σὺν τῇ φωλεᾷ, ἀφανὴς γέγονε. Ἡ δὲ στραφεῖσα εἶπε τῷ συνεύνῳ αὐτῆς· 'Ἐγὼ μὲν προέγνωκα ταῦτα, σὺ δὲ ἠγνόησας, καὶ διὰ τοῦτο ἐπῆλθεν ἡμῖν ἡ λύπη αὕτη.' Ὁ δὲ ἁλκυὼν ἔφη αὐτῇ· 'Ἀληθῶς εἶπας, ἀλλ᾽ εἰπόν σοι ὅτι ἐὰν πάθωμέν τι ἐναντίον παρ᾽ αὐτῆς δείξω σοι τὴν ἀντιπάθειαν, καὶ ἄρτι ὄψει αὐτήν.' Ἀπελθὼν οὖν εὐθὺς πρὸς τοὺς συγγενεῖς καὶ φίλους αὐτοῦ, ἐγνώρισεν αὐτοῖς πάνθ᾽ ὅσα πέπονθε παρὰ τῆς νηρηίδος, καὶ εἶπεν αὐτοῖς· 'Δέομαι ὑμῶν τοῦ

poor me, I have no other means of living. So pick me up and take me away from here with you." And they said, "Unless you swear to us first that you won't say a single word while we're carrying you, we won't move you or take you to live somewhere else." The turtle promised. And so, the ducks took hold of a straight stick and instructed the turtle to bite onto the middle of it, and each duck took hold of one end of the stick, and in this way they raised the turtle into the air from there. Some people happened to be passing down below and were amazed when they saw the turtle hanging there. They said, "Look at that great wonder, a turtle is being carried through the air between two ducks." And when the turtle heard this, she said, "I'm flying up high away from you." And as she was about to say this, she opened her mouth, fell to the ground, and was smashed. That's what happens to someone who doesn't listen to a person who gives them good advice.'

"The male kingfisher said, 'I understand what you're say- 48
ing to me, but you must just lay your eggs and not fear the sea nymph.' So she produced her young there, but the sea nymph came, took her chicks along with the nest, and vanished. She turned to her mate and said, 'I foresaw that this was going to happen, but you didn't understand, and that's why this grief has come upon us.' The kingfisher said to her, 'What you say is true, but I said to you that if we suffered any hostility from her, I'd show you my retribution, and now you're going to see it.' So he went off immediately to his relatives and friends and informed them about everything he had suffered from the sea nymph; and he said to them, 'I'm

συνεργῆσαι καὶ ἀντιλαβέσθαι μοι κατ' αὐτῆς, ἅτε ὁμογενεῖς καὶ ὁμοιοπαθεῖς τυγχάνοντες, μήποτε καὶ ὑμεῖς πάθητε ὡς κἀγώ.' Οἱ δὲ εἶπον αὐτῷ· ''Ημεῖς μὲν συνεργοί σοι καὶ ἐπίκουροι πρὸς τοῦτό ἐσμεν, τί δ' ἄρα σοι ὠφελήσωμεν οὐκ οἴδαμεν, οὐδὲ γὰρ φοβεῖται τὴν παρ' ἡμῶν βλάβην.' Ὁ δὲ ἁλκυὼν εἶπεν αὐτοῖς· 'Ἀπέλθωμεν τοίνυν καὶ δεηθῶμεν τοῖς πετεινοῖς πᾶσιν ὅπως συνεργήσωσιν ἡμῖν.'

49 "Ἀπελθόντες οὖν ἐκεῖνοι εἶπον πᾶσι τοῖς πετεινοῖς ταῦτα, τὰ δὲ πετεινὰ ἔφησαν· 'Βουλόμεθα μετὰ πάσης ἡμῶν προθυμίας συνελθεῖν ὑμῖν πρὸς βοήθειαν, ἀλλ' οὐδέν σοι ὠνήσομεν.' Ὁ δὲ ἁλκυὼν ἔφη αὐτοῖς· 'Δέομαι ὑμῶν τοίνυν ἀπελθεῖν πρὸς τὸν βασιλέα ἡμῶν φοίνικα, καὶ μετὰ κραυγῆς δεηθῶμεν αὐτῷ πάντες, καὶ οὕτως ἐκδίκησιν ποιήσηται πρὸς ἡμᾶς.' Ἀπελθόντες οὖν πάντες πρὸς τὸν βασιλέα αὐτῶν καὶ βοήσαντες ἐφάνη αὐτοῖς καὶ ἀνήγγειλαν αὐτῷ πάντα καὶ ᾐτήσαντο αὐτῷ ἵνα ποιήσηται αὐτοῖς τὴν ἐκδίκησιν. Ὁ δὲ βασιλεὺς ἐκεῖνος ὑπέσχετο ἐκδικῆσαι αὐτοῖς· ἀκούσασα δὲ ταῦτα ἡ νηρηὶς καὶ φοβηθεῖσα τὴν ἀντιπαράταξιν τοῦ βασιλέως, ὑπέστρεψε τοὺς νεοττοὺς τῆς ἁλκυόνος.

"Καὶ ταῦτά σοι διεξῄειν ἵνα γνῷς ὅτι οὐ συμφέρει σοι ἡ ἀντιπαράταξις τοῦ λέοντος, οὐδὲ συναινῶ σοι εἰς τοῦτο."

50 Ὁ δὲ ταῦρος ἔφη· "Οὐχ οὕτως ἀναιδῶς ἐπιχειρήσω τῇ ἀπωλείᾳ τοῦ λέοντος." Ὁ δὲ Ἰχνηλάτης εἶπεν· "Εἰ ἴδῃς ἐν τῷ λέοντι τοιαῦτα σημεῖα ὀργῆς, οἷον ὀφθαλμοὺς ἀγρίους καὶ αἱματώδεις, καὶ ὁρμὴν ἀκατάσχετον καὶ κίνησιν τῆς κέρκου συνεχῆ καὶ ταχεῖαν, τὰ λεγόμενα πληροφορήθητι."

begging you to work with me and help me against her, as you belong to the same family as I do and sympathize with me, so that you too don't suffer the same as me.' They said to him, 'We are indeed your coworkers and your allies in this, but we don't know how to help you, as she's not afraid of being hurt by us.' The kingfisher said to them, 'Well then, let's go and ask all the birds if they'll help us.'

"So they went and told all the birds about it, and the birds 49
said, 'With all our hearts we want to join up with you to help, but we won't do you any good.' The kingfisher said to them, 'Then I beg you to go to our king, the phoenix, and with our cries let us all implore him to avenge us.' So they all went to their king, and when they called him, he showed himself to them; they told him everything and asked him to avenge them. The king promised to avenge them, and when the sea nymph heard this, she was afraid of the king's retaliation, and returned the kingfisher's young.

"And I've told you this," said Ichnelates, "so you may understand that it isn't beneficial for you to retaliate against the lion, and that I don't agree with you on this."

And the bull said, "I won't recklessly attempt to destroy 50
the lion like that." And Ichnelates said, "If you see signs of rage in the lion, such as wild and bloodshot eyes, uncontrolled motion, and a continuous and rapid movement of the tail, you should be convinced by what's been said." Then

Εἶτα εἰσῆλθεν ὁ ταῦρος πρὸς τὸν λέοντα καὶ ἰδὼν τοῦτον ἠλλοιωμένον καὶ ἃ προεῖπεν αὐτῷ ὁ Ἰχνηλάτης σημεῖα ἐμφαίνοντα, θυμοῦ πλησθεὶς εἶπεν· "Κρεῖττόν ἐστιν φωλεῷ ὄφεως παροικεῖν ἢ βασιλεῖ," καὶ διανέστη πρὸς τὴν τοῦ λέοντος ἀντιπαράταξιν. Ἰδὼν δὲ ὁ βασιλεὺς λέων τὸ τοιοῦτον, συνεπλάκη αὐτῷ καὶ αὐτὸς τῷ λέοντι.

51 Παρὼν δὲ καὶ ὁ Στεφανίτης τηνικαῦτα, ἔφη τῷ Ἰχνηλάτῃ· "Ἴδε τὸν δόλον ὃν συνέρραψας, καὶ τὰ τῆς ἀποβάσεως σκόπησον. Τὸν γὰρ λέοντα κατῄσχυνας καὶ τὸν ταῦρον ἀπώλεσας καὶ τὴν ὁμόνοιαν τῶν συστρατιωτῶν διεσκέδασας. Ἢ οὐκ οἶσθα, ὡς ὁ συνετώτατος τοῦ βασιλέως πρωτοσύμβουλος οὐκ ἐᾷ τοῦτον πολέμου προκατάρξασθαι, ἔνθα δι' εἰρήνης τὸ πάθος ἰαθῆναι δύναται, καὶ εἰ δυνατώτεροι οἱ ἐχθροὶ εἶεν, διὰ μεθοδείας ἡττῆσαι τούτους; Ἡ γὰρ φρόνησις τὰς τῶν πολλῶν χεῖρας νικᾷ. Ἔγωγε οὖν ὁρῶν σου ἀεὶ τὴν οἴησιν καὶ τὴν πλεονεκτικὴν γνώμην, ἔγνων ὡς καὶ τὸ τοιοῦτον ἔργον κατατολμήσεις. Οὐδὲν γὰρ ἕτερον ἀπόλλυσι τοὺς ἐξουσιαστὰς ὡς τὸ ἀκούειν καὶ δέχεσθαι λόγους παρὰ τῶν τοιούτων, οἷος καὶ σύ. Κοσμεῖ γὰρ λόγον μὲν σύνεσις, ῥητορείαν δὲ δικαιοσύνη, μετάδοσιν δὲ ἱλαρότης, εἶδος δὲ ψυχῆς ὡραιότης, πλοῦτον δὲ ἡ πρὸς τοὺς δεομένους μετάδοσις, καὶ ὑπόσχεσιν ἡ ἀφοσίωσις, καὶ ζωὴν ἡ ὑγεία καὶ ἡ εὐφροσύνη. Ἴσθι δὲ πρὸς τούτοις, ὡς διὰ τῆς γνώσεως νήφει μὲν ὁ συνετός, μεθύσκεται δὲ ὁ ἀσύνετος, καθάπερ πάσχει τὰ τῶν νυκτερίδων ὄμματα πρὸς τὸ φέγγος τὸ καθ' ἡμέραν.

the bull went to the lion, and when he saw that he was changed and was showing the signs which Ichnelates had foretold to him, he was filled with anger and said, "It is better to live next to the den of a snake than to a king," and he braced himself for the lion's retaliation. When the lion king saw this, he himself engaged with the bull and the bull with him.

Stephanites, who was also there then, said to Ichnelates, 51
"Look at the treachery you've contrived, and consider the outcome. For you've shamed the lion, killed the bull, and broken up the unity of our fellow soldiers. Don't you know that the king's most intelligent first minister doesn't allow him to begin a war when the injury can be healed through peaceful means, and that, if his enemies are more powerful, he should overcome them through craft? For good sense defeats weight of numbers. As for myself, since I always see your self-conceit and greedy attitude, I knew that you'd recklessly try something like this. For nothing destroys those in power like listening to and accepting words from people like you. For intelligence adorns speech, justice adorns rhetoric, cheerfulness adorns giving, spiritual beauty adorns appearance, sharing with the needy adorns wealth, commitment adorns a promise, and health and happiness adorn life. And you should know that, in addition to these things, the intelligent man is sober because of his understanding, but the stupid man gets drunk, and he suffers just as the eyes of bats do in the light of midday.

52 “Καὶ ὁ βασιλεὺς ὁ περὶ αὐτὸν τοιούτων εὐπορῶν ὑπηκόων ἔοικεν ὕδατι πάνυ καθαρωτάτῳ καὶ διειδεῖ κροκοδείλων δὲ πλήρει, ᾧ τις ἂν πλησιάσειεν, κἂν δίψει καταφλέγοιτο, οὐ δυνήσαιτο πιεῖν. Σὺ οὖν οὐδένα ἠθέλησας πλὴν σοῦ οἰκειωθῆναι τῷ λέοντι, ἀλλ’ ἡ βασιλεία διὰ τῶν περὶ αὐτὴν συνίσταται, ὡς ἡ θάλασσα διὰ τῶν ἑαυτῆς κυμάτων· ἐν τούτοις γὰρ καὶ φοβερὰ τοῖς πλέουσι καθίσταται. Ἀνόητον δὲ πάντῃ τὸ ἐπιπολαίως φιλεῖν καὶ τὰ εἰκότα τῇ φιλίᾳ μὴ τηρεῖν καὶ τὸ δι’ ἑτέρων βλάβης οἰκείαν ἐπισπᾶσθαι ὠφέλειαν. Πρὸς τούτοις οἶδα τὰ τοιαῦτά σοι παραινῶν, ὡς ἀνηνύτοις ἐπιχειρεῖν με. Φησὶ γάρ τις τῶν σοφῶν· *Μὴ ἔλεγχε μωροὺς ἵνα μὴ μισήσωσί σε.* Ὥσπερ ἀπώλεσαν οἱ πίθηκες τὸν κόρακα ἐλέγχοντα αὐτούς.”

53 *Περὶ πιθήκων καὶ κόρακος.*

“Λέγεται γὰρ ὥς τινες πίθηκες ἔν τινι τόπῳ τῶν ὀρέων καθ’ ὥραν χειμέριον διατρίβοντες, καὶ σφοδρῷ ῥίγει συσχεθέντες, καί τι ζωύφιον περιφαὲς εὑρόντες, ὑπέλαβον πῦρ εἶναι καὶ ἐνεφύσων αὐτῷ ἱκανῶς. Κόραξ δέ τις ἰδὼν τούτους κενῶς πονοῦντας, ἔφη· ‘Μὴ πλανᾶσθε, ὦ οὗτοι, οὐ γὰρ πῦρ ἐστι τὸ προκείμενον ὑμῖν.’ Ὡς οὖν τούτου οὐκ ἤκουον, κατῆλθεν ἐπ’ αὐτούς. Ἰδὼν δέ τις αὐτὸν κατερχόμενον, εἶπεν· ‘Ὦ κόραξ, μὴ μάτην κοπία, μηδ’ ἐπιχείρει τὸν σκολιὸν εὐθύνειν καὶ τὸν ἀσύνετον συνετίζειν. Οὐδεὶς γὰρ τὴν ἑαυτοῦ σπάθην ἐπὶ πέτρας δοκιμάζει ἀτόμου.’ Ὁ δὲ κόραξ μὴ ἐπιστραφεὶς πρὸς τὸν παραινοῦντα προσήγγισε τοῖς πίθηξιν. Οἳ καὶ συλλαβόντες αὐτὸν διεσπάραξαν.

"The king who has many such subjects surrounding him is like water that is very pure and clear, but full of crocodiles: if someone were to go near it, even if he were dying of thirst, he would not be able to drink it. You wanted nobody but yourself to be close to the lion, but a kingdom is made up of those who compose it, just as the sea is made up of its waves, and it is the waves that make it fearsome to sailors. It is foolish in every way to love in a superficial way, not to seek out that which promotes friendship, and to pursue one's own advantage by harming others. In addition, I know that, in advising you of such things, I am attempting something that is impossible for me to achieve. For one of the wise men says, *do not correct those who are* stupid*, so that they will not hate you.* Just as the apes destroyed the crow who criticized them." 52

About apes and a crow. 53

"For it is said that some apes spent every winter somewhere in the mountains, suffering from extreme cold, and when they found an insect that glowed, they supposed it was fire and kept blowing on it. A crow saw them toiling in vain and said, 'Don't be deceived, you apes, for what's lying in front of you isn't fire.' Then, as they didn't listen to him, he went down to them. Someone saw him come down and said, 'Crow, don't labor in vain, or try to straighten what is crooked, or make the unintelligent intelligent. For no one tests his sword on rock which cannot be cut.' But the crow did not turn back to the person giving him this advice and went up to the apes. And they grabbed hold of him and tore him to pieces.

"Οὕτω δὴ κἀμοὶ τὰ τοιαῦτά σοι παραινοῦντα δοκεῖ εἶναι, ἀλλὰ καὶ σὺ τῇ φιλαυτίᾳ καὶ τῇ πονηρίᾳ ἡττώμενος οὐκ ἀκούεις μου τῆς παραινέσεως καὶ ταὐτόν τι πείσῃ τῷ τοῦ πονηροῦ ἀνδρὸς τοῦ κοινωνοῦ τοῦ σχολαστικοῦ."

54 *Περὶ πονηροῦ ἀνδρὸς καὶ σχολαστικοῦ.*

"Λέγεται γὰρ ὡς πονηρός τις ἀνὴρ καὶ ἄλλος σχολαστικὸς κοινωνίαν πρὸς ἀλλήλους συνεστήσαντο, καί ποτε ἀλλήλοις συμπεριπατοῦντες εὗρον χρυσίου τάλαντα χίλια. Ὁ δὲ σχολαστικὸς εἶπε τῷ πονηρῷ· 'Διάνειμαι τὸ ἕρμαιον ἐπ' ἴσης.' Ὁ δὲ πονηρὸς εἶπεν· 'Οὐχί, ἀλλ' ὅσον ἐξ αὐτοῦ νῦν βουλόμεθα, ἀναλαβώμεθα καὶ τὸ λοιπὸν ὑπὸ γῆν συγκαλύψωμεν, καὶ ὅτε δεηθῶμέν τινος, ἐλευσόμεθα καὶ κατὰ μικρὸν τὸ αὔταρκες ἐξαντλήσομεν. Τούτῳ γὰρ τῷ τρόπῳ, ἡ κοινωνία ἐπὶ πολὺν διαρκέσει χρόνον, καὶ διὰ τῆς κοινωνίας ἡ φιλία.' Καὶ ἐπείσθη ὁ σχολαστικὸς τῇ παραινέσει αὐτοῦ, καὶ ὑπό τι δένδρον μέγα τε καὶ συνηρεφὲς τὸν χρυσὸν κατορύξαντες ἔκρυψαν. Μετὰ δέ τινας ἡμέρας λάθρα ἐξελθὼν ὁ πονηρὸς ἐσφετερίσατο τὸν τεθησαυρισμένον ὅλον χρυσόν.

55 "Μετὰ δέ τινα χρόνον ἔφη ὁ σχολαστικὸς πρὸς αὐτόν· 'Ἀπέλθωμεν, εἰ δοκεῖ, καὶ ἀναλαβώμεθα μέρος τι τοῦ ὑπὸ γῆν χρυσοῦ.' Καὶ ἐξελθόντες καὶ τὴν γῆν ἀνορύξαντες, ὡς οὐδὲν εὗρον, ἤρξατο ὁ πονηρὸς τίλλειν τὰς τρίχας καὶ τύπτειν τὸ στῆθος αὐτοῦ καὶ καταβοᾶν τοῦ σχολαστικοῦ ὡς τὸν θησαυρὸν ὑποκλέψαντος. Ὁ δὲ σχολαστικὸς μυρίοις τοῦτον ἐβεβαίου ὅρκοις, ὡς οὐδὲν τοιοῦτον ἔδρασε. Τέως

"Giving such advice to you," continued Stephanites, "seems to be the same to me, and as you, too, are overcome by selfishness and wickedness, you don't listen to my advice, and you will suffer the same fate as the wicked man who was the lawyer's companion."

About a wicked man and a lawyer. 54

"For it is said that a wicked man and another who was a lawyer became companions, and that once, while they were walking around together, they found a thousand talents of gold. The lawyer said to the wicked man, 'Let's divide the windfall equally.' But the wicked man said, 'No, let's take as much as we want of it now and bury the rest in the ground. When we need some of it, we'll come and, little by little, take out just enough. For in this way our companionship will last a long time, and, through companionship, friendship.' The lawyer was persuaded by his advice, and they hid the gold by burying it under a large shady tree. But some days later the wicked man went out secretly and took for himself all the gold they had hoarded.

"Sometime later, the lawyer said to him, 'If you like, let's 55
go and dig up some of the buried gold.' They went off and, when they had dug up the ground, as they found nothing, the wicked man started to tear his hair and beat his breast and loudly accuse the lawyer of having stolen the treasure. The lawyer swore countless oaths to assure him he had done no such thing. In the meantime, the wicked man dragged

καὶ πρός τινα τοῦτον εἵλκυσε τῶν κριτῶν. Ὁ δὲ κριτὴς εἶπεν· "Ὁ ἐνάγων βαρύνεται ταῖς ἀποδείξεσι, καὶ δεῖ σε λοιπὸν τὸ τοιοῦτον ἡμῖν δεῖξαι.' Ὁ δὲ εἶπε· 'Τὸ δένδρον αὐτὸ μαρτυρήσει μου τὴν ἀλήθειαν, εἰ καὶ ἄφωνόν ἐστι.' Καὶ ἀπελθὼν εἰς τὸν ἴδιον πατέρα ἀνήγγειλεν αὐτῷ τὰ κατ' αὐτόν, καὶ ἠξίωσεν εἰς τὸ δένδρον ἐκεῖνο ὑπεισελθεῖν καὶ προς τὸν ἐρωτῶντα ἀποκρίνεσθαι ὡς ὁ σχολαστικὸς τὸν θησαυρὸν ἐσύλησεν. Ὁ δὲ εἶπεν· ''Εγὼ μὲν οὖν τοῦτο ποιήσω, ἀλλ' ὅρα μὴ ταῖς ἰδίαις ἄρκυσι σαγηνευθῇς, καὶ πάθῃς ὅπερ ὁ κύκνος ἔπαθεν.'"

56 *Περὶ κύκνου καὶ ὄφεως καὶ καρκίνου.*

"'Λέγεται γὰρ ὡς κύκνος τις <ἦν> φωλεύων ἔν τινι τόπῳ πλησίον ὄφεως καὶ ἐν τῷ γεννᾶν τὸν κύκνον ἤσθιεν ὁ ὄφις τοὺς νεοττοὺς αὐτοῦ. Ὁ δὲ κύκνος διὰ τὴν τῆς κατοικίας γλυκύτητα οὐκ ἠβούλετο μετοικῆσαι τοῦ τόπου. Γνοὺς οὖν τὴν αὐτοῦ βλάβην καὶ δυσφορῶν ἐπὶ τῇ τοιαύτῃ δυστυχίᾳ, καρκίνος τις προσῆλθε τῷ κύκνῳ καὶ εἶπεν αὐτῷ· "Τί σε βλέπω ἀδημονοῦντα;" Ἀνήγγειλε δὲ αὐτῷ ὁ κύκνος πάντα τὰ κατ' αὐτὸν καὶ ἅπερ παρὰ τοῦ ὄφεως πέπονθεν. Ὁ δὲ καρκίνος, δείξας αὐτῷ τὴν ὀπὴν ἄντικρυς τῆς καταδύσεως τοῦ ὄφεως, λέγει αὐτῷ· "Τίς ἡ ὀπὴ ἐστιν αὕτη;" Ὁ δὲ εἶπε· "Τῆς νύμφης ἡ ὀπή ἐστιν." Ὁ δὲ καρκίνος ἔφη· "Ἡ νύμφη μεγίστην ἔχθραν ἔχει μετὰ τοῦ ὄφεως, ἄπελθε οὖν καὶ λαβὼν ἰχθύας, θὲς αὐτοὺς ἀναμεταξὺ τῆς ὀπῆς τοῦ ὄφεως καὶ τῆς νύμφης, ὅπως ἐξέλθῃ ἡ νύμφη φαγεῖν τοὺς ἰχθύας, καὶ εὑροῦσα τὴν ὀπὴν τοῦ ὄφεως ἀποκτενεῖ

him in front of one of the judges. The judge said, 'The burden of proof is on the plaintiff, so then, you must prove it to me.' And the wicked man said, 'The tree itself, even though it can't speak, will testify to the truth for me.' And he went off to his father and told him about his situation, and asked him to secretly climb into the tree and to reply, to the person who asked, that the lawyer had stolen the treasure. His father said, 'I will do this, but see that you don't get caught in your own nets, and suffer what the swan did.'"

About a swan, a snake, and a crab. 56

"'For it is said that a swan nested in a place near a snake, and when the swan produced her young, the snake ate the cygnets. The swan, because it was pleasant where they lived, did not want to move from the place. While she was thinking about the harm she had suffered and angry at this misfortune, a crab approached the swan and said to her, "Why do I see you are distressed?" And the swan told him everything that had happened to her and what she had suffered because of the snake. The crab showed her a hole right opposite the snake's burrow and said, "What's that hole?" And the swan replied, "It belongs to a nymph." And the crab said, "The nymph really hates the snake, so go and get some fish and put them between the snake's hole and the nymph, so that when the nymph comes out to eat the fish and finds the

τοῦτον." Ὁ δὲ κύκνος οὕτω ἐποίησεν, καὶ ἐξελθοῦσα ἡ νύμφη καὶ τοὺς ἰχθύας φαγοῦσα, κατήντησε μέχρι καὶ τῆς τοῦ ὄφεως καταδύσεως, καὶ εἰσελθοῦσα ἀπέκτεινεν αὐτόν. Τῇ δὲ ἑξῆς πάλιν ἡ νύμφη ἐξελθοῦσα κατὰ τὸ εἰωθὸς καὶ τὸν κύκνον εὑροῦσα, ἔφαγε καὶ αὐτὸν καὶ τοὺς νεοσσοὺς αὐτοῦ.

"'Ταύτην οὖν σοι τὴν παραβολὴν διεξῄειν, ὦ τέκνον, ἵνα γνῷς ὡς ὁ ἐπιβουλεύων τινὶ μετὰ ἀφροσύνης τῇ ἰδίᾳ πονηρίᾳ ἁλίσκεται.'

57 "Ὁ δὲ υἱὸς αὐτοῦ εἶπεν· 'Μὴ φοβοῦ, πάτερ, τὴν τοιαύτην παραβολήν, ἵνα κερδήσωμεν τὰ τάλαντα.' Ὁ δὲ πατὴρ πεισθεὶς τῷ υἱῷ αὐτοῦ καὶ ἀπελθὼν ὑπεισέδυ ἐκεῖνος τοῦ δένδρου. Τοῦ δὲ κριτοῦ ἐκεῖσε παραγενομένου καὶ τὸ δένδρον ἐπερωτήσαντος, τίς τὸν χρυσὸν ἀφείλατο, φωνὴ ἀνεδίδοτο ὡς ὁ σχολαστικὸς ἔκλεψεν τὸν θησαυρόν. Ταῦτα οὖν ὁ κριτὴς ἀκούσας, τὸν δόλον ἐφώρασε καὶ προσέταξε πυρὶ τὸ δένδρον ἀποτεφρωθῆναι. Τούτου οὖν γενομένου, καὶ τοῦ πυρὸς ἀναφθέντος, ὡς ἐπ' αὐτὸν ἀνῆλθεν ὁ καπνός, εὐθὺς ἐφώνησε. Καὶ ἐκβληθείς, τὸν δόλον καθωμολόγησε καὶ σφοδρῶς παρὰ τοῦ κριτοῦ τιμωρηθεὶς σὺν τῷ υἱῷ, ἀφῃρέθησαν ἅπαντα τὸν χρυσόν, ὃς δὴ καὶ ἐδόθη μόνῳ τῷ σχολαστικῷ. Τοιαύτη οὖν ἐστιν ἡ τοῦ μοχθηροῦ καὶ δολίου ἀνδρὸς ἀπόβασις."

Ἔφη δὲ ὁ Στεφανίτης τῷ Ἰχνηλάτῃ· "Ἐγὼ μὲν οὖν ἀεί σου τὴν γλῶτταν ἐπτοούμην, ὦ Ἰχνηλάτα, ὡς τὸν ὀδόντα τοῦ ὄφεως, ἐπεὶ καὶ ἀμφοῖν ἰὸς ἀποστάζεται. Καλῶς γὰρ εἴρηκεν ὁ εἰπών· 'Φευκτέον τοὺς πονηροὺς ἄνδρας, κἂν

snake's hole, she'll kill him." The swan did this, and when the nymph came out and ate the fish, she also came to the snake's burrow, went in, and killed it. But the next day the nymph came out again as usual, found the swan, and ate both it and its cygnets.

"'So, my child,' the wicked man's father concluded, 'I've gone through this analogy so that you may understand that someone who plots in a foolish way against someone else gets caught by his own wickedness.'

"His son said to him, 'Don't be frightened by this analogy, 57
father, so that we may get the talents.' And the father, persuaded by his son, went off and got into the tree. When the judge arrived there and asked the tree who had taken the gold, a voice answered that the lawyer had stolen the treasure. But when the judge heard this, he saw through the trick and ordered the tree to be set on fire and reduced to ashes. While this was happening, and when the fire had been lit, the father cried out as soon as the smoke reached him. He fell out of the tree, confessed to the trick, and was severely punished by the judge, along with his son. All the gold was taken from them and given to the lawyer alone. Such is the outcome for a nefarious and treacherous man."

And Stephanites also said to Ichnelates, "So, I'm thus always as nervous of your tongue, Ichnelates, as I am of a snake's fang, since both drip venom. For the man spoke well who said, 'One must flee from wicked men even if they are

συγγενεῖς κἂν ἀγχιστεῖς ὦσιν.' Ταὐτὸν γάρ τι πεποιήκας τῷ τοῦ ἐμπόρου."

58 *Περὶ παρακαταθήκης ἐμπόρου.*

"Λέγεται γὰρ ὡς ἔμπορός τις μέλλων ἀποδημεῖν παρεκατέθετό τινι τῶν φίλων αὐτοῦ λάμνας σιδήρου ἑκατόν. Καὶ ἐπαναζεύξας παρεγένετο πρὸς τὸν τὴν παρακαταθήκην λαβόντα, ἤδη ἀπογνόντα τὴν ἐπιστροφὴν τοῦ ἐμπόρου, καὶ τὸν σίδηρον πωλήσαντα, καὶ εἶπεν αὐτῷ· 'Ἀντίστρεψόν μοι, ὃν παρεθέμην σοι σίδηρον.' Ὁ δὲ ἔφη· '"Εν τινι γωνίᾳ τῆς οἰκίας μου τοῦτον τέθεικα καὶ κατέφαγον αὐτὸν οἱ μῦες. Ἀλλὰ μηδέν σοι μελήσῃ περὶ αὐτοῦ, ἐπειδὴ σῶος πρὸς ἡμᾶς ἐπανῆκες. Ἀλλ' ἐλθὲ σήμερον καὶ συνεστιάσθητι ἡμῖν μετὰ περιχαρείας καὶ τελέσωμέν σοι τὰ εἰσιτήρια.' Ὁ δὲ κατένευσε, καὶ εἰσελθὼν ἐντετύχηκε τῷ υἱῷ αὐτοῦ, καὶ συλλαβὼν τοῦτον ἀπήγαγεν ἐπὶ τὴν οἰκίαν αὐτοῦ· καὶ ἀποκρύψας ὑπέστρεψε· καὶ εὑρὼν τοῦτον ἐπερωτῶντα περὶ τοῦ παιδὸς αὐτοῦ, εἶπεν· 'Εἶδον τοῦτον παρὰ ἱέρακος εἰς ἀέρα αἰρόμενον.' Ὁ δὲ φωνήσας ἔφη τοῖς ἐκεῖσε· '"Ιδετέ ποτε ἱέρακα ἀνθρώπους εἰς ὕψος αἴροντα;' Ὁ δὲ κύριος τοῦ σιδήρου ὑπολαβὼν ἔφη· 'Ναί, ἔνθα μῦες σίδηρον τοσοῦτον ἐσθίουσιν, ἐκεῖσε οἱ ἱέρακες καὶ ἐλέφαντα αἴρουσιν.' Ὁ δέ, αἰσχυνθεὶς ἐπὶ τούτῳ, δέδωκεν αὐτῷ τὸν σίδηρον, ὅσον ἀφείλατο, καὶ τὸν οἰκεῖον παῖδα παρέλαβεν.

59 "Οὕτως ἄρα καὶ σὺ καταισχυνθήσῃ ψευδεῖς λόγους πλαττόμενος. Ἀλλ' ὁ κακὸς οὐδὲν ἄλλο πλὴν κακός. Καὶ γὰρ ὁ πικρὸς καρπός, κἂν πολλάκις ἐπιχρισθῇ μέλιτι, οὐκ

kinsfolk and close family.' For you've done something like the merchant."

About a merchant's deposit. 58

"For it is said that a merchant who was about to go abroad deposited one hundred bars of iron with one of his friends. Upon his return he went to the recipient of the deposit, who by now had despaired of the merchant's return and had sold the iron. The merchant said to him, 'Give me back all the iron I deposited with you.' And he said, 'I stored it in a corner of my house and the mice ate it. But don't concern yourself about it, seeing that you have come back to us safely. Come and dine with us today with great happiness, and let's celebrate your return.' He nodded in agreement and went in. But he came across the man's son, and, grabbing him, took him off to his own house. He concealed him there and returned. When he found the man was asking about his son, he said, 'I saw him being taken up into the air by a hawk.' And the man called out to the people who were there, 'Have you ever seen hawks carrying people up into the air?' The owner of the iron replied, 'Yes, where mice eat that much iron, hawks even carry off elephants.' The man was ashamed at this, gave him the same amount of iron as he had taken, and got his child back.

"So you too will be disgraced for inventing false stories. 59
An evil person is nothing but evil. For bitter fruit, even if it is often mixed with honey, does not change its natural bit-

οἶδεν μετατρέπειν τὴν οἰκείαν πικρότητα εἰς γλυκύτητα. Ἀνθεκτέον οὖν τῆς τῶν ἀγαθῶν ἀνδρῶν ξυναυλίας καὶ φευκτέον τοὺς πονηρούς. Ὥσπερ γὰρ μεταλαμβάνει ὁ πνέων ἀὴρ ἀπὸ τῆς δυσωδίας δυσωδιῶν καὶ ἐκ τῆς εὐωδίας εὐωδιῶν, ἐφ' ᾧ τινι ἂν τούτων τύχῃ πεπνευκώς, οὕτω μεταδίδωσιν ἡ τῶν φαύλων καὶ σπουδαίων ἀνδρῶν ὁμιλία τῷ προσομιλοῦντι. Οἶδα γὰρ πρὸς τούτοις, ὡς καὶ πάνυ σοι φορτικὸς παραινῶν ταυτὶ καταφαίνομαι. Ἀεὶ γὰρ φορτικοί εἰσι τοῖς ἀνοήτοις ἀνδράσιν οἱ συνετοί, καὶ τοῖς ἀπαιδεύτοις οἱ πεπαιδευμένοι, τοῖς δὲ φειδωλοῖς οἱ εὐμετάδοτοι, καὶ τοῖς προπετέσιν οἱ ἀνεξίκακοι, καὶ τοῖς στρεβλοῖς οἱ εὐθεῖς."

60 *Περὶ τῆς ἀναιρέσεως τοῦ ταύρου.*

Τούτων δὲ λεγομένων μεταξὺ Ἰχνηλάτου καὶ Στεφανίτου, τὸν ταῦρον ὁ λέων ἀνῄρηκεν ὁ βασιλεύς, καὶ εὐθὺς μετεμελήθη ἐπὶ τῇ ἀναιρέσει αὐτοῦ. Ὁ δὲ Ἰχνηλάτης ἀπελθὼν πρὸς τὸν λέοντα καὶ σύννουν αὐτὸν θεασάμενος, ἔφη· "Τί μετάμελος ἐπὶ τῇ ἀναιρέσει τοῦ ταύρου γέγονας; Οὐκ οἶσθα, ὡς εἰ δηχθῇ τις ὑπὸ ἐχίδνης τὸν δάκτυλον, ἐκτέμνει τοῦτον καὶ τὸ οἰκεῖον μέλος ἀθετεῖ ὡς ἀλλότριον, ἵνα μὴ δι' αὐτοῦ ὁ ἰὸς τῆς ἐχίδνης ἐπὶ τὸ σύμπαν σῶμα ἀναδοθῇ;" Καὶ ἀκούσας ὁ λέων ἐπίστευσε τοῖς λόγοις αὐτοῦ καὶ παρεκλήθη.

61 Οὕτως ἄρα ὁ φιλόσοφος ἐν τῷ πρώτῳ τμήματι ἔφη ὡς· "Ὁ κακὸς καὶ μοχθηρὸς ἀνήρ, ὅτε μεταξὺ δύο τινῶν ἀλλήλοις ἀντιφιλούντων ἑαυτὸν παρεμβάλλει, κινδύνους καὶ θορύβους ἐμποιεῖ καὶ τοὺς φίλους διΐστησιν."

terness into sweetness. One must thus keep to the company of good men and flee the wicked. For just as air gets a bad smell from blowing over things that smell bad and a sweet smell from those which smell sweet, whichever it happens to blow over, in the same way, the conversation of both good and bad men is shared with the person who converses with them. And I know this as well, that I also appear exceedingly tiresome to you in giving you this advice. For the intelligent are always tiresome to unintelligent men, as well-educated men are to the ignorant, the generous to the thrifty, the patient to the reckless, and the straightforward to the devious."

About the killing of the bull. 60

While these things were being said between Ichnelates and Stephanites, the bull was killed by the lion king, and he immediately regretted killing him. But Ichnelates then went over to the lion, and having noticed that he was worried, said, "Why do you regret killing the bull? Don't you know that if someone has been bitten on the finger by a viper, he cuts it off and gets rid of his own limb as something hostile, so that the viper's venom won't spread throughout his whole body because of it?" And when the lion heard this, he believed his words, and was consoled.

And this, then, is how, in the first chapter, the philosopher said that, "When an evil and wicked man insinuates himself between two people who are friends with each other, he causes danger and confusion and divides the friends." 61

[Chapter 2]

Ἀρχὴ τοῦ δευτέρου τμήματος.
Προλογίζει ὁ βασιλεύς.

Πάλιν ὁ βασιλεὺς τῷ φιλοσόφῳ εἶπεν· "Ἀνάγγειλόν μοι, ὅπως ἀπέβη τὰ κατὰ τὸν Ἰχνηλάτην ἐκεῖνον μετὰ τὴν τοῦ ταύρου ἀναίρεσιν." Ὁ δὲ φιλόσοφος ὑπολαβὼν ἔφη·

2 Μετὰ τὴν τοῦ ταύρου ἀναίρεσιν, ἐξῆλθε μιᾷ τῶν νυκτῶν λεοντόπαρδος, ὃς διδάσκαλος ἦν τῷ λέοντι καὶ πιστὸς σύμβουλος, καὶ προσελθὼν τῇ τοῦ Ἰχνηλάτου πύλῃ, εὗρε τὸν Στεφανίτην κατονειδίζοντα τοῦτον ὑπὲρ ὧν εἰς τὸν ταῦρον ἔδρασε, καὶ ὡς οὐ διεκφύγει φάσκοντα τὰς τοῦ λέοντος χεῖρας, μαθόντος τὸν συρραφέντα δόλον παρ' αὐτοῦ. Καὶ ἀκούσας τοῦτο εἰσῆλθε πρὸς τὴν μητέρα τοῦ λέοντος καὶ ἀνήγγειλεν αὐτῇ ὅσα ἀκήκοεν.

3 Ἡμέρας δὲ ἐπιφωσκούσης παρεγένετο αὕτη πρὸς τὸν λέοντα· καὶ ἰδοῦσα τοῦτον σκυθρωπὸν καὶ κατηφῆ καὶ μετάμελον ἐπὶ τῇ τοῦ ταύρου ἀπωλείᾳ ἔφη· "Ὦ τέκνον, ὁ μετάμελος καὶ ἡ φροντὶς οὐδὲν ἄλλον ἐργάζονται ἀλλ' ἢ τοῦ σώματος τηκεδόνα καὶ τοῦ νοὸς ζόφον. Ἀλλ' *ἐξαύδα μὴ κεῦθε νόῳ ἵνα εἴδομεν ἄμφω.* Ἀλλ' οἶδα καὶ πρὸ τοῦ

Chapter 2

BEGINNING OF THE SECOND CHAPTER.
THE KING SPEAKS FIRST.

The king said again to the philosopher, "Tell me how things turned out for that Ichnelates after the killing of the bull." And the philosopher replied:

After the killing of the bull, a leopard, who was the lion's 2
teacher and his faithful adviser, came out and went to Ichnelates's gate one night. He found Stephanites taking him to task for what he had caused to happen to the bull, and telling him that he would not escape the lion's clutches if the latter discovered the trick he had contrived. When the leopard heard this, he went to the lion's mother and told her what he had heard.

At daybreak, she went to the lion. When she saw him 3
looking sad, dejected, and regretful over the slaughter of the bull, she said, "My child, regret and anxiety accomplish nothing, except wasting away the body and darkening the mind. So *speak up, do not conceal it in your mind, so that we both may know,* although I am aware, even before you speak, that

εἰπεῖν σε, ὡς διὰ τὸν ταῦρον ἀθυμεῖς, ὃν ἀναιτίως ἀνῄρηκας. Καὶ εἴ γε δίκαιος ᾖς, ἔδει σε τῇ πρὸς αὐτόν σου διαθέσει τὴν ἐκείνου πρὸς σὲ διακρῖναι διάθεσιν. Λέγεται γὰρ ὡς ἀνταμείβουσιν ἀλλήλαις αἱ καρδίαι. Εἰπὲ οὖν μοι, ὅπως διέκεισο πρὸς τὸν ταῦρον." Ὁ δὲ λέων εἶπεν· "Ἀεί μοι ὁ ταῦρος φίλος ἦν καὶ ἐπίστευον αὐτῷ ἐν πᾶσι καὶ τὰς αὐτοῦ παραινέσεις ἐδεχόμην, καὶ οὐδεμία μοὶ περὶ αὐτὸν ὑπόληψις ἐναντία ὑπέδραμεν. Καὶ νῦν πάνυ μεταμεμέλημαι ἐπὶ τῷ θανάτῳ αὐτοῦ καὶ περιώδυνός εἰμι αἰσθόμενος ὡσανεὶ εἶναι τοῦτον ἀθῷον τῶν κατ' αὐτοῦ ἐγκληθέντων. Ἀλλ' ἠπατήθην τοῖς τοῦ δολίου Ἰχνηλάτου λόγοις καὶ τοῖς ψευδέσιν αὐτοῦ συλλογισμοῖς. Ἀνάγγειλόν μοι οὖν, εἴπερ τι τοιοῦτον ἀκήκοας· ἡ γὰρ ἀληθὴς ὑπόληψις βεβαιοῦται καὶ διὰ τῶν ἔξωθεν ἐρχομένων ἀγγελιῶν."

4 *Περὶ τῆς φανερώσεως τοῦ Ἰχνηλάτου τερατουργήματος.*

Ἡ δὲ τοῦ λέοντος μήτηρ φησίν· "Ἀκήκοα παρά τινος τῶν πιστοτάτων ὡς διὰ φθόνον ὁ Ἰχνηλάτης πρὸς σὲ τοῦ ταύρου κατεψεύσατο." Ὁ δὲ λέων εἶπεν αὐτῇ· "Καὶ τίς ἐστιν ὁ ἀναγγείλας σοι τὸ τοιοῦτον;" Ἡ δὲ μήτηρ αὐτοῦ ἔφη· "Δεῖ τὰ μυστήρια τῶν φίλων τηρεῖν· ὁ γὰρ τοῦτο μὴ ποιῶν διαφθείρει τὴν ἰδίαν πιστότητα." Ὁ δὲ λέων· "Ἐν ἄλλοις δεῖ τὸ τοιοῦτον παρατηρεῖν, ἔνθα δὲ σκοπός ἐστιν τῆς ἀληθείας ἡ φανέρωσις καὶ τοῦ ἡμαρτημένου ἡ ἐκδίκησις, οὐ δεῖ συγκαλύπτειν τὸ ἁμάρτημα. Ὁ γὰρ δίκαιος βασιλεὺς οὐχ ὑπολήψει τιμωρεῖ, οὐδ' ἂν ᾖ τι ἀμφιβαλλόμενον

you are depressed about the bull, whom you have killed unjustly. But if you were indeed just, you should have decided your attitude toward him based on his attitude toward you. For it is said that hearts answer to one another. So tell me how you felt about the bull." And the lion said, "The bull was always my friend and I trusted him in everything, I accepted his advice and no sense of hostility about him ever occurred to me. Now I very much regret his death, and I am extremely sad, feeling, as it were, that he was innocent of the charges against him, and that I was deceived by the words of the treacherous Ichnelates and by his false arguments. Tell me, then, if you have heard any such thing; for the truth of a suspicion is also confirmed by the messages which come from others."

About the disclosure of Ichnelates's monstrous behavior. 4

And the lion's mother said, "I have heard from someone who is most trustworthy that Ichnelates told you lies about the bull out of jealousy." And the lion said to her, "Who told you this?" His mother said, "The secrets of friends must be kept, for someone who does not do this destroys their own trustworthiness." But the lion said, "It may be necessary to observe this in other cases, but where the aim is revealing the truth and bringing an offender to justice, one shouldn't cover up the offense. For the just king does not punish on the basis of suspicion, nor yet if there may be some doubt

τῆς ὑποθέσεως· δέδοικα γάρ, μήπως τὰ ὅμοια μεταμεληθῶ ὡς τῇ τοῦ ταύρου ἀναιρέσει καὶ ἐπὶ τῇ τοῦ Ἰχνηλάτου." Ἡ δὲ μήτηρ αὐτοῦ ἔφη· "Οὐχ ὑπελάμβανόν σε, τέκνον, ἐνδοιάζειν τὰ περὶ ἐμοῦ." Ὁ δὲ λέων εἶπεν· "Οὐκ ἐνδοιάζω, μῆτερ, ἀλλὰ βούλομαι τὴν ἀλήθειαν εἰς φῶς ἀγαγεῖν." Ἡ δὲ μήτηρ αὐτοῦ ἔφη· "Δέδοικα μή, τοῦτο ποιήσασα, ἀσυνείδητος ἀποδειχθῶ."

5 *Ἐξέτασις πρώτη τοῦ Ἰχνηλάτου.*

Ταῦτα ἀκούσας ὁ λέων παρὰ τῆς μητρὸς αὐτοῦ, παρέστησεν αὐτῷ ἅπαντας τοὺς ὑπ' αὐτόν· μετεκαλέσατο δὲ καὶ τὸν Ἰχνηλάτην. Ἰδὼν οὖν τοῦτον κατηφῆ, ὁ Ἰχνηλάτης εἶπεν πρὸς τοὺς πλησίον· "Τί ὅτι ὁρῶ τὸν λέοντα στυγνὸν καὶ κατηφείας πλήρη;" Ὑπολαβοῦσα δὲ ἡ μήτηρ τοῦ λέοντος ἔφη· "Οὐ διά τι ἕτερον κατηφιᾷ ἀλλ' ἢ τὸ μέχρι τοῦδε ἐᾶσαί σε τοῖς ζῶσι συναναστρέφεσθαι πείσαντα τοῦτον δόλῳ καὶ πανουργίᾳ τὸν ἄθλιον ταῦρον ἀνελεῖν." Ὁ δὲ Ἰχνηλάτης εἶπεν· "Ὁρῶ, ὡς πᾶς ὁ σπεύδων ἐπὶ τὸ ἀγαθὸν ἕτοιμός ἐστι πρὸς ὑποδοχὴν τῶν συμφορῶν μᾶλλον, ἢ τῶν εὐποιϊῶν· ἐπὶ τούτῳ γὰρ οἶμαι καὶ τοὺς ἀσκητάς, χαίρειν εἰπόντας τῇ τῶν ἀνθρώπων ἀναστροφῇ, τὰς ἐρήμους διώκειν. Ἐγὼ δὲ εὔνους περὶ τὸν βασιλέα διακείμενος ἀνέφερον αὐτῷ τὰ κατὰ τὸν ταῦρον καὶ ἐξεφαύλισα τὴν ἐπιβουλὴν αὐτοῦ. Εἰ οὖν ἀκριβῶς ἐξετάσεις τὰ παρ' ἐμοῦ ἀνενεχθέντα αὐτῷ, εὑρήσεις πάντως ἀληθῆ μου τὴν ἀναφοράν· τὸ γὰρ ἐνοικουροῦν πῦρ τῷ λίθῳ καὶ τῷ ξύλῳ μεθόδῳ τινὶ φανεροῦται καὶ τὰ ἐγκλήματα ἐξεταζόμενα

about the case; for I am afraid that I will perhaps regret the killing of Ichnelates in a similar way as I do that of the bull." And his mother said, "I didn't suppose that you, my child, would have doubts about me." And the lion said, "I'm not doubting you, mother, but I want to bring the truth to light." And his mother said, "I'm afraid that if I were to do this, I might appear unscrupulous."

The first investigation of Ichnelates. 5

When the lion had heard this from his mother, he summoned all his subjects and sent for Ichnelates as well. When Ichnelates saw that the lion was dejected, he said to those nearby, "Why do I see that the lion is so gloomy and so dejected?" And the lion's mother replied and said, "The only reason he's dejected is for allowing you to continue among the living until now after you persuaded him through trickery and cunning to kill the poor bull." Ichnelates said, "I see that anyone who strives for good must be ready to accept misfortune rather than recognition for their good deeds, and I think this is why ascetics have said farewell to human society and have sought the desert. Since I am well-disposed toward the king, I reported to him about the bull and ruined the latter's plot. So, if you investigate carefully what I reported to him, you will find that my report was completely true: for the fire that is present in flint and in wood reveals itself in some way, and when crimes that are

καὶ ἐρευνώμενα μᾶλλον ἀποκαλύπτεται, τῇ ἀληθείᾳ φανερούμενα, παραπλησίως τῇ δυσώδει ὕλῃ ταραττομένῃ.

6 "Εἰ μὲν οὖν συνεγίνωσκον ἐμαυτῷ ἁμαρτήματι, οὐκ ἂν ἐνταῦθα προσαφικόμην, ἀλλ' ἔν τινι τόπῳ τῆς *εὐρείας χθονὸς* τὴν ἀναστροφὴν ἐποιησάμην. Ἀξιῶ δέ σου τὴν βασιλικὴν μεγαλειότητα ἐξετάσαι ἀκριβῶς τὰ κατ' ἐμὲ διά τινος δικαιοτάτου διαιτητοῦ, μὴ τὴν ἀλήθειαν παραχαράττοντος, μήτε μὴν πρόσωπον λαμβάνοντος, μήτε πρὸς τοὺς φθονοῦντας τὰ ὦτα κλίνοντος, ἐπεὶ πολλοί μοι πάρεισιν οἱ τοιοῦτοι, δι' ἣν εἶχε πρός με ὁ βασιλεὺς ἀγαθὴν διάθεσιν. Εἰ δὲ μὴ τοῦτο ποιήσῃ, οὐκ ἔχω πρὸς ὅντινα καταφεύξομαι, ἀλλ' ἢ πρὸς τὴν τοῦ Θεοῦ εὐσπλαγχνίαν τοῦ *καρδίας καὶ νεφροὺς ἐτάζοντος*. Πρὸς δὲ τούτοις οὐ πτοοῦμαι τὸν θάνατον· οἶδα γὰρ τοῦτον ὡρισμένον καὶ ἀπαραίτητον παντὶ ζῴῳ θνητῷ, καὶ εἰ *μυρίας ἔχοντι ψυχάς*."

7 *Περὶ τῆς μοιχαλίδος γυναικός.*

"'Ερρέθη τοίνυν παρὰ σοφῶν, ὡς ὁ πιστεύων τὰ παρόμοια τῶν πραγμάτων, ταὐτόν τι παθεῖν τῷ τῆς ἀσυνέτου γυναικός, ἥτις ἠχρείωσεν ἑαυτὴν μετὰ τοῦ ἑαυτῆς δούλου. Λέγεται γὰρ ὡς ἔν τινι πόλει ἦν ἔμπορός τις ἔχων γυναῖκα πάνυ ὡραίαν. Ἡ δὲ γυνὴ ἐφίλει τινὰ ζωγράφον· λέγει οὖν ἡ γυνὴ τῷ μοιχῷ αὐτῆς ζωγράφῳ· 'Οὐ δύνασαί τι τεχνάσασθαι ἵνα ἐρχομένου σου πρός με, θεωροῦσά σε ἐξέρχομαι ἄνευ φωνῆς;' Ὁ δὲ εἶπε· 'Δύναμαι τοῦτο ποιῆσαι πάνυ εὐκόλως.' Καὶ λαβὼν σινδόνα, ἀνιστόρησε τὸ ὁμοίωμα αὐτῆς· καὶ ἐξελθών, πρὸς αὐτὴν ἀπῆλθε τῇ νυκτὶ ἐκείνῃ,

being investigated and inquired into become more fully known, they are truly disclosed, just as when evil-smelling material is disturbed.

"If I were aware of being at fault in this, I would not have 6
come here, but would have made a life for myself somewhere in the *wide earth*. So I think your royal majesty should carefully investigate the case against me through some arbiter who is very just, does not falsify the truth, and shows no partiality nor lends his ear to those who are jealous, since there are many such people around me because the king used to be well-disposed toward me. And if you will not do this, I have no other recourse except the compassion of God, who *tries hearts and minds*. In addition to this, I am not afraid of death, for I know it is determined and inevitable, and that every living being is mortal, even if he *has ten thousand souls*."

About an adulterous wife. 7

"Moreover, wise men have said that someone who trusts in the resemblance of things will suffer what the foolish woman did, who let herself be molested by her own slave. For it is said that there was a merchant in some city who had a very beautiful wife. But the wife was in love with a painter, and so she said to her lover, the painter, 'Can't you make something, so that, when you are coming to me, I will see it and come out without us speaking?' He said, 'I can do that very easily.' He took a scarf and painted it with her likeness and, going out, he went to her that night and showed it to

καὶ ὑπέδειξεν αὐτῇ ταύτην, καὶ ἐγένετο αὕτη περιχαρής. Λέγει οὖν ὁ ζωγράφος πρὸς αὐτήν· 'Ὅταν ἴδῃς με ταύτην τὴν σινδόνα φοροῦντα, γίνωσκε ὅτι ἐγώ εἰμι, καὶ ἀνενδοιάστως ἐξέρχου πρός με.'

8 "Ἔσχε δὲ ὁ ἔμπορος δοῦλον, καὶ εἰσελθὼν ἄφνω ἐπηκροάσατο ἅπερ πρὸς ἀλλήλους ἔλεγον. Μιᾷ δὲ τῶν ἡμερῶν παραγενομένου τοῦ ζωγράφου ἐν τῷ παλατίῳ, ἀπῆλθεν ὁ δοῦλος αὐτῆς πρὸς τὴν τοῦ ζωγράφου παιδίσκην, καὶ λέγει αὐτῇ· 'Ερωτῶ σε ὅπως μοι ἐπιδώσῃς τὴν σινδόνα τοῦ αὐθέντου σου, καὶ συντόμως σοι ταύτην ἐπαναστρέψω.' Ἡ δὲ δούλη, διὰ ἀκακίαν ἣν εἶχε, δέδωκεν αὐτῷ τὴν σινδόνα. Λαβὼν δὲ ὁ δοῦλος τὴν σινδόνα καὶ φορέσας αὐτὴν εἰσῆλθε πρὸς τὴν κυρίαν αὐτοῦ νυκτός. Ἡ δὲ ἰδοῦσα τὴν σινδόνα καὶ ὑπολαβοῦσα τὸν ζωγράφον εἶναι κατὰ τὸ σύνθημα, προσελθοῦσα μετὰ σπουδῆς, συνεγένετο αὐτῷ. Ὁ δὲ ἐξελθών, ὑπέστρεψε τὴν σινδόνα εἰς τὴν τοῦ ζωγράφου παιδίσκην. Ὁ δὲ ζωγράφος ἐλθὼν καὶ τὴν σινδόνα βαλών, εἰσῆλθεν πρὸς τὴν φιλουμένην αὐτῷ τῇ νυκτὶ ἐκείνῃ κατὰ τὸ εἰωθός. Ἐξελθοῦσα δὲ αὕτη λέγει αὐτῷ· 'Τί οὕτως σπουδαίως ὑπέστρεψας ἐν μιᾷ νυκτί, ὅπερ οὐκ ἔδρασας ἄλλοτε;' Καὶ ὁ ζωγράφος ἀκούσας ταῦτα, περίλυπος γέγονε, τὸν δόλον διαγνούς. Καὶ στραφεὶς πρὸς τὸν οἶκον αὐτοῦ, ἔτυψεν ἀφειδῶς τὴν παιδίσκην αὐτοῦ, καὶ καθωμολόγησεν αὐτῷ πάντα. Καὶ λαβὼν τὴν σινδόνα κατέκαυσεν αὐτὴν πυρί."

9 Ταῦτα διεξιὼν ὁ Ἰχνηλάτης πρὸς τὴν λέαιναν ἔφη αὐτῇ· "Ὦ κυρία μου, δίκαιόν ἐστιν τὴν βασιλικήν σου μεγαλειότητα μὴ πιστεύειν ἅπερ ἀκήκοεν κατ' ἐμοῦ. Πέφυκε γάρ

her, and she was delighted. So the painter said to her, 'When you see me wearing this scarf, you will know that it's me, and come out to me without hesitation.'

"But the merchant had a slave who came in unexpectedly 8
and overheard what they were saying to each other. One day, when the painter was at the palace, this slave went to the painter's maid and said to her, 'I'm asking you to give me your master's scarf; I'll bring it back to you right away.' And the maid, as she was naive, gave him the scarf. The servant took the scarf, put it on, and went to his master's wife that night. When she saw the scarf, she assumed it was the painter, according to their agreed signal, and went eagerly to him and had intercourse with him. The servant left and returned the scarf to the painter's maid. But the painter came and, throwing on the scarf, went to his beloved that same night, as usual. She came out and said to him, 'Why have you come back again so eagerly like this in one night, which you've never done before?' When the painter had heard these words, he became very sad, realizing the trick. He went back to his house, beat his maid mercilessly, and she confessed everything to him. Then he took the scarf and burned it in a fire."

While Ichnelates was relating these matters to the lion- 9
ess, he said to her, "My lady, it is only fair that your royal majesty should not believe what you have heard about me.

τοι καὶ τὰ ψευδῆ τῇ ἀληθείᾳ παρομοιοῦσθαι. Ἐγὼ δὲ οὐ φείδομαι ἐμαυτοῦ διὰ τὴν τοῦ βασιλέως ἀρέσκειαν." Ὑπολαβὼν δέ τις τῶν στρατιωτῶν ἔφη αὐτῷ· "Οὐ φθέγγῃ τὰ τοιαῦτα διὰ τὴν φιλικὴν πρὸς τὸν βασιλέα διάθεσιν, οὔτε μὴν διὰ τὸ πρὸς αὐτὸν σέβας, ἀλλ' ἢ διὰ σεαυτόν, ὑπεραπολογούμενος, ὧν παρηνόμησας." Ὁ δὲ Ἰχνηλάτης εἶπεν· "Οὐκ οἶσθα, ὦ ἄφρον, ὡς οὐ μεμπτέον ἐστὶ τὸ τοιοῦτον ἔργον; Καὶ τί ἕτερον τῷ ζῴῳ τῆς ἑαυτοῦ ψυχῆς τιμιώτερον; Εἰ γὰρ μὴ ἑαυτοῦ ἀπολογήσεταί τις, σχολῇ ἂν ἑτέρου ὑπερασπίσεται; Καὶ γὰρ ἐφανέρωσας τὸν φθόνον τὸν ἐνδομυχοῦντά σοι, καὶ ἀνεγνώρισας πᾶσιν, ὡς ἄφιλος εἶ καὶ ἀβέβαιος. Ἄφες οὖν τὸ προσανέχειν σε τῇ βασιλικῇ πύλῃ· ἀνάξιον γάρ ἐστι τὸ τοιοῦτόν σε ὄντα βασιλεῦσι προσεγγίζειν." Ταῦτα ἀκούσας ἐκεῖνος ἐξῆλθε κατηφής.

10 Ἡ δὲ τοῦ λέοντος μήτηρ ἔφη πρὸς τὸν Ἰχνηλάτην· "Ἄγαμαί σου τὸ προπετές, Ἰχνηλάτα, καὶ ὅπως τοιούτου κατατολμήσας ἔργου, τοιούτοις ἡμῖν καταναιδεύει τοῖς ῥήμασιν." Ὁ δὲ Ἰχνηλάτης ὑπολαβὼν εἶπε· "Ἵνα τί με δι' ἑνὸς ὄμματος ὁρᾷς, ὦ κυρία μου; Οὐχ οἶσθα, ὡς *στρεπταὶ αἱ τῶν ἐσθλῶν φρένες* εἰσίν, κατὰ ποίησιν; Ἀλλ' ὁρῶ, ὡς *πάντες* κατὰ τὸν προφήτην *ἐξέκλιναν, ἅμα ἠχρειώθησαν,* καὶ οὐδεὶς ὁ τὴν ἀλήθειαν ἀσπαζόμενος, τοῦ βασιλέως δι' ὑπερβολὴν ἀγαθότητος μήτε ἐκδειματοῦντός τινα, μήτε ἐπιπλήττοντος." Ἡ δὲ μήτηρ τοῦ λέοντος ἔφη· "Ἴδετε τὸν πονηρότατον τοῦτον καὶ ἀσεβέστατον, πῶς τοιαῦτα πράξας ἀνομήματα καὶ μεγάλοις περιπεσὼν ἐγκλήμασι, παραχαράττειν ἐπιχειρεῖ τὴν ἀλήθειαν, καὶ συλλογισμοῖς ψευδέσι, μᾶλλον δὲ παραλογισμοῖς ἀπατᾶν ἅπαντας;" Ὁ δὲ Ἰχνηλάτης·

For falsehood indeed naturally tends to assume the form of truth. But I do not spare myself because of my desire to please the king." But one of the soldiers said to him in reply, "You aren't saying this because you have a friendly attitude toward the king, nor actually out of respect for him, but because you're defending yourself for the crimes you've committed." Ichnelates said, "Don't you know, you fool, that such an action would not be blameworthy? What else is more precious to a living creature than his own life? For if someone will not defend himself, he will hardly be protected by anyone else. You've revealed the envy lurking within you, and made it known to everyone that you're hostile and unreliable. So you should give up loitering at the king's gate, for someone like you isn't worthy to be anywhere near kings." When he had heard this, the soldier left, looking dejected.

The lion's mother said to Ichnelates, "I am astonished at 10
your recklessness, Ichnelates, and how, after having dared to do this, you're insulting us with such words." But Ichnelates replied, "Why are you looking at me through one eye, my lady? Don't you know that *the minds of good people* are *easily swayed,* according to poetry? But I see that *all,* according to the prophet, *have turned aside, together they have gone wrong,* and there is no one who will welcome the truth, if the king, out of an excess of goodness, neither terrifies nor punishes anyone." And the lion's mother said, "Look how this most wicked and impious creature, who has committed such offenses and who is faced with serious charges, is trying to twist the truth and deceive everyone with lies, or rather with fallacious arguments." But Ichnelates said, "Someone

"Τοιοῦτός ἐστι, ὦ κυρία μου, ὁ τὰ μυστήρια ἐκφαυλίζων, καὶ ὁ γυναικείοις τρόποις ἀνὴρ χρώμενος καὶ ἡ ἀνδρείοις χρωμένη γυνή, καὶ ὁ λέγων ξένος ἑαυτὸν κύριον τῆς οἰκίας, καὶ ὁ παρὰ βασιλεῖ ἀπολογούμενος περὶ ὧν οὐκ ἐρωτᾶται."

11 Ἡ δὲ μήτηρ τοῦ λέοντος ἔφη· "Οὐκ οἶδας, ὦ Ἰχνηλάτα, ὅσα σὺ εἰργάσω δεινά;" Ὁ δὲ Ἰχνηλάτης εἶπεν· "Ὁ δεινὰ ἐργαζόμενος οὐκ εὐνοεῖ πρός τινα οὐδ' ἀποτρέπει μελλούσας κακίας." Ἡ δὲ μήτηρ τοῦ λέοντος ἔφη· "Μὴ ὑπολάβῃς, ὦ ἀσεβέστατε, ὡς ἐκφεύξῃ τὴν ἐκ τῆς καταδίκης τιμωρίαν διὰ τῶν ψευδῶν σου τούτων παραλογισμῶν." Ὁ δὲ Ἰχνηλάτης εἶπε· "Τοιοῦτοί εἰσιν οἱ τὰ ψευδῆ διαπλαττόμενοι καὶ τὸ δίκαιον ἐκκλίνοντες καὶ μήτε τοῖς λόγοις μήτε τοῖς ἔργοις στέργοντες." Ἰδοῦσα δὲ ἡ τοῦ λέοντος μήτηρ τὸν λέοντα μηδὲν πρὸς τὰ τοιαῦτα ἀπολογούμενον, ἔφη ἐν ἑαυτῇ· "Ἴσως κατεψεύσαντο τοῦτον οἱ διαβάλλοντες. Δοκεῖ γὰρ ἀληθῆ φθέγγεσθαι ὁ ἐπὶ μέσου τοῦ θεάτρου καὶ ἐνώπιον βασιλέως παρρησιαζόμενος καὶ παρὰ μηδενὸς ἀνατρεπόμενος." Τηνικαῦτα οὖν ὁ λέων προσέταξεν καθειρχθῆναι καὶ δεσμευθῆναι τὸν Ἰχνηλάτην, ἄχρις ἂν τὰ κατ' αὐτὸν ἐξετάσῃ. Μετὰ δὲ τὸ δεσμευθῆναι καὶ φρουρηθῆναι τοῦτον, καθωμολόγησε τῷ λέοντι ἡ μήτηρ αὐτοῦ τὸν εἰπόντα, ὡς ὁ λεοντόπαρδος ἦν. Ὁ δὲ λέων εἶπεν πρὸς αὐτήν· "Ἔασον τοῦτον, ὄψει γὰρ ἃ πείσεται."

12 Νυκτὸς δὲ ὁ Στεφανίτης πρὸς τὸν Ἰχνηλάτην παραγενόμενος καὶ δέσμιον τοῦτον θεασάμενος ἔκλαυσε καὶ ἔφη· "Ταῦτά εἰσιν, ἅπερ σοι προέλεγον, καὶ τῇ οἰήσει καὶ τῇ

like that, my lady, is a person who disparages the sacred mysteries, a man who adopts the manners of a woman, a woman who misuses those of a man, a guest who says that he is the master of the house, and someone who speaks in his own defense before a king concerning things about which he is not being questioned."

The lion's mother said, "Don't you know, Ichnelates, how 11
many terrible things you've done?" But Ichnelates replied, "Someone who does terrible things doesn't show goodwill to someone, or avert bad things that are about to happen." But the lion's mother said, "Don't assume, you most impious creature, that you can escape your condemnation and punishment through these lying fallacies of yours." But Ichnelates said, "People like that are those who concoct falsehoods, who distort what is right, and who are discontented in both their words and deeds." But when the lion's mother saw that the lion was offering nothing in defense against these points, she said to herself, "Perhaps those who cast doubt on Ichnelates were speaking falsely. For someone who speaks freely in the middle of the assembly and in the presence of the king, and who does not change his story for anyone, would appear to be telling the truth." Then the lion gave orders for Ichnelates to be locked up and bound until he could investigate the allegations against him. And after Ichnelates had been bound and imprisoned, the lion's mother confessed to him that it was the leopard who had spoken to her. But the lion said to her, "Let him be, for you will see what will happen to him."

Stephanites went to Ichnelates that night and, when he 12
saw he was a prisoner, he wept and said, "This is what I warned you about, but you were overcome by your conceit

φιλαυτίᾳ ἡττώμενος οὐ προσεδέχου. Ὅρα οὖν τὴν ἀπόβασιν." Ὁ δὲ Ἰχνηλάτης εἶπεν· "Ἀληθῶς εἶπας· οὐ γὰρ διέλειπες παραινῶν μοι τὰ συμφέροντα, ἀλλ' ἐγώ σου οὐχ ὑπήκουον ἀπληστίαν νοσῶν ὁ ἄθλιος. Πέπονθα γὰρ ταὐτόν τι τῷ τῶν νοσούντων, οἵτινες εἰδότες ὡς βλάπτονται παρά τινος τῶν ἐδεσμάτων, οὐκ ἀπέχονται τούτου. Καὶ νῦν οὐ δι' ἐμαυτὸν ἀλύω, ἀλλὰ δέδοικα περὶ σοῦ, μήποτε διὰ τὴν μεταξὺ ἡμῶν φιλίαν συλληφθήσῃ καὶ σὺ καὶ καταναγκασθήσῃ καὶ καθομολογήσῃς τὰ κατ' ἐμέ, καὶ θάνατόν μοι καταψηφίσονται ἄωρον, καὶ συναναιρεθῇς μοι τότε καὶ σύ." Ὁ δὲ Στεφανίτης εἶπε· "Κἀγὼ ταῦτα διελογησάμην, ἀλλὰ συναινῶ σοι ἅπαν ὁμολογῆσαί σου τὸ ἁμάρτημα· κρεῖττον γάρ σοι κολασθῆναι ἐνταῦθα προσκαίρως ἢ ἐκεῖ αἰωνίως." Ὁ δὲ Ἰχνηλάτης εἶπεν· "Ἀνέξομαι, μέχρις ἂν ἴδω, εἰς τί καταντήσει τὰ κατ' ἐμέ." Ὁ δὲ Στεφανίτης ὁμοῦ περίδειλος καὶ περίλυπος γεγονώς, ἀπαλλαγεὶς πέπωκε δηλητήριον καὶ ἐξέπνευσε.

13 *Ἐξέτασις δευτέρα τοῦ Ἰχνηλάτου.*

Τῇ δὲ ἐπαύριον προσεκαλέσατο ὁ λέων τόν τε κριτὴν καὶ τὸν λεοντόπαρδον καὶ τὸν Ἰχνηλάτην ὥστε ἐπὶ μέσου κριθῆναι. Καὶ συνελθόντων ἁπάντων ἔφη ὁ λεοντόπαρδος· "Ὁ βασιλεύς, ὦ συστρατιῶται, οὐ διαλείπει φροντίζων περὶ τῆς τοῦ ταύρου ἀναιρέσεως καὶ τῆς τοῦ Ἰχνηλάτου κακίστης προαιρέσεως. Εἴ τις οὖν λοιπὸν ἐξ ὑμῶν συνεῖδέ τι περὶ αὐτοῦ, ἀναφερέτω τὸ τοιοῦτον τῷ βασιλεῖ· οὐ γὰρ βούλεται ἀνεξέταστον τὴν δίκην ἐπενεγκεῖν." Ὁ δὲ

and selfishness and took no notice. Now look at the result." And Ichnelates said, "You spoke the truth, for you never stopped advising me of what was in my interest, but I, wretch that I am, did not listen to you, as I was sick with greed. For I have suffered the same thing as sick people who, although they know they are harmed by a particular kind of food, still do not avoid it. And now I'm not worried for myself, but I am afraid for you, in case you are arrested because of our friendship, and you too are tortured, and you confess about me, and they condemn me to an untimely death, and you also are then killed alongside me." And Stephanites said, "I've thought about that too, but I advise you to confess all your offenses; for it's better for you to be punished here on this one occasion than there, in the other world, forever." But Ichnelates said, "I'll hold on until I see how the case against me turns out." And Stephanites, who was terribly afraid and very sad, went off, drank poison, and died.

Ichnelates's second investigation. 13

The following day the lion summoned the judge, the leopard, and Ichnelates, so that Ichnelates could be tried in public. When everyone had gathered, the leopard said, "My fellow soldiers, the king never stops thinking about the killing of the bull, and about Ichnelates's most evil conduct. So then, if any one of you knows anything about him, let him report it to the king, for the lion does not wish to pass judgment without an investigation." The judge said, "The leop-

κριτὴς εἶπεν· "Καλῶς οὗτος ἔφη, ὦ βασιλεῦ, καὶ εἴ τις ἔγνω τι περὶ ταύτης τῆς ὑποθέσεως, ἀναγγειλάτω. Πονηροῦ γὰρ ἀνδρὸς ἀναιρουμένου συστολὴ τοῦ κακοῦ γίνεται, καὶ πρὸς τὸ συμφέρον ὁρᾷ τὸ τοιοῦτον τῆς πολιτείας." Οἱ δὲ ἀκούσαντες ἐσιώπησαν, ὁ δὲ Ἰχνηλάτης εἶπεν· "Ἵνα τί σιωπᾶτε, ὦ οὗτοι; Εἴ τις ἐξ ὑμῶν οἶδέ τι περὶ ἐμοῦ, λαλησάτω, κἀγὼ ὑπεραπολογήσομαι. Ὁ γὰρ τὰ ψευδῆ λέγων, ταὐτόν τι πείσεται τῷ τοῦ ἀμαθοῦς ἰατροῦ."

14 *Περὶ ἀμαθοῦς ἰατροῦ.*

"Λέγεται γὰρ ὅτι τις τοιοῦτος ἰατρὸς ἐπεδήμησέ τινι πόλει· ἔτυχε δὲ τὴν θυγατέρα τοῦ ἐξουσιαστοῦ τῆς πόλεως ἐκείνης νόσῳ περιπεσεῖν καὶ διωρίσατο σοφός τις ἰατρὸς τυφλὸς χρήσασθαι ταύτην ἀδιάντῳ. Προσεκλήθη οὖν ὁ ξένος ἰατρὸς ὥστε διακρῖναι τὸ ἀδίαντον ἐκ τῆς φαρμακοφόρου κύστιδος, καὶ τοῦτο ἀγνοῶν ἐντεριώνην ἀντ' αὐτοῦ προσελάβετο καὶ δέδωκε πιεῖν τῇ γυναικί. Ἡ δὲ πιοῦσα τὸ τοιοῦτον καὶ δυσεντερίᾳ περιπεσοῦσα ἐτελεύτησεν. Ἐβιάσθη οὖν ὁ ἀμαθὴς ἰατρὸς παρὰ τοῦ πατρὸς τῆς κόρης ἐκ ταύτης πιεῖν, καὶ πιὼν περὶ τὸ ζῆν ἐκινδύνευσεν.

"Οὕτως οὖν ὁ ποιῶν καὶ λέγων, ἃ οὐκ οἶδε, πείσεται."

15 Ἀναστὰς δὲ ὁ πρωτομάγειρος εἶπεν· "Ἀκούσατέ μου τῶν λόγων, ὦ συστρατιῶται, φυσιογνώμων γάρ εἰμι, καὶ προδήλως μοι ὁ Ἰχνηλάτης καταφαίνεται δόλιός τε καὶ μοχθηρότατος. Λέγεται γὰρ ὡς ὁ ἔχων τὸν ἀριστερὸν ὀφθαλμὸν τῷ μεγέθει βραχύτατον καὶ εὐκινητότατον, καὶ

ard has spoken well, my king, and if anyone knows anything about this case, let him speak up. For if a wicked man is destroyed, evil will be curtailed, and this may be seen as being to the benefit of the state." The audience kept silent, but Ichnelates said, "Why are you silent? If any one of you knows anything about me, let him speak, and I will defend myself. For someone who lies will suffer the same fate as the ignorant physician."

About an ignorant physician. 14

"For it is said that a physician of this sort went to live in a city; it happened that the daughter of the ruler of that city fell sick, and a wise physician, who was blind, prescribed that she should take maidenhair fern. So the foreign physician was summoned to identify the maidenhair fern from the bag containing the drugs, and as he did not know this plant, took out a laxative instead of it and gave it to the woman to drink. After she had drunk this, she fell ill with dysentery and died. So the ignorant physician was forced by the girl's father to drink from this potion, and when he drank it, put his own life in danger.

"That, then," said Ichnelates, "is what someone who does and says things that he does not understand will experience."

The chief cook stood up and said, "Listen to my words, 15
my fellow soldiers, for I can judge a man from his features, and Ichnelates appears clearly to me to be someone who is both treacherous and a real villain. For it is said that the sort of man who has a left eye that is very small and constantly

τὰς ὀφρύας ἀλλήλων διεστηκυίας, καὶ ἐν τῷ βαδίζειν τὴν κεφαλὴν κλίνων, συκοφάντης ὁ τοιοῦτός ἐστι καὶ πονηρότατος. Ὁρῶμεν δὲ τοιοῦτον καὶ τοῦτον τὸν ἄθλιον.” Ὁ δὲ Ἰχνηλάτης ὑπολαβὼν ἔφη· “Πάντες ἐσμὲν ὑπὸ τὸν οὐρανὸν καὶ οὐδεὶς ἡμῶν ὑπερβαίνει τοῦτον, καὶ οὗτος ὁ ταῦτα λέγων δοκεῖ σώφρων εἶναι. Εἰ οὖν, ὥς φησιν, *αἱ ψυχικαὶ δυνάμεις ἕπονται ταῖς τοῦ σώματος κράσεσι,* τί δεῖ κολάζειν τοὺς βίᾳ παρανομοῦντας, ἢ βραβεῖα χορηγεῖν τοῖς ὀρθῶς πολιτευομένοις; Ἔοικάς μοι, ὦ ἄφρον, *τὴν μὲν ἐν τῷ ὀφθαλμῷ σου δοκὸν μὴ κατανοεῖν, τὸ δὲ κάρφος τὸ ἐν τῷ ὀφθαλμῷ* τοῦ πλησίον *σου* διακρίνειν, ταὐτόν τι πεπονθὼς τῇ ἄφρονι ἐκείνῃ γυναικί.”

16 *Περὶ ἄφρονος γυναικός.*

“Λέγεται γὰρ ὡς δύο γυναῖκες μετὰ καὶ ἀνδρὸς ἔκ τινος αἰχμαλωσίας διαδράντες γυμνοὶ συνηυλίζοντο τῷ χώρῳ· καὶ ξύλα συλλέγοντες, ἡ μία ἐξ αὐτῶν ῥάκει τινὶ προστυχοῦσα τὴν ἰδίαν αἰσχύνην τούτῳ περιεκάλυψεν. Ἐπιστραφεῖσα δὲ πρὸς αὐτὴν ἡ ἑτέρα εἶπεν· ‘Οὐκ αἰσχύνῃ γυμνὴ βαδίζουσα;’ Πρὸς ἣν ὁ ἀνὴρ ἔφη· ‘Κατέλιπες, ὦ ἀσύνετε, τὸ τὴν ἰδίαν ὁρᾷν γυμνητείαν καὶ ὀνειδίζεις ταύτην ἐπὶ τούτῳ;’

“Τοιοῦτος οὖν καὶ σύ, ὦ πρωτομάγειρε, καθέστηκας καὶ σαυτὸν οὐ περισκοπεῖς δυσώδεις ἔχων ἐν τῇ σαρκὶ μώλωπας, καὶ κατατολμᾷς παρίστασθαι βασιλεῖ καὶ τὴν τούτου δίαιταν μεταχειρίζεσθαι;” Ταῦτα ἀκούσας ὁ πρωτομάγειρος μετεμελήθη ἐφ’ οἷς εἶπε καὶ ἔκλαυσε καὶ ἀναμαθὼν παρά τινος ὁ λέων τὰ λεχθέντα ἐξεδίωξε τοῦτον.

moving, who has eyebrows set apart from each other, and who walks with a bent head, is a slanderer and extremely wicked. And we see that this wretch is of that sort." But Ichnelates replied, "We all live under the sky and none of us can pass beyond it, so someone who says these things appears to be wise. If, therefore, as it says, the *spiritual faculties follow the temperaments of the body,* why is it necessary to punish those who are forced to break the law, or to reward those who lead an upright life in society? You seem to me, you fool, not to notice *the beam in* your own *eye* but to make out *the speck of sawdust in the eye of your* neighbor, and so suffer what that foolish woman did."

About a foolish woman. 16

"For it is said that two women and a man had escaped naked from some captivity and were living rough together in the country. While they were gathering wood, one of the women came across a rag, and covered her shame with it. And, turning toward the other woman, she said, 'Aren't you ashamed to be walking around naked?' And the man said to her, 'Have you forgotten seeing your own nakedness, you stupid woman, and are now reproaching her for this?'

"You're just such a person, chief cook," said Ichnelates, "for while you're standing there do you not see that you yourself have stinking sores on your body, and yet dare to serve a king and manage his diet?" When he had heard this, the chief cook regretted what he had said and wept, and when the lion learned from someone what had been said, he banished him.

17 Καὶ ἐσημειώθη ἐν γραφῇ τὰ τῆς δίκης καὶ αὖθις καθείρχθη ὁ Ἰχνηλάτης. Ἕτερος δέ τις φίλος τοῦ Ἰχνηλάτου παρεγένετο πρὸς αὐτὸν καὶ ἀνήγγειλεν αὐτῷ τὸν τοῦ Στεφανίτου θάνατον, ἐφ' ᾧ πάνυ λυπηθεὶς καὶ πικρῶς κλαύσας ἔφη· "Τί με δεῖ ζῆν ἔτι; ἀσπάσασθε σήμερον στερηθέντα φίλου τοιούτου, φιλτάτου τε καὶ εὐγνώμονος! Κάλλιστα οὖν ἔφησεν ὁ εἰπὼν ὡς ἐν καιρῷ πειρασμοῦ συρρέει πανταχόθεν τὰ δεινά." Εἶτα καὶ αὖθις παρέστη τῷ δικαστηρίῳ καὶ ἰδὼν τοῦτον ὁ στρατηγὸς ἔφη· "Ἔγνων, ὦ Ἰχνηλάτα, τὰ ἔργα σου καὶ οὐ καταλέλειπταί τι σημεῖον περὶ σοῦ ἀμφιβολίας, καὶ εἰ μὴ ἦν ἡ τοῦ βασιλέως εὐσπλαγχνία μεγίστη καὶ ἄπειρος, οὐκ ἂν μέχρι τοῦδέ σε ζῆν εἴασεν." Καὶ ὁ Ἰχνηλάτης εἶπεν· "Εἰ καὶ πολλὴ καὶ ἄπειρος ἡ ἐκείνου εὐσπλαγχνία, ἀλλὰ νικᾷ ἡ ἀνεξίτητός σου ἀπήνεια καὶ σκληροκαρδία. Ὁρῶ γάρ σε τῶν σῶν θελημάτων ἀνδράποδον, καὶ πρὸ τῆς καταδίκης μου βίαιον καταψηφιζόμενον θάνατον· καὶ οὐ μέμφομαί σοι τοῦδε τοῦ τρόπου· ἀεὶ γὰρ οἱ φαῦλοι τοῖς σπουδαίοις ἀντικαθίστανται."

18 Ὁ δὲ κριτὴς ὑπολαβὼν ἔφη· "Δεῖ τοὺς ἄρχοντας ἐπ' ἀληθείᾳ παρρησιάζεσθαι καὶ ἐλέγχειν καὶ ἐπιτιμᾶν τοῖς ἀπαιδεύτοις ἀνδράσιν. Ἀλλὰ συναινῶ σοι, ὦ Ἰχνηλάτα, προαιρεῖσθαί σε ἐνταῦθα κολασθῆναι ἢ ἐν τῷ μέλλοντι αἰῶνι παρὰ τοῦ Θεοῦ· καθομολόγησον τοίνυν τὴν ἀλήθειαν." Ὁ δὲ Ἰχνηλάτης εἶπεν· "Καλῶς ἔφης, ὦ δικαστα, δεῖ γὰρ ἅπαντα νουνεχῆ τῶν προσκαίρων προκρίνειν τὰ ἀΐδια. Ἀλλ' ἀθῷός εἰμι τοῦδε τοῦ ἐγκλήματος καὶ οὐ δεῖ με κοινωνὸν γενέσθαι ὑμῖν τῆς ὑπὲρ τοῦ αἵματός μου νῦν ἀντεκτίσεως. Εἰ γὰρ ὁ ἑτέρου καταψευδόμενος ἀσύνετος

The details of the trial were recorded in writing, and Ichnelates was once again imprisoned. Another of Ichnelates's friends came to him and told him of Stephanites's death. He was greatly saddened by this and, after weeping bitterly, he said, "Why should I go on living? Embrace me, for I have today been deprived of this most beloved and kind friend! He who said that, in trying times, bad things flow together from all directions, spoke very well." Then, when Ichnelates was present in court again, the general saw him and said, "Ichnelates, I know what you do, and there remains not a shadow of a doubt about you, and if the king's mercy were not vast and boundless, he would not have allowed you to live this long." And Ichnelates said, "Although his mercy is indeed great and boundless, your inexorable cruelty and hardness of heart conquers it. For I see that you are a slave to your wishes, and a violent death is being decreed before my condemnation. And I don't blame you for acting this way, for bad people always oppose good people." 17

The judge replied, "Rulers must speak the truth openly, and refute and reprove ignorant men. But I advise you, Ichnelates, to choose to be punished here and now, rather than in the future by God; so now, confess the truth." But Ichnelates said, "You have spoken well, judge, for every sensible person should prefer the eternal to the transitory. But I am innocent of the charge, and I should not now make myself your accomplice in seeking retribution with my blood. For if someone who slanders another person is reckoned to be stupid, then how much more is someone who 18

λογίζεται, πόσῳ μᾶλλον ὁ ἑαυτοῦ; Ἴδετε οὖν, μήπως μεταμεληθήσεσθε, ὁπότε μὴ λυσιτελῇ ὁ μετάμελος, καὶ ἴδετε, μὴ ταὐτόν τι πείσεσθε τῷ ἀμαθῶς λέγοντι καὶ ἃ μὴ οἶδε μαρτυροῦντι."

19 *Περὶ ψεύστου.*

"Λέγεται γὰρ ὥς τις ἱερακάριος ἠράσθη τῆς γυναικὸς τοῦ κυρίου αὐτοῦ· ἡ δὲ ἀπεστρέφετο τούτου. Καὶ ὀργισθεὶς ἐπὶ ταύτῃ, ἐθήρευσεν ἐν μιᾷ τῶν ἡμερῶν κίσσας δύο καὶ ἐδίδαξε τὴν μὲν μίαν λέγειν τῇ Περσίδι διαλέκτῳ ὡς· 'Εἶδον τὴν κυρίαν μου συγγινομένην τῷ πυλωρῷ·' τὴν δὲ ἑτέραν ὡς· ''Εγὼ οὐδὲν λέγω.' Μιᾷ δὲ τῶν ἡμερῶν ἔτυχεν τὸν κύριον αὐτοῦ Πέρσαις τισὶ συνδιαιτᾶσθαι· οἳ δὴ καὶ ἀκούσαντες τῶν κισσῶν ᾐδέσθησαν, εἶτα καὶ αὐτά, ἅπερ αἱ κίσσαι ἔλεγον, ἀνήγγειλαν. Ὁ δὲ ἱερακάριος ἔξωθεν παρεστηκὼς ἔφη· 'Κἀγὼ συμμαρτυρῶ, ὡς καὶ τὸ τοιοῦτον εἶδον οὐχ ἅπαξ ἀλλὰ καὶ πολλάκις.' Ὁ δὲ θυμοῦ πλησθεὶς ἔμελλε τὴν ἰδίαν γυναῖκα ἀποκτεῖναι· ἡ δὲ τῷ ἰδίῳ ἀνδρὶ τὰ περὶ τοῦ ἱερακαρίου ἀνήγγειλε καὶ ὡς δόλον ὁ τοιοῦτος κατ' αὐτῆς συνέρραψε διὰ τὸ μὴ πεισθῆναι αὐτῷ περὶ τὴν αἰσχρουργίαν, καὶ ὡς οὐχ ἑτέραν λέξιν Περσικὴν οἴδασιν αἱ κίσσαι πλὴν τοῦ λόγου, οὗ ἐδιδάχθησαν. Καὶ ἐπερωτήσαντες οἱ Πέρσαι τὰς κίσσας περί τινων ἑτέρων ὑποθέσεων εὗρον αὐτὰς μηδὲν ἕτερον μαθούσας ἢ τὸ αἰσχρὸν ἐκεῖνο ἀπόφθεγμα. Ἐλθοῦσα δὲ ἡ γυνὴ πρὸς τὸν ἱερακάριον ἔφη· 'Οὐ φοβῇ τὸν Θεόν, τοιαῦτά μου καταμαρτυρῶν; Οὕτως ἔχει τὸ πρᾶγμα;' Ὁ δὲ εἶπε· 'Ναί, οὕτως

slanders himself? So make sure you don't feel regret when regret is of no use, and make sure you don't suffer the fate of someone who speaks in ignorance and testifies to things he didn't see."

About a liar. 19

"For it is said that a falconer fell in love with his master's wife, but she rejected him. As he was angry with her, he caught two jays one day and taught one of them to say in Persian, 'I saw my lady sleeping with the doorkeeper,' and the other to say, 'I'm saying nothing.' One day his master was dining with some Persians, and when they had heard the jays, they were embarrassed and then told the master what the jays were saying. And the falconer, who was standing outside, said, 'I too bear witness with them, and I saw this not once but often.' Filled with rage, the husband was about to kill his wife, but she told him about the falconer, and that he had treacherously devised this trick against her because she had not been persuaded by him to act shamefully, and that the jays knew no other Persian expression than the phrase that they had been taught. When the Persians questioned the jays about some other subjects, they found that they had learned nothing except that shameful assertion. The wife went up to the falconer and said, 'Don't you fear God in testifying against me about this? Is this what really happened?' And he said, 'Yes, it is.' And while he

ἔχει.' Καὶ ταῦτα αὐτοῦ πρὸς τὴν γυναῖκα λέγοντος ἄφνω ὁ ἱέραξ ἐκπηδήσας τοὺς ὀφθαλμοὺς αὐτοῦ ἐξεκέντησεν.

"Οὕτως ἄρα καὶ ὑμεῖς πείσεσθε, εἰ ψευδῶς μου καταμαρτυρήσετε."

20 *Περὶ ἐγκαθείρξεως τρίτης τοῦ Ἰχνηλάτου καὶ τῆς αὐτοῦ ἀναιρέσεως.*

Μηδενὸς οὖν τὸν Ἰχνηλάτην καταδικάσαι ἐξ ἐκείνων ἰσχύσαντος αὖθις ἐφρουρήθη ἐφ' ἡμέρας ἑπτά. Ἡ δὲ μήτηρ τοῦ λέοντος ἐν τῷ μεταξὺ πρὸς τὸν λέοντα ἔφησεν· "Εἰ τὸν ἀσεβέστατον τοῦτον τοῦ ἐγκλήματος ἀπολύσεις, ἴσθι ὡς ἕκαστος τῶν ὑπὸ σέ, ὅπερ κἀκεῖνος βούλεται, ἀνυποστόλως διαπράξεται, πληροφορούμενος τὸ μὴ εὐθύνας ἀπαιτηθῆναι ὧν διεπράξατο." Ἰδὼν οὖν ὁ λέων τὴν ἔνστασιν τῆς ἰδίας μητρὸς προσέταξέ τινι τῶν ὑπηρετῶν αὐτοῦ τὸν Ἰχνηλάτην ἀναιρεθῆναι. Καὶ οὕτως ἀμοιβαῖον τέλος τῶν ἔργων αὐτοῦ ὁ Ἰχνηλάτης ἐδέξατο.

Εἶτα ὁ φιλόσοφος εἶπεν· "Σκοπητέον τὰ τοιαῦτα καὶ συγγνωστέον, ὡς πᾶς τις ἀνὴρ δόλον καθ' ἑτέρου συρράπτων, ἐμπεσεῖται εἰς βόθρον, ὃν εἰργάσατο."

was saying this to the wife, the falcon suddenly leaped up and pecked out his eyes.

"And that's what you will suffer too," said Ichnelates, "if you testify falsely against me."

About Ichnelates's third imprisonment 20
and his killing.

As none of them was able to convict Ichnelates, he was again imprisoned for seven days. Meanwhile the lion's mother said to the lion, "If you acquit that most impious creature from the charge, you should know that each of your subjects will do whatever he wants without fear, being fully assured that he will not be called to account for what he has done." When the lion understood his mother's position, he gave orders to one of his officers for Ichnelates to be killed. And in this way Ichnelates received his just deserts for his actions.

Then the philosopher said, "One must consider these matters carefully and bear in mind that everybody who contrives a trap for someone else is going to fall into the pit which he has made."

[Chapter 3]

Ἀρχὴ τοῦ τρίτου τμήματος.

Καὶ πάλιν ὁ βασιλεὺς τῷ φιλοσόφῳ εἶπεν· "Διέγνων τὰ τοιαῦτα παραδείγματα, λοιπὸν οὖν ἀνάγγειλόν μοι ὑπόδειγμά τινων ἀντιφιλούντων ἀλλήλοις καὶ τῇ φιλίᾳ ἀεὶ συστοιχούντων." Ὑπολαβὼν δὲ ὁ φιλόσοφος εἶπε·

Φίλου πιστοῦ οὐκ ἔστιν ἀντάλλαγμα τῶν ὄντων οὐδὲν καὶ δεῖγμα τοῦτο σαφέστατον τὸ τοῦ κόρακος καὶ τοῦ μυὸς καὶ τῆς δορκάδος καὶ τῆς χελώνης.

2 *Περὶ κόρακος καὶ μυὸς καὶ χελώνης καὶ δορκάδος.*

Λέγεται γὰρ ὡς ἔν τινι πόλει τόπος ἦν τις πρὸς θήραν ἐπιτήδειος, ἐφ' ᾧ τις τῶν θηρευτῶν συχνῶς παρεγένετο. Ἦν δὲ ἐκεῖσε καὶ δένδρον ὑψιπέτηλον καὶ συνηρεφές, καὶ ἐνεφώλευε τούτῳ κόραξ. Μιᾷ δὲ τῶν ἡμερῶν εἶδέ τινα θηρευτὴν ἐκ τοῦ δένδρου δυσειδῆ, τῷ μὲν τραχήλῳ δίκτυον ἐπιφερόμενον, ῥάβδον δὲ τῇ χειρὶ κατέχοντα. Καὶ τοῦτον ἰδὼν ἐδειλίασε καὶ διελογίσατο ἐν ἑαυτῷ ἐμμεῖναι τῷ οἰκείῳ φωλεῷ καὶ θεάσασθαι, τί μέλλει ὁ τοιοῦτος ποιῆσαι· ὁ δὲ θηρευτὴς τὸ δίκτυον ἐξήπλωσε καὶ ἐπ' αὐτῷ σίτου

Chapter 3

BEGINNING OF THE THIRD CHAPTER.

Again, the king said to his philosopher, "I have understood these lessons, so now give me an example of people who are friends with each other and who always support each other in their friendship." And the philosopher said in reply:

There is nothing in existence that is a substitute for a faithful friend, and the clearest example of this is the story of the crow, the mouse, the gazelle, and the turtle.

About a crow, a mouse, a turtle, and a gazelle. 2

For it is said that in a certain city there was a place that was well suited for hunting, and which a hunter used to visit frequently. There was a tall, shady tree there, and a crow used to nest in it. One day, he saw from the tree an unpleasant-looking hunter carrying a hunting net around his neck and holding a stick in his hand. When the crow saw him, he was afraid and said to himself that he should stay in his own nest and see what this man was going to do. The hunter spread out the net and scattered grains of corn over it. One dove,

κόκκους ἀπέρριψε. Περιστερὰ δέ τις τῶν ἄλλων προκριτωτέρα τοὺς μὲν κόκκους ἰδοῦσα τὸ δὲ δίκτυον μὴ θεασαμένη ἐμπέπτωκεν αὐτῷ μετὰ τῶν λοιπῶν περιστερῶν τῶν ὑπ' αὐτῇ. Ὁ δὲ θηρευτὴς ηὐφράνθη τὰ μέγιστα· ἤρξαντο δὲ αἱ περιστεραὶ συνταράττεσθαι καὶ ἑκάστη τὴν ἰδίαν πραγματεύεσθαι σωτηρίαν. Ἡ δὲ τούτων κυρία ἔφη· "Μὴ θορυβῆσθε, ἀλλ' ὁμοῦ ἀλλήλαις συνασπισώμεθα εἴποτε δυνηθείημεν ἆραι τὸ δίκτυον." Καὶ τοῦτο ποιήσασαι ἦραν εἰς ἀέρα τὸ δίκτυον.

3 Ὅπερ ἰδὼν ὁ θηρευτὴς ἐθαύμασε μέν, οὐκ ἀπέγνω δέ, ἀλλ' ἠκολούθει μακρόθεν ταύταις ἐπὶ προσδοκίᾳ τοῦ μὴ ἐπὶ πολὺ προήκειν. Ὁ δὲ κόραξ δεῖν ἔγνω ἕψεσθαι ταύταις καὶ ἰδεῖν ὅποι καταντήσει τὰ κατ' αὐτάς. Ἡ δὲ κυρία τῶν περιστερῶν ἰδοῦσα τὸν θηρευτὴν ταύταις ἑπόμενον εἶπε πρὸς αὐτάς· "'Ὁ ἁλιεὺς' οὗτος ἕπεται ἡμῖν, καὶ εἰ κατὰ πεδίον τὴν πτῆσιν ποιησόμεθα, οὐκ ἀπόσχηται ἀκολουθεῖν. Εἰ δ' ἐπ' ὀρέων καὶ δυσβάτων τόπων τὴν πτῆσιν ποιησόμεθα, τάχιστ' ἂν ἡμῶν ἀπογνῷ. Πρὸς δὲ τούτοις ἔχω κατὰ ταύτην τὴν ὁδὸν μῦν φίλον, καὶ εἴ γε εἰς τοῦτον καταντήσομεν, τοὺς περιδέσμους ἡμῶν τοῖς ὀδοῦσι διαρρήξει καὶ ἡμᾶς τοῦ θανάτου ἐλευθερώσει." Ἰδὼν οὖν ὁ θηρευτὴς ταύτας τοιάνδε τὴν βουλὴν διαπραξαμένας, ἀπέγνω καὶ ὑπέστρεψεν.

4 Ὁ δὲ κόραξ ἠκολούθησε ταύταις, ἅμα τε τὸν τρόπον τῆς αὐτῶν σωτηρίας μαθησόμενος, καὶ τὸν φίλον αὐτῶν, τὸν μῦν, θεασόμενος. Ὡς οὖν ἐπὶ τῷ φωλεῷ αὐτοῦ γεγόνασιν, κατῆλθον ἐπὶ τὴν γῆν. Ὁ δὲ μῦς ἐξελθὼν καὶ ἰδὼν τὴν περιστερὰν περιχαρῶς ὑπεδέξατο καὶ εἶπεν· "Τίς σε

who was the leader of the others, saw the grains but did not notice the net, and fell into it with the other doves that were her followers. The hunter was extremely pleased, but the doves became agitated and each tried to save herself. But their mistress said, “Don’t panic, but let’s all work together so that we may perhaps be able to lift up the net.” They did this, and lifted the net into the air.

When the hunter saw this, he was amazed but did not 3
give up, and he followed them at a distance, expecting they would not go far. And the crow decided he should follow them, to see how things would turn out for them. When the mistress of the doves saw the hunter following them, she said to them, “This ‘fisherman’ is following us, and if we fly at the speed he is walking, he won’t stop pursuing us. But if we direct our flight toward mountains and inaccessible places, he may soon give up on us. In addition, I have a mouse friend along this road, and if we can reach him, he will gnaw through our bonds with his teeth and will set us free from death.” When the hunter saw them following this plan, he gave up and turned back.

But the crow followed them so that he would learn the 4
means of their escape and see their friend, the mouse. So when the doves had reached his nest, they landed on the ground. The mouse came out and, when he saw the dove, he welcomed her very happily and said, “My dear friend, who

τοῖς τοιούτοις δεινοῖς, ὦ φιλτάτη, περιέπλεξεν;" Ἡ δὲ ἔφη· "Οὐκ οἶσθα, ὡς τἀγαθὰ καὶ τὰ φαῦλα τῶν πραγμάτων πέπρωται; Ἡ εἱμαρμένη με τοῖς τοιούτοις περιέπλεξε καὶ πρὸς τοὺς κόκκους τοῦ σίτου ὡδήγησε καὶ ἀβλεψίᾳ τοῦ δέοντος περιέπειρεν ὥστε με τῷ δικτύῳ περιπλακῆναι. Οὐκ οὖν θαυμαστὸν τὸ τοιούτῳ περιπεσεῖν με συμπτώματι, μείζονες γὰρ ἢ ἔγωγε μείζοσι περιέπεσον· ὅ τε γὰρ ἥλιος τῇ σελήνῃ ἐπισκοτούμενος ἐκλείπει καὶ ἡ σελήνη τῇ σκιᾷ τῆς γῆς συγκαλύπτεται, καὶ ὁ θαλάττιος ἰχθὺς ἐκ βάθους τῷ κλύδωνι συναρπάζεται καὶ τὰ πετεινὰ ἐξ ἀέρος κατάγεται, ὅταν ὁρισθῇ τούτοις. Καὶ δι' οὗ πολλάκις ὁ ἀσύνετος τυγχάνει τῶν ἐφετῶν, δι' αὐτοῦ ἐκείνου ὁ ἐχέφρων ἀποτυγχάνει τῶν κατὰ σκοπόν."

5 Ταῦτα εἰπούσης τῆς περιστερᾶς, ἤρξατο ὁ μῦς τοὺς δεσμοὺς κατεσθίειν καὶ λύειν τῆς κυρίας τῶν περιστερῶν. Ἡ δὲ περιστερὰ ἔφη· "Ἄρξαι πρῶτον ἐλευθεροῦν τὰς ὑπ' ἐμέ, εἶτα ἐμέ·" ὁ δὲ μῦς, μὴ ἐπιστραφεὶς τῶν αὐτῆς λόγων πλέον ἐπέκειτο τοῦ ἀπολῦσαι αὐτήν. Ὡς οὖν ἐπὶ μακρὸν τὸν λόγον ἐκτείνασα οὐκ ἠκούετο, ἔφη τῷ μυΐ· "Μὴ μέμφου μοι, ὦ μῦ, ὑπὲρ ὧν σοι προστάσσω. Ἐπεὶ γὰρ δέδωκέ μοι ὁ Θεὸς τὴν κατ' αὐτῶν ἐξουσίαν, ἐποφείλεται παρ' ἐμοῦ ταύταις ἡ τούτων πρόνοια, ἐπεὶ καὶ εὐγνωμόνως μοι αὗται καθυπηρέτησαν, καὶ διὰ τῆς τούτων συμμαχίας καὶ συναντιλήψεως ὁ Θεὸς ἡμᾶς τῶν τοῦ θηρευτοῦ παγίδων ἠλευθέρωσεν. Δέδοικα δὲ πρὸς τούτοις μήπως εἰ πρότερόν με λύσῃς καὶ πρός τινας τούτων καταντήσας ἀπείπῃς, καὶ ὡς δειλιῶν ἐάσῃς ταύτας δεσμίας καὶ ἀνεκλύτους. Εἰ γὰρ ἔγωγε μόνη καταλειφθείην, διὰ τὴν φιλίαν ἣν ἔχομεν ἴσως

entangled you in this terrible mess?" But she said, "Don't you know that both good and bad things are fated? Destiny entangled me in them, and led me to the grains of corn, and afflicted me with blindness, as had to happen for me to get entangled in the net. It's not surprising I met with this mishap, for those greater than me have met with worse: for the sun is left in the dark by the moon, and the moon is hidden by the shadow of the earth; the fish is plucked from the depths of the sea by a wave; and the birds are brought down from the sky whenever it is ordained for them. And for the very reason that the foolish man often gets what he wants, for that same reason the wise one fails to attain his goals."

When the dove had said this, the mouse began to gnaw 5
through the cords and to free the mistress of the doves first. But she said, "Start by freeing the doves who are my subjects first, and then me." But the mouse did not listen to her words and pressed on even more to set her free. So, when she was not heeded, despite having repeated her request many times over, she said to the mouse, "Don't find fault with me, mouse, for what I told you to do. For since God has given me authority over them, I owe them my care, because they gladly assisted me, and, through their alliance and support, God delivered us from the traps of the hunter. But I'm also worried that, if you free me first, when you get to some of them, you'll give up and, becoming discouraged, you'll leave them still prisoners and not freed. However, if I alone am left, you'll have to release me from my bonds because of

ἀναγκασθήσῃ τῶν δεσμῶν ἀπολύειν με.” Ὁ δὲ μῦς ὑπολαβὼν λέγει αὐτῇ· “Οὗτοί σου οἱ λόγοι ἐπὶ πλέον σε φιλεῖν τοὺς ὑπὸ σὲ καὶ τοὺς οἰκείους διερεθίζουσι.” Καὶ ταῦτα εἰπὼν ἔλυσε πάσας τῶν δεσμῶν καὶ λυθεῖσαι ἀπηλλάγησαν.

6 Ἰδὼν οὖν ὁ κόραξ τότε τὸ πραχθέν, κατῆλθεν ἐπὶ τὴν τοῦ μυὸς πρόσδυσιν καὶ ἐφώνησε τοῦτον. Ὁ δὲ μῦς εἶπε· “Τίς εἶ, σὺ φίλτατε;” Ὁ δὲ κόραξ ἔφη· “Ἐγώ εἰμι ὁ κόραξ, καὶ ἰδών σου τὴν πρὸς φίλους διάθεσιν, ἠθέλησα καὶ αὐτὸς φιλιωθῆναί σοι, καὶ ἐπὶ τούτῳ προσῆλθόν σοι.” Ὁ δὲ μῦς εἶπε· “Τί κοινὸν ἐμοί τε καὶ σοί; Δεῖ γὰρ τὸν νουνεχῆ τὰ δυνατά, οὐ τὰ ἀδύνατα ἐπιζητεῖν· ὁ γὰρ τοιούτοις ἐπιχειρῶν, ἔοικε τῷ καθ’ ὕδατος ἐλαύνοντι ἅμαξαν, ἐπὶ δὲ ξηρᾶς πλοῖον. Πῶς γάρ σοι καὶ ἔσομαι φίλος βρῶσις ὑπάρχων σοι;” Ὁ δὲ κόραξ ἔφη· “Διάκρινε ἐν τῷ σῷ λογισμῷ τὰ εἰκότα· οὐδὲν γάρ μοι λυσιτελεῖ τὸ διὰ σοῦ τραφῆναι· πόσῳ γάρ μοι τούτου ὠφελιμώτερον τὸ τοῖς ζῶσι συνεῖναί σοι καὶ συνεργεῖν μοι ἐν ἅπασιν; Οὐ δεῖ σε οὖν κενόν με ἀποπέμψασθαι τῶν ἐλπίδων· πεπληροφόρημαι γάρ σου τὴν περὶ τοὺς φίλους εὔνοιαν, κἂν μή συ ταύτην μοι ὑπέδειξας. Ἡ γὰρ τοῦ σπουδαίου ἀρετὴ τῇ τοῦ μόσχου ἔοικεν εὐωδίᾳ, ἥτις καὶ συγκαλυπτομένη διαχεῖται καὶ τοῖς πᾶσι κατάδηλος γίνεται.”

7 Ὁ δὲ μῦς εἶπε· “Μεγίστη ἐστὶν ἡ οὐσιώδης ἔχθρα, αὕτη δὲ διττή ἐστιν· ἡ μὲν ἀντεριστικὴ λεγομένη, ὡς ἡ τοῦ λέοντος καὶ τοῦ ἐλέφαντος, ἡ δὲ φευκτή τε καὶ διωκτική, ὡς ἡ τῆς κάττης καὶ τοῦ μυός. Καὶ οὐ δεῖ πιστεύειν ἐχθροῖς· τὸ γὰρ ὕδωρ κἂν τῷ πυρὶ θερμανθῇ, ἀλλ’ οὐ τὴν οἰκείαν

our friendship." The mouse said to her in reply, "These words of yours encourage your subjects and their relatives to love you even more." And when he had said this, he freed them all from their bonds, and they went off.

So, when the crow saw what the mouse had done, he went 6
down to his hole and called to him. The mouse said, "Who are you, my friend?" And the crow said, "I'm the crow and, since I've seen your attitude toward friendship, I too want to become your friend; and that's why I've come to you." And the mouse said, "What do you and I have in common? For a smart person should desire what is possible, not what is impossible; someone who tries the latter is like a person pulling a wagon across water and a ship over dry land. For how will I be your friend, when I'm food for you?" And the crow said, "Think about what's likely to happen, for it's of no benefit to me if I feed on you. How much better would it be for you to be alive and helping me in everything? You shouldn't send me away with my hopes unfulfilled; for I'm fully convinced of your affection for your friends, even if you haven't shown it to me. For the virtue of a good person is like the fragrance of musk, which, even when it is covered up, spreads and becomes known to everyone."

The mouse said, "Natural enmity is very powerful, and 7
this is twofold: on the one hand there is what is called enmity of competition, like that between the lion and the elephant, and on the other, the enmity of the pursued and the pursuer, like that between the cat and the mouse. And no one should trust their enemy; for water, even if heated on the fire, does not lose its own nature, and still extinguishes

φύσιν ἀποβάλλει, ἐπεὶ καὶ τῷ πυρὶ ἐπιχεόμενον σβέννυσι τοῦτο." Ὁ δὲ κόραξ ἔφη· "Ἔγνων ἃ λέγεις, ἀλλ' ἡ πρός σέ μου φιλία οὐ τοιαύτη γενήσεται, ἀλλὰ στερέμνιος καὶ παγία. Ὥσπερ γὰρ τὸ χρυσοῦν ἀγγεῖον δυσκέδαστόν ἐστι καὶ εὐκατασκεύαστον, τὸ δὲ ὀστράκινον εὔθραυστον μέν, δυσανάκτιστον δέ, οὕτω καὶ ἡ εἰλικρινὴς φιλία δυσμετάβλητός ἐστι καὶ εὐανάδοτος, ἡ δὲ μὴ καθαρὰ εὔφθαρτος καὶ δυσίατος."

8 Ὁ δὲ μῦς εἶπεν· "Δέχομαί σου τὴν φιλίαν, ἐπεὶ οὐδέποτέ τινα τῶν δεομένων μου κενὸν ἀπέπεμψα, ἀλλὰ τούτοις τοῖς λόγοις ἐμαυτῷ μᾶλλον ἀπόλογον ποιῆσαι ᾑρετισάμην ἢ σοί. Εἰ γάρ ποτε καιροῦ ἀνατρέψεις τὰς ἡμετέρας συνθήκας, οὐκ ἂν ἔχοις εἰπεῖν· 'Εὗρον τὸν μῦν ἀσύνετον καὶ ἠπάτησα τοῦτον καὶ ἐδελέασα.'" Εἶτα προέκυψε τῆς οἰκείας καταδύσεως, ὁ δὲ κόραξ ἔφη· "Τί μὴ τέλεον ἐξέρχῃ πρός με;" Ὁ δὲ μῦς εἶπεν· "Οἱ ἐν τῷ βίῳ ἀναστρεφόμενοι κατὰ δύο τρόπους ἀλλήλους ἀντιφιλοῦσιν· οἱ μέν ψυχικῶς, οἱ δὲ χρειωδῶς. Καὶ ψυχικῶς μὲν φιλοῦσιν ὅσοι μὴ δι' ἄλλο τι τὸν φίλον ἀσπάζονται, ἢ διὰ τὴν ἑαυτῶν ψυχήν· οἱ δὲ χρειωδῶς φιλοῦντες ἕνεκά τινος ἑτέρου τῶν βιωτικῶν πραγμάτων τὴν φιλίαν συνιστῶσι. Καὶ ἐοίκασιν οὗτοι τῷ θηρευτῇ, ὃς ὑπορρίπτει τὸν σῖτον δέλεαρ κάτωθεν τοῖς πτηνοῖς, οὐ ταῦτα φιλοτιμούμενος ἀλλ' ἑαυτῷ τὸ συμφέρον ποιούμενος. Ἔγωγε οὖν οὐ δι' ἄλλο τι ἢ διὰ σεαυτὸν ἐφιλιώθην σοι καὶ οὐδὲν ἕτερον κωλύει με τῆς πρὸς σὲ ἐξελεύσεως ἀλλ' ἢ τὸ δεδοικέναι τοὺς ὁμοειδεῖς καὶ ὁμοουσίους σοι, οἳ κατὰ μὲν τὴν οὐσίαν καὶ τὸ εἶδος κοινωνοῦσί σοι, κατὰ δὲ τὴν γνώμην διαλλάττουσιν." Ὁ

the fire when poured onto it." And the crow said, "I understand what you're saying, but my friendship toward you will not be like that, but rather will be firm and steadfast. For just as a gold vessel is hard to break but easy to make, an earthenware pot is easily damaged but hard to mend. In the same way the sincerest friendship is hard to change, but that which is not pure is easily damaged and difficult to repair."

The mouse said, "I accept your friendship, since I have 8
never sent anyone who asked me for something away empty-handed, but with these words I have chosen to create a defense for myself rather than for you. For if at some time you should overturn our agreement, you would not be able to say, 'I discovered the mouse was a fool, and I deceived and entrapped him.'" Then he peeped out from his nest and the crow said, "Why won't you come out to me completely?" And the mouse said, "While leading their lives, people love each other in two ways: some do so spiritually, others out of need. Those who love spiritually, embrace their friend for nothing other than their own soul's sake; but those who love out of need establish the friendship on account of some other material reasons. The latter are like the hunter, who throws down grain for the birds as bait, not out of generosity but doing it for his own benefit. So the only reason I myself have become your friend is for your own sake, and the only thing that prevents me from coming out to you is the fear of those who are of the same shape and the same kind as you—those who share their kind and shape with you, but

δὲ κόραξ ἔφη· "Μὴ φοβοῦ τούτου ἕνεκα· τῆς γὰρ εἰλικρινοῦς φιλίας τεκμήριον τὸ φιλιοῦσθαι τῷ φίλῳ τοῦ φίλου καὶ ἐχθραίνεσθαι τῷ ἐχθρῷ αὐτοῦ. Κἀμοῦ σε ποθοῦντος καὶ οἱ μετ' ἐμοῦ σε συμποθήσουσι." Ταῦτα εἰπόντος τοῦ κόρακος ἐξῆλθεν ὁ μῦς καὶ ἡ φιλία μεταξὺ τούτων ἐπαγιώθη.

9 Μιᾷ δὲ τῶν ἡμερῶν ὁ κόραξ ἔφη· "Ὁρῶ σου τὴν κατάδυσιν πλησίον τῆς ὁδοῦ καὶ δέδοικα μὴ δι' ἐμοῦ διαγνωσθῇ σου ἡ κατοίκησις. Ἀλλ' οἶδα τόπον κεχωρισμένον, ἐν ᾧ ἰχθύες ἱκανοὶ καὶ ἕτεραι διατροφαὶ δαψιλεῖς ὑπάρχουσιν. Ἔστι δέ μοι ἐν αὐτῷ καὶ φίλη χελώνη καὶ βούλομαι ἐκεῖσε ἀπελθεῖν καὶ ἀναστρέφεσθαι." Ὁ δὲ μῦς εἶπε· "Συμπορεύσομαί σοι κἀγώ, ἐμίσησα γὰρ τὴν ἐνταῦθα διαγωγήν, δι' ἃς μέλλω σοι ἀφηγήσασθαι αἰτίας περί τινος ἄλλου τόπου διαγωγήν, ὅτε τὸν τόπον ἐκεῖνον καταλήψομαι." Λαβὼν οὖν ὁ κόραξ τὸν μῦν διὰ τῆς οὐρᾶς ἀπήγαγεν τοῦτον ἐπὶ τὴν πηγήν, ἐν ᾗ ἡ χελώνη διῆγεν. Ὡς οὖν εἶδεν αὐτὴ τὸν κόρακα μῦν ἐπιφερόμενον, ἔδοξε ἀλλότριον τοῦτον εἶναι καὶ δειλιάσασα ὑπεκρύβη τῷ ὕδατι. Θεὶς οὖν ὁ κόραξ τὸν μῦν ἐπὶ τῆς γῆς, ὀνομαστὶ τὴν χελώνην προσεκαλέσατο. Ἡ δὲ χελώνη τὴν τούτου φωνὴν γνωρίσασα ἐξῆλθε πρὸς αὐτὸν καὶ ἠρώτησε πόθεν παρεγένετο. Ὁ δὲ ἀνήγγειλεν αὐτῇ ἅπαντα τὰ γενόμενα καὶ πρὸς τὸν μῦν ἔφη· "Ὑπέσχου μοι ὡς, ὅτε τὰ ἐνταῦθα καταλάβομεν, ἀναγγεῖλαί μοι περί τινων τῶν κατὰ σέ."

differ in their thinking." And the crow said, "Don't be afraid of that: becoming friends with the friend of a friend is proof of sincere friendship, as is being at enmity with his enemy. And since I want to be friends with you, those with me will want to be friends with you too." When the crow said this, the mouse came out and the friendship between them was established.

One day the crow said, "I see that your nest is near the 9
road, and I'm afraid that where you live may become known because of me. But I know a secluded place, where there are plenty of fish and an abundance of other food. I am also friends with a turtle there, and I want to go and live there." And the mouse said, "I will travel with you. For I have hated my life here, for reasons related to my life in another place, which I will explain to you when I arrive at our destination." So the crow took the mouse by the tail and carried him off to the spring where the turtle was living. When the turtle saw the crow bringing a mouse, she assumed he was a stranger and hid under the water, as she was frightened. The crow put the mouse on the ground and called the turtle by name. As she recognized his voice, she came out to him and asked him where he had come from. The crow told her everything that had happened, and said to the mouse, "You promised me that when we arrived here you would tell me some things about yourself."

10 *Περὶ μοναχοῦ.*

Ὁ δὲ μῦς εἶπεν· "Ἐγὼ τὴν πρώτην ἐποιησάμην οἴκησιν παρά τινι μοναχῷ καὶ ἤσθιον λάθρα, ἃ ἡτοίμαζεν ἑαυτῷ ἐδέσματα, καὶ κορεννύμενος ἐλάμβανον τὰ περιττὰ καὶ τοῖς λοιποῖς παρετίθουν μυσί· καὶ πολλάκις ὁ μοναχὸς ἄνωθεν ἀναρτήσας τὴν οἰκείαν τροφὴν οὐκ ἠδυνήθη τὴν ἐξ ἐμοῦ βλάβην διεκφυγεῖν. Μιᾷ δὲ τῶν ἡμερῶν ξένος τις κατέλυσε παρ' αὐτῷ καὶ ἤρξαντο ἀλλήλοις προσομιλεῖν. Διὰ μέσου δὲ ὁ μοναχὸς τὰς χεῖρας ἐκρότει ἐμὲ ἐκφοβῶν. Ὁ δὲ ξένος εὐθὺς ἠρώτησεν ὡς 'Διατί οἱ κρότοι γίνονται;' Καὶ ὁ μοναχὸς ἔφη· ''Ερωτᾶς με δι' ἣν αἰτίαν ποιῶ τοὺς κρότους, κἀγὼ ἀναγγελῶ σοι. Ἐν τῇ οἰκίᾳ μού ἐστι μῦς καὶ βλάπτομαι παρ' αὐτοῦ τὰ μέγιστα· καὶ ἐσθίει τὸ βρῶμά μου καὶ διαφθείρει αὐτό.' Ὁ δὲ ξένος εἶπε πρὸς αὐτόν· 'Εἷς μῦς ὑπάρχει ἢ καὶ ἄλλοι πολλοί;' Ὁ δὲ μοναχὸς ἔφη· 'Οἱ μῦες πολλοί εἰσιν, ἀλλὰ παρ' ἑνὸς βλάπτομαι τὰ μέγιστα.' Καὶ ἀνήγγειλεν αὐτῷ τὰ κατ' ἐμέ. Ὁ δὲ ξένος εἶπεν· 'Οὗτος ὁ μῦς αἰτίαν τινὰ ἔχει· καὶ γὰρ μέμνημαι ἀνθρώπου τινὸς εἰπόντος μοι περὶ μιᾶς γυναικός, ἧστινος κατελύσαμεν ἐν τῇ οἰκίᾳ, ὅτι ἡ γυνὴ αὕτη δι' αἰτίαν τινὰ συνήλλαξε τὸν κεκαθαρισμένον σήσαμον αὐτῆς πρὸς ἀκαθάριστον.' Ο δὲ μοναχὸς ἔφη· 'Καὶ πῶς ἦν τοῦτο;' Ὁ δὲ ξένος εἶπε· 'Μιᾷ τῶν ἡμερῶν ἐγώ τε καὶ ὁ ἄνθρωπος ἐκεῖνος μετὰ καὶ ἑτέρων κατελύσαμεν πρός τινα ἐν τῇ πόλει· καὶ δειπνήσαντες ἐκοιμήθημεν. Ἦν δὲ ἀναμεταξὺ ἡμῶν σκέπη· ἤκουσα δὲ τοῦ οἰκοδεσπότου πρὸς τὴν γυναῖκα αὐτοῦ λέγοντος· "Βούλομαι ἐγὼ αὔριον καλέσαι τινὰς τοῦ δειπνῆσαι σὺν

CHAPTER 3

About a monk. 10

The mouse said, "I made my first home with a monk and would secretly eat the food he prepared for himself, and when I had my fill, I would take the leftovers and serve them to the rest of the mice; and often the monk, even though he had hung up his food, was unable to escape the damage I did. But one day a stranger stayed with him, and they began to talk to each other. During the course of their conversation the monk began to clap his hands to frighten me. The stranger immediately asked, 'Why are you clapping?' And the monk said, 'You ask me the reason why I am clapping, and I will tell you. In my house there is a shameless mouse, and I am being badly hurt by it. It's eating my food and spoiling it.' The stranger said to him, 'Is there one mouse or are there many others?' And the monk said, 'There are many mice, but I'm being harmed most by the one.' And he told him about me. The stranger said, 'This mouse has a reason for doing this. I'm reminded of a man who told me about a woman, in whose house we lodged, and how this woman for some reason mixed up her cleaned and uncleaned sesame.' And the monk said, 'How was that?' The stranger said, 'One day, I and that man, along with some others, lodged for some reason in the city, and after we had eaten, we went to bed. There was a screen between us and I heard the owner of the house say to his wife, "I want to ask some people to

ἐμοί." Ἡ δὲ λέγει πρὸς αὐτόν· "Πῶς δύνασαι τοῦτο ποιῆσαι μηδὲν περισσευόμενος, μηδὲ ἔχων τροφὴν ἐν τῷ οἴκῳ σου, ἀλλὰ πάντοτε πάντα καταναλίσκεις;" Ὁ δὲ ἀνὴρ αὐτῆς τότε λέγει πρὸς αὐτήν· "Μή σοι μέλει περὶ τῶν ἐξοδιασθέντων παρ' ἡμῶν· καὶ γὰρ οἱ θησαυρίζοντες ἄνθρωποι καὶ πλεονεκτοῦντες ἴσως ἀπολέσουσιν ἑαυτούς, ὡς ὁ λύκος."""

11 *Περὶ λύκου.*

"""Λέγεται γὰρ ὥς τις θηρευτὴς ἐξῆλθε τοῦ θηρεῦσαι θηρία ἔχων μεθ' ἑαυτοῦ τὸ τόξον αὐτοῦ καὶ τὰ βέλη. Καὶ συναντήσας δορκάδος ἔτρωσεν αὐτὴν καὶ ἄρας ταύτην ὑπέστρεφεν εἰς τὸν οἶκον αὐτοῦ. Καὶ πάλιν συναντήσας χοίρου, ἔρριψε κατ' αὐτοῦ τὸ βέλος· ὁ δὲ χοῖρος πηδήσας ἔτρωσε τὸν θηρευτήν, καὶ πεσόντες ἀμφότεροι τεθνήκασιν. Ἔπεσε δὲ καὶ τὸ τόξον, ὅπερ ἦν παλέστρα, πλῆρες μετὰ βέλους. Κατὰ συγκαιρίαν δὲ λύκος τις ἐλθών, καὶ ἰδὼν τούτους τεθνηκότας, πάνυ δὲ λιπαροὺς καὶ παχεῖς, εἶπεν ἐν ἑαυτῷ· 'Φυλάξω τούτους ἐμαυτῷ κατὰ δύναμιν καὶ μὴ φανοῦμαι ἀμελής, μᾶλλον δὲ καὶ τὴν σήμερον γαστρίμαργος· καὶ ταῦτα γὰρ τὰ εὑρεθέντα μοι βρώματα θησαυρίσω καὶ αὐταρκεσθῶ ἐν ταύτῃ τῇ ἡμέρᾳ τοῦ φαγεῖν μόνον τὴν τοῦ τόξου χορδήν·' καὶ μεταχειρισάμενος τοῦ φαγεῖν αὐτὴν ἀπεπήδησε τὸ βέλος καὶ ἔτρωσεν αὐτὸν κατὰ τὴν καρδίαν καὶ πεσὼν ἀπέψυξεν. Οὕτως ἄρα καὶ οἱ πλεονέκται διὰ μόχθου τινὸς ἀποτελευτῶσιν."

""Ἡ δὲ λέγει αὐτῷ· "Ἄπελθε λοιπὸν καὶ κάλεσον ὅσους βούλει· καὶ γὰρ ἔχω ὀρύζην καὶ σήσαμον ἓξ ἀνδρῶν καὶ

dine with me tomorrow." But she said to him, "How can you do this when there is nothing to spare, and you have nothing to eat in your house but everything has been used up?" And her husband said to her, "Don't worry yourself about our expenses, for people who are hoarders and who are greedy will probably destroy themselves like the wolf."'"

About a wolf 11

"'"For it is said that a hunter went out to hunt wild animals and took his bow and arrows with him. When he came across a gazelle, he mortally wounded her, picked her up, and returned home. Again, he came across a pig and shot an arrow at it, but the pig sprang up and mortally wounded the hunter, and both of them fell down and died. And the bow, which was a crossbow, also fell down, loaded with an arrow. By chance, a wolf came along and, seeing them dead and that they were very fat and plump, said to himself, 'I'll keep them for myself as best I can and not appear careless, rather than being a glutton today; for I'll hoard what I've found as food for myself, and today I'll satisfy myself by eating only the bowstring.' And, as he was trying to eat this, the arrow shot off and wounded him in the heart and he fell down and expired. So that's how those who are greedy end up after all their hard work."

"'And she said to him, "Go and invite whoever you want, for I have rice and sesame for six men, and I will go and get

ἀπέρχομαι εὐτρεπίσαι αὐτά.” Καὶ τῇ ἐπαύριον καθαρίσασα τὴν σήσαμον, ἥπλωσεν αὐτὴν ἐν τῷ ἡλίῳ τοῦ ξηρανθῆναι, καὶ ἀπῆλθεν εἰς τὴν ἰδίαν ὑπηρεσίαν. Κατὰ συγκαιρίαν δέ, ἐλθών τις κύων οὔρησεν ἐν αὐτῇ τῇ σησάμῳ· καὶ ἰδοῦσα τὸ τοιοῦτον αὕτη ἡ γυνὴ ἐβδελύχθη, καὶ λαβοῦσα τὴν σήσαμον, κατήλλαξε πρὸς ἀκαθάριστον ἐπ’ ἴσης. Ἐγὼ δὲ πάντα ἔβλεπον παρὼν ἐκεῖσε· καὶ ἤκουσά τινος ὑπὸ τῶν σὺν ἐμοὶ λέγοντος· “Αὕτη ἡ γυνὴ δι’ αἰτίαν τινὰ κατήλλαξε τὴν καθαρὰν αὐτῆς σήσαμον ἐπ’ ἴσης πρὸς ἀκαθάριστον.” Οὕτω καὶ ὁ μῦς οὗτος ὁ ἀναιδὴς οὐκ ἄνευ αἰτίας τῶν τοιούτων κατατολμᾷ, ἀλλὰ ἐρευνήσωμεν ὁμοῦ τὰ κατ’ αὐτὸν καὶ κατορύξωμεν τὴν εἴσδυσιν αὐτοῦ.’

12 “ Ἔτυχον δὲ ἐγὼ τηνικαῦτα ἐν ἑτέρᾳ ὀπῇ ἀκούων τῶν λεγομένων παρ’ αὐτῶν. Ὑπῆρχον δὲ ἐν τῇ ἐμῇ καταδύσει νομίσματα χίλια, ἅτινα ὑπεστρώννυον ἐμαυτῷ καὶ μέγα ἐπὶ τούτοις ἐφρόνουν. Καὶ κατορύξαντες ἐκεῖνοι τὴν κατάδυσιν καὶ εὑρόντες τὸν χρυσὸν ἀφείλαντο τοῦτον καὶ εἶπον· ‘Ὁ χρυσὸς οὗτος διηρέθιζε τὸν μῦν καὶ διανίστα ὡς τῶν τοιούτων κατατολμᾶν, καὶ ὄψει, <ὡς> ἀπό γε τοῦ παρόντος ἀνίσχυρος ὁ μῦς καὶ ἀδύνατος γενήσεται.’ Καὶ εὐθέως ἀφηρέθη τὸ θράσος καὶ κατεβλήθη μου ἡ ἔπαρσις καὶ ἀπέλειψέ μοι ἡ οἴησις καὶ κατεφρονήθην καὶ παρωράθην ὑπὸ τῶν μυῶν. Καὶ μέλλων τῇ ἐπαύριον ἐπεισπηδῆσαι τῷ ταλάρῳ τῶν ἐδεσμάτων, οὐκ ἠδυνήθην, καὶ διὰ τοῦτο ἀντέστησαν οἱ λοιποὶ μῦες καὶ ἐχθροί μου ἐγένοντο. Ἐγὼ δὲ ἐθαύμαζον, ὅπως διὰ τοῦ χρυσοῦ καὶ οἱ φίλοι καὶ οἱ συγγενεῖς καὶ οἱ ὑπήκοοι συνίστανται, ἀλλ’ οὐδ’ αὕτη ἡ

it ready." The following morning when she had cleaned the sesame, she spread it in the sun to dry, and went off to do her work. But by chance a dog came and urinated on the sesame. The woman was disgusted when she saw this, so she took the sesame and exchanged it for the same amount that had not been cleaned. And I saw everything, as I was present there, and I heard one of the men who were with me say, "This woman had a reason for changing her clean sesame for the same amount of uncleaned seed." So, this shameless mouse also doesn't dare to do such things without a reason, but let's look together for signs of him and dig up where he's getting in.'

"At that time I was in another hole listening to what 12
they were saying. But in my hole there were a thousand *nomismata,* out of which I had made a bed for myself and of which I was very proud. After they had dug out the hole and found the gold, they took it away and said, 'This gold was provoking the mouse and inciting him to dare to do such things, and you'll see that from now on he'll become weak and powerless.' And immediately my courage was taken away, my high spirits were cast down, my self-confidence deserted me, and I was despised and slighted by the other mice. On the next day, when I was going to leap into the food basket, I was unable to do so, and because of this the other mice turned against me and became my enemies. I was astonished at how, on account of gold, friends, relatives, and subjects are brought together, but not even a good conscience

ἀγαθὴ συνείδησις δείκνυται εἰ μή γε διὰ τοῦ χρυσίου. Καὶ μὴν ὁ λογισμὸς καὶ ἡ ἰσχὺς δι' αὐτοῦ ἐπιγίνονται· ὁ δὲ τούτου ἀπορῶν οὐ δύναταί τι καταλήψεσθαι τῶν ἐφετῶν. Καὶ ἀνεμνήσθην, ὡς καλῶς ἔφησεν ὁ εἰπών, ὅτι *δεῖ χρημάτων καὶ ἄνευ τούτων οὐδέν ἐστι γενέσθαι τῶν δεόντων,* καὶ *ὡς χρὴ πενίην φεύγοντα καὶ ἐς μεγακήτεα πόντον ῥιπτεῖν καὶ πετρῶν, Κύρνε, κατ' ἠλιβάτων.*

13 "Καὶ ὥσπερ τὸ ὀλίγον ὕδωρ οὐ δύναται τὸν οἰκεῖον τόπον—ἤγουν τὴν θάλασσαν—καταλαβεῖν ἀνιμώμενον ὑπὸ τοῦ ἀέρος καὶ τῇ γῇ ξηραινόμενον, οὕτω καὶ ὁ μὴ εὐπορῶν πλούτου καταλαβεῖν ἐφετὸν οὐ δύναται. Ὁ γὰρ πενίᾳ συζῶν κινδύνων κατατολμᾷ καὶ ἐφαμάρτοις ἐπιχειρεῖ, δι' ὧν καὶ πολλάκις ἀπόλλυσι καὶ τὴν ἐνταῦθα ζωὴν καὶ τὴν ἐκεῖθεν ἀπόλαυσιν. Ὁ γὰρ τῶν ἀναγκαίων ἐπιδεὴς λυπηρὸς γίνεται, καὶ τοιοῦτος γενόμενος μισεῖται καὶ μισούμενος ἐπὶ πλεῖον λυπεῖται καὶ λυπούμενος οὐκ εὐφρονεῖ, καὶ μὴ οὐκ εὐφρονῶν τὰ συμφέροντα ἑαυτῷ οὐκ ἐργάζεται. Εἶδον δὲ καὶ ὅσα παρὰ τοῖς πλουσίοις εἰσὶν ἐπαινετὰ παρὰ τοῖς πένησι τὰ αὐτὰ καὶ μεμπτά. Εἰ γὰρ ὁ πένης ἀνδρεῖός ἐστι, θρασὺς καὶ ῥιψοκίνδυνος ὀνομάζεται, εἰ δὲ καὶ εὐμετάδοτος, ἀναλωτὴς καὶ δάπανος, εἰ δὲ καὶ πρᾷος καὶ προσηνής, ἀδύνατος, εἰ δ' εἰδήμων, ἠλίθιος, εἰ δὲ λόγιος, φλύαρος, εἰ δὲ σιωπηλός, ἀνόητος. Καὶ *ἄμεινον τοῦ βίου προαπελθεῖν ἢ τὸν ἥλιον,* κατὰ τὸν εἰπόντα, *αἰσχύνης κτήσασθαι μάρτυρα,* καὶ μάλιστα εἰ πρός τινάς τις τῶν φειδωλῶν ποιεῖται τὴν αἴτησιν.

14 "Ταῦτα διαλογιζόμενος εἶδον τὸν ξένον, ὅτε τὴν τοῦ χρυσοῦ ἐποιεῖτο διαίρεσιν, ἔν τινι βαλαντίῳ τὴν ἰδίαν

itself is demonstrated except on account of gold; indeed, even reason and strength derive from it, and someone who lacks it is unable to attain what he wants. And I was reminded that he spoke well who said that *money is necessary, and without it nothing may be done that ought to be,* and that *someone fleeing poverty should throw himself into the yawning depths of the sea, Cyrnos, or from precipitous rocks.*

"And just as a drop of water is unable to reach its rightful 13
place—that is, the sea—when it is evaporated by the air and dried out by the earth, so also someone who does not have great wealth is unable to attain his goal. Someone who lives in poverty ventures rashly into dangers and wrongly seeks them out, and, as a result, often loses both his life here and his enjoyment of the one to come. For someone who lacks the bare necessities becomes miserable, and, when that happens, he is hated, and being hated he becomes even more aggrieved, and being aggrieved he is depressed, and being depressed, does not work at things that are advantageous for him. And I have also seen that what is seen as praiseworthy for the rich is seen as being worthy of blame for the poor. For if a poor man is brave, he is called rash and foolhardy; if he is generous, a spendthrift and a profligate; if he is gentle and kindly, weak; if he is knowledgeable, foolish; if he is eloquent, a babbler; and if he is quiet, stupid. And *it is better to depart life,* according to the saying, *than have the sun as a witness to your shame,* especially if one is making the request of misers.

"While I was considering these things, I saw that the 14
stranger, when he was dividing the gold, had put his own

μοῖραν ἐμβαλόντα καὶ τῇ τούτου κεφαλῇ ὑποκρύψαντα καὶ δεῖν ᾠήθην τοῦτο λάθρα ἑλκύσαι, δοκῶν τοῦτον τῷ ὕπνῳ κατεχόμενον. Ὁ δὲ ξένος ἔξυπνος ὢν ἔλαβε τῇ χειρὶ κλάδον τινὰ αὐτῷ παρακείμενον καὶ ἔτυψέ με κατὰ κεφαλῆς καὶ ἀλγήσας ὑπέστρεψα. Εἶτα πάλιν τοῦ βαλαντίου κατετόλμησα. Καὶ πάλιν ἰδὼν ἔτυψέ με τῷ κλάδῳ καὶ αὖθις κατὰ κεφαλῆς σφοδρότερον. Καὶ εὐθὺς αἷμα ἐξερρύη τῶν ῥινῶν μου καὶ λιποθυμία μοι ἐγένετο. Καὶ μόλις ἕλκων ἠρέμα ἐμαυτὸν κατέλαβον τὴν ὀπήν, ἐν ᾗ ἐτύγχανον οἰκῶν καὶ ἄφωνος ἐκείμην ὥρας ἱκανάς. Καὶ τοσοῦτον ἐμίσησα τὸν χρυσὸν ὡς οὐδὲ μνείαν ἀνέχεσθαί με ἀκοῦσαι τοῦ χρυσοῦ. Καὶ ἔγνων ὡς πάντων αἴτιον τῶν κακῶν ἐν τῷ βίῳ ἡ πλεονεκτικωτάτη γνώμη, καὶ ὡς ὁ ἔχων ταύτην ῥᾷον ἂν κινδύνων κατά τε τὴν γῆν καὶ θάλασσαν κατατολμήσειεν, εἴπερ ὁ λελογισμένος οὐκ ἐπιχειρήσει λαβεῖν ἑτοίμου προκειμένου χρυσοῦ.

15 "Ἐπληροφορήθην δὲ καὶ ὡς οὐκ ἔστι μεῖζον τῆς αὐταρκείας ἀγαθόν, καὶ ὡς ἐκείνῃ μάλιστα ἡ καρτερία τε καὶ ἡ ὑπομονὴ ἕπεται καὶ ἐπαινεῖται, ἐν οἷς οὐκ ἔστι πόρον ἢ δίοδον εὑρεῖν. Λέγεται γάρ, ὡς πρώτη ἀρετὴ ἡ ἐλεημοσύνη, καὶ ἐξαίρετον χρῆμα τῆς φιλίας τὸ ἁπλοϊκῶς φέρεσθαι, καὶ ἀρχὴ φρονήσεως τὸ γνῶναι τὰ ἐσόμενα καὶ μή, καὶ μεγίστη εὐθυμία τὸ μὴ ἀδυνάτοις ἐπιχειρεῖν. Διὰ ταῦτα οὖν μετήμειψα τὸν βίον τὸν ἐρημικόν, ἀνταλλαξάμενος τοῦ ἐν οἰκήμασιν. Εἶχον δὲ καὶ φίλην περιστεράν, ἥτις πρὸ τοῦ κόρακος ἐφιλιώθη μοι, ἐπεὶ οὐδεμία τέρψις ἐστὶν ἐν τῷ βίῳ τῇ τῶν φίλων ξυναυλίᾳ παρόμοιος. Ἔγνων γὰρ ἐγὼ διὰ πείρας ὡς οὐ δεῖ τὸν ἐχέφρονα πλείονα ἐν τῷ βίῳ

share into a purse and hidden it under his head, and I thought I would pull the purse out secretly, supposing that the man was fast asleep. But the stranger was awake, and he took a stick that was lying next to him and struck me on the head with it; as I had been hurt, I turned and fled. Then I made another desperate attempt on the purse. And when he saw me again, he suddenly struck me on the head again with the stick even harder. Immediately, blood flowed from my nostrils and I felt faint. I dragged myself along with difficulty and slowly reached the hole in which I was living; and I lay speechless for a long time. And I hated the gold so much that I could not even bear to hear a mention of gold. I realized that a very greedy character is the cause of all the evils in life and that a man with such a character would more readily brave dangers by land and sea, even if a rational person would not try to take gold lying ready to hand.

“And I was also convinced that there is no greater good 15
than self-sufficiency, and that patience and perseverance follow this and are especially recommended in circumstances in which there is no pathway or route. For it is said that the first virtue is mercy, that a particular duty of friendship is to behave straightforwardly, that good sense begins with recognizing what the future may or may not hold, and that not attempting the impossible is a great joy. For these reasons, then, I turned to the eremitical life, and left behind the one lived indoors. I was also friends with a dove, with whom I became friends before the crow here, since there is no joy in life equal to the company of friends. For I, on my part, have learned from experience that a smart person does not seek

τῶν ἀρκούντων ἐπιζητεῖν. Ῥᾴδια γὰρ ταῦτα τῷ βουλομένῳ παντί, ὡς τῆς μακαρίας φύσεως δαψιλῶς παραγούσης αὐτά—τὴν ἀναγκαίαν, φημί, τροφὴν καὶ τὸ ὕδωρ. Εἰ γὰρ ὑποθώμεθά τινα τοῦ κόσμου παντὸς κυριεύσαντα, οὐκ ἂν οὗτος πάντων τούτου ἀπώνατο πλὴν τῶν ἐλαχίστων. Ταῦτα διαλογιζόμενος τῷ κόρακι συνωδοιπόρησα καί σε αὖθις φίλην προσελαβόμην."

16 Ἡ δὲ χελώνη ὑπολαβοῦσα εἶπεν· "Ἔγνων, ἃ ἐξέφρασας κάλλιστά τε καὶ τελεώτατα· ἀλλ' εἶδόν σε ἔναυλον διατηροῦντα τὴν τούτων μνήμην τῶν ἐπιγινομένων σοι δεινῶν. Καὶ δεῖ σε εἰδέναι, ὡς κοσμεῖ τοὺς λόγους ἡ πρᾶξις, καὶ ὁ ἄρρωστος εἰ μὴ χρήσεται, οἷς οἶδεν ἑαυτὸν ὠφελεῖσθαι, εἰς κενὸν ἂν αὐτοῦ ἡ γνῶσις ἔνεστι μὴ δυναμένου διὰ ταύτης τῆς νόσου ἐφευρεῖν κουφισμόν. Μὴ οὖν φρόντιζε οἴκου πλοῦτον· ὁ γὰρ μεγαλόνους ἀνὴρ καὶ χωρὶς τούτου σεβάζεται παρὰ πάντων, ὡς ὁ κοιμώμενος λέων, ὥσπερ πάλιν ὁ ἀσύνετος πλούσιος ἀτιμάζεται καὶ παρορᾶται, [καὶ] ὡς ὁ περιδέραια χρυσᾶ περικείμενος κύων. Μήτε μὴν περὶ τῆς ξενιτείας σου διαλογίζου καὶ ἀλαζονεύου, οὐδεὶς γὰρ τῶν συνετῶν ξένος· μὴ οὖν μνημόνευε τῶν προτέρων λόγων, ὡς ἦσθά ποτε ὄλβιος, καὶ γέγονας ἠπορημένος. *Τὰ γὰρ ἐν γενέσει καὶ φθορᾷ ἐν ῥοῇ ἐστι καὶ ἀπορροῇ*, καθάπερ τις σφαῖρα, τάχιστα μετακινουμένη καὶ μεταρριπτουμένη. Λέγεται γάρ, ὡς ταῦτα τῶν ἄλλων εἰσὶ ἀστατώτερα, τὸ τοῦ νέου φρόνημα καὶ ἡ τῶν μοχθηρῶν ἀνδρῶν φιλία καὶ ὁ τῶν γυναικῶν ἔρως καὶ ὁ ψευδὴς ἔπαινος καὶ ὁ πλοῦτος. Ὁ δὲ ἐχέφρων καὶ ὁ νουνεχὴς οὔτε τοῦ πλούτου τῇ δαψιλείᾳ ἐπιτέρπεται οὔτε μὴν ἀλύει τῇ ὀλιγότητι." Ὡς οὖν

more in life than is sufficient, for these things are easy to obtain by anyone who wants them, as blessed nature provides them in abundance—I mean the food and water one needs. For if we imagine someone being lord of the whole world, he would have no joy from this at all except for these most insignificant things. When I considered all this, I traveled with the crow and, in turn, took you as my friend."

The turtle said in reply, "I understand what you've de- 16
scribed so eloquently and in such great detail, but I see that you're keeping the memory of the bad things that happened to you fresh in your mind. And you should know that action adorns words, and that, if someone who is sick does not make use of what benefits him, the knowledge he has is worthless, as he is unable to find relief from his sickness through it. So don't worry about the wealth of your house. For, even without this, a magnanimous man is respected by everyone, like a sleeping lion, just as also a rich fool is disrespected and ignored, like a dog wearing a golden collar. And don't keep talking and going on about your having to live somewhere else, for no one who is smart is a stranger. Forget your earlier words that you were once prosperous but are now poor. *For things that are born and die are always in a state of ebb and flow,* just like a ball, being moved about and turned upside down very swiftly. For it is said that the following things are more unstable than others: the mind of a youth, the friendship of bad men, the love of women, false praise, and wealth. But the intelligent and smart person doesn't delight in an abundance of wealth, nor is troubled by the lack

ἤκουσεν ὁ κόραξ τὴν τῆς χελώνης διάλεξιν ηὐφράνθη ἐπὶ ταύτῃ καὶ εἶπεν ὡς· "Οὐδὲν ἕτερόν ἐστι κρεῖττον τῆς τῶν φίλων συναντιλήψεως καὶ συναγαλλιάσεως. Οὐδεὶς γὰρ ἕτερος τοῦ σπουδαίου ἀνδρὸς ἀντέχεται εἰ μή γε σπουδαῖος, ὥσπερ οὐδὲν ἕτερον ἐγείρει πεσόντα τὸν ἐλέφαντα εἰ μὴ μόνος ἐλέφας."

17 Ταῦτα καὶ τὰ τούτοις παραπλήσια τοῦ κόρακος λέγοντος, δορκάς τις ἄφνω παρεγένετο, ἣν ἰδὼν ὁ κόραξ ἐπὶ [τὸ] δένδρον ἐξέπτη καὶ ἡ χελώνη τῷ ὕδατι περιεκαλύφθη καὶ ὁ μῦς ὑπεισῆλθεν καταδύσει τινί. Ἡ δὲ ὀλιγοστοῦ μεταλαβοῦσα ὕδατος ἔστη περίδειλος ἔνθεν κἀκεῖθεν τοὺς ὀφθαλμοὺς περιστρέφουσα. Ὁ δὲ κόραξ ἐφ' ὕψους ἀρθεὶς περιεσκόπει, εἴ ποτέ τι τὴν δορκάδα καταδιώκει θηρίον. Πανταχόθεν τοίνυν περιβλέψας, ὡς οὐδὲν ἐθεάσατο, κατῆλθε καὶ τὴν χελώνην καὶ τὸν μῦν ἐκάλεσεν, ἀναγνωρίσας ὡς οὐδὲν δεινὸν ἐποπτεύεται. Ἡ δὲ χελώνη ἐξελθοῦσα καὶ τὴν δορκάδα θεασαμένη τοῦ πιεῖν μὴ κατατολμῶσαν, πείθει πιεῖν ταύτην καὶ εἶπε· "Πίε, φιλτάτη, οὐδεὶς γὰρ ἐνταῦθα νυνὶ καταλαμβάνει. Ἀνάγγειλον δέ μοι, πόθεν ἥκεις." Ἡ δὲ δορκὰς ἔφη· "Ἐδιωκόμην μέχρι τοῦ νῦν παρὰ τῶν θηρευτῶν τόπον ἐκ τόπου ἀμείβουσα καὶ ἐνταῦθα κατήντησα." Ἡ δὲ χελώνη εἶπεν· "Θάρρει, φιλτάτη, οὐδέποτε γὰρ παρ' ἡμῖν θηρευτὴς ἐπεδήμησε, καὶ ὁμοζώει μεθ' ἡμῶν. Ἰδοὺ γάρ σοι πρόκειται τροφὴ δαψιλὴς καὶ ὕδατος νᾶμα διαφανές." Ἡιρετίσατο οὖν ἡ δορκὰς τὸ συνδιαιτᾶσθαι καὶ συνδιάγειν αὐτοῖς, καὶ ἐποιοῦντο ἑκάστοτε τὴν πανδαισίαν καὶ τὴν ὁμιλίαν παρά τινι δένδρῳ συνηρεφεῖ. Μιᾷ δὲ τῶν ἡμερῶν ὁ κόραξ καὶ ὁ μῦς καὶ ἡ χελώνη

of it." When the crow had heard the turtle's speech, he was delighted by it and said, "Nothing else is better than the mutual support of friends and the happiness they find in each other. For no one else helps a good man except another good man, just as only an elephant can raise a fallen elephant."

While the crow was saying these and similar things, a ga- 17
zelle suddenly appeared; when they saw her, the crow flew off into the tree, the turtle hid in the water, and the mouse slipped into a hole. But the gazelle, after taking a very small sip of water, stood there terrified, turning her eyes this way and that. The crow, soaring high above her, was looking around in case some wild beast was pursuing the gazelle. So, when he had looked all around, and because he saw no one, he came down and called the turtle and the mouse, as he realized there was nothing frightening to be seen. When the turtle emerged and saw the gazelle not daring to drink, she persuaded her to drink and said, "Drink, my dear, for there is no one following you here now. But tell me where you've come from." And the gazelle said, "Up until now I was being chased by hunters, moving from place to place, and I ended up here." The turtle said, "Take courage, my dear, for no hunter has ever visited us or lived here with us. For look, there's plenty of food lying in front of you, and a clear stream of water." So the gazelle decided to live there and spend her life with them, and every day they feasted and talked beside a shady tree. But one day the crow, the mouse, and the turtle

συνελθόντες κατὰ τὸ εἰωθὸς καὶ τὴν δορκάδα προσδεχόμενοι, ὡς οὐ κατέλαβεν ἐστοχάσαντο ὡς παγίδι περιέπεσε. Καὶ ἀναπτὰς ὁ κόραξ εἶδε ταύτην σχοινίοις ἐμπεπλεγμένην παγίδος τινὸς θηρευτοῦ, καὶ ὑποστρέψας ἀνήγγειλε τὸ θεαθέν. Ἡ δὲ χελώνη πρὸς τὸν μῦν ἔφη· "Ἐν σοὶ ἄρτι ἡ τῆς ἡμετέρας δορκάδος κεῖται σωτηρία."

18 Ὁ δε μῦς ᾗ τάχος εἶχε δραμών, τὴν δορκάδα κατέλαβε καὶ εἶπεν αὐτῇ· "Πῶς συνετωτάτη οὖσα, ὦ φίλη, τοῖς τοιούτοις δεινοῖς σεαυτὴν περιέπλεξας;" Ἡ δὲ ἔφη· "Καὶ τίς ἂν ἀπόναιτο τῆς οἰκείας συνέσεως, ὅτε δεῖ τὸ ὡρισμένον τελεσθῆναι;" Ταῦτα λεγούσης αὐτῆς, κατέλαβεν καὶ ὁ κόραξ ὁμοῦ καὶ ἡ χελώνη. Ἡ δὲ δορκὰς πρὸς τὴν χελώνην εἶπε· "Τί ἔδρασας ἐλθοῦσα ἐνταῦθα; Ἐγὼ γὰρ λυθεῖσα τῶν δεσμῶν παρὰ τοῦ μυὸς δραμοῦσα διαδράσω, ὡσαύτως καὶ ὁ κόραξ δι' ἀέρος καὶ ὁ μῦς εὑρήσει κατάδυσίν τινα, σὺ δὲ μόνη καταλειφθήσῃ τῷ θηρευτῇ παρανάλωμα." Ἡ δὲ ὑπολαβοῦσα ἔφη· "Ἀβίωτος ὁ μετὰ τὴν τῶν φίλων στέρησιν βίος, καὶ τίς ἑτέρα ἐν τούτῳ τέρψις καταλιμπάνεται;" Ταῦτα διαλεγομένης τῆς χελώνης, ἐπῆλθεν ὁ θηρευτὴς ἅμα τῷ τὴν δορκάδα λυθῆναι παρὰ τοῦ μυὸς καὶ ἀποδρᾶσαι· καὶ ὁ μὲν κόραξ εἰς τὸν ἀέρα ἀπέπτη, ὁ δὲ μῦς καταδύσει τινὶ ἀπεκρύβη· καὶ θαυμάσας ὁ θηρευτὴς τὸ γεγονός, εἶδε μόνην τὴν χελώνην, καὶ συλλαβὼν ἐκεῖνος ταύτην κατέδησεν.

19 Ὁ δὲ κόραξ καὶ ὁ μῦς καὶ ἡ δορκὰς ἰδόντες τὸ γεγονὸς σφόδρα περιαλγεῖς γεγόνασι καὶ ὁ μῦς ἔφη· "Ἴδε, πῶς τὰ τοῦ βίου ἐξετράπη ἡμῖν. Καλῶς γὰρ ἔφησεν ὁ εἰπών, ὡς ὅτε τις πρὸς ἅπαξ προσκόψει, πολλάκις περιπίπτει

gathered as usual and were waiting for the gazelle; as she did not arrive, they guessed that she had fallen into a trap. The crow flew up and saw her entangled in the ropes of a hunter's trap, and when he returned, he told them what he had seen. And the turtle said to the mouse, "Our gazelle's safety now lies with you."

The mouse ran as fast as he could, reached the gazelle and 18
said to her, "How is it, my friend, though you are so intelligent, that you have entangled yourself in such a terrible situation?" And she said, "Who can benefit from their intelligence, when what has been fated must come to pass?" While she was saying this, the crow arrived at the same time as the turtle. The gazelle said to the turtle, "What have you done, coming here? For when I've been freed from my bonds by the mouse, I'll run off and escape, and so too the crow will fly through the air and the mouse will find some hole, but you alone will be left as prey for the hunter." But the turtle said in reply, "A life after one is deprived of friends is no life; what other enjoyment is left in it?" While the turtle was saying this, the hunter arrived at the moment the gazelle was set free by the mouse and ran off, the crow flew up into the air, and the mouse hid in a hole. The hunter, who was astonished by what had happened, saw only the turtle and, having taken hold of her, tied her up.

The crow, the mouse, and the gazelle became terribly up- 19
set when they saw what had happened, and the mouse said, "See how life has changed for us. For he spoke well who said that when someone stumbles once, he frequently meets

συμπτώματι. Οὐκ ἤρκει μοι τὸ τῆς πατρίδος καὶ τῶν συγγενῶν καὶ τοῦ πλούτου ἀποπεσεῖν, ἀλλ' ἐστερήθην νῦν καὶ τῆς φιλτάτης μοι χελώνης, ἥτις οἶδε θεσμοὺς φιλίας τηρεῖν. Ἀλλ' ἐρρέτω τὸ θνητὸν τοῦτο σῶμα, καὶ μυρίοις περιεστοιχισμένον δεινοῖς καὶ μηδέποτε μένον ἐπὶ τὸ αὐτό, ἀλλ' ἀλλοιούμενον διηνεκῶς καὶ καταβαλλόμενον. Καὶ ὥσπερ ὁ ἀστὴρ ἀνατέλλων οὐ προσμένει τῇ ἀνατολῇ, ἀλλὰ περιφερόμενος διὰ τάχους δύνει καὶ ὁ ἑῷος ἑσπέριος γίνεται καὶ τὸ ἐν τῇ ἀνατολῇ μέρος δύνει καὶ τὸ δῦνον ἀνατέλλει, οὕτως τὰ παρ' ἡμῖν ἀεί εἰσιν εὐμετάβλητα. Ἀνεμνήσθην οὖν ἔγωγε τῶν προτέρων μου συμφορῶν διὰ τῆς παρούσης λύπης, καθάπερ ἡ ἐκ τραύματος ἐνσκιρρωθεῖσα οὐλή, ὅτε πληγῇ, ὁμοῦ τε τῆς ἐκ πλήξεως ἀλγηδόνος ἐπαισθάνεται καὶ τὸ πρότερον τραῦμα αὖθις ὡς ἔκ τινος ἑτέρας ἀρχῆς ἀνακαινίζεται."

Ἡ δὲ δορκὰς ὑπολαβοῦσα ἔφη· "Ἡ ἡμετέρα ἄρτι λύπη καὶ οἱ σοὶ περιώδυνοι λόγοι, εἰ καὶ ῥητορείας ἔχονται, τὴν χελώνην οὐκ ὠφελοῦσιν, ἀλλ' ἔασον ταῦτα καὶ εὑρὲ πόρον αὐτῇ σωτηρίας. Λέγεται γὰρ ὡς ὁ μὲν ἀνδρεῖος ἐν καιρῷ συμπλοκῆς δοκιμάζεται, ὁ δὲ πιστὸς ἐν ταῖς δόσεσι καὶ λήψεσι, καὶ οἱ φίλοι *ἐν καιρῷ πειρασμοῦ*." Ὁ δὲ μῦς εἶπε· "Κρίνω νῦν συμφέρον τὸ ἀπελθεῖν σε τὴν δορκάδα καὶ ὡς νεκρὰν πεσεῖν ἐν τῇ ὁδῷ τοῦ θηρευτοῦ, καὶ ἐπιμαρτυρῆσαί σου τὴν νέκρωσιν τὸν κόρακα τῷ ἐπικαθῆσθαί σοι καὶ ὑποκρίνεσθαι κατεσθίειν τὰς σάρκας σου. Οἶμαι γάρ, ὡς τοῦτο ἰδὼν ὁ θηρευτὴς ἀποθήσει τὸ τόξον αὐτοῦ καὶ τὴν φαρέτραν καὶ πρὸς σὲ ἐπελεύσεται. Ὅταν οὖν ἴδῃς τοῦτον προσεγγίσαντα, ἀνάστα καὶ σχολαιότερον δράμε ἐλπίδι

with mishaps. The loss of my homeland, my family, and my wealth was not enough for me, but I have now even been deprived of the turtle, who is most dear to me and who knows how to observe the bonds of friendship. But, away with this mortal body, beset as it is by countless terrible things and which never stays the same, but rather is continuously being changed and laid low! Just as the rising star does not remain in the east, but, wheeling round, quickly sets, and daybreak becomes evening, and the part that was in the east sets, and that which was setting rises, so too our circumstances are always easily changed. So I myself am reminded simultaneously of my former misfortunes by my present grief, just as, when the hardened scar of a wound is struck, one simultaneously feels both the pain of the blow and that of the earlier wound again, which is renewed as though from the start."

But the gazelle said in reply, "Our present grief and your 20
most painful words, even if they possess rhetorical virtue, will not help the turtle; so leave that be and find a way to save her. For it is said that the brave person is put to the test in trying circumstances, the trustworthy one in their receipts and payments, and friends *at a time of temptation.*" And the mouse said, "I think it would be helpful if you, gazelle, went off and fell down as if you were dead in the path of the hunter, and that the crow should provide evidence of your death by settling on you and pretending to eat your flesh. For I think that, when the hunter sees this, he will put down his bow and quiver, and will go toward you. So, when you see that he has come close to you, get up, and run away quite

τοῦ καταλαβεῖν σε αὐτὸν ὑποσαίνουσα. Καὶ καταλαμβάνοντος τούτου, χρῷ ἐπὶ πλέον τῇ τῶν ποδῶν ὠκύτητι. Διὰ μέσου γὰρ ἔγωγε τῶν δεσμῶν τὴν χελώνην ἀπολύσω." Ἡ δὲ δορκὰς τὸ προσταχθὲν ἐποίησε καὶ διὰ τοῦ τοιούτου τρόπου ἐλύθη παρὰ τοῦ μυὸς ἡ χελώνη, καὶ σῶοι ἅπαντες οἴκαδε ἐπανέζευξαν.

Οὕτως ἄρα οἱ ὀρθῶς φιλοῦντες ἀεὶ τῶν οἰκείων φίλων ἀντέχονται· καὶ ὑπὲρ περισσοῦ τὴν φιλίαν φυλάττουσιν ἄχρι τῶν συμπερασμάτων αὐτῶν.

slowly, enticing him with the hope that he will catch up with you. And when he does catch up, use your swiftness of foot to the full. In the meantime, I will free the turtle from her bonds." The gazelle did as she had been told and in this way the turtle was freed by the mouse, and they all returned home, safe.

This is how those who are truly friends always support their friends; and, even more remarkably, how they preserve their friendship until their deaths.

[Chapter 4]

Ἀρχὴ τοῦ τετάρτου τμήματος.

Μετὰ δὲ ταῦτα ὁ βασιλεὺς πρὸς τὸν φιλόσοφον ἔφη· "Ἔγνων διὰ τούτου τοῦ παραδείγματος τὰ τῆς εἰλικρινοῦς φιλίας· λοιπὸν οὖν ἀνάγγειλόν μοι ὑπόδειγμα πῶς δεῖ τινα παρατηρεῖν τὸν ἐχθρόν, τὴν εὔνοιαν ἐπιδεικνύμενον." Ὁ δὲ φιλόσοφος εἶπεν·

2 *Περὶ κοράκων καὶ γλαυκῶν.*

Ὁ ἐχθρῷ καταπιστευόμενος πείσεται τὸ τῶν γλαυκῶν. Λέγεται γὰρ ὡς ἔν τινι ὄρει ἐν δένδρῳ ὑπερμεγέθει κόρακες διῆγον χίλιοι, ὧν ἦρχε κόραξ εἷς. Ἦσαν δὲ καὶ ἐν ἑτέρῳ τόπῳ πλησίον δένδρα πολλὰ ἐν οἷς διῆγον γλαῦκες χιλίαι, παρ' ἑνὸς καὶ αὐταὶ κυριευόμεναι, καὶ πρὸς τοὺς κόρακας ἀεὶ ἐχθρωδῶς διακείμεναι. Μιᾷ γοῦν τῶν νυκτῶν ἐπῆλθον τοῖς κόραξι καὶ πολλοὺς μὲν ἀπέκτειναν ἑτέρους δὲ ἐτραυμάτισαν.

3 Ἕωθεν δὲ ὁ τῶν κοράκων βασιλεὺς τοὺς ὑπ' αὐτὸν ἐπισυνάξας καὶ συνέδριον ποιήσας εἶπεν· "Εἴδετε, ἃ τὸ τῶν γλαυκῶν γένος εἰς ἡμᾶς ἔδρασε, καὶ ὅπως τὴν ἡμετέραν

Chapter 4

BEGINNING OF THE FOURTH CHAPTER.

After this, the king said to the philosopher, "I have understood through this last lesson the characteristics of true friendship; so now give me an example of how someone should watch out for his enemy, when the enemy makes a display of goodwill." And the philosopher said:

About crows and owls. 2

Someone who trusts in his enemy will suffer the fate of the owls. For it is said that on a mountain in an enormous tree there lived a thousand crows, ruled by one crow. In another place nearby there were many trees in which lived a thousand owls, who were also ruled by one of their number, and they were always hostile toward the crows. One night they attacked the crows; they killed many and wounded others.

At daybreak the king of the crows, once he had gathered 3
his subjects together and convened a council, said, "See what the race of owls has done to us, how they've put our

δύναμιν κατετροπώσατο, καὶ ὅσους μὲν ἀπέκτεινεν ὅσους δὲ ἐτραυμάτισε καὶ τὰ πτίλα ἀπέτιλλε. Ὧν δὴ πάντων χείριστον ὅτι ὅλως ἡμᾶς κατετόλμησαν κυριεῦσαι καὶ διὰ πείρας καταφρονῆσαι. Ταῦτα γνόντες, θεάσασθε καὶ τὰ ἑπόμενα."

4 *Περὶ τῶν πέντε πρωτοσυμβούλων τῶν τοῦ βασιλέως κοράκων.*

Ἦσαν δὲ ἐκεῖσε παρὰ τῷ τοιούτῳ βασιλεῖ πρωτοσύμβουλοι πέντε, ὧν ὁ εἷς ὑπολαβὼν εἶπεν· "Οὐδὲν ἕτερον σώσει ἡμᾶς ταύτης τῆς ἐπιδρομῆς ἀλλ' ἢ τὸ φυγεῖν καὶ τὴν ἐνταῦθα διατριβὴν καταλιπεῖν, καὶ τὸν ἐπὶ ξένοις βίον ἀσπάζεσθαι, μὴ ἐξὸν πρὸς τοὺς πολεμίους ἀντιπαρατάττεσθαι." Ὁ δὲ ἕτερος ἔφη· "Οὐ κρίνω συμφέρον εἶναι ἐπὶ τοσοῦτον ὑπὸ μιᾶς προσβολῆς ταπεινωθῆναι ἡμᾶς ὡς τὴν πατρίδα καταλιπεῖν καὶ τὸν ἐπὶ ξένοις βίον ἀσπάσασθαι, ἀλλ' ἑτοιμάζεσθαι, καὶ παρασκευάζεσθαι, καὶ ἀγῶνας ὑποδύεσθαι, καί, εἴ ποτε οἱ ἐχθροὶ ἐπελεύσονται, συμπλακῆναι τούτοις καὶ φυλάττεσθαι τὸ εἰσδῦναι τούτους ἐν μέσῳ ἡμῶν. Καὶ εἰ μὲν ἡττήσομεν τούτους τῷ Θεῷ δόξα, εἰ δ' οὖν ἄμεμπτοι τὴν πρώτην προσβολὴν τελέσομεν." Ὁ δὲ τρίτος εἶπεν· "Οὐ καλῶς, ὦ βασιλεῦ, οὗτοι λέγουσιν, ἀλλὰ δεῖ ἡμᾶς ἀκριβῶς ἀναμαθεῖν, εἰ βούλονται οἱ ἐχθροὶ ἡμῶν φιλιωθῆναι ἡμῖν καὶ σπονδὰς εἰρηνικὰς ποιήσασθαι διὰ δώρων ὑπαγόμενοι, ἃ δὴ καὶ στελοῦμεν αὐτοῖς, καὶ ἀμέριμνον βίον βιώσωμεν. Ἀεὶ γὰρ οἱ βασιλεῖς περὶ τὰς οἰκείας χώρας δεδιότες καὶ πρὸς τοὺς ἐχθροὺς ἀδυνατοῦντες

force to flight, and how many they've killed and how many wounded, and how they've plucked our feathers. And the worst thing of all is that they've presumed to dominate us completely, and, through this experience, have come to despise us. When you've reflected upon these matters, also consider the consequences."

About the five chief counselors 4
of the king of the crows.

There were five chief counselors there with this king, one of whom said in reply, "Nothing else will save us from this attack but taking flight, abandoning our life here, and embracing a life among strangers, since it's not possible to withstand our enemies." But another said, "I don't think it useful for us, because of one attack, to be so humiliated that we leave our homeland behind and embrace a life among strangers. But instead we should ready ourselves, prepare ourselves, and engage in contests, and if our enemies ever attack, engage them and prevent them from getting in among us. And if we defeat them, glory be to God, but if not, we will not be to blame for having attempted the first assault." The third said, "These men, my king, aren't speaking well. Rather, we should inquire carefully whether our enemies wish to become friends with us and make peace treaties, encouraged by means of gifts we send them, and we will then live our life without any care. For kings are always fearful for their own territories and, when they are powerless toward

ἀντάλλαγμα ποιοῦνται τὸν χρυσόν, δι᾽ οὗ συντηροῦσιν τοὺς ὑπ᾽ αὐτούς.”

5 Ὁ δὲ τέταρτος ἔφη· “Οὐ καλῶς καὶ οὗτος βουλεύῃ, ἀλλὰ κρεῖττόν ἐστι στενοῦσθαι τῷ βίῳ καὶ περιωδυνᾶσθαι ἢ τοσοῦτον τοῖς ἐχθροῖς ὑποπεσεῖν, ὧν κρείττονές ἐσμεν καὶ τιμιώτεροι. Ἀλλ᾽ εἰ καὶ τοῦτο, ᾧ συναινεῖς ἐπιχειρήσομεν, οὐκ ἀρκεσθήσονται τοῖς ὀλίγοις, ἀλλὰ τὰ ὑπὲρ δύναμιν ἐπιζητήσουσιν. Λέγεται γὰρ ὡς δεῖ πρὸ τῆς χρείας τὸν ἐχθρὸν διὰ μετρίων δώρων ἐφέλκεσθαι πρὸς φιλίαν, μὴ μέντοι διὰ πολλῶν. Τοῦτο γὰρ τὴν μὲν ἐκείνου δύναμιν ἐπιτείνει, τὴν δὲ ἡμετέραν ἐκλύει· τῆς γὰρ ἐν ἡλίῳ ἱσταμένης ῥάβδου ἡ μετρία κλίσις τὴν σκιὰν ἐπιτείνει, ἡ δ᾽ ἄμετρος ταύτην συστέλλει. Δεῖ οὖν καὶ τὴν ὑπομονὴν ἀσπάζεσθαι καὶ τὸ πολεμεῖν.”

6 Ὁ δὲ πέμπτος εἶπεν· “Καλῶς ἔλεξας πάντα, ἀλλ᾽ οὐ δυνατὸν ἡμῖν ἐστι τὸ πολεμεῖν. Ἐπικρατέστεροι γὰρ ἡμῶν οἱ ἐχθροί· ὁ γὰρ ἑαυτὸν ἀγνοῶν καὶ πρὸς τοὺς κρείττονας ἀντιφερίζων ἑαυτὸν μᾶλλον ἢ τοὺς ἐναντίους ἔβλαψεν· εἰ τάχα ὁ συνετὸς οὐκ ἀδύνατόν ποτε λογίζεται τὸν ἐχθρόν, ἔγωγε οὖν καὶ νῦν τε καὶ πρότερον τὸν ἐχθρὸν δέδοικα καὶ πρὸ τούτου ἐδεδοίκειν. Οὐδεὶς γὰρ ἐχέφρων ἀνὴρ τὸν ἴδιον ἐχθρὸν περιφρονεῖ, κἂν καὶ πόρρω διάγει, καὶ ὁ ἄριστος στρατηγὸς ἑτέρας μηχανῆς προκειμένης οὐχ αἱρεῖται τὸν πόλεμον. Πᾶσαι γὰρ ἐν τοῖς ἄλλοις αἱ δαπάναι περὶ τὸν πλοῦτον καταγίνονται καὶ τοὺς λόγους, ἐν δὲ τῷ πολέμῳ περὶ αὐτὰς τὰς ψυχάς.”

7 Ὁ δὲ βασιλεὺς εἶπεν· “Εἰ τῷ πολεμεῖν οὐ συναινεῖς τί ἕτερον προτρέπεις;” Ὁ δὲ εἶπε· “Δεῖ σε, ὦ βασιλεῦ,

their enemies, they make an exchange of gold, by means of
which they keep their subjects safe."

And the fourth said, "You're not advising well either, for 5
it's better to be impoverished in life and to suffer hardship
than to cower so much before our enemies, when we're su-
perior and worthier than them. Even if we were to try what
you are suggesting, they won't be satisfied with trifles but
will demand what is beyond our means. For it's said that one
ought to lead one's enemy toward friendship before it be-
comes a necessity, and by means of moderate gifts and not
many. For that increases the other's power, but weakens
one's own; for when a rod is stood up in the sun, a moderate
inclination increases the shadow, but an extreme one de-
creases it. Therefore, we should embrace both endurance
and going to war."

And the fifth said, "You've put it well, but it is not possi- 6
ble for us go to war. For our enemies are more powerful than
we are: someone who does not know himself, and who sets
himself against those who are stronger, hurts himself rather
than his opponents. If a smart person probably never con-
siders his enemy to be powerless, I myself not only fear the
enemy now more than before, but I also used to fear him
then. For no intelligent man underestimates his enemy, even
if he lives far away; and the best general does not choose war
if another means is available. For in other circumstances all
the costs relate to wealth and words, but in war they relate
to lives themselves."

The king said, "If you don't agree with going to war, what 7
else do you recommend?" And he said, "My king, you must

συμβούλοις χρᾶσθαι τοῖς ὑπὸ σὲ ἐχέφροσιν· ἡ γὰρ ἀρίστη βουλὴ μυρίων στρατευμάτων καὶ παρασκευῶν ἐπικρατεστέρα ἐστί, καὶ προστίθησιν αὕτη σκοποὺς ὀνησίμους τῷ βασιλεῖ, ὥσπερ οἱ ποταμοὶ τῷ θαλαττίῳ ὕδατι. Καὶ οὐδέποτε ὁ νουνεχὴς τὴν τοῦ ἐχθροῦ δύναμιν καὶ πονηρίαν ἐπὶ βλάβῃ ἀγνοεῖ, καὶ ὅσα καὶ οἷα βουλεύεται, καὶ οἷς πρὸς αὐτὸν στρατεύμασι χρήσεται καὶ ἐπιτηδεύμασι καὶ ἑτοιμασίαις. Ἐπεὶ οὖν μοι συμβούλῳ ἐχρήσω, ὦ βασιλεῦ, βούλομαί σοι διηγήσασθαι ἰδίᾳ τε καὶ δημοσίᾳ προσομιλῆσαι, καὶ δημοσίᾳ μὲν λέγω σοι ὅτι, ὥσπερ οὐ συνορῶ λυσιτελὲς τὸ πολεμεῖν, οὕτως οὐδὲ τὸ φόρους τελεῖν καὶ ὑπόπτωσιν τοιαύτην ἀσπάζεσθαι. Ὁ γὰρ μεγαλόνους ἀνὴρ αἱρεῖται μᾶλλον τὸν μετὰ δόξης θάνατον ἢ τὴν ἐν ἀτιμίᾳ ζωήν. Μὴ οὖν ἀμελήσῃς καὶ ἀναβάλῃς περὶ τὰ τοιαῦτα· *αἰεὶ γὰρ ἀμβολίεργος ἀνὴρ ἄτῃσι παλαίει,* κατὰ τὸν ποιητήν.

8 "Ἰδίᾳ δέ σοι διαλέξομαι, ὅτι ἀκήκοα τῶν πάλαι λεγόντων ὡς οἱ βασιλεῖς τροπαιοῦχοι γίνονται διὰ τῆς ἀρίστης οἰκονομίας. Ἡ δὲ ἀρίστη οἰκονομία ἐπιγίνεται διὰ τῆς πολυειδοῦς βουλῆς, ἡ δὲ βουλὴ ἐνεργεστέρα γίνεται, ὅτε μὴ ἐκφαυλισθῇ. Ἐκφαυλίζεται δὲ τὰ μυστήρια ἑξαχῶς· ἢ παρὰ τοῦ προσκαλοῦντος εἰς τὴν συμβουλήν, ἢ παρὰ τῶν προσκαλουμένων, ἢ διὰ τῶν ταῦτα συνεργούντων, ἢ ἐπί τινων εἰς πρεσβείαν ἀποστελλομένων, ἢ παρὰ τῶν τὰ ἑπόμενά τισι τῶν προδήλων ἔργων τηρούντων, ἢ παρὰ τῶν συλλογιζομένων ὀρθῶς καὶ στοχαζομένων. Ὁ δὲ τὸ οἰκεῖον μυστήριον συντηρῶν κατὰ δύο τρόπους ὠφελεῖται· ἢ γὰρ τυγχάνει τοῦ ἐφετοῦ καὶ ἐπὶ τῷ ἰδίῳ φρονήματι γέγηθεν ἢ ἀποτυχὼν τὴν ἐπὶ τῇ ἀτυχίᾳ μέμψιν ἐκφεύγει. Οὐ δεῖ δὲ

consult with those of your counselors who are clever, for the best advice is superior to countless armies and weapons, and it provides a king with useful perspectives, just as rivers provide the sea with water. Someone who is sensible is never ignorant of his enemy's strength and of his evil proclivity for harm, of how much and what kind of things he wants, and of what sort of armies and tactics and equipment he will use against him. So, since you employed me as a counselor, my king, I wish to explain things to you in private and speak to you in public, and in public I am telling you that, just as I do not think going to war is advantageous, the same goes for paying tribute and embracing such submission. A magnanimous man prefers death with glory to life with dishonor. So don't be careless and delay in these matters: for *a man who has not received advice is always his own enemy,* according to the poet.

"But I will have a discussion with you in private, because 8
I have heard it said of old that kings triumph through excellent government. And excellent government comes about through varied advice, and advice is more effective when it is not scorned. Secrets are broken in six ways: by the person who asks for the advice; by those who are asked for it; by those who are assisting in the matters; by those who are sent out on an embassy; by those who watch the outcomes of things people do openly; or by those who correctly draw conclusions and make guesses. The person who keeps his own secret safe will benefit in two ways: for either he reaches his goal and has been made happy in his own mind, or, if he fails, he avoids blame for the mishap. And someone who

τὸν προσκαλοῦντα εἰς τὴν συμβουλήν, συνετώτατον ὄντα, τῶν προσκαλουμένων τοὺς λογισμοὺς περιφρονεῖν, ὅτι βεβαιοῦται πολλάκις καὶ προτίθεται ἐκ τούτων ἡ τοῦ λογισμοῦ αὐτοῦ ἀκρίβεια.

9 "Εἰ δὲ ὁ βασιλεὺς συντηρεῖ τὰ οἰκεῖα μυστήρια καὶ τοῖς νουνεχέσι ἀνδράσι πρὸς τὰς οἰκονομίας κέχρηται, καὶ φοβερὸς τοῖς πᾶσι τυγχάνει, καὶ ἀκατάληπτος τὴν διάνοιαν, καὶ εἰ μὴ τὴν τοῦ εὐνοοῦντος καὶ εὐγνωμονοῦντος ἐνέργειαν παρορᾷ, μήτε τὰ παρά τινος ἡμαρτημένα παρατρέχει, οὗτος ἐν πᾶσιν εὐοδωθήσεται καὶ κράτιστος ἔσται. Τάξις δέ ἐστιν καὶ ἐν τοῖς μυστηρίοις· τὰ μὲν γὰρ δύο, τὰ δὲ καὶ ἐπέκεινα ἀκουστὰς ἐπιδέχεται. Ἐν ᾧ δέ σοι μέλλω ἀναγγεῖλαι, στόματα δύο καὶ ὦτα τέσσαρα συνδραμεῖν βούλομαι."

10 *Περὶ γένους πτηνοῦ τοῦ ἀναγορεύσαντος τὴν γλαῦκα βασιλέα.*

Ταῦτα ἀκούσας ὁ βασιλεὺς ἀνέστη καὶ καταμόνας αὐτῷ προσωμίλησε καὶ ἐπηρώτησε περὶ τῆς αἰτίας τῆς μεγίστης ἔχθρας. Ὁ δὲ πρωτοσύμβουλος εἶπεν ὅτι· "Ἀρχὴ τῆς διενέξεως ταύτης οὕτως ἐστίν· λέγεται γὰρ ὅτι πτηνῶν ποτε γένος τι συναθροισθέντων ἀνηγόρευσε γλαῦκά τινα ἑαυτοῖς βασιλέα. Κόραξ δέ τις ἐκεῖσε παρατυχὼν ἔφη· 'Εἰ μή τι τῶν τιμιωτέρων κατελείφθη πτηνῶν ὡς ταώς τε καὶ γέρανος καὶ νῆττα καὶ περιστερά, οὐκ ἔδει ἡμᾶς τὸ δυσειδέστατον τοῦτο καὶ σαπρὸν ζῷον οὕτω τιμῆσαι καὶ ἀναγορεῦσαι βασιλέα. Ὁμοῦ τε γὰρ καὶ τὸ τῆς ψυχῆς κάλλος

asks for advice, if he is very smart, should not ignore the reasoning of those who have been asked, since often the correctness of his own reasoning is confirmed and advanced by them.

“If a king keeps his own secrets, has appointed intelligent 9
men to his government, is feared by all, keeps his thoughts to himself, and if he neither ignores the actions of a person who is loyal and dutiful, nor overlooks someone’s offenses, such a man will be successful in all things and will be very powerful. There is a ranking in secrets too: for some allow for two listeners, and others for more. But for what I am going to tell you, I want two mouths and four ears to be present.”

About a group of birds who proclaimed the owl as king. 10

When the king had heard this, he rose, spoke with the fifth counselor alone, and asked him about the cause of the great enmity. And the chief counselor said, “The start of this disagreement was this: for it is said that once a group of birds assembled and proclaimed an owl as their king. But a crow that happened to be there said, ‘Unless some of the more respected birds, such as the peacock, the crane, the duck, and the dove, should have become extinct, we should not honor this most ugly and unwholesome creature in this way and proclaim it king. For as well as being devoid of any

ἀφήρηται, καὶ ἄνουν ἐστὶ καὶ ἀσύνετον, ὀργίλον τε καὶ ἄστεγκτον, καὶ ὄψεως ἡμερινῆς ἐστερημένον, δόλιόν τε καὶ πανοῦργον, ὃ δὴ πάντων χείριστον.' Καὶ ὅτι· 'Οὐ δύναταί τι τῶν πτηνῶν προσεγγίσαι αὐτῷ διὰ τὴν αὐτοῦ οἴησίν τε καὶ ὑπερηφανείαν καὶ πονηρίαν. Καὶ γὰρ ὁ βασιλεὺς εἰ τύχει καὶ ἀσύνετος εἶναι, οἱ δὲ ἐγγὺς καὶ πλησιάζοντες αὐτῷ νουνεχεῖς καὶ σώφρονες, ἡ βασιλεία αὐτοῦ μένει ἀπαρασάλευτος καὶ ἀπαράλλακτος, καὶ εὐθύνονται τὰ πράγματα αὐτοῦ, ὥσπερ ἐκείνου τοῦ λαγωοῦ τοῦ πορευθέντος ἀφ' ἑαυτοῦ πρὸς τοὺς ἐλέφαντας ἐκ προσώπου τοῦ φέγγους, καὶ κατορθωκότος τὰ πράγματα τοῦ βασιλέως αὐτοῦ σὺν πᾶσι τοῖς ὑπ' αὐτόν.' Τὰ δὲ πτηνὰ εἶπον πρὸς αὐτόν· 'Καὶ πῶς συνέβη τὰ κατ' αὐτόν; Ἀνάγγειλον ἡμῖν.'"

11 *Περὶ ἐλεφάντων καὶ λαγωῶν.*

"Ὁ δὲ κόραξ ἔφη πρὸς αὐτοὺς αὖθις· 'Λέγεται γάρ, ὥς ποτε τῶν καιρῶν γέγονεν ἀνομβρία καὶ λεῖψις τῶν πηγαίων ὑδάτων, ὥστε ξηρανθῆναι τὰ φυτὰ πάντα. Ἐστενοχωρήθησαν οὖν πάντα τὰ ζῷα, ἐξαιρέτως δὲ οἱ ἐλέφαντες, καὶ προσελθόντες εἶπον τῷ βασιλεῖ αὐτῶν· "Δέον ἡμᾶς ἐστιν, ὦ βασιλεῦ, μετοικῆσαι ἐν ἄλλῳ τινὶ τόπῳ χλοηφόρῳ καὶ ὑδατώδει, μήπως τεθνήξωμεν ἐνθάδε." Ὁ δὲ βασιλεὺς αὐτῶν ἔστειλέ τινας ἐξ αὐτῶν ἐφευρεῖν τόπον αὐτοῖς δέοντα. Οἱ δὲ ἀπελθόντες εὗρον τόπον καὶ ὑποστρέψαντες ἀνήγγειλαν τῷ βασιλεῖ, λέγοντες· "Ἐν τῷ δεῖνι τόπῳ ἔστι πηγὴ ὕδατος καὶ χλόη δαψιλής." Καὶ εὐθὺς μετοικήσαντες

spiritual beauty, it is both foolish and stupid, irritable and insufferable, deprived of sight during the day, deceitful and cunning, and the worst of all the birds.' The crow also said, 'No bird can approach it because of its self-conceit, its arrogance, and its wickedness. For even if the king is unintelligent, but his associates are sensible and prudent, his kingdom remains unshaken and unchanged and his affairs are well directed. Just as when that hare decided to go himself to the elephants as a representative of the moon, and set right the affairs of his king and all his subjects.' The birds said to him, 'How did his affairs turn out? Tell us.'"

About elephants and hares. 11

"The crow said to them again, 'For it is said that once upon a time there was a drought and the springs ran dry, so that all the plants withered. All the animals were hard pressed, but especially the elephants, who went to their king and said to him, "We need to move, your majesty, to another place where there is vegetation and water, so that we don't die here." Their king sent some of them to find a suitable place for them. When they had found a place and came back, they told the king, "In such and such a place there is a spring of water and plentiful vegetation." And they left there at once

κατέλυσαν ἐκεῖσε. Ἦσαν δὲ ἐν τῷ τόπῳ ἐκείνῳ ὀπαὶ λαγωῶν, καὶ προσελθόντες οἱ ἐλέφαντες κατεπάτησαν ἐκεῖσε τοὺς λαγωοὺς καὶ ἀπέκτεινάν τινας ἐξ αὐτῶν.

12 "'Ἐν δὲ τῷ ὑποστρέψαι αὐτοὺς συνήχθησαν οἱ λαγωοί, καὶ προσελθόντες τῷ βασιλεῖ αὐτῶν, ἀνήγγειλαν αὐτῷ ὅσα πεπόνθασι παρὰ τῶν ἐλεφάντων, καὶ ᾐτήσαντο αὐτῷ ὅπως γένηταί τις μηχανὴ παρ' αὐτῶν τοῦ λυτρωθῆναι τῆς ἐπηρείας τῶν ἐλεφάντων. Ἀναστὰς οὖν ἐξ αὐτῶν τις λαγωός, ἔφη· "Ἐγὼ ἀπελθὼν πρὸς τοὺς ἐλέφαντας ποιήσω τοῦτο, συνελθέτω δέ μοι καί τις τῶν λαγωῶν, ἵνα ἀκούσηται ὅσα πρὸς αὐτοὺς διαλέξομαι." Ὁ δὲ βασιλεὺς τῶν λαγωῶν εἶπε· "Σὺ πιστὸς εἶ, καὶ οὐ δεῖταί σου μαρτυρία τῆς πράξεως, καὶ γὰρ ἔγνων σου τὴν πρὸς τὸ ὁμόφυλον εὐγνωμοσύνην. Ἄπελθε οὖν καὶ ποίει καὶ λέγε ἃ βούλει." Ἀνατείλαντος δὲ τοῦ φέγγους, προσῆλθεν ὁ λαγωὸς τοῖς ἐλέφασι, καὶ φοβηθεὶς μήποτε καταπατηθῇ παρ' αὐτῶν, ἀνῆλθεν ἐπί τινα βουνὸν ὑψηλόν.

13 "'Καὶ κράξας φωνῇ μεγάλῃ, εἶπεν· "Ὦ βασιλεῦ τῶν ἐλεφάντων, πρέσβυς πρὸς σὲ ἀπεστάλην παρὰ τοῦ φέγγους. Σὺ δὲ οἶδας ὅτι ὁ ἀπεσταλμένος ἀβλαβὴς μένει, κἂν θρασυλογῇ. Καὶ γὰρ λέγει σοι τὸ φέγγος ὅτι· 'Ἄτακτον καὶ μεμπτέον ἐστὶν τὸ πολεμεῖν τὸν δυνατὸν τὸν ἀδύνατον, ἐπαινετώτερον δὲ τὸ πολεμεῖν τὸν ἰσοδύναμον. Σὺ δὲ ἐλθὼν ἐν τῷδε τῷ τόπῳ ἀδικεῖς καὶ καταβλάπτεις τοὺς ὑπ' ἐμὲ λαγωούς, οἳ καὶ ἀσθενέστεροι πάντων τῶν ζῴων πεφύκασι. Καὶ ἀπέκτεινας αὐτούς, καὶ κατέλυσας αὐτῶν τὰς ὀπάς, καὶ ἐθόλανας τὸ ὕδωρ ἐν ᾧ εἰμι. Ἀλλ' ἰδοὺ κἀγὼ διὰ ταῦτα, ἃ πεποίηκας πρὸς αὐτοὺς ἀδίκως, σβεννύω τοὺς

and migrated. But there were holes where hares lived in that place and when the elephants arrived, they trampled the hares there and killed some of them.

"'The hares gathered together as they retreated, went to 12
their king and told him what they had suffered from the elephants, and asked him if there was some way for them to be rescued from the elephants' abuse. Then one of the hares stood up and said, "I'll go to the elephants and do this, but let one of the other hares also come with me so that you can hear what I'm going to say to them." But the king of the hares said, "You're trustworthy, and there's no need of a witness for your actions, for I know your loyalty toward your fellow hares. Go then, and do and say what you want." And when the moon rose, the hare approached the elephants, and fearing that he would be trampled by them, he went up onto a high hill.

"'Shouting very loudly, he said, "King of the elephants, I 13
have been sent by the moon as a messenger to you. And you know that someone who has been sent, even if he should speak boldly, is to remain unharmed. For the moon tells you, 'It is inappropriate and wrong for someone who is powerful to go to war against someone who is powerless, and more laudable to go to war with someone of equal power. But you, by coming to this place, are wronging and harming the hares who are my subjects, and who are by nature the weakest of all living creatures. You have killed them, you have destroyed their holes, and you have disturbed the water in which I am. But see, because of what you have unjustly done

ὀφθαλμοὺς ὑμῶν καὶ ἀποκτενῶ ὑμᾶς. Καὶ εἰ ταῦτα ἀπιστεῖς, βασιλεῦ, ἐλθὲ πρὸς τὴν πηγὴν καὶ ὄψει με.'"

14 "'Ἀκούσαντες δὲ ταῦτα ὁ τῶν ἐλεφάντων βασιλεὺς καὶ οἱ σὺν αὐτῷ πάντες παρὰ τοῦ λαγωοῦ, ὡς ἐκπροσώπου τοῦ φέγγους, ἐθαύμασαν. Καὶ ὁ ἐλέφας προσκαλεσάμενος τὸν λαγωὸν ἀπῆλθεν πρὸς τὴν πηγὴν σὺν αὐτῷ. Ὁ δὲ λαγωὸς ὑποδείξας τῷ ἐλέφαντι πρὸς τὴν πηγὴν τὸ τοῦ φέγγους ἐκτύπωμα, εἶπεν αὐτῷ· "Νίψαι ἐκ τοῦδε τοῦ ὕδατος καὶ πρόσευξαι, ὅπως ἀξιωθῇς τῆς ὁμιλίας αὐτοῦ." Ὁ δὲ βασιλεὺς τῶν ἐλεφάντων τοῦτο ποιήσας, ἐταράχθη τὸ ὕδωρ τῆς πηγῆς καὶ ἦν μὴ φαινόμενον τὸ τοῦ φέγγους ἐκτύπωμα. Ὁ δὲ λαγωὸς τότε φησὶ πρὸς αὐτόν· "Εἶδες, βασιλεῦ, πῶς ὠργίσθη κατὰ σοῦ εἰς ὃ ἔδρασας;" Ὁ δὲ βασιλεὺς τῶν ἐλεφάντων φοβηθεὶς εἶπεν· "Ὦ κύριέ μου, μὴ ὀργίζου κατ' ἐμοῦ ἔτι, ἀλλὰ σύγγνωθί μου τῷ πταίσματι, ὅτι ἀπάρτι οὐκ ἐλεύσομαι ἐνθάδε, οὐδέ τις τῶν ὑπ' ἐμέ." Καὶ διὰ τοῦ τοιούτου τρόπου ἀπηλλάγησαν οἱ λαγωοὶ τῆς τῶν ἐλεφάντων βλάβης.

"'Καὶ ταῦτα ὑμῖν διεξῄειν διὰ τὴν ὀξυθυμίαν καὶ μεγαλαυχίαν καὶ πονηρίαν τῆς γλαυκός, καὶ ὅτι οὐ δύναταί τις προσεγγίσαι αὐτῇ ἢ συμβουλεύσασθαι ἢ ὁμιλῆσαι, διότι οὐκ ἔστιν ἐξ αἵματος βασιλικοῦ. Πάλιν δὲ οἱ προβάλλοντες μετὰ τοῦ κακοῦ βασιλέως διαβολάς τινας καὶ ἀδικίας καὶ πονηρίας, πείσονται τὸ τοῦ λαγωοῦ καὶ τοῦ σκιούρου, καὶ τοῦ κάττου, οἵτινες ἠρέσθησαν κριθῆναι παρὰ τούτου τοῦ πανούργου καὶ πονηροῦ.' Τὰ δὲ πτηνὰ εἶπον· 'Καὶ πῶς ἦν τοῦτο;'"

to the hares, I am going to put out your eyes and kill you. If you do not believe this, king, go to the spring and you will see me.'"

"'When the king and all those who were with him heard 14
the hare's words as the moon's representative, they were amazed. And the elephant, after he had called the hare to him, went to the spring with him. When the hare had shown the elephant the reflection of the moon in the spring, he said to him, "Cleanse yourself in this water and pray, so that you may be worthy of his address." And when the king of the elephants had done this, the water of the spring was troubled, and the reflection of the moon was not visible. Then the hare said to him, "Do you see, king, how he is angry with you for what you have done?" And the king of the elephants was afraid, and said, "My lord, do not be angry with me anymore, but forgive me for my sin, because from now on I will not come here, nor will any of my subjects." And in this way the hares were rid of the harm done by the elephants.

"'And I've been through all this for you because of the owl's short temper and arrogance and wickedness, and because no one can approach or give advice or speak with it, because it is not of royal blood. And again, those who are putting forward any slanders and wrongs and wickedness in favor of the evil king will suffer what the hare and the squirrel and the cat did, when they chose to be judged by this crafty and wicked creature.' And the birds said, 'And how was that?'"

15 *Περὶ λαγωοῦ, σκιούρου, καὶ κάττου.*

"Ὁ δὲ κόραξ ὑπολαβὼν πάλιν ἔφη· 'Ἦν πλησίον τινὸς δένδρου ὀπὴ σκιούρου, ἦν δέ μοι ὁ σκίουρος ἀγαπητὸς καὶ ποθητὸς καὶ φίλτατος πάνυ. Μιᾷ δὲ τῶν ἡμερῶν ἀπελθὼν ὁ σκίουρος, κατέλιπεν τὴν ὀπὴν αὐτοῦ μόνην· ἐγὼ δὲ ἀπελθὼν ἐν αὐτῇ καὶ μὴ εὑρὼν τοῦτον, ἐξεδεχόμην αὐτὸν πάνυ καὶ οὐχ ὑπέστρεψε, καὶ μεγάλως ἐθλίβην περὶ αὐτοῦ. Ἐλθὼν δὲ λαγωός τις ἐξ ἄλλου τινὸς τόπου, κατῴκησεν ἐν τῇ ὀπῇ αὐτοῦ. Μετὰ δὲ ταῦτα, στραφεὶς ὁ σκίουρος, εἶδε τὸν λαγωὸν ἐν τῇ ὀπῇ αὐτοῦ, καὶ εἶπεν αὐτῷ· "Ἔξελθε ἐκ τῆς οἰκίας μου." Ὁ δὲ λαγωὸς μὴ θέλων ἐξελθεῖν εἶπεν αὐτῷ· "Οὗτος ὁ τόπος ἐμὸς ἦν τὸ πρότερον, καὶ εἰ βούλῃ, δικασθῶμεν." Ὁ δὲ σκίουρος ἔφη· "Ἔχω περὶ τούτου μάρτυρας." Καὶ ὁ λαγωός· "Ὅταν εὑρήσῃς δικαστήν, παράγαγε τοὺς μάρτυρας." Ὁ δὲ εἶπεν· "Πλησίον ἡμῶν ἐστιν ὁ δικαστής." Καὶ ὁ λαγωός· "Καὶ τίς ἐστιν οὗτος;" Ὁ δὲ σκίουρος· "Κάττης τις ἀσκητὴς παρὰ τῷ αἰγιαλῷ θεοσεβής, καὶ δίκαιος, μὴ ὀργιζόμενός ποτέ τινος." Ὁ δὲ λαγωὸς ἔφη· "Ἀπέλθωμεν λοιπὸν πρὸς αὐτόν."

16 "'Ὁ δὲ κάττης τούτους ἰδὼν πρὸς αὐτὸν ἐρχομένους, ἤρξατο εὔχεσθαι ὑποψιθυρίζων καὶ γονυκλιτῶν, ὅτι φύσει πανοῦργος ἦν, καὶ ὅτι ἐβουλεύσατο ἵνα καταφάγῃ αὐτούς. Ὃ καὶ ἐποίησεν. Οἱ δὲ ἐγγίσαντες αὐτοῦ, ἤρξαντο ἀντιλέγεσθαι καὶ ἀντιμάχεσθαι δεινῶς. Ὁ δὲ κριτὴς εἶπεν αὐτοῖς· "Ἵνα τί, ἀδελφοί, οὕτως ἀντιμάχεσθε; Ἐγγίσατε πρός με, ἵνα ἀκούσωμαι ὑμῶν, ὅτι γεγήρακα καὶ τετύφλωμαι, καὶ τοῖς ὠσὶν οὐκ ἀκούω. Ἐγγίσατέ μοι οὖν πλησίον καὶ ἄρατε τὰς φωνὰς ὑμῶν, ὅπως νοήσω τὰ λεχθέντα παρ' ὑμῶν." Οἱ

CHAPTER 4

About a hare, a squirrel, and a cat. 15

“And the crow said again, ‘Near a tree there was a squirrel’s hole, and the squirrel was my beloved and very dear and close friend. One day the squirrel went off and left his hole empty. And when I went into it and didn’t find the squirrel, I waited a long time for him, but he didn’t come back and I was very worried about him. Then a hare arrived from somewhere else and took up residence in his hole. Later on, when the squirrel returned, he saw the hare in his hole and said to him, “Get out of my house!” But the hare didn’t want to leave and said to him, “This was my hole before; if you want, let’s get a judgment.” And the squirrel said, “I have witnesses to this.” And the hare said, “When you’ve found a judge, bring your witnesses along.” And he said, “There’s a judge close by.” And the hare said, “Who’s that?” And the squirrel replied, “There’s a cat at the beach who’s a monk; he’s devout and just, and never gets angry with anyone.” And the hare said, “All right, let’s go to him.”

“‘When the cat saw them coming toward him, he began 16
to pray, whispering and genuflecting, because he was crafty by nature and because he was planning to eat them. Which, indeed, he did. When they approached him, they began to argue and quarrel fiercely. And the judge said to them, “Why are you quarreling like this, brothers? Come close to me so that I can hear you, because I’m old and blind and I can’t hear with my ears. Come right up close to me and raise your voices so that I can understand what you’re saying.” And

δὲ ὡς ἄφρονες τοῦτο ἐποίησαν. Ἀκούσας δὲ τὰ λεχθέντα παρ' αὐτῶν, ἤρξατο ἐκεῖνος παραινεῖν αὐτούς. Οὗτοι δὲ ἀκούσαντες τὰς παραινέσεις αὐτοῦ θαρσαλέως προσήγγισαν αὐτῷ. Ὁ δὲ εἰσπηδήσας ἀπέκτεινεν αὐτούς.

"'Καὶ ταύτην τὴν παραβολὴν διεξῄειν ὑμῖν, ὦ οὗτοι, ὅτι ἡ γλαῦξ πανοῦργος τυγχάνει καὶ σαρκοφάγος καὶ οὐ δεῖ ὑμᾶς καταπιστεῦσαι αὐτῇ.'"

17 *Περὶ τῆς καθαιρέσεως τῆς γλαυκὸς ἀπὸ τῆς ἀρχῆς τῶν πτηνῶν.*

"Ταῦτα ἀκοῦσαν τὸ πτηνὸν γένος ἐκεῖνο καθεῖλον τῆς ἀρχῆς τὴν γλαῦκα. Καθαιρεθεῖσα δὲ ἡ γλαῦξ εἶπε πρὸς τὸν κόρακα· 'Οὐ σύνοιδα ἐμαυτῇ, ὦ κόραξ, ὡς ἔδρασά ποτε εἴς σέ τι ἐναντίον, ἵνα τοιαύτην πρός με ποιήσῃς ἀντέκτισιν. Ἀλλ' ἴσθι, ὡς τὸ τεμνόμενον διὰ τῆς ἀξίνης δένδρον καὶ αὖθις φύει καὶ τὸ τραῦμα τὸ διὰ ξίφους γινόμενον συνουλοῦται καὶ ἐνσκιρροῦται. Ἡ δὲ τῆς γλώττης δῆξις ἀνίατός ἐστιν ὡς ἁπτομένης μέσης αὐτῆς τῆς καρδίας. Καὶ γὰρ τὸ πῦρ σβέννυσι τὸ ὕδωρ, καὶ τὸ δηλητήριον φαρμάκοις τισὶν ἀντικρούεται καὶ ὁ ἔρως τῇ ἐπιτυχίᾳ παύεται. Τὸ δὲ τῆς μνησικακίας πῦρ ἀείζωόν ἐστιν. Καὶ ὃ ἐνεσπάρη μέσον ἡμῶν καὶ ὑμῶν, ὦ κόραξ, δένδρον γενήσεται μηδέποτε ἐκριζούμενον.' Ταῦτα εἰποῦσα ἡ γλαῦξ ἀπηλλάγη θυμοῦ πνέουσα, καὶ ὁ κόραξ μετεμελήθη, ἐφ' οἷς κατηναιδεύσατο. Αὕτη οὖν ἐστιν ἡ μεγίστη ἔχθρα καὶ οὐκ ἄλλη."

Ὁ δὲ βασιλεὺς ἔφη· "Ἔγνων τὰ τοιαῦτα, λοιπὸν οὖν εἰπὲ περὶ τῶν προκειμένων καὶ τῶν ἀναγκαίων ἡμῖν, καὶ τί

being foolish, they did so. When the cat heard what they were saying, he began to give them advice; and they listened to his advice and confidently went up to him. But he sprang on them and killed them.

"'I've been through this lesson for you,' said the crow, 'because the owl is crafty, and a meat eater, and you shouldn't trust it.'"

About the overthrow of the owl from 17
power over the birds.

"When the group of birds heard this, they overthrew the owl from power. And when it had been overthrown, the owl said to the crow, 'I'm not aware, crow, of ever having done anything hostile to you for you to take such revenge on me. But you should know both that a tree which has been felled by an ax grows again, and that a wound from a sword heals over and becomes hardened; but the bite of the tongue is incurable, as the heart is gravely affected by it. For water quenches fire, and a poison is stopped by drugs, and desire is ended by fulfillment. However, the fire of resentment is everlasting. And that which has been sown between us and you, crow, will become a tree that will never be uprooted.' When the owl had said these things, it went away, seething with anger, and the crow regretted having been so insulting. So that, and nothing else, is the great enmity."

And the king said, "I understand this, but speak about the present situation, what we need, and what has to be

δεῖ ἄρτι ποιεῖν.” Ὁ δὲ πρωτοσύμβουλος εἶπε· “Τὰ περὶ τοῦ πολέμου οὐ συναινῶ, οὐδὲ προτρέπω τοῦτο, ἀλλ' ἴσως δυνηθείημέν τι διά τινος μηχανῆς ἑτέρας κατορθῶσαι, μεγάλως γὰρ αὕτη δύναται, καθάπερ ἐμηχανήσαντο καί τινες κατά τινος ἀσκητοῦ.”

18 *Περὶ ἀσκητοῦ.*

“Λέγεται γὰρ ὡς ἀσκητής τις ἠγόρασε τράγον καὶ ἀπήρχετο εἰς τὸν οἶκον αὐτοῦ. Ἰδόντες δὲ αὐτόν τινες συνεβουλεύσαντο ἆραι ἀπ' αὐτοῦ τὸν τράγον διὰ μηχανῆς τινος. Ἐγγίσαντες οὖν πρὸς αὐτόν, εἶπεν ὁ πρῶτος αὐτῶν· ‘Θεωρεῖτε πῶς σύρει οὗτος ὁ ἀσκητὴς τὸν κύνα τὸν μιαρόν;’ Ὁ δὲ δεύτερος ἔφη· ‘Θεωροῦμεν ἀσκητήν, ἔργον δὲ ἀσεβοῦς· εἰ γὰρ ἦν ἀσκητής, οὐκ ἂν ἔσυρε τὸν κύνα, ἀλλ' ἀπέλυσεν αὐτὸν καὶ ἐκάθητο ὡς ἀσκητής.’ Καὶ ὁ τρίτος εἶπεν· ‘Ὦ ἀσκητά, πωλεῖς τὸν κύνα;’ Ὁ δὲ ἀσκητὴς ταῦτα παρ' αὐτῶν ἀκούσας ἐπείσθη, καὶ ἐνόμισε τὸν τράγον ἀληθῆ κύνα εἶναι, καὶ ἀπέλυσεν αὐτόν· καὶ ἀπελθὼν ἔπλυνε τὰ ἱμάτια αὐτοῦ ἐν τῷ ποταμῷ, καὶ ἐκαθαρίσθη. Οἱ δὲ λαβόντες τὸν τράγον ἔσφαξαν καὶ διεμερίσαντο αὐτὸν ἐν ἑαυτοῖς.

“Καὶ ταύτην σοι ἐκδιεξῄειν τὴν παραβολήν, ἵνα ἐπιγνῷς ὁμολογουμένως, ὡς ἄνω μοι εἴρηται, ὅτι ἡ μηχανὴ μεγάλα δύναται ποιῆσαι.

19 “Κρίνω οὖν συμφέρον εἶναι ὀργισθῆναί σου τὴν μεγαλειότητα κατ' ἐμοῦ πάντων ὁρώντων καὶ προστάξαι τοῖς στρατιώταις τυφθῆναί με ἀφειδῶς ἐπὶ μέσου ὥστε αἱματωθῆναί με τῷ πλήθει τῶν αἰκισμῶν, εἶτα καὶ τὰ πτερά μου

done right now." The chief counselor said, "I don't agree on the matter of war, nor do I encourage it, but perhaps we could achieve something by some other means, for that could achieve a lot, just as the ruse some people devised against an ascetic did."

About an ascetic. 18

"For it is said that an ascetic bought a goat and was taking it home. Some people who saw it made a plan to take the goat from him by a ruse. They went up to him, and the first one said, 'Do you see how this ascetic is dragging the dirty dog along with him?' And the second said, 'We see an ascetic, but what he's doing is sacrilegious. For if he were an ascetic, he wouldn't be dragging the dog around but would get rid of it and would live as an ascetic.' And the third said, 'Ascetic, will you sell the dog?' And when the ascetic heard them saying all this, he was convinced and thought the goat really was a dog and he got rid of it. Then he went and washed his clothes in the river and was purified. But they took the goat and slaughtered it and shared it between them.

"And I've been through this lesson in detail for you, so that you may know without doubt that, as I said before, a ruse can achieve a lot.

"So I believe it would be advantageous for your majesty 19
to be extremely angry with me, with everyone watching, and for you to order the soldiers to set upon me without mercy in public, so that I start bleeding from so much mistreatment, then also that my feathers and my tail itself

τίλλεσθαι καὶ αὐτὴν τὴν οὐρὰν καὶ ῥιφῆναι πλησίον τούτου τοῦ κέδρου. Εἶτα, τούτου γενομένου, ἀπᾶραί σε μετὰ τῶν ὑπό σε ἐπί τινα τόπον, καὶ ἐᾶσαί με κείμενον." Ὃ δὴ καὶ ποιήσας, ὁ βασιλεὺς τῶν κοράκων μετὰ τῶν ὑπ' αὐτὸν ἀπεδήμησε.

20 Νυκτὸς δὲ αἱ γλαῦκες ἐπὶ τῷ δένδρῳ παραγενόμεναι, οὐκ εἶδόν τινα ἐν αὐτῷ εἰ μὴ μόνον τὸν τυφθέντα κόρακα κείμενον, καὶ ἀνήγγειλαν τοῦτο τῷ οἰκείῳ αὐτῶν βασιλεῖ. Ὁ δὲ προσεγγίσας τούτῳ ἐπηρώτησε τοῦτον πόθεν τέ ἐστι καὶ ὅπῃ οἱ λοιποὶ ἐτράπησαν κόρακες. Ὁ δὲ κόραξ εἶπεν· "Ἐγώ εἰμι ὁ δεῖνα, ὁ τοῦ δεῖνος, ὅπου δὲ οἱ λοιποὶ κόρακες ἐτράπησαν οὐκ ἴσημι. Πῶς γὰρ οὑτωσὶ διακείμενος τὰ ἐκείνων ἐπίσταμαι μυστήρια;" Ὁ δὲ βασιλεὺς ἔφη· "Τῷ ὄντι οὗτός ἐστιν ὁ πρωτοσύμβουλος τοῦ τῶν κοράκων ἀρχηγοῦ· ἐπερωτήσατε οὖν αὐτὸν διὰ ποίαν αἰτίαν τοιαῦτα πέπονθε δεινά."

21 Ὁ δὲ κόραξ εἶπεν· "Ἡ ἐμὴ κακοβουλία τοιούτοις με κακοῖς περιέπλεξεν. Ὅτε γὰρ ἡττήθησαν παρ' ὑμῶν οἱ κόρακες, βουλευτήριον τούτοις συνέστη παραυτίκα καὶ ἕκαστος, ὡς εἶχε σκέψεως, ἐφθέγξατο καὶ συνεβούλευσε καὶ ἀπεφθέγξατο. Ἐγὼ δὲ ἐπαρρησιάσθην ὑπὲρ ὑμῶν καὶ εἶπον ὡς· 'Ἀδυνατώτεροί ἐστε τῶν γλαυκῶν καὶ ἀσθενέστεροι, καὶ διὰ τοῦτο δεῖ μὴ ἀντιπράττειν αὐτοῖς, ἀλλὰ τὴν εἰρήνην ζητῆσαι καὶ φόρους τελέσαι, οὕσπερ, εἰ δέξοιντο, καὶ ἀσπάζεσθαι καὶ στέργειν καὶ τῷ Θεῷ χάριν ἕνεκα τούτου ἀπονέμειν. Τῷ γὰρ ἐπικρατεστέρῳ ἐχθρῷ δεῖ τὸν ἐχέφρονα ὑπείκειν ὥστε τὴν ἐκ τούτου βλάβην διεκφεύγειν. Ἢ οὐχ ὁρᾶτε ὅπως ὁ σφοδρὸς ἄνεμος τὰ μὲν ὑπερμεγέθη

be plucked out, and I be thrown out near this cedar tree. Then, once this has happened, you should go somewhere else with your subordinates, and let me lie there." So the king of the crows did this and went away with his subordinates.

That night, when the owls arrived at the tree, they saw no 20
one in it, only the crow which had been beaten and was lying there, and they reported this to their own king. The king went up to the crow, and asked him where he was from and where the other crows had gone. And the crow said, "I'm so-and-so, son of so-and-so, but as to where the rest of the crows have gone, I don't know. For how would I know their secrets, when I'm in such a state?" And the king said, "Actually, this one is the chief counselor to the leader of the crows, so ask him why he has suffered such terrible things."

And the crow said, "My bad advice got me involved in this 21
trouble. For when the crows were defeated by you owls, a council about these things was called immediately, and each spoke and gave his advice and expressed himself according to his opinion. I spoke freely about you, and I said, 'You crows are less powerful than the owls and weaker, and, because of this, you should not offer them any resistance but should seek peace and pay tribute; and, if they accept it, you should be glad and content, and should give thanks to God as a result. For someone who's smart must yield to an enemy who's superior so as to escape harm from him. Do you not see how a violent wind uproots and splits very large trees,

τῶν δένδρων ἐκριζοῖ καὶ συνθραύει, τὰ δὲ χθαμαλώτερα καὶ ἀδρανῆ τῶν φυτῶν τούτῳ συμπεριφερόμενα οὔτε καταβάλλει οὔτε ἐκριζοῖ;' Ταῦτα ἀκούσαντες οἱ κόρακες ὑπώπτευσαν ὡς διά τινα τρόπον εὐνοϊκῶς τὰ πρὸς ὑμᾶς διακείμενος ταῦτα φθέγγομαι, καὶ θυμοῦ πλησθέντες τοιαύτῃ με καταδίκῃ ὑπέβαλον, τὸ πολεμεῖν τοῦ εἰρηνεύειν προαιρούμενοι."

22 *Περὶ τῶν πρωτοσυμβούλων τῶν τοῦ βασιλέως γλαυκῶν.*

Ταῦτα ἀκούσας ὁ βασιλεὺς ἔφη πρός τινα τῶν πρωτοσυμβούλων αὐτοῦ· "Τί δεῖ ἡμᾶς περὶ τούτου ποιῆσαι;" Ὁ δὲ εἶπεν· "Τάχιον ἀναιρεθήτω. Τρόπαιον γὰρ ἡμῖν γενήσεται μέγιστον ἡ τούτου ἀναίρεσις· ἀπαλλαγησόμεθα γὰρ αὐτοῦ τῶν σκαιωριῶν καὶ μηχανῶν, ἃς ὑπὲρ τῶν κοράκων συρράπτειν οὐ παύεται. Λέγεται γὰρ ὡς ὁ ἀμελῶν περί τι τῶν πρακτέων τῶν ἀξιολόγων πραγμάτων ἤδη ἐν χερσὶ τοῦτο ἔχων, καὶ ἀπολέσας τοῦτο, οὐ ῥᾳδίως ἄλλοτε αὐτοῦ τεύξεται. Καὶ ὁ τὸν ἐχθρὸν αὐτοῦ ἐν ἀδυναμίᾳ εὑρίσκων καὶ μὴ ἀναιρῶν αὐτόν, ἐς νέωτα μεταμεληθήσεται ἰσχυροποιούμενον τοῦτον καὶ ἐνδυναμούμενον ὁρῶν."

23 Ἕτερος δέ τις τῶν τοῦ βασιλέως πρωτοσυμβούλων ὑπολαβὼν ἔφη· "Οὐ δεῖ τοῦτον ἀναιρεθῆναι, γέγραπται ὡς, *κάλαμον συντετριμμένον οὐ κατεάξει καὶ λίνον τυφόμενον οὐ σβέσει·* ἐλεεῖν δὲ μᾶλλον τοῦτον δεῖ καὶ οἰκτείρειν, ὅτι τοιάσδε ὑπέστη συμφορὰς καὶ τοιαῦτα ῥαπίσματα. Δεῖ οὖν τὸν τοιοῦτον περιέπειν καὶ θάλπειν· τὸ γὰρ διαφέρεσθαι μᾶλλον τοὺς ἐχθροὺς πρὸς ἀλλήλους καὶ ἐριστικῶς

but does not topple nor uproot the lower-growing and flimsy plants that adapt themselves to it?' When the crows had heard this, they suspected that I was saying such things because I was somehow friendly to you; they were filled with anger and subjected me to this sentence, as they preferred making war to peace."

About the chief counselors of the king of the owls. 22

In response to this the king of the owls said to one of his chief counselors, "What should we do about this crow?" He said, "Get rid of him quickly. For killing him will be a great sign of victory for us; for we will be rid of the treachery and ruses which he never ceases contriving for the crows. For it is said that someone who is careless about something which is important to do when he already has it in his hand, will not easily get it back another time, once he has lost it. And someone who finds his enemy is powerless and does not kill him, will regret it next year when he sees him invigorated and revitalized."

But another of the king's chief counselors said in reply, 23
"He should not be killed, as it has been written, *do not break a reed that has been crushed and do not extinguish smoldering flax.* One should rather take pity on him and show him compassion, considering the kind of mistreatment and beating he's undergone. So we should treat him well and take care of him, for having one's enemies divided among each other and

διακεῖσθαι μέγιστόν ἐστιν εὐτύχημα, καὶ ὅμως ἴσως ὠφεληθείημεν ἐξ αὐτοῦ, ὥσπερ ὁ ἔμπορος παρὰ τοῦ κλέπτου."

24 *Περὶ ἐμπόρου βδελυττομένου παρὰ τῆς γυναικὸς αὐτοῦ.*

"Λέγεται γὰρ ὡς ἔμπορός τις γηραιός, πολύολβος ὢν καὶ ἔχων γυναῖκα νέαν, ἐπόθει αὐτὴν λίαν. Αὕτη δὲ αὐτὸν ἀπεστρέφετο. Μιᾷ δὲ νυκτὶ κοιμωμένων αὐτῶν, εἰσῆλθε κλέπτης τοῦ συλῆσαι τὴν οἰκίαν αὐτοῦ. Ἡ δὲ γυνὴ τοῦτον ἰδοῦσα καὶ φοβηθεῖσα συνεσφίχθη τῷ στήθει τοῦ ἀνδρὸς αὐτῆς. Ἔξυπνος δὲ γενόμενος ὁ ἀνὴρ αὐτῆς, εἶπεν αὐτῇ· 'Πόθεν μοι τοῦτο; Καὶ τίς ἡ εὐσπλαγχνία αὕτη;' Καὶ ἀναβλέψας εἶδε τὸν κλέπτην καὶ ἔγνω ὅτι δι' αὐτοῦ ἐστιν ἡ εὐσπλαγχνία αὕτη τῆς γυναικὸς αὐτοῦ πρὸς αὐτόν, καὶ εἶπε πρὸς τὸν κλέπτην· 'Λάβε ἐκ τοῦ οἴκου μου ὅσα θέλεις ἀκωλύτως, διὰ τὸ πεποιηκέναι σε πρός με τοῦτο τὸ ἀγαθόν· καὶ γὰρ διὰ σοῦ περιεπλάκη μοι ταύτῃ τῇ νυκτὶ ἡ περιπόθητός μου γυνή, ἡ πολλά με μισοῦσα.'

"Οὕτω καὶ ἡμεῖς ἴσως ἐξ αὐτοῦ ὠφεληθῶμεν." Ἄλλος δέ τις πρωτοσύμβουλος τοῦ βασιλέως εἶπε· "Καλῶς ἔφη οὗτος, ὦ βασιλεῦ· καὶ γὰρ ὁ νουνεχὴς ὅταν εὕρῃ τὸν φίλον τοῦ ἐχθροῦ αὐτοῦ τυφθέντα καὶ μαστιχθέντα παρ' αὐτοῦ, δεῖ αὐτὸν εὐεργετῆσαι, καὶ ἴσως ἂν ὠφεληθήσεται παρ' αὐτοῦ, ὥσπερ ὁ μοναχὸς ὁ λυτρωθεὶς ἐκ τοῦ θανάτου διὰ τῆς μάχης τοῦ δαίμονος καὶ τοῦ κλέπτου."

in conflict is a great stroke of luck, and at the same time we may perhaps benefit from him, just like the merchant did from the thief."

About a merchant who was detested by his wife. 24

"For it is said that a merchant, who was old and very wealthy, had a young wife whom he desired very much. But she rejected him. One night, while they were sleeping, a thief came in to rob his house. But the wife saw him and, terrified, pressed herself to her husband's chest. Her husband woke up and said to her, 'Where's this coming from? What's this affection?' And looking up he saw the thief and understood this was the reason for his wife's affection toward him. So he said to the thief, 'Take what you like from my house without any hindrance because you've provoked this love for me, and because of you my wife, whom I really desire but who really hates me, embraced me tonight.'

"So we also may perhaps benefit from the crow." And another of the owl king's chief counselors said, "This one speaks well, my king. For an intelligent man, whenever he finds his enemy's friend beaten and whipped by him, should look after him, and perhaps he will be helped by him, just like the monk who was saved from death by the fight between the demon and the thief."

25 *Περὶ ἀσκητοῦ, καὶ κλέπτου καὶ διαβόλου.*

“Λέγεται γὰρ ὡς ἀσκητής τις θεάρεστος εἶχε δάμαλίν τινα ἔν τινι τόπῳ. Ἰδὼν δὲ αὐτὴν κλέπτης τις, ἠβουλήθη αὐτὴν κλέψαι μετὰ πανουργίας. Συνοδοιπορήσας ὅλως μετ’ αὐτοῦ, εἶτα ἐφάνη ὁ διάβολος ἐν μορφῇ ἀνθρώπου. Ὁ δὲ κλέπτης πρὸς τὸν διάβολον ἔφη· ‘Πόθεν ἔρχῃ καὶ ποῦ πορεύῃ; Καὶ τί βούλει ποιεῖν;’ Ὁ δὲ εἶπεν· ‘Διάβολός εἰμι καὶ βούλομαι τὸν ἀσκητὴν τοῦτον ἀποπνῖξαι.’ Ὁ δὲ κλέπτης εἶπεν πρὸς αὐτόν· ‘Κἀγὼ βούλομαι τὴν δάμαλιν αὐτοῦ κλέψαι.’ Ἀμφότεροι δὲ ἠκολούθησαν ἐκεῖσε τῷ μοναχῷ μέχρι τοῦ οἴκου αὐτοῦ. Ὁ δὲ μοναχὸς βαλὼν τὴν δάμαλιν αὐτοῦ εἰς τὸν οἶκον αὐτοῦ εἰσῆλθεν τοῦ δειπνῆσαι. Ὁ δὲ κλέπτης εἶπεν ἐν ἑαυτῷ· ‘Ἐὰν εἰσέλθῃ ὁ διάβολος πνῖξαι τὸν ἀσκητήν, ἴσως ἀναφωνήσῃ, καὶ συναχθέντος τοῦ λαοῦ ἀποτύχω τῆς ἐμῆς προσδοκίας.’ Καὶ εὐθὺς ἔφη πρὸς τὸν διάβολον· ‘Βλέπε ἀκριβῶς, ἕως οὗ πρότερον εἰσέλθω ἐγώ, καὶ λάβω τὴν δάμαλιν, καὶ ἔσται ἡμῖν κοινή.’ Ὁ δὲ διάβολος φοβηθεὶς μήπως ἐν τῷ εἰσελθεῖν τὸν κλέπτην τοῦ λαβεῖν τὴν δάμαλιν, νοηθῇ παρὰ τῶν ἀνθρώπων καὶ ἀστοχήσωσιν ὁμοῦ, εἶπε τῷ κλέπτῃ· ‘Ἄνεσχε ἕως ἂν ὑπνώσωσιν πάντες, καὶ εὐθέως τύχομεν ὁμοῦ, ὅπερ βουλόμεθα ἀμφότεροι.’ Ὁ δὲ κλέπτης εἶπεν· ‘Οὐχί.’ Καὶ ἤρξαντο μάχεσθαι πρὸς ἀλλήλους, ἕως οὗ ἐφώνησεν ὁ κλέπτης τῷ μοναχῷ καὶ εἶπεν· ‘Οὗτος ὁ διάβολος βούλεταί σε πνῖξαι·’ καὶ ὁ διάβολος πάλιν φωνήσας τῷ μοναχῷ ἔφη· ‘Καὶ οὗτος ὁ κλέπτης, βούλεταί σου κλέψαι τὴν δάμαλιν.’ Ὁ δὲ ἀσκητὴς ἀφυπνώσας, ἐδίωξεν αὐτοὺς καὶ ἐρρύσθη ἀπὸ τοῦ θανάτου.

About an ascetic, a thief, and the devil. 25

"For it is said that a devout ascetic, who was pleasing to God, had a heifer somewhere. A thief saw this and planned to steal it by cunning. The devil, who traveled everywhere with him, then appeared in the form of a man. The thief said to the devil, 'Where have you come from and where are you going? What do you want to do?' He said, 'I'm the devil, and I want to choke this ascetic.' The thief said to him, 'And I want to steal his heifer.' Both of them followed the monk from there to his home. The monk put the heifer in his house and went in to have his meal. The thief said to himself, 'If the devil were to go in to choke the ascetic, he might perhaps call out, and that would attract people and I would fail in what I want to do.' So, right away, he said to the devil, 'You keep watch carefully while I go in first and take the heifer, and we'll share it.' But the devil was afraid that, by going in to take the heifer, he would be noticed by people and they would fail altogether, so he said to the thief, 'Hold off until everyone's asleep and we'll immediately both get what we want, at the same time.' But the thief said, 'No!' And they began to quarrel with each other until the thief called out to the monk and said, 'This devil wants to choke you.' And the devil called out to the monk, 'And this thief wants to steal the heifer.' And the ascetic woke up and chased them away and was delivered from death.

"Ταῦτα ὑμῖν διηγησάμην, ἵνα γνῷτε, ὅτι δεῖ τὸν ἐχέφρονα τιμῆσαι καὶ εὐεργετῆσαι τὸν φίλον τοῦ ἐχθροῦ αὐτοῦ, καὶ ἴσως ὠφεληθήσεται ἐξ αὐτοῦ, ὥσπερ ὁ τοιοῦτος ἀσκητής." Ὁ δὲ τὴν ἀναίρεσιν αὐτοῦ συναινέσας εἶπεν· "Ὦ βασιλεῦ, τάχιον ἀναιρεθήτω, καὶ μὴ πιστεύσῃς τοὺς λόγους αὐτοῦ τοὺς ψευδεῖς. Ὁ γὰρ ἐχέφρων ἀνὴρ οὐ πιστεύει τὰ ψευδοῦς· ὁ δὲ ἄνθρωπος ὁ πιστεύων τὰ μὴ ἀληθῆ, ὅμοιός ἐστι τῷ τέκτονι τῷ ἀπιστήσαντι ἃ εἶδε, καὶ πιστεύσαντι ἃ ἤκουσε."

26 *Περὶ πεπλανημένου τέκτονος.*

"Λέγεται γάρ, ὡς τέκτων τις εἶχε γυναῖκα πάνυ ὡραίαν καὶ περικαλλῆ. Ἡ δὲ γυνὴ αὐτοῦ ἐφίλει τινὰ γείτονα αὐτῆς. Οἱ δὲ συγγενεῖς τοῦ τέκτονος νοήσαντες τοῦτο, ἀνήγγειλαν αὐτῷ τὰ περὶ τούτου. Ὁ δὲ εἶπεν αὐτοῖς· '*Ἐὰν μὴ ἴδω* τοῖς ὀφθαλμοῖς μου, *οὐ πιστεύσω* τοῦτο.' Καὶ θέλων δοκιμάσαι τὴν ἰδίαν γυναῖκα, εἶπεν αὐτῇ· 'Βούλομαι ἀπελθεῖν ἐν τῷ δεῖνι τόπῳ, ὅπως οἰκοδομήσω οἶκον τῷ βασιλεῖ. Ἑτοίμασον οὖν μοι τὴν τῆς ὁδοῦ δαπάνην.' Ἡ δὲ ἐποίησε τοῦτο συντόμως· καὶ ἐξελθὼν ὁ ἀνὴρ αὐτῆς παρήγγειλεν αὐτῇ λέγων· 'Κλεῖσαι τὴν θύραν σου καὶ τήρησον τὸν οἶκόν σου ἄχρι τῆς ἐλεύσεώς μου.' Ἀπελθὼν δὲ μικρὸν τόπον, ἐπανουργεύσατο καὶ στραφεὶς ἐκρύβη ὑποκάτω τοῦ κραββάτου αὐτοῦ. Ἡ δὲ γυνὴ αὐτοῦ ἀπέστειλε πρὸς τὸν φίλον αὐτῆς λέγουσα· ''Ελθὲ τὸ τάχιον πρός με· ὁ γὰρ ἀνήρ μου ἀπεδήμησε ἔν τινι τόπῳ μακρῷ εἴς τινα δουλείαν.' Καὶ ὁ φίλος αὐτῆς ἐλθὼν ἔμεινε παρ' αὐτῇ. Ὁ δὲ

"I've been through all this for you so that you may know that a smart man, who honors and looks after his enemy's friend, will perhaps be helped by him, just as this ascetic was." But the owl who favored killing the crow said, "My king, he must be killed quickly. Don't believe his lying words, for a smart man doesn't believe lies, and the man who believes what is not true is like the builder who did not believe what he saw but believed what he heard."

About a builder who was led astray. 26

"For it is said that a builder had a wife who was very beautiful and good looking. But the wife loved one of her neighbors. The builder's relatives knew this and told him about it, but he said to them, '*Unless I see* this with my own eyes, *I will not believe* it.' Wishing to test his wife, he said to her, 'I want to go away to such and such a place, so that I may build a house for the king. So get the provisions for my journey ready.' She promptly did this. When he was leaving, he instructed her and said, 'Shut your door and look after the house until I arrive back.' He went off a little way, but then devised a plan and, returning, hid under his bed. His wife sent a message to her lover, saying, 'Come to me quickly, for my husband has gone somewhere a long way away for his work.' Her lover came and stayed with her. The builder, who

τέκτων ἀκούων καὶ βλέπων τὰ παίγνια αὐτῶν καὶ τὰς ὁμιλίας αὐτῶν ὕπνωσεν ἐν ᾧ ἦν τόπῳ καὶ ἥπλωσεν τὸν πόδα αὐτοῦ ἔξωθεν τῆς κλίνης. Ἐκείνων δὲ κοιμωμένων καὶ συγγινομένων, στραφεῖσα ἡ τούτου γυνὴ καὶ βλέψασα τὸν πόδα τοῦ ἀνδρὸς αὐτῆς ἐξηπλωμένον, εἶπε τῷ φίλῳ αὐτῆς· 'Φώνησόν μοι, ἐρωτῶν με, "Τίνα φιλεῖς πλέον, τὸν ἄνδρα σου ἢ ἐμέ;"' Ὁ δὲ εἶπε τοῦτο τὸ ἐρώτημα πρὸς αὐτήν. Ἡ δὲ γυνὴ εἶπε πρὸς αὐτόν· 'Τί σοι χρεία περὶ τοῦ ἐρωτήματος τούτου; Οὐκ οἶσθα ὅτι οὐ προκρίνω τινὸς κρείττονος τοῦ ἀνδρός μου ἢ τοῦ ποδὸς αὐτοῦ ἐπὶ τῆς γῆς; Καὶ γὰρ αἱ γυναῖκες ἐὰν κτήσωνται φίλους, διὰ μικρὰν ἡδονὴν καὶ χρήματα τοῦτο ποιοῦσιν· ὁ γὰρ νόμιμος ἀνὴρ κρείττων ἐστὶν χιλίων φίλων, καὶ αὐτῶν τῶν γονέων καὶ ἀδελφῶν καὶ τέκνων· καὶ γὰρ ὁ κόπος αὐτοῦ καὶ ὁ μόχθος τῆς γυναικὸς αὐτοῦ ἐστι· καὶ εἰ τάχα φιλῶ σε, ἀλλ' οὖν δάκτυλον ἕνα ἐκ τῶν ποδῶν τοῦ ἀνδρός μου κρείττονα ἔχω ἢ σέ.' Διυπνισθεὶς δὲ ὁ ἀνὴρ αὐτῆς καὶ ἀκούσας ταῦτα πάντα, εἶπεν ἐν ἑαυτῷ· 'Ὄντως ἀληθῶς ἡ ἀγάπη τῆς γυναικός μου πρός με πολλὴ καὶ στερεά ἐστι.' Πρωίας δὲ γενομένης ἀνέστη καὶ ἀπῆλθεν ὁ φίλος αὐτῆς. Ἡ δὲ ἀπεκοιμήθη ἐν τῷ κοιτῶνι αὐτῆς, καὶ ἀναστὰς ὁ ἀνὴρ αὐτῆς τότε, ἤρξατο ῥιπίζειν αὐτὴν μετὰ τοῦ ῥιπιστηρίου ὅτι θέρος ἦν. Καὶ ἐξυπνισθείσης αὐτῆς, ἔφη πρὸς αὐτὴν ὁ ἀνὴρ αὐτῆς· 'Ὦ φιλτάτη ἀναπαύου· καὶ γὰρ ταύτῃ τῇ νυκτὶ πολλὰ ἠγρύπνησας.' Διὰ γὰρ τὴν ἀφροσύνην αὐτοῦ, ἠπίστησεν ἃ εἶδεν εἰς αὐτήν, καὶ ἐπίστευσεν ἃ ἤκουσε παρὰ τῆς γυναικὸς αὐτοῦ.

heard and saw their games and what they were saying to each other, fell asleep where he was, and stuck his feet out from under the bed. And while they were lying there and having sex, the man's wife turned over and saw her husband's foot sticking out. She said to her lover, 'Call out to me, and ask me, "Who do you love more, your husband or me?"' He asked her this question. The woman said to him, 'What need is there for you to ask about that? Don't you know that I prefer no one on earth more than my husband, or even just his foot? For wives, even if they take lovers, do this for a little pleasure and money. But a lawful husband is better than a thousand lovers and, indeed, than parents and brothers and children. For his toil and hard work belong to his wife. And if perhaps I love you, I still consider that one toe of my husband's foot is better than you.' Her husband, who had woken up and heard all this, said to himself, 'Really and truly, my wife's love for me is deep and strong.' In the morning her lover got up and left, but she stayed asleep in her bed. Her husband got up then and began to fan her with the fan because it was summer. When she woke up, her husband said to her, 'Rest, my dearest, for you spent a lot of the night awake.' For, in his foolishness, he did not believe what he saw, but believed what he had heard from his wife.

"Καὶ ταύτην σοι διεξῄειν τὴν παραβολήν, ὦ βασιλεῦ, ἵνα μὴ πιστεύσῃς τοὺς λόγους τοῦ κόρακος, τοὺς λήρους καὶ ψευδεῖς, ἀλλ' ἀναιρεθήτω ταχέως."

27 Ὁ δὲ βασιλεὺς τῶν γλαυκῶν διὰ τὴν ἄνοιαν καὶ μωρίαν αὐτοῦ, οὐκ ἤκουσεν τοῦ πρώτου συμβούλου αὐτοῦ, ἀλλὰ προσέταξε διὰ τιμῆς καὶ αἰδοῦς ἄγεσθαι τὸν κόρακα. Ὁ δὲ τὴν ἀναίρεσιν αὐτοῦ συναινέσας ἔφη· "Ἐπεὶ τοῦτον οὐκ ἀπεκτείνατε, κἂν ἔστω ἐν παραφυλακῇ, καὶ διαγέτω παρ' ἡμῖν ὡς ἐχθρὸς παρατηρητέος· δεινὸς γάρ ἐστιν ὁ κόραξ καὶ δόλιος καὶ οἶμαι τοῦτον διὰ πανουργίαν καὶ ἀπάτην ἐνταῦθα παραγενέσθαι." Ἤρξατο οὖν ὁ κόραξ ἔκτοτε ταῖς γλαυξὶ προσομιλεῖν καταμόνας καὶ οἰκειοῦσθαι ταύταις καὶ συμφιλιοῦσθαι. Μιᾷ δὲ τῶν ἡμερῶν εἶπε πρὸς αὐτάς· "Ἀκήκοα τῶν παλαιῶν λεγόντων ὡς, εἴ τις ἑαυτὸν τῷ πυρὶ ἀφειδῶς παρεμβάλῃ, τηνικαῦτα ὃ ἐὰν αἰτήσηται παρὰ Θεοῦ δοθῆναι, δοθήσεται αὐτῷ. Βούλομαι οὖν κᾀγὼ τοιοῦτόν τι διαπράξασθαι καὶ καταδυσωπῆσαι τὸ Θεῖον μεταβαλεῖν μου τὴν φύσιν εἰς γλαῦκα, ὡς ἂν τοῖς κόραξι πολεμήσω μεθ' ὑμῶν καὶ ἀμύνωμαι τούτους, ὑπὲρ ὧν εἰς ἐμὲ ἔδρασαν." Παρὼν δὲ τηνικαῦτα ὁ τὴν ἀναίρεσιν αὐτοῦ προτρεψάμενος, ἔφη· "Ἐοίκασιν οἱ λόγοι οὗτοι πόματι διειδεῖ δηλητηρίου μεστῷ, <οὗ> οὔ τις ἂν γεύσοιτο, εἰ καὶ δίψῃ συνέχοιτο. Εἰ γὰρ καὶ πυρίκαυστόν σε διαθήσομεν, οὐκ ἄν σου δυνησώμεθα τὴν γνώμην διαλαβεῖν ἢ τὴν φύσιν μεταβαλεῖν, ἀλλ' οὖν εἰς τὸ ἀρχαῖόν σου πλάσμα στραφήσῃ, ὡς ἡ μῦς ἡ στραφεῖσα ἐν τῇ ἰδίᾳ φύσει καὶ συζευχθεῖσα τῷ μυῒ τῷ ὁμογενεῖ αὐτῆς, τὸν δὲ ἥλιον καὶ τὴν σελήνην καὶ τὰ λοιπὰ κτίσματα ἐβδελύξατο πάνυ." Ὁ δὲ

"And I have been through this lesson, my king, so that you may not believe the crow's idle, lying words, but may kill him quickly."

But the king of the owls in his ignorance and stupidity 27
did not listen to his chief counselor, but ordered the crow to be treated with respect and honor. But the one who favored killing him said, "Since you did not put him to death, let him be kept under guard and spend his time treated by us as an enemy: a crow is clever and deceitful, and I think this one has come here for the sake of trickery and treachery." So, from that time on, the crow began talking to the owls individually, making them his friends, and endearing himself to them. One day he said to them, "I have heard from those who spoke long ago that if someone throws himself recklessly into a fire, then whatever he asks God to give him will be given to him. I too wish to do something like this, and entreat God to transform my nature into that of an owl, so that I can fight the crows alongside you and take my revenge on them for what they did to me." The one who had urged that the crow should be killed was present at that time, and he said, "Your words are like a clear drink that is full of poison which no one would taste, even if they were tormented by thirst. For even if we arranged for you to be burned, we would not be able to affect the way you think or alter your nature. You would return to your original shape, like the mouse who returned to her own nature and married the mouse who was of the same kind as her, but detested the sun

βασιλεὺς τῶν γλαυκῶν ἔφη· “Καὶ πῶς ἦν τοῦτο;” Ὁ δὲ πρωτοσύμβουλος αὐτοῦ εἶπε·

28 *Περὶ ἀσκητοῦ καὶ μυός.*

“Λέγεται γὰρ ὡς ἀσκητής τις θεάρεστος ἵστατο παρὰ τὸν ποταμὸν εὐχόμενος· καὶ ἰδοὺ νίβλα βαστάζουσα μῦν ὑπὸ τοὺς πόδας αὐτῆς, [καὶ] ἐλθοῦσα πλησίον τοῦ ἀσκητοῦ ἔρριψεν αὐτὴν ἡμιθανῆ. Ὁ δὲ ἀσκητὴς λαβὼν ταύτην καὶ σπλαγχνισθεὶς ἐπ’ αὐτήν, ᾐτήσατο τὸν Θεὸν τοῦ μεταστρέψαι αὐτὴν εἰς κοράσιον καὶ αὖθις ἐγένετο τὸ αἴτημα αὐτοῦ. Καὶ λαβὼν ταύτην ἀπῆλθεν εἰς τὸ κελλίον αὐτοῦ καὶ ἀνέθρεψεν αὐτήν. Αὐξησάσης δὲ ταύτης καὶ γενομένης ἐννόμου ἡλικίας, ἠβουλήθη ὁ μοναχὸς συζεῦξαι αὐτήν. Μιᾷ οὖν τῶν ἡμερῶν, ἐλθὼν πρὸς αὐτὴν εἶπε· ‘Βούλομαί σε συζεῦξαι· εἰπὲ οὖν μοι τίνα θέλεις συζευχθῆναι αὐτῷ.’ Ἡ δὲ εἶπε· ‘Ζεῦξαί μοι ὅνπερ γινώσκεις δυνατώτερον πάντων τῶν κτισμάτων.’ Ὁ δὲ μοναχὸς ἔφη αὐτῇ· ‘Οὐ γινώσκω εἶναί τινα δυνατώτερον τοῦ ἡλίου.’ Ἡ δὲ μῦς εἶπε πρὸς αὐτόν· ‘Ναὶ θέλω.’ Καὶ ἀπελθὼν ὁ μοναχὸς πρὸς τὸν ἥλιον, ᾐτήσατο αὐτὸν τοῦ συζευχθῆναι μετ’ αὐτῆς. Ὁ δὲ ἥλιος εἶπεν· ‘Κἀγὼ δυνατός εἰμι· πλὴν τὸ νέφος σκέπει τὸ φῶς μου.’ Ἐλθὼν δὲ πάλιν ὁ μοναχὸς πρὸς τὸ νέφος ᾐτήσατο αὐτὸ τοῦ συζευχθῆναι μετ’ αὐτῆς τῆς μυός. Τὸ δὲ νέφος εἶπε· ‘Καὶ ἐγὼ δυνατόν εἰμι, ἀλλ’ ὁ ἄνεμος δυνατώτερός μού ἐστι· καὶ γὰρ διώκει καὶ σκορπίζει με.’ Εἶτα πάλιν ἐλθὼν ὁ μοναχὸς πρὸς τὸν ἄνεμον, ᾐτήσατο καὶ αὐτὸν ὁμοίως. Ὁ δὲ ἄνεμος ἔφη· ‘Κἀγὼ δυνατός εἰμι, ἀλλὰ τὸ

and the moon and the rest of creation." And the king of the owls said, "And how was that?" His chief counselor said:

About an ascetic and a mouse. 28

"For it is said that an ascetic, who was pleasing to God, was standing beside a river and praying when, lo and behold, a hawk carrying a mouse in its feet came close to the ascetic and put her down, half dead. The ascetic picked her up and, feeling sorry for her, asked God to transform her into a little girl, and at once he got his request. Taking her with him, he went to his cell and looked after her. She grew up and, when she came of legal age, the monk wanted her to get married. So one day he came to her and said, 'I want you to get married; tell me who you want to marry.' And she said, 'Marry me to whoever you know who is more powerful than any other creature.' The monk said to her, 'I don't know anyone more powerful than the sun.' The mouse said to him, 'Yes, I want that.' So the monk went off to the sun and asked him to marry her. But the sun said, 'I am indeed powerful, but the cloud covers my light.' Again, the monk went to the cloud and asked him to marry that mouse. But the cloud said, 'I, too, am powerful, but the wind is more powerful than me, for he chases and scatters me.' Then again, the monk went to the wind and asked him the same thing. But the wind said, 'I am powerful also, but the mountain is more powerful

ὄρος δυνατώτερόν μού ἐστιν, διότι οὐ δύναμαι αὐτὸ παρασαλεῦσαι.' Καὶ ὁ μοναχὸς πάλιν ἐλθὼν πρὸς τὸ ὄρος, ᾐτήσατο καὶ αὐτὸ ὁμοίως. Τὸ δὲ ὄρος ἀπεκρίθη λέγον· 'Ἐγὼ μὲν δυνατόν εἰμι, ἀλλ' ὁ μῦς δυνατώτερός μού ἐστι· καὶ γὰρ κατατρυπᾷ με ἔνθεν κᾀκεῖθεν, καὶ οὐ δύναμαι ἀποφυγεῖν τὴν βλάβην αὐτοῦ.' Ἀπῆλθεν δὲ καὶ πρὸς τὸν μῦν ὁμοίως λέγων. Ὁ δὲ μῦς ἔφησεν αὐτῷ· 'Ἐγὼ μέν εἰμι μικρός, αὕτη δέ ἐστι μεγάλη τὴν ἡλικίαν καὶ οὐ χωρεῖ εἰς τὴν ἐμὴν κατάδυσιν.' Ὁ δὲ ἀσκητὴς στραφεὶς πρὸς τὴν κόρην ἀνήγγειλεν αὐτῇ πάντα, ὅσα εἶδε καὶ ὅσα ἤκουσε παρὰ τῶν κτισμάτων, ὁμοίως καὶ τὰ λεχθέντα παρὰ τοῦ μυός. Ἡ δὲ εἶπεν αὐτῷ· 'Λοιπόν, αἴτησαι τὸν Θεόν σου, ὅπως μεταστρέψῃ με εἰς τὸ παλαιὸν καὶ ἀρχαῖόν μου σχῆμα.' Ὁ δὲ μοναχὸς ᾐτήσατο τὸν Θεὸν καὶ εἰσήκουσεν αὐτοῦ καὶ μετεστράφη εἰς τὴν ἀρχαίαν αὐτῆς φύσιν, καὶ συνέζευξεν αὐτῇ τὸν μῦν.

"Ἀλλὰ ταῦτά σοι διεξῄειν, ὦ βασιλεῦ, ἵνα γνῷς ὅτι κἂν τῷ πυρὶ κατακαυθήσεται, πάλιν εἰς τὴν ἰδίαν γνώμην καὶ φύσιν στραφήσεται." Ὁ δὲ βασιλεὺς τῶν γλαυκῶν οὐκ εἰσήκουσεν αὐτοῦ τὰ τοιαῦτα λαλοῦντος, ἀλλ' εἴασε τὸν κόρακα ἐκεῖσε.

29 *Περὶ τῆς φυγῆς κόρακος ἀπὸ τῶν γλαυκῶν.*

Ὁ δὲ κόραξ διέμεινε κατανοούμενος τὰ τῶν γλαυκῶν ἅπαντα, καὶ κατανοήσας τὴν αὐτῶν φρόνησιν καὶ δύναμιν διέμεινεν ἀμέριμνος μετ' αὐτῶν. Καὶ ἐπαχύνθη καὶ ἐλιπάνθη καὶ ἐνεφύη τούτῳ πτερά. Καί ποτε καιροῦ

than me, because I am unable to move it.' And once again the monk went to the mountain and asked it the same thing. But the mountain replied and said, 'I am powerful, but the mouse is more powerful than me, for he makes holes in me here and there and I am unable to escape the damage he does.' He went to the mouse and said the same thing to him. The mouse said, 'I am small, and she is big and does not fit into my hole.' The ascetic went back to the girl and told her everything he had seen and heard from the creatures, and likewise what the mouse had said. She said to him, 'All right, ask your God to turn me back into my old, original shape.' The monk asked God and he was heard by him and she was turned back into her original nature; and he married the mouse to her.

"I've been through this for you, my king, so that you may know that even if the crow is burned by the fire, he will revert to his own way of thinking and nature." But the king of the owls did not listen to what he was saying, but left the crow alone there.

About the crow's escape from the owls. 29

The crow stayed on, observing everything about the owls; and when he had observed the way they thought and their power, he went on living a life of ease with them. He became fat and sleek, and his feathers grew. Sometime later he seized

δραξάμενος ἐπιτηδείου ἀπέδρα καὶ πρὸς τοὺς κόρακας παραγενόμενος ἔφη τῷ τούτων ἡγεμόνι· “Χαίροις, ὦ βασιλεῦ· ἰδοὺ γάρ σοι τετέλεκα τὸ κατὰ σκοπόν. Λείπεται οὖν τὸ διαστῆναι ἡμᾶς καὶ πέρας αἴσιον τῇ καλῇ ἐπιθεῖναι ἀρχῇ. Ἰδοὺ γὰρ ἅπασαι αἱ γλαῦκες τῷ δεῖνι ἄντρῳ ὑπεκρύβησαν· ἀναλαβέτω οὖν ἕκαστος ἡμῶν ἐκ τῆσδε τῆς ὕλης ὅσα δύναται φέρειν τῶν ξυλίσκων καὶ περιθήσωμεν ταῦτα πρὸς τῷ τοῦ ἄντρου στόματι. Καὶ πῦρ ὑπανάψωμεν καὶ ταῖς πτέρυξι τοῦτο διαφυσήσωμεν ἐν τοσούτῳ ὡς ἀέριον τὴν φλόγα ἀπεργάζεσθαι. Τούτῳ γὰρ τῷ τρόπῳ αἱ μὲν ἔνδοθεν τῷ καπνῷ συμπνιγήσονται, αἱ δὲ ἔξωθεν ἐρχόμεναι καταφλεγήσονται κακιγκάκως.” Ὃ δὴ καὶ ποιήσαντες οἱ κόρακες τέλεον τοὺς ἐχθροὺς αὐτῶν ἐξηφάνισαν.

Καὶ ἐπανέζευξεν ὁ τῶν κοράκων βασιλεὺς τροπαιοῦχος πρὸς τὴν ἰδίαν κατοίκησιν, καὶ ἔφη πρὸς τὸν κόρακα· “Πῶς ἠνέσχου τῆς τῶν γλαυκῶν ὁμιλίας καὶ πονηρίας;” Ὁ δὲ κόραξ εἶπεν· “Ὁ νουνεχὴς ἀνὴρ δεινοῖς περιπεσὼν ὑπείκει τοῖς εὐτελέσιν, ἄχρις οὗ τὸ οἰκεῖον ἐφετὸν καταλήψεται.” Ὁ δὲ βασιλεὺς ἔφη· “Ἀνάγγειλόν μοι τὰ τῶν γλαυκῶν φρονήματα οἷά εἰσιν.” Ὁ δὲ κόραξ· “Οὐκ εἶδον ἐν αὐταῖς συνετωτέραν τῆς τὴν ἀναίρεσίν μου συμβουλευσαμένης γλαυκός, αἱ δὲ λοιπαὶ πόρρω που τοῦ δέοντος ἐξετρέποντο. Δεῖ γὰρ τοὺς βασιλεῖς τὰ οἰκεῖα τηρεῖν μυστήρια ἐν ἑαυτοῖς καὶ μὴ ἐᾶν ἀλλότριόν τινα ταῖς οἰκείαις γραφαῖς πλησιάσαι ἢ τῷ ὕδατι δι’ οὗ μέλλουσιν ἀπονίψασθαι, ἢ τῇ στρωμνῇ ἢ τοῖς ἀμφιάσμασιν ἢ τοῖς ὅπλοις ἢ τῇ βρώσει καὶ πόσει ἢ τοῖς ὑποζυγίοις ἢ τοῖς μύροις. Ἀλλ’ οὐδὲ ἦν δυνατὸν ὑπερηφάνους ὄντας τοὺς ἡμετέρους

a suitable opportunity and escaped. When he had returned to the crows, he said to their ruler, "Greetings, my king: see, I have completed my spying mission for you. So what remains is for us to make our move and add a happy ending to the good beginning. For you see, all the owls have hidden themselves in such and such a cave; so let's each take as many sticks as he can carry from this wood and place them in front of the mouth of the cave. Then let's light a fire, and fan it with our wings so as to make the flames rise up into the air. That way, those who are inside will be choked by the smoke and those who come out will be burned in the worst way." The crows did this and completely destroyed their enemies.

The king of the crows returned in triumph to his own 30
home, and said to the crow, "So how did you stand the company and wickedness of the owls?" And the crow replied, "When a sensible man falls into a dangerous situation, he submits to his inferiors until he gets what he himself wants." And the king said, "Tell me what the owls' minds are like." And the crow replied, "I did not see one among them who was smarter than the owl who advised that I should be killed; the rest were far from where they should be. For kings should keep their secrets to themselves and not allow some stranger to access their private documents, nor get near the water with which they are about to wash themselves, nor to their beds, their clothes, their weapons, their food and drink, their pack animals, nor their perfumes. Nor was it possible for our enemies, being so arrogant, to prevail.

ἐχθροὺς νικᾷν. Σπανίως γάρ τις τρόπαιον συνιστᾷ ὑπερήφανος, καὶ σπανίως ἀδηφάγος μέχρι τέλους ἄνοσος διατελεῖ. Καὶ οὐ ῥᾳδίως ὁ ἀσυνέτοις συμβούλοις χρώμενος τῆς ἀπωλείας σῴζεται. Ἔγωγε οὖν ὑπετάγην καὶ ἐταπεινώθην τοῖς ἐχθροῖς, ἵνα τύχω τοιούτου κατορθώματος καθάπερ ὁ ὄφις ὁ τῷ βατράχῳ ἐκείνῳ τοῦ λιμνηδίου ὑποπεσών."

31 *Περὶ ὄφεως καὶ βατράχων.*

"Λέγεται γὰρ ὡς ὄφις τις παρηβηκὼς καὶ γεγηρακὼς πρὸς τὴν θηρείαν ἠτόνησε καὶ τῆς ἀναγκαίας ἠπορεῖτο τροφῆς. Ἕρπων δὲ κατέλαβε λιμνήδιον βατράχων πολλῶν μεστόν, ἐξ οὗ τὴν ἀρχὴν ἤγρευεν, καὶ σκυθρωπὸς καὶ κατηφὴς ἑαυτὸν ἐκεῖσε πλησίον ἐξήπλωσε. Βάτραχος δέ τις εἶπε πρὸς αὐτόν· 'Τί, ὄφι, ἀλύεις οὕτως ἐνταῦθα καὶ κατηφιᾷς;' Ὁ δὲ ἔφη· 'Καὶ πῶς οὐ σκυθρωπάσω; Ἀεὶ γὰρ ἀπὸ ταύτης τῆς λίμνης τῆς πρὸς τὸ ζῆν ἀναγκαίας ἐποριζόμην τροφῆς ἄνευ κόπου και φροντίδος. Νῦν δέ τινός μοι τῶν ἀσκητῶν ἐπαρασαμένου, οὐκέτι δύναμαι πρὸς ὑμᾶς, καὶ βούλομαι ὑποζύγιον ἔσεσθαι τῷ βασιλεῖ ὑμῶν.' Ταῦτα ἀκούσας ὁ τῶν βατράχων βασιλεὺς προσελάβετο τοῦτον καὶ ἐπέβαινεν αὐτῷ καὶ δύο βατράχους ἐδίδου τούτῳ καθεκάστην ἡμέραν πρὸς διατροφήν. Οὕτω κἀγὼ διὰ τὸ τοιοῦτον τέλος πρόσκαιρα ὑπέστην ἀλγεινά."

32 Ὁ δὲ βασιλεύς ἔφη· "Ὁρῶ τὴν δι' ὑπουλότητος καὶ μηχανῆς εὐόδωσιν καὶ νίκην κρείττονα οὖσαν τῆς δι' ἀντερίσεως. Τὸ μὲν γὰρ πῦρ θερμότατον καὶ ὀξύτατον ὂν μόνα

For seldom does an arrogant man manage to win, and seldom does the glutton remain healthy until death. And someone who employs foolish counselors does not easily escape destruction. So I for my part subordinated myself and was humble before our enemies, so that I might enjoy the same success as that of the snake who fawned upon the frog in that pond."

About the snake and the frogs. 31

"For it is said that a snake, past his prime and too old for hunting, was exhausted and did not have enough food to eat. Slithering along, he came to a pond filled with many frogs in which he originally used to hunt, and, sad and miserable, he stretched himself out somewhere there. A frog said to him, 'Why are you lying about like this and looking miserable, snake?' And he replied, 'How can I not be miserable? For I have always provided myself from this pond with the food I need to live on without toil or anxiety. But now I've been cursed by some ascetic, and I no longer have power over you, and I wish to be a donkey for your king to ride on.' When the king of the frogs heard this, he welcomed him, rode upon him, and gave him two frogs every day as food. So I too, for the sake of achieving this outcome, submitted to temporary suffering."

And the king said, "I see that progress and victory 32
through treachery and trickery are better than through contention. For the hottest and fiercest fire only destroys what

τὰ ὑπὲρ γῆν ἀπόλλυσι· τὸ δὲ ὕδωρ ψυχρὸν ὂν καὶ γαληνὸν καὶ κάτωθεν αὐτῆς διεισδύνει καὶ ἐκριζοῖ τὰ ἐν αὐτῇ. Λέγεται γὰρ ὡς οὐ δεῖ καταφρονεῖν τινος τουτωνὶ τῶν τεσσάρων καὶ εἰ ἐλάχιστα πάντη εἰσί—λέγω δή, πυρός, νόσου, ἐχθροῦ καὶ χρέους—καὶ τὰ τοιαῦτα φοβοῦ." Ὁ δὲ κόραξ εἶπεν· "Ὅσα κατώρθωται διὰ τῆς σῆς ἐστιν εὐτυχίας, ὦ βασιλεῦ. Ὅτε γὰρ δύο τινὲς ἐπιζητοῦσι τρόπαιον, ὁ κρείττων τούτων κατὰ τὴν συνείδησιν τεύξεται τούτου, εἰ δὲ ἐξισοῦνται κατὰ ταύτην, ὁ νουνεχέστερος, εἰ δὲ κατὰ τοῦτο παρομοιοῦσιν, ὁ κρειττόνων εὐπορῶν ὑπηκόων, εἰ δὲ καὶ κατὰ τοῦτο ἰσάζουσιν, ὁ εὐτυχέστερος."

33 Ὁ δὲ βασιλεὺς ἔφη· "Εὗρόν σε τοῖς ἔργοις αὐτοῖς τὴν εὔνοιαν ἐπιδεικνύμενον, τοὺς δὲ λοιποὺς λόγοις μόνοις ἀνηνύτοις θεραπεύοντας κατανενόηκα. Διὰ σοῦ γὰρ μεγίστη χάρις νῦν ἐπεγένετο ἡμῖν, καὶ ἡ δείπνου καὶ τροφῆς ἡδονὴ διὰ σοῦ προσεπορίσθη ἡμῖν. Λέγεται γὰρ ὡς ἄνεσιν μεγίστην εὑρίσκει ὁ ἐκ πυρετοῦ ἀνακαλούμενος, καὶ ὁ βαρὺ φορτίον ἀποτιθείς, πρὸς τούτοις καὶ ὁ τῆς τῶν ἐχθρῶν ἀπαλλαγεὶς ἐπιβουλῆς." Καὶ αὖθις ὁ βασιλεὺς εἶπε· "Ἀνάγειλλον οὖν ἡμῖν πῶς ἐθεάσω τὴν τοῦ γλαυκῶν βασιλέως διαγωγήν;" Ὁ δὲ κόραξ εἶπε· "Μοχθηρὰν καὶ πονηρὰν καὶ ἀνώμαλον καὶ ἄτακτον καὶ τοὺς ὑπ᾽ αὐτὸν ὁμοίους αὐτῷ, ἐκτὸς μόνου τοῦ τὴν ἐμὴν ἀναίρεσιν συναινέσαντος· οὗτος γὰρ πάντων ὤφθη μοι συνετώτατος." Ὁ δὲ βασιλεὺς ἔφη αὐτῷ· "Καὶ τί σοι ἐφάνη ἐκ τῆς συνέσεως αὐτοῦ καὶ οὕτω μεγάλως ἐπαινεῖς αὐτόν;" Καὶ ὁ κόραξ εἶπεν· "Ἦν οὖν, βασιλεῦ, εὐθὺς ἐν τῷ λέγειν, ταχὺς εἰς τὸ ἀκοῦσαι, ὀξὺς εἰς τὸ νοῆσαι, πάσης δὲ παιδεύσεως πλήρης,

is on the surface of the earth, but water, being cool and calm, flows down through it and uproots what is in it. For it is said that someone should not disregard the following four things, no matter how insignificant they are—I mean fire, disease, an enemy, and debt—but should fear them." And the crow said, "Whatever has been achieved is through your good fortune, my king. For when two people compete for a trophy, the one who is the better informed of the two will win it, but if they are equal in that respect, then the one who is smarter will do so, and if they are also alike in this, then the one who has better subjects, and if in this too they are equal, then the one who has better luck."

And the king said, "I've discovered that you demonstrate 33
your goodwill through actual deeds, but have observed that the others only serve me with unrealistic words. For thanks to you a most considerable benefit has now come to us, and you have provided us with the pleasure of sleeping and eating. For it is said that someone who recovers from a fever finds great relief, and also someone who puts down a heavy burden, and, in addition, someone who is rid of his enemies' plots." And again the king said, "So, tell us, what did you think of the owl king's way of life?" And the crow said, "Wretched, wicked, disorderly, and undisciplined, and his subordinates were like him, with the sole exception of the one who advised that I should be killed. Rather, he seemed to me more intelligent than all the others." And the king said to him, "And what struck you about his intelligence, and why did you find him so admirable?" And the crow said, "He was, my king, swift in hearing, sharp in understanding,

ἁπάντων γνωστικότατος, τῷ βασιλεῖ αὐτῶν εὐγνωμονέστατος καὶ πάσης ἀρετῆς ἔμπλεως καὶ ἐμοὶ ἀγνωμονέστατος."

Οὕτως οὖν οἱ πονοῦντες ὡς οἱ γλαῦκες καὶ μὴ ὀρθῶς φρονοῦντες πείσονται.

very well educated, wiser than anyone, very frank with their king, filled with every virtue, and very hard-hearted toward me."

So those who toil like the owls and do not think correctly will suffer what they did.

[Chapter 5]

Ἀρχὴ τοῦ πέμπτου <τμήματος>.

Καὶ πάλιν ὁ βασιλεὺς τῷ φιλοσόφῳ εἶπεν· "Ἔγνων τὸ ῥηθέν σοι παράδειγμα. Λοιπὸν ἀνάγγειλον μοι, πῶς πολλάκις ἐπιτυγχάνων τις τοῦ ἐφετοῦ, καὶ μήπω καλῶς τὸ ἐπικτηθὲν τηρεῖν δυνάμενος, ἀπόλλυσιν τοῦτο." Ὁ δὲ φιλόσοφος ὑπολαβὼν εἶπεν·

2 *Περὶ πιθήκου καὶ χελώνης.*

Λέγεται λόγος ὥς τινες πίθηκοι βασιλέα ἔχοντες παρηβηκότα ἤδη τῷ χρόνῳ καὶ ὑπέργηρων, τοῦτον διὰ τὸ γῆρας τῆς οἰκείας αὐτοῦ ἀρχῆς ἐξεδίωξαν. Ὁ δὲ παντελεῖ συσχεθεὶς ἀπορίᾳ ἐπί τινα συκῆν τῶν παραλίων ἐπὶ τὴν θάλασσαν ἐξέχουσαν παρεγένετο καὶ κατῴκησεν ἐν αὐτῇ, καὶ ἤσθιεν τὸν καρπὸν αὐτῆς. Μιᾷ δὲ τῶν ἡμερῶν ἐσθίοντος πέπτωκε ἀπὸ τῆς χειρὸς αὐτοῦ συκῆ μία, ἣν ἀρρενικὴ χελώνη λαβοῦσα ἔφαγεν. Ἐφ' ᾧ ὁ πίθηξ γελάσας ἡδέως οὐ διέλιπε τὴν χελώνην συκίζων. Ἡ δὲ χελώνη ἡδυτάτην εὑροῦσα τὴν τροφήν, τῆς ἰδίας ἐπελάθετο οἰκίας καὶ διὰ τοῦτο ἡ σύζυγος αὐτῆς ἀθυμοῦσα ἦν τὰ μέγιστα καὶ

Chapter 5

BEGINNING OF THE FIFTH CHAPTER.

And again, the king said to the philosopher, "I understand the example you have described. Now tell me how someone often gets what he wants but then loses it, as he is not yet able to take care of what he has acquired." And the philosopher replied and said:

About an ape and a turtle. 2

A story is told that some apes, who had a king who had already become advanced in years and extremely old, drove him out of his own kingdom because of his age. Suffering from absolute poverty, he came to a fig tree on the beach overhanging the sea and lived in it; and he used to eat its fruit. One day, as he was eating, a fig fell from his hand, which a male turtle took and ate. The ape laughed happily at this and carried on fattening the turtle with figs. As the turtle found the food very sweet, he forgot about his own home and, because of this, his wife became very depressed and

μηχανὴν ἐζήτει, δι’ ἧς τὸν μὲν πίθηκα ἀπολέσῃ, τὸν σύζυγον δὲ ἀπολάβῃ.

3 Μιᾷ δὲ τῶν ἡμερῶν ἡ χελώνη οἴκαδε ἐπανιοῦσα καὶ περίλυπον τὴν σύζυγον εὑροῦσα, εἶπε πρὸς αὐτήν· “Τί ὅτι σκυθρωπὴν ὁρῶ σε καὶ νοσεράν;” Ἡ δὲ σύζυγος αὐτοῦ ἔφη· “Νόσῳ δεινῇ περιπέπτωκα ἡ ταλαίπωρος καὶ οὐκ ἔστιν ἄλλως ἴασιν εὑρεῖν με, εἰ μή καρδίαν πίθηκος φάγομαι, καθάπερ οἱ ἰατροί μου ἀνήγγειλαν.” Ὁ δὲ σύνευνος αὐτῆς ἀπορήσας καθ’ ἑαυτὸν διελογίζετο τὴν τοῦ ζητουμένου δυσχέρειαν, καὶ ὡς οὐχὶ ἑτέραν καρδίαν εὑρήσει εἰ μή γε τὴν τοῦ ἑταίρου αὐτοῦ. Τοῦτο δὲ παράβασιν καὶ ἀθέτησιν τῆς φιλίας εἶναι κατανοῶν, παντοίοις ἐπάλαιε λογισμοῖς.

4 Ὅθεν καὶ ἀπελθὼν ἐκεῖνος πρὸς τὸν πίθηκα προσηγόρευσεν αὐτόν. Ὁ δὲ πίθηξ τὴν χελώνην περὶ τῆς βραδυτῆτος αὐτῆς ἐπηρώτησε, καὶ ἡ χελώνη ἀπεκρίνατο, ὡς οὐ δι’ ἄλλο τι ὑστέρησεν εἰ μή γε διὰ τὴν πρὸς τοῦτον αἰδῶ, μὴ ἀξίαν τὴν ἀντέκτισιν τῆς εὐποιΐας δυναμένη ἐργάσασθαι. Ὁ δὲ πίθηξ ἔφη· “Μὴ ὑπολάμβανε τοιαῦτα, οὐ γὰρ ἔγωγε τοιοῦτός εἰμι ὥστε ἀμοιβὰς παρὰ φίλων ζητεῖν. Μᾶλλον γὰρ σύ μοι εὐεργέτης ἐχρημάτισας, τοιαύταις συμφοραῖς περιεστοιχισμένῳ καὶ τοιούτοις δεινοῖς πεπτωκότα παραμυθουμένη τὰ μέγιστα.” Ἡ δὲ χελώνη εἶπε· “Βούλομαι καὶ ἔτι παγιωθῆναι καὶ βεβαιωθῆναι τὴν μεταξὺ ἡμῶν φιλίαν. Ἑδραιοῦται δὲ αὕτη διὰ τῶν τριῶν τούτων, ἤγουν διὰ τῆς εἰς τὴν οἰκίαν τοῦ φίλου εἰσελεύσεως, καὶ τῆς τῶν συγγενῶν θέας καὶ ἐπισκέψεως, καὶ τῆς τῶν ἄλλων κοινωνίας.”

sought a means by which she could get rid of the ape and get her husband back.

One day, when the turtle returned home, he found his 3
wife looking very sad, and he said to her, "Why do I see you looking miserable and sick?" And his wife said to him, "Poor me, I've caught a terrible sickness, and there's no cure to be found for me, unless I eat an ape's heart, just as the physicians told me." Her husband was quite at a loss, for he was pondering the difficulty of getting what was being sought, as he would not find any heart other than that of his companion; and as he considered this to be a betrayal and a rejection of his friendship, he was wrestling with all sorts of thoughts.

So he went to the ape and greeted him. The ape asked 4
him about his slowness, and the turtle answered that he was only late out of a sense of shame toward him, as he was unable to properly repay him for his kind treatment. The ape said, "Don't think anything of the sort, for I'm not the kind of person to seek recompense from friends. Rather, it's you who have been my benefactor, giving me great encouragement when I've been beset by such disasters and caught up in such terrible things." The turtle said, "I want the friendship between us to be made even more firm and secure. And friendship is strengthened by these three things, namely, entering the house of a friend, seeing and visiting family, and enjoying the companionship of others."

5 Ὁ δὲ πίθηξ ἔφη· “Ὦ φιλτάτη, οὐ ταῦτα συνιστῶσιν τὴν ἀκραιφνῆ φιλίαν, ἀλλ’ ἡ εἰλικρινεστάτη διάθεσις. Τὸ γὰρ ὁρᾶν συγγενεῖς ἔστι καὶ τοῦ σκηνίτου· τὸ δὲ ὁμοδίαιτον ἔστι καὶ πολλοῖς τῶν ἀλόγων ζῴων καὶ ἡμιόνων καὶ ἄλλων τινῶν· ἡ δὲ πρὸς τὴν οἰκίαν εἰσέλευσις ἔστι καὶ τῶν ληστευομένων.” Ἡ δὲ χελώνη ὑπολαβοῦσα εἶπεν· “Ἀληθῶς εἶπας. Δεῖ γὰρ τὸν φίλον μόνην φιλίαν παρὰ τῶν φίλων ἀπαιτεῖν. Ὁ δὲ δι’ ἄλλο τι τῶν βιωτικῶν πραγμάτων τὴν φιλίαν συνιστῶν, ἐπ’ ἀδρανοῦς θεμελίου ταύτην ἀνοικοδομεῖ. Λέγεται γὰρ ὡς οὐ δεῖ παρὰ τῶν φίλων περιττὰ ἐπιζητεῖν. Ὁ γὰρ μόσχος, ὅτε πλέον τοῦ δέοντος τὴν μητέρα θηλάσῃ, παροργίζει αὐτὴν ὥστε διώκεσθαι ὑπ’ αὐτῆς. Ἐγὼ δέ σε βούλομαι ἐλθεῖν εἰς τὴν οἰκίαν μου· οἰκῶ γὰρ ἐν νήσῳ τινὶ ποηφόρῳ τε καὶ χλοηφόρῳ καὶ μυρίων πληθούσῃ τῶν καρπῶν. Ἐγὼ δέ σε ἐπὶ τῶν ὤμων φέρουσα ἐκεῖσε ἀπαγάγω.”

6 Πεισθεὶς οὖν ὁ πίθηξ ἐπέβη τῆς χελώνης καὶ ἐφέρετο παρ’ αὐτῆς ἐν τῷ πελάγει. Ἡ δὲ χελώνη τῷ κλύδωνι μέσῳ περιπεσοῦσα ἔστη, διαλογιζομένη ὅπως ποντίσῃ τὸν πίθηκα. Ἰδὼν δὲ ὁ πίθηξ τὴν τῆς χελώνης βραδυτῆτα ὑπώπτευσε τἀναντία καὶ καθ’ ἑαυτὸν ἐλογίζετο λέγων· “Μήποτε κατ’ ἐμοῦ ἐβουλεύσατο ἡ χελώνη τι τῶν ἀποτροπαίων; Οἶδα γάρ, ὡς οὐδὲν καρδίας εὐαλλοιοτώτερον καὶ εὐμεταβλητότερον. Δεῖ γὰρ τὸν νουνεχῆ μὴ ἀμελεῖν ποτε, ἀλλ’ ἐξετάζειν τὰς τῶν συγγενῶν καὶ φίλων καρδίας καὶ τεκμαίρεσθαι τούτων διά τε τῶν λόγων αὐτῶν καὶ τῶν πέριξ λοιπῶν.” Εἶτα πρὸς τὴν χελώνην ἔφη· “Ὁρῶ σε σύννουν

But the ape said, "My dearest friend, it's not these things 5
that create pure friendship but having a most sincere disposition. After all, seeing family is what someone who shares a tent does; living together is what even many animals like horses and mules and other creatures do; and entering a house is also what burglars do." The turtle replied, "What you've said is true. For a friend should demand steadfast friendship from his friends. And someone who creates a friendship for some other reason to do with worldly affairs establishes that friendship on a weak foundation. For it is said that one should not make excessive demands on friends. The calf provokes its mother when it suckles more than it should from her, so that she chases it away. But I would like you to come to my house, for I live on a grassy and leafy island that is full of countless fruits. Let me take you there by carrying you on my back."

So the ape was persuaded, climbed onto the turtle, and 6
was carried by him into the sea. But the turtle stopped when he encountered the waves, pondering how he should drown the ape. But when the ape noticed the turtle's slowness, he suspected hostile intent and said to himself, "Perhaps the turtle has decided to do something terrible to me? For I know that nothing is more easily swayed and changed than a heart. A smart man should never be negligent but should examine the hearts of his family and friends and judge them by both their words and other things about them." Then he said to the turtle, "I see that you're thoughtful and anxious,

καὶ ἔμφροντιν, καὶ δέδοικα διὰ τοῦτο. Τί οὖν, ὦ φίλη, ἐστὶ τὸ τῆς μερίμνης ταύτης αἴτιον;"

7 Ἡ δὲ χελώνη εἶπε· "Φροντίς μοι μεγίστη ἐστι, μήποτε καταλαβὼν τὴν οἰκίαν μου οὐκ ἐντύχῃς ἅπασιν, ὡς βούλομαι· κλινοπετὴς γὰρ καὶ περιαλγὴς ἡ ἐμὴ ὁμευνέτις ἐστίν." Ὁ δὲ πίθηξ ἔφη· "Μὴ μερίμνα περὶ τούτου· οὐδὲν γὰρ λυσιτελήσει ἡ μέριμνα, ἀλλὰ φρόντισον αὐτῇ ἀκεσωδύνων φαρμάκων." Ἡ δὲ χελώνη εἶπε· "Φασὶν ἰατρῶν παῖδες τὴν τοῦ πίθηκος καρδίαν ἰᾶσθαι τὴν νόσον αὐτῆς." Τοῦτο ἀκούσας ὁ πίθηξ καθ' ἑαυτὸν τὴν οἰκείαν ἀπωδύρετο ἀπώλειαν, λέγων· "Φεῦ τῆς ἐμῆς ἀβελτηρίας, ὅπως ἡ πλεονεκτική μου γνώμη, γηραιὸν ὄντα, τοῖς τοιούτοις με κακοῖς περιέπειρεν. Ὁ γὰρ τοῖς ὀλίγοις ἀρκούμενος ἄνετον βιοῦται ζωήν· ὁ δὲ πλεονεκτικὴν ἔχων τὴν γνώμην ἐν μόχθοις ἀεὶ καὶ πόνοις τῶν ἡμερῶν αὐτοῦ διαπεραιοῦται τὸν δίαυλον."

8 Εἶτα πρὸς τὴν χελώνην ἔφη· "Διὰ ποῖον λόγον, ὦ φιλτάτη, οὐκ ἐδήλωσάς μοι τὸ τοιοῦτον πρὶν ἢ τὴν οἰκίαν με καταλιπεῖν, ὥστε μου τὴν καρδίαν ἀναλαβέσθαι σὺν ἐμοί; Νενομισμένον γάρ ἐστιν ἡμῖν, ὅτε πρὸς φίλον ἀπίωμεν, τὴν καρδίαν οἴκαδε καταλιμπάνειν διὰ τὸ μὴ ὑπολαβεῖν τι περὶ τοῦ φίλου ἐναντίον." Ταῦτα ἀκούσασα ἡ χελώνη ὀπισθόπους χαίρουσα ἔπλει καὶ τὸν πίθηκα τῷ αἰγιαλῷ προσώρμισεν. Ὁ δὲ τῆς χέρσου ἐπιβὰς δρομαῖος ἐπὶ τὴν συκῆν ἀνῆλθεν. Ἡ δὲ χελώνη κάτωθεν ἐβόα· "Κάτελθε διὰ τάχους, ἑταῖρε, ἵν' ἀπέλθωμεν οἴκαδε, καὶ ἔνεγκε σύν σοι καὶ τὴν καρδίαν σου." Ὁ δὲ πίθηξ ὑπολαβὼν ἔφη· "Εἰ

and I'm frightened by this. So what's the reason for your worry, my friend?"

The turtle said, "My greatest concern is that, when you 7
reach my house, you may not find everything as I would wish; for my spouse is bedridden and in great pain." And the ape said, "Don't worry about that, for worry is of no use; but see about getting painkilling medicines for her." The turtle said, "The physicians say the heart of an ape will cure her illness." When the ape had heard this, he bitterly lamented his own destruction, saying, "How stupid I have been, as my greedy disposition, in my old age, has got me caught up in this mess. For someone who's content with only a few things lives a relaxed life, but someone who has a greedy disposition always spends his days in hard work and toil."

Then he said to the turtle, "Why didn't you let me know 8
this, dearest one, before I left home, so that I could have brought my heart with me? For it's our custom, when we go to a friend's, to leave our heart at home, so as not to suspect anything bad about a friend." When the turtle had heard this, he happily swam back and landed the ape on the shore. But he, when he set foot on dry land, climbed up the fig tree at full speed. The turtle called up to him from below, "Come down quickly, my friend, so that we may set off for home, and bring your heart with you too." But the ape replied and

τοῦτο ποιήσω καὶ πλανηθῶ ἐκ δευτέρου, ὅμοιος ἔσομαι τῷ ὄνῳ τῷ πλανηθέντι παρὰ τῆς ἀλώπεκος."

9 *Περὶ ὄνου καὶ ἀλώπεκος.*

"Λέγεται γὰρ ὡς λέων τις ᾤκει ἔν τινι τόπῳ· ἦν δὲ μετ' αὐτοῦ ἀλώπηξ τις τρεφομένη ἐκ τῶν περισσευμάτων αὐτοῦ. Ψωριάσας οὖν ὁ λέων ἠδυνάτησεν καὶ τὰ πρὸς τὴν θήραν ἠτόνησεν. Ἡ δὲ ἀλώπηξ ἔφη αὐτῷ· 'Τί ὅτι ὁρῶ σε ἐν ἀδυναμίᾳ καὶ ταλαιπωρίᾳ πολλῇ;' Ὁ δὲ λέων ἔφη αὐτῇ· 'Ἀπὸ τῆς κατεχούσης με ταύτης ἀσθενείας, ἣν βλέπεις· καὶ αὕτη ἡ ἀσθένεια οὐκ ἄλλως ἰᾶται εἰ μή γε μόνον διὰ τῆς καρδίας τοῦ ὄνου καὶ τῶν ὤτων αὐτοῦ.' Ἡ δὲ ἀλώπηξ ἔφη· 'Καὶ τοῦτο εὔκολόν μοί ἐστι τοῦ ποιῆσαί σοι· καὶ γὰρ πλησίον ἡμῶν ἐστι πηγή, ἐν ᾗ κναφεὺς ἔρχεται καθεκάστην σὺν τῷ ὄνῳ αὐτοῦ. Ἀλλ' ἀπέρχομαι καὶ προσφέρω σοι τοῦτον.' Ὁ δὲ λέων ἔφη αὐτῇ· 'Καὶ εἰ τοῦτό μοι ποιήσεις, χάριν μεγίστην ἕξεις παρ' ἐμοῦ.' Ἀπελθοῦσα οὖν ἡ ἀλώπηξ πρὸς τὸν ὄνον ἔφη αὐτῷ· 'Τί ὁρῶ σε στυγνὸν καὶ πεπτωχευμένον;' Ὁ δὲ ὄνος λέγει αὐτῇ· 'Ἀπὸ τῆς κακίας τοῦ δεσπότου μου· καὶ γὰρ φορτοῖ με βαρέως, καὶ ὀλιγοτροφεῖ με, καὶ δεδεμένον με ἵστησιν ὅλην τὴν ἡμέραν.' Ἡ δὲ ἀλώπηξ· 'Καὶ ὑπομένεις σὺ ταῦτα πάντα;' Ὁ δὲ ὄνος· '"Οπου δ' ἂν ἀπέλθω, ἕτερος ἄνθρωπος λαβών με, ὁμοίως με βασανίσει.' Καὶ ἡ ἀλώπηξ· 'Καὶ λοιπὸν ἄπελθε μετ' ἐμοῦ· καὶ γὰρ γινώσκω τόπον χλοηφόρον καὶ ὑδατώδη. Ἔστι δὲ ἐκεῖ ἄλλη ὄνος νεμομένη, καὶ ἔσῃ ἄφοβος, ὡς ἐμοὶ δοκεῖ, μετ' αὐτῆς, ὅτι οὐδέποτε πλησιάζει ἐκεῖσε ἄνθρωπος.'

said, "If I were to do that, I would have been led astray twice, and I would be like the donkey who was led astray by the fox."

About a donkey and a fox. 9

"For it is said that a lion lived somewhere, and there was a fox with him who fed off his leftovers. As the lion had mange, he lacked strength and was too exhausted to hunt. The fox said to him, 'Why do I see that you are weak and in such a wretched state?' And the lion said to her, 'It's due to this illness that I have, which you see. And this illness can only be cured by the heart and ears of a donkey.' And the fox said, 'That's easy for me to do for you. For there's a spring near us to which a fuller comes every day with his donkey. I'll go and bring it to you.' And the lion said, 'If you do this for me, I'll be very grateful to you.' So the fox went off to the donkey and said to him, 'Why do I see you are sad and destitute?' And the donkey said to her, 'Because of my master's wickedness. He loads me heavily and doesn't feed me much and keeps me tied up all day.' The fox said, 'Do you put up with all this?' The donkey said, 'Wherever I went, another man would take me and mistreat me in the same way.' And the fox said, 'All right, come with me, for I know a place that's leafy and well watered. There's another female donkey grazing there, and you won't be afraid, I think, with her, because no man never goes near there.'

10 “Ταῦτα ἀκούσας ὁ ὄνος, ἠκολούθησεν αὐτῇ ἄχρι τοῦ λέοντος. Ἐγγίσας οὖν αὐτὸς πρὸς τὸν λέοντα, ἐπεπήδησεν ὁ λέων κατ’ αὐτοῦ. Διὰ δὲ τὴν ἀδυναμίαν, ἀπέδρασεν ἐκ τῶν χειρῶν αὐτοῦ ὁ ὄνος. Ταῦτα ἰδοῦσα ἡ ἀλώπηξ εἶπε πρὸς τὸν λέοντα· ‘Διατί ἀπέλυσας αὐτόν; Καὶ εἰ μὲν ἑκουσίως τοῦτο ἐποίησας, τί δ’ ἂν κόπους παρέσχες μοι, εἰ δ’ ἀκουσίως, φεῦ ἐμοῦ καὶ τῆς ζωῆς μου.’ Ὁ δὲ λέων μὴ θέλων φανερῶσαι τὴν ἀδυναμίαν αὐτοῦ, εἶπεν· ‘Ἀνάγαγέ μοι τοῦτον ἐκ δευτέρου εἰ δύνασαι, καὶ εἴπω σοι διὰ ποίαν αἰτίαν ἐγὼ τοῦτο ἐποίησα καὶ αὐτὸν κατέλιπον ἀβλαβῆ.’

11 “Ἡ δὲ κερδὼ πάλιν στραφεῖσα πρὸς τὸν ὄνον ἔφη αὐτῷ· ‘Δι’ ἥντινα αἰτίαν ἔφυγες ἀπὸ τῆς ὄνου; Καὶ γὰρ ἐκείνης ἀπὸ τῆς χαρᾶς μελλούσης περιπλέκεσθαί σοι, σὺ ἀπέδρασας αὐτῆς.’ Ὁ δὲ ὄνος μὴ εἰδώς ποτε λέοντα, ἐπίστευσεν τῇ ἀλώπεκι, καὶ ὑπέστρεψε μετ’ αὐτῆς πρὸς αὐτόν, καὶ ἤγγισεν πάλιν τῷ λέοντι. Ἐκπηδήσας δὲ ὁ λέων κατ’ αὐτοῦ ἀπέκτεινε τοῦτον. Εἶτα λέγει πρὸς τὴν ἀλώπεκα· ‘Πρόσεχε αὐτὸν ἕως οὗ ἀπελθὼν πρὸς τὴν πηγὴν νίψομαι.’ Ἐξελθόντος οὖν τοῦ λέοντος, ἔφαγεν ἡ ἀλώπηξ τὰ ὦτα τοῦ ὄνου καὶ τὴν καρδίαν αὐτοῦ. Καὶ στραφεὶς ὁ λέων ἐκ τῆς πηγῆς λέγει τῇ ἀλώπεκι· ‘Ποῦ εἰσιν, ὦ ἀλώπηξ, τὰ ὦτα καὶ ἡ καρδία αὐτοῦ;’ Ἡ δὲ ἀλώπηξ ἔφη· ‘Εἰ εἶχεν ὁ ὄνος καρδίαν καὶ ὦτα τοῦ ἀκούειν, οὐκ ἂν ἐστρέφετο ἐκ δευτέρου πρός σε, ἰδὼν τὴν πρώτην ἀνάγκην, ὁπότε ἐκ σοῦ ἀπέδρασε.’

“Ταῦτά σοι διηγησάμην, ὦ χελώνη, ἵνα γνῷς, ὅτι οὔκ εἰμι ἄφρων καθάπερ ὁ ὄνος· εἰ γὰρ τοῦτο ποιήσω, καρδίας

"When the donkey heard this, he followed the fox as far as the lion, and when he drew close, the lion leaped on him. But because of the lion's weakness, the donkey escaped from his clutches. The fox saw this and said to the lion, 'Why did you let him go? If you did this on purpose, why did you let me go to that trouble, but if it was not on purpose, it's goodbye to me and my life.' But the lion did not want to reveal his weakness, so he said, 'Bring him to me a second time if you can, and I'll tell you the reason why I did this and let him get away unharmed.' 10

"The wily fox returned to the donkey and said to him, 'Why did you flee from the female donkey? For she was going to embrace you out of joy, and you ran away from her.' And the donkey, who had never experienced a lion, believed the fox and went back with her to him. He approached the lion again, and the lion jumped on him and killed him. Then he said to the fox, 'Watch over him while I go to the spring to wash.' Then, while the lion was away, the fox ate the donkey's ears and heart. The lion returned from the spring and said to the fox, 'Fox, where are his ears and heart?' And the fox said, 'If the donkey had had a heart and ears with which to hear, he would not have come back to you a second time, knowing the first trouble he had, when he ran away from you.' 11

"I've told you this, turtle," said the ape "so that you may know that I am not a fool like the donkey. For if I were to do

ὄντως τέλεον οὐκ εὐπορήσω." Οὕτως καὶ οἱ καιροῦ εὐθέτου δραξάμενοι καὶ μὴ τὸ κατὰ σκοπὸν ἐκπληροῦντες, ἀλλὰ τοῦτο παραδραμόντες, πάντῃ τοῦ ἔργου ἀποτυγχάνουσιν.

this, I really would end up with no heart." Thus, those who have seized the right moment but do not fulfill their intention, when the moment has passed, fail completely in their undertaking.

[Chapter 6]

Ἀρχὴ τοῦ ἕκτου τμήματος.

Ὁ δὲ βασιλεὺς τῷ φιλοσόφῳ εἶπεν· "Ἔγνων τὸ τοιοῦτον παράδειγμα. Λοιπὸν ἀνάγγειλόν μοι, τίνι ἔοικεν ὁ σπεύδων ἐπί τι ἔργον καὶ μὴ ἀνεχόμενος τοῦτο πρὸ τῆς ἐπιχειρήσεως καταμαθεῖν." Ὁ δὲ φιλόσοφος ὑπολαβὼν ἔφη·

2 *Περὶ τοῦ ἀνδρὸς καὶ τοῦ τέκνου αὐτου.*

Λέγεται γάρ ποτε ὥς τις ἀνὴρ τῇ ἰδίᾳ ὁμευνέτιδι καταμόνας συζῶν εἶπε πρὸς αὐτήν· "Εὔελπίς εἰμι, ὦ γύναι, ὡς ἄρρην ἡμῖν παῖς τεχθήσεται, ὃς ἡμῖν προθύμως ἐκδουλεύσει. Λοιπὸν οὖν σκεψώμεθα, τί τούτῳ τῶν ὀνομάτων ἐπιθήσομεν." Ἡ δὲ τούτου ὁμευνέτις ὑπολαβοῦσα ἔφη· "Παῦσαι, ἄνερ, τοῦ λήρου. Ἡδὺς γὰρ εἶ τοιαῦτα φθεγγόμενος καὶ περὶ τῶν ἀδήλων ἀποφαινόμενος, καὶ ἔοικας ἐκείνῳ τῷ ἀνδρὶ τῷ τὸ μέλι καὶ τὸ βούτυρον καταχύσαντι."

Chapter 6

BEGINNING OF THE SIXTH CHAPTER.

And the king said to the philosopher, "Indeed, I have understood this example. Now tell me what someone resembles who does something hastily and doesn't have the patience to think carefully before acting." And the philosopher said in response:

About the man and his child. 2

For it is said that, once upon a time, a man who lived alone with his spouse, said to her, "I have good hopes, my wife, that we will have a male child, who will be eager to serve us. So, then, let's think carefully about what name we'll give him." But his spouse replied, "Husband, stop this idle chatter. For you're taking pleasure in talking about this and making assertions about what is still uncertain, and so you're like that man who spilled his butter and honey."

3 *Περὶ ἄφρονος ἀνδρὸς τοῦ ἐλπίζοντος ὃ οὐκ ἔστι δυνατὸν λαβεῖν.*

"Λέγεται γὰρ ὥς τις ἀνὴρ τῶν πενήτων βούτυρον καὶ μέλι ἔν τινι ἀγγείῳ ἔνθα ἐκάθευδε πλησίον εἶχε. Μιᾷ δὲ τῶν νυκτῶν καθ' ἑαυτὸν ταῦτα διελογίζετο λέγων· 'Μέλλω τὸ τοιοῦτον μέλι καὶ τὸ βούτυρον πωλῆσαι νομίσματος τὸ ἐλάχιστον καὶ δι' αὐτοῦ ἀγοράσαι αἶγας δέκα, αἵτινες ἀποτέξουσιν ἑτέρας τοσαύτας διὰ πέντε μηνῶν, καὶ διὰ πέντε ἐνιαυτῶν περιστήσονται εἰς τετρακοσίας, δι' ὧν ἐξωνήσομαι βόας ἑκατόν, καὶ δι' αὐτῶν ἄρουραν σπείρω. Καὶ ἐκ τῶν ἐπιγεννημάτων ὁμοῦ καὶ τῶν καρπῶν, δι' ἑτέρων πέντε ἐτῶν *ῥυδὸν ἀφνειὸς* γενήσομαι. Καὶ οἰκίαν ἐγερῶ τετραώροφον καὶ χρυσώροφον καὶ δούλους παντοδαποὺς ἐξωνήσομαι καὶ ὁμευνέτιδι συζευχθήσομαι, ἥτις καὶ παῖδά μοι τέξεται, καὶ καλέσω τοῦτον Πάγκαλον καὶ παιδεύσω τοῦτον ὡς δεῖ, καὶ εἴπερ ἀμελοῦντα θεάσομαι, ταύτῃ τῇ ῥάβδῳ οὑτωσὶ τύψω.' Καὶ λαβὼν τὴν παρακειμένην αὐτῷ ῥάβδον καὶ τὸ ἀγγεῖον ταύτῃ διακρούσας τοῦτο διέρρηξε· τὸ δὲ μέλι καὶ τὸ βούτυρον τῷ ἰδίῳ πώγωνι κατέχυσεν. Οὕτω καὶ σὺ ὡς ἐκεῖνος ὁ ἄνους καὶ ἄγνωστος ἀνὴρ τὰ τοιαῦτα φθέγγῃ."

4 Εἶτα ἔτεκε παῖδα ἡ τούτου ὁμευνέτις. Καὶ μετά τινας ἡμέρας εἶπεν ἡ γυνὴ πρὸς τὸν ἄνδρα αὐτῆς· "Προσανάσχου μοι ἐνταῦθα παρὰ τῷ παιδί, ἄχρις ὅτου ἀπελθοῦσα διὰ τόδε ὑποστρέψω ἐνταῦθα." Καὶ ταύτης ἀπιούσης προσεκλήθη παρὰ τοῦ ἀρχηγοῦ ὁ ἀνὴρ αὐτῆς. Ἔτυχε δὲ

CHAPTER 6

About a foolish man who hopes for what it is impossible to get. 3

"For it is said that a poor man kept butter and honey in a jar close to where he slept. One night he was thinking about them, and said to himself, 'I'm going to sell this honey and butter for at least one *nomisma,* and with it I'll buy ten goats, who in five months will give birth to as many again, and in five years they will become four hundred; with them, I'll purchase one hundred oxen, and with them I'll sow some arable land. And thanks to their young, along with the harvests, in another five years I will become *abundantly rich.* And I'll build a four-story house with a golden roof, and I'll purchase all kinds of slaves, and I'll get married to a wife, who will also bear me a child whom I'll call Pankalos, and I'll bring him up properly, and if I see him being negligent, I'll beat him with this stick, just like this.' And, taking the stick that was lying next to him, he hit the jar and broke it; and the butter and honey poured out over his beard. You're being like that stupid ignorant man when you say this."

Then the man's wife had a baby. Some days later, the 4
woman said to her husband, "Take care of the child for me here, while I go out for this, until I get back here." And while she was away, the man was summoned by his superior.

τηνικαῦτα, ἀμφοῖν ἀπόντοιν ὄφιν ἐπὶ τὸν παῖδα ἑρπύσαι, ὅν τις νύμφη ἐπεισπηδήσασα κατέκοψεν. Ὑποστρέψας δὲ ὁ ἀνήρ, καὶ ταύτην θύραθεν ἰδὼν καθῃμαγμένην τῷ τοῦ ὄφεως αἵματι, ἔδοξε τὸν παῖδα ταύτην λαφύξαι. Καὶ μὴ ἀνασχόμενος ἄχρι τῆς τοῦ παιδὸς θέας, κατὰ κεφαλῆς ταύτην ἔτυψεν ἀφειδῶς καὶ ἀπέκτεινεν. Εἰσελθὼν δὲ καὶ σῶον εὑρὼν τὸν παῖδα καὶ τὸν ὄφιν ἀνῃρημένον, σφόδρα μετάμελος γέγονε καὶ ἔκλαυσε πικρῶς.

Οὕτως ἄρα καὶ οἱ σπεύδοντες περὶ τὰ πολλὰ τῶν πραγμάτων σφάλλονται ὡς μὴ ἀνεχόμενοι.

But then it happened that, while they were both away, a snake crawled onto the baby, and a nymph jumped on it and killed it. When the husband returned and saw the nymph outside all bloody with the blood of the snake, he presumed that she had eaten the baby. And he did not wait until he had seen the baby, but struck her mercilessly on the head and killed her. So then, when he entered the house and found the baby unharmed and the snake dead, he was filled with regret and cried bitterly.

This is how those who act hastily make mistakes about many things, because they are impatient.

[Chapter 7]

Ἀρχὴ τοῦ ἑβδόμου τμήματος.

Πάλιν ὁ βασιλεὺς ἐφθέγξατο· "Ἔγνων καὶ τὸ τοιοῦτον· λοιπὸν ἀνάγγειλόν μοι, πῶς ἔνεστι τὸν βασιλέα τὴν οἰκείαν βασιλείαν τηρεῖν ἀβλαβῆ, καὶ ἐν τίνι μᾶλλον; Τῇ ἀνεξικάκῳ γνώμῃ, ἢ τῇ ἀγαθῇ συνειδήσει ἢ τῇ μεταδόσει;" Ὁ δὲ φιλόσοφος ὑπολαβὼν ἔφη·

2 Πάντων κρείττων ἡ φρόνησις καὶ ἡ ἀνοχὴ καὶ πρὸς τούτοις ἡ τῶν συνετῶν συμβούλων σύνεσις, εἶτα καὶ ἡ ἀρίστη καὶ φρονιμωτάτη γυνή. Ἔστι δὲ τούτου καὶ παράδειγμα τὸ εἴς τινα τῶν Ἰνδῶν βασιλέα συμβάν.

3 *Περὶ τοῦ βασιλέως καὶ τῶν ὀνείρων οὓς ἐθεάσατο.*

Λέγεται γὰρ ὡς οὗτος ὁ βασιλεὺς ἐν μιᾷ τῶν νυκτῶν ὀκτὼ ὀνείρους φοβεροὺς ἰδὼν ἐταράχθη καὶ ἐθροήθη καὶ ἀφυπνώσας προσεκαλέσατο πάντας τοὺς φιλοσοφοῦντας, καὶ ἃ εἶδε καθ' ὕπνους διηγήσατο αὐτοῖς. Οἱ δὲ φιλόσοφοι εἶπον αὐτῷ· "Ὀπτασίας ἑώρακας ἀξιοθαυμάστους, καὶ δεῖ ἡμᾶς ἑπτὰ ἡμέρας τὰ περὶ τούτων σκοπῆσαι, εἴ ποτέ σε δυνηθείημεν τῆς βλάβης ἀναγαγεῖν."

Chapter 7

BEGINNING OF THE SEVENTH CHAPTER.

The king spoke once more: "I have understood this too. So now, tell me, how can a king keep his kingdom safe from harm, and which way is preferable? Through a tolerant disposition, or through good counsel, or the distribution of benefits?" And the philosopher replied:

Good sense and restraint are superior to all things, and in 2
addition to these the intelligence of intelligent counselors, then also an excellent and most sensible wife. And what happened to one of the kings of the Indians is an example of this.

About the king and the dreams that he saw. 3

For it is said that one night this king was upset and frightened after seeing eight disturbing dreams. When he woke up, he summoned all his philosophers and described to them what he had seen in his dreams. And the philosophers said to him, "You have seen wondrous visions, and we must spend seven days considering the details of them if we are ever going to be able to keep you from harm."

4 *Περὶ μηχανουργίας τῶν φιλοσόφων τοῦ ἀνελεῖν τὸν βασιλέα καὶ τοὺς ὑπ᾽ αὐτόν.*

Καὶ ἐξελθόντες διηλέχθησαν πρὸς ἀλλήλους καὶ εἶπον· "Οὐ πολὺς παρῳχήκει καιρὸς ἐξ ὅτου ὁ δεινὸς οὗτος βασιλεὺς ἀνήρηκε μυρίους ἐξ ἡμῶν. Νῦν οὖν τὸ Θεῖον ἡμῶν προνοούμενον ἐνέβαλε τοῦτον ταῖς ἡμετέραις χερσί, καὶ δεῖ ἡμᾶς τοῦτον ἀπολέσαι· ταῦτα οὖν δεῖ συναινεῖν αὐτῷ εἰπεῖν ἡμᾶς ἵνα· 'Τὴν σὴν ὁμευνέτιν ἀναιρήσῃς, ὦ βασιλεῦ, καὶ τὸν υἱὸν αὐτῆς. Πρὸς τούτοις καὶ τὸν σὸν υἱόν, καὶ τὸν σὸν πρωτοσύμβουλον, ἔτι δὲ καὶ τὸν λευκὸν ἐλέφαντα, ἐφ᾽ ὃν ἐπιβαίνεις, καὶ τοὺς ἑτέρους σου δύο μεγίστους ἐλέφαντας, καὶ τὸν ἵππον, καὶ τὴν κάμηλον, καὶ τὸ αἷμα τούτων ἐν φιάλῃ ἀποθήσῃς, δι᾽ οὗ σε καὶ ἀποπλύνομεν καὶ ἐπᾴσομεν ἀκεσωδύνους ἐπῳδάς, καὶ ἀναρρύσομεν τῶν μελλόντων σοι ἐπισυμβαίνειν ἀνιαρῶν.'"

5 Καὶ ταῦτα σκεψάμενοι προσῆλθον τῷ βασιλεῖ καὶ εἶπον· "Ἐρευνήσαμεν ἐν ταῖς γραφαῖς καὶ εὕρομεν τάδε καὶ τάδε, ὡς οὐκ ἔστι σοι, ὦ βασιλεῦ, πόρος σωτηρίας ἕτερος, πλὴν διὰ τοῦ ποιῆσαι ταῦτα." Ὁ δὲ βασιλεὺς εἶπε· "Βούλομαι ἐγὼ τούσδε σώους εἶναι κᾀμὲ ἀπολέσθαι." Οἱ δὲ φιλόσοφοι πρὸς αὐτὸν εἶπον· "Μηδέν τι τῆς ἑαυτοῦ προέλῃ ψυχῆς, πάντα γὰρ ταύτης ὑποδεέστερα." Ἀκούσας οὖν τὰ τοιαῦτα ὁ βασιλεὺς καὶ περίλυπος γεγονὼς ἐπὶ τῆς ἰδίας κλίνης πέπτωκε πρηνὴς διαλογιζόμενος, τί ἐργάσηται.

6 Διεδόθη οὖν ἡ φήμη πανταχοῦ περὶ τῆς τοῦ βασιλέως ἀθυμίας. Καὶ μαθὼν τοῦτο ὁ πρωτοσύμβουλος αὐτοῦ καὶ τὸν δόλον φωράσας, οὐκ ἔγνω δεῖν παρευθὺς αὐτοψεὶ

CHAPTER 7

About the philosophers' plot to get rid of the king and his subjects. 4

When they had left, they spoke to one another and said, "Not much time has passed since this dreadful king killed countless of us. So now our provident God has put this man into our hands, and we should get rid of him. So we should agree to say something like this to him: 'O king, you must kill your wife and her son. And, along with them, your son and your chief counselor, and the white elephant you ride, and your other two enormous elephants, and your horse, and camel, and put their blood into a bowl. We will bathe you with this and chant healing incantations, and we will avert the bad things which are going to happen to you.'"

After they had plotted these things, they went to the king 5
and said, "We have searched in the scriptures and have found such and such passages, so that there is no other way to save you, O king, than to do these things." But the king said, "I want them be alive and well, and for me to die instead." And the philosophers said to him, "Do not prefer anything to your own life, as everything is less important than that." When he heard this, the king was very sad and fell facedown on his bed, wondering what he should do.

News of the king's despair spread everywhere. And his 6
chief counselor, when he learned of it and detected the trick, decided that he ought not to speak to the king in

προσομιλῆσαι περὶ τούτου τῷ βασιλεῖ, ἀλλὰ τῇ τούτου πρότερον ὁμευνέτιδι, καὶ προσελθὼν εἶπεν αὐτῇ· "Ὁρῶ τὸν βασιλέα περίλυπον καὶ δέδοικα, μήποτε οἱ ψευδεῖς οὗτοι φιλόσοφοι δόλον κατ' αὐτοῦ συνέρραψαν διὰ μνησικακίαν, τοῦτον τέλεον ἐξολοθρεῦσαι βουλόμενοι. Ἀλλ' ἐπερώτησον αὐτῷ τὴν αἰτίαν δι' ἣν ἐπὶ τοσαύταις ἡμέραις ἀθυμεῖ, καὶ ταύτην μαθοῦσα ἐμοὶ ἀποκάλυψον."

7 Ἡ δὲ βασιλὶς εἰσελθοῦσα πρὸς αὐτὸν καὶ καθίσασα πρὸς τῇ κεφαλῇ αὐτοῦ ἔφη· "Ἀνάγγειλόν μοι, ὦ βασιλεῦ, τί συνεβουλεύσαντο οἱ φιλόσοφοι οὗτοι;" Ὁ δὲ βασιλεὺς εἶπεν αὐτῇ· "Μὴ προσθήσῃς τοῖς μώλωψί μου μώλωπας. Οὐ δεῖ γάρ σε τὰ τοιαῦτα πυνθάνεσθαι διὰ τὸ μὴ τὴν τούτων ὑποσχεῖν κακίαν." Ἡ δὲ βασιλὶς ἔφη· "Οὐκ ἤλπιζόν σέ ποτε μυστήριον ἐξ ἐμοῦ ἀποκρύψαι. Εἰ μὴ γὰρ ἐμοὶ ἀποκαλύψῃς τὸ τοιοῦτον εὐνοούσῃ σου σχολῇ γ' ἂν ἑτέροις πιστεύσῃς." Ὁ δὲ βασιλεύς· "Τί με ἐπερωτᾷς, ὦ γύναι, περὶ τῆς σῆς ἀπωλείας καὶ πάντων τῶν ἐμοὶ φιλτάτων;" Ἡ δὲ βασιλὶς ἔφη· "Ἐγὼ μὲν καὶ οἱ λοιποὶ οὐκ ἐκφευξούμεθα τοῦ μὴ γενέσθαί σοι ἀντάλλαγμα. Τί γάρ σου ἡμῖν τιμιώτερον; Ἀλλὰ δέομαί σου, ὦ βασιλεῦ, μετὰ τὴν ἐμὴν τελευτήν, τινὶ τουτωνὶ τῶν φιλοσοφούντων μὴ πιστεῦσαι, ἔτι δὲ μὴ ἀναιρῆσαι ἕτερον πρὶν ἢ τοῖς ὑπὸ σὲ εὐνοηταῖς ἀνακοινῶσαι τὸ βούλευμα. Οὐκ οἶδας, ὡς ἐχθρωδῶς πρός σε οἱ φιλοσοφοῦντες διάκεινται, ὡς πλήθη ἱκανὰ ἐξ αὐτῶν πρὸ ὀλίγου ἀνῃρηκότα; Μὴ οἴου τοίνυν τούτους τοῦ φόνου ἐπιλαθέσθαι. Ἔδει γάρ σε μηδὲ τὴν ἀρχὴν τούτοις τὸν ὄνειρον διηγήσασθαι, ἀλλ' εἴ μοι πείθῃ, ἐπερώτησον τὸν παρ' ἡμῖν ἀσκητὴν γέροντα τὰ περὶ τοῦ ὀνείρου."

person about this immediately but first speak to his wife. So he went to her and said, "I see that the king is extremely sad and I fear that those false philosophers have devised some trick against him out of malice, as they want to destroy him completely. But ask him the reason why he has been in despair for so many days, and when you have learned what it is, let me know."

The queen went to the king, sat by his head, and said, 7
"Tell me, my king, what those philosophers have advised?" And the king said, "Do not add wounds to my wounds. You mustn't ask about these things, because their evil is unbearable." The queen said, "I didn't ever expect you to keep a secret from me. For if you don't reveal the secret to me, when I'm your friend, you'll hardly be able to trust other people." The king said, "Why are you asking me, my wife, about your own destruction, and that of all who are dearest to me?" The queen said, "I and the others will not run away to avoid taking your place. For what is more precious to us than you? But I beg you, my king, that after my death you will not put your trust in any of those philosophers, and also that you will not have anyone killed before communicating the decree to those of your subjects who wish you well. Don't you know that the philosophers are hostile toward you because you killed a lot of them a short time ago? Don't imagine they have forgotten about that massacre. You shouldn't have described the dream to them to begin with, but instead, if you take my advice, ask our old ascetic about the dream."

8 *Περὶ τῆς ἐξηγήσεως τῶν ὀνείρων τοῦ βασιλέως παρὰ τοῦ ἀσκητοῦ.*

Ὁ δὲ βασιλεὺς εὐθὺς τοῦ ἵππου ἐπιβὰς ἀπῄει πρὸς τὸν τοιοῦτον ἀσκητήν, καὶ ἅπερ εἶδε, τούτῳ ἀνήγγειλεν. Ὁ δὲ ἀσκητὴς εἶπεν αὐτῷ· "Μὴ πτοηθῇς, ὦ βασιλεῦ περὶ τούτου, οὐδὲν γάρ σοι ἀνιαρὸν ἐπισυμβήσεται. Δηλοῦσι γὰρ οἱ δύο ἰχθύες, οὓς ἑώρακας ἐπὶ τῶν οὐραίων βαδίζοντας, ὡς πρέσβυς σοι ἥξει ἔκ τινος τῶν μεγιστάνων δύο ἐλέφαντας τῶν πολυτίμων ἐπαγόμενος. Αἱ δὲ δύο νῆτται, ἃς περιπετομένας σοι ἑώρακας, σημαίνουσιν ὡς καὶ Περσῶν ἥξει σοι πρέσβυς δύο ἵππους τῶν γενναίων ἐπιφερόμενος. Ὁ δὲ ἕρπων ἐπὶ σὲ ὄφις δηλοῖ τὸ ἐνεχθῆναί σοι σπάθην τινά, οἵαν οὐδεὶς ἑώρακε πώποτε. Τὸ δὲ δι' αἵματος βαπτίζεσθαί σε ἐμφαίνει τὸ πεμφθῆναί σοι δεξίωμα ἱμάτιον πορφυροῦν λάμπον ἐν τῇ σκοτίᾳ. Τὸ δὲ ὕδατι ἀποπλύνεσθαί σε προμηνύει τὸ διαφόροις σε στολαῖς δεξιωθῆναι. Τὸ δὲ ἐπ' ὄρους σε λευκοῦ βεβηκέναι τεκμήριον ἐναργές ἐστι τοῦ ἐπὶ ἐλέφαντος λευκοῦ ἐποχηθῆναί σε. Τὸ δὲ ἐπὶ τῆς κεφαλῆς σου πῦρ προϋπογράφει σοι τὸ δέξασθαί σε στέφανον πολυτελῆ παρά τινος τῶν μεγίστων βασιλέων. Περὶ δὲ τοῦ τὴν κεφαλήν σου τύπτοντος ὀρνέου ἄρτι οὐδὲν ἀποφαίνομαι· δηλοῖ γὰρ μερικήν τινα λύπην καὶ ἐπιστροφὴν ποθουμένου προσώπου. Καὶ ταῦτα πάντα ἐπιγενήσεταί σοι μεθ' ἡμέρας ἑπτά." Ἃ δὴ καὶ κατὰ τὴν ἑβδόμην ἡμέραν γέγονεν καὶ ἧκον κατὰ ταύτην οἱ πρέσβεις, πάντα ὅσα ὁ ἀσκητὴς προεῖπεν, ἐπιφερόμενοι.

9 Ἅπερ ἰδὼν ὁ βασιλεὺς καὶ ἔκθαμβος γεγονὼς εἶπε· "Δεῖ

About the explanation of the king's dreams by the ascetic. 8

The king immediately got on his horse, went off to this ascetic, and told him what he had seen. And the ascetic said to him, "Don't be afraid about this, my king, for nothing bad is going to happen to you. For the two fish you saw walking on their tails indicate that an ambassador will come from one of the notables, bringing two valuable elephants. And the two ducks you saw flying around you signify that ambassadors will also come from Persia, bringing you two thoroughbred horses. The snake crawling on you indicates that a sword will be brought to you, the like of which no one has ever seen. Your being baptized in blood represents a purple robe that shines in the dark being sent to you as a pledge of friendship. Your being washed clean in water predicts that you will receive a pledge in the form of special garments. Your walking on a white mountain is a clear sign of you being carried upon a white elephant. And the fire on your head signifies to you that you will receive a sumptuous crown from one of the greatest kings. But as for a bird striking you on the head, I reveal nothing just now, for it indicates some particular grief and the return of a beloved person. And all these things will happen to you after seven days." And they did indeed happen on the seventh day, and on that day the ambassadors came, bringing all the things that the ascetic had foretold.

When the king saw all this, he was amazed and said, "A 9

τὸν νουνεχῆ παρὰ μόνων δέχεσθαι λόγους τῶν φιλτάτων.” Εἶτα ἰδὼν τὰ δῶρα ἔφη· “Οὐ δεῖ μέ τι ἐξ αὐτῶν σφετερίζεσθαι, ἀλλ’ ἀναλάβετε ὑμεῖς ταῦτα ἅμα τῇ εὐνουστάτῃ μου ὁμευνέτιδι· τὰς γὰρ ὑμετέρας ψυχὰς ὑπὲρ ἐμοῦ τεθείκατε.” Ὁ δὲ πρωτοσύμβουλος ὑπολαβὼν ἔφη· “Οὐ δεῖ ἡμᾶς τοὺς ὑπηκόους τὰ τοιαῦτα δῶρα λαμβάνειν· δικαιότεροι γὰρ ταῦτα παρὰ σοῦ λαμβάνειν οἱ κατὰ τὸ γένος σοι προσήκοντες.” Ὁ δὲ βασιλεὺς εἶπεν· “Σὺ τῆς ἐμῆς πρωταίτιος γέγονας σωτηρίας καὶ μυρίων ἄξιος εἶ τῶν εὐεργετημάτων, ὦ Παλλάριε” (τοῦτο γὰρ ὄνομα αὐτῷ). Εἶτα ἔλαβεν ὁ βασιλεὺς ἐν ἑαυτῷ τὸν λευκὸν ἐλέφαντα, καὶ δέδωκε καὶ τῷ υἱῷ αὐτοῦ ἕνα τῶν ἵππων, τῷ δὲ πρωτοσυμβούλῳ τὴν πολύτιμον σπάθην, τῷ δὲ ἀσκητῇ ἔπεμψε τὰ λοιπὰ πολυτελῆ ἐνδύματα. Τὰ δὲ λοιπὰ προσέταξε τῷ πρωτοσυμβούλῳ αὐτοῦ φέρειν μεθ’ ἑαυτοῦ ἐπὶ τὰς γυναῖκας· ἦσαν δὲ τούτῳ τῷ βασιλεῖ φίλταται δύο, ἥ τε συναινέσασα τούτῳ τὸν ἀσκητὴν περὶ τῶν ὀνείρων ἐπερωτῆσαι, ᾗ ὄνομα Πελάς, καὶ ἑτέρα φιλτάτη.

10 Ὁ δὲ πρωτοσύμβουλος παρέθηκε ταύταις τὸν στέφανον καὶ τὴν πορφύραν, ὡς ἂν διέλωνται ταῦτα. Ὁ δὲ βασιλεὺς εἶπε πρὸς τὴν Πελάδα τὴν σύμβουλον· “Ἐπίλεξαι τῶν δύο ἕνα ὃ προαιρῇ, ἢ τὸ στέμμα ἢ τὴν πορφύραν, ὡς ἂν ἡ ἑτέρα γυνὴ λάβῃ τῶν χαρισμάτων τὸ καταλειφθέν.” Ἡ δὲ βασιλὶς ἀποροῦσα ὁποῖον προαιρεῖται, εἶδε πρὸς τὸν πρωτοσύμβουλον. Ὁ δὲ ἔνευσε ταύτῃ προκρῖναι τὸν ἱματισμόν. Ἔτυχε δὲ τηνικαῦτα τὸν βασιλέα τοὺς ὀφθαλμοὺς αὐτοῦ ἆραι καὶ ἰδεῖν τὸν πρωτοσύμβουλον τῇ γυναικὶ προσνεύοντα περὶ τοῦ ἱματισμοῦ. Ἡ δὲ γνοῦσα ὡς οὐ

sensible man should only accept the words of those who are most dear to him." Then, when he saw the gifts, he said to the chief counselor, "I should not take any of these for myself, but you, together with my most loyal wife, should take them, for you laid down your lives for me." But the chief counselor replied, "We subjects should not receive such gifts, for it is more fitting for members of your family to receive them from you." But the king said, "You are the principal reason for my safety, and are worthy of countless benefactions, Pallarios" (for this was his name). Then the king took the white elephant for himself, gave one of the horses to his son, the valuable sword to his chief counselor, and sent the remaining sumptuous garments to the ascetic. The rest he ordered his chief counselor to take, along with himself, to his wives. The king had two who were very dear to him: the one who had advised him to consult the ascetic about his dreams, who was called Pelas, and another very dear one.

The chief counselor presented the crown and the purple 10
robe to them, so that they could decide on them. The king said to Pelas, the one who had advised him, "Choose which one of the two you prefer, either the crown or the purple robe, so that my other wife may receive the gift that is left." As the queen did not know which one to pick, she looked at the chief counselor. He indicated with a wink to her to select the garment. However, the king happened at that moment to look up and see the chief counselor winking at the woman about the garment. When she realized that the wink

διέλαθεν αὐτὸν τὸ νεῦμα, τὸν στέφανον ἀνελάβετο. Ὁ δὲ πρωτοσύμβουλος ἔκτοτε τὸν ὀφθαλμὸν αὐτοῦ ἔκλινεν ἐπὶ τεσσαράκοντα ἔτεσιν, ἵνα ἐκ τούτου ὑπολάβῃ ὁ βασιλεύς, ὡς ὁ ὀφθαλμὸς αὐτοῦ πάθος εἶχε τοιοῦτον καὶ οὐ νεῦμα ἦν τὸ πρὸς τὴν γυναῖκα γενόμενον. Καὶ εἰ μὴ τοῦτο ἔδρασε, περὶ τὸ ζῆν ἂν ἐκινδύνευσε.

11 Μιᾷ δὲ τῶν ἡμερῶν ἡ τὸν στέφανον λαβοῦσα, τούτῳ ταινιωθεῖσα προσήνεγκε τῷ βασιλεῖ ὄρυζαν ἐπὶ πίνακι. Ἰδοῦσα δὲ ταύτην ἡ ἑτέρα γυνὴ τὴν πορφύραν ἐνεδύσατο καὶ εἰσελθοῦσα ἔπλησε φωτὸς τὸν τόπον ἐκεῖνον. Ὡς οὖν εἶδε ταύτην ὁ βασιλεύς, ἐπόθησε αὐτὴν καὶ εἶπε πρὸς τὴν ἑτέραν· "Τί παθοῦσα τὴν τοιαύτην πορφύραν κατέλιπες, καὶ τὸν στέφανον προέκρινας;" Ἡ δὲ βασιλὶς θυμοῦ πλησθεῖσα ἔρριψε τὸν πίνακα κατὰ τῆς κεφαλῆς τοῦ βασιλέως καὶ ἐπεχύθη τούτῳ ἡ ὄρυζα. Ἐφ' ᾧ πάνυ ὀργισθεὶς ὁ βασιλεὺς προσέταξε τῷ πρωτοσυμβούλῳ αὐτοῦ ταύτην καρατομῆσαι καὶ μηδόλως αὐτῆς φείσασθαι. Ὁ δὲ ταύτην παραλαβὼν καὶ ἐξελθὼν διελογίσατο καθ' ἑαυτόν, μήποτε ὁ βασιλεὺς μετάμελος ἐπὶ τῇ ἀναιρέσει αὐτῆς γενήσεται. Καὶ διὰ τοῦτο ταύτην γυναιξί τισι λάθρα παραδοὺς διὰ πάσης τιμῆς ἄγεσθαι ἐκέλευσεν ταύτην.

12 Ὁ δὲ βασιλεὺς μετάμελος σφόδρα γεγονὼς καὶ ἀναμιμνησκόμενος τῆς εὐνοϊκῆς αὐτῆς πρὸς αὐτὸν διαθέσεως ἠθύμει τὰ μέγιστα. Ἔγνω οὖν ὁ πρωτοσύμβουλος αὐτοῦ τὴν τοῦ βασιλέως ἀθυμίαν καὶ εἶπε πρὸς αὐτόν· "Οὐδεμία ὄνησις ἐπιγίνεταί τινι ἐκ μερίμνης καὶ φροντίδος, ἀλλὰ σαρκὸς ἔκτηξις, ὥς τις ἔφησε τῶν σοφῶν· *νοῦς ἐμμέριμνος*

had not escaped the king's notice, she took the crown. From then on, the chief counselor kept his eye closed for forty years, so that the king would suppose from this that his eye was afflicted in this way, and that he had not winked at the king's wife. If he had not done this, his life would have been in danger.

And one day the wife who had taken the crown was wear- 11
ing it when she brought rice to the king on a platter. But when the other wife saw her, she put on the purple robe and, when she entered, she filled the place with light. So, when the king saw her, he was filled with desire for her and said to the other one, "What was wrong with you, that you left a purple robe like this and preferred the crown?" But the queen was filled with rage and threw the platter at the king's head, and the rice went all over him. The king became extremely angry at this, and ordered his chief counselor to cut off her head and not to spare her for any reason. But the chief counselor took her and left, wondering to himself whether the king would later regret her execution. And for this reason, he secretly handed her over to some women, and ordered them to treat her with great respect.

And the king became deeply regretful, and, remembering 12
her kindly affection for him, was in great despair. His chief counselor noticed the king's despair, and said to him, "No one gets any benefit at all from anxiety and worry, they just wither the flesh; as one of the wise men said, *an anxious mind*

σῆς βιβρώσκων ὀστέα. Παρακλήθητι οὖν, ὦ βασιλεῦ, ἐφ' οἷς οὐκ ἔστιν ἀνάκλησις, μὴ ταὐτόν τι πάθῃς τῷ τῶν περιστερῶν."

13 *Περὶ περιστερῶν.*

"Λέγεται γὰρ ὡς ἄρρην τις καὶ θήλεια περιστερὰ τὴν οἰκείαν ἐνέπλησαν φωλεὰν σίτου ὑγροτάτου καὶ συνεῖδον ἄμφω μὴ πρότερον ἀπογεύσασθαι ἐκεῖνοι τοῦ ἀποταμιευθέντος σίτου πρὶν ἢ τὰς θύραθεν ἐπιλεῖψαι διατροφάς. Θέρους δὲ καταλαβόντος καὶ τοῦ ἡλίου τὴν ἐν τῷ σίτῳ ὑγρότητα ἀνιμήσαντος εἰς μικρὰν ὄγκωσιν κομιδῇ ὁ τούτου συνεστάλη ὄγκος. Ὅπερ ἰδοῦσα ἡ ἄρρην περιστερὰ ὑπείληφε τὴν θήλειαν τοῦτον καταφαγεῖν, καὶ διὰ τοῦτο οὐ διέλιπε ταύτην τύπτων ἀφειδῶς, ἄχρις ὅτου ἀπέκτεινε ταύτην. Χειμῶνος δὲ καταλαβόντος καὶ τοῦ σίτου αὖθις ὀγκωθέντος ἔγνω ἡ περιστερά, ὡς ἀδίκως τὴν σύζυγον ἀπέκτεινε, καὶ διὰ τοῦτο ἐθρήνει διηνεκῶς καὶ ὑπὸ τῆς λύπης ἐξέπνευσεν.

"Οὕτως οἱ μὴ ἀνεχόμενοι καὶ τοῦ θυμοῦ μὴ κυριεύοντες πάσχουσι."

14 *Περὶ πίθηκος λαβόντος φακόν.*

"Ἐρρέθη δὲ πάλιν, ὡς ἄνθρωπός τις ἐβάσταζε σάκκον γέμοντα φακῆς, καὶ κοπιάσας ἐκεῖνος τῆς ὁδοιπορίας, τέθηκεν αὐτὸν ὑπὸ τοῦ δένδρου καὶ ἀνεπαύθη μικρόν. Ἰδὼν δὲ ταύτην πίθηξ τις, ἐλθὼν ἔλαβε ἐκ τοῦ σάκκου τῆς φακῆς

is a worm eating away one's bones. So take comfort, my king, about those things for which there is no remedy, so that you do not also suffer the same thing as the doves."

About doves. 13

"For it is said that a male and a female dove filled their nest with very damp grain, and they both agreed not to touch the hoarded grain until the food outside had run out. But when summer came and the sun dried up the moisture in the grain, its mass was reduced to a tiny amount. When the male dove saw this, he assumed the female had eaten it, and for this reason he kept pecking her cruelly until he had killed her. But when winter arrived and the grain swelled up again, the dove realized that he had killed his spouse unjustly, and because of this he mourned ceaselessly and expired from grief.

"This is how those who are impatient and do not control their anger will suffer."

About an ape taking a lentil. 14

"For it has been said again that a man was carrying a bag full of lentils; when he grew tired of walking, he set it down under a tree, and had a little rest. But an ape saw it and came and took a handful of lentils from the sack. While the ape

αὐτῆς δράκα μίαν. Καὶ ἀνερχόμενος ἐπί τινος δένδρου πέπτωκεν ἐκ τῆς χειρὸς αὐτοῦ φακὸς εἷς· ὁ δέ, ἁπλώσας τὴν χεῖρα τοῦ λαβεῖν τὸν φακόν, ἐκπεπτώκασι καὶ οἱ λοιποί.

"Τί δέ σοι πρὸς τούτοις μέλλει, ὦ βασιλεῦ, περὶ μιᾶς γυναικός, ἔχοντι τῶν μυρίων ἐπέκεινα καὶ εἴασας τὸ ταύταις ἐφήδεσθαι καὶ κενῶς τὴν ἀποιχομένην ὀδύρῃ οὑτωσίν;"

Ὡς οὖν ταῦτα ὁ βασιλεὺς ἤκουσεν, περίλυπος γέγονε μήποτε τὴν γυναῖκα ἀνῄρηκε, καὶ πρὸς αὐτὸν εἶπεν· "Οὕτως δι' ἑνός μου ῥήματος τὸ τοιοῦτον μῦσος ἔδρασας;" Ὁ δὲ πρωτοσύμβουλος εἶπε· "Τοῦ νουνεχοῦς ὁ εἷς λόγος ἀμετάτρεπτος." Ὁ δὲ βασιλεὺς ἔφη πρὸς αὐτόν· "Περίλυπός εἰμι περὶ τῆς εὐνουστάτης μου γυναικός, ὦ Παλλάριε." Ὁ δὲ Παλλάριος ἔφη αὐτῷ· "Δύο ἀνθρώπους δεῖ λυπεῖσθαι, τὸν μήποτε ἀγαθοεργήσαντα, καὶ τὸν μὴ μνημονεύσαντα τῆς ἐσχάτης ἡμέρας." Ὁ δὲ βασιλεὺς εἶπεν· "Ἐὰν ἴδω τὴν Πελάδα, οὐκέτι μέλλει μοι περί τινος." Ὁ δὲ Παλλάριος ἔφη· "Δύο ἄνδρας οὐ δεῖ λυπεῖσθαι, τὸν ἀγαθοποιὸν καὶ τὸν μὴ ἁμαρτήσαντά ποτε." Ὁ δὲ βασιλεὺς εἶπε πρὸς αὐτόν· "Οὐκέτι βλέπω τὴν Πελάδα·" Καὶ ὁ Παλλάριος· "Δύο εἰσὶν οἱ μὴ βλέποντες, ὁ τυφλὸς καὶ ὁ ἄνους· ὥσπερ γὰρ οὐ βλέπει τὸν οὐρανὸν ὁ τυφλός, οὔτε γινώσκει τὰ πόρρω ἐκ τῶν ἐγγύς, οὕτως οὐδὲ ὁ ἄνους διακρίνει τὸ πονηρὸν ἐκ τοῦ ἀγαθοῦ." Ὁ δὲ βασιλεὺς εἶπεν· "Οὐκ ἐπλήσθην τῆς Πελάδος ἐγώ ποτε·" Ὁ δὲ Παλλάριος ἔφη· "Δύο ἄνθρωποι οὐ πλησθήσονται εἰς τὸν αἰῶνα, ὁ φιλάργυρος καὶ ὁ ἀκόρεστος·" Καὶ ὁ βασιλεὺς εἶπε πρὸς

was climbing up into a tree, one of the lentils fell out of his hand and when he opened his hand to catch the lentil, the others fell out.

"Why do you care about these matters, my king, and about one woman, when you have countless others besides her? Why have you given up enjoying the others, and pointlessly mourn like this the one who is dead?"

When the king heard this, he became very sad that he had perhaps killed his wife, and said to his chief counselor, "So you did such a foul thing because of one word from me?" And the chief counselor said, "A single word from a sensible man cannot be changed." But the king said to him, "I am very sad, Pallarios, about my loyal wife." And Pallarios said to him, "One should grieve for two kinds of person: one who has never done good deeds and one who has not been mindful of the last judgment." And the king said, "If I were to see Pelas, I wouldn't be worried about anything anymore." And Pallarios said, "One should not grieve for two kinds of men: one who has done good and one who has never sinned." And the king said to him, "I no longer see Pelas." Pallarios said, "There are two kinds of men who don't see, the blind man and the fool. For just as the blind man doesn't see the sky, nor can tell what is close from what is far away, so too the fool does not distinguish good from evil." The king said, "I could never have enough of Pelas." But Pallarios said, "There are two types of men who never have enough, the avaricious and the insatiable." Then the king said to him, "I need to get

αὐτόν· "Δεῖ με μακρυνθῆναι ἀπὸ σοῦ·" Ὁ δὲ Παλλάριος ἔφη· "Μακρυνθῆναί σε δεῖ ἀπὸ τὸν ἀσεβῆ τὸν μὴ φρονοῦντα, μηδὲ ὁμολογοῦντα τὴν κρίσιν καὶ τὴν ἀνταπόδοσιν, καὶ ἀπὸ τὸν μὴ κυριεύοντα τὰς ὀρέξεις καὶ τὰς ἐπιθυμίας τὰς αὐτοῦ." Ὁ δὲ βασιλεὺς εἶπεν αὐτῷ· "Ἐστερήθην ὁ οἶκός μου ἀπὸ τῆς Πελάδος." Καὶ ὁ Παλλάριος ἔφη· "Τέσσαρές εἰσιν οἱ ἐστερημένοι, ὁ ἄνυδρος ποταμός, ἡ ἀβασίλευτος γῆ, ἡ ἄνευ ἀνδρὸς γυνή, καὶ ὁ ἄνθρωπος ὁ μὴ γινώσκων τὸ ἀγαθὸν διακρίνειν ἐκ τοῦ πονηροῦ." Ὁ δὲ βασιλεὺς εἶπεν αὐτῷ· "Ἀπώλετο ἡ Πελάς, ὦ Παλλάριε, ἀδίκως, καὶ ἄξιος εἶ πολλῶν βασάνων πεῖραν λαβεῖν." Καὶ ὁ Παλλάριος λέγει· "Οἱ βασάνων πολλῶν ἄξιοι τρεῖς εἰσιν· ὁ ἀδικῶν τὸν ἀναίτιον, ὁ εἰσερχόμενος ἐν δείπνῳ ἀκάλεστος, καὶ ὁ ἁρπάζων τὰ μὴ ἴδια." Καὶ ὁ βασιλεὺς εἶπε πρὸς αὐτόν· "Ἔδει σε μακροθυμῆσαι εἰς αὐτὴν ἕως οὗ ἀποστραφῇ ὁ θυμός μου." Ὁ δὲ Παλλάριος ἔφησε· "Τρεῖς δεῖ μακροθυμεῖν· τὸν ἀνερχόμενον ἐπὶ τοῦ ὄρους, τὸν ἐσθίοντα τοὺς ἰχθύας, καὶ τὸν ἐργαζόμενον δυνατὸν πρᾶγμα." Ὁ δὲ βασιλεὺς εἶπεν αὐτῷ· "Πολλά με καταφρονεῖς, ὦ Παλλάριε, ἀντιλέγων μοι τὰ τοιαῦτα." Ὁ δὲ Παλλάριος ἔφη· "Οἱ καταφρονοῦντες τὸν βασιλέα εἰσὶν οὗτοι· ὁ πολύλαλος, ὁ λαλῶν ἐν οἷς οὐκ ἐρωτᾶται, καὶ ὁ λέγων ἅπερ οὐ γινώσκει, καὶ ὁ πλούσιος δοῦλος, ὁ μὴ περιποιούμενος τὸν ἴδιον δεσπότην, ἀλλὰ μαχόμενος καὶ ἕλκων αὐτὸν ἐν δικαστηρίῳ."

16 Ὁ δὲ βασιλεὺς εἶπε πρὸς αὐτόν· "Ἔσαλσας, ὦ Παλλάριε, τοιαῦτα λέγων·" Ὁ δὲ Παλλάριος ἔφη· "Σαλός ἐστιν

away from you." And Pallarios said, "You need to get away from the impious man, from the one who does not believe in judgment and retribution, and from the one who does not control his own appetites and desires." The king said, "My house has been deprived of Pelas." And Pallarios said, "There are four things that are deprived: a waterless river, a land without a king, a woman without a man, and the man who cannot distinguish good from evil." The king said to him, "Pelas died unjustly, Pallarios, and you deserve to experience many torments." And Pallarios said, "Those who deserve torments are three: someone who wrongs the innocent, someone who comes to dinner uninvited, and someone who takes what is not his." The king said to him, "You should have been patient with Pelas until my wrath abated." And Pallarios said, "Three people should be patient: someone climbing a mountain, someone eating fish, and someone doing a mighty deed." The king said to him, "You are seriously disrespecting me, Pallarios, answering back to me like this." But Pallarios said, "Those who disrespect the king are these: someone who says too much, someone who speaks when he has not been questioned, someone who says something he does not know, and the rich servant who does not take care of his own master, but quarrels with him and takes him to court."

The king said to him, "You've gone crazy, Pallarios, saying 16
such things." Pallarios said, "A crazy man is someone who

ὁ διδάσκων μωρόν, καὶ ἀντιλέγων σοφῷ, καὶ ὁ συναναστρεφόμενος τοῖς ἀχρειολόγοις, καὶ μιμούμενος αὐτούς, καὶ ὁ πιστεύων γυναικὶ πόρνῃ ἐν τοῖς λόγοις αὐτῆς, καὶ ὁ φανερῶν τὸ μυστήριον αὐτοῦ τῷ μὴ πιστῷ." Ὁ δὲ βασιλεύς· "Ἄτακτα πεποίηκας, ὅτι ἐφόνευσας τὴν Πελάδα." Καὶ ὁ Παλλάριος· "Ἄτακτός ἐστιν ὁ ψεύστης, ὃς οὐ ποιεῖ κατὰ τοὺς λόγους αὐτοῦ, καὶ ὁ νέος ὁ μολύνων τὸν θυμὸν αὐτοῦ καὶ ἔχων ἔρωτα ἐν γυναικὶ παλλακίδι καὶ νικᾶται πρὸς τὰς ἀκορεσίας αὐτῆς, καὶ ὁ βασιλεύς, ὁ ἐγχειρίσας πρᾶγμα μέγιστον, καὶ μὴ συμβουλεύων τοῖς ἑαυτοῦ συμβούλοις." Ὁ δὲ βασιλεὺς εἶπεν αὐτῷ· "Ταπεινὲ Παλλάριε δεῖ σε φοβεῖσθαί με." Ὁ δὲ ἔφη· "Τέσσαρές εἰσιν οἱ φοβούμενοι ἐν οἷς οὐκ ἔστιν φόβος· ὁ πετεινός, ὁ ὑψῶν τοὺς πόδας αὐτοῦ ἐπὶ τὸν οὐρανόν, μήπως ὁ οὐρανὸς πέσῃ κατ' αὐτοῦ, ὁ γερανός, ὁ ἱστάμενος δι' ἑνὸς ποδὸς καὶ φειδόμενος μήπως διὰ τοῦ ἑτέρου γένηται χάσμα ἐν τῇ γῇ, ὁ σκώληξ, ὁ ἐσθίων τὸν χοῦν καὶ μὴ χορταζόμενος ἐξ αὐτοῦ, ἀλλὰ φοβεῖται μήπως ἐκκοπῇ ὁ χοῦς ἐκ τῆς γῆς, καὶ ἡ νυκτερίς, ἡ πετομένη ἐν τῇ νυκτὶ ἐν δὲ τῇ ἡμέρᾳ κρυπτομένη καὶ φοβουμένη μήπως θηρευθῇ διὰ τὴν ὡραιότητα καὶ τὸ κάλλος αὐτῆς." Καὶ ὁ βασιλεὺς εἶπεν· "Οὐκέτι εἶδον ἐν γυναιξὶν ὁμοίαν τῆς Πελάδος." Καὶ ὁ Παλλάριος· "Τέσσαρές εἰσιν οἱ ἀμετάτρεπτοι· ἡ γυνή, ἡ ἐθισθεῖσα εἰς τοὺς πολλοὺς ἄνδρας, <ἣ> καὶ ἕνα καθ' ἕνα παραβλέπει ὡς μυκτηριζομένη, ὁ ἀνήρ, ὁ τὸ ψεῦδος ἐθίσας, ὁ ὑψηλόφρων ἀνήρ, καὶ ὁ κακόγνωμος, καὶ ὁ ἀνὴρ ὁ πονηρὸς καὶ δόλιος καὶ πλεονέκτης καὶ συκοφάντης." Ὁ δὲ βασιλεὺς εἶπεν·

teaches a moron, who disputes a wise man, who converses with men whose talk is useless and follows them, who believes the words of a prostitute, and who reveals his secret to an untrustworthy person." The king said, "You behaved inappropriately in murdering Pelas." And Pallarios said, "A liar is inappropriate, who does not keep his word; and so is a youth who defiles his soul with passion, lusts after a concubine, and is conquered by her insatiable desires; as again is the king who attempts a great enterprise without taking the advice of his counselors." The king said to him, "Lowly Pallarios, you should fear me." But he said, "There are four examples of being fearful when there is no need to be: the rooster who raised his feet to the sky in case the sky should fall on him; the crane who stood on one leg because he was taking care the other one didn't create a chasm in the ground; the worm who ate dirt and never had its fill because it was afraid the dirt would be eradicated from the earth; and the bat which flew in the night and hid in the day because she was afraid she might be hunted for her prettiness and beauty." And the king said, "I've never seen another woman like Pelas." And Pallarios, "There are four unchangeable things: a woman accustomed to many men, who despises them and turns her nose up at them one after another; a man accustomed to lying; a proud and malevolent man; and a wicked, crafty, greedy and extortionate man." The

“Οὐκ ἐξέρχεται ἡ λύπη τῆς καρδίας μου ποτέ, ὦ Παλλάριε, ἕνεκα τῆς Πελάδος.” Ὁ δὲ ἔφη αὐτῷ· “Δεῖ σε λυπεῖσθαι, βασιλεῦ, τὴν γυναῖκα τὴν ἔχουσαν πέντε ἀρετάς, ἤγουν τὴν σώφρονα, τὴν νουνεχῆ, τὴν κεκρατημένην ἐν τοῖς λόγοις αὐτῆς, τὴν εὐγενῆ καὶ εὔμορφον, καὶ τὴν ὑποτασσομένην τῷ ἀνδρὶ αὐτῆς καὶ ποθοῦσαν αὐτόν.” Ὁ δὲ βασιλεύς· “Ἐφύτευσας ἐν τῇ καρδίᾳ μου μεγίστην λύπην, ὦ Παλλάριε, καὶ ἔχθραν κατὰ σοῦ διὰ τὸ ἀποκτεῖναί σε τὴν πεποθημένην μου Πελάδα δεινῶς.” Ὁ δέ φησιν· “Οἱ ἀληθῶς ἐχθραίνοντες πρὸς ἀλλήλους εἰσὶν οὗτοι· ὁ λύκος καὶ τὰ πρόβατα, ὁ μῦς καὶ ἡ γαλῆ, ὁ ἱέραξ καὶ ὁ πέρδιξ, ὁ κόραξ καὶ ἡ γλαῦξ, ὁ καρκίνος καὶ ὁ ὄφις· ὡσαύτως καὶ οἱ φίλοι, ὅταν τῆς φιλίας ἐκπέσωσιν, μεγάλως ἐχθραίνονται πρὸς ἑαυτούς.”

17 Καὶ ὁ βασιλεύς· “Οὐ πλησθήσομαι ἔτι ὕπνου ἀπὸ τῆς λύπης τῆς Πελάδος.” Ὁ δὲ Παλλάριος· “Ὀκτώ εἰσιν οἱ μὴ ὑπνοῦντες· ὁ πολύολβος ἄνθρωπος ὁ μὴ ἔχων πιστὸν δοῦλον, ὁ βουλόμενος ἀποκτεῖναι τὸν αὐτοῦ φίλον, ὁ ἔχων πόθον πρὸς γυναῖκα, ὁ ψευδῆ καταλαλῶν, ὁ ἄπορος ὁ ἀπαιτούμενος ἃ μὴ ἔχει, ὁ κείμενος ἐν ἀσθενείᾳ δεινῇ καὶ μὴ ἔχων ἰατρόν, ὁ ἔχων γυναῖκα πόρνην, ὁ πλούσιος καὶ φειδόμενος περὶ τῆς πτωχείας, καὶ ὁ ζητῶν πρᾶγμα ὃ οὐ δύναται καταλαβεῖν.” Ὁ δὲ βασιλεὺς λέγει πρὸς αὐτόν· “Ἀπὸ τοῦ νῦν οὐ δύναμαι ὁμιλεῖν μετὰ σοῦ.” Ὁ δὲ Παλλάριος ἔφη· “Οἱ ἀνάξιοι τῆς ὁμιλίας οὗτοί εἰσιν· ὁ διὰ ψεῦδος μισῶν τὸν ἀδελφὸν αὐτοῦ, ὁ ὑπερήφανος καὶ ἀκατάδεκτος, ὁ προκρίνων τὸν πλοῦτον κρείττονα τῆς ψυχῆς αὐτοῦ, καὶ ὁ ἀντιλέγων τοῦ κυρίου καὶ τοῦ διδασκάλου αὐτοῦ.” Καὶ

king said, "The grief I feel over Pelas is never leaving my heart, Pallarios." He said to him, "You should grieve the wife who has five virtues, that is to say, chastity, intelligence, restraint in her speech, good breeding and a good body, and obedience to her husband and desire for him." The king said, "You have planted the deepest grief in my heart, Pallarios, and hostility toward you, since you killed Pelas, whom I desired so much." He said, "Those who are truly hostile to each other are these: the wolf and the sheep, the mouse and the cat, the hawk and the dove, the crow and the owl, the crab and the snake. But the same goes for friends; when their friendship fails, they are very hostile to each other."

And the king said, "I will not be able to sleep any more 17
from my grief for Pelas." And Pallarios said, "There are eight who do not sleep: the very wealthy man who does not have a trustworthy slave; the man who wants to kill his friend; the man who desires a woman; the slanderer; the poor man who is asked to pay what he doesn't have; the man who lies badly sick and does not have a physician; the man who has a licentious wife; the rich man who is afraid of poverty; and the man who seeks something he cannot get." The king said, "From now on I cannot talk with you." And Pallarios said, "Those not worth talking to are these: someone who hates his brother falsely; someone who is proud and haughty; someone who prefers wealth more than his soul; and someone who contradicts his master and his teacher." And the

ὁ βασιλεὺς πάλιν λέγει· “Οὐδεὶς ἐν πᾶσιν ἀναμάρτητος, καὶ τὸ τέλειον παρ’ οὐδενὶ τῶν ἀνθρώπων ἐστί.” Καὶ μετὰ τὰς πολλὰς διαλέξεις καὶ τὴν τοῦ βασιλέως ἀπόγνωσιν, στεφηφοροῦσαν αὐτῷ προσήνεγκε τὴν ὁμευνέτιν ὁ Παλλάριος. Καὶ ταύτην ἰδὼν ὁ βασιλεὺς καὶ πάνυ περιχαρὴς γεγονὼς πολυτελέσι τοῦτον δεξιώμασιν ἐφιλοτιμήσατο. Τοὺς δὲ φιλοσόφους ἐκείνους τοὺς μεριμνήσαντας τὸν αὐτοῦ θάνατον, συναγαγὼν ὁμοῦ πάντας ἀπέκτεινεν ἐνώπιον αὐτοῦ. Οὕτως ἄρα τῇ φρονήσει καὶ τῇ ἀνοχῇ καὶ τῇ τῶν συνετῶν συμβούλων συνέσει, καὶ τῇ φρονίμῳ γυναικί, φυλάττει ὁ βασιλεὺς ἀβλαβῆ τὴν οἰκείαν βασιλείαν, ὅλως ἀσάλευτον.

king said again, "No one is faultless in every respect, and perfection is to be found in no man." After this long debate and despair on the part of the king, Pallarios brought him his wife, wearing the crown. And when he saw her, the king was overjoyed, and presented him with extravagant tokens of friendship. As for those philosophers who plotted his death, he gathered them all together and had them killed in his presence. Thus, by the care and forbearance and intelligence of intelligent counselors, and by the prudence of his wife, the king kept his kingdom free from harm, completely undisturbed.

[Chapter 8]

Ἀρχὴ τοῦ ὀγδόου τμήματος.

Ὁ δὲ βασιλεὺς τῷ φιλοσόφῳ εἶπεν· "Ἔγνων δὴ τὸ τοιοῦτον παράδειγμα. Λοιπὸν ἀνάγγειλόν μοι, πῶς δύο ἐχθροὶ φιλοῦνται τοιούτως ἐν περιστάσει, καὶ πάλιν λυτροῦνται ἀμφότεροι ἐκ τῶν κινδύνων;" Σταθεὶς δὲ πάλιν ὁ φιλόσοφος ἔμπροσθεν τοῦ βασιλέως ἔφη οὕτως·

Οὐ πᾶσα, βασιλεῦ, φιλία συνίσταται εἰς ὠφέλειαν, διὰ τὴν τῶν καιρῶν ἀπαλλαγὴν καὶ ἀποτροπήν. Ὁ δὲ νουνεχὴς ἐξετάζει τὸν καιρὸν καὶ ἐν περιστάσει φιλιοῦται τῷ ἐχθρῷ αὐτοῦ διὰ τὴν ἑαυτοῦ σωτηρίαν, καθὼς ὁ μῦς καὶ ἡ γαλῆ πεποιήκασι.

2 *Περὶ μυὸς καὶ γαλῆς.*

Λέγεται γάρ, ὡς ἦν δένδρον παμμεγεθέστατον ἔν τινι τόπῳ· ἐν δὲ τῇ ῥίζῃ αὐτοῦ ἦν κατάδυσις μυὸς καὶ πλησίον αὐτοῦ ὀπὴ γαλῆς. Μιᾷ δὲ τῶν ἡμερῶν ἐξῆλθέ τις θηρευτὴς καὶ ἥπλωσε τὰ δίκτυα αὐτοῦ πλησίον τοῦ δένδρου. Ἐξελθοῦσα δὲ καὶ ἡ γαλῆ ζητοῦσα βρῶσιν, συνεπλάκη τοῖς δικτύοις. Ἐξῆλθε δὲ καὶ ὁ μῦς βοσκηθῆναι καὶ θεωρήσας

Chapter 8

BEGINNING OF THE EIGHTH CHAPTER.

The king said to the philosopher, "I have understood this example. Now tell me, how may two enemies be friends in an emergency and, again, rescue each other from danger?" The philosopher stood before the king once more and said this:

My king, not every friendship is established for the benefit of averting and escaping times of crisis. An intelligent man examines the situation and, in an emergency, makes friends with his enemy for his own safety, just as the mouse and the weasel did.

About a mouse and a weasel. 2

For it is said that there was an enormous tree somewhere, and in its roots there was a mouse's hole and, nearby, a weasel's hole. One day a hunter came and spread his nets near the tree. When the weasel came out in search of food, she was entangled in the nets. The mouse also came out to feed

τὴν γαλῆν τοῖς βρόχοις περιπεπλεγμένην, μεγάλως ἐπὶ τοῦτο περιχαρὴς ἐγένετο. Καὶ στραφεὶς ὄπισθεν αὐτοῦ θεωρεῖ νύμφην καταλαβοῦσαν τὴν αὐτοῦ κατάδυσιν· ἐν δὲ τῇ κορυφῇ τοῦ δένδρου γλαῦκά τινα παρακαθημένην. Φόβῳ δὲ μεγάλῳ συσχεθείς, εἶπεν ἐν ἑαυτῷ· "Εἰ ζητήσω τὴν κατάδυσίν μου ἀπολοῦμαι παρὰ τῆς νύμφης· εἰ δὲ πάλιν φύγω δεξιᾷ ἢ ἀριστερᾷ ἁρπαγήσομαι παρὰ τῆς γλαυκός· εἰ δὲ καὶ πρὸς τὴν γαλῆν ἀπέλθω, βρωθήσομαι ὑπ' αὐτῆς. Ἀλλὰ σκέψομαι μηχανήν τινα, δι' ἧς σωθήσομαι· καὶ γὰρ δεῖ τὸν νουνεχῆ μὴ θροηθῆναι ἐν περιστάσει. Ἀλλ' οὐχ ὁρῶ πόρον σωτηρίας ἕτερον, εἰ μὴ διὰ τῆς τῆς γαλῆς φιλίας· καὶ γὰρ καὶ αὐτὴ ἐν δεινῇ περιστάσει ὑπάρχει, καὶ ἀγωνίσομαι εἴποτε δυνηθῶ λυτρῶσαι ταύτην τῶν βρόχων τοῦ θηρευτοῦ· οἶμαι γὰρ διὰ τοῦτο αὕτη διώξει τὴν νύμφην ἐκ τῆς ὀπῆς μου εἰς τὸ φαγεῖν αὐτήν, κἀγὼ σωθήσομαι, καὶ ἕξω τὴν ταύτης φιλίαν."

3 Καὶ προσελθὼν ὁ μῦς πρὸς τὴν γαλῆν εἶπεν αὐτῇ· "Πῶς διάγεις" Ἡ δὲ γαλῆ ἔφη πρὸς αὐτόν· "Ἐν λύπῃ καὶ στενοχωρίᾳ καθὼς θέλεις συ καὶ ποθεῖς." Καὶ ὁ μῦς· "Ἀληθῶς ἔφης· ἀλλ' οὖν κἀγὼ συγκοινωνός σοι ἄρτι γέγονα ἐν περιστάσει πεσών. Καὶ γὰρ σὺ ὁρᾷς τὴν νύμφην, πῶς τὴν ὀπήν μου κατέλαβε, καὶ τὴν γλαῦκα ζητοῦσάν με ἁρπάσαι· καὶ γὰρ καὶ αὐτοὶ ἀμφοτέρων ἡμῶν δύο ἐχθροί εἰσιν. Ἀλλ' οὖν δεῖ ἡμᾶς διαλλαγῆναι, καὶ φιλικὰς συνθήκας ποιῆσαι, ὅπως κἀγὼ διὰ σοῦ ῥυσθήσομαι τῆς βλάβης αὐτῶν. Κἀγὼ δὲ κόψω τοὺς δεσμούς σου καὶ λυτρώσω σε πάντως τοῦ θηρευτοῦ, σὺ δὲ ἐκδιώξεις τῆς ὀπῆς μου τὴν νύμφην." Ταῦτα ἀκούσασα ἡ γαλῆ παρὰ τοῦ μυὸς περιχαρὴς ἐγένετο,

and when he saw the weasel entangled in the mesh, he was very happy about this. When he turned around, he saw that a nymph had occupied his nest, and an owl was perching in the crown of the tree. He was terrified and said to himself, "If I try to get to my hole, I will be killed by the nymph, but if I run away to either the right or the left, I will be grabbed by the owl, and if I go toward the weasel, I'll be eaten by her. But I will think of a stratagem by which I may save myself, for someone who's intelligent should not panic in an emergency. I see no other way to be safe except for the weasel's friendship. She's in a real emergency, and so I will do what I can to release her from the hunter's nets; for I think, as a result, she will chase the nymph out of my hole so as to eat it, and I will be saved and will have her friendship."

The mouse went to the weasel and said to her, "How are 3
you doing?" The weasel said to him, "As you see and wish, I'm in a bad way and in trouble." The mouse said, "That's true, but then I too share with you in having an emergency right now. For you see how the nymph has occupied my hole and the owl wants to grab me, and the two of them are enemies of us both. But we should reconcile and make a pact of friendship, so that I may be freed by you from their harm. I will cut your bonds and save you completely from the hunter, but you will chase the nymph out of my hole." When the weasel heard the mouse suggest this, she was delighted

καὶ εἶπε πρὸς αὐτόν· "Εἰ τοῦτο ποιήσῃς, μεγάλην χάριν ἕξεις παρ' ἐμοῦ, μᾶλλον δὲ καὶ ἀντάμειψιν."

4 Καὶ τότε προσελθὼν ὁ μῦς πρὸς αὐτήν, γέγονεν ἡ φιλία μεταξὺ τούτων. Καὶ εὐθὺς ὁ μῦς ἤρξατο κατεσθίειν τοὺς δεσμοὺς αὐτῆς, κατέλιπε δὲ ἕνα δεσμόν, φοβούμενος μήπως ἀθετήσει ἡ γαλῆ τοὺς ὅρκους· ἡ δὲ γαλῆ ἔφη αὐτῷ· "Τί βραδύνεις, μὴ γὰρ ἐτράπη ἡ πρός με φιλία σου;" Ὁ δὲ μῦς εἶπεν· "Ἡ ἐμὴ φιλία οὐκ ἐτράπη, ἀλλὰ φοβοῦμαι μὴ τὴν σὴν φιλίαν τραπῆναι· τὸ γὰρ ἐκ φύσεως οὐκ ἀφίσταται, καὶ ἐὰν ἀφίσταται, οὐ μεθίσταται, εἰ δὲ καὶ μεθίσταται, οὐδὲ συνίσταται. Διὰ τοῦτο κατέλιπον τὸν ἕνα δεσμόν, ἕως οὗ εὕρω καιρὸν ἐπιτήδειον τοῦ κόψαι καὶ αὐτόν." Πρωΐας δὲ γενομένης, κατέλαβε καὶ ὁ θηρευτὴς πρὸς αὐτούς. Ἰδὼν δὲ αὐτὸν ὁ μῦς μακρόθεν εἶπε τῇ γαλῇ· "Τοίνυν ὁ καιρὸς κατέλαβε τοῦ τὰς συνθήκας πληροῦσθαι, ἀλλ' οὖν ἐγὼ οὐκ ἀθετῶ τὰς συνθήκας," καὶ κόψας ὁ μῦς τὸν καταλειφθέντα δεσμόν, ἔφυγεν. Ἡ δὲ γαλῆ τότε διὰ τὸν φόβον τοῦ θηρευτοῦ, διώξασα τὴν νύμφην εἰς τὸ δένδρον ἀνῆλθεν, καὶ ὁ μῦς εἰσῆλθεν εἰς τὴν κατάδυσιν αὐτοῦ. Ὁ δὲ θηρευτὴς λαβὼν τὰ δίκτυα κενὸς ἐξ αὐτῶν ἀνεχώρησε.

5 Μιᾷ δὲ τῶν ἡμερῶν ἐξῆλθεν ὁ μῦς τοῦ βοσκηθῆναι, καὶ ἰδὼν τὴν γαλῆν μακρόθεν, οὐκ ἠθέλησε πλησιάσαι αὐτῆς. Ἡ δὲ γαλῆ πρὸς αὐτὸν ἔφη· "Πρόσελθε, ὦ φίλτατε, πρός με, ὅπως ἀνταμείψωμαι ὑπὲρ ὧν ἐποίησας εἰς ἐμὲ ἀγαθῶν." Καὶ ὁ μῦς· "Ἡ ἡμετέρα φιλία οὐ δέεται ἐγγύτητος· πῶς γὰρ ἐγγίσω σοι βρῶσίς σοι ὑπάρχων; Οὐ δεῖ γὰρ τὸν ἀδύνατον πλησιάσαι τῷ δυνατωτέρῳ αὐτοῦ ἐχθρῷ· ἡ γὰρ

and said to him, "If you do this, you'll have my thanks, or rather, my reward as well."

Then the mouse went to her, and there was friendship 4
between them. The mouse immediately began to gnaw her bonds, but left one rope, as he was afraid the weasel would not honor their oaths. But the weasel said to him, "Why are you delaying? You haven't changed your mind about your friendship with me, have you?" The mouse said, "I haven't changed my mind about my friendship, but I'm afraid you may have changed you mind about yours. For what is there by nature does not go away, and, even if it does go away, it doesn't change, and even if it does change, it doesn't do so permanently. That's why I've left the one rope until I find the right time to cut that as well." When morning came, the hunter approached them. When the mouse saw him in the distance, he said to the weasel, "The time has come to fulfill our pact, so I am going to honor it," and the mouse cut the remaining rope and ran away. And the weasel, out of fear of the hunter, chased the nymph away and went up into the tree, and the mouse went into his hole. But the hunter took his empty net and went away from them.

One day, the mouse went out to feed and saw the weasel 5
in the distance but did not want to go near her. The weasel said to him, "Come here to me, my dear, so that I can pay you back for the good turn you did for me." But the mouse said, "Our friendship does not need to be too close. How can I be close to you when I'm your food? Someone who's weak should not get close to a more powerful enemy. The

προλαβοῦσα ἡμῶν φιλία, ἀναγκαία γέγονε διὰ τὴν τῶν ἀμφοτέρων ὠφέλειαν καὶ σωτηρίαν. Ἀπὸ τοῦ νῦν δὲ ἔστω ἡμῶν ἡ φιλία μακρόθεν· τὸ γὰρ ἐγγίσαι με πρός σε, ἀδύνατόν ἐστιν."

"Οὕτως ἄρα," ὁ φιλόσοφος εἶπε, "δύο ἐχθροὶ ἐν ἀνάγκῃ τινὶ φιλοῦνται, καὶ ἀμφότεροι τῶν κινδύνων ἐλευθεροῦνται, καὶ οὐ πάντοτε."

friendship we established earlier was necessary for the benefit and safety of both of us, so, from now on, let our friendship be at a distance, because it's impossible for me to be close to you."

"In this way, then," said the philosopher, "two enemies may become friends out of necessity, and both may be freed from danger, but not all the time."

[Chapter 9]

Ἀρχὴ τοῦ ἐννάτου τμήματος.

Καὶ αὖθις ὁ βασιλεὺς τῷ φιλοσόφῳ ἔφη· "Ἔγνων καὶ τὸ τοιοῦτον παράδειγμα. Λοιπὸν ἀνάγγειλόν μοι πῶς δεῖ τὰς ἔχθρας εὐλαβεῖσθαί τινα καὶ τὰς μνησικακίας παρατηρεῖν." Ὁ δὲ φιλόσοφος ὑπολαβὼν ἔφη·

2 *Περὶ βασιλέως καὶ ψιττακοῦ.*

Βασιλεύς τις εἶχε ψιττακὸν ἐχέφρονά τε καὶ ὡραῖον, ἔχοντα καὶ οἰκεῖον νεοττόν, οὓς καὶ προσέταξεν ὁ βασιλεὺς συνδιαιτᾶσθαι τῷ ἰδίῳ παιδί. Συνέπαιζον οὖν ἀλλήλοις οἷα εἰκὸς καὶ πάντοτε τῆς αὐτῆς μετελάμβανον τροφῆς. Ὁ δὲ ψιττακὸς ὁσημέραι ἐπί τι ὄρος ἀνήρχετο καὶ δύο τινὰς καινὰς ὀπώρας μετεκόμιζεν καὶ ἐδίδου, τὴν μὲν μίαν τῷ οἰκείῳ νεοττῷ, τὴν δὲ ἑτέραν τῷ τοῦ βασιλέως παιδί, δι' ὧν ταχίστη ἀμφοτέρων ἐγένετο <ἡ> αὔξησις καὶ ἡ τῆς ἰσχύος ἐπίδοσις καὶ ἡ ἀκμὴ τῆς ἡλικίας. Μιᾷ οὖν τῶν ἡμερῶν ἀποδημοῦντος τοῦ ψιττακοῦ, ὁ νεοσσὸς αὐτοῦ ἐπί τι πτηνὸν τῷ τοῦ βασιλέως παιδὶ προσφιλὲς [αὐτῷ] ἐπεισπηδήσας, ἐτραυμάτισεν, ἐφ' ᾧ δὴ καὶ ὁ παῖς ὀργισθεὶς τοῦτον ἀπέκτεινεν.

Chapter 9

BEGINNING OF THE NINTH CHAPTER.

The king again said to the philosopher, "I understand this example. So now, tell me how one should respect one's enemies and watch out for the grudges they hold." And the philosopher responded:

About a king and a parrot. 2

A king had a parrot that was clever and beautiful and which had a chick of its own, and he ordered that they should live with his son. They used to play with each other, as it seems, and always shared the same food. But the parrot would fly up to a mountain every day and bring back two strange fruits which it would give them, one to its own chick, the other to the king's son, as a result of which both grew very quickly, increased in strength, and reached the flower of youth. But one day, while the parrot was away, its chick leaped upon a bird which the king's son liked. It wounded it and, as a result, the boy became angry and killed the chick.

3 Ὁ οὖν ψιττακὸς παραγενόμενος καὶ τὸν οἰκεῖον νεοττὸν ἀνῃρημένον θεασάμενος καὶ περίλυπος πάνυ γεγονώς, ἔφη· "Οὐαὶ τοῖς βασιλεῦσι, τοῖς μήτε συνθήκας τηροῦσι, μήτε φιλίας θεσμούς. Οὐαὶ δὲ καὶ τοῖς ἐξυπηρετοῦσιν αὐτοῖς, οἳ οὔτε τιμῶσιν, οὔτε τηροῦσί τινα, εἰ μή γε πολλάκις ἐπιδεεῖς αὐτῶν γίνονται, ὅτε δὲ οὐκ ἐπιδέονται τούτων, οὐδὲ προσφωνοῦσιν αὐτοῖς, μὴ εἰδότες ἀρετῆς ἀμοιβήν, μήτε συγγνώμην ἁμαρτημάτων, οἱ πᾶν πλημμέλημα ἐργαζόμενοι καὶ μηδαμινὸν τοῦτο λογιζόμενοι." Εἶτα εἶπεν· "Ἀμυνοῦμαι σήμερον τοῦτον τὸν παλαμναῖον καὶ ἀλιτήριον καὶ πρὸς οἶκτον ἀκαμπῆ καὶ τῆς συναυλίας ἀθετητήν, καὶ τῆς συνδιαιτήσεως ἐπιλήσμονα." Καὶ ἐπεισπηδήσας τῷ τοῦ παιδὸς προσώπῳ, ταῖς οἰκείαις ὄνυξι τὰς κόρας τῶν ὀφθαλμῶν αὐτοῦ κατώρυξε. Καὶ τὸ τοιοῦτον οὗτος κατατολμήσας ἐπί τινα ὑψηλότατον καὶ ὀχυρώτατον τόπον ἀνῆλθεν.

4 Ὁ οὖν βασιλεὺς τὸ γενόμενον ἀναμαθὼν καὶ θυμοῦ πλησθείς, ἀπῆλθε πρὸς τὸν ψιττακόν, καὶ προσεκαλεῖτο αὐτόν. Ὁ δὲ ψιττακὸς ἔφη· "Γίνωσκε, ὦ βασιλεῦ, ὡς ὁ τῶν συνθηκῶν παραβάτης, εὐάλωτός ἐστι τῇ οἰκείᾳ παραβάσει, καὶ εἰ πρός τινα καιρὸν ἀνέξεται τούτου ἡ θεία πρόνοια, οὐκ ἀπολυθήσεται τῆς καταδίκης, ἀλλ' εἰς αἰῶνας κολασθήσεται. Διαβαίνει δὲ ἡ κόλασις καὶ ἐπὶ υἱοὺς καὶ υἱωνοὺς καὶ εἰς τὸ ἑξῆς. Ὁ γοῦν σὸς υἱὸς τὴν ἀντέκτισιν τῆς δίκης ταχεῖαν εἴληφεν." Ὁ δὲ βασιλεύς· "Καλῶς εἶπας, καὶ οὐδὲν ἀμφίβολον καταλέλειπται. Τὸ λοιπὸν κάτελθε ἀνενδοιάστως." Ὁ δὲ ψιττακός· "Οὐ δεῖ με τοῦτο ποιεῖν· οἱ γὰρ ἐχέφρονες παραινοῦσιν ἀεὶ παρατηρεῖσθαι τὸν

When the parrot returned and saw its chick lying dead, it 3
became very upset and said: "Alas for kings, who do not hold to their agreements nor the bonds of friendship. And alas for those who serve these kings, who do not respect nor pay any attention to anyone unless, perhaps, they need them, and then, when they're not necessary to them, neither summon them, nor think to reward their virtue, nor forgive their faults, when they themselves commit every kind of fault and think nothing of it." Then it said, "Today I'm paying back the guilty murderer, who is unmoved by pity, despises companionship, and forgets the time we lived together." And the parrot leaped up at the boy's face and with its claws gouged out the pupils of his eyes. And after it had perpetrated this attack, it flew up to a very high and secure place.

When the king learned what had happened, he was filled 4
with anger and went up to the parrot and called it. The parrot said, "My king, you must know that someone who violates agreements is easily led to his own downfall by his transgression, and if for some time divine Providence spares him, he will never be released from his sentence and will be punished forever. And that punishment passes on to his sons and his sons' sons forever. Your son has received the swift retribution of justice." The king said, "What you say is true, and there's no doubt about it. So you should come down now without any hesitation." The parrot said, "I should not do that. For smart people urge one to always be

μνησίκακον, καὶ ὅσον ὁ τοιοῦτος ὑποκολακεύει καὶ ὑποσαίνει, τοσοῦτον φευκτέος καὶ παρορατέος, καὶ οὐκ ἄλλως τις ἐκφεύξεται τὴν ἐξ αὐτοῦ βλάβην, εἰ μή γε τῇ τούτου ἀποχῇ καὶ τῇ τῶν οἰκείων συντηρήσει. Λέγεται γὰρ ὡς δεῖ τὸν νουνεχῆ, τοὺς μὲν γονεῖς λογίζεσθαι φίλων τάξιν ἐπέχειν, τοὺς δ' ἀδελφοὺς συνοδοιπόρων, τὰς δ' ὁμευνέτιδας συνήθων, τοὺς δὲ υἱοὺς μνήμης ἕνεκα προσειλημμένους, τὰς δὲ θυγατέρας ἀντιδίκους, τοὺς δὲ συγγενεῖς δανειστὰς καὶ χρεῶν ἀπαιτητάς, ἑαυτὸν δὲ μεμονωμένον καὶ πάσης συγγενείας ἔρημον. Κἀγὼ οὖν τῇ τοιαύτῃ παραινέσει ἑπόμενος, ἤδη μεμόνωμαι." Ὁ δὲ βασιλεύς· "Εἰ μὲν σὺ πρῶτος κατήρξω τῆς ἡμετέρας βλάβης, ἔδει σε ἡμᾶς παραφυλάττεσθαι· ἐπεὶ δὲ ἡ προκάταρξις ἀφ' ἡμῶν γέγονε, τί σοι πάρεστιν ἔμποδον ἐν τούτοις τοῦ μὴ πιστεύειν ἡμῖν;" Ὁ δὲ ψιττακὸς ἔφη· "Αἱ μνησικακίαι μέγιστα πάθη περὶ τὰς καρδίας ἐργάζονται καὶ αἱ γλῶσσαι οὐκ ἐμφαίνουσιν ἀληθέστατα τὰ τῶν ψυχῶν διανοήματα καὶ τῶν καρδιῶν. Ἀξιοπιστότεραι αἱ μαρτυρίαι κατὰ τὰ τῶν καρδιῶν ὑπὲρ τὰς γλώσσας· οὔτε οὖν ἡ ἐμὴ καρδία μαρτυρεῖ σῇ τῇ γλώσσῃ, οὔτε ἡ σὴ καρδία τῇ ἐμῇ μαρτυρεῖ γλώσσῃ."

5 Ὁ δὲ βασιλεύς· "Οὐκ οἶσθα, ὦ ψιττακέ, ὡς ὁ ἐχέφρων ἀνὴρ σπεύδει τὴν μνησικακίαν ἐξολοθρεῦσαι μᾶλλον, ἢ αὐξῆσαι;" Ὁ δὲ ψιττακός· "Ἔστι τοῦτο, ὦ βασιλεῦ, καθὼς εἶπας, ἀλλ' οὐ δεῖ τὸν ἐχέφρονα ἄνδρα ὑπολαμβάνειν ὡς ὁ ἐχθρὸς αὐτοῦ τῆς προκειμένης μεταξὺ ἐπιλέλησται ἀμφισβητήσεως, ἀλλὰ παρατηρεῖσθαι τὸ ἀπατᾶσθαι· πολλοὶ γὰρ μὴ δυνάμενοι τῇ βίᾳ ἡττηθῆναι, τοῖς ἀπατηλοῖς ἔργοις καὶ λόγοις ἑάλωσαν, καθάπερ ὁ ἄγριος ἐλέφας διὰ τοῦ

on one's guard against someone who bears a grudge, and the more someone flatters and fawns, the more they should be avoided and ignored; one will not otherwise escape harm from a person like this, except by keeping away from him and looking after one's own interests. For it is said that an intelligent person considers his parents as being on the same level as his friends, his brothers on that of companions, his wives on that of acquaintances; he treats his sons as a way of being remembered, his daughters as plaintiffs, his relatives as creditors and debt collectors, and himself as living alone, isolated from any kin. And so, I am following this advice and already living alone." The king said, "If it was you who started the harm I've suffered, you should be on your guard, but since the beginning of the problem was mine, what reason is there for you not to believe me?" But the parrot said, "Grudges produce great passion in people's hearts, and tongues do not express very clearly the thoughts of people's hearts and souls. The confirmation of the heart is more trustworthy than that of the tongue; my heart does not confirm what your tongue is saying nor does your heart confirm what my tongue says."

The king said, "Don't you know, parrot, that a smart man 5
is keen to get rid of a grudge rather than exacerbate it?" And the parrot said, "What you say, my king, is indeed the case, but a smart man should not assume that his enemy has forgotten the earlier dispute that existed between them, but should, rather, watch out for being deceived. For many who cannot be defeated by force have succumbed to deceitful deeds and words, just as the wild elephant succumbs to the

ἡμέρου ἁλίσκεται.” Ὁ δὲ βασιλεύς· “Ὁ ἐλευθέριος ἀνὴρ οὐ μεταλλάττει τὸν τρόπον· τοῦτο γὰρ ἔργον ἀνδρῶν τὸ φρόνημα χθαμαλῶν.” Ὁ δὲ ψιττακός· “Αἱ μνησικακίαι πᾶσαι ἐπισφαλεῖς καὶ τῶν λοιπῶν ἐπισφαλέστεραι, καὶ μᾶλλον ἐν ταῖς τῶν βασιλέων ψυχαῖς, οἳ δὴ λογίζονται τὴν ἀντέκτισιν τρόπαιόν τε καὶ καύχημα· ἔοικε γὰρ ἡ μνησικακία, ἄνθραξιν ἐν τῇ καρδίᾳ ἀνημμένοις, οἷς ὅτε ἐπιτηδεία ὕλη πρὸς ἔξαψιν προσεγγίσει, τὸν πυρσὸν ἀέριον ἀπεργάζεται καὶ τὴν φλόγα δυσκατάσβεστον· οὔτε γὰρ δυσωπήσεσιν ὁ μνησίκακος ὑπείκει, οὔτε ταῖς ἱκεσίαις μαλθακίζεται. Πολλάκις δὲ ὁ μνησικακούμενος, δυνάμενος ἰᾶσθαι τὸν μνησίκακον διά τινων εὐνοιῶν καὶ ὠφελειῶν δυναμένων ἀπαλεῖψαι τὰ ἐν ταῖς καρδίαις ἐνσκιρρωθέντα, ἐπιστρέφει πρὸς τὸν μνησίκακον· ἀλλ᾽ ἐγὼ ἀδυνάτως ἔχω τοιούτοις πρὸς σὲ χρήσασθαι· ἀλλ᾽ εἰ καθαρὰν διάθεσιν πρός με διατηρεῖς, ἄγνωστον τοῦτο ἐμοί, καὶ περιδεὴς ἔσομαι κατὰ πάντα τὸν τῆς συναυλίας καιρόν. Οὐδὲν οὖν ἄλλο καταλέλειπται σκοποῦ ἐχόμενον ὀρθοῦ, ἀλλ᾽ ἢ τὸ ἀποσχισθῆναί σου καὶ ἀποχωρισθῆναι καὶ ἀπομηκισθῆναι. Λοιπὸν οὖν μοι ἔρρωσο.”

6 Ὁ δὲ βασιλεύς· “Οἶδα ὡς ἀδυνάτως ἔχει ἕκαστος τοῦ ὠφελεῖν καὶ βλάπτειν καὶ ὡς οὐδέν ἐστι τῶν ὄντων, ἢ μεῖζον ἢ ἔλαττον, ὃ μὴ καθ᾽ εἱμαρμένην καὶ πεπρωμένην μοῖράν τινα γίνεται· καὶ ὥσπερ οὐκ αἴτιός τίς ἐστι τῶν ἀνθρώπων τῆς γενέσεως τῶν γινομένων, οὕτως οὐδὲ τῆς φθορᾶς τῶν φθειρομένων. Οὐδὲν οὖν ἔγκλημα προσάπτεταί σοι ἕνεκεν τῆς τοῦ υἱοῦ μου πηρώσεως, οὐδὲ ἐκείνῳ ἕνεκεν τῆς τοῦ νεοττοῦ σου ἀναιρέσεως· εἵμαρται γὰρ

tamer." The king said, "The free man does not change his way of life; that's what people with a humble mind-set do." But the parrot said, "All grudges are dangerous, and more dangerous than anything else, especially in the souls of kings who consider revenge a victory and something to boast about. For a grudge is like charcoal glowing in the heart, which, when the wood necessary for kindling is present, is set alight by the air, and its flame is hard to extinguish. For the person who holds a grudge neither yields to persuasion, nor is softened by entreaties. Often someone against whom a grudge is held may be able to pacify the holder of the grudge through some kindnesses and benefits which, if they can expunge the things that have hardened in his heart, may change the mind of the bearer of the grudge. But I can't treat you like that, and, even if you do have a pure attitude toward me, that will be unknown to me and I will always be very frightened of your company. So there is nothing else for it but to separate myself from you and go away as far as possible. So say goodbye to me."

The king said, "I know that each of us is powerless to help 6
or harm and that there is nothing in existence, greater or smaller, which is not subject to fate and what fortune has ordained, just as no human being is the cause of the coming into being of the things that are, nor also of the passing of the things that pass away. So you are not to blame for my son's blinding, nor is he to blame for the killing of your

τάδε γενέσθαι καὶ συνεργοὶ ἡμεῖς τῇ τῆς εἱμαρμένης ἀνάγκῃ ἐχρηματίσαμεν."

7 Ὁ δὲ ψιττακός· "Ἀληθῶς εἶπας περὶ τῆς εἱμαρμένης, ἀλλὰ δεῖ τὸν ἐχέφρονα παρατηρεῖν τὰ ἐπισφαλῆ καὶ παραφυλάττεσθαι καὶ μὴ πιστεύειν τῇ εἱμαρμένῃ· ὑπέρτερον δὲ ταύτης τὸν οἰκεῖον δοξάζειν λογισμόν. Ἔγωγε οὖν οἶδα, ὡς ἡ *γλῶσσα ὀμώμοκεν, ἡ δὲ φρὴν ἀνώμοτος*· σὺ οὖν τὴν ἐμὴν ψυχὴν ἐκζητεῖς καὶ αἱ ψυχαὶ τὸν θάνατον ἀπαναίνονται. Λέγεται δὲ ὡς ἡ πενία καὶ ἡ λύπη καὶ ἡ τῶν φιλτάτων στέρησις, μέγισται συμφοραί εἰσι, καὶ ὁ ταῦτα μαθών, ἀκριβέστερον οἶδε τὰς τῶν παθόντων ἀλγηδόνας. Κᾀγὼ οὖν ἔχω τινὰ παρὰ τῇ ἐμῇ ψυχῇ ὑποδείγματα, τῶν ἐν τῇ σῇ ψυχῇ παθημάτων, καὶ ἀσύμφορον ἔσται μοι τὸ συνέπεσθαί σοι· ὅσον γὰρ ἀπομνημονεύεις σὺ τὸ τοῦ υἱοῦ σου πάθος, κᾀγὼ τὸ τοῦ ἐμοῦ νεοττοῦ, ἀλλοίωσις [γὰρ] μεγίστη περὶ τὰς καρδίας γίνεται."

8 Ὁ δὲ βασιλεύς· "Οὐκ ἀγαθὸς ὁ μὴ δυνάμενος ἀπαλεῖψαι τὰ ἐν τῇ ψυχῇ παθήματα, ἀλλὰ μνημονεύει τινὰ ἐξ αὐτῶν." Ὁ δὲ ψιττακός· "Ὁ τὸν πόδα ἀλγῶν, εἰ καὶ ἐπιτηδεύσεται τάχιον βαδίζειν, οὐκ ἀνάλγητος διαμένει, καὶ ὁ ὀφθαλμιῶν εἰ πρὸς ἀνέμων ἀντωπήσει πνοάς, πάντως ἀμβλυωπήσει, καὶ ὁ μνησίκακος, εἰ πρὸς τὸν μνησικακούμενον διαλέξεται πάθος τῷ πάθει προστίθησι. Δεῖ οὖν τὸν ἐχέφρονα, πόρον σωτηρίας εὑρίσκοντα, διέρχεσθαι τοῦτον· κᾀμοὶ πολλοὶ πόροι σωτηρίας πρόκεινται. Λέγουσι δὲ οἱ φιλόσοφοι, ὡς πέντε τινὰ ἤθη δοξάζουσι τὸν ἄνδρα· τὸ μὴ βλάπτειν, τὸ πεπαιδευμένον εἶναι, τὸ τὰς ἐναντίας ὑπολήψεις ἐκφεύγειν, τὸ προσηνὲς καὶ φιλότιμον ἐν τοῖς ἤθεσι

chick. For these things were fated to happen, and we have simply been the assistants to the necessity of fate."

The parrot said, "What you have said about fate is true, 7
but the smart man should watch out for dangers and protect himself and not believe in fate, and he is better off giving credit to his own power of reasoning than to it. For I know that *it was my tongue that swore, not my mind.* So you are seeking to take my life, but life rejects death. For it is said that poverty, grief, and deprivation of friends are great calamities, and someone who has acquaintance with these understands more clearly the pain of those who suffer them. And I have examples in my life of the misfortunes in yours, and so it will be bad for me to live with you, for as long as you remember the suffering of your son and I remember that of my chick, the distance between our hearts will become very great."

The king said, "Someone who cannot remove the things 8
that he has suffered from his heart but who clings to some of them is not virtuous." But the parrot said, "A man with a painful foot will eventually manage to walk faster, but the pain will still persist; and if someone with poor eyesight looks into a gust of wind, he will become completely blind; and if the person who holds a grudge talks to the person against whom the grudge is held, he piles passion on passion. The smart man who finds a safe way should follow it. And many safe ways lie before me. The philosophers say that five practices bring credit to a man: not causing harm, being educated, avoiding hostile suspicions, being pleasant and generous in his habits, and being impressive in his

καὶ τὸ μεγαλοπρεπὲς ἐν τοῖς ἔργοις. Καὶ <ὁ> φρόνιμος, ὅτε δέδοικε περὶ ἑαυτοῦ ἀποσχοινίζεται τῶν συγγενῶν, καὶ τῶν υἱῶν, καὶ τῆς πατρίδος, καὶ τοῦ πλούτου· ἁπάντων τούτων ἀντάλλαγμα εὑρήσει, τῆς δὲ ψυχῆς οὔ. Λέγεται δὲ ὡς χείρων πλοῦτος τῶν ἄλλων ὁ μὴ μεταδιδόμενος, καὶ χείρων ὁμευνέτις ἡ μὴ τῷ ἀνδρὶ εὐνοοῦσα, καὶ χείρων παῖς ὁ ἀπειθής, καὶ χείρων ὁ βασιλεύς, <ὃς> οὐ πτοεῖται ἀθῴους, καὶ χείρων φίλος ὁ ἄπιστος καὶ ἀβέβαιος, καὶ χείρονες χῶραι αἱ περίφοβοι καὶ ἐπισφαλεῖς. Κᾀγὼ οὖν εἰ πεισθήσομαί σοι ἀεὶ περίδειλος ἔσομαι.” Καὶ ταῦτα εἰπὼν ἀπηλλάγη.

Οὕτως ἄρα δεῖ τινα, ὡς τὸν ψιττακόν, εὐλαβεῖσθαι καὶ παρατηρεῖν τὰς μνησικακίας.

actions. And when the prudent man fears for himself, he separates himself from his relatives, his sons, his homeland, and his wealth. And he can find a substitute for all these things, but not for his soul. For it is said that wealth that is not shared is worse than all other wealth, and worse too is a spouse who does not agree with her husband, and a disobedient child, and a king who does not respect the innocent, and a faithless and untrustworthy friend, and fearsome and dangerous regions. So I will always be very wary of trusting you." And when it had said this, the parrot went away.

Thus one should be wary, like the parrot, and watch out for grudges.

[Chapter 10]

Ἀρχὴ τοῦ δεκάτου <τμήματος>.

Ὁ δὲ βασιλεὺς πάλιν τῷ φιλοσόφῳ εἶπε· "Τὸ μὲν παράδειγμα τῶν πρὸς ἀλλήλους ἀπεχθανομένων διέγνων. Παραδειγμάτισαι δέ μοι, ὅπως δεῖ τοὺς βασιλεῖς ἐπιστρέφειν πρὸς ἑαυτοὺς τοὺς οἰκείους, οὓς ἀδίκως καὶ κατὰ λήθην ποτὲ ἐτιμώρησαν καὶ ἀπεσόβησαν." Ὁ δὲ φιλόσοφος ὑπολαβὼν εἶπε·

2 *Περὶ θωός.*

Λέγεται δὲ ὡς ἔν τινι τόπῳ θώς τις διῆγεν, καὶ ἦν ὁ τοιοῦτος σώφρων καὶ ἐπιεικὴς παρά τε τοῖς ὁμογενέσι καὶ ταῖς ἀλώπεξι, καὶ τοῖς λοιποῖς, μήτε ποιῶν τὰ ἔργα αὐτῶν, μήτε αἷμα ἐκχέων ἀθῶον, μήτε κρεωφαγῶν. Ἐφ' ᾧ τὰ ἄλλα θηρία ὀργισθέντα εἶπον αὐτῷ· "Γίνωσκε θώς, ὡς ἀπαρεσκόμεθά σου τῇ διαγωγῇ καὶ τῷ βίῳ, ὃν προείλου· οὐδὲν γάρ σοι λυσιτελοῦσιν αἱ ἀρεταί, ἐπεὶ ἀδύνατον συμβαδίζειν σε ἡμῖν." Ὁ δὲ θὼς εἶπεν· "Ἡ μὲν ὑμετέρα ὁμιλία καὶ συνοδοιπορία, οὐδὲ ἓν ἁμάρτημά μοι προξενεῖ, ἐπεὶ μηδὲ οἱ τόποι καὶ αἱ συναυλίαι τυποῦσι τὰ ἁμαρτήματα, ἀλλ' αἱ

Chapter 10

BEGINNING OF THE TENTH CHAPTER.

The king again said to the philosopher, "I've paid attention to the example of those who hate each other. But now give me an example of how kings should behave toward their own people whom they have punished or exiled unjustly and by mistake." And the philosopher responded:

About a jackal. 2

For it is said that there was a jackal living somewhere, and it was thoughtful and courteous to its own kind, and to the foxes and the other animals, and in not doing what jackals do, nor shedding blood unjustly, nor eating meat. The other animals were angry at this and said to him, "You know, jackal, we don't like the conduct and way of life you've chosen. These virtues are not doing you any good, for it's impossible for you to go on being with us." And the jackal said, "Being in your company and traveling around with you doesn't make me sin, since neither place nor company

καρδίαι καὶ τὰ ἔργα· πλὴν εἰ συναυλίζομαι ὑμῖν τῷ σώματι, τῇ δὲ ψυχῇ πόρρω ἀπῴκισμαι." Ἐπέμεινεν οὖν ὁ τοιοῦτος θὼς τῇ ἀρετῇ οὕτως καὶ διαβόητος ἐγένετο ἐπὶ ταύτῃ.

3 *Περὶ λέοντος.*

Λέων δέ τις βασιλεὺς τῶν θηρίων ἀναμαθὼν τὰ κατ' αὐτὸν προσεκαλέσατο τοῦτον καὶ εἶπε πρὸς αὐτόν· "Μεγάλη μου ἡ δυναστεία καὶ εὐρύχωροι αἱ χῶραι, καὶ δέομαι πιστοτάτου ὑπηρέτου· καὶ ἤκουσταί μοι τὰ περὶ σοῦ καὶ τῶν σῶν ἀρετῶν, καὶ βούλομαί σε δοξάσαι, καί τινά σοι ἀρχὴν ἐγχειρίσαι μεγάλην." Ὁ δὲ θὼς ἔφη· "Δεῖ τοὺς βασιλεῖς τοὺς ἑκόντας ἐπιλέγεσθαι καὶ τούτοις παραδιδόναι τὰς ἀρχάς· ἐπεὶ εἴ τις ἀκουσίως μεταχειρίζεταί τι τῶν ἔργων, οὐ προθύμως αὐτῷ μέτεισι. Κἀγὼ οὖν τὰς ἐξουστικὰς ἀεὶ ἀποτρέπομαι μεταχειρίσεις ἄπειρος ὢν τῶν τοιούτων· καί σοι, ὦ βασιλεῦ, πάρεστι πολλὰ θηρίων γένη καὶ περὶ πᾶν ἔργον προθυμότατα, ἃ δὴ καὶ σὲ ἀποθεραπεύσει ὡς δεῖ, καὶ ἑαυτὰ ὠφελήσει πρεπόντως." Ὁ δὲ λέων· "Ἄφες ἄρτι, οὐ γὰρ ἐάσω σε τοῦ ἔργου."

4 Ὁ δὲ θώς· "Δύο τινὲς μόνοι δύνανται τοῖς ἐξουσιασταῖς δουλεύειν· ὅ τε δόλιος ἀνὴρ ὁ συγκαλύπτων τὰ ἔργα αὐτοῦ διὰ δώρων καὶ μεταδόσεων, καὶ ὁ ἠλίθιος καὶ δυσαίσθητος τοσοῦτον ὡς διὰ τῆς οἰκείας ἠλιθιότητος ἐκφεύγειν τὸν τῶν πολλῶν φθόνον· ὁ δὲ σωφρόνως καὶ εὐσεβῶς ἐκδουλεύειν πειρώμενος σπανίως τὰς ἔχθρας καὶ τὸν φθόνον ἐκφεύγει· ὅ τε γὰρ ἐχθρὸς τοῦ ἐξουσιαστοῦ ἀπεχθάνεται πρὸς τοῦτον ὡς εὐνοοῦντα πρὸς αὐτόν· καὶ ὁ φίλος

determine sins, but hearts and deeds; even if I live alongside you in my body, I dwell far away in my heart." So this jackal persisted in his virtue in this way and became famous for it.

About a lion. 3

And a lion, who was king of the beasts, when he learned about the jackal, summoned him and said to him, "My power is great and my lands are wide, and I have need of a most faithful servant. The report of you and your virtues has reached me, and I want to honor you and entrust you with a great office." But the jackal said, "Kings should select those who want this and give offices to them, since if someone is put in charge of one of these jobs without wanting to be, they will not enter into it eagerly. I always avoid positions of authority, as I have no experience in such matters. You, my king, have many kinds of animals who are very eager for every job, who will serve you with honor as they should, and will benefit themselves appropriately." And the lion said, "Leave it now, I won't let you off doing the job."

The jackal said, "Only two kinds of people are able to 4
serve rulers: the crafty man, who conceals what he does with gifts and favors, and the man who is so foolish and dim that he avoids the envy of the majority through his own foolishness. The man who attempts to serve prudently and conscientiously, however, seldom avoids enmity and envy, for the enemy of the ruler hates him because the ruler is well-disposed toward him, and the friend of the ruler competes

ἐρίζει βουλόμενος οἰκειότερος τούτου ἔσεσθαι. Ἕτοιμος οὖν ἐστιν ὁ τοιοῦτος διὰ ταῦτα ἀπολέσθαι." Ὁ δὲ λέων· "Μή σοι μελέτω ἕνεκεν τῶν ἐμῶν ὑπηκόων· ὑπέρτερον γάρ σε τούτων τῇ τιμῇ ἀναδείξω." Ὁ δὲ θώς· "Μεγάλη σου ἡ εὐεργεσία πρός με, ὦ βασιλεῦ, τὸ ἐᾶσαί με ἐν ταύτῃ τῇ ἐρήμῳ ἀδεῶς διαιτᾶσθαι ἀρκούμενον τῇ τῆς χλόης καὶ τοῦ ὕδατος μεταλήψει. Ἀκούω γὰρ ὡς ἐν μιᾷ καιροῦ ῥοπῇ ὁ τοῖς βασιλεῦσιν ὑπηρετῶν πάσχει τὴν ψυχὴν ὑπὸ τοῦ δέους τοσοῦτον, ὅσον ἕτερος παρ' ὅλην αὐτοῦ τὴν ζωὴν οὐχ ὑφίσταται· καὶ ὁ μετρίως ζῶν καὶ ἡδέως κατὰ πολὺ κρείττων τοῦ ἐν δόξῃ καὶ μυρίαις φροντίσιν." Ὁ δὲ λέων· "Ἔγνων ἅπερ εἶπας καὶ μὴ φοβοῦ τοιούτως· ἀναγκαῖον γάρ ἐστι τὸ ἐκδουλεῦσαι ἡμῖν."

5 Ὁ δὲ θώς· "Ἐπεὶ ἀδύνατόν ἐστι γενέσθαι μου τὸ αἴτημα, λοιπὸν ἀξιῶ εἴ τις τῶν ὑπό σε κατηγορήσει μου, μὴ συναπαχθῆναί σε τοῖς τούτου λόγοις εὐθύς, ἀλλ' ἀνέχεσθαι καὶ μετὰ τὴν ἔρευναν τὴν δίκην ἐπενεγκεῖν. Φιλία γὰρ ἄκαιρος, ἴσον ἐστὶ τῷ μισεῖν, καὶ βουλευόμενος μετά τινος περὶ τῶν σεαυτοῦ, σκόπει πρῶτον πῶς ἐκεῖνος τὰ οἰκεῖα διῴκησεν· ὁ γὰρ κακῶς ὑπὲρ τῶν οἰκείων διανοηθείς, οὐδέπω καλῶς βούλεται περὶ τῶν ἀλλοτρίων. Καὶ τὸν προσομιλοῦντά σοι τριχῇ δεῖ σκοπεῖν· ἢ ὡς μείζονα, ἢ ὡς ἐλάττονα, ἢ ὡς ἴσον· καὶ εἰ μὲν μείζων σου, δεῖ ἀκούειν καὶ πείθεσθαι αὐτῷ, εἰ δὲ ἥττων, πείθειν, εἰ δὲ ἴσος, συμφωνεῖν, καὶ οὐδέποτε ἐκπέσεις εἰς φιλονικίαν ὅλως." Ὁ δὲ βασιλεὺς λέων τὸ τοιοῦτον πληροφορήσας τὸν θῶα, παρέδωκεν αὐτῷ τὰ οἰκεῖα ταμεῖα, καὶ παρὰ πάντας προέκρινε καὶ

with him as he himself wants to be closer to the ruler; such a man is thus almost certain to perish as a result.” The lion said, “Don’t concern yourself with my subordinates. I will appoint you to a higher position than them.” The jackal said, “Your kindness to me, my king, is great, to allow me to live in this desert without fear, satisfied by my enjoyment of the foliage and water. For I hear that in a brief period of time a king’s servant suffers emotional stress of a kind that an ordinary person never experiences in his life. Someone who lives modestly and gladly is much better off than living in honor but with countless cares.” And the lion said, “I understand what you’ve said, and you mustn’t fear that. You have to serve me.”

And the jackal said, “Since it is impossible to have my re- 5
quest, I thus ask that if one of your subordinates should accuse me, you are not immediately convinced by his words, but hold back and impose punishment only after investigation. For an untimely friendship is the same as hating, and if you consult with someone about your affairs, you must first consider how he looks after his own affairs; for someone who understands his own affairs poorly, by no means gives good advice about the affairs of others. And you need to consider someone who speaks with you in three ways: either as better, inferior, or equal. If he is better than you, you should listen to him and be persuaded by him; if he is inferior, persuade him; and if you are equal, you should agree and you will never get into an argument.” When the lion king had fully satisfied the jackal about this, he entrusted his personal treasury to him, preferred him to everyone else,

συμβούλῳ ἐχρήσατο· καὶ δι' αἰδοῦς καὶ σεβασμοῦ τοῦτον ἦγεν.

6 Οὐ πολὺ δὲ τὸ ἐν μέσῳ καὶ ἀγανακτήσαντες οἱ περὶ τὸν λέοντα καὶ φθόνου πλησθέντες ἐβουλεύσαντο ἵνα διεγείρωσι τὸν θυμὸν τοῦ λέοντος δολίως κατὰ τοῦ θωός. Καὶ δὴ μιᾷ τῶν ἡμερῶν τοῦ λέοντος τροφὴν ἡδίστην παραγγείλαντος εἰς τὴν αὔριον τηρηθῆναι, [καὶ] λαθόντες ταύτην ἔκλεψαν <καὶ ἐν τῇ οἰκίᾳ τοῦ θωὸς κατέκρυψαν>. Ἣν καὶ ὁ λέων ἐπιζητήσας καὶ μὴ εὑρὼν πάνυ ἐπλήσθη θυμοῦ, ὁ δὲ θὼς τηνικαῦτα ἐκεῖσε οὐ παρῆν, ἐκεῖνοι δὲ μόνοι παρῆσαν, οἱ τὸν δόλον συρράψαντες· οἵπερ θυμωθέντα τὸν λέοντα θεασάμενοι πρὸς ἀλλήλους ἔφασκον· "Ἀναγκαῖόν ἐστιν ἡμᾶς τοῦ ἀναγγεῖλαι τῷ βασιλεῖ τὰ ὠφελοῦντα τοῦτον καὶ βλάπτοντα, εἰ καὶ δυσχεραίνουσί τινες ἐπὶ τοῦτο. Ἀνεμάθομεν γὰρ ὡς ὁ θὼς ἐπὶ τὴν ἰδίαν οἰκίαν τὴν τροφὴν τοῦ βασιλέως ἀνήγαγε." Καί τις ἐξ αὐτῶν ἔφη· "Καὶ ἔοικεν ἡ πρᾶξις αὕτη ἐκείνου ὑπάρχειν· ἀλλ' ἐρευνήσατε ἀκριβῶς περὶ τούτου." Ἄλλος δὲ εἶπεν· "Εἰ τὸ τοιοῦτον φανῇ ἐργασάμενος, ἀληθῆ πάντα εἰσὶν ὅσα κατ' αὐτοῦ ἐλέγετο." Ἕτερος δὲ ἔφη· "Οὐδεὶς δόλιος ὑπάρχων ἀνὴρ καὶ πανοῦργος δύναται λαθεῖν." Ἄλλος δὲ εἶπε· "Περὶ τοῦ τοιούτου θωὸς μέγιστόν μοι ἔγκλημα ἠνώτιστο, ἀλλ' οὐκ ἐπίστευσα τούτῳ ἄχρις ὅτου τὸν ὑμέτερον λόγον νυνὶ ἀκήκοα." Ἕτερος δὲ ἔφη· "Οὐ λέληθέ μοι ὁ τοιοῦτος ἅμα τῷ πρῶτον αὐτὸν θεάσασθαι. Πολλάκις τε εἶπον πρός τε τὸν δεῖνα καὶ τὸν δεῖνα, ὅτι πάντα τὰ κατ' αὐτὸν ὑποκρίσεις μόναι εἰσίν." Ἄλλος δὲ εἶπεν· "Εἰ τοῦτο φανῇ ἀληθῶς, οὐ κλοπή ἐστι μόνον τὸ ἔργον, ἀλλὰ καὶ ἀσέβεια καὶ

and made him his counselor. And he showed him respect and honor.

Not long after, the lion's courtiers were annoyed and, full 6
of envy, developed a plot through which the lion's anger might be cunningly aroused against the jackal. And one day, when the lion had given orders for his favorite food to be kept for the next day, they secretly stole it and concealed it in the jackal's house. When the lion looked for it and did not find it, he was extremely angry. The jackal was not there then, however, and the only ones present were those who had contrived the plot. When they saw the lion was angry, they started saying to each other, "It's our duty to tell the king both what is helpful and harmful, even if some are displeased by this. So, we've learned that the jackal took the king's food to his own house." And one of them said, "It seems this action of his is real, but you must investigate this carefully." And another said, "If it becomes clear that he has done this, all the things that were said about him are true." And a different one said, "No crafty and deceitful man can avoid detection." And another said, "I have been made aware of a serious accusation against this jackal, but I didn't believe it until I heard what you just said." And a different one said, "It was obvious the first time I saw him, and I've often said to someone or other that everything about him is just a pretense." And another said, "If this turns out to be true, the action is not just theft but disloyalty and arro-

θρασύτης.” Ἕτερος δέ ἔφη· “Ὁ βασιλεὺς εἰ ψηλαφήσει τὴν οἰκίαν αὐτοῦ, εὑρήσει τὴν ἀλήθειαν.” Ἄλλος δὲ εἶπεν πρὸς αὐτούς· “Λοιπὸν τάχιον γενέσθω ἡ ψηλάφησις.” Καὶ ἕτερος ἔφη· “Οἶδα ὡς ὁ θὼς τὴν οἰκείαν πανουργίαν καὶ αὖθις χρήσεται, καὶ κεναῖς ἀπολογίαις πείσει τὸν βασιλέα.” Καὶ διελέγοντο οὑτωσὶ πρὸς ἀλλήλους ἄχρις οὗ τὸν λέοντα <πρὸς θυμὸν> ἐκίνησαν.

7 Καὶ προσεκαλέσατο ὁ λέων τὸν θῶα, καί ἐπηρώτησε τοῦτον περὶ τοῦ ἐδέσματος τί γέγονεν. Ὁ δὲ θὼς ἔφη· “Τῷ δεῖνι τοῦτο ἐπιδέδωκα τοῦ φυλάξαι αὐτό.” Ἐκεῖνος δὲ ἐρωτηθεὶς ἠρνήσατο· συνόμοιος γὰρ ἦν τῶν συκοφαντῶν. Ἀπεστάλησαν δέ τινες παρὰ τοῦ βασιλέως ἐπὶ τὴν τοῦ θωὸς οἰκίαν, καὶ εὗρον ἐν αὐτῇ τὸ ἔδεσμα. Καὶ λαβόντες αὐτὸ τῷ βασιλεῖ προσήνεγκαν. Παρῆν δ’ ἐκεῖσε λύκος τις ἀγαθὸς τοῖς ἄλλοις λογιζόμενος καὶ δίκαιος, ὃς τηνικαῦτα προσεγγίσας εἶπεν· “Οὐ δεῖ σε, ὦ βασιλεῦ, ἀπονεῖμαι συγγνώμην τῷ ἀλιτηρίῳ τούτῳ· εἰ γὰρ οὗτος τῆς δίκης ἀφεθῇ, οὐδεὶς ἔτι τολμήσει δόλον τινὸς ἀποκαλύψαι τῷ κράτει σου φανερῶς.”

8 Προσέταξεν οὖν ὁ λέων τὸν θῶα τηρεῖσθαι ἀκριβῶς ἐν παραφυλακῇ. Καί τις τῶν συγκαθέδρων αὐτοῦ ἔφη· “Θαυμάζω ὅπως λέληθεν ὁ τοιοῦτος ἄχρι τοῦ νῦν τὴν τοῦ λέοντος ἀγχίνοιαν, πανοῦργος ὢν καὶ δόλων ἀνάπλεως.” Ἕτερος δὲ εἶπε· “Θαυμαστότερον τούτου εἰ ἐρευνᾶν μέλλει μετὰ τὴν τοῦ ἐγκλήματος φανέρωσιν.” Ἐξαπέστειλεν οὖν ὁ λέων τινὰς ἐπὶ τὸν θῶα ἐπερωτήσοντας αὐτὸν ὅπως ἔχει. Οἱ δὲ ὑποστρέψαντες ἐπλάσαντό τινας λόγους ὡς ἀπὸ τοῦ

gance." And a different one said, "If the king searches the jackal's house, he will discover the truth." And another said to them, "So let the search happen quickly." And another said, "I know that the jackal will use his own cunning once again and persuade the king with empty excuses." And they went on discussing with each other in this way until they roused the lion to anger.

The lion summoned the jackal and asked him what had 7
happened to his food. The jackal said, "I gave it to so-and-so to guard." But when that one was asked, he denied it, because he was on the same side as the slanderers. When some were sent by the king to the jackal's house, they found the food there, and they took this and brought it to the king. And there was a wolf there who was held to be good and just by the others. He came close then and said, "My king, you should not grant forgiveness to this wicked creature, for if he should escape punishment, no one will again openly dare to reveal someone's treachery to your majesty."

So the lion ordered the jackal to be held under close 8
guard. And one of his advisors said, "I'm amazed how this creature has escaped the lion's notice until now, as he's full of craft and treachery." And another said, "It will be even more amazing if there's going to be an investigation after the announcement of the charge." So the lion sent some people to the jackal to ask him how he was, but when they returned they concocted some speech, supposedly from the

θωὸς πρὸς θυμὸν τὸν λέοντα παροξύνοντας· οὓς ἀκηκοὼς ὁ λέων ἀναιρεθῆναι τὸν θῶα παραυτίκα προσέταξεν.

9 Ὅπερ μαθοῦσα ἡ τοῦ λέοντος μήτηρ, τὸ σκαιώρημα διαγνοῦσα, ἀναβαλέσθαι τὴν τοῦ θωὸς ἀναίρεσιν διετάξατο, καὶ πρὸς τὸν λέοντα παραγενομένη ἐπηρώτησε· "Δι' ἣν αἰτίαν ἀναιρεῖς τὸν θῶα;" Ὁ δὲ λέων εἶπεν αὐτῇ τὰ γεγονότα. Ἡ δὲ ἔφη· "Ἔσπευσας, τέκνον, περὶ τὸ ἔργον· καὶ οὐ δεῖ τὸν νουνεχῆ σπεύδειν, ὡς ἂν ἐκφύγῃ τὸν ἐς νέωτα μετάμελον. Καὶ δεῖ ὑπὲρ πάντας τοὺς βασιλεῖς ἀνέχεσθαι καὶ μὴ σπεύδειν· ἥ τε γὰρ γυνὴ διὰ τοῦ οἰκείου ἀνδρὸς συνίσταται, καὶ ὁ παῖς διὰ τῶν γονέων, καὶ ὁ μαθητὴς διὰ τοῦ διδασκάλου, καὶ ὁ στρατὸς διὰ τοῦ στρατηγοῦ, καὶ ὁ ἀσκητὴς διὰ τῆς πίστεως, καὶ ὁ κοινὸς λαὸς διὰ τοῦ βασιλέως, καὶ ὁ βασιλεὺς διὰ τοῦ νόμου, καὶ οἱ νόμοι διὰ τῆς φρονήσεως, καὶ ἡ φρόνησις διὰ τῆς ἀνοχῆς· <καὶ ἡ ἀνοχὴ διὰ τῆς συνέσεως>· καὶ ἀρχὴ συνέσεως βασιλέως τὸ γινώσκειν τοὺς ὑπ' αὐτόν, καὶ ἑκάστῳ τὴν κατ' ἀξίαν ἀπονέμειν τιμήν. Καὶ εἰδέναι ὡς οὐ παύσονται οὗτοι πρὸς ἀλλήλους ἐρίζοντες, καὶ ἀλλήλους κατηγοροῦντες.

10 "Καὶ σὺ οὖν ἐδοκίμασας πολλάκις τὸν θῶα καὶ εὑρὼν τοῦτον πιστότατον, ἀρτίως δι' εὐτελῆ τροφὴν βιοθάνατον ἀπεργάζει διὰ κατηγορίαν τινῶν μοχθηρῶν; Ἢ ἀγνοεῖς ὡς οἱ βασιλεῖς ὅτε ἑτέροις ἐπιτρέπουσιν, ἃ αὐτοὶ ὀφείλουσιν δι' ἑαυτῶν μετέρχεσθαι, ἀπόλλυνται; Ἢ οὐχ ὁρᾷς τοὺς τὸν οἶνον ἐξωνουμένους ὅπως ἀκριβολογοῦνται περὶ τὴν χρόαν αὐτοῦ καὶ τὴν γεῦσιν καὶ τὴν ὀσμήν, μήπως ἀδικηθῶσιν; Πόσῳ γε δεῖ μᾶλλον τοὺς βασιλεῖς ἀκριβολογεῖσθαι ἕνεκα τῶν προκειμένων μεγίστων ἔργων; Δεῖ οὖν

jackal, that aroused the lion's anger; and, when he heard this, the lion immediately ordered that the jackal should be executed.

But when the lion's mother learned this, she realized the 9
plot, gave instructions for the jackal's execution to be delayed, and went to the lion and asked, "Why are you executing the jackal?" The lion told her what had happened, but she said, "My child, you're being hasty in doing this. An intelligent person is not hasty, so that he may avoid a new reason for regret. Kings, above all, need to be patient and not be hasty, for the wife is supported by her husband, and the child by its parents, and the student by the teacher, and the army by the general, and the ascetic by his faith, and the common people by their king, and the king by the law, and the laws by sense, and sense by tolerance, and tolerance by understanding. And the beginning of understanding for a king is to know his subordinates and to give each the honor that is his due; and also to realize that such people never cease quarreling with each other and accusing each other.

"You have tested the jackal many times and found him 10
trustworthy, so why now, on account of some trifling food, are you putting him to death based on the accusation of some bad people? Don't you know that kings are destroyed when they allow others to attend to things which they ought to do themselves? Don't you see how those buying wine carefully examine its color, its taste, and its smell so that they are not mistaken? How much more do kings need to examine carefully the very important matters that are presented to them? So you, my king, need to consider more

σε, βασιλεῦ, διασκέψασθαι περὶ τοῦ θωὸς ἀκριβέστερον. Θαυμάζω γὰρ ὅπως ὁ τοιοῦτος τὸν τοσοῦτον χρόνον κρεῶν ἀπεχόμενος, μικρὸν ἔδεσμα νυνὶ ἐσφετερίσατο φαγεῖν. Πόθεν οὖν οἶδας, εἰ οἱ κατήγοροι τὸ ἔδεσμα λάθρα ἐν τῇ οἰκίᾳ αὐτοῦ ἀπέκρυψαν διὰ φθόνον; Ἢ οὐχ ὁρᾷς τὸν γύπα ὅταν πτῶμα ἐφεύρῃ ὑπὸ τῶν πολλῶν πτηνῶν ὑπὲρ τούτου συμπολεμούμενον; Καὶ τὸν κύνα ὅταν δράξηται ὀστοῦν ὑπὸ πολλῶν κυνῶν καθυλακτούμενον; Δύο γάρ εἰσιν αἱ μέγισται βλάβαι τοῖς τε ἄρχουσι καὶ τοῖς ὑπηκόοις καὶ μάλιστα τοῖς βασιλεῦσι, τό τε στερηθῆναι συμβούλων καὶ φίλων ἀγαθῶν, καὶ τὸ εὐπορεῖν συμβούλων καὶ φίλων πονηρῶν. Ὁ οὖν τοιοῦτος θὼς ὅλος σοι προσανακείμενος καὶ μηδέν σου ἀποκρύπτων, ἔργον φθόνου γέγονεν."

11 Ταῦτα τῆς μητρὸς τοῦ λέοντος δημηγορούσης, εἰσῆλθέ τις τῶν πονηρῶν ἐκείνων καὶ συνωμοτῶν, καὶ ἀνήγγειλεν τῷ λέοντι ἅπαν τὸ σκαιώρημα. Ὅπερ διαγνοῦσα ἡ μήτηρ τοῦ λέοντος ἔφη πρὸς αὐτόν· "Ἐπειδὴ ἔγνως τὴν ἀλήθειαν, ἀποδίωξον τοὺς ἀλιτηρίους τούτους καὶ συκοφάντας, καὶ μὴ καταφρονήσῃς τούτων ὡς μηδαμινῶν, ὁ γὰρ ἀσθενὴς χόρτος συνδεδεμένος σχοῖνον ἀποτελεῖ δυνάμενον τὸν παμμεγέθη συνέχειν ἐλέφαντα. Καὶ οἰκείωσον αὖθις τὸν θῶα· πρὸς γὰρ τὴν προτέραν ἀποκαταστήσεταί σοι εὔνοιαν." Ὁ δὲ βασιλεὺς λέων, ἐνθυμηθεὶς τῶν ῥημάτων τοῦ θωὸς εἰπόντος αὐτῷ ὡς εἴ τις κατηγορήσειεν αὐτοῦ μὴ ἀκοῦσαι τοὺς λόγους αὐτοῦ, ἀλλὰ μετὰ τὴν ἔρευναν τὴν δίκην αὐτῷ ἀποδοῦναι, μετεκαλέσατο αὐτὸν καὶ ὑπέσχετο τούτῳ ὡς διὰ τιμῆς πλείονος τοῦτον ἕξει.

carefully about the jackal. I'm surprised that someone who has abstained from meat for so long would take some to eat now. How do you know the accusers didn't secretly conceal the meat in his house out of envy? Don't you see how the vulture, when it finds a carcass, gets involved in a fight with all the other birds over it? And the dog, when it gets a bone, is barked at by lots of other dogs? There are two things which cause the greatest harm to rulers and their servants, and especially to kings: being deprived of good counselors and friends, and having a lot of wicked counselors and friends. So, because this jackal is totally devoted to you and hides nothing from you, he has become a victim of envy."

After the lion's mother had made this public, one of those 11
wicked conspirators came and revealed the whole plot to the lion. When the lion's mother discovered this, she said to him, "Now you know the truth, banish these guilty slanderers, and don't just overlook them as nuisances, for feeble grass, when woven into a rope, ends up being able to restrain an enormous elephant. And make friends with the jackal again and restore his previous goodwill toward you." And the lion king remembered the words the jackal had said to him, that if someone accused him, he should not listen to their words but only pass sentence after an investigation, and so he recalled him and promised him that he would treat him with even more respect.

12 Ὁ δὲ θὼς εἶπε· "Γίνωσκε, βασιλεῦ, ὡς μέγιστον προτέρημά ἐστι τὸ ἀνέχεσθαι τὸν ἄρχοντα τοῦ ὑπηκόου παρρησιαζομένου τὴν ἀλήθειαν. Κἀγὼ οὖν εὐνοϊκῶς λέγω, ὡς οὐ δεῖ σε καὶ εἰς ἔτι ὑπουργῷ μοι χρήσασθαι. Δεῖ γὰρ τοὺς βασιλεῖς παρατηρεῖσθαι τοὺς παρ' αὐτῶν ἀδίκως βλαφθέντας, καὶ τοὺς πλοῦτον ὁμοίως ἀφαιρεθέντας, καὶ τούς ποτε οἰκείους καὶ ἀναιτίως ἀπομακρυνθέντας καὶ τοὺς στερηθέντας μισθοῦ τινος καὶ τοὺς πλεονέκτας καὶ ἀπλήστους καὶ λογιζομένους τὴν τῶν βασιλέων ὠφέλειαν, οἰκείαν βλάβην καὶ τὴν βλάβην ἐκείνων, οἰκείαν ὠφέλειαν. Οὗτοι γὰρ πάντες ἐχθρῶν τάξιν ἐπέχουσι, καὶ φευκτέοι <τοῖς ἐχέφροσίν εἰσιν. Οὐκ οὖν κἀμε χρὴ φευκτέον> λογίζεσθαι. Καὶ πρὸς τούτοις δέδοικα μήπως πάλιν τὸ πονηρὸν τοῦτο ἄθροισμα συρράψει καὶ αὖθις κατ' ἐμοῦ δόλον καὶ—τῇ παρούσῃ ὑπολήψει—συνεργῷ πρὸς τοῦτό σε χρήσεται."

13 Ὁ δὲ λέων ἔφη· "Ἔγνων σου τὴν φύσιν ὡς ἀγαθή ἐστι καὶ πάσης ἐναντίας ἐστερημένη ὑπολήψεως· καὶ τὸν ἀγαθὸν ἄνδρα μία εὐεργεσία μυρίων ἐπιλαθέσθαι ἁμαρτημάτων παρασκευάζει. Λοιπὸν προθύμως ἡμῖν ὑπούργει." Ἀπεκατεστάθη οὖν ὁ θὼς εἰς τὴν προτέραν αὐτοῦ ὑπεροχὴν καὶ τιμήν.

Οὕτως δεῖ τοὺς βασιλεῖς ἐπιστρέφειν πρὸς τοὺς ἑαυτῶν φίλους, οὓς ἀδίκως ποτὲ ἐδίωξαν καὶ ἀπεσόβησαν.

The jackal said, "You know, my king, that it is a very great advantage for a ruler to tolerate a subject who speaks the truth frankly to him. So I say respectfully that you should not employ me as your minister any longer. For kings should keep a close eye on those who have been unjustly harmed by them, and likewise on those who have been dispossessed of their wealth, those who were once intimates but who have been distanced from them without cause, and those deprived of some reward; and also on those who are greedy and insatiable and who consider the benefit of kings as their own harm, and the kings' harm as their own benefit. For all these make up a category of enemies whom sensible people should avoid. I shouldn't be considered part of it but, in addition, I am afraid that this wicked gang will once more concoct a plot against me and they—based on the present incident—will use you again as an accomplice to their plot." 12

The lion said, "I know that your nature is good and precludes any hostile suspicion; also that one good deed prepares a good man to forget myriad offenses. So please be willing to serve me." So the jackal was reinstated in his former position and honor. 13

This is how kings should turn back to their friends whom they once unjustly banished and drove away.

[Chapter 11]

Ἀρχὴ τοῦ ἑνδεκάτου τμήματος.

Ἔφη ὁ βασιλεὺς πάλιν τῷ φιλοσόφῳ· "Ἔγνων δὴ καὶ τὸ τοιοῦτον ὑπόδειγμα. Λοιπὸν ἀνάγγειλόν μοι παράδειγμα τίνα δεῖ τὸν βασιλέα εὐεργετεῖν καὶ ὡς δεῖ καταπιστεύεσθαι." Ἄρξας οὖν πάλιν ὁ φιλόσοφος τοιαῦτα ῥήματα τῷ βασιλεῖ προσαγορεύειν, ἔφη·

Δεῖ τὸν βασιλέα εὐεργετεῖν τοὺς εὐχαρίστους καὶ ἀξίους τῆς εὐεργεσίας καὶ μὴ προκρίνειν αὐτῶν τοὺς συγγενεῖς αὐτοῦ καὶ φίλους καὶ πλουσίους, τοὺς δὲ πένητας καταφρονεῖν, ἀλλ᾽ οὖν καὶ τὸν νουνεχῆ καὶ φρόνιμον εὐεργετεῖν τε καὶ προσδέχεσθαι τοὺς εὐγνώμονας καὶ πιστοὺς καὶ οὕσπερ εἰσὶν ἐκ τῶν χρηστοτέρων· καὶ γὰρ [ὅπως] ἐν καιρῷ ἀνάγκης ἀνταμείψονται αὐτόν· ὥς φασί τις τῶν σοφῶν· ἄνθρωπος ἀνθρώπου τὴν ἀπαντὴν προσποιεῖται· ἀλλ᾽ οὔτε γὰρ ὄρους τὴν ἀπαντὴν [οὐ] δύναται ποιῆσαι. Ἀλλ᾽ οὖν ἄνθρωπον ἀχάριστον μὴ φείδεσθαι μηδὲ καταπιστεύειν αὐτῷ. Καὶ φέρω σοι παράδειγμα τοιοῦτον <παρὰ> τῶν ἀλόγων ζῴων.

Chapter 11

BEGINNING OF THE ELEVENTH CHAPTER.

The king again said to the philosopher, "I understand this illustration also. So now, give me an example of whom a king should reward and trust." The philosopher thus started again to address these words to the king, and said:

A king should be kind to those who are grateful and worthy of kindness, and he should not prefer his relatives, his friends, and the wealthy over them, but should concentrate on the poor; he should also show kindness to someone who is intelligent and sensible, and welcome those who are honest and loyal, and those who are among the more virtuous. For in a time of need they will return the favor. As one of the wise men says, men can meet men, but mountains are unable to meet. The king should therefore not have consideration for an ungrateful man nor trust him. And I bring you this example from the irrational animals.

2 *Περὶ χρυσοχόου καὶ πίθηκος, δράκοντός τε καὶ ὄφεως καὶ ἐρημίτου.*

Λέγεται γὰρ ὡς ὤρυξάν τινες λάκκον τοῦ θηρεῦσαι λέοντα. Ἔτυχε δὲ πεσεῖν ἐν αὐτῷ ἄνθρωπόν τινα χρυσοχόον, καὶ πίθηκα, καὶ δράκοντα, καὶ ὄφιν. Ἰδὼν δὲ αὐτούς τις ἐρημίτης εἶπεν ἐν ἑαυτῷ· "Προξενήσω τῇ ψυχῇ μου μισθὸν αἰώνιον διὰ τὸ λυτρῶσαί με τὸν ἄνθρωπον ἐκ τῶν θηρίων τούτων." Εὐθὺς οὖν χαλάσας τὸ σχοινίον, πρῶτος ὁ πίθηξ κρατήσας ἀνῆλθεν. Ὁ δὲ ἀσκητὴς πάλιν χαλάσας αὐτὸ ἐκ δευτέρου, ἀνῆλθεν ὁ δράκων. Καὶ πάλιν αὐτὸς ἐκ τρίτου χαλάσας τοῦτο, ὁ ὄφις ἀνῆλθεν. Ἀνελθόντα οὖν τὰ τρία ζῷα αὐτά, εὐχαρίστησαν τῷ ἀσκητῇ μεγάλως. Καὶ εἶπον αὐτῷ· "Κατάλειψον τὸν ἄνθρωπον τοῦτον ἐν τῷ λάκκῳ ὅτι ἀχάριστός ἐστιν." Εἶτα λέγει αὐτῷ ὁ πίθηξ· "Ἐγὼ κατοικῶ πλησίον τῆς πόλεως Ζαντζούρ." Ὁ δὲ δράκων εἶπε· "Καὶ ἐγὼ κατοικῶ ἐν τοῖς τείχεσι τῆς αὐτῆς πόλεως," καὶ ὁ ὄφις ὁμοίως ὡς ὁ δράκων ἔφη. Εἶτα εἶπον αὐτῷ πάντες· "Εἰ συμβῇ διαβῆναί σε ἐκεῖθεν ἀνταμειψόμεθά σοι κατὰ τὴν σὴν πρὸς ἡμᾶς ἣν ἐποίησας εὐεργεσίαν καὶ καλλιεργασίαν."

3 Εἶτα ὁ ἐρημίτης μὴ ἀκούσας αὐτῶν, ἐχάλασε πάλιν τὸ σχοινίον καὶ ἀνήγαγε καὶ τὸν χρυσοχόον. Ὁ δὲ χρυσοχόος εὐχαριστήσας καὶ προσκυνήσας αὐτῷ ἔφη· "Κἀγὼ οἰκῶ ἐν τῇ πόλει Ζαντζούρ, καὶ εἴπερ ἐλεύσει ἐκεῖ, ἐρώτησον τὰ περὶ ἐμοῦ, ὅπως ἀνταμείψομαί σοι ὑπὲρ ὧν ἐποίησας εἰς ἐμὲ ἀγαθῶν." Καὶ παρευθὺς ἀπῆλθον ἕκαστος εἰς τὰ ἴδια. Ὁ δὲ ἀσκητὴς ἦν διατρίβων ἐν τῇ ἐρήμῳ, καὶ συνέβη

CHAPTER II

About a goldsmith and an ape, 2
a serpent and a snake, and a hermit.

For it is said that some people dug a pit to catch a lion. But a man who was a goldsmith happened to fall into it, along with an ape, a serpent, and a snake. A hermit saw them and said to himself, "I will gain eternal reward for my soul by saving the man from those wild animals." As soon as he let down the rope, the ape got hold of it first and climbed up. When the ascetic let it down again for a second time, the serpent came up, and on the third occasion he let it down, the snake came up. So, after they had come up, the three animals thanked the ascetic very much. And they said to him, "Leave that man in the pit because he is ungrateful." Then the ape said to him, "I live near the city of Zantzour." And the serpent said, "And I live in the walls of the same city," and the snake said the same thing as the serpent. Then they all said to him. "If you happen to travel there, we will all pay you back for the kindness you have done to us and for your good deed."

The hermit didn't listen to them, but lowered the rope 3
again and brought up the goldsmith. The goldsmith thanked him and venerated him and said, "I too live in the city of Zantzour, and if you ever come there, ask for me, so that I may pay you back for the good you have done for me." And each of them went off at once to their own places. The ascetic was living in the desert and he happened to go into the

αὐτὸν εἰσελθεῖν εἰς τὴν πόλιν. Καὶ συναντήσας ὁ πίθηξ ἔξω τῆς πόλεως καὶ χαιρετήσας, εἶπεν αὐτῷ· "Ἀνάσχου μοι μικρὸν ἐνταῦθα ἕως οὗ ὑποστρέψω." Καὶ ἀπελθὼν ἐκεῖνος προσήνεγκεν αὐτῷ ὀπώρας παντοδαπάς. Ὁ δὲ μοναχὸς φαγὼν τὰς ὀπώρας ἐκείνας ἐποίει χώραν ἐκεῖσε. Συναντήσας δὲ αὐτῷ καὶ ὁ δράκων, καὶ περιχαρὴς γενόμενος ἔφη αὐτῷ· "Ἀνάσχου μοι μικρὸν ἕως οὗ ἀπελθὼν ὑποστρέψω." Καὶ ἀπάρας ἐκεῖθεν ὁ δράκων, ἀπέκτεινε τὴν θυγατέρα τοῦ βασιλέως καὶ ἤγαγε τὰ κόσμια αὐτῆς καὶ δέδωκε τῷ ἐρημίτῃ. Ὁ δὲ ἐρημίτης λαβὼν τὰ κόσμια εἰσῆλθεν εἰς τὴν πόλιν, καὶ ἐπερωτήσας εὗρε τὸν χρυσοχόον. Ὁ δὲ ὑπεδέξατο αὐτόν, καὶ ἰδὼν τὰ κόσμια καὶ γνωρίσας αὐτὰ ἀπῆλθεν πρὸς τὸν βασιλέα καὶ εἶπεν αὐτῷ· "Εὗρον τὸν ἀποκτείναντα τὴν σὴν θυγατέρα καὶ λαβόντα τὰ κόσμια αὐτῆς. Ἀπόστειλον οὖν τινας εἰς τὸν οἶκόν μου, ὅπως κρατήσωσιν αὐτόν."

4 Ο δὲ βασιλεὺς ἀποστείλας, ἐκράτησαν αὐτὸν καὶ ἤγαγον αὐτὸν εἰς τὸν οἶκον τὸν βασιλικὸν ἐνώπιον αὐτοῦ. Καὶ ἰδὼν αὐτὸν ὁ βασιλεὺς καὶ τὰ κόσμια προσέταξεν αὐτὸν τυφθῆναι ἀφειδῶς. Ὁ δὲ ἐρημίτης τυπτόμενος ἔκραζεν· "Εἰ ἤκουον τοῦ πίθηκος καὶ τοῦ δράκοντος καὶ τοῦ ὄφεως, οὐκ ἂν ἔπασχον τὰ τοιαῦτα." Ὁ δὲ ὄφις ἀκούσας τῆς φωνῆς τοῦ ἀσκητοῦ περίλυπος ἐγένετο σφόδρα, καὶ ἀπελθὼν ἔκρουσε τὴν χεῖρα τοῦ υἱοῦ τοῦ βασιλέως ἰσχυρῶς. Ἐλθόντες δὲ οἱ σοφοὶ καὶ οἱ ἰατροὶ τοῦ θεραπεῦσαι αὐτὸν οὐκ ἠδυνήθησαν. Εἶπε δὲ πρὸς αὐτοὺς ὁ παῖς τοῦ βασιλέως· "Οὐ θεραπευθήσομαι παρά τινος εἰ μὴ διὰ τῆς εὐχῆς τοῦ ἐρημίτου· καὶ γὰρ ὁ πατήρ μου ἀδίκως αὐτόν, καὶ λίαν,

city. The ape met him outside the city and, after greeting him, said to him, "Wait here for me a little, until I come back." He went off and brought back all kinds of fruit for him. After he had eaten this fruit, the monk made a place for himself there. The serpent met him and was overjoyed; he said to him, "Wait here for me a little, while I go off and come back." The serpent went away, killed the king's daughter, and brought her jewelry, which he gave to the hermit. The hermit took the jewelry and went into the city and asked where he might find the goldsmith. This man welcomed him, but when he saw the jewelry, he recognized it and went to the king and said to him, "I've found the man who killed your daughter and took her jewelry. Send some men to my house so that you may arrest him."

The king sent them, and they arrested the hermit and 4
took him to the palace and into the king's presence. When the king saw him and the jewelry, he ordered him to be beaten without mercy. And while the hermit was being beaten, he cried out, "If I had listened to the ape and the serpent and the snake, I wouldn't be suffering this." The snake heard the ascetic's voice and became very upset, so he went and badly bit the hand of the king's son. The wise men and the physicians came, but they were unable to cure him. The king's son said to them, "I won't be cured by anyone except through the prayer of the hermit, for my father punished him unjustly and severely." When the king heard this,

ἐτιμώρησεν." Ἀκούσας δὲ ταῦτα ὁ βασιλεὺς ἤγαγεν αὐτὸν πρὸς τὸν υἱὸν αὐτοῦ. Ἐλθὼν οὖν ὁ ἐρημίτης ἐπὶ μέσου πάντων ἀνήγγειλεν αὐτοῖς πάντα τὰ περὶ αὐτοῦ καὶ τῶν θηρίων τὴν καλλιεργασίαν καὶ τοῦ χρυσοχόου τὰ κατορθώματα. Καὶ εὐθὺς ὁ ἀσκητὴς δεηθεὶς καὶ τὴν χεῖρα αὐτοῦ θεὶς ἐπὶ τὸν υἱὸν τοῦ βασιλέως ἐκείνου εἶπε· "Κύριε Ἰησοῦ Χριστέ, εἰ ἀληθῆ εἰσιν ἅπερ λέγω ἐγὼ ὁ δοῦλός σου, ἰαθήτω ὁ υἱὸς τοῦ βασιλέως." Καὶ παρευθὺς ἔστη ὁ υἱὸς τοῦ βασιλέως ὑγιής, μηδὲν κακὸν ἔχων. Ὁ δὲ βασιλεὺς τιμήσας ἐνδόξως τὸν ἐρημίτην, καὶ δώσας αὐτῷ ἱκανὰ χρήματα ἀπέλυσεν αὐτὸν μετ' εἰρήνης, ὡς δίκαιον. Τὸν δὲ χρυσοχόον ἀπέκτεινε διὰ τὴν συκοφαντίαν αὐτοῦ.

Εἶτα ὁ φιλόσοφος τῷ βασιλεῖ εἶπεν· "Οὕτως ἄρα δεῖ τινα τοὺς καλοὺς εὐεργετεῖν καὶ καταπιστεύεσθαι, καὶ μὴ ὡς τὸν ἐρημίτην καλοποιεῖν τὸν ἄδικον καὶ ἀχάριστον ἄνθρωπον."

he took the hermit to his son. So the hermit came into the middle of them all and told them all about himself, and the good deed he did for the animals and his virtuous actions toward the goldsmith. Then the ascetic prayed right away and, placing his hand on the king's son, said, "Lord Jesus Christ, if what I, your servant, say is true, heal the king's son." And straight away the king's son was well again and had nothing wrong with him. The king honored the hermit splendidly, gave him a lot of money, and sent him away in peace, as was right. But he killed the goldsmith for his slander.

Then the philosopher said to the king, "So that's why one should be kind to good people and trust them, and not, like the hermit, do good to an unjust and ungrateful man."

[Chapter 12]

Ἀρχὴ τοῦ δωδεκάτου τμήματος.

Μετὰ δὲ τὸ τοιοῦτον παράδειγμα, ἔφη πάλιν ὁ βασιλεὺς τῷ φιλοσόφῳ· "Ἔγνων καὶ τὸ τοιοῦτον. Λοιπὸν ἀνάγγειλόν μοι πῶς συμβαίνει τινὶ καὶ πλουτεῖ ἀπὸ πτωχείας καὶ εὐημερεῖ ἀπὸ δυστυχίας;" Ἐπιδείξας οὖν πάλιν ὁ φιλόσοφος τοῖς προτέροις ῥήμασιν ῥήματα, τῷ βασιλεῖ ἔφη·

Ἀκατάληπτον πρᾶγμα ἠρώτησας, ὦ βασιλεῦ· καὶ γάρ τινες πλουτοῦσιν ἀπὸ συμβεβηκότος κόπου ἢ εὐτυχίας, τινὲς δὲ ἀπὸ πείρας καὶ τέχνης, ἄλλοι δὲ ἀπὸ δυνάμεως καὶ πονηρίας, ἕτεροι δὲ ἀπὸ πορνείας, ἄλλοι δὲ ἀπὸ εὐγενείας, καὶ ἄλλοι ἀπὸ πραγματείας, καὶ ἕτεροι ἀπὸ ἀλλοτρίου κόπου, καὶ ἄλλοι ἀπὸ εὑρέματος.

2 *Περὶ δυστυχῶν ἀνδρῶν.*

Καὶ γὰρ ἐρρέθη ὡς τέσσαρές τινες ἄνδρες δυστυχήσαντες ἡνώθησαν ἐν ὁδῷ. Ἦν δὲ ὁ εἷς ἐξ αὐτῶν βασιλέως υἱός, ὁ δὲ δεύτερος ἐνδόξου καὶ εὐγενοῦς υἱὸς καὶ λίαν ἦν εὐειδής· ὁ δὲ τρίτος ἐμπόρου υἱός, ὁ δὲ τέταρτος γεωργοῦ

Chapter 12

BEGINNING OF THE TWELFTH CHAPTER.

After this example, the king again said to the philosopher, “I understand this. So now, tell me how someone becomes wealthy from poverty and successful from misfortune.” So, once more adding words to his earlier words, the philosopher said to the king:

My king, you have asked about something that is incomprehensible. For some people become wealthy by hard work or good fortune, others from their experience and skill, others again through their power and wickedness, others through prostitution, others by their noble birth, others from their occupations, others from the toil of others, and others, again, from what they find.

About unfortunate men. 2

For it has been said that four unfortunate men were traveling together. One of them was a king’s son; the second was the son of a famous and noble man and was very good-looking; the third was the son of a merchant; and the fourth,

τινος υἱός. Καὶ ἐν τῷ ὁδεύειν αὐτούς, εἶπεν ὁ υἱὸς τοῦ βασιλέως· "Πάντα τὰ τοῦ βίου τούτου προωρισμένα εἰσι καὶ εἱμαρμένα." Ὁ δὲ υἱὸς τοῦ ἐμπόρου εἶπεν· "Ἡ φρόνησις κρείττων ἐστὶ πάντων τῶν πραγμάτων." Ὁ δὲ υἱὸς τοῦ εὐγενοῦς εἶπεν· "Τὸ κάλλος τοῦ ἀνθρώπου κρεῖττόν ἐστι ὑπὲρ ὧν εἴπατε." Ὁ δὲ υἱὸς τοῦ γεωργοῦ ἔφησεν οὕτως· "Ὁ ἀγὼν καὶ ὁ κόπος καὶ ὁ μόχθος κρείττων ἐστὶ τούτων πάντων."

3 Πλησιάσαντες δέ ἐν πόλει τινὶ καὶ μὴ ἔχοντές τι φαγεῖν, εἶπον πάντες τῷ υἱῷ τοῦ γεωργοῦ "Ἄπελθε καὶ ἔνεγκαι ἡμῖν σήμερον βρώματα διὰ τοῦ σοῦ ἀγῶνος καὶ μόχθου." Ὁ δὲ υἱὸς τοῦ γεωργοῦ ἀπελθὼν ἐν τῷ ὄρει καὶ καταγαγὼν ξύλα πέπρακεν <αὐτὰ> ἐν ταύτῃ τῇ πόλει, καὶ διὰ <τῆς> τιμῆς ἐξωνήσατο αὐτοῖς τροφάς, καὶ ἀπ' ἀλλήλων ἐτράφησαν. Καὶ ἐξελθὼν τῇ πύλῃ τῆς πόλεως ἔγραψεν ἐν αὐτῇ· "Ὁ ἀγὼν μιᾶς ἡμέρας, ἐκόρεσεν ἄνδρας τέσσαρας." Τῇ δὲ ἐπαύριον εἶπον τῷ υἱῷ τοῦ εὐγενοῦς καὶ ὡραίῳ· "Ἄπελθε καὶ σὺ σήμερον καὶ ἔνεγκαι ἡμῖν διὰ τοῦ σοῦ κάλλους τροφὰς τῇ ἡμέρᾳ ταύτῃ, ὅτι μεγάλως πενόμεθα." Ὁ δὲ ἀπελθὼν διελογίζετο ἐν ἑαυτῷ λέγων· "Τέχνην οὐ γινώσκω, καὶ κενὸς πάλιν πρὸς τοὺς ἐμοὺς συντρόφους ὑποστρέψαι οὐ δύναμαι." Ἠβουλήθη οὖν καταλιπεῖν αὐτοὺς καὶ μὴ ὑποστρέψαι πρὸς τούτους. Καὶ ἐν τῷ διαλογίζεσθαι τὰ τοιαῦτα, ἰδού, κόρη τις τῶν εὐγενῶν ἰδοῦσα αὐτὸν ἄνωθεν <ἐκ τοῦ οἴκου αὐτῆς>, ἔστειλε τὴν δούλην αὐτῆς, καὶ προσεκαλέσατο αὐτόν. Ἑνωθεῖσα δὲ ὅλην τὴν ἡμέραν αὐτῷ, ἤσθιε καὶ ἔπινεν μετ' αὐτοῦ. Ὀψίας δὲ γενομένης δέδωκεν αὐτῷ νομίσματα πεντακόσια. Ὁ δὲ

the son of a farmer. While they were on their way, the king's son said, "Everything in this life is preordained and fated." But the merchant's son said, "Good sense is better than anything else." The son of the noble said, "A man's beauty is better than what you say." And the farmer's son said this: "Effort and labor and toil are better than all those things."

When they approached a city, because they had nothing 3
to eat, all of them said to the farmer's son, "Go and bring us food today through your effort and toil." The farmer's son went off onto the mountain, brought down wood, and sold it in the city. With the money he made, he bought food for them and they all shared it. As he was coming out of the city gate, he wrote on it, "One day's effort satisfied four men." The next day they said to the handsome son of the nobleman, "You go today and bring us food for the day through your beauty, because we're destitute." As he was on his way, he thought to himself, "I know no skill and I can't go back to my companions again empty-handed." So he was planning to leave them and not go back to them. But while he was thinking such things, lo and behold, a noble girl saw him from above from her house, sent her maid, and invited him in. She spent the whole day intimately with him, and she ate and drank with him. When evening came, she gave him five

λαβὼν αὐτὰ ἔθρεψε καὶ αὐτὸς τούτους. Καὶ ἐξελθὼν ἔγραψε καὶ αὐτὸς ἐν τῇ πύλῃ τῆς πόλεως ὅτι· "Κάλλος μιᾶς ἡμέρας προεξένησε νομίσματα πεντακόσια."

4 Τῇ ἐπιούσῃ δὲ παλιν εἶπον τῷ υἱῷ τοῦ ἐμπόρου· "Ἄπελθε καὶ σὺ σήμερον καὶ διοίκησον ἡμᾶς τῇ σῇ γνώσει καὶ φρονήσει {σου}." Ὁ δὲ ἀπελθὼν πρὸς τὸν λιμένα τῆς πόλεως {καὶ} θεωρεῖ σκάφην ἔχουσαν πραγματείας ἱκανάς. Ἐξελθόντων δὲ τῶν πραγματευτῶν τῆς πόλεως καὶ μηδὲν ἀγορασάντων, ἔσχατος ἀνῆλθεν καὶ αὐτός, καὶ ἀπέκοψε μετὰ τοῦ ναυκλήρου τὴν τιμὴν πάσης τῆς πραγματείας εἰς ἑκατὸν χιλιάδας μιλιαρήσια. Ὁ δὲ λαβὼν ταῦτα ἀπῆλθεν πρὸς τοὺς ἑαυτοῦ συντρόφους· ἐξελθὼν δέ, τῇ πύλῃ τῆς πόλεως ἔγραψε καὶ αὐτός· "Ἡ φρόνησις καὶ ἡ πραγματεία ἡμέρας μιᾶς ὠφέλησε δέκα μυριάδας μιλιαρήσια·" καὶ ἐτρύφησαν τῇ ἡμέρᾳ ἐκείνῃ καλῶς. Τῇ δὲ ἐπαύριον εἶπον τῷ υἱῷ τοῦ βασιλέως· "Ἄπελθε καὶ σὺ ποίησον κατὰ δύναμιν ὅπερ δύνασαι." Ὁ δὲ ἀπελθὼν ἐκάθησεν παρὰ τῇ πύλῃ τῆς πόλεως μετὰ περιχαρίας, ἀγνοῶν ἐν ἑαυτῷ τί διαπράξεται. Συνέβη δὲ τῇ ἡμέρᾳ ἐκείνῃ τελευτῆσαι τὸν βασιλέα τῆς τοιαύτης πόλεως ἄτεκνον, καὶ μὴ καταλιπόντα κληρονόμον τῆς αὐτοῦ βασιλείας. Ἐξερχόμενοι δὲ τοῦ κηδεῦσαι αὐτὸν ἅπαντες, θεωροῦσι τὸν νέον καθεζόμενον χαίροντά τε καὶ μὴ λυπούμενον· καὶ εὐθὺς ἐνεβριμήσαντο αὐτῷ καὶ ἀτιμήσαντες ἀπήγαγον αὐτὸν ἐν παραφυλακῇ.

5 Κηδεύσαντες δὲ τὸν βασιλέα αὐτῶν, καὶ στραφέντες συνεβουλεύσαντο τίνα καταστήσουσι βασιλέα. Ὁ δὲ πρόεδρος τούτων εἶπεν αὐτοῖς· "Ἀγάγετε τὸν νέον ἄνθρωπον

hundred *nomismata.* He took this and provided for the others. And, as he was coming out, he too wrote on the city gate, "One day's beauty procured five hundred *nomismata.*"

On the following day, again, they said to the son of the 4
merchant, "You go today and provide for us through your knowledge and good sense." He went to the town's harbor and saw a small boat containing a lot of merchandise. After the traders had come out of the city but not bought anything, he came up last and did a deal with the shipowner for all the merchandise for a hundred thousand *miliaresia.* He took them and went back to his companions. But as he was leaving, he too wrote on the city gate, "One day's good sense and merchandise gained ten times ten thousand *miliaresia.*" And that day they feasted well. And the next day they said to the king's son, "You go and do whatever you can through your abilities." He went and sat happily by the city gate, not knowing what he would do. And it happened that the king of that city died that day, childless and without leaving an heir to his kingdom. While everyone was coming out to bury him, they saw the young man sitting there happily and not grieving. They immediately scolded him and, as they disapproved of him, took him into custody.

When they had buried their king, they returned and dis- 5
cussed whom they should make king. Their leader said to them, "Bring that young man here and ask him where he's

ἐκεῖνον, καὶ ἐξετάσωμεν αὐτὸν πόθεν ἐστί, μήπως κατάσκοπος παρεγένετο ἐν τῇ πόλει ἡμῶν." Ἀχθεὶς οὖν καὶ ἐρωτηθεὶς παρ' αὐτῶν εἶπεν αὐτοῖς· "Ἐγώ εἰμι υἱὸς Σανταμᾶν Βασιλέως· καὶ τελευτήσαντος τοῦ πατρός μου, κατεκράτησε τῆς βασιλείας αὐτοῦ ὁ ἀδελφός μου· ἐγὼ δὲ φοβηθεὶς ἀπέδρασα ἀπ' αὐτοῦ καί εἰμι τὰ νῦν ἐν ἐσχάτῃ πτωχείᾳ καὶ ταλαιπωρίᾳ πολλῇ καὶ κακῇ."

6 Ἀκούσαντες δὲ ταῦτα οἱ πολῖται καὶ γνωρίσαντες τοὺς λόγους αὐτοῦ, ἔστεψαν αὐτὸν βασιλέα τῆς πόλεως αὐτῶν, καὶ καθίσαντες αὐτὸν ἐπὶ τοῦ ἐλέφαντος ἐποίησαν αὐτῷ προπομπὴν ἐν πάσῃ τῇ χώρα ἐκείνῃ. Ἐλθὼν οὖν καὶ αὐτὸς ἐν τῇ πύλῃ τῆς πόλεως, καὶ ἰδὼν καὶ ἀναγνωρίσας τῶν ἑταίρων αὐτοῦ τὰς γραφάς, προσέταξε γραφῆναι καὶ τὰ αὐτοῦ γράμματα. Οἱ δὲ ἔγραψαν οὕτως· "Ὁ ἀγών, καὶ τὸ κάλλος, καὶ ἡ γνῶσις, καὶ πᾶν ἀγαθόν, ἐκ τῆς τοῦ Θεοῦ Προνοίας ἐστίν." Εἶτα ἀπελθὼν εἰς τὰ βασίλεια προσεκαλέσατο τοὺς συνοδοιπόρους αὐτοῦ καὶ δέδωκεν αὐτοῖς χρήματα ἀπὸ τῶν βασιλείων ἱκανά, καὶ μεγάλως τιμήσας αὐτοὺς ἀπέλυσεν ἐν εἰρήνῃ. Καὶ ἐδόξασαν τὸν Θεόν, τὸν διδόντα καὶ εὐεργετοῦντα ἑκάστῳ κατὰ τὴν Πρόνοιαν αὐτοῦ.

Οὕτως ἄρα πλουτοῦσι, βασιλεῦ, ἐκ τῆς ἰδίας τύχης καὶ Προνοίας τοῦ Θεοῦ καὶ εὐγενείας καὶ γνώσεως καὶ δυνάμεως.

from, in case he's a spy who has come to our city." So, after they had brought him and asked him about this, he said, "I'm the son of King Santaman. When my father died, my brother took control of his kingdom and, because I was afraid, I ran away from him, and now I'm in a state of complete poverty, in a lot of trouble, and in a bad way."

When they heard this and had verified his words, the citi- 6
zens crowned him king of their city. Then they sat him on the elephant and made a procession for him through that whole country. So, when he too came to the city gate and saw and read the writing of his companions, he ordered his own words to be written also. And they wrote this: "Effort, beauty, knowledge, and everything good is from the Providence of God." Then he went to the palace and summoned his fellow travelers. He gave them a lot of money from the royal treasury, honored them greatly, and let them go in peace. And they glorified God, who had provided for and benefitted each of them in his Providence.

Thus, my king, men are wealthy from their own good fortune, from the Providence of God, and from noble birth, good sense, and power.

[Chapter 13]

Ἀρχὴ δὲ τοῦ τρισκαιδεκάτου <τμήματος>.

Ὁ δὲ βασιλεὺς εἶπεν πάλιν· "Ἔγνων καὶ τὸ τοιοῦτον. Λοιπὸν ἀνάγγειλόν μοι πῶς καταλιμπάνει τις τὴν βλάβην τῶν ἑτέρων διὰ τὴν εἰς αὐτὸν [μὴ] ἐπιγενομένην βλάβην, καὶ γίνεται αὐτῷ παραίνεσις καὶ παιδεία;" Εὐθέως οὖν πάλιν ὁ φιλόσοφος εἶπε·

Πᾶς ὁ ἐγχειρίσας βλάβην ἑτέρῳ, πρὸς τὴν ἑαυτοῦ ὠφέλειαν, ἄφρων ἐστὶ καὶ ἀσύνετος. Καὶ ὁ μὴ ἔχων εἰς νοῦν τὴν τοῦ ἀδικήματος ἀντέκτισιν, καὶ τῆς τελευταίας ἡμέρας τὴν ἀντάμειψιν, πάσχει κακῶς, καὶ ἴσως μετανοεῖ καὶ οὐδὲν ὠφελεῖται· καὶ ἴσως πάλιν παιδεύεται διὰ τὴν εἰς τὸν ἕτερον ἐπιγινομένην βλάβην, ὥσπερ ἡ λέαινα ἔπαθε.

2 *Περὶ λεαίνης.*

Λέγεται γὰρ ὡς λέαινά τις εἶχε δύο σκύμνους καὶ ἐξελθοῦσα πρὸς θήραν κατέλιπεν αὐτοὺς ἐν καλαμῶνί τινι. Διελθὼν δὲ διὰ τοῦ δρυμῶνος θηρευτής τις, καὶ εὑρήσας τούτους ἀπέκτεινε· καὶ ἄρας τὰ δέρματα αὐτῶν ἀπῆλθεν. Ἐλθοῦσα δὲ ἡ λέαινα, καὶ ἰδοῦσα τὸ γεγονός, ἐλυπήθη

Chapter 13

BEGINNING OF THE THIRTEENTH CHAPTER.

The king said again, "I've understood this. So now, tell me how someone stops harming others because of the harm which befalls him, and how this is an encouragement and a lesson for him." So again, the philosopher immediately said:

Everyone who causes harm to another for his own benefit is a fool and stupid. Someone who is not mindful of the consequence of a crime, and the retribution of the last judgment, suffers badly, and equally, if he repents, is not helped at all; but equally, again, he may be educated through the harm that happens to another, just as the lioness experienced.

About a lioness. 2

For it is said that a lioness had two cubs. When she went out to hunt, she left them in a reedbed, but a hunter came through the thicket and, when he found them, killed them. He took their skins and went away. When the lioness came back and saw what had happened, she was very upset and

σφόδρα, καὶ διὰ τοῦτο ἔκλαιεν ἀπαραμυθήτως. Ἀκούσασα δέ τις ἄρκαινα τὸν κοπετὸν αὐτῆς, καὶ ἐλθοῦσα παραμυθήσασθαι αὐτήν, ἔφη αὐτῇ· "Τί ὁρῶ σε περίλυπον; Καὶ τί ἐστι τὸ γεγονὸς πρός σε;" Ἡ δὲ λέαινα εἶπε πρὸς αὐτήν· "Καὶ πῶς μὴ κλαύσω ἢ μὴ θρηνήσω ἢ μὴ στενάξω καὶ κόψωμαι, ὅτι τοὺς δύο μου σκύμνους οὓς εἶχον κρυπτοὺς ἐν καλαμῶνι θηρευτής τις τούτους εὑρών, ἀπέκτεινεν αὐτοὺς καὶ ἐκδάρας, ἦρε τὰ κῴδια αὐτῶν καὶ ἀπῆλθεν;" Ἡ δὲ ἄρκαινα λέγει πρὸς αὐτήν· "Μὴ λυποῦ μηδὲ κλαῖε· καὶ γὰρ ἔπαθες ὅπερ ἔπραττες. Τὸ λοιπὸν μὴ θλίβου· καὶ γὰρ πολλὰς σὺ ἔθλιψας καὶ ἀτέκνους ἐποίησας. Καὶ γὰρ γέγραπται· *ἐν τῷ μέτρῳ ᾧ μετρήσεις, ἀντιμετρηθήσεταί σοι,* καὶ ὅπερ ποιήσεις, πάθῃς, καὶ ὅπερ *σπείρεις, τοῦτο καὶ θερίσεις,* καὶ πᾶς ὅστις κατὰ τοῦ ἑτέρου δόλον συρράψει, αὐτὸς εἰς αὐτὸν ἐμπεσεῖται, καθὼς καὶ ἀλλαχοῦ λέγεται· *μὴ κρίνετε, ἵνα μὴ καὶ ὑμεῖς κριθῆτε·* ταὐτόν τι καὶ σὺ ποιήσασα πέπονθας."

3 Ἡ δὲ λέαινα εἶπε πρὸς αὐτήν· "Καὶ ὑπόδειξόν μοι τοῦτο πῶς ἐστιν." Ἡ δὲ ἄρκαινα· "Πόσα ἔτη ἔχεις διατρίβουσα ἐν τῇ ζωῇ σου;" Ἡ δὲ λέαινα ἔφη· "Ἄπειρα." Καὶ ἡ ἄρκαινα λέγει αὐτῇ· "Καὶ τί ἤσθιες τὸν τοσοῦτον χρόνον;" Ἡ δὲ λέαινα· "Σάρκας ζῴων ἤσθιον." Καὶ ἡ ἄρκαινα· "Καὶ τίς ἐδίδου τὰς σάρκας τῶν ζῴων ὧν ἤσθιες;" Ἡ δὲ λέαινα· "Ἐγὼ μόνη ἐθήρευον αὐτὰ ἐκ τῶν ὀρέων." Καὶ ἡ ἄρκαινα· "Ἀλλ' οὐκ εἶχον γονεῖς τὰ ζῷα, ἤ τινας συγγενεῖς;" Ἡ δὲ λέαινα ἔφη· "Ναί, εἶχον." Καὶ ἡ ἄρκαινα· "Καὶ πῶς οὐχ ὁρῶμεν πενθοῦντας ἐκείνους, ὥσπερ σε πενθοῦσαν πικρῶς

wept inconsolably as a result. A female bear heard her lament and came to comfort her. She said to her, "Why do I see you are so sad? What's happened to you?" The lioness said to her, "How would I not weep and wail, and groan, and beat my breast, when a hunter found my two cubs which I had hidden in a reedbed, killed them, skinned them, took their pelts, and left?" The bear said to her, "Don't grieve, don't cry, for you've experienced what you yourself have done to others. So, now, don't distress yourself, for you've distressed many others and left them childless. For it has been written, *by the measure you give, you will be measured;* and what you do, you will experience; and what *you sow, you will reap;* and every trap that you contrive for someone else, you will fall into yourself; just as it is written elsewhere, *do not judge, so that you are not yourself judged.* For you have experienced what you did yourself."

The lioness said to her, "Show me how that's so." And the 3
bear said, "How long have you been alive?" And the lioness said, "A long time." And the bear said to her, "What were you eating all that time?" And the lioness said, "I've been eating the flesh of animals." And the bear said, "Who has been giving you the flesh of the animals which you ate?" And the lioness replied, "I've been hunting them myself in the mountains." And the bear said, "But didn't the animals have parents and relatives?" And the lioness said, "Yes, they did." And the bear said, "So why don't we see them grieving in the same way you are bitterly grieving for your own children? So

τὰ ἴδια τέκνα; Ἀλλ' ὅπερ ἔπραττες, τοῦτο καὶ ἔπαθες, διὰ τὸ μὴ ἐνθυμεῖσθαί σε τὴν ἀντάμειψιν."

4 Ἀκούσασα δὲ ταῦτα ἡ λέαινα, καὶ γνοῦσα ὅτι αὐτὴ προεξένησεν ἑαυτῇ τὰ τοιαῦτα κακά, μετάμελος γέγονε σφόδρα, καὶ καταλείψασα τότε τὴν σαρκοφαγίαν, ἡσύχασε πάνυ. Ἐτρέφετο δὲ ἐκ τῶν καρπῶν τῶν δενδρων, παρ' ὅλην αὐτῆς τὴν ζωήν.

Εἶτα ὁ φιλόσοφος εἶπε τῷ βασιλεῖ· "Οὕτω δεῖ καὶ τὸν ἄνθρωπον καταλιπεῖν τὴν βλάβην τῶν ἑτέρων, διὰ τὴν εἰς αὐτόν, καὶ ζητεῖν τὰ αἰώνια. Λέγεται γὰρ ὡς, καθὼς θέλεις ἵνα ποιῶσιν οἱ ἄνθρωποι πρὸς σέ, καὶ σὺ ποίει ὁμοίως αὐτοῖς. Τοῦτο γὰρ καὶ Θεῷ εὐάρεστόν ἐστι καὶ ἀνθρώποις."

you're now experiencing what you've been doing yourself, because you were not considering the consequence."

When the lioness heard this and realized that she had 4
brought these evils on herself, she become very remorseful and stopped eating meat and lived a peaceful life. She fed on the fruits of the trees for the rest of her life.

Then the philosopher said to the king, "So a person should stop harming others, because of the harm he is doing to himself, and seek the eternal things. For it is said that you should do to people what you want them to do to you. For that is pleasing to both God and men."

[Chapter 14]

Ἀρχὴ [δὲ] τοῦ τεσσαρεσκαιδεκάτου <τμήματος>.

"Κατέλαβον δὲ καὶ τὸ τοιοῦτον," εἴρηκεν ὁ βασιλεύς. "Μόνο ὑποδειγμάτισόν μοι καὶ τοῦτο· πῶς δεῖ τοὺς βασιλεῖς προσλαμβάνεσθαι συμβούλους εὐνοϊκούς, καὶ τίς ἡ ἐκ τούτων ὠφέλεια." Ὁ δὲ φιλόσοφος ὑπολαβὼν ἔφη·

Τὸ τούτου παράδειγμα, ὡς εἴς τινα βασιλέως μυῶν πρωτοσύμβουλον γενόμενον, ὅστις ἦν συνέσει καὶ ἀγχινοίᾳ κεκοσμημένος, δι' ἣν καὶ οἰκεῖος τῷ βασιλεῖ ἐχρημάτισεν· οὗ ταῖς ὑποθήκαις καὶ ταῖς παραινέσεσι τὰ μέγιστα, ὅ τε βασιλεύς καὶ οἱ ὑπ' αὐτὸν ὠφελήθησαν.

2 *Περὶ μυῶν.*

Λέγεται γὰρ ὡς ἔν τινι ἐρήμῳ πόλις τις ἦν ἀσφαλῶς κατωχυρωμένη ἐν ᾗ ἦρχέ τις μῦς Τρωγλοδύτης ἐπονομαζόμενος. Εἶχε δὲ τρεῖς πρωτοσυμβούλους, ὄνομα τῷ ἑνὶ Τυροφάγος, τῷ δὲ ἄλλῳ Κρεωβόρος, τῷ δὲ ἑτέρῳ Ὀθονοφάγος· ἐξ ὧν ἦν ὁ Τυροφάγος λίαν ἐχέφρων καὶ σοφώτατος. Διὰ δὲ τὴν οἰκείαν σοφίαν ᾠκειώθη πλέον τῷ

Chapter 14

BEGINNING OF THE FOURTEENTH CHAPTER.

"I have understood this one, too," said the king. "Just illustrate this for me also: how kings should choose favorable counselors and what their benefit is." And the philosopher responded:

This example is about a chief counselor of the king of the mice. This counselor was adorned with intelligence and wisdom and, as a result, was reckoned as a friend by the king; and the king and his subjects were helped greatly by his suggestions and encouragement.

About mice. 2

For it is said that there was a securely fortified city in a desert, in which a mouse called Troglodytes ruled. He had three chief counselors, one called Tyrophagos, the other Kreoboros, and the other Othonophagos. Of these, Tyrophagos was very smart and wise, and, because of his wisdom, was closer

βασιλεῖ. Μιᾷ οὖν τῶν ἡμερῶν ὁμοῦ συνελθόντες οἱ εἰρημένοι ἅμα τῷ βασιλεῖ, ἐμακάριζον τὸν ἑαυτῶν βίον, καὶ τὴν παροῦσαν αὐτοῖς εὐδαιμονίαν. Διηγοῦντο δέ, μηδὲν ἕτερον λέγοντες ἔμποδον αὐτοῖς τῆς ἡδονῆς γενέσθαι ἢ τὸ πλῆθος τῶν κρειττόνων, καὶ βουλεύσασθαί τι περὶ αὐτῶν καιριώτερον προτρέποντες.

3 Ὁ δὲ βασιλεὺς Τρωγλοδύτης ὑπολαβών, εἶπε· "Δεῖ τὸν βασιλέα τὸ οἰκεῖον πρότερον ἐπιτηδεύεσθαι ἀγαθόν, εἶτα καὶ τὸ τῆς ἰδίας ποίμνης, ἔπειτα φροντίσαι τῆς σωτηρίας τῶν παίδων καὶ τῶν συγγενῶν, καὶ πρὸς δύο σκοποὺς ἐφορᾶν, πρός τε τὴν τοῦ ἀγαθοῦ ἐπίκτησιν καὶ τὴν τοῦ κακοῦ ἀποδίωξιν· δεῖ οὖν καὶ ἡμᾶς τὸ ἐπισκοτοῦν τῷ φωτὶ τῆς ἡμετέρας εὐημερίας κακὸν πάθος παρ' ἡμῶν ἀποσοβῆσαι." Ὑπολαβόντες οὖν ὅ τε Κρεωβόρος καὶ ὁ Ὀθονοφάγος εἶπον αὐτῷ· "Χαίροις, ὦ βασιλεῦ, ὡς καλῶς πάνυ ἐσκόπησας καὶ φιλαγάθως τῆς οἰκείας προενοήσω ποίμνης· γέγραπται γὰρ ὅτι δεῖ πρὸς τὴν κυβέρνησιν ἐχέφρονος ἀνδρὸς καὶ συνετοῦ καὶ τύχης δεξιᾶς. Καὶ ἡμεῖς οὖν πάντες σοῦ ἀνηρτήμεθα καὶ τῆς σῆς εὐστόχου συνέσεως· καὶ δεῖ πάντας τοὺς μύας συνδραμεῖν καὶ τῶν κόπων καὶ τῶν μόχθων μεταλαβεῖν, ὥστε κατορθωθῆναι τὸ μέγιστον τοῦτο ἐπιχείρημα."

4 Ταῦτα εἰπόντων τῶν δύο πρωτοσυμβούλων, ὁ Τυροφάγος ἐσιώπα, μηδόλως φθεγγόμενος· πρὸς ὃν ὁ βασιλεὺς ἔφη· "Ἵνα τί σιωπᾷς καὶ οὐ τὸ δοκοῦν σοι ὑποφαίνεις ἡμῖν; Ἢ οὐκ οἶσθα ὡς οἱ ἄνθρωποι βουλευτήρια συνιστῶσι καὶ περὶ τῶν μελλόντων βουλεύονται καὶ περὶ τῶν πρακτέων,

to the king. So one day, the said mice were meeting with the king, and were extolling their life and their present happiness. And they were explaining this, saying that there was no other impediment to their pleasure except the horde of creatures who were stronger than them, and they were encouraging him to plan some quite serious harm for them.

King Troglodytes replied, "The king should take care of 3
his own good first, then that of his flock, then look after the safety of his children and relatives; and he should keep two aims in view, acquiring the good and eliminating the bad. We should thus drive off the evil passion darkening the light of our happiness." Kreoboros and Othonophagos replied and said to him, "May you rejoice, my king, as you have been very attentive and benignly solicitous for your flock. For it has been written that administration needs a sensible, intelligent man, and good fortune. And we all depend on you and your well-directed intelligence. All the mice should gather and share in the toil and labor so that this great enterprise may be brought to a successful conclusion."

But while the two chief counselors were saying this, Ty- 4
rophagos stayed silent, and didn't say a word. So the king said to him, "Why are you silent, and why do you not reveal your opinion to me? Or do you not know that men hold councils and make plans for the future and about what needs

καὶ οὐδὲν αὐτοῖς ὄνειδος, ἤ τις ὑπόπτωσις ἐκ τοῦ βουλεύεσθαι ἐπιγίνεται;" Ταῦτα ἀκούσας ὁ Τυροφάγος εἶπε· "Μὴ μέμψῃ μοι, κραταιότατε βασιλεῦ, τῆς σιωπῆς· δι' οὐδὲν ἕτερον ἐσιώπησα ἢ διὰ τὸ λογίζεσθαι ὃ καὶ ἀποκρινοῦμαί σοι. Γίνωσκε οὖν, βασιλεῦ, ὡς τὸ ἔργον τοῦτο δυσχερές ἐστι καὶ διὰ τὴν τούτου δυσχέρειαν οὔτε οἱ πρόγονοι ἡμῶν οὔτε ἕτεροι τοῦτο ἐπεχείρησαν ὡς ἀδύνατον παριδόντες."

Οὕτω δεῖ τοὺς βασιλεῖς ἔχειν τοιούτους συμβούλους, ὡς τὸν μῦν τοῦτον τὸν Τυροφάγον, καὶ πάνυ ὠφεληθήσονται.

to be done, and there is no disgrace in it? What problem is there with planning?" When Tyrophagos heard this, he said, "Do not find fault with my silence, most mighty king; I was only silent because I was considering what to reply to you. So you must know, my king, that this is a difficult task, and due to its difficulty, neither our forebears nor others have attempted it since they saw that it was impossible."

Thus, kings should have counselors like that mouse Tyrophagos, and they will be given much help.

[Chapter 15]

Ἀρχὴ τοῦ πεντεκαιδεκάτου τμήματος.

Ὁ δὲ βασιλεὺς τῷ φιλοσόφῳ εἶπεν· "Ἔγνων δὴ καὶ τὸ τοιοῦτον παράδειγμα. Λοιπὸν τοῦτο τὸ ἔσχατον ἀνάγγειλόν μοι περὶ τοῦ ζητοῦντος πρᾶγμα ὃ οὐ δύναται καταλαβεῖν, [ἵνα μὴ] καὶ ὃ ἔχει ἀπόλλυσι ἐξ αὐτοῦ." Ἐσχάτως πάντων ὁ φιλόσοφος πάλιν τῷ βασιλεῖ εἶπεν οὕτως·

2 *Περὶ ἀσκητοῦ καὶ μωροῦ.*

Λέγεται ὡς ἦν ἔν τινι τόπῳ ἀσκητής τις εὐλαβὴς καὶ φοβούμενος τὸν Θεόν. Μιᾷ οὖν τῶν ἡμερῶν κατέλυσε παρ' αὐτῷ ξένος τις λίαν μωρός. Ὁ δὲ ἀσκητὴς παρέθηκεν αὐτῷ τράπεζαν καὶ προσέφερεν αὐτῷ ἄρτους, καὶ φοίνικας, καὶ ὕδωρ. Ὁ δὲ ξένος φαγών, εἶπε τῷ ἀσκητῇ· "Γλυκέα μοι ἐφάνησαν ταῦτα, καὶ οὔκ εἰσιν ἐν τῇ χώρᾳ ἡμῶν, ἤγουν οἱ φοίνικες· ἀλλ' οὖν ἔχομεν ἑτέρας ὀπώρας γλυκείας, ἤγουν ἰσχάδας καὶ σταφίδας καὶ ἕτερά τινα, δι' ὧν αὐταρκούμεθα, μὴ ζητοῦντες φοίνικας, ἀλλὰ ταῦτα ἤρεσάν μοι, καὶ θέλω ἐκ τούτων κτήσασθαι." Ὁ δὲ ἀσκητὴς ἔφη αὐτῷ· "Καλῶς ἔφησας, ἀλλ' οὖν ἡ ἀπληστία τοῦ

Chapter 15

BEGINNING OF THE FIFTEENTH CHAPTER.

The king said to the philosopher, "I've understood this example. So, lastly, tell me about someone who is seeking something which he cannot grasp and, in addition, is deprived of what he has." Last of all, the philosopher again said this to the king:

About an ascetic and a stupid man. 2

For it is said there was an ascetic somewhere who was devout and God-fearing. One day a stranger, who was very stupid, stayed with him. The ascetic set a meal before him and offered him bread and dates and water. While he was eating, the stranger said to the ascetic, "These things seem sweet to me and we don't have them in my country, I mean, dates. But we do have other sweet fruit, I mean dried figs, raisins, and other such, with which we're satisfied without wishing to have dates, but I do like these and I want to get some for myself." The ascetic said to him, "You've said it well, but

ἀνθρώπου ἀκόρεστον αὐτὸν ποιεῖ καὶ οὐκ αὐταρκεῖται ἐν οἷς ἔχει, ἀλλ' ἐπιθυμεῖ τὰ ξένα καὶ διὰ τοῦτο ἀγωνίζεται καὶ κοπιᾷ ὑποκτήσασθαι ὅπερ οὐκ ἔχει καὶ ἕνεκεν τούτου ἀπόλλυσιν ὃ ἐκτήσατο."

3 Ὁ δὲ ξένος λέγει τῷ μοναχῷ· "Ἤκουσα παρά σου ἑβραϊκὴν [τινα] λέξιν καὶ θαυμαστή μοι ἐφάνη· εἰ οὖν βούλει, δίδαξόν με ταύτην· καὶ γὰρ κἀγὼ ἐπιθυμῶ αὐτὴν κτήσασθαι, καὶ ταχέως δύναμαι μαθεῖν." Ὁ δὲ ἀσκητὴς λέγει αὐτῷ· "Μὴ βουληθῇς καταλιπεῖν τὴν σὴν λέξιν καὶ ζητεῖν ἑτέραν, ἣν οὐ δύνασαι καταλαβεῖν, μήπως πάθῃς τὸ τοῦ κόρακος."

4 *Περὶ κόρακος.*

"Λέγεται γὰρ ὡς κόραξ τις ἰδὼν πέρδικα περιπατοῦσαν, ἠβουλήθη μαθεῖν τὸ αὐτῆς περιπάτημα· γυμνάσας οὖν ἑαυτὸν οὐκ ἠδυνήθη μαθεῖν αὐτό, ἀλλὰ καὶ τὸ ἴδιον ἀπώλεσεν. Διὰ τοῦτο κατελείφθη ἠπορημένος μήτε τὸ ἴδιον ἔχων μήτε τὸ ζητούμενον καταλαβών. Ἰδὼν δὲ αὐτὸν ἕτερος κόραξ ἔφη πρὸς αὐτόν· 'Ὦ ἀνόητε, εἰς τί σου ἡ κενὴ ταύτη καὶ ματαία διατριβή; Καὶ τί οὕτως σεαυτὸν ἀπώλεσας; Ἔπαθες γὰρ τὸ τοῦ μωροῦ ἱερακαρίου. Λέγεται γὰρ ὡς ἱερακάριός τις κρατῶν ἐν τῇ χειρὶ αὐτοῦ ἱέρακα, εἶδεν ἕτερον ἱέρακα ἐν τῷ ἀέρι πετόμενον, καὶ ἐφάνη αὐτῷ ὅτι μείζων ὑπῆρχε ὁ ἐν τῷ ἀέρι πετόμενος τοῦ ἐν τῇ χειρὶ αὐτοῦ κρατουμένου, καὶ ἀπολύσας ὃν ἐκράτει, ἐδίωκε συλλαβεῖν τὸν πετόμενον, ὅνπερ μὴ δυνηθεὶς πιᾶσαι ἀπώλεσε καὶ ὃν ἐκράτει, καθὼς πέπονθας καὶ σύ, ἄθλιε· ἄρτι γὰρ καὶ τὸ ἴδιον ἀπώλεσας καὶ τὸ ζητούμενον οὐ κατέλαβες.'

man's greed makes him insatiable, and he is not satisfied with what he has but desires novel things; on this account he struggles and toils to get what he does not have and, as a result of this, destroys what he already possesses."

The stranger said to the monk, "I have heard you use the 3
Hebrew language, and I was amazed by it. Please teach me this, for I desire to acquire it, and I'm a quick learner." And the ascetic said to him, "You shouldn't want to leave your own language and seek another which you are unable to understand, so that you don't suffer what the crow did."

About a crow. 4

"For it is said that a crow saw a partridge walking about and wanted to learn its way of walking. He trained himself, but he was unable to learn it and he also ruined his own way of walking. As a result, he was left confused, as he had grasped neither his own nor what he sought. When another crow saw him, he said to him, 'You idiot, what was this pointless and foolish waste of time for? Why have you ruined yourself? You've suffered what the stupid falconer did. For it is said that a falconer was holding his hawk on his hand when he saw another hawk flying in the air, and the one flying in the air seemed bigger to him than the one he was holding on his hand, so he let the one he was holding go and pursued the one that was flying, and when he was unable to catch it, he also lost the one he was holding. That's just what you've suffered too, you poor thing, for now you've ruined your own way of walking and not grasped the one you sought.'

"Ταύτην δέ σοι διεξῄειν τὴν παραβολήν, ὦ ἄνθρωπε, ἵνα μὴ καταλιπὼν τὴν ἰδίαν λέξιν, μηδὲ τὴν ἑτέραν δυνηθῇς μαθεῖν, καὶ μείνῃς καὶ τῶν δύο ἐστερημένος. Λέγεται γὰρ ὡς ἄφρων λογίζεται ὁ καταλιπὼν ὃ ἔχει καὶ ζητῶν τὰ μὴ αὐτῷ πρέποντα καὶ ἀναγκαζόμενος εἰς ἃ οὐ μὴ δύναται καταλαβεῖν οὔτε τις τῶν πατέρων αὐτοῦ ἢ πάππων κατέλαβεν."

Ταῦτα δὲ ἐσχάτως εἰπὼν ὁ φιλόσοφος ἐσίγησεν. Μετὰ δὲ ταῦτα εἶπεν τῷ βασιλεῖ· "Εἰς τὸν αἰῶνα ζῆθι, βασιλεῦ· καὶ γὰρ ἐν σοὶ πεπλήρωται πᾶσα ἀρετὴ καὶ δόξα καὶ τιμὴ καὶ προσκύνησις. Ἀλλ' ἐγὼ περὶ τῶν σῶν ὑποθέσεων ἀπεκρίθην καὶ ἡρμήνευσα κατὰ τὴν ἐμὴν γνῶσιν καὶ δύναμιν. Ἐγὼ δὲ ζητῶ πρὸς τούτοις τὴν σὴν θεραπείαν καὶ τὴν ἐμὴν παρὰ σοῦ ἐλεημοσύνην τε καὶ εὐεργεσίαν. Ἀμήν."

Τέλος τοῦ *Στεφανίτου*
καὶ Ἰχνηλάτου.

"I've been through this illustration for you, my man," said the ascetic, "so that you don't give up your own language and, when you are unable to learn the other, end up deprived of the two. For it is said that someone is thought a fool who gives up what he has and seeks what is not suitable for him, and forces himself into things which he himself is not able to understand nor which any of his fathers or grandfathers understood."

When he had finally said this, the philosopher fell silent. And then he said to the king, "May you live forever, king, for in you every virtue, and glory, and honor, and worship has been made complete. But I have responded to the subjects you proposed and have explained them according to my knowledge and ability. And I seek for them your care and my alms and benefit from you. Amen."

THE END OF *STEPHANITES AND ICHNELATES.*

Abbreviations

EI2 = *The Encyclopaedia of Islam,* 2nd ed., 13 vols. (Leiden, 1960–2005)

LbG = Erich Trapp et al., eds., *Lexikon zur byzantinischen Gräzität: Besonders des 9.–12. Jahrhunderts* (Vienna, 1994)

ODB = Alexander P. Kazhdan, Alice-Mary Talbot, Anthony Cutler, Timothy E. Gregory, and Nancy P. Ševčenko, eds., *Oxford Dictionary of Byzantium,* 3 vols. (New York, 1991)

PG = Jacques-Paul Migne, *Patrologiae cursus completus: Series graeca,* 161 vols. (Paris, 1857–1866)

Note on the Text

A text of *Stephanites and Ichnelates* has already appeared twice in print: Vittorio Puntoni, ed., *Stephanites kai Ichnelates: Quattro recensioni della versione greca del "Kitab Kalila wa-Dimna"* (Florence, 1889), and Lars-Olof Sjöberg, ed., *Stephanites und Ichnelates: Überlieferungsgeschichte und Text* (Uppsala, 1962). More recently, Marc Lauxtermann has published a study of the introductory prologues and paratextual material to the Eugenian recension of the work, which includes a new edition of this small part of the text: Marc Lauxtermann, "The Eugenian Recension of *Stephanites and Ichnelates:* Prologue and Paratexts," *Νέα Ῥώμη* 15 (2018): 100–106.

The Greek text of our volume represents a substantially new edition of the Eugenian recension, although it still cannot be considered a critical one. (A more detailed study of the manuscript tradition of this text is being prepared by A. Alexakis.) The current edition is based on four manuscripts: Paris, Supplementum graecum 692; Vatican, codex Barberinianus Graecus 172; Leiden, codex Bonaventurae Vulcanii 93; and Oxford, codex misc. 272 (Bodleian Auct. T. 5. 10); with the sigla P, B, L, and O, respectively.

Manuscript P (available online at https://gallica.bnf.fr/ark:/12148/btv1b110001438) dates to the year 1586 and consists of

92 folios, of which fols. 1r–3r hold a list of contents, drawn up by the copyist Konstantinos Mavromates. This list provides the headings of particular stories, usually repeated verbatim or slightly altered in the relevant margins of the stories themselves within the manuscript. Sometimes these headings point to a small fraction of text (even just one line), and for this reason they have been relegated to the Notes to the Text. Folio 91 is missing, resulting in the loss of the last story listed in the contents on fol. 3r (περὶ κόρακος, "about a crow"; see 15.4). The beginnings of the chapters are indicated with small decorations, framing in most cases on the right and the left side the words "Ἀρχὴ τοῦ (δευτέρου, τρίτου, etc.) τμήματος," that is, "Beginning of the (second, third, etc.) chapter."

Manuscript P was ignored by Puntoni and Sjöberg, but it seems that it might be the closest one to the Eugenian recension (or at least the closest compared to the manuscripts used by them). It provides a number of better readings compared to all other manuscripts used by both Puntoni and Sjöberg, as is, for example, the Homeric ῥυδὸν ἀφνειὸς (abundantly rich) in chapter 6.3 against ῥοιζηδὸν ἀφνειὸς (rich all of a sudden) of all other manuscripts. Despite some lacunose segments, it usually provides a more complete text and its stylistic level is higher than that of BL and O, although in some sections, as in parts of chapters 2 and 3, it is also lower (obviously the result of contamination). For these reasons this manuscript has been given preferential treatment in our edition. We have based the edition of chapters 10 to 15 exclusively on P, and the missing text of its lost fol. 91 has been supplemented by the text of Florence, Bi-

blioteca Medicea Laurenziana (BML) Plut. 57. 30 (F), folios 77v–78v.

The paper manuscript B is of the late sixteenth to early seventeenth century and preserves our text in folios 5r–64v. Most of the folios have large empty spaces intended for illustrations, but only eight of them were executed and one was left unfinished, in the pencil-sketching stage. The scribe has provided a text with egregious misspellings and errors in punctuation and separation of words. According to PINAKES, this scribe was a certain Ματθαῖος μητροπολίτης Μυρέων (Matthew metropolitan of Myra, see https://pinakes.irht.cnrs.fr/notices/cote/64720/). The contents of B are the eight original chapters of L, the three additional chapters and extra stories added by the second hand of L (all of these also being in O), and another additional three chapters. The beginnings of the chapters are marked by either a letter or a word indicating their order (for example, λόγος β′ or λόγος δεύτερος). A facsimile of B is available online at https://digi.vatlib.it/view/MSS_Barb.gr.172.

Manuscript L dates from the first half of the fifteenth century, although the original text, copied by a certain Gerardos (Γηράρδος—the Greek form of the name is very unusual), has been supplemented by different hands; see https://pinakes.irht.cnrs.fr/notices/cote/64720/. The main hand is responsible for the preface, prologues, and eight chapters; toward the end of the work another hand has added extra stories and an additional three chapters in the margins and spaces for illustrations. On account of innumerable common spelling errors, it seems possible this other hand might have copied the text of B for the stories

added in the margins of L. This hand is very small, cramped, and difficult to read. Yet another hand, probably the scribe of O, has added throughout many corrections to spellings and accents in the margins.

Manuscript O dates from the sixteenth century and is a copy of L, although with minor differences. It contains the expanded version of L as provided by both hands: the preface, prologues, and the eight original chapters of the main hand, plus the extra stories and the three additional chapters.

For the fifteen chapters of the main text, Puntoni abandoned manuscripts B and L, which he had used for the prefatory section, and turned to Florence, Biblioteca Medicea Laurenziana Plut. 57. 30, with very rare references to B and L and, once, to Vaticanus gr. 949. (Note that the chapter arrangement in Puntoni's edition varies slightly from that of P followed by our edition: chapter 11 of Puntoni corresponds to chapter 14 in the present edition, and chapters 12–14 to chapters 11–13, respectively). Puntoni believed that Seth's original translation, which he was trying to reestablish, was represented by the manuscripts offering the fullest version of the text (three prologues and fifteen chapters), and this is not the case for B and L. Sjöberg, who in contrast believed that Seth's original translation was represented by the manuscripts containing an abbreviated version of the text (no prefaces or prologues, the first seven chapters—some of which were shorter than in Puntoni's edition—and the ninth left unfinished), did not use L and B for his edition either. Sjöberg's view has prevailed, and his edition is generally accepted as the closest to Seth's.

The present edition, however, in seeking to establish the

Eugenian recension of *Stephanites and Ichnelates,* assumes that what Lauxtermann proposes for the prefatory texts is equally valid for the remainder of the entire work, and thus takes as granted two major points. The first is that

> Bε [that is, the version transmitted by BLO and P and five more manuscripts of no particular importance to our edition] is the closest we can get to the Eugenian recension, but since the two principal Bε manuscripts, L and B, are clearly inserting Eugenian material rather than transmitting the Eugenian recension in its full glory and since the other Bε manuscripts . . . show clear signs of contamination, the sad conclusion must be that we do not possess a single manuscript that preserves the authentic Eugenian recension. Its beauty can only be glimpsed at, but through a glass and darkly. In fact, as will become abundantly clear when we turn to the prefatory material in Bε manuscripts, Bε is at several removes from the Eugenian archetype.
>
> (Lauxtermann, "The Eugenian Recension," 59)

The second point is that P is a manuscript that, despite the signs of contamination, is perhaps the witness most closely related to the hyparchetype on which BLO are also dependent; see Lauxtermann, "The Eugenian Recension," 71, where the relevant *stemma codicum* is provided.

Where a suitable reading was not offered by manuscripts PBL and O, one has been taken either from Puntoni's edition or from Sjöberg's. On occasion the editors (*AA* = Alexander Alexakis and Alison Noble) have provided a reading. Although there is considerable variance between the manu-

scripts we have used, much of it is minor. Following established practice in the series, the Notes to the Text have thus been kept to an absolute minimum. They are confined only to variants—either variants from P or those contained in it—that significantly affect the translation or illustrate why the chosen reading has been preferred on a particular point. The vast majority of variant readings have, necessarily, thus been excluded, such as those indicating exchange of phrases (for instance, ὁ μὲν ἔφη for καὶ ὁ Ἰχνηλάτης εἶπεν), the use of similar pronouns (αὐτοῦ/ἑαυτοῦ, τοῦτος/τοιοῦτος, etc.), verbs in different tenses or moods (ἐλάμβανον/ἔλαβον), variant composite verbs (ὑπέλαβε/ἀπέλαβε), the omission of single words or of short phrases, and different word order.

The start of the text, consisting of prefatory material and three distinct prologues, provides a particular set of problems. Puntoni, in his edition, published the text of the preface and prologues as he found it in B and L, although he omitted nine sections of text from Prologue A. Eight of these were published by Sjöberg in his edition. More recently Lauxtermann, "The Eugenian Recension," has edited all the paratexts, rubrics, and scholia found in the preface and Prologue A. This part of our present edition is mostly based on Lauxtermann's study, which divides the prefatory material, minus the scholia, into five paratexts; of these he thinks it likely that only Eugenius's introduction formed part of the original version. The heading, the dedicatory epigram, Eugenius's introduction, and the summary of contents (Lauxtermann's paratexts 1–3 and 5) are to be found in our text, while the image caption (paratext 4) is in the Notes to the Translation. The nine rubrics, which offer a commen-

tary on the text of the first prologue and are unlikely to have formed part of the original Eugenian version, together with the three *scholia* that Lauxtermann identifies as not forming part of the original version of the preface, are also to be found in these Notes. Both the rubrics and the scholia would have found their way into the text at an early stage through scribal errors and reworkings. We have used the contents list of manuscript P to provide the paragraph headings throughout the text.

Sigla

< > = added by editors

[ ] = secluded by editors

<. . .> = lacuna

B = Vatican, codex Barberinianus Graecus 172, paper, late 16th to early 17th century, fols. 5r–64v

F = Florence, Biblioteca Medicea Laurenziana (BML) Plut. 57. 30, paper, 16th century, fols. 77v–78v (only for the last two paragraphs of chapter 15)

L = Leiden, codex Bonaventurae Vulcanii 93, paper, 15th century, fols. 1r–112v

O = Oxford, codex misc. 272 (Bodleian, Auct. T. 5. 10), paper, 16th century, fols. 2r–144r

P = Paris, Bibliothèque nationale de France, codex Supplementum graecum 692, paper, 1586, fols. 1r–92r

X = Marc Lauxtermann, "The Eugenian Recension of *Stephanites and Ichnelates:* Prologue and Paratexts," *Νέα Ῥώμη* 15 (2018): 55–106 (only for the prefaces and the paratexts)

Pu = Vittorio Puntoni, *Stephanites kai Ichnelates: Quattro recensioni della versione Greca del "Kitab Kalila wa-Dimna"* (Florence, 1889)

Sj = Lars-Olof Sjöberg, *Stephanites und Ichnelates: Überlieferungsgeschichte und Text* (Uppsala, 1962)

AA = reading provided by editors where readings from BLOPXPuSj rejected

Notes to the Text

Preface

title P *in the upper margin has*: φυσιολογικὸν βιβλίον . . . Στεφανίτης καὶ Ἰχνηλάτης

1 πόνος BLP: ΠΟΝΟΝ O

μετασχηματισθέντες BLP: ΜΕΤΑΣΧΗΜΑΤΙΣΘΈΝΤΩΝ O

2 πρὸς βιωτικοὺς καὶ βαρβαρώδεις ὕθλους P: πρὸς βιωτικὴν ὠφέλειαν ἀνθρώπων X, πρὸς βιωτικὴν συντείνουσα τὰς πράξεις BLO

μεταβληθεῖσα X: ἣ μεταβληθεῖσα BLOP

after Ἑλλήνων BLO *add*: ἐξ ἀραβικοῦ καὶ βαρβαρώδους ὕθλου,

τοῦ X: καὶ BLOP

3 τῷ μὴ ζῶντι X: τὸν μὴ ζῶντα BLOP

μετενέγκαι *AA*: μὴ ἐνεγκέναι BLOP, μετενεγκέναι X

κτᾶσθαι X: κτᾶται BLOP

δι' *added* X

εἰδόσι X: εἰδότας BLOP

4 *after* ῥητόρων BLOP *add* χορὸς

ὅτι *added* X

ἀνάξιον *AA*: ἀναξίως BLO, ἀναξίους PX

δεῖ *added* X

6 ἀποστολὴ X: ἐπιστολὴ BLOP

καὶ διάγνωσις τῶν ἐκεῖσε X: *omitted* BLOP

περιτραχήλιον P: περιτραχήλιος BLO

καὶ ὅσα περιέχουσι X: περιέχουσι δὲ BLOP

after μυθεύματα BLO *add*: + ἀπὸ τῶν ὧδε ἄρχεται τὸ βιβλίον, P *adds* ἀρχὴ τοῦ (πρώτ)ου βιβλίου τῶν ιε′ τμημάτων

Prologue A

1 Καϊδὰδ LO: καὶ δαβὶδ BP

ἀπέκειτο *AA*: ἐπέκειτο BLOP

4 Ἰνδὺς P: ἰνδῆς B, ἰνδὴς LO

ὑπέπλασας *AA*: ὑπέπλευσας BLOP

πειραθῆναι Pu *in the apparatus*: περαιωθῆναι BLOP

ἢ *added* Pu

5 *heading* P *fol. 1r*

P *in margin of fol. 7r has*: ἐνταῦθα δείκνυσιν ὁ φίλος τοῦ Περζουὲ πόσαι ἀρεταί εἰσιν, ἃς ὀφείλει διατηρεῖν ὁ καλὸς ἄνθρωπος αἵτινές εἰσιν αὗται

6 Ἰνδεῖ BLO: ἰνδῷ P

7 *heading* P *fol. 1r* Περὶ τοῦ οἰκοδομοῦντος τὴν οἰκίαν ἐπὶ στερεὰν πέτραν

8 πεποιθὼς P *in margin of fol. 7r*: πεποιηκὼς BLO

9 Ἀνασουράνον P: Ἀσουροάνον BL, ἀσουράνον O

μακροημερίας P *in margin of fol. 8r*: περημερίας B, περιμερίας LO

10 διὰ γλώττης . . . πετεινῶν P *as correction in margin of fol. 8v*: τῶν ἑτερογλώσσων οὗτος LOP: τῶν ἑτέρων γλωσσῶν οὗτος B

11 πῆχυν (πύχην) P *over* μίαν: *omitted* BLO

12 καὶ Πασχητικῆς P *in margin of fol. 9r*: *omitted* BLO

13 ἀναφέρεσθαι P *in margin of fol. 9r*: ἀναφέρεται BLO

15 ἀδυνατεῖ P: ἀγανακτεῖ BLO

Prologue B

heading Ἑλλάδα BLO: ἑλληνικὴν P

P *in margin of fol. 9v has*: ἀρχὴ τοῦ πρώτου βιβλίου ἔχοντος πρόσρρημα τοῦ Συμεὼν Μαγίστρου

αὐτῶν *AA*: αὐτοῦ BLOP

2 καὶ δι᾽ ἣν . . . κεφάλαιον P *in margin of fol. 10r*: *omitted* BLO

ἃ ἀναγινώσκει *AA*: εἰ ἀναγνώσκει BOP

ἀνάγνωσις P: διάγνωσις BLO

after διάγνωσις P *has in margin of fol. 10r*: Παραβολὴ (πρώτ)η περὶ ἄφρονος, O *has* παραβολή

3 *heading* P *fol. 1r*

Οὐχὶ . . . μερίσαι P: *omitted* BLO

4 χαρὰν μεγάλην BP: χαρᾷ μεγάλῃ LO

τὸ προσταχθὲν ποιήσωμεν P: ποιήσωμεν ὅπερ προσετάχθημεν BLO

<ἵνα μὴ . . . θησαυρόν>: *added by* Pu *from cod. Laurentianus Plut. 57.30 and cod. Upsaliensis 8*

ἵνα μηδεὶς . . . ὤληται P: ἵνα μηδεὶς ἐξ ὑμῶν ἀπώληται BLO

5 τὸν ἀναγινώσκοντα *AA*: οἱ ἀναγινώσκοντες O, τῶν γινωσκόντων P, γινώσκοντα L

καὶ τὴν τοῦ O: καὶ τὸ τοῦ LP, καὶ τῶτε καὶ B

γνῷ LO: γνῶναι BP

ὠνηθήσεται O: *omitted* BLP

6 *heading* P *fol. 1r*: παραβολὴ (δευτέρ)α περὶ τοῦ ἀμαθοῦς P *in margin of fol. 11v*

7 *heading* P *fol. 1r*: (τρίτ)η περὶ ἀμερίμνου P *in margin of fol. 11v*, Περὶ τοῦ οἰκοδεσπότου καὶ τοῦ κομπτώματος τῶν κλεπτῶν B *fol. 10v*

συνάξῃ BP: συνάξω LO

8 <ὃς> *added AA*

καταλείψας O: καλύψας BLP

τινὲς *AA*: τινῶν BLOP

9 πράττει O: πράττειν BLP

10 περὶ . . . σησαμοπρατῶν B *fol. 11r* P *in margin of fol. 12v and in fol. 1r*: *omitted* LO

συλῆσαι P: κλέψαι BLO

καὶ ἔσται . . . κοινόν P: *omitted* BLO

11 κοσμοῦσι P: κοσμίζουσι BLO

12 Περὶ . . . κλέπτου P *in margin of fol. 13r and in fol. 1r*: περὶ τοῦ πένητος καὶ τοῦ κλέπτου B *fol. 11v*, *omitted* LO

βαλεῖν σῖτον P: *omitted* BLO

κύριος τοῦ οἴκου P: οἰκοκύριος BLO

13 *transmitted only by* P

heading P *in margin of fol. 14v and in fol. 1r*

<ἀπ>ελπίζειν Pu: ἐλπίζειν P

ὠφελεῖ *see* Pu: ὀφείλει P

14 ζήσεται Pu: ζητήσει P

δοξασθήσεται Pu: κολασθήσεται P

15 ὁμοιωθῆναι *AA*: ὁμοιωθήσεται P

Prologue C

title in P *fol. 15r*, *omitted* BLO

1 Περζουέ BLO: Περζωέ P

τὸν πλοῦτον . . . μισθόν: *omitted* BLO

τὸν μισθὸν P: ταῦτα, ὁ τε πλοῦτος, αἱ ἡδοναί, ἡ ἐξουσία, καὶ τὸ ἔσχατον ὁ μισθός BLO

3 ἐπεθύμησε *AA*: ἐπιθυμήσασα BLOP

4 ἐξαιρουμένῳ Pu: ἐξερούμενον B, ἐξαιρούμενον LOP

τρέφοντι Pu: τρέφοντα BLOP

στρέφων *AA*: στρέφοντες BLOP

ἐλπίζει *AA*: ἐλπίζειν BLOP

5 *heading* P *in margin of fol. 17r and in fol. 1r*: Περὶ ἐμπόρου πωλήσαντος δαμάσκηνα

διαπιπράσκῃ *AA*: διαπράσσῃ BLOP

ἐν ἀποθήκῃ *AA*: ἀποθήκην BLOP

6 καὶ παραινέσας . . . ψυχήν: *omitted* BO

ἀποδρᾶσαι *AA*: ποῦ δρᾶσαι BLOP

ὑστερήθην *AA*: ἠστερήθην BLOP

7 Μαθὼν . . . ἐπιστήμην: *omitted* BLO

ἑκάστῳ Pu: ἕκαστον BLOP

8 *heading* P *in margin of fol. 17v and in fol. 1r*: Περὶ τοῦ πλανηθέντος κλέπτου B *fol. 13r*

σὺ δέ με Pu: σὺ δέ μοι BLOP

Ἐμοῦ P: ἐγὼ BLO

9 Τοιοῦτο . . . ἀκολουθήσω: *omitted* BLO

11 *heading* P *in margin of fol. 19r and in fol. 1r*: Περὶ τῆς πόρνης B *fol. 14r*

ἀνὴρ αὐτῆς P: οἰκοκύριος BLO

12 *after* εἶναί P *adds* με

τῶν πονηρῶν Pu: τοῖς πονηροῖς BLOP

οὐ συμπαλαιοῦται Pu: οὐ *omitted* BLOP

Εὗρον Pu: εὑρὼν BLOP

13 *heading* P *in margin of fol. 19v and in fol. 1r*: Περὶ τῶν μαργαρήτων B *fol. 14v*

σεῖστρα *AA*: σύστρα BLOP

Ὡς οὐκ ἐποίησας . . . αὐτῷ: *omitted* BLO

ὡς προσέταξας P: ὥσπερ προσέταξας BLO

14 *heading* B *fol. 14v*

ἀένναον P: αἰώνιον BLO

after ἔσομαι P *in margin of fol. 20r has* παράδειγμα: P *fol. 1r*: Περὶ παραδείγματος κυνὸς καὶ ἑτέρων

<οὐκ> *added AA*

15 ὅπερ εὑρὼν ὁ κύων *AA*: εὑρὼν δὲ αὐτὸ ὁ κύων P, ὅπερ ὁ κύων BLO

ἤ ἡ ἐνίβλα P: *omitted* BLO

τῆς μετάξης P *in margin of fol. 20v*: τοῦ μεταξίου BLOP

ἔξοδος . . . ἐργασίας P: ἐργασία BLO

ὅταν ἐννοήσῃς . . . μακρυνθῆναι P: ὅταν ἐννοῇς τοὺς κόπους καὶ τὴν στένωσιν ἣν ἔχει, οὐδὲ πάλιν τοῦ βίου μακρυνθήσει. Ὅταν ἐννοήσεις τὰς ἐν αὐτῷ (ἑαυτῶν B) πονηρίας, οὐδὲ τότε δυνήσῃ ἐκφυγεῖν BLO

16 ἑκατὸν ἔτη P: ἑκατὸν BLO

ζῆσαι P: ἠτήσαι B, ζητῆσαι LO

<οὐκ ἂν> *added AA*

τὸ κρύος . . . γήρως καὶ P: τῆς γερουσίας BLO

πολυετῆσαι δεινόν P: τὴν πολυετίαν BLO

ἐν τῷ βίῳ τούτῳ P: ἐκ τοῦ κόσμου τούτου BLO

ἔσχατον δὲ πάντων P: ἔπειτα BLO

καὶ ἐν . . . ῥεούσαις P: εἰς τὰς αὐτοῦ ἡδονὰς τὰς φθειρομένας καὶ ῥεούσας BLO

βλαβερῶν P: θλιβερῶν BLO

17 θαύματος *AA*: θαυμάσας BLOP

after θαύματος εἶπον B *fol. 15v adds heading* Περὶ τοῦ βίου τοῦ ἀνθρώπου: περὶ ὡραίου παραδείγματος P *in fol. 1r*, ὅρα ὡραῖον παράδειγμα P *in margin of fol. 22r*

δεινοῦ μονοκέρωτος . . . ἀπορίᾳ P: δεινοῦ· ἐντυχὼν δὲ λάκκῳ ἔχοντι ἐν τῷ χείλει δένδρον, ἐκρεμάσθη ἐν αὐτῷ· κρατῶν δὲ κλάδους δύο τοῦ δένδρου ταῖς χερσίν, ἔθηκε τοὺς πόδας

αὐτοῦ ἐν τόπῳ τινὶ τοῦ στερεωθῆναι ἐν αὐτῷ. Ἦσαν δὲ ὄφεις τέσσαρεις ἐκβάλλοντες τὰς ἑαυτῶν κεφαλὰς ἐκ τῶν τρωγλῶν αὐτῶν. Παρακύψας δὲ κάτωθεν εἶδε δράκοντα ἀνεῳγμένον ἔχοντα τὸ στόμα, καὶ δύο μύας, λευκὸν καὶ μέλανα, ἐσθίοντας τὰς ῥίζας τῶν κλάδων ὧν ἐκράτει. Ἐν ἀπορίᾳ . . . BLO

18 *text given as in* P *fols. 21v–22r*

τῇ προσκαίρῳ . . . ταύτῃ *AA*: τὴν πρόσκαιρον ζωὴν ταύτην P

τῇ ἡμέρᾳ . . . νυκτί *AA*: τὴν ἡμέραν τε καὶ τὴν νύκτα P

19 *text given as is in* P *fol. 22v*

Chapter 1

heading Ἀρχὴ σὺν . . . Δίμνε: *added* P

Ἀρχὴ . . . Λόγος πρῶτος: *added* B *fol. 16r*

1 αὐτὸν Pu: αὐτῶν BLO, αὐτοῦ P

2 *heading* P *fol. 1r*: Περὶ τοῦ ἐμπόρου καὶ τῶν τέκνων αὐτοῦ· λόγος πρῶτος B *fol. 16r*

Λέγεται L *(in margin)* P: *omitted* BO

εὐπορῶν P: ἀπορῶν BLO

3 τινι BLO: τῇ P

Εἰ γὰρ . . . δυνηθείη P: Καὶ γὰρ εἰ μὴ βίου εὐπορήσει, οὐκ ἂν δυνηθῇ περὶ τὸν βίον ἀναστραφῆναι οὔτε τινὰς εὐεργετῆσαι BLO

βίον P: πλοῦτον BLO

τὸ στίμμι Sj: στόμμι LOP, στόματι B

οὐδ᾽ ἔνθα δεῖ καταβληθῇ BLO: ἔνθεν κἀκεῖθεν P

καὶ αἴτιος . . . εὐπορίας P (εὐπορίας Sj *in the apparatus*: ἀπορίας P): καὶ αἴτιον τοῦτο ἔσται τῷ τὸν πλοῦτον ἔχοντι παντελοῦς ἀπορίας BLO

μὴ . . . εὑρίσκει P: πόρον οὐχ εὑρίσκει BLO

4 *heading* P *in margin of fol. 23v and in fol. 1r*

συμποδισθῆναι P: ἐκπεσεῖν BLO

Ἐφ᾽ ᾧ ὁρμηθεὶς ὁ ἔμπορος P: Ἀλλ᾽ οὗτος ὁρμήσας BLO

after πηλοῦ BLO *add* καὶ ἀνείλκυσε παραυτίκα

περαιτέρω προχωρεῖν μὴ δυνάμενος P: πρότερον μὴ δυνηθεὶς διὰ τὴν ἀνάγκην προχωρῆσαι BLO

Καὶ παντελεῖ . . . βαδίσας P: Ἀλλ' ὕστερον ἠρέμα χωρήσας καὶ κατὰ μικρὸν προϊὼν BLO

5 *heading* P *in margin of fol. 24r and in fol. 1r*

Διῆγε P: ἦν BLO

λέοντές τε . . . ἕτερα εἴδη P: ἄρκοι τε καὶ λέοντες, πάνθηροί τε καὶ λύκοι καὶ ἀλώπεκες, καὶ ἕτερα τινὰ γένη θηρίων BLO

καὶ . . . φρόνησιν P: ἀλλὰ τὸ φρόνημα ἐλλιπῶς ἐτύγχανεν BLO

Καὶ ἀκούσας . . . φανερῶσαι P: ἀκούσας γὰρ τὸν τοῦ ταύρου μηκυθμόν, ἐδειλίασε παραχρῆμα, ἅτε δὴ ἄπειρος ὢν καὶ ἀνήκοος τοῦ τοιούτου ἤχου, πλὴν οὐκ ἠβουλήθη τὴν τοιαύτην δειλίαν τοῖς τότε παρατυχοῦσι θηρίοις φανερὰν ποιήσασθαι BLO

6 *heading* P *in margin of fol. 24r and in fol. 1r*

καὶ πλεῖον . . . καταλήψεως P: ὁ Ἰχνηλάτης BLO

after καταδυναστεύοντα BLO *add* τῶν ἄλλων κατὰ τὸ σύνηθες

ἡμῖν πρόσεστιν P: τι πεπόνθαμεν BLO

after ἀνιαρὸν BLO *add* ἐξ αὐτοῦ

προσκαρτεροῦμεν . . . βασιλέως P: τούτου προσκαθήμενοι BLO

ποριζόμενοι P: καθεκάστην ἐκεῖθεν ποριζόμεθα BLO

περὶ P: τὰ τῶν BLO

διαλέγεσθαι P: ἡμῶν ἐρευνᾶν πράγματα ἢ BLO

τὰ τούτων περισκοπεῖν P: πολυπραγμονεῖν BLO

Παῦσον οὖν . . . ἴσθι P: Λοιπὸν οὖν παῦσαι τοῦ τοιούτου ἐπιχειρήματος, εἰδὼς BLO

ἀνοικείοις P: τοῖς μὴ ἀνήκουσιν BLO

πιθήκου P: πίθηκος πείσεται BLO

7 *heading* P *in margin of fol. 24r and in fol. 1r*: Περὶ τοῦ τέκτονος καὶ τοῦ πίθηκος B *fol. 17v*

ἀφαιροῦντα . . . προσπηγνῦντα BLO: ἀφαιρεῖν καὶ πηγνύειν τὸν ἕτερον P

ὁ δὲ πίθηξ τοῦ ξύλου P: τοῦ ξύλου (*omitted* B) καὶ αὐτὸς BLO

after ὅμοια BLO *add* ἐκείνου

ῥήγματι συμπιεσθέντων P: σχίσματι συσχεθέντων BLO

8 πρόσεισιν P: πρόεισιν BLO

ἀρκεῖσθαι τοῖς τυχοῦσι P: μετρίοις ἀρκεῖσθαι BLO

heading Περὶ κυνὸς P *in margin of fol. 24v*

καταδιώκει P: διώκει καὶ ἁρμοδίως BLO

heading λέοντος P *in margin of fol. 24v*

heading κυνὸς P *in margin of fol. 24v*

ὅτου τὸ τρύφος Sj: ὅτου τῆς τρυφῆς P, ἂν τὸ κόμμα BLO

heading ἐλέφαντος P *in margin of fol. 24v*

heading καλοῦ ἀνδρὸς P *in margin of fol. 24v*

Καὶ . . . μεγαλόθυμος P: Ὁ γὰρ μεγαλόνους BLO

μεταλλάξει P: ἀνύσει BLO

heading πτωχοῦ P *in margin of fol. 24v*

ἀπορίᾳ P: ταλαιπωρίᾳ BLO

ἑτέρους ὠφελῶν P: ἄλλους θέλων ὠφελεῖν BLO

βραχύβιος . . . γῆρας P: εἰ καὶ εἰς βαθὺ καταντήσει γῆρας, βραχύβιός ἐστι καὶ ὀλιγοχρόνιος BLO

9 ποιεῖται τὴν ἄνοδον P: τὴν ὁδὸν ἐπιζητεῖ BLO

heading λίθου P *in margin of fol. 25r*

ἐπιζητεῖν ὅσον τὸ κατὰ δύναμιν P: ἐπινοεῖσθαι ὅση δύναμις BLO

οἰκείῳ μέτρῳ P: παρόντι BLO

ἐξὸν Sj: ἐξ ὧν ἀεὶ BLOP (*omitted* ἀεὶ)

10 Οἶδα, φησίν, τὸν τούτου P: φησίν· ἔγνων τούτου τὸν BLO

αὐτὸς . . . παιδείας P: βασιλικῆς ὁμιλίας τε καὶ παιδεύσεως BLO

οἷς . . . ἔχει P: τοῖς ἀπείροις αὐτοῖς BLO

τύχην P: τέχνην BLO

ἀλλὰ καὶ . . . παρομοιούμενος P: ἀλλὰ τὸν πλησιέστερον τῶν ἄλλων παρομοίως BLO

heading P *in margin of fol. 25v*: περὶ τῆς ἀμπέλου

τῶν κάτωθεν εἰς ὕψος μέγα BLO: κάτωθεν P

τοιούτοις ἐπιχειρῆσαι BLO: οὕτως ἐπιχειρήσασθαι P

11 ὑπόθου P: πόθον LO, πόθεν B

after αὐτοῦ BLO *add* δύναμιν καὶ τὴν

Μεταχειριζομένῳ Sj: μεταχειριζόμενον BLO, μεταχειριζομένου P

τινος *AA*: τι P, τινι BLO

ἐγκαταλείψει P: καταλήψει BLO

λυσιτελὲς P: ἀλυσιτελές BLO

heading γραφέως P *in margin*

12 *after* βούλει BLO *add* καὶ θέλεις

τοῦ ταῖς γυναιξὶ πιστεύειν μυστήρια *AA*: τοῦ τῶν γυναικῶν πιστεύειν μυστήρια P, τοῖς τῶν γυναικῶν μυστηρίοις LO, *omitted* B

heading περὶ βασιλέως P *in margin of fol. 26r*

ὑπηρεσίας P: ὑπουργίας BLO

heading περὶ μεγαλόφρονος P *in margin of fol. 26r*

παρὰ . . . διατριβαί P: τῶν ἀσκητῶν διαγωγαὶ καὶ τριβαί BLO

13 ἐπηρώτησε αὐτὸν P: ἠρώτησε τοῦτον BLO

πραγμάτων P: μεγάλων BLO

συμμεταλήψεως P: συνεργίας καὶ ἀντιλήψεως BLO

πολλοὶ τῶν P: ἡ BL, οἱ O

κνησμονήν BLO: κνησμὸν P

ἀνὴρ P: ἄνθρωπος BLO

τῆς ὁμιλίας P: ὁμιλίας αὐτοῦ BLO

αὐτοῦ BP: αὐτῶν ἔργων LO

ἔργων LO: λόγων P

after ἐστιν BLO *add* ἕκαστος

δείκνυται P: ἀποδείκνυται BLO

after συμπλέκων BLO *add* τε καὶ προσμιγνύων

λογικοὺς BLO: λογίους P

14 τρόπαια BLO: ἐπιχειρήματα P

αὐτὸν *AA*: αὐτῶν BLO, αὐτοῦ P

μόνον προσάγεσθαι P: προσοικειοῦσθαι BLO

τὰ πορρωτέρω φάρμακα P: πονηρότερα φάρμακα BLO

παρορᾶν P: μὴ παρορᾶν BLO

15 Ἰδὼν οὖν P: γνοὺς τοίνυν BLO

εὐμενῆ τὴν P: ὡς εὐμενής ἐστιν ἡ BLO

ὅτι οὐ . . . ἤδη BLO: ὅτι ἐπὶ πολὺν ἤδη καιρὸν ἔμεινας ἀκίνητος, μὴ μεταβαίνων ἐπὶ τόπον ἕτερον; P

Καὶ ὁ . . . ἔφη BLO: ἠβουλήθη οὖν ὁ λέων τὴν ἑαυτοῦ δειλίαν ἀποκαλύψαι, ἀλλ' ἔφθησε τῷ μεταξὺ μηκυθμὸν ἀκοῦσαι τοῦ ταύρου, καὶ ἔτι περίτρομος γεγονώς, ἔφη P

16 *heading* P *in margin of fol. 27v and fol. 1r*: Περὶ τῆς ἀλόπεκος καὶ τοῦ τιμπάνου B *fol. 19v*

προστετύχηκεν . . . διέρρηξεν αὐτό P: εἶδε κατά τινα ὕλην τύμπανον δένδρῳ ἀπηωρημένον καὶ ὑπὸ ἀνέμων παρακινούμε-

νον, ἀλαλαγμὸν δέ τινα ἀποτελοῦν μέγιστον ἐκ τῆς τῶν κλόνων κινήσεως. Τοῦτο οὖν ἰδοῦσα ἐπτοήθη πλησιάσαι τῷ πράγματι, ἀλλὰ τῷ λιμῷ καὶ τῇ πείνῃ κατεχομένη κατετόλμησε τούτου, καὶ πλησιάσασα πολλοῖς πιμελῆς καὶ κρέασι λιπαροῖς ἐντυχεῖν, καὶ τῷ μεγέθει τοῦ τυμπάνου τὴν ὄψιν καταπλαγεῖσα (-αν BL). Διὸ καὶ πάντα κάλων κινήσασα διέρρηξε τοῦτο BLO

17 τοῦτο . . . ἀπελθόντος P: ὁ βασιλεὺς ἐπένευσε τοῦτο γενέσθαι· ἐπεὶ δὲ ἀνεχώρησε BLO

ἀπλήστῳ P: ἀπίστῳ BLO

ἐκολάκευέ P: ἐκδουλεύσει BLO

οἰκείως . . . τοιούτοις P: τὴν οἰκείαν γνώμην καὶ πίστιν καθαρὰν ἀποδείξαντι BLO

ἐκ πολλοῦ . . . πρὸς P: πλοῦτον καὶ δόξαν ἀφηρημένος BLO

after ἐλαττώματα BLO *add* καὶ ἔκτοτε οὐ πιστῶς ἐκδουλεύσει μοι

καὶ τὰ . . . λέοντος P: δὲ αὐτοῦ διαλογιζομένου BLO

Ὡς . . . λέων P: Καὶ ὁ λεὼν ἰδὼν τοῦτον BLO

ἐπεγένετο ἐξ αὐτοῦ P: ἐξ αὐτοῦ περιεγένετο BLO

ὑψιπέτηλα P: ὑψίκομα BLO

ἐκτίλλει (ἐκτεῖλαι) P: ἀνασπᾷ BLO

Εὐφρανθεὶς P: ἐχάρη BLO

18 αὐτῷ P: ταύρῳ BLO

πρὸς . . . ἐκείνου P: τὴν πρὸς αὐτὸν BLO

με . . . σε P: ἐμέ σε ἐξαπέστειλεν BLO

after ἐστι BLO *add* πάντων

δειλιάσας P: εἰ καὶ δεδειλίακεν, ἀλλ᾽ οὖν BLO

after λέοντος P *adds* σὺν τῷ Ἰχνηλάτῃ

Καὶ . . . ἰδών P: Ὃν ἰδὼν ὁ λέων BLO

ἐπηρώτησε . . . αὐτὸν P: τὰ περὶ αὐτοῦ ἐπηρώτα BLO

ἀνέθηκεν αὐτῷ *AA*: ἀνέθηκεν ἐπ᾽ αὐτῷ P, ἀνέθετο εἰς αὐτὸν BLO

ὑπ᾽ αὐτόν P: λοιπῶν BLO

19 καθυστερήσαντα . . . ἀξίᾳ P: ὑπηρετήσαντά O: ὑπερτερήσαντα BL

after νουνεχῆ BLO *add* ἄνδρα πάντα ταῦτα μεταχειρίζεσθαι, ἅπερ πρότερον ἔπαθεν, ἀγαθά τε καὶ ἐναντία *and continue with*

the narrative Περὶ ἀσκητοῦ, *while the entire part of paragraph from* βούλομαι *is inserted below in section 27 after* εἶπεν (ἡττήθησαν *in the present edition)*

καὶ σπεύδειν . . . φαῦλα P: ἀποστρέφεσθαι BLO

καὶ οὐχ . . . ἀλλ' ἢ P: καὶ ἄλλον τινὰ πόρον εἰς τὴν τοιαύτην ἐπάνοδον οὐχ εὗρον ἢ

ἀποκτεῖναι P: ἀναιρεῖν BLO

παραγκωνισάμενος P *in margin of fol. 29v*: περιφρονήσας BLOP

καὶ καθαιρεῖται P: ἐλαττοῦται BLO

τῷ P: τοῦ BLO *(throughout the present paragraph)*

δεινότητος P: αὐστηρίας BLO

τοὐναντίον P: ἐκεῖθεν BLO

πρὸς . . . πᾶσι P: ἔτι δε BLO

ταῦρον P: βασιλέα BLO

δυνατώτερον P: ἰσχυρότερον BLO

ἀπίδης P: ἐπείδης BLO

τυχόντων P: ἀδυνάτων BLO

20 *heading* P *in margin of fol. 29r and in fol. 1r*, Περὶ τοῦ ἀσκοιτοῦ καὶ τῶν ἱφασμάτων B *fol. 20v*

πολύτιμα BLO: πολλὰ P

μεθ' ἡμέρας BLO: μετ' οὐ πολὺ P

ὀπίσω αὐτοῦ BLO: τούτου P

ὁδεύειν P: διώκειν BLO

ἕλκη P: σκέλη BLO

συγκρούσαντες P: προσκρούσαντες BLO

21 *heading* P *in margin of fol. 29v and in fol. 1v*

καλάμῳ BP: καλάμη LO

καὶ θήσασα . . . αὐτόν P: ὃ καὶ φυσήσασα κοιμωμένῳ ἐν τῷ ἀφεδρῶνι αὐτοῦ εἰς τὸ εἰσελθεῖν ἔνδον τῶν ἐγκάτων αὐτοῦ καὶ ἀποθανεῖν BLO

ταύτην BLO: αὐτὴν ὁλοτελῶς τὸ φάρμακον P

22 *heading* P *in margin of fol. 29r and in fol. 1v*

αὐτοῦ . . . γυνὴ αὐτοῦ P: αὕτη μαυλίστριαν αὐτῆς καθυπερετοῦσαν αὐτῇ ἐξ ἔθους πρὸς τῷ μοιχῷ. Ἡ δὲ γυνὴ τοῦ σκυτοτόμου εὐκαιρίαν ἤδη λαβοῦσα ἔφη BLO

καὶ ἔνεγκε P: κάλεσον BLO

ἔξω μένει P: ἐξώκοιτος γίνεται BLO

ἐν . . . ἔδησε P: οἴκοι κατέδυσε BLO

23 Καὶ λέγει . . . γυνή BLO: ἡ δὲ λέγει αὐτῇ P

ὁρᾷς BLO: βλέπεις P

βλέπεις . . . αὐτῷ P: ὁρᾷς, (ὦ φίλη μου *omitted* P), τὸ συμβάν μοι· ἀλλ' οὖν δέομαί σου, λύσασά με, δέσμευσον σεαυτὴν τῷ στύλῳ (τῷ στύλῳ *omitted* P), ἕως ἀπελθοῦσα τῷ ἐραστῇ μου συνομιλήσω BLO

ἐξυπνισθεὶς P: διυπνισθεὶς BLO

μήπως γνωρίσῃ αὐτήν P: μήποτε τῷ σκυτοτόμῳ γνωρισθῇ BLO

ῥῖνα P: μύτην BLO

ἐν . . . αὐτοῦ BLO: ἐκεῖ P

24 ταύτην . . . καὶ P: τὴν μαυλίστριαν BLO

ῥῖνα P: μύτην BLO

βοᾶν P: καταβοᾶν BLO

κολληθήτω . . . γενηθήτω BLO: στραφήτω ἡ ῥίν μου ἠγιὴς P

καὶ τὴν . . . γενομένην P: πρὸς ἐμέ BLO

κατέστησεν P: ἀπεκατέστησεν BLO

εἶδεν P: ἐθεάσατο BLO

ἐφ' οἷς . . . σφάλματος BLO: ἤρξατο παρακαλεῖν τοῦ διαλλαγῆναι αὐτῇ P

25 *text given as is in* P, *for the* BLO *version see Notes to the Translation*

26 *text given as is in* P, *for the* BLO *version see Notes to the Translation*

καὶ ἐρρύσατο . . . τιμωρίας Pu *cited in the apparatus from manuscript Vatic. gr. 949*

27 Οὕτω . . . βλάψεις P: Εἶπε δὲ ὁ Στεφανίτης τῷ Ἰχνηλάτῃ· Οὕτω καὶ σὺ σεαυτὸν ἔβλαψας BLO

εἴπερ . . . κακόν P: ἀλλὰ τί βούλει ποιεῖν BLO

heading P *in margin of fol. 31r and in fol. 1v*

θῶς P: λυκοπάνθηρος BLO

28 *heading* P *in margin of fol. 31r and in fol. 1v*

Παρά . . . λίμνῃ P: περὶ λίμνην BLO

P *has in margin of fol. 31v, and in fol. 1v*: Περὶ κύκνου καὶ ἰχθύων

παρήδρευον *AA*: παρέδρευον LOP, παρεδρεύων B

τῇ λίμνῃ ταύτῃ P: ἐν τῇδε τη λίμνῃ BLO

ἱκανῶν P: πολλῶν BLO

παραγενομένους . . . διαλεγομένους P: δύο εἰς τοῦτον τὸν ποταμὸν ἀφικομένους καὶ διασκεπτομένους καὶ μελετῶντας BLO

σαγηνεύσωσιν P: ἀγρεύσωσιν BLO

μεταστῆναι P: μεταθῆναι BLO

after ἁλιεῖς BLO *add* καὶ κατάσχουσιν

29 τοῦ ὄρους BLO: τοιοῦτον P

μετοικίζονται BLO: μετακομίζονται P

next to μετακομίζονται P *in margin of fol. 31v has* ὅρα τὸν τοῦ κύκνου θάνατον

κρημνὸν P: τόπον BLO

βιοθανατήσει P: βιαίως καὶ αὐτὸς τελευτήσει BLO

βιοθανατήσει . . . καὶ P: κἄντε συμπλακείῃ πρὸς μάχην, κἄντε ὑποταγείῃ αὐτῷ· ὅμως BLO

ὑποστῆναι P: ὑπομεῖναι BLO

καλῶς τεθνηκέναι BL: κακῶς τεθνηκέναι PO

διεξῆλθον BLO: διεξίην P

next to διεξίην P *has in margin of fol. 32r* καὶ τὸν τοῦ ὄφεως θάνατον

ἐπιβουλεύων τίς τινι P: τις τῶν ἐπιβουλευόντων τισί BLO

οἰκείαις ἄρκυσιν P: ἰδίαις νάρκυσιν BLO

δύνῃ . . . τιμιώτερον P: δυνήσει, ὀξυπέτης ὢν καὶ ὀξυωπήσας κάτωθεν κατόπτευσον, στοχασάμενος γυναικὸς κόσμου τῶν τιμιωτέρων BLO

ἀναιροῦσιν P: ἀνέλουσι BLO

after ἀπηλλάγη P *adds* παντελῶς ἐξ ἐκείνου

30 ἐπικρατεστέρα P: ἐπικρατερῶς BLO

τῇ ἀνδρείᾳ P: τῇ σῇ ἀνδρείᾳ BLO

ἐνεχώρει ἂν BLO: ἐνεχειρήσω P

31 *heading* P *fol. 1v*: Περὶ τοῦ λέοντος καὶ τῶν ἄλλων ζώων B *fol. 24r*, ὅρα πανουργίαν τοῦ λαγωοῦ πρὸς τὸν λέοντα P *in margin of fol. 32r*

ὑδατῶδες πεδίον P: ὑδατώδη παράδεισον BLO

εὐμοιροῦντα *AA*: εὐμοιρούντων P, ἔχοντα BLO

παρενοχλούμενα P: συνεχόμενα BLO

μόχθῳ P: κόπῳ BLO

περίδειλοι P: περίτροποι LO, περίτρο B
ὁσημέραι διατελοῦμεν P: ἐσμέν BLO
εἰσπεσόντα P: ὑποβαλλόμενον BLO
αὐτόν Sj: ἡμᾶς BLO, *omitted* P

32 βραδυτέρᾳ . . . ἐχρήσατο P: βραδύτερον τὴν πορείαν ἐχρῆτο BLO
ἐβράδυνας BLO: ἐσχόλασας P
εἱλκόμην BLO: ἐφελκόμην P
αὐτῷ P: ἐμοῦ BLO
ἐπιφωνησαμένου P: προφωνησαμένου BLO
προδιαμαρτυρουμένου P: διαμαρτυρουμένου BLO
ἐπέμφθη P: προεπέμφθη BLO
εἰσηκούσθην P: εἰσήκουσέ μου BLO
ὥστε P: καὶ BLO
Ἰδοὺ BLO: Οὗτός ἐστιν P
ὧν P: οὗ BLO
πλανηθεὶς P: ἀπατηθεὶς BLO
φρέατι BLO: ὕδατι P
δύνασαι τὸν P: δυνατόν σοι BLO
ἕτεροι πλεῖστοι P: ἄλλοι πολλοὶ BLO
διὰ τῆς P: διὰ τελῶν B, διατελῶν LO
παρασπόνδησις Sj: παρασπούδησις BLOP

33 *heading* P *fol. 1v*, P *in margin of fol. 33v has* κατασκευὴ τοῦ Ἰχνηλάτου πρὸς τὸν λέοντα περὶ τοῦ ἀναιρεθῆναι τὸν ταῦρον
συνέβη P: συμβέβηκε πάθος BLO
ἐπαίσθηται Sj: ἀπέστηται P, ἔσθηται BLO
οὐ . . . κατατολμᾷ P: σιωπᾷ καὶ οὐ τολμᾷ τι λέγειν BLO
συνέσει BLO: εὐνοίᾳ P
δόξαντος P: νομίζοντος
νοῶ BLO: διανοοῦμαι P
διαλογίζομαι δὲ πάλιν BLO: ἀλλὰ πάλιν διαλογίζομαι P

34 αὐτὸν . . . τούτοις P: ἐν πᾶσιν BLO
Καὶ . . . προοιμίων P: Καὶ ἀκούσας ταῦτα, ἀνακαλύπτω σοι ὅτι ἐκ τῶν τοιούτων ῥημάτων BLO
τὴν τούτου . . . παρασπόνδησιν BLO: τῆς τούτου ἀσεβείας καὶ τῆς παρασπονδήσεως P
after ὑψώσαντος BLO *add* εἰς μέγα ὕψος ἄραντος

διενοήθη τῆς σῆς περιδράξασθαι (ἐπιδρ. P) ἀρχῆς P: ἐκεῖνος πονηρὰ κατὰ σοῦ ἐμελέτησε καὶ τῆς σῆς ἀρχῆς περιδράξασθαι ἐνενόησεν BLO

προκαταβάλλειν P: προκαταλαμβάνειν BLO

ἐπὶ μέγα . . . κακόν BLO: τὰ τῆς ἐφέσεως ἐπὶ μεῖζον ἀρθῇ P

ἀνέγκλητα . . . συμπτώματα P: ἀδρανέστερα ἴσως γενήσονται τὰ μελετώμενα κακά BLO

μὴ ἐμπεσεῖν P: μηδ' ὅλως ἐμπίπτειν (ἐπίμπτειν L) BLO

after ἴσως BLO *add* περιπετείαις

ἄλλοι πάντῃ P: πάντα BLO

35 *heading* Περὶ τῶν τριῶν ἰχθύων B *fol. 25v* P *fol. 1v*, ὅρα παράδειγμα τῶν τριῶν ἰχθύων P *in margin of fol. 33v*

διῃτῶντο P: διέτριβον BLO

πρὸς ἐκεῖνον P: εἰς BLO

ἀμελήσαντες . . . προσεκαρτέρησαν P: ἔμενον ἐκεῖσε ἀμελήσαντες BLO

ἀβλεψίᾳ P: ἀφρονησίᾳ BLO

ἀμελούντων ἀπόβασις P: μελλόντων ἀπόφασης BLO

καὶ καιρίως P: τι καίριον BLO

ὑπεκρίθη τοῦ P: ὑπέθετο BLO

εἰσπηδήσας ἐσώθη P: προσπηδήσας ἔσωθεν διεσώθη BLO

36 σου τὸ ὑπόδειγμα P: ὅπερ εἶπας BLO

ἐναντίον P: δεινὸν BLO

δόλιον P: δολιώτατον BLO

ἀσυνείδητος BLO: εὐσυνείδητος P

Καὶ τ. καταλαβών P: Εἰς τ. δὲ φθάσας BLO

σπουδαίως φαίνεσθαι P: σπουδαῖον εἶναι BLO

καταλήψεως P: ἐπιτυχίας BLO

ἐπανακάμπτει P: ἐπανακύπτει BLO

φαίνεται P: φέρεται BLO

χρῆσιν P: δόσιν BLO

37 τῆς εὐνοίας ἀντιποιούμενος P: μὴ κατέχων καὶ ἀποκρύπτων εὔνοιαν BLO

Λέγεται . . . ὡς P: Ἐπεὶ BLO

ἐπιβαίνειν P: καθεύδειν BLO

after τινὰ BLO *add* καὶ ὕπνου σπᾶν

συνοικεῖν τινι P: τινος προσεγγίζειν BLO

after τῶν BLO *add* περὶ αὐτὸν

χλοηνόμος P: χλοηφόρος BLO

ὑπάρχοντος P: τυγχάνοντος BLO

38 *heading* P *in margin of fol. 35r and in fol. 1v*

Λέγεται . . . χρόνῳ P: Φθὴρ γάρ τις τοῖς ὅ φασι δεμνίοις τινὸς τῶν μεγίστων ἐπὶ μύκηστον ἐκρύπτετο χρόνον BLO

ἀφόρητος ἦν P: ὑπνώττοντι ἐτρέφετο ἐκ τοῦ αἵματος αὐτοῦ BL (*omitted* αἵματος αὐτοῦ) O

ἐξύπνησε P: διύπνωσεν BLO

39 σεσημμένος P: τετριμμένος BLO

διαφθαρείσης τροφῆς P: φθαρείσης ψυχῆς BLO

Δηλώσω . . . τούτῳ P: Ἐπιτάξω τοῦτον BLO

ἀναιδείᾳ χρήσεται BLO: ἐχθρὸς γενήσεται P

παρασκευασθήσεται P: χωρήσει BLO

ἁμαρτήσαντα BLO: πταίσαντα P

ἀδήλως P: ἀφανῶς ἐπταικότα BLO

δειχθῇ P: ἀποδειχθῇ BLO

ὑπόληψις P: ὑπόθεσις BLO

after μᾶλλον BLO *add* ἔβλαψε καὶ

ἕτοιμος ἔσο· ἐκ γὰρ P: διασκόπησον ἀκριβῶς, καὶ ἐκ BLO

ὀφθαλμῶν ἐπιβολῆς P: προσβολῆς BLO

ἐπὶ . . . εἰρημένοις BLO: τὰ εἰρημένα ῥήματα P

40 *heading* P *fol. 1v*: ἐπέλευσις ἰχνηλάτου πρὸς τὸν λέοντα P *in margin of fol. 35v*

after καὶ BLO *add* καὶ προσωμιλῆσαι αὐτὸν τοῦ

καὶ συνεῖδε . . . εἶπεν P: καὶ ὅτι εἰ μάθοι τοῦτο, ὁ λέων ὑποπτεύσει τὸν δόλον, εἶπεν οὕτως BLO

αὐτὸν P: ταῦρον BLO

μοι . . . πρώτης P: με ἡ τούτου ἐπίνοια ἑκάστης BLO

Ὁ δὲ . . . εἰσῆλθε P: Καὶ προσέταξεν ὁ λέων τοῦτο γενέσθαι, καὶ εἰσῆλθε πρὸς τὸν ταῦρον οὕτω BLO

ἐπηρώτησε . . . εἶπε P: ἠρώτα BLO

Πάντως P: καὶ εἰ BLO

πάρεστιν P: πρόσεστιν BLO

ἑτέρῳ . . . ἀβεβαίῳ P: ὑφ᾽ ἑτέρου ἀγόμενος ἀπίστου καὶ ἀβεβαίου BLO

οἰκειώσεως BLO: ἀφίξεως P

heading P *fol. 1v* Περὶ τῆς διαβολῆς τοῦ Ἰχνηλάτου πρὸς τὸν ταῦρον κατὰ τοῦ λέοντος: διαβολὴ Ἰχνηλάτου πρὸς τὸν ταῦρον κατὰ τοῦ λέοντος P *in margin of fol. 35v*

after διὰ τὸ BLO *add* παχυνθῆναι καὶ

τὸν σκοπὸν αὐτοῦ P: τὸ πρᾶγμα BLO

σεαυτῷ τὸ *AA*: σεαυτῷ αὐτῷ P, σεαυτὸν τὶ BLO

41 τινι τῶν περὶ αὐτόν BLO: πρός τινα τῶν ὑπ' αὐτόν P

πονηροὶ BLO: φθονεροὶ P

κατεψεύσαντό μου P: ψευδῆ κατ' ἐμοῦ ἐμελέτησαν καὶ οἱ BLO

after φερόμενοι BLO *add* τοιαῦτα δεδράκασι

πονηρῶν P: μοχθηρῶν BLO

ταύτης . . . διαθέσεως P: τῆς τοιαύτης κατά σου μελέτης καὶ ἐπιβουλῆς BLO

ἄστατος . . . ἀγνώμων BLO: ἄστατος, ἄφιλος, ἀγνώμων, ἀβέβαιος P

πρότερον καὶ P: κατ' ἀρχάς, εἶτα BLO

πικροῦ τούτου Sj: πικροῦ P, πικροτάτου BLO

χλοηνόμον ὄντα *AA*: χλοηνόμος ὢν P, χλοηνόμενος ὢν BLO

after ὄντα BLO *add* καὶ ταῖς πόαις τρεφόμενον

τοῖς νυμφαί(ε P)οις ἄνθεσιν P: τοῖς τῆς νυμφαίας ἄνθεσιν Sj: ταῖς τῆς νυμφαίας ἄνθεσιν BLO

συμμυόντων P: συμμιγενούντων BL, συμμιγνύντων O

δένδροις . . . ἄνθεσιν P: τοῖς τῶν δένδρων ἄνθεσιν BLO

ἐλέφαντος BLO: λεοντος P

Ἄφες . . . μόρου P: Σκόπει τὰ καίρια, βουλὴν δὲ ἐφευρὼν ἀρίστην, σῶσον σεαυτὸν ἐκ θανάτου BLO

ἀκέραιος P: ἀκαίρως BLO

ᾗ P: ἐστι BLO

κατὰ . . . λέοντα B: εἰς τὴν κάμηλον P: εἰς τὸν λέοντα LO

42 *heading* P *fol. 1v*: ὅρα ἀναίρεσιν καμήλου παρὰ τῶν τριῶν ζώων P *in margin of fol. 36v*, Περὶ τοῦ λύκου καὶ τοῦ λεόντος καὶ τοῦ κόρακος καὶ θωὸς καὶ καμήλου B *fol. 27r*

βούλει P: στέργεις BLO

συναυλίαν . . . τοῦτο P: συμβουλίαν, ἐφεῖταί σοι τόπος ἐνταῦθα χλοηφόρος, ἐν ᾧ BLO

πολλῇ BLO: σου P

ἡ κάμηλος . . . θήραν P: ἄχρι τινὸς ἡ κάμηλος. Μιᾷ δὲ τῶν ἡμερῶν ἐξελθὼν ἐπὶ θήρᾳ BLO

after ὑπέστρεψε BLO *add* καὶ μεμωλωπισμένος καὶ

μεταβῆναι P: παραβῆναι BLO

ἔγνω P: ἐπέγνω BLO

ἀλύομεν P: ἀλλοιούμεθα BLO

43 εὑρήσετε . . . μοί P: εὑρεῖν δυνηθείητε τὰ αὐτάρκως ἐμοῦ τε καὶ ὑμῖν BLO

ἔγγιον P: μικρὸν BLO

χλοηνόμῳ P: χλοηφόρῳ BLO

Καὶ ὁ μὲν θὼς P: Ὁ δὲ λυκοπάνθηρος BLO

καὶ . . . κᾀκεῖνον P: ἐμὲ δὲ κᾀκεῖνον ἐάσατε BLO

Εἶτα ὁ κόραξ (θὼς P) . . . λέοντα P: Καὶ εἰπὼν ἀπηλλάγη BLO

Ἄραγε P: Τί τοῦτο; BLO

ἐπήσθου *AA*: ὑπήσθου P, ἐπύθου BLO

διέγνως P: ἐπέγνως τι BLO

Καὶ BLO: ἐκεῖνος P

διαγνώσεται BLO: γινώσκεις P

δυνάμεθα P: εἰ δυνηθείημεν BLO

ἀνακληθῆναι BLO: ἀνακλίναι P

ἐπακούσεις ἡμῖν BLO: ὑπακούσεις ὑμῶν P

μέσῳ BLO: μεταξὺ P

ὀργισθεὶς εἶπε P: μετ' ὀργῆς ἔφη BLO

ἀπηνείας P: ἀπονίας BLO

44 εἴρηκας P: ἔκρινας BLO

σὺν σοὶ κατατρυχόμεθα νῦν BLO: συγκατατρυχόμεθα σήμερον P

ὑπέρτερος BLO: ἀνώτερος P

after ἑαυτὸν BLO *add*: καὶ ἀναθῆναι τῷ λέοντι

σκαιωρήσαντες P: μηχανησάμενοι τὸ σκαιώρημα BLO

εὐπραγίαι P: εὐεργεσίαι γενόμεναι BLO

ἀλλ' . . . προσοίσω P: καὶ οὐκ ἔχω ὅ τι προθεῖναί BLO

ἔσομαι P: προθήσομαι BLO

ἔσομαι BLO: εἰμί P

ὁμοῦ . . . ἐβόησαν P: εἶπον BLO

45 ταὐτὸν P: τὰ ὅμοια BLO

τοῦ λέοντος BLO: αὐτοῦ P

Οὐ γὰρ LO: ὁ γὰρ B, οὕτω γὰρ P

ἱλαρῷ δότῃ BLO: ἱλαροδότῃ P

κινδυνώδει πράγματι Sj: κινδυνώδη πράγματα BLOP

δι' ἑαυτοῦ προσπλακῆναι P: ἀπροόπτως περιπλέκεσθαι BLO

ὕστερον ἐπιχειρεῖ P: χωρεῖ BLO

εὐνοϊκῶς σοι BLO: εὐνοϊκώτατα P

τοῦ ἀλκυόνος P: τῆς νειραΐδος BLO

46 *heading* P *in margin of fol. 38r and in fol. 1v* : Περὶ τῆς νηραΐδος καὶ τοῦ ἀλκύωνος B *fol. 28v*

Ἡ . . . ἐγγίσασα *AA*: τῆς δὲ συνεύνου ἐγγισάσης P, τῇ δὲ συνεύνῳ ἐγγισάσῃ BLO

Εἰ εὑρήσεις . . . ἐστι P: Ἑτοίμασόν μοι τόπον ἐπιτήδειον καὶ ὀχυρὸν ἤδη πρὸς τὸ τεκεῖν BLO

ἔλθῃ P: ἐπέλθῃ μοι BLO

νηρὴς P: νειραῒς BLO *(throughout this fable)*

λάβῃ ἡμῶν P: ἀφέληταί μου BLO

Τέξαι ἐνθάδε P: Ἐνθάδε τοῦ τεκεῖν σε κρεῖττον ἐστί BLO

Λοιπὸν . . . πρόσεχε P: Εἰπόν σοι εὐνοϊκῶς προσσχεῖν ἡμᾶς τὴν τῶν νεοττῶν ὠφέλειαν BLO

Ὡς . . . ποιησαι P: Οἶμαι ὅτι οὐκ ἐπιχειρήσει BLO

εἶπε P: πάλιν BLO

λέγων καὶ φοβερίζων P: λέγειν, καὶ ἀπειλεῖσθαι BLO

οἶσθα P: ἐπίστασαι BLO

Οἱ γὰρ . . . πείσονται BLO: ὁ γὰρ μὴ ἀκούων παρὰ τοῦ εὐνοϊκῶς βουλεύοντος, πείσεται P

47 *heading* P *in margin of fol. 38v and in fol. 1v* : Περὶ τῆς χελώνης καὶ τῶν δύο νηττῶν B *fol. 28v*

δεῖν . . . μεταστῆναι P: διενοήθησαν ἀπὸ τὰ ἐκεῖθεν διαναστῆναι BLO

ἀπᾶραι BLO: μεταστῆναι P

λείψεως BLO: μεταλήψεως P

ξύλον P: ξυλάριον BLO

συλλαβοῦσαι P: λαβοῦσαι BLO

Εἰς . . . ἄνωθεν: πάντως καὶ BLO

48 λέγεις P: διεσαφήσω BLO

σὺ τέξαι P: τεκεῖν δεῖ σε BLO
αὕτη ἐκεῖσε . . . γέγονε P: ἀνῆλθεν ἡ θάλασσα καὶ ἀφείλετο ἡ νειραῗς τὰ νοσσία αὐτῆς ἐν τῇ φωλεῷ ταύτης, καὶ ἀφανὴς ἐγεγόνει BLO
δὲ στραφεῖσα . . . συνεύνῳ P: δ' ἀλκυὼν ἔφη τῷ ὁμοζύγῳ BLO
προέγνωκα BLO: ἔγνων P
ἐπῆλθε . . . αὕτη BLO: οὕτως πεπόνθαμεν P
Ἀληθῶς . . . δείξω σοι P: Οὐκ εἶπόν σοι ὅτι ὄψει BLO
αὐτήν BLO: τοῦτο P
πάνθ' ὅσα πέπονθε BLO: πάντα, ἅπερ ἔπαθε P
τοῦ P: ὅπως BLO
τυγχάνοντες BLO: ὄντες ὑμεῖς P
μὲν P: δὲ . . . καὶ BLO
τί δ' . . . βλάβην BLO: ἀλλ' οὖν τί δυνάμεθα βλάψαι αὐτήν; P
τοίνυν BLO: πάντες P
ὅπως . . . ἡμῖν P: καὶ χρησώμεθα αὐτοῖς βοηθόν BLO
49 τὰ . . . ἔφησαν P: ἔφη οὖν καὶ τὰ πετεινά BLO
Βουλόμεθα . . . πρὸς ἡμᾶς BLO: ἡμεῖς μετὰ προθυμίας βουλόμεθα βοηθῆσαι ὑμῖν, μόνον ὁ βασιλεὺς ἡμῶν θελησάτω· καὶ P
ἀντιπαράταξιν P: παράταξιν BLO
50 ἐν . . . σημεῖα BLO: σημεῖα τοῦ λέοντος τοιαύτης P
κέρκου BLO: οὐρᾶς P
προεῖπεν BLO: εἶπεν P
φωλεῷ BLO: ἰλεῷ ἤτοι φωλεᾷ P
51 ἀπώλεσας P: ἐφόνευσας BLO
συστρατιωτῶν P: στρατιωτῶν BLO
ὁ συνετώτατος . . . τοῦτον BLO: οἱ συνετώτατοι βασιλέων πρωτοσύμβουλοι οὐκ ἐῶσιν τούτους P
προκατάρξασθαι BLO: κατάρξασθαι P
ἔνθα . . . εἶεν BLO: ἔνθα δ' εἰρήσεις τὸ πάθος ἰαθῆναι δύναται· καὶ εἴπερ δυνατώτεροι εἶεν οἱ ἐχθροί P
διὰ μεθοδείας . . . τούτους Sj: *omitted* BLOP
καθ' ἡμέραν P: μεθημερινόν BLO
52 διειδεῖ P: διηκεῖ BOL
ἐπιπολαίως P: ἐπὶ πολέμου BLO
ὡς ἀνηνύτοις ἐπιχειρεῖν με P: ὡς ἂν εἴ τις ἐπιχειρῶν BLO

μωρούς P: κακούς BLO

53 *heading* P *in margin of fol. 40r and in fol. 1v*: Περὶ τοῦ κοράκου καὶ τῶν πιθήκων B *fol. 30r*

τόπῳ τῶν ὀρέων BLO: ὀρεινῶν δένδρων καὶ τόπων P

καί τι . . . αὐτῷ BLO: καί τινα λίθον στίλβοντα εὑρόντες, ἐπέλαβον πῦρ εἶναι, καὶ κατεφύσων αὐτὸν P

κενῶς πονοῦντας BLO: ἱκανῶς ποιοῦντας P

ἐπιχείρει *AA*: ἐπιχειρήσῃς BLO, ἐπεχείρει P

πρὸς . . . παραινοῦντα P: τῆς ἑαυτοῦ παραινέσεως BLO

τῷ τοῦ *AA*: τὸ τοῦ BLO, *omitted* P

54 *heading* P *in margin of fol. 40v and in fol. 1v*: Περὶ τοῦ πονηροῦ κινωνοῦ τοῦ σχολαστηκοῦ B *fol. 30r*

ὅσον BLO: ὅσα P

κατορύξαντες ἔκρυψαν BLO: κρύψαντες ὑπέστρεψαν P

55 ἐξελθόντες P: ἀπελθόντες BLO

Τέως BLO: Τέλος P

μου . . . ἀλήθειαν BLO: τῇ ἀληθείᾳ P

εἰς τὸ . . . ἐκεῖνο P: τῷ δένδρῳ BLO

πρὸς τὸν ἐρωτῶντα ἀποκρίνεσθαι P: προσερωτῶντι ἐκείνῳ ἀποκρίνασθαι BLO:

καὶ πάθῃς . . . ἔπαθεν P: παθὼν οἷα καὶ ὁ κύκνος ἐπεπόνθει O, *omitted* BL

Ὁ δὲ εἶπεν LP: Ἔφη τῷ πονηρῷ ἀνδρὶ ὁ πατὴρ αὐτοῦ B, *transferred by* O *after* σαγηνευθῇς

56 *heading* P *in margin of fol. 41r and in fol. 1v*: Περὶ τοῦ κύκνου καὶ τοῦ ὄφεως B *fol. 31r*

<ἦν> φωλεύων *AA*: ἐμφολεύων BLO, φωλεύων P

τὸν P: τὴν BLO

προσῆλθεν . . . αὐτῷ BLO: προσελθὼν τῷ κύκνῳ εἶπε P

Τί σε . . . αὐτῷ P: Ὁρῶ σε ἀδημονοῦντα καὶ λυπούμενον ἤδη. Ἴσθι οὖν ταχεῖαν ἀπαλλαγὴν τοῦ δεινοῦ." Καὶ ἀνήγγειλεν ὁ κύκνος αὐτῷ, ὅσα ἐξ ἀρχῆς παρὰ τοῦ ὄφεως πέπονθεν BLO

Ὁ δὲ εἶπε . . . νύμφη P: Καὶ ὁ κύκνος· "Νύμφης ἑρπυστικῆς παρ' αὐτῇ οἰκούσης, ἥτις BLO

ἔχει P: κέκτηται BLO

ἐποίησεν καὶ *AA*: ποιήσας BLOP

ἀπέκτεινε αὐτὸν P: τὸν ὄφιν ἀπέκτεινε BLO

57 *after* παραβολήν P *adds* μᾶλλον δὲ

ὑπεισέδυ . . . δένδρου P: ὑπεισῆλθεν (εἰσῆλθεν B) εἰς τὸ δένδρον BLO

τίς (οἷος L) τὸν χρυσὸν ἀφείλατο BLO: *omitted* P

Ταῦτα . . . ἀκούσας *AA*: Ταῦτα . . . ἀκούσαντος BLO, οὗπερ ἀκούσαντος P

ὃς δὴ L: οἱ δὲ B, ὃν δὴ O, ὃς P

μοχθηροῦ καὶ δολίου BLO: πονηροῦ καὶ μοχθηροῦ P

ἀμφοῖν . . . ἀποστάζεται P: ἀμφότερα ἰὸν ἀποστάζουσι BLO

κἂν[2] P: ἢ BLO

τῷ *AA*: τὸ BLO, *omitted* P

58 *heading* P *in margin of fol. 41v and in fol. 1v*: Περὶ τοῦ ἐμπόρου καὶ τοῦ σιδήρου καὶ τοῦ φίλου αὐτοῦ B *fol. 32r*

ἐπιστροφὴν BLO: ἀποστροφὴν P

τοῦ ἐμπόρου BLO: αὐτοῦ P

πωλήσαντα P: ἐμπολήσαντα BLO

καὶ . . . αὐτῷ P: Ἔφη αὐτῷ ὁ ἔμπορος BLO

ὃν P: ὅσον BLO

τέθεικα P: κατέθηκα BLO

Ἀλλὰ P: Καὶ BLO

ἐπανῆκες BLO: ἐπανῆλθες P

καὶ συνεστιάσθητι *AA*: συνεσθιάθητι BLO, συνεσθίασον P

Καὶ εἰσελθὼν P: Μετὰ δὲ τὸ ἐσθιαθῆναι μέλλων ἐξέρχεσθαι BLO

καὶ ἀποκρύψας . . . εὑρὼν P: ἀπέκρυψε· καὶ ὑποστρέψας εὗρε BLO

αἰρόμενον LO: φερόμενον B, ἐρχόμενον P

παρέλαβεν P: ἀπέλαβεν BLO

59 ἄρα BLO: ἔτι P

οὐκ οἶδεν . . . εἰς P: οὐ μετατρέπει τὴν ἰδίαν φύσιν πρὸς γλυκύτητα BLO

σπουδαίων BLO: πονηρῶν P

γὰρ . . . τούτοις P: καὶ τοῦτο BLO

πεπαιδευμένοι P: σοφοὶ BLO

60 *heading* P *fol. 1v*: ἀναίρεσις ταύρου P *in margin of fol. 42v*

τὸν ταῦρον . . . βασιλεύς P: ἀνήρηται ὁ ταῦρος παρὰ τοῦ λέοντος BLO

αὐτὸν θεασάμενος BLO: ἰδὼν P

τῇ . . . ταύρου BLO: τῷ ταύρῳ P

εἰ P: ὅτε BLO

δηχθῇ P: δαχθῇ BLO

61 παρεμβάλλει *AA*: παρεμβάλλων BLO, παραβάλλει P

after διΐστησιν P *adds* Τέλος τοῦ πρώτου Τμήματος

Chapter 2

heading P *fol. 42v*

1 ὅπως ἀπέβη BLO: πῶς ἐπέβη P

2 τὴν . . . ἀναίρεσιν P: τὸ ἀναιρεθῆναι τὸν ταῦρον BLO

φάσκοντα *AA*: φάσκοντος BLO, *omitted* P

3 Ἀλλ' ἐξαύδα P: Εἰπὲ οὖν ἡμῖν BLO

ἀναιτίως P: ἀρτίως BLO

τῇ . . . διαθέσει P: τὴν . . . διάθεσιν BLO

φίλος P: φιλητὸς BLO

πάνυ BLO: πάλιν P

τῷ θανάτῳ P: τῇ ἀναιρέσει BLO

συλλογισμοῖς BLO: διαλογισμοῖς P

τι τοιοῦτον P: ψευδόν τι BLO

4 *heading* P *fol. 1v*: φανέρωσις τὸ τοῦ Ἰχνηλάτου τερατούργημα P *in margin of fol. 43r*

κατεψεύσατο BLO: διεψεύσατο P

after λέων BLO *add* ἔφη· 'Ἀλλ'

ἡμαρτημένου P: ἐκδικημένου BLO

ἂν ᾖ τι ἀμφιβαλλόμενον P: ἔτι ἀμφιβαλλομένης BLO

εἰς φῶς ἀγαγεῖν P: σαφῶς παραγαγεῖν BLO

μὴ . . . ποιήσασα P: εἰ τοῦτο ποιήσω, μὴ BLO

5 *heading* P *in margin of fol. 43v*: Περὶ τῆς πρώτης αὐτοῦ ἐξετάσεως P *fol. 1v*

τὸ μέχρι Sj: τοῦ μέχρι BLOP

σπεύδων ἐπὶ BLO: βλέπων περὶ P

καὶ τοὺς ἀσκητάς P: πολλοὺς BLO

ἐνοικουροῦν P: ἐνοικοῦν BLO
τῷ λίθῳ BLO: καὶ τοῖς λίθοις P
ἀποκαλύπτεται P: ἀνακαλύπτεται BLO
6 προσαφικόμην P: προσανεχόμην ἀναστρέφεσθαι BLO
κλίνοντος P: ἐγκλίνοντος BLO
καταφεύξομαι P: νῦν καταφυγεῖν BLO
ἐτάζοντος BLO: ἐξετάζοντος P
παντὶ . . . θνητῷ P: καὶ πᾶν ζῷον θνητόν BLO
7 *heading* P *in margin of fol. 44r and in fol. 1*: Περὶ τοῦ ζωγράφου καὶ τῆς πόρνης B *fol. 34r*
δούλου P: δόλου BLO
8 Μιᾷ . . . παλατίῳ P: Ὁ δὲ ζωγράφος ἐν τῷ παλατίῳ μιᾷ τῶν ἡμερῶν προσελθὼν BLO
παραγενομένου τοῦ ζωγράφου *AA*: παραγενόμενος ὁ ζωγράφος P
ἐπιδώσης BLO: δώσης P
αὐθέντου BLO: κυρίου P
ἀκακίαν P: ἐκκακίαν BLO
Ὁ . . . ἐλθὼν BLO: ἐλθὼν δὲ αὐτὸς P
οὕτως σπουδαίως P: ὅτι συντόμως BLO
δόλον P: δοῦλον BLO
9 ἀκήκοεν *AA*: ἀκήκοας BLOP
αὐτῷ BLO: πρὸς αὐτὸν P
ζῴῳ BLO: ζῶντι P
σχολῇ *AA*: σχολῆς P, σχολήσι B, σχολήσει LOP *in margin*
ὑπερασπίσεται P: ὑπερασπίζεσθαι BLOP *(in margin of fol. 45r)*
φθόνον . . . σοι P: ἐνμοιχοῦντά σοι δόλον BLO
10 τοιούτου . . . ἔργου BLO: τοιούτων κατετόλμησας ἔργων P
καταναιδεύει P: κατενεδρεύεις BLO
ἐσθλῶν P: ἀθλῶν LBO
κατὰ ποίησιν BLO: ὡς τὸν ποιητὴν P
χρωμένη P: ἀπεχρωμένη BLO
ὁ λέγων ξένος ἑαυτὸν κύριον τῆς οἰκίας P: ὁ ξένον ἑαυτὸν κύριον ὢν τοῖς οἰκείοις BLO
11 ὅσα σὺ (σοι) P: πόσα BLO
μήτηρ . . . λέοντος ἔφη P: εἶπε BLO
ψευδῆ διαπλαττόμενοι P: ψευδὰ πραττόμενοι BLO

ἐκκλίνοντες P: ἐγκλίνοντες BLO

ἀπολογούμενον BLO: ἀποκρινόμενον P

κατεψεύσαντο τοῦτον BLO: κατεψηφίσαντο τούτου P

διαβάλλοντες P: ἐνδιαβάλλοντες BLO

μεσου τοῦ θεάτρου P: μέσον πολλῶν BLO

ἐγκάθειρξις ἰχνηλάτου P *adds in margin of fol. 45v*: Περὶ τῆς ἐγκαθείρξεως πρώτης τοῦ Ἰχνηλάτου P *in fol. 1v*

ἀνατρεπόμενος P: ἀποτρεπόμενος BLO

ἂν τὰ P: ὅτου BLO

τοῦτον P: τὸν Ἰχνηλάτην BLO

ἃ P: ὅπερ BLO

12 τῷ *AA*: τὸ P, τὰ BLO

ὡς βλάπτονται P: ὡς οὐ βλάπτονται BLO

τινὸς τῶν P: τῶν BLO

ἀπέχονται BLO: ἀπόσχονται P

συλληφθήσῃ . . . καθομολογήσῃς P: συλληφθεὶς καὶ βασανιστεῖς καὶ ὁμολογήσεις BLO

διελογισάμην P: διενοησάμην BLO

ἅπαν . . . ἁμάρτημα P: καθομολογῆσαί σου τὰ ἁμαρτήματα BLO

καταντήσει P: καταντήσω σοι BLO

13 *heading* P *in margin of fol. 46r*: Περὶ τῆς ἐξετάσεως δευτέρας τοῦ Ἰχνηλάτου P *in fol. 1v*

after περὶ BLO *add* ἁπάντων, καὶ

ὁρᾷ τὸ τοιοῦτον P: πραχθήσεται BLO

τὰ ψευδῆ λέγων P: μὴ εἰδὼς ἃ λέγει BLO

14 *heading* P *in margin of fol. 46v and in fol. 2r*: Περὶ τοῦ ἀμαθῆ ἰατροῦ B *fol. 35v*

ὅτι τις BLO: ὁ P

κύστιδος BLO: κύστης P

πατρὸς τῆς κόρης P: ἐξουσιαστοῦ BLO

15 φυσιογνώμων P: φυσιογνωμονῶν BLO

P *in margin of fol. 46v has* σημεῖα ἀνδρὸς δολίου, P *fol. 2r has* Περὶ σημείων ἀνδρὸς δολίου

τὰς . . . διεστηκυίας BLO: τοὺς ὀφθαλμοὺς ἀλλήλων διεστηκότας P

καὶ οὗτος P: οὕτω δεῖ καὶ BLO

δεῖ P: δοκεῖ BLO

κατανοεῖν BLO: ὁρᾶν P

16 *heading* P *in margin of fol. 47r and in fol. 2r*

προστυχοῦσα P: περιτυχοῦσα BLO

ἐν τῇ σαρκὶ P: ἐν σαρκίῳ BLO

17 Τί με . . . τε καὶ P: Τί με δεῖ τὸ ζῶ ἀσπάζεσθαι στερηθέντα φίλου φιλτάτου καὶ BLO

Εἶτα . . . στρατηγὸς P: Καὶ αὖθις ὁ δικάζων ἀνακαλεσάμενος παρέστη τῷ δικαστηρίῳ καὶ ἰδὼν αὐτὸν BLO

ἡ τοῦ βασιλέως . . . ἄπειρος P: βασιλέως πολλή τις καὶ ἄπειρος ἦν ἡ μακροθυμία BLO

νικᾷ . . . σου (σοι P) P: ἀνεκδιήγητος ἡ σὴ BLO

καὶ πρὸ BLO: πρὸς P

καταψηφιζόμενον P: ψηφιζόμενον BLO

18 ἐπ' ἀληθείᾳ BLO: τὴν ἀλήθειαν P

τοῖς . . . ἀνδράσιν BLO: τοὺς ἀπαιδεύτους ἄνδρας P

παρὰ τοῦ Θεοῦ P: ἐκείνῳ ἐμβληθῆναι εἰς γέενναν (πυρὸς *added* O) BLO

ἀΐδια BLO: αἰώνια P

πόσῳ P: πῶς οὐ LO, πῶς οὖν B

οἶδε P: θεασαμένῳ BLO

19 *heading* P *in margin of fol. 48r and in fol. 2r*: Περὶ τοῦ ἱερακαρίου, καὶ τῆς γυναικὸς τοῦ κυρίου αὐτοῦ B *fol. 36v*

ἀπεστρέφετο τούτου BLO: οὐκ ἐπιστρέφετο τούτου ὅλως P

συγγινομένην P: συγκυμωμένην BLO

πυλωρῷ P: θυρωρῷ BLO

συνδιαιτᾶσθαι P: συνεσθι(η B)ᾶσαι BLO

εἶτα καὶ αὐτά P: καὶ εἶπον αὐτῷ BLO

παρεστηκὼς BLO: ἑστηκὼς P

after ἰδίαν P *adds* ὡς ἤκουσεν

δόλον P: δολίως BLO

ἐπερωτήσαντες BLO: ἐρωτήσαντες P

ἔχει P: ἐστίν BLO

after λέγοντος P *adds* ἐν ἐκείνοις

20 *heading* P *fol. 2r*: P *in margin of fol. 48v has* ἐγκάθειρξις τρίτη τοῦ Ἰχνηλάτου

τὸν Ἰχνηλάτην P: τοῦ Ἰχνηλάτου BLO

ἀπαιτηθῆναι . . . διεπράξατο BLO: ἀποτίσαι εὐθύνας ὧνπερ ἔπραξεν P

ἀναιρεθῆναι P: ἀποκτανθῆναι BLO

P *in margin of fol. 48v has* ἀναίρεσις Ἰχνηλάτου

Σκοπητέον . . . εἰργάσατο P: Σκεπτέον τοίνυν τῷ τὰ τοιαῦτα ἀναγινώσκοντι, ὅτι ὁ κατορύσσων τῷ πλησίον αὐτοῦ βόθρον, καὶ δόλους αὐτῷ συρράπτων, ἀθρόως τοῖς αὐτοῖς ἐκπεσεῖται· καὶ οὐκ ἐπιγνώσεται πόθεν ἥξει αὐτῷ BLO

after ἐμπεσεῖται P *adds* Τέλος τοῦ δευτέρου τμήματος

Chapter 3

1 *heading* P *in fol. 48v*: λόγος β′ B *in margin of fol. 37r*

Καὶ πάλιν . . . εἶπεν P: Ὁ οὖν βασιλεὺς τῶν Ἰνδῶν ἔφη πάλιν τῷ φιλοσόφῳ αὐτοῦ BLO

τὰ τοιαῦτα P: σου πάντα τὰ BLO

after μοι BLO *add* καὶ ἕτερα

2 *heading* P *in margin of fol. 48v and in fol. 2r*: Περὶ τῶν περιστερῶν B *in margin of fol. 37r*

συχνῶς P: συνεχῶς BLO

ὑψιπέτηλον P: ὑψηλὸν BLO

τραχήλῳ BLO: δακτύλῳ P

θορυβῆσθε P: φοβεῖσθε ἐπὶ τοσοῦτον θορυβούμεναι BLO

ὁμοῦ . . . συνασπισώμεθα P: συναπίπτασθέ μοι BLO

3 Ὅπερ P: Καὶ τοῦτο BLO

μακρόθεν BLO: δὲ P

προήκειν P: προσήκειν BLO

δεῖν ἔγνω ἕψεσθαι P: διέγνω ἀναστῆναι καὶ συνέπεσθαι BLO

ἰδεῖν P: θεάσασθαι BLO

ἁλιεὺς BLO: θηρευτὴς P

ἕπεται ἡμῖν P: οὐκ ἀφίσταται ἀφ᾽ ἡμῶν BLO

πεδίον . . . ἀκολουθεῖν P: πόδας αὐτοῦ διϊπτάμεθα περιγένηται ἡμῖν BLO

τὴν . . . ποιησόμεθα BLO: τρέξομεν P

Πρὸς . . . ἔχω P: Ὑπάρχει δέ μοι καὶ BL, Ὑπάρχει δέ μοι O

κατὰ LO: ὑπὸ P, καταυτὴν B
εἰς τοῦτον P: πρὸς αὐτὸν BLO
βουλὴν . . . καὶ P: πτῆσιν ποιησαμένας καὶ ἀπογνοὺς μετὰ λύπης BLO
4 ἠκολούθησε ταύταις P: συνέπετο αὐταῖς BLO
μαθησόμενος P: μαθεῖν γλιχόμενος BLO
τῷ φωλεῷ αὐτοῦ P: τὴν φωλεὰν τοῦ μυὸς BLO
τὴν περιστερὰν P: ταύτας BLO
Τίς σε . . . περιέπλεξεν P: Ὦ φίλαι, τίς ὑμῖν τὸν τοιοῦτον δόλον συνέρραψεν BLO
Ἡ δὲ ἔφη P: Αἱ δὲ εἶπον BLO
πέπρωται LO: πέπρατε B, πέπρωνται P
με . . . περιέπλεξε P: τοιούτοις τοῖς ἄρκυσι προσέπλεξε BLO
περιπλακῆναι P: τούτῳ περιπεσεῖν BLO
Οὐκ οὖν P: Οὐκ οὖν οὐ δὴ L, Οὐκ οὖν οὐ δὲ BO
τὸ . . . συμπτώματι P: εἰ τοιούτοις περιπεπτώκαμεν BLO
μείζονες . . . περιέπεσον P: ὅτι καὶ μείζονες ὑπὲρ ἡμῶν τοιαῦτα πεπόνθασιν BLO
ὅ τε γὰρ . . . συγκαλύπτεται P: ἥλιος γὰρ καὶ σελήνη τοῦ φωτὸς πρὸς ὥραν στερίσκονται BLO
ἐπισκοτούμενος *AA*: ἐπισκοτουμένη P
Καὶ . . . πολλάκις P: Ἔστιν δ' ὅτε καὶ BLO
δι' αὐτοῦ . . . ἀποτυγχάνει P: καὶ ἀποτυγχάνειν τὸν ἐχέφρονα BLO
5 εἰπούσης τῆς περιστερᾶς P: αἱ περιστεραὶ ἐξειποῦσαι BLO
τοὺς δεσμοὺς . . . περιστερῶν P: ἤρξατο ὁ μῦς κατεσθίειν καὶ λύειν τὰς περιστερὰς ἀπὸ τῶν κειρίων ὧν κατεδέσμηντο, ἡ δὲ προσέχουσα τῶν ἄλλων περιστερῶν ἔφη τῷ μυΐ BLO
πρῶτον . . . ἐμέ P: πρότερον τὰς ὑπ' ἐμὲ περιστερὰς διαλύειν, μετ' αὐτὰς δὲ καμέ BLO
μέμφου *AA*: μέμφω BLO, μέμφη P
μῦ . . . προστάσσω P: φίλε, προστάσσοντί σοι πρότερον ἀπολύειν αὐτάς BLO
δέδωκέ P: πεπίστευκέ BLO
ἐξουσίαν P: προστασίαν BLO
τοῦ θηρευτοῦ BLO: τοὺς θησαυροὺς P

ἠλευθέρωσεν P: ἐρρύσατο BLO
μήπως . . . λύσῃς P: μήποτε λύσας ἐμὲ πρότερον BLO
τινας *AA*: τινα BLOP
ἀνεκλύτους *AA*: ἀνεγκλύτους P, ἀνέκλυτον BLO
ἀναγκασθήσῃ . . . ἀπολύειν P: αἰδεσθῇς τῶν δεσμῶν ἀπολύσεις BLO
6 τότε . . . πραχθέν P: τὸ γεγονὼς BLO
πρόσδυσιν P: ὀπὴν BLO
μῦς εἶπε P: ἐξελθὼν λέγει BLO
σὺ φίλτατε P: καὶ πόθεν μου ἐπὶ τὴν ὀπὴν παραγέγονας BLO
σου τὴν . . . διάθεσιν P: ἣν πρὸς τοὺς φίλους τοὺς σοὺς εἰλικρινῆ διάθεσιν κέκτησαι BLO
ἐπὶ . . . σοι P: διὰ τοῦτο ἦλθον πρός σε BLO
τὰ δυνατά . . . πλοῖον P: μὴ τοῖς ἀδυνάτοις ἐπιχειρεῖν· ἔοικεν ὁ τὰ τοιαῦτα δρῶν ὡς τῷ ἐπὶ τὴν θάλασσαν ἕλκοντι ἅμαξαν, κατὰ δὲ τὴν ξηρὰν πλοῖον BLO
λυσιτελεῖ . . . τραφῆναι P: λυσιτελὲς τραφήσεσθαι διὰ σοῦ BLO
πόσῳ . . . τὸ P: ὀνησιμώτερον δε μοι τῷ BLO
Οὐ P: Ὅθεν καὶ BLO
κενὸν . . . ἐλπίδων P: μὴ τῶν ἐλπίδων κενὸν ἐκπεμφθῆναί με BLO
πεπληροφόρημα . . . ὑπέδειξας P: εἰδότα τὴν πρὸς τοὺς φίλους σου εὔνοιαν, ἀλλὰ νῦν μοι ταύτην ὑπόδειξον BLO
Ἡ . . . ἀρετὴ P: Τῶν γὰρ σπουδαίων ἡ ἀρετὴ BLO
καὶ συγκαλυπτομένη P: κεκαλυπτομένη BLO
7 αὕτη . . . ἐστιν P: ἡ δὲ τοιαύτη διττή BLO
κάττης P: κάτας BLO
οὐ . . . ἐχθροῖς P: οὐδεὶς πιστεύειν ἐχθρῷ πέφυκεν BLO
κἂν . . . θερμανθῇ P: διὰ τοῦ πυρὸς θερμαινόμενον BLO
ἐπεὶ . . . τοῦτο P: ἐκχεόμενον δ' αὐτὸ τῷ πυρὶ τοῦτο σβέννυσι BLO
γενήσεται P: ἔσεται BLO
δυσκέδαστόν P: εὔχρηστόν BLO
8 τινα . . . δεομένων P: τὸν δεόμενον BLO
after οὐκ BLO *add* ἀτιμώρητον ἐάσῃς με. Ὁ δὲ κόραξ εἶπεν· Ἐν τούτῳ ἔχεις εἶπειν ὡς

Εὖρον Sj: εὑρὼν BLOP
βίῳ P: βορίῳ BLO
συνιστῶσι P: καθιστῶσι BLO
φιλοτιμούμενος P: περιποιούμενος BLO
ἐξελεύσεως BP: ἐπεξελεύσεως LO
μετ' ἐμοῦ συμποθήσουσι Pu: μετ' ἐμὲ συμποθήσουσι P, μὲν ἐμὲ ποθοῦσι BLO

9 διαγνωσθῇ P: γνωσθῇ BLO
ἱκανοὶ BLO: πολλοὶ P
ἀφηγήσασθαι BLO: ὑφηγήσασθαι P
περί τινος . . . καταλήψομαι P: ὅτε περὶ τὸν τόπον ἐκεῖνον καταλήψομεν BLO
καταλήψομαι *AA*: καταλείψομαι P, καταλήψομεν BLO
τὴν πηγήν P: τὴν γῆν BLO
τῆς γῆς, ὀνομαστὶ P: τῆν γῆν, ὀνομαστὴν BLO
καὶ . . . ἔφη P: ὁ δὲ κόραξ εἶπε πρὸς τὸν μῦν BLO

10 *heading* P *in margin of fol. 51v and 2r*
after Ὁ δὲ ξένος BLO *add* ἐρωτήσας τὴν αἰτίαν ἀνέμαθεν, ὡς δι' ἐμὲ οἱ κρότοι γίνονται, καὶ εἶπεν· *and omit the text down to* οὕτω καὶ, P *is our only witness to this part*

11 *heading* P *in margin of fol. 52r and in fol. 2r*
παλέστρα *AA*: παλαίστρα P
φανοῦμαι *AA*: φανεροῦμαι P
ὀρύζην Pu: ὀρίδνην P
ἓξ *AA*: ἐξ P
lacuna of BLO *stops at* Οὕτω καὶ ὁ μῦς
ἐρευνήσωμεν P: εὑρήσωμεν BLO

12 Ὑπῆρχον BLO: ἦσαν P
νομίσματα χίλια BLO: χρυσοῦ τάλαντα χίλια P
ὑπεστρώννυον P: ὑπεχώννυον BLO
ὡς τῶν . . . κατατολμᾶν P: πρὸς τὰ τοιαῦτα BLO
ὡς Pu: *omitted* BLOP
ταλάρῳ Pu: σπατάλῳ BLOP *in margin*, ταρτάρῳ P
τῶν ἐδεσμάτων . . . ἠδυνήθην P: ἐν ᾧ τὰ ἐδέσματα ἐτύγχανον οὐκ ἴσχυσα BLO
διὰ τοῦ χρυσίου BLO: δι' αὐτοῦ P

after χρημάτων BLO *add* τὰ πάντα κατορθοῦται
ἐστι γενέσθαι P: γίνεται BLO
πενίην Sj: πενίαν BLOP
φεύγοντα BLO: ἐκφεύγοντα P
13 ὥσπερ BLO: ὅτι P
οὐ δύναται P: ἀδύνατον LO, ἀδυνάτων B
ἐφαμάρτοις P: ἐφ' ἅρματος BLO
λυπηρὸς P: ἀνέκφραστος BLO
εὐφρονεῖ P: ἐγχεφρονεῖ BLO
εὐφρονῶν P: ἐγχεφρονῶν BLO
παρὰ P: πάντα BLO
τὰ αὐτὰ καὶ μεμπτά P: καταμεμφόμενα BLO
φειδωλῶν BLO: ἐξουσιαστῶν P
14 ὑποκρύψαντα BLO: ἀποκρύψαντα P
δεῖν ᾠήθην P: διενοήθην BLO
κατεχόμενον P: κατισχυμένον BLO
τῷ κλάδῳ P: ἄφνω BLO
ἐξερρύη . . . ῥινῶν μου BLO: ἐρρύη μοι ἐκ τῶν ῥινῶν
ὡς . . . μνείαν P: ὥστε μηδὲ BLO
με *AA*: μοι BLO, μου P
Καὶ ἔγνων . . . καὶ ὡς P: Ἔγνων δὲ ὅμως ὡς πάντων αἴτιον τῶν κακῶν τὸ χρυσίον, μᾶλλον δὲ καὶ αὐτῶν τῶν καλῶν. Αἴτιον δὲ καὶ ἡ πλεονεκτικὴ γνώμη ἐστὶ καὶ BLO
λελογισμένος P: ἐλεύθερος BLO
προκειμένου BLO: προσκειμένου P
χρυσοῦ P: χρυσίου BLO
15 ἐκείνῃ P: ἐκείνης B, ἐκείνοις LO
μεγίστη BLO: πρωτίστη P
after ἐν τῷ βίῳ BLO *add* τῶν ἀρκούντων
after φημί BLO *add* τῆς συντόνου εὐχαριστείας
ὑποθώμεθά P: Εἰ γὰρ ὑποθέμεθά BLO
16 ἃ ἐξέφρασας P: ἅπερ ἐξέφθασας BLO
διατηροῦντα P: ποιοῦντα BLO
αὐτοῦ P: αὐτῷ BLO
δυναμένου P: δυνάμενος B, δυναμένης LO
οἴκου πλοῦτον P: περὶ πλούτου BLO

σεβάζεται P: εὐφροσύνας ἕξει BLO
χρυσᾶ BLO: χρυσοῦ P
ὡς ἦσθα *AA*: ὡς ἧς P, ὧν ἧς BLO
φθορᾷ LOP: φθονερᾷ B
τις σφαῖρα P: τὰ τῆς σφαίρας BLO
μετακινουμένη καὶ μεταρριπτουμένη P: μετακυβ(δ B)ευόμενα καὶ μεταρριπτούμενα BLO
νέου φρόνημα P: νέφους σκίασμα BLO
φιλία BLO: ὁμιλία P
πλούτου BLO: τούτου P
Ὡς οὖν ἤκουσεν P: Συνήκουσεν BLO
κρεῖττον BLO: βήου P
ἀντέχεται P: συνέχεται BLO
γε P: ὁ BLO
17 περιεκαλύφθη P: συνεκαλύφθη BLO
καταδύσει τινὶ P: εἰς τὴν κατάδυσιν BLO
ὀλιγοστοῦ BLO: ὀλίγου ἐξ αὐτῶν P
Πανταχόθεν τοίνυν BLO: Καὶ πανταχόθεν P
περιβλέψας P: περιβλεψάμενος BLO
ἐποπτεύεται BLO: ὑποπτεύεται P
after ὑποπτεύεται P *adds* καὶ πρὸς τὴν δορκάδα εἶπεν, ἀναγνωρίσας ὡς οὐδέν τι τῶν θηρίων εἶδεν
καὶ ὁμοζώει P: ἀλλ' ὁμόζει BLO
τροφὴ δαψιλὴς P: χλόης δαψίλεια BLO
συνδιάγειν αὐτοῖς BLO: διάγειν μετ' αὐτῶν P
προσδεχόμενοι BLO: προσδεξάμενοι P
ὡς . . . κατέλαβεν BLO: καὶ ἰδόντες P
ἐστοχάσαντο P: ἔγνωσαν BLO
περιέπεσε P: περιπλακεῖσαν αὐτὴν BLO
ἀναπτὰς BLO: ἀναστὰς P
σχοινίοις BLO: σχοίνοις P
ἄρτι *AA*: αὕτη BLO, *omitted* P
δορκάδος κεῖται σωτηρία P: δορκάδος σωτηρία BLO
18 ᾗ τάχος εἶχε *AA*: ᾗ τάχους εἶχε P, ὡς τάχος ἔχον BLO
αὐτῇ BLO: πρὸς αὐτὴν P
τίς ἂν *AA*: τίς P, τίς ἄν τις BLO

ὁ μετὰ τὴν τῶν φίλων στέρησιν βίος P: ἡ μετὰ τῶν φίλων στέρησις βιωτὴ BLO
διαλεγομένης . . . ἐπῆλθεν P: διαλεγομένων ἐπεισῆλθεν BLO
καὶ ἀποδρᾶσαι (ἀποδρᾶσαν) P: ἐθαύμασε BLO
θαυμάσας P: ἡ δορκὰς ἀπέδρασε. Εὕρων δὲ BLO
19 μῦς ἔφη BLO: κόραξ ἔφη P
ὅτε τις . . . συμπτώματι P: ὅταν τις ἅπαξ προσκόψει, πολλάκις ἀλλ' ἐπαλλήλων προσκόψει πολλάκις BLO
πλούτου P: τοιούτου BLO
after θνητὸν BLO *add* καὶ δεινὸν
δεινοῖς P: κακοῖς BLO
καταβαλλόμενον P: μεταβαλλόμενον BLO
τὸ δῦνον P: τὸν ἥλιον BLO
μου P: ὁμοῦ BLO
τῆς ἐκ πλήξεως ἀλγηδόνος P: ἐκ τῆς πλήξεως ὀδύνης BLO
ἀρχῆς ἀνακαινίζεται P: ἀρχῆς ἀναγκάζεται BLO
20 Ἡ δὲ δορκὰς ὑπολαβοῦσα P: Ὁ δὲ κόραξ ὑπολαβὼν BLO
ἄρτι λύπη P: αὕτη λύπη BLO
δοκιμάζεται BLO: ἑτοιμάζεται P
λήψεσι P: θλίψεσι BLO
P *in margin of fol. 56r has* ὅρα τέρας τοῦ μυὸς
κατεσθίειν BLO: ἐσθίειν P
ἀνάστα καὶ SjP: ἀναστᾶσα BLO
προσταχθὲν P: ἐπιταχθὲν BLO
after ἀντέχονται P *adds* Τέλος τοῦ τρίτου τμήματος
καὶ ὑπὲρ . . . αὐτῶν: *omitted* P

Chapter 4

heading P *fol. 56v*: Λόγος γ' Περὶ τῶν βούφων καὶ τῶν κοράκων, διάλεξις βασιλικὴ πρὸς φιλόσοφον B *fol. 41v* L *fol. 87v*, λόγος γ' O *fol. 97r*
1 Μετὰ . . . ταῦτα ὁ P: Ὁ δὲ BLO
τὴν P: ὅταν BLO
2 *heading* P *in margin of fol. 56v and in fol. 2r*
καταπιστευόμενος P: ἐμπιστευόμενος BLO

γλαυκῶν P: βούφων BLO

ἐν . . . ὑπερμεγέθει P: δένδρον ἦν παμμεγέθες τε καὶ ὑψηλὸν ἐν ᾧ BLO

ὧν ἦρχε P: οὓς εἶχε BLO

Ἦσαν . . . γλαῦκες P: Διέκειτο δὲ αὐτοῦ πλησίον ὄρος ἐν ᾧ βοῦφοι διῆγον BLO

ἀεὶ ἐχθρωδῶς διακείμεναι P: ἀεὶ ὁ ἐχθρωδῶς διέκειτο BLO

ἑτέρους P: οὐκ ὀλίγους BLO

3 γλαυκῶν P: βούφων BLO

πτίλλα ἀπέτιλε BLO: πτερὰ ἔτειλεν P

Ὧν δὴ P: Καὶ τὸ BLO

ὅτι ὅλως . . . θεάσασθε BLO: τὸ κατατολμῆσαι καὶ καταφρονῆσαι. Εἴδετε P

4 *heading* P *in fol. 2r*: περὶ τῶν πέντε πρωτοσυμβούλων τοῦ κόρακος P *in margin of fol. 56v*

next to ἕτερον P *has in margin of fol. 56v* (πρῶτ)ος

μὴ ἐξὸν P: ἐπεὶ οὐκ ἔξεστι BLO

next to ἀντιπαρατάττεσθαι P *has in margin of fol. 56v* (δεύτερ)ος

ἀλλ' ἑτοιμάζεσθαι . . . ἡμῶν P: Ἀλλ' ἑτοιμάσθητε καὶ παρασκευάσθητε ἅπαντες καὶ πρὸς ἀγῶνας χωρήσατε, ὡς ἂν εἴ ποτε οἱ ἐχθροὶ ἐπελεύσονται, συμπλακείημεν τούτοις καὶ φυλαξώμεθα τὸ κατὰ δύναμιν ἑαυτούς, καὶ κωλύσωμεν τὴν τούτων παρείσδυσιν BLO

δόξα P: χάριτι BLO

τὴν . . . τελέσομεν P: διατηρησώμεθα BLO

next to οὗτοι P *has in margin of fol. 57r* (τρίτ)ος

δεδιότες P: φοβούμενοι BLO

5 καὶ οὗτος B: καὶ οὕτως LO, *omitted* P

next to βουλεύῃ ἀλλὰ P *has in margin of fol. 57r* (τέταρτ)ος

στενοῦσθαι P: ὑστερεῖσθαι BLO

ἐφέλκεσθαι P: ἄγειν BLO

ἐκλύει P: διαλύειν BLO

6 *next to* πολεμεῖν P *has in margin of fol. 57r* (πέμπτ)ος

πρὸ τούτου P: τοὺς περὶ τοῦτον BLO

περιφρονεῖ P: παραφρονεῖ BLO

πᾶσαι . . . ἄλλοις P: Ἐν γὰρ ταῖς ἄλλαις περιστάσεσιν BLO

7 τῷ πολεμεῖν *AA*: τὸ πολ. BLOP

συμβούλοις . . . ἐχέφροσιν P: συμβουλεύειν τοὺς ὑπὸ σὲ ἐχέφρονας BLO
βασιλεῖ BLO: βίῳ P
after νουνεχὴς BLO *add* οὐκ ἀγνοεῖ
ἐπὶ . . . βλάβη P: καὶ ὁπόθεν τοῦτο ἐπιγίνεται BLO
ἀγνοεῖ BLO: ἐπάγεται P
ἐπιτηδεύμασι BLO: ἐπιτηδείοις P
καὶ ἑτοιμασίαις Sj: ἑτοιμάσμασιν P, *omitted* BLO
ἀμβολίεργος . . . παλαίει P: ἀνὴρ ἀσύμβουλος καθ' ἑαυτοῦ πολέμιος BLO

8 ἑξαχῶς P: πενταχῶς BLO
τῶν προσκαλουμένων *AA*: τῶν καλουμένων P, τοῦ προσκαλουμένου BLO
ταῦτα συνεργούντων P: ταῦτα ὑπηρετούντων οἱονεὶ ἐνεργούντων BLO, ταύτην ἐνεργούντων οἱονεὶ ὑπηρετούντων Pu
παρὰ τῶν τὰ ἑπόμενα SjPu: περὶ BLOP
καὶ ἐπὶ . . . φρονήματι γέγηθεν Pu (γεγήθη) BLO: *omitted* P
Οὐ δεῖ δὲ P: Δεῖ γὰρ BLO
ὄντα P: εἶναι ἴσως BLO
τοὺς λογισμοὺς περιφρονεῖν P: μὴ κατεπαίρεσθαι ποτε καὶ καταφρονεῖν BLO
προτίθεται ἐκ BLO: προστίθεται διὰ P

9 τοῖς νουνεχέσι P: φρονίμοις BLO
πᾶσι τυγχάνει BLO: πολλοῖς ὑπάρχει P
εἰ μὴ P: μηδὲ BLO
εὐνοοῦντος P: ἀγνοοῦντος BLO
παρά . . . ἡμαρτημένα P: ὑπηκόων ἁμαρτήματα καὶ παραβλέπειν καὶ
παρατρέχει Sj: παρατρέχειν BLO, διατρέχει P
στόματα . . . συνδραμεῖν P: στόματι· δύο ὦτα παρασυνδραμεῖν BLO

10 *heading* P *fol. 2r and in margin of fol. 58v*
Ἀρχὴ . . . ποτε P: Αἴτιον ἀρχῆθεν τῆς μεγάλης μάχης καὶ διενέξεως τοῦτο ἐστίν, ὅτι τὸ τῶν πτηνῶν BLO
πτηνῶν P: τινὰ ὀστᾶ BLO
ταώς τε Sj: τάων τε P, ταοῦ BLO
δυσειδέστατον BLO: δυσῶδες P

ἄστεγκτον BLO: ἄτακτον P

ὃ . . . πάντων χείριστον P: καὶ τῶν ἄλλων χειρίστατον BLO

after πονηρίαν BLO *add* ταῦτα ἀκούσαντα τὰ πτηνὰ παραυτίκα καθεῖλον τὴν τῆς γλαυκὸς ἀρχήν

νουνεχεῖς BLO: ἐὰν νουνεχεῖς ὦσι P

συνέβη . . . ἡμῖν BLO: ἦν τοῦτο P

11 *heading* P *in margin of fol. 58v and in fol. 2r*: Περὶ τοῦ λαγωοῦ καὶ τῶν ἐλεφάντων B *fol. 43r*

The text is given in the P *version. Although both versions provide almost exactly the same meaning, the variant readings are disproportionately frequent to be included in the Notes to the Text. The* BLO *version and its translation are included in the Notes to the Translation.*

δεῖνι *AA*: ὁδεῖνι P

12 ὑποστρέψαι P: ὑποστρέφειν BLO

προσελθόντες P: προσῆλθον BLO

βασιλεῖ αὐτῶν P: πρωτοσυμβούλῳ αὐτῶν καὶ προέχοντι καὶ BLO

ὅσα πεπόνθασι BLO: τὰ πεπονθότα P

τῶν ἐλεφάντων P: αὐτῶν BLO

τοὺς ἐλέφαντας . . . διαλέξομαι BLO: αὐτοὺς πείσω τούτους ἀπελθεῖν ἐκ τοῦ τόπου ἡμῶν· στείλατε οὖν τινας μετ' ἐμοῦ ὅπως ἀκούσωσι τοὺς λόγους μου, οὓς μέλλω εἰπεῖν πρὸς αὐτούς P

βασιλεὺς τῶν λαγωῶν εἶπε P: πρωτοσύμβουλος τούτων ἔφη BLO

οὐ δεῖταί . . . ὁμόφυλον BLO: οὐκ ἔστιν ἡμῖν χρεία τις κατὰ σοῦ τοῦ πέμψαι μάρτυρα· καὶ γὰρ εἶδον τὴν σὴν πρὸς ἡμᾶς P

καὶ λέγε ἃ P: ὃ BLO

προσῆλθεν . . . ἐλέφασι BLO: ἀπῆλθεν ὁ λαγωὸς πρὸς τοὺς ἐλέφαντας P

τινα βουνὸν LO: τι βουνὸν B, τι ὄρος P

13 φωνῇ μεγάλῃ P: μεγίστῃ φωνῇ BLO

ἀβλαβὴς . . . θρασυλογεῖ P: κἂν θρασύλογος πέφυκεν, ἀλλ' ἀπήμαντος διατηρεῖται BLO

το πολεμεῖν . . . ἐπαινετώτερον P: τοὺς ἰσχυροὺς πρὸς τοὺς χθαμαλοὺς καὶ ἀδρανεῖς ἀντιφέρεσθαι. Οὐ μεμπτέον BLO

πεφύκασι BLO: εἰσί P

Καὶ ἀπέκτεινας . . . εἰμι P: Σὺ δὲ ἀποκτείνας αὐτούς, ἠφάνησας καὶ τὰς καταδύσεις αὐτῶν, καὶ ταράξας δὲ καὶ τὸ ὕδωρ αὐτῶν καὶ τεθόλωκας BLO

ἰδοὺ . . . ὑμῶν P: ἤδη καὶ ἐγὼ ἔγνων ὅσα παραλόγως ἐποίησας πρὸς αὐτούς. Διὰ τοῦτο καὶ τοὺς ὀφθαλμοὺς ἡμῶν σβέσω BLO

after ἀποκτενῶ BLO *add* καὶ πρὸς τούτῳ

14 Ἀκούσαντες (ἀκούσας P) . . . ὡς P: Ταῦτα ἀκούσαντες ὅ τε βασιλεὺς καὶ οἱ ἐλέφαντες, οἱ ὄντες σὺν αὐτῷ BLO

ὁ ἐλέφας προσκαλεσάμενος BLO: εὐθὺς καλέσας αὐτὸς P

καὶ ἣν μὴ . . . ἐκτύπωμα BLO: σὺν τῷ ἐκτυπώματι τοῦ φέγγους P

τότε . . . αὐτόν P: ἔφη BLO

κύριέ μου P: κύριόν μου φέγγος BLO

ὅτι . . . ἐνθάδε BLO: οὐ γὰρ ἔρχομαι ἔτι ἐνθάδε P

ὀξυθυμίαν . . . βασιλικοῦ BP: τῆς γλαυκὸς ἀρχήν, καὶ μάλιστα τὴν οἴησιν καὶ ὑπερηφάνειαν, ὥστε διὰ ταῦτα ἐκπεσεῖν τῆς ἀρχῆς L *crossed out in pencil, whereas* BOP *continue with the text that follows down to section 17*, L *inserts it in the margin of fol. 93v*

διὰ τὴν . . . πονηρίαν τῆς γλαυκός P: γλαυκὸς ἀρχὴν BLO

after συμβουλεύσασθαι B *adds* μετ' αὐτῶν, LO μετ' αὐτοῦ

προβάλλοντες O: προσβάλλοντες BLP

πείσονται O: πάθοσιν BL, πάθουσι P

ἠρέσθησαν P: εὑρέθησαν BLO

15 *heading* P *fol. 2r and in margin of fol. 60r*, Περὶ τοῦ λαγωοῦ τοῦ σκιόρου καὶ τοῦ κάτου B *fol. 44v*, L *in the margin of fol. 93v*

Μιᾷ δὲ BO: Μετὰ δέ τινας P

ἐξεδεχόμην P: περιέμηνεν BL, περιέμεινον O

ἐθλίβην περὶ P: ἐθληβόμην παρ' αὐτοῦ BL, ἐθλιβόμην παρ' αὐτῷ O

θεοσεβὴς P: εὐσεβὴς BLO

μὴ ὀργιζόμενός ποτέ P: μὴ γεωργὴν ἐπάγων BLO

16 κάττης OP: κάτος BL

ὑποψιθυρίζων καὶ γονυκλιτῶν BLO: καὶ ὑποψιθυρίζειν καὶ γονυκλιτεῖν P

ἀντιλέγεσθαι P: διαλέγεσθαι BLO

κριτὴς BLO: κάττης P

Ἵνα . . . ἀδελφοὶ P: τὶ ἆδε λέγειν BL, τί ἀδελφοὶ O

Ἀκούσας . . . παραινεῖν P: καὶ αὐτῶς ἤρξατο παραινεῖν B, καὶ αὐτὸς παραινεῖ LO

τυγχάνει P: ἐστι BLO

17 *heading* P *fol. 2r and in margin of fol. 60v*

Ταῦτα ἀκοῦσαν . . . γλαῦκα P: ἀκούσαντα (ἄσαντα BL) δὲ ταῦτα τὰ πτηνὰ καὶ πιστεύσαντες καθεῖλον τὴν τῆς (τοῦ BL) γλαυκὸς ἀρχήν. ταῦτα καὶ πλείονα τοῦ κόρακος παραδειγματίζοντος πρὸς διερέθησιν τῶν πτηνῶν BLO

Οὐ . . . ὡς ἔδρασά P: Οὐκ οἶδα, ὦ κόραξ, δρᾶσαί O, οὐκ οἶδας, ὦ κόραξ, μὴ δρᾶσαί BL

ἵνα . . . ποιήσῃς ἀντέκτισιν P: καὶ οὐκ οἶδ' ὅ τι παθῶν τοιαύτην μοι ἐποιήσω τὴν ἀντέκτισιν BLO

δένδρον BLO: ξύλον P

διὰ P: ἐκ τοῦ BLO

μέσης P: μετ' BL, κατ' O

after δηλητήριον BLO *add* φάρμακον ἑτέροις

ὦ κόραξ . . . μηδέποτε P: κοράκιδες ὡς δένδρον μήδε ποτε BL, *omitted* O

ἀπηλλάγη P: ἀνεχώρησεν BLO

πνέουσα P: γέμουσα BLO

ἐφ' οἷς BLO: καὶ P

κατηναιδεύσατο P: ἠνεσχύντικε κατ' ἐκείνης BLO

Ἔγνων . . . οὖν P: Ἔα μοι ταῦτα, ἀλλ' LO, Ἔα μοι . . . δύνανται *is transferred in* BO *after section 18*

συναινῶ P: συνετά BLO

ἀλλ' ἴσως . . . κατορθῶσαι P: ἀλλὰ διά τινος μηχανῆς ἑτέρας δυνησόμεθα ἐφευρεῖν τὸ συνοῖσον BLO

18 *heading* P *in margin of fol. 61r and in fol. 2r*, Περὶ τοῦ ἀσκητοῦ καὶ τοῦ τράγου καὶ τῶν κλεπτῶν B *fol. 45v*. Ὁ δὲ πρωτοσύμβουλος ὑπολαβὸν πάλιν ἔφη BOL *in margin of fol. 94r*

σύρει (αἴρει P) . . . μιαρόν P: πῶς σύρει τὸν τράγον ὡς κύνα μιαρὸν BLO

ἀσκητήν . . . ἀσεβοῦς P: ἀσκητοῦ ἔργον δι' ἀσεβοῦς BO

ἐκάθητο P: ἐκαθέζετον BLO

ταῦτα . . . ἐπείσθη καὶ P: ἀκούσας καὶ πεισθεὶς τὰ παρ’ αὐτῶν BO

καὶ ἀπελθὼν . . . ἐκαθαρίσθη P: καὶ ἐκαθέζετον ὡς ἀσκητὴς, πλύνας καὶ τὰ ἱμάτια αὐτοῦ ἐν τῷ ποταμῷ καὶ καθαρισθείς (καθαρίσας O) BLO

ἐκδιεξῄειν P: ἐξεῖπον BLO

19 αἰκισμῶν *AA*: ἐκκεντήσεων BLO, αἰκίσεων P

κέδρου P: δένδρου BLO

ἀπᾶραί σε μετὰ τῶν P: σὲ μὲν ἀπᾶραι τῶν ὧδε καὶ τοῖς BLO

ἀπεδήμησε P: ὑπεχώρησε BLO

20 αἱ BLO: οἱ P

προσεγγίσας P: πλησιάσας BLO

οὐκ ἴσημι P: ἀγνοῶ BLO

ἐπίσταμαι P: οἶδα BLO

21 συνέστη P: συνεστήσαντο BLO

after ἕκαστος BLO *add* τὴν οἰκείαν βουλὴν

ὑπὲρ BLO: περὶ P

ὡς ἀδυνατώτεροί ἐστε τῶν γλαυκῶν καὶ ἀσθενέστεροι BLO: ὡς δυνατώτεροί ἐστε τῶν κοράκων καὶ εὐσθενέστεροι P

ἀντιπράττειν αὐτοῖς *AA*: ἀντιπράττειν αὐτούς BLO, ἀντιπαρατάξασθαι πρὸς ὑμᾶς P

ζητῆσαι BLO: ἐπιζητεῖν P

καὶ ἀσπάζεσθαι καὶ στέργειν P: ἀσπάζεσθαί τε ταύτην καὶ στέργειν ἐπ’ αὐτὴν BLO

ὑπώπτευσαν . . . διακείμενος (διακείμενον BLO) φθέγγομαι BLO: ὕποπτόν με ὡς κατά τινα τρόπον εὐνοϊκὸν ὑμῖν τὰ τοιαῦτα διαλέγομαι P

καταδίκῃ ὑπέβαλον P: συμφορᾷ καθυπέβαλον BLO

τοῦ εἰρηνεύειν P: οὐ τὸ εἰρηνεύειν BLO

22 *heading* P *in fol. 2r and in margin of fol. 62r*

Ταῦτα ἀκούσας P: Πρὸς ταῦτα BLO

P *in the margin of fol. 62r has* (πρῶτ)ος

Τάχιον . . . μηχανῶν P: Ἀναιρεθήτω τάχιστα ὁ κατάρατος. Οὐ γάρ ἐστιν ἡμῖν κάλλιόν τι τῆς τούτου ἀναιρέσεως, ἀπαλλαγησομένοις τῶν συμβουλιῶν τούτου καὶ μηχανῶν BLO

ἃς ὑπὲρ P: ὧν ὑπὲρ BLO

συρράπτειν P: συνάπτειν BLO
after παύεται BLO *add* καθ' ἡμῶν δὲ ἐπινοεῖσθαι
ἄλλοτε αὐτοῦ τεύξεται P: ἄλλο τεύξεται τούτων BLO
ἀδυναμίᾳ P: ἐσχάτῃ ἀσθενείᾳ BLO
νέωτα P: νέῳ πολλὰ BLO
ἰσχυροποιούμενον . . . ὁρῶν BLO: μὴ δυναμένου τότε αὐτοῦ P

23 P *in margin of fol. 62r has* (δεύτερ)ος
τῶν . . . πρωτοσυμβούλων P: σύμβουλος BLO
οὐ κατεάξει / οὐ σβέσει: *emended on the basis of the biblical passage*, μὴ κατεάξειν / μὴ σβέσειν BLO, μὴ κατεάξῃς P
ἐλεεῖν . . . οἰκτείρειν BLO: μᾶλλον γὰρ οἰκτείρειν δικαιότατον P

24 *heading* P *in margin of fol. 62v*: Περὶ ἐμπόρου μισουμένου ἀπὸ τῆς γυναικὸς αὐτοῦ P *fol. 2r*, Περὶ τοῦ ἐμπόρου καὶ τῆς γυναικὸς αὐτοῦ καὶ τοῦ κλέπτου B *fol. 47r*, L *in margin of fol. 95v*
ὢν . . . ἔχων P: ὃς εἶχεν BLO
Ἄλλος . . . βασιλέως P: ἕτερος δὲ τῶν συμβούλων (τις σύμβουλος O) αὐτοῦ BLO
τὸν φίλον . . . εὐεργετῆσαι P: αὐτοῦ μαστιχθέντα καὶ βασανισθέντα δι' αὐτόν, χρὴ εὐεργετῆσαι, ὡσαύτως καὶ τὸν ἐχθρόν BLO
μοναχὸς BLO: ἄνθρωπος P

25 *heading* P *in fol. 2r and in margin of fol. 62v*, Περὶ τοῦ μοναχοῦ καὶ τοῦ δέμονος καὶ τοῦ κλέπτου B *fol. 47r*
Εἶτα ἐφάνη P: συνόδευσε δὲ αὐτὸν (αὐτῷ LO) καὶ BLO
ἐκεῖσε . . . μέχρι P: ὁμοῦ ἄχρι BLO
βαλὼν . . . τοῦ BLO: αὐτὸς λαβὼν τὴν δάμαλιν αὐτοῦ εἰσῆλθεν ἐν τῷ οἴκῳ αὐτοῦ τοῦ P
ἀναφωνήσῃ *AA*: ἂν φωνήσῃ BLOP
οὗ πρότερον BLO: ἂν πρῶτον P
οὐχὶ καὶ / ἕως οὗ P: οὐχὶ ἕως οὗ / καὶ B, οὐχὶ ἕως οὗ / ἕως οὗ LO
τῷ μοναχῷ καὶ εἶπεν P: τὸν μοναχὸν λέγων BLO
τῷ μοναχῷ / τῷ μοναχῷ P: τὸν μοναχὸν / τὸν μοναχὸν BLO
ἀφυπνώσας P: γρηγορήσας BLO
ὑμῖν / γνῶτε P: σοι / γνῷς BLO
after ἀσκητὴς BLO *add* Προσέταξεν οὖν ὁ βασιλεὺς δι' αἰδοῦς καὶ τιμῆς ἄγεσθαι τὸν κόρακα

συναινέσας εἶπεν P: προξενήσας ἔφη BLO

Ὦ βασιλεῦ . . . ἀναιρεθήτω P: Ἐπεὶ τοῦτον οὐκ ἀπεκτείνατε, κἂν ἔστω ἐν φυλακῇ, καὶ παρατηρεῖτε αὐτὸν ὡς ἐχθρόν· ὅτι (ὁ B) δεινός ἐστιν ὁ κόραξ καὶ δόλιος καὶ οἶμαι τοῦτον διὰ πανουργίαν καὶ ἀπάτην ἐνταῦθα παραγενέσθαι BLO, *which is inserted by* P *below at the beginning of section 27*

πιστεύων BLO: προσέχων P

26 *heading* P *in margin of fol. 63v and in fol. 2v*, Περὶ τοῦ τέκτονος καὶ τῆς γυναικὸς αὐτοῦ μετὰ τοῦ μιχοῦ B *fol. 47v*, L *preserves this fable in the margin of folios 95v and 96r*

αὐτῷ τὰ P: τῷ ἀνδρὶ αὐτῆς BO, τὸν ἄνδρα αὐτῆς L

δεῖνι P: ὀδύνη BL, ὁδεῖνι O

Κλεῖσαι (κλύσαι P) τὴν θύραν P: ἀσφάλισαι τὸν οἶκον σου BO, ἀσφάλησον L

τὸν οἶκον . . . ἐλεύσεώς μου P: αὐτὸν ἕως οὗ ὑποστρέψω BLO (ἐπιστρέψω O)

Ἐκείνων . . . συγγινομένων *AA*: ἐκεῖνοι δὲ κοιμώμενοι καὶ συγγινόμενοι P, *omitted* BLO

Ὁ δὲ . . . αὐτήν P: ὁ δὲ ἠρότησεν αὐτὴν μεγάλῃ τῇ (τῇ *omitted* O) φωνῇ BLO

ἡ δὲ . . . περὶ P: ἡ δὲ εἶπεν αὐτῷ· καὶ τίς ἡ χρεία BLO

τέκνων P: φίλων BLO

κόπος . . . ἐστι BLO: σκοπὸς αὐτῶν καὶ μόχθος οὐδέν ἐστι P

ὄντως ἀληθῶς P: οὗτος εἶ ἀληθὸς B, οὑτωσῖ ἀληθῶς, O, οὗ η L

ῥιπιστηρίου P: ῥιπιδίου BLO

θέρος O: θέρμη P, θερμὸς B, θερμὸν L

Καὶ ἐξυπνισθείσης αὐτῆς / πρὸς αὐτὴν P: ἐξυπνισθεῖσα δὲ αὐτῇ / αὐτῇ (*omitted* L) BL, ἐξυπνήσασα δὲ αὐτή / αὐτῆς O

27 τοῦ πρώτου συμβούλου P: αὐτὸν BLO

διὰ . . . ἄγεσθαι P: μετὰ τιμῆς καὶ αἰδοῦς (ἔδει BL) εἶναι BLO

Ὁ δὲ τὴν ἀναίρεσιν . . . παραγενέσθαι P: BLO *place this passage above in the end of section 25*

συναινέσας P: προξενήσας BLO

παραφυλακῇ P: φυλακῇ BLO

διαγέτω παρ' ἡμῶν P: παρατηρεῖτε αὐτὸν BLO

παραγενέσθαι BLO: παρεμβαλεῖν P

ἀφειδῶς P: ἐκφειδῶς BLO

οὖν . . . τι P: δὲ καὶ αὐτὸς τοῦτο BLO
καταδυσωπῆσαι / μεταβαλεῖν BLO: ἀξιῶσαι / μετατρέψαι P
τούτους P: τοὺς κόρακας BLO
προτρεψάμενος ἔφη BLO: συμβουλευσάμενος εἶπεν P
<οὗ> *added AA*
διαθήσομεν P: ποιήσομεν BLO
from ἀλλ' εἰς τὸ ἀρχαῖον L *continues with the text written in the margin of fol. 96r–v*
τῷ μυῒ τῷ ὁμογενεῖ BL: τὸν μῦν τὸν ὁμοιογενῆ P, μετὰ τοῦ ὁμογενοῦς O
πῶς ἦν / πρωτοσύμβουλος αὐτοῦ P: πῶς ἔστι / γλαὺξ BLO

28 *heading* P *in margin of fol. 64v and in fol. 2v*: Περὶ τοῦ μυὸς καὶ τοῦ μοναχοῦ B *fol. 48v*; L *preserves this fable in the margin of folios 96r and 96v*
νίβλα P: ἐνίβλα P *fol. 20v*, νύβλα B, νήβλα LO
αὐτὴν *AA*: αὐτὸν BLOP
ἀπῆλθεν P: ἀνῆλθεν BLO
Ζεῦξαί μοι ὅνπερ P: ζεῦξον μοι εἰ BLO
τὸ P: μικρὸν BLO
Ἐλθὼν δὲ . . . ᾐτήσατο P: ὁ δὲ μοναχὸς ἦλθεν εἰς τὸ νέφος καὶ εἶπεν αὐτῷ BLO
ᾐτήσατο καὶ αὐτὸ P: εἶπεν αὐτῷ BO
ὅσα εἶδε . . . λεχθέντα P: ὅσα ἤκουσε BO

29 *heading* P *fol. 2v*: φυγὴ τοῦ κόρακος P *in margin of fol. 65v*
Ὁ δὲ κόραξ . . . αὐτῶν P: Καὶ ἦν ὁ κόραξ ἔκτοτε κατανοῶν καὶ περισκοπῶν κατὰ τῶν γλαυκῶν ἅπαντα BLO
τούτῳ P: αὐτοῦ τὰ BLO
ἀπέδρα BLO: διέδρασε P
ἡγεμόνι BLO: βασιλεῖ P
καλῇ . . . ἀρχῇ BLO: καταρχῇ ἐπιθεῖναι P
ἀναλαβέτω οὖν P: ἀλλὰ λαβέτω BLO
διαφυσήσωμεν P: ἀναφυσήσωμεν BLO
ἀέριον P: ἀνέριον BLO
ἀπεργάζεσθαι P: γενέσθαι BLO
ἔξωθεν . . . κακιγκάκως P: ἐξερχόμεναι παρ' ἡμῶν θανατωθήσονται BLO

CHAPTER 4

heading P *in fol. 2v* Περὶ τῆς ἀναιρέσεως τῶν γλαυκῶν παρὰ τῶν κοράκων, *and in margin of fol. 65v* ἀναίρεσις τῶν γλαυκῶν

30 Πῶς . . . πονηρίας P: Καὶ πῶς ἠνέσχου τὴν τῶν γλαυκῶν πονηρίαν καὶ μοχθηρίαν ὁρᾶν BLO

δεινοῖς περιπεσὼν P: ὅταν δεῖ τινι περιπεσεῖν BL, ὅταν δ' εἴ τινι περιπεσεῖν O

εὐτελέσιν P: ἐχθροῖς καὶ ὑπόκειται BLO

συνετωτέραν . . . λοιπαὶ P: συνετόν τινα ἄλλον ἢ τὸν τὴν ἐμὴν ἀναίρεσιν ἐπισπεύδοντα, καὶ ὁ μὲν τοῦτο συμβουλευσάμενος ἐπαινετός μοι δοκεῖ· οἱ δὲ λοιποὶ BLO

οἰκείαις . . . πλησιάσαι P: μυστικαῖς αὐτῶν πλησιάζειν γραφαῖς BLO

τῷ ὕδατι P: τοῦ ὕδατος ἅπτεσθαι BLO

μύροις P: δώροις BLO

Ἀλλ' οὐδὲ . . . νικᾶν P: Τέως δὲ ἀνέκδετον ἦν ἵνα νικήσωσιν ἡμᾶς οἱ ἐχθροί, ἀλαζόνες ὄντες καὶ ὑπερήφανοι BLO

συνιστᾷ τρόπαιον P: εἰς τὰ τρόπαια BLO

καὶ σπανίως ἀδηφάγος μέχρι P: ὅτι καὶ ὁ ἀδηφάγος οὐ μέχρι BLO

Καὶ οὐ P: ὁ δὲ BLO

τῆς ἀπωλείας σῴζεται P: τὸ ἐναντίον ἀποφεύγει BLO

ἵνα τύχω τοιούτου κατορθώματος P: τοῦ τοιούτου κατορθώματος ἐπιτύχοιμι BLO

31 *heading* P *in margin of fol. 66r and in fol. 2v*: Περὶ τοῦ ὄφεως καὶ τῶν βατράχων B *fol. 50r*

τῶν ἀσκητῶν P: πάντως BLO

πρὸς ὑμᾶς P: γενναῖόν τι ποιεῖν BLO

ὑμῶν P: τῶν βατράχων BLO

τὸ τοιοῦτον τέλος P: τὸ τοιούτου τυχεῖν τέλους BLO

32 δι' ἀντερίσεως P: ἐριστικῆς καὶ μαχίμου BLO

τὰ ὑπὲρ γῆν P: τὰ ὑπὸ γῆν BLO

Λέγεται . . . ὡς P: καὶ BLO

after δεῖ BLO *add* τινι

καὶ εἰ . . . εἰσι P: καὶ τὸ ἐλάχιστον BLO

Ὅσα . . . εὐτυχίας P: τὰ κατορθώματα ἃ γέγονεν BLO

after βασιλεῦ BLO *add* πάντως διὰ τῆς εὐτυχίας γεγόνασιν

τεύξεται BLP: τοξεύεται O

33 ἀνηνύτοις BLO: ἀνοήτοις P

καὶ ἡ ὕπνου καὶ τροφῆς ἡδονὴ διὰ σοῦ προσεπορίσθη ἡμῖν P: ἤγουν τὸ ἡδέως ὑπνεῖν καὶ τρυφῆς γλυκείας μεταλαμβάνειν BLO

after ἀποτιθεὶς BLO *add* ἔκ τινος

τῆς τῶν . . . ἐπιβουλῆς (βουλῆς B) BLO: τῆς ἐξ ἐχθροῦ βλάβης ἀπαλλαγείς P

συναινέσαντος P: συνεργήσαντος BLO

Ὁ δὲ βασιλεὺς . . . ἔμπλεως L *in margin of fol. 99r*

οὕτω μεγάλως P: ὅτι οὕτως (οὗτος B) BLO

ὀξὺς εἰς τὸ BLO: καὶ P

ἁπάντων γνωστικότατος P: πάντων δὲ λογιώτατος BLO

after πείσονται P *adds* τέλος τοῦ (τετάρ)του τμήματος

Chapter 5

heading P *fol. 67r*: Περὶ τῶν πιθήκων λόγος τέταρτος B *fol. 50v*, λόγος δ' O *fol. 117v*

2 *heading* P *in margin of fol. 67r and in fol. 2v*

λόγος LO: γὰρ B, *omitted* P

ἐξεδίωξαν P: κατεβίβασαν BLO

ἐξέχουσαν P: προκύπτουσαν οἰκεῖν BLO

τὸν καρπὸν P: ἐκ τῶν καρπῶν BLO

ἀρρενικὴ BLO: ἀγρία P

ἦν P: ἡ BLO

μηχανὴν / δι' ἧς BLO: πόρον / δι' οὗ P

3 Μιᾷ . . . χελώνη P: Καὶ ποτὲ ὁ ἄρρηκτος BLO

ἐπανιοῦσα P: ἀπιὼν BLO

σύζυγον εὑροῦσα P: τὴν χελώνην εὑρὼν BLO

νοσεράν P: πάνυ σερράν BL, πάνυ σειριᾶν O

μὴ BLO: μήπως τύχω P

ἀπορήσας . . . δυσχέρειαν P: ἀκούσας, διηπόρει καθ' ἑαυτὸν διαλογιζόμενος ὡς τὸ πρᾶγμα δυσχερές ἐστι, καὶ τὸ ζητούμενον δυσεύρετον BLO

εἰ μή γε P: ἢ BLO

ἑταίρου αὐτοῦ P: φίλου πίθηκος BLO

Τοῦτο δὲ παράβασιν . . . λογισμοῖς BLO: ὃ καὶ παράβασιν εἶναι διανοούμενος παντοίων ἐγένετο λογισμῶν P

4 προσηγόρευσεν BLO: ἐφώνησεν P

πίθηξ (πίθηκος P) τὴν χελώνην P: τοῦτον BLO

ὑστέρησεν *AA*: ὑστέρησα P, ὑστέρημα BLO

ἐργάσασθαι LO: ἐργάζεσθαι P, ἐργάσθαι B

εἰμι ὥστε BLO: οἷος P

τοιούτοις . . . μέγιστα BLO: ἔκπτωτον P

πεπτωκότα BL: περιπεπτοκότα O

5 ἀκραιφνῆ φιλίαν P: κοινωνίαν BLO

6 πεισθεὶς BLO: δησθεὶς P

ἔστη BLO: ἔτι P

ἐβουλεύσατο BLO: ἐλογίσατο P

ἀλλ' BLO: τοῦ P

τε τῶν λόγων αὐτῶν καὶ P: τε λόγων καὶ BLO

φίλη BLO: χελώνη P

τῆς μερίμνης BLO: τοιαύτης μερίμνης P

7 καταλαβὼν SjPu: καταλαβοῦσα BLO, καταλαβεῖν P

ἐντύχῃς BLOPu: ἐντυχεῖν P

κλινοπετὴς P: κλινοπετὸς BLO

ὁμευνέτις P: εὐμενέτης BLO

ἐστι BLO: ὑπάρχει P

8 λόγον P: σκοπὸν BLO

τὸ τοιοῦτον P: τοῦτο BLO

ἢ . . . οἰκίαν BLO: τὰ οἰκεῖα P

ἀπίωμεν *AA*: ἐπίωμεν P, ἀπέλθωμεν BLO

after ὁ δὲ P *adds* πίθηκος

ἵν' ἀπέλθωμεν οἴκαδε BLO: ἵνα οἴκαδε ἀπελευσώμεθα P

καὶ ἔνεγκε P: ἕνεκεν δὲ BL, ἔνεγκε δὲ O

καὶ πλανηθῶ . . . ἀλώπεκος BL *in margin of fol. 101v* P: ὄντως καρδίαν τέλεον οὐκ εὐπορήσω . . . ἀποτυγχάνουσιν BL (ὄντως . . . εὐπορήσω *omitted* O)

9 *heading* P *in margin of fol. 69v and in fol. 2v*, Περὶ τοῦ ὄνου καὶ τῆς ἀλόπεκος καὶ τοῦ λέοντος B *fol. 51v*

τινι τόπῳ P: δάσει τινὶ BLO

Ἡ δὲ . . . αὐτῷ P: ἐν μιᾷ οὖν τῶν ἡμερῶν ἔφη αὐτῷ ἡ ἀλώπηξ BLO

τοῦ ποιῆσαι P: εἰς τὸ (ὥστε BL) ποιῆσαί σοι BLO

ἀπέρχομαι P: ἀπέλθω BLO

ἕξεις παρ' ἐμοῦ BLO: παρέξεις P

στυγνὸν καὶ πεπτωχευμένον P: πτωχὸν καὶ πεπληγμένον BLO

φορτοῖ με βαρέως P: βαρειφορτείη με BLO

ὄνος / δ' ἂν P: ἔφη / γὰρ BLO

ἐκεῖ P: καὶ BLO

νεμομένη BLO: δεδεμένη P

καὶ ἔσῃ P: ἔσῃ δὲ καὶ σὺ BLO

10 αὐτῇ . . . λέοντος P: ἐκεῖ BL, τῇ ἀλώπεκι O

ἐπεπήδησε P: ἐπήδησε BLO

διὰ δὲ τὴν ἀδυναμιαν . . . {11} κατ' αὐτοῦ: *omitted* O

ἀπέλυσας αὐτόν B: ἐποίησας οὕτως P

τῆς ζωῆς *AA*: τὴν ζωὴν BLP

11 Δι' ἥντινα αἰτίαν P: διατί BL

ἐκείνης *AA*: ἐκείνη BLP

μελλούσης *AA*: μέλλουσα BLP

ἤγγισεν . . . Ἐκπηδήσας P: ἐγγείσασα οὖν πάλιν τὸ λέοντι, ἐπίδησε BL

ἕως οὗ ἀπελθὼν πρὸς τὴν πηγὴν P: ἕως ἂν ἀπέλθω πρὸς τὴν πηγὴν καὶ BL, ἕως ἂν ἀπέλθω ἐν τῇ πηγῇ καὶ O

ἐξελθόντος . . . τοῦ λέοντος *AA*: ἐξελθὼν . . . ὁ λέων BLOP

ἂν ἐστρέφετο P: ἀνεστρέφετο πάλιν BLO

after ἀποτυγχάνουσιν P *has* Τέλος τοῦ πέμπτου τμήματος

Chapter 6

heading P *fol. 70*: λόγος πέμπτος B *fol. 52v* O *fol. 121v*

1 τίνι BLO: περὶ τοῦ τίνος P

2 *heading* B *fol. 52v*

τέκνου αὐτοῦ *AA*, τιαύτου B

Λέγεται γάρ B: Λέγεται δέ O, Λέγεται LP

after συζῶν P *adds* ποτε δὲ καιροῦ

ἄρρην παῖς *AA*: ἄρρεν παιδίον BL, ἄρρεν παιδίον O, ἄρρεν παῖς P

Ἡδὺς γὰρ εἶ τὰ P: Οὐδεὶς γάρ ἐστιν BLO

τῶν ἀδήλων P: τοιούτων BLO

3 *heading* P *in margin of fol. 70v and in fol. 2v*

τὸ τοιοῦτον P: τῷ τοιούτῳ BLO

ἑτέρας P: ἄλλας BLO

ἐνιαυτῶν P: ἐτῶν BLO

τετρακοσίας P: διακοσίας BLO

σπείρω P: κατασπείρω BLO

ῥυδὸν P: ῥοιζηδὸν BLO

4 ἀπόντοιν *AA*: ἀπόντες BLO, ἀποδημεῖν P

ἐπεισπηδήσασα BLO: ἐπιπηδήσασα P

after σφάλλονται P *has* Τέλος τοῦ ἕκτου τμήματος

ὡς μὴ ἀνεχόμενοι: *omitted* P

Chapter 7

heading P *fol. 71r*: Λόγος ἕκτος B *fol. 53r* O *fol. 123r*

1 Πάλιν . . . ἐφθέγξατο P: Ὁ δὲ βασιλεὺς εἶπε BLO

τῇ ἀνεξικάκῳ γνώμῃ P: ἐν τῇ ἀρχῇ BLO

τῇ ἀγαθῇ P: ἐν τῇ ἀγαθωτάτῃ BLO

2 συνετῶν LO: ἀγαθῶν καὶ P

σύνεσις LO: φρόνησις P

3 *heading* B *fol. 53r*

οὗτος ὁ P: τις BLO

4 *heading* P *fol. 3v*, ὅρα τὴν τῶν φιλοσόφων μηχανουργίαν P *in margin of fol. 71r*

ὅτου ὁ δεινὸς οὗτος BLO: ὅτε οὗτος ὁ P

ἵνα P: ὡς δὴ BLO

after πρωτοσύμβουλον BLO *add* αὐτοῦ, καὶ τὸν πρωτονοτάριον

σου P: αὐτοῦ BLO

σε P: τοῦτον BLO

καὶ ἀναρρύσομεν P: ὡς δῆθεν ἀναρρυσσόμενοι τούτων BLO

ἐπισυμβαίνειν ἀνιαρῶν P: ἐπισυμβῆναι δεινῶν BLO

5 τάδε . . . ταῦτα P: ὡς οὐκ ἔστι πόρος ἕτερος σωτηρίας πλὴν διὰ τοῦ ποιῆσαι τάδε καὶ τάδε BLO

7 ὑποσχεῖν P: ὑπερβολὴν καὶ BLO

τὸ τοιοῦτον . . . σου PL *(correction in margin)*: μυστήριον τῇ σῇ εὐνοούσῃ BLO

πιστεῦσαι / ἀναιρῆσαι BLO: πιστεύσῃς / ἀναιρήσῃς P

τοῖς Sj: τῶν P, τοὺς BLO

εὐνοηταῖς P: εὐνοϊκῶς διακειμένους BLO

ἐπιλαθέσθαι P: ἐπιλαβέσθαι BLO

πείθῃ Sj: πείθει BLO, πείθεις P

8 *heading* P *fol. 2v*: ἐξήγησις τῶν ὀνείρων τοῦ βασιλέως παρὰ τοῦ ἀσκητοῦ P *in margin of fol. 72v*

τῶν πολυτίμων ἐπαγόμενος P: πολυτίμους (τιμίους *correction in margin* L) ἐπαγόμενοι BLO

πρέσβυς / ἐπιφερόμενος P: πρέσβεις / σοι ἐπικομιζόμενοι BLO

ἀποπλύνεσθαί P: ἀπολουθῆναι BLO

ἐπιστροφὴν (ἀπο P) . . . προσώπου P: καὶ ἐπιστροφὴν πρὸς ποθουμένου ἀνθρώπου πρόσωπον BLO

ταύτην BLO: τὴν ἑβδόμην BLO

9 λόγους τῶν φιλτάτων P: τοὺς λόγους οὓς φιλεῖ καὶ παρ' ὧν φιλεῖται B

δικαιότεροι . . . προσήκοντες P: δικαιότερον γὰρ ταῦτα τοῖς κατὰ γένος προσήκουσί σοι δοθῆναι

ὦ Παλάριε· τοῦτο γὰρ ὄνομα αὐτῷ BL *(in margin)* O: *omitted* P

καὶ δέδωκε . . . αὐτοῦ P: τῷ δὲ υἱῷ αὐτοῦ δέδωκε BLO

φέρειν P: ἀγαγέσθαι αὐτὰ BLO

after γυναῖκας P *adds* ἦν δὲ τῷ πρωτοσυμβούλῳ ὄνομα Παλλάριος

φιλτάτη P: μία BLO

10 εἶπε πρὸς τὴν Πελάδα τὴν σύμβουλον Pu: εἶπε πρὸς τὸν πρωτοσύμβουλον P, καὶ εἶπε πρὸς τὴν Παλάδα B, *omitted* LO

ἐπίλεξαι (ἕνα B) / ὃ προαιρῇ P: ἐπήλεξον ἕνα/ ὃν προήρησε B, *omitted* LO

προαιρεῖται P: προέληται BLO

τῇ γυναικὶ . . . ἱματισμοῦ BLO: πόρρω νεύοντα τοῦτον περὶ τοῦ λαβεῖν τὸν ἱματισμόν P

ἔκλινεν P: οὐκ ἔκλινεν BLO

ἵνα . . . τοιοῦτον BLO: ὥστε γνῶναι τὸν βασιλέα πάθος ἔχειν τὸν ὀφθαλμὸν τοιόνδε P

11 ὄρυζαν P: ὀρύζιον BLO

next to ἔρριψε P *has* ὅρα τόλμην βασιλίδος *in margin which corresponds to the heading* Περὶ τῆς τόλμης τῆς βασιλίδος κατὰ τοῦ βασιλέως *in* P *fol. 2v*

13 *heading* P *in margin of fol. 74r*, Περὶ τῶν δύο περιστερῶν B *fol. 55v*, περὶ περιστερῶν P *fol. 2v*

τὴν οἰκείαν . . . φωλεὰν BLO: τὸν οἰκεῖον . . . φωλεὸν P

συνεῖδον P: συνειδοῦσα BLO

ἀπογεύσασθαι ἐκεῖνοι P: ἅψασθαι BLO

πρὶν ἢ P: ἕως ἂν BLO

ἐπιλεῖψαι P: ἀπολεῖψαι BLO

μικρὰν ὄγκωσιν BL: μακρὰν ὄγκωσιν O, μικρὸν ὄγκον P

ἰδοῦσα . . . ὑπείληφε P: ἰδὼν ὁ ἄρρην ὑπέλαβε BLO

καταλαβόντος P: ἐπιγενομένου BLO

14 *heading* P *in margin of fol. 74r and in fol. 2v*: Περὶ τοῦ ἀνθρώπου τοῦ βαστάζοντος τὴν φακὴν καὶ τοῦ πίθηκος B *fol. 55v*

Ἐρρέθη . . . οἱ λοιποί L *preserved in the lower margin of fol. 107r, almost illegible*

after μικρὸν BLO *add* ἐκ τῆς ὁδοιπορίας

φακὸς P: κόκος BL

τὸ ταύταις ἐφήδεσθαι B: τὸ ταύτας ἐφήδεσθαι L τοσαύτας ἐφήδεσθαι O, τοσαύταις φείδεσθαι P

15 *The text from* ἔφη περίλυπος *down to* δικαστηρίῳ *is preserved in* L *in the margin of fol. 107v.*

τοῦ νουνεχοῦς ὁ εἷς λόγος ἀμετάτρεπτος P: τοῦ μὴ ἀνεχοὺς ὁ εἷς λόγος ἀμετάτρεπτος L

after λυπεῖσθαι BL *add* τὸν πόρνον καὶ

Πελάδα P: Παλ(λ)άδα BLO *throughout sections 15–17*

ἄνδρας P: ἀνθρώπους BLO

πονηρὸν ἐκ τοῦ ἀγαθοῦ P: καλὸν ἐκ τοῦ πονηροῦ BLO

ἐστερημένοι P: ὑστερούμενοι BLO

ἄνευ ἀνδρὸς *AA*: ἄνανδρος BLO, ἄνυδρος P

τὸ ἀγαθὸν . . . πονηροῦ P: τὸ καλὸν καὶ τὸ πονηρόν BLO

μὴ ἴδια P: ἴδια BLO

16 *The text of this paragraph is preserved in L in the margin of fol. 107v.*

ἔσαλσας P *(it is a hapax)*: ἐσέλησας BL, ἐσέλλισας O

ἐγχειρίσας P: ἔχων BLO

φόβος BLO: ἀφοβία P

ἐκκοπῇ . . . γῆς P: ἐκλείψει ἡ γῆ BLO

τὴν ὡραιότητα . . . κάλλος P: τοῦ κάλους BLO

εἶδον BLO: ἴδω P

ἐθισθεῖσα P: ἐστήσα BLO

ἕνα . . . μυκτηριζομένη P: ἕνα παρ' ἕνα παριδίως μυκτηρίζουσα BLO

ἐθίσας *AA*: εἰθίσας P, ἠθήσας BLO

after ὁ δὲ βασιλεύς BLO *add* ἔφη τῷ Παλαρίῳ (Παλαρεῖ LO)

γαλῆ P: κάτα BL, κάττης O

L *stops after* ὁ γλαῦξ

τῆς φιλίας ἐκπέσωσιν BO: πέσωσιν εἰς φιλίαν P

17 κείμενος B: κοιμώμενος PO

φειδόμενος . . . πτωχείας P: ὁ φοβούμενος πτωχείαν B, ὁ φοβούμενος πτωχῆσαι O

δύναμαι BO: δεῖ με P

after ἀδελφὸν αὐτοῦ BLO *add*: καὶ ὁ βασιλεὺς περίλυπος γεγονὼς μήποτε τὴν γυναῖκα ἀνήρηκε καὶ πρὸς αὐτὸν εἶπεν· οὕτως δι' ἑνὸς ῥήματος τὸ τοιοῦτον ἔδρασας; ὁ δέ φησι· τοῦ μὴ ἀνεχοῦς ὁ εἷς λόγος ἀμετάτρεπτος, *which is part of section 15*

τοὺς δὲ φιλοσόφους . . . ἀπέκτεινεν *marginal addition* L, P *has in margin of fol. 76r* ἀναίρεσις τῶν φιλοσόφων *and in fol. 2v* Περὶ τῆς ἀναιρέσεως τῶν φιλοσόφων

τοὺς μεριμνήσαντας . . . θάνατον BLO: οἳ εἰς αὐτὸν τὴν μνησικακίαν ἐμερίμνησαν P

after ἀσάλευτον P *adds* Τέλος τοῦ ἑβδόμου τμήματος

Chapter 8

heading P, λόγος ἕβδομος B *fol. 57r*, O *fol. 131v*

1 ἔγνων δὴ P: ἐπέγνων σου LO, ἔγνων B

λυτροῦνται P: λυτροῦσθαι O, τηροῦνται BL

ὠφέλειαν BLO: φιλίαν P

ἐξετάζει P: ἐξαγοράζει BLO

γαλῆ P: κάτα B, κάττης LO

2 *heading* P *in margin of fol. 76v and fol. 2v*, περὶ τοῦ μυὸς καὶ τῆς κάτας B *fol. 57r*

τόπῳ P: χώρᾳ BLO

ὀπὴ γαλῆς P: ἣν κάτας BL, (κάττου) O ὀπή BLO (κάτα *throughout this chapter* BL, κάττης O)

κατάδυσιν P: ὀπήν BLO

δεξιᾷ ἢ ἀριστερᾷ P: δέδοικα μήπως LO, δια ἤ αρα B

γαλῆν / ὑπ' αὐτῆς P: κάταν / παρ' αὐτῆς BL, κάττην / παρ' αὐτοῦ O

πόρον . . . ἕτερον P: πόρον τῆς ἐμῆς σωτηρίας BLO

τῆς τῆς γαλῆς φιλίας *AA*: τὴν τῆς γαλῆς φιλίαν P, διὰ τὴν τῆς κάτας φιλίαν BL, διὰ τὴν τῆς τοῦ κάττου φιλίας O

ὑπάρχει P: εὑρίσκεται BLO

ἕξω P: εὑρήσω BLO

3 κἀγὼ . . . γέγονα P: συσκηνῶσαι σοι ἄρτι παραγέγονα BLO

εἰσιν P: πεφύκασιν BLO

καὶ λυτρώσω σε πάντως P: λυτρώσομαί σε BLO

ταῦτα . . . γαλῆ / ἐγένετο P: ἀκούσας δὲ ἡ κάτα (ὁ κάττης O) / γέγονε BLO

4 Καὶ τότε P: οὖν BLO

αὐτὴν P: τὴν κάτα BL, τὸν κάττην O

καὶ ἐὰν . . . συνίσταται P: εἰ δὲ καὶ μεθίσταται, οὐ συνίσταται καὶ LO, μᾶλλον δὲ καὶ σινήσταται, εἰ δὲ καὶ μεθίσταται οὐ σινήσταται καὶ B

πληροῦσθαι P: ποιῆσθαι BLO

ἔφυγεν P: δρομαῖος εἰς τὴν κατάδυσιν αὐτοῦ ἐπεισῆλθεν BLO

τοῦ θηρευτοῦ P: αὐτοῦ BLO

5 τὴν γαλῆν / αὐτῆς P: τὴν κάταν / αὐτήν BL, τὸν κάττην / αὐτόν O

δυνατωτέρῳ P: δυνατῷ BLO

after πάντοτε P *adds* τέλος τοῦ ὀγδόου τμήματος

Chapter 9

The last chapters are exlusively based on P *with few additions from* Pu. *For the* BLO *version of this chapter, see Notes to the Translation.*

heading P *in margin of fol. 78r and in fol. 2v*

4 ἀποχῇ *AA*: ἀπαρχῇ P

τὰς δ' ὁμευνέτιδας *AA*: τοὺς δ' ὁμευνέτιδας

μαρτυρεῖ σῇ *AA*: μαρτυρούσῃ P

5 καρδίᾳ Pu; κακίᾳ P

ἀπαλεῖψαι Pu: ἀπολεῖψαι P

ἐχόμενον *AA*: ἐρχόμενον P

6 τοῦ ὠφελεῖν Pu: τῷ ὠφελεῖν P

γίνεται *AA*: γίνετο P

7 τὸ συνέπεσθαί *AA*: τῷ συνέπαισθαί P

8 μνημονεύει *AA*: μνημονεύειν P

ἀντωπήσει *AA*: ἐν τῷ πίσειν P

<ὁ> *added AA*

ὃς οὐ πτοεῖται ἀθώους *AA*: ὃς πτοεῖται ἀθώους Pu: οὐ ποιεῖται ἀθῶος P

BLO version

2 *heading* Περὶ τῆς κίσσης καὶ τοῦ βασιλεώς B

ἤνεγκε Sj: ἐνέγγασα B, ἐνέγκασα LO, Pu *worded differently*

3 τοῖς βασιλεῦσιν Sj: μετὰ βασιλέων BLO, Pu *worded differently*

πρὸς ἑαυτήν *AA*: πρὸς αὐτήν BLO, Pu *worded differently*

5 συγγενεῖς δανειστὰς καὶ Sj: συγγενεῖς καὶ BLO, Pu *worded differently*

παρ' ὑμῶν Sj: τὴν παρ' ὑμῶν BLO

ἐν ὄρεσι καὶ τόποις δυσβάτοις BO: *added in* L *in later hand*

Chapter 10

heading P *fol. 80v*

2 *heading* P *in margin of fol. 80v and in fol. 2v*

ὃν *AA*: ᾧ P

3 *heading* P *in margin of fol. 81r and in fol. 2v*
μεταχειρίζεταί τι Pu: μεταχειρίζεσθαι P
αὐτῷ Pu: αὐτὰ P

4 ἐκφεύγει *AA*: ἐκφεύγειν P

5 συναπαχθῆναί σε Pu: συναπαχθῆναι σοι P
βουλευόμενος Pu: βουλόμενος P
ἦγεν Pu: διῆγεν P

6 <καὶ ἐν . . . κατέκρυψαν> *added from* Pu
οἵπερ θυμωθέντα *AA*: ὑπερθυμωθέντα P

8 ἐπερωτήσοντας *AA*: ἐπερωτήσαντας P
<πρὸς θυμὸν> *added from* Pu

9 ἀναβαλέσθαι *AA*: ἀναλαβέσθαι P
τοῦ νόμου *AA*: τὸν νόμον P
<καὶ ἡ ἀνοχὴ . . . συνέσεως> *added from cod. Paris. Suppl. gr. 1233 fol. 95r*

10 ἐπιτρέπουσιν *Paris. Suppl. gr. 1233 fol. 95r*: ἐπιστρέψουσιν P

12 <τοῖς . . . φευκτέον> *added from* Pu

13 *after* ἀπεσόβησαν P *adds* τέλος τοῦ δεκάτου τμήματος

Chapter 11

heading P *fol. 84v*

1 προκρίνειν αὐτῶν *AA*: προκρίνει αὐτὸν P
οὗσπερ *AA*: εἴπερ P
ἄνθρωπος ἀνθρώπου . . . δύναται ποιῆσαι P: βουνὸς τοῦ βουνοῦ τὴν ἀπαντὴν οὐ δύναται ποιῆσαι, ἄνθρωπος δὲ ἀνθρώπου τὴν ἀπαντὴν προσποιεῖται, ἀλλ᾽ οὖν εἰς πολλοὺς τῶν ἀνθρώπων τὰ τοιαῦτά εἰσιν Pu, ἄνθρωπος ἀνθρώπου τὴν ἀπάτην προσποιεῖται, ἀλλ᾽ οὔτε γὰρ βουνὸς τοῦ βουνοῦ τὴν ἀπάτην ποιῆσαι δύναται BO, ἄνθρωπος δὲ ἀνθρώπῳ τὴν ἀπαντὴν προσποιεῖται, οὐ γὰρ ὄρει τὴν ἀπαντὴν ποιῆσαι δύναται *Paris. Suppl. gr. 1233 fol. 96v*
αὐτῷ *AA*: αὐτὸν P
<παρὰ> *added from* Pu

2 *heading* P *in margin of fol. 84v and in fol. 2v*

πεσεῖν Pu: πεσὼν P

ἀνελθόντα . . . αὐτὰ *AA*: ἀνελθόντων οὖν τῶν τριῶν ζώων αὐτῶν P

3 συνέβη αὐτὸν *AA*: συνέβη αὐτῷ P

4 ἤγαγον Pu: ἤγαγεν P

after ἄνθρωπον P *adds* τέλος τοῦ ἑνδεκάτου τμήματος

Chapter 12

heading P *fol. 86r*

2 *heading* P *in margin of fol. 86r and in fol. 2v*

3 <αὐτὰ> *added from* Pu

<τῆς> *added AA*

ὡραίῳ *AA*: ὡραίου P

πενόμεθα: ἢ πεινῶμεν P *in margin of fol. 86v*

<ἐκ τοῦ οἴκου αὐτῆς> *added from* Pu

4 σκάφην ἔχουσαν *AA*: σκάφη ἔχοντα P

ἔσχατος *AA*: ἐσχάτως P

after χιλιάδας μιλιαρίσια Pu *adds* Ἀκούσαντες δὲ οἱ πραγματευταὶ τῆς πόλεως ἦλθον πρὸς αὐτὸν καὶ ὠφέλησαν αὐτὸν ἑκατὸν μιλιαρίσια

ἐνεβριμήσαντο Pu: ἐνεμβρυμήσαντο P

5 Σανταμάν P: Σαρταβὰν Pu

τελευτήσαντος τοῦ πατρός *AA*: τελευτήσας ὁ πατήρ P

6 *after* δυνάμεως P *fol. 87v adds* τέλος δωδεκάτου, ἀρχὴ δὲ τοῦ τρισκαιδεκάτου

Chapter 13

heading P *fol. 87v*

1 ἑτέρῳ *AA*: ἑτέρου P

ἀδικήματος Pu: ἐκδικήματος P

2 *heading* P *in margin of fol. 88r and in fol. 2v*

ἐκδάρας Pu: ἐκδορήσας P

3 καταλιπεῖν *AA*: καταλιπὼν P

after ἀνθρώποις P *adds* τέλος τοῦ τρισκαιδεκάτου

Chapter 14

heading P *fol. 88v*

2 *heading* P *in margin of fol. 89r and in fol. 3r*

βουλεύσασθαι Pu: βούλεσθαι P

καὶ συνετοῦ: *added from* Pu

4 *after* ὠφεληθήσονται P *adds* τέλος καὶ τοῦ δεκάτου τετάρτου

Chapter 15

heading P *fol. 90r*

1 τοῦτο τὸ *AA*: τοῦτο ἦν P

ἀπόλλυσιν Pu: ἀπολέσει P

2 *heading* P *in margin of fol. 90r and in fol. 3r*

ἤρεσάν μοι *AA*: ἤρεσάν με P

3 *heading* P *in fol. 3r*

P *stops at* ὁ δὲ ἀσκητὴς *the remainder of the text is provided by* F *fol. 78r–v*

4 *heading* P *in fol. 3r*

ζητῶν *AA*: ζητεῖ F

Notes to the Translation

Preface

1 After the three opening lines the following comment is inserted in manuscripts LBP, *Bucharest* 292, and *Athous Iveron* 1132: Τὸ παρὸν βιβλίον ἐγράφη κατασκευὴν ὅτι καὶ πλείστην ἔχον ἐντός· καὶ γὰρ τοῖς ἁπλουστέροις μῦθοι μὲν λογισθήσονται καὶ ὕθλοι [καὶ] πρὸς οὐδὲν ὀνήσιμον ἐφοδιάζοντες· τοῖς δὲ νουνεχέσι καὶ ἐχεμύθοις εἰκότως ἂν προσδεχθήσονται διὰ τὴν ἐκ τούτων προσγινομένην ὠφέλειαν. "The present book was written in a most artful way. For these stories will be considered by simpler people as fables and nonsense that offer nothing useful, but they will probably be favorably received by those who are sensible and discerning on account of the benefit to be derived from them." This is Lauxtermann's scholion 1; Marc Lauxtermann, "The Eugenian Recension of *Stephanites and Ichnelates:* Prologue and Paratexts," *Νέα Ῥώμη* 15 (2018): 104. There is a wordplay in the Greek on μύθοι (fables) and ἐχεμύθοις (discerning), which it is impossible to render in English.

2 *the admiral of the king of Sicily*: For the rank and title of the office of "emir" (ἀμηρᾶ or, in its Latin form, *amiratus*), here translated as "admiral," see Jeremy Johns, *Arabic Administration in Norman Sicily: The Royal Diwan* (Cambridge, 2002), 68–74. See also *ODB,* vol. 1, p. 690.

After these verses the following comment is inserted in manuscripts LBP and *Bucharest* 292: Ἐκ τοῦ προλόγου τοῦ πάροντος βιβλίου· ἡ τοῦ τοιούτου προλόγου κατασκευὴ δείκνυσιν

ἡμῖν ὅτι τῷ ἀναγινώσκοντι καὶ πειθομένῳ παντὶ βιβλίῳ—λέγω δὴ καὶ τῶν μὴ καθ' ἡμᾶς φιλοσόφων—ὠφέλειά τε ἐκ τοῦ πείθεσθαι τούτῳ προσγίνεται, ἡ πρὸς παιδείαν καὶ γνῶσιν τοῦτον συντείνουσα, ὡς τῇ μελίσσῃ προσεοικότα ἐκ παντὸς φυτοῦ καὶ βοτάνης τὰ κρείττονα συλλεγούσῃ. "From the prologue of the present book: the argument of this prologue shows us that there is a benefit for someone who reads and is convinced by the whole book—and I dare say even one of the secular philosophers—for it leads him to education and knowledge, inasmuch as he resembles the bee, who gathers what is best from every plant and herb." This is Lauxtermann's scholion 2; "The Eugenian Recension," 104.

3 *You should make use . . . from the Egyptians*: An almost direct quotation from Gregory of Nazianzos, *Orations* 45.20 *(In sanctum pascha);* PG 36:652A. The references to the actions of Jacob and Rachel in the following sentence are drawn somewhat less directly from the same oration, 45.21; PG 36:652C.

Jacob . . . stole her father's idols: See Genesis 31:17–21.

Rachel, the patriarch's soul: Gregory of Nazianzos, *Orations* 45.21 *(In sanctum pascha);* PG 36:652B.

The author of Proverbs refers us to the bee: Proverbs 6:8.

4 *if the person who says the following is to be believed*: Following this statement (probably as a marginal note on it), a comment is inserted in the text of manuscripts LB and P: Ἐν τῷδε τῷ βιβλίῳ <τὴν> προκειμένην ἔννοιαν καὶ σοφίαν καὶ τὴν τούτου ἀκρόασιν ἀνακόπτων οὐκ ἔλαθε φιλοδοξίαν νοσῶν, ὑφ' ἧς ἁλισκόμενος μυρίους προβάλλεται δρόμους καὶ περιδρόμους προτάσσων ὡς τὸν εἱρμὸν τῶν ἡγουμένων διαστῆσαι βουλόμενος. Ὁ γὰρ ποιητὴς τῶν παρόντων οὐ διδάσκει τὰ μὴ ὁρίσμενα, ἀλλὰ πρὸς τοὺς ἐρωτῶντας περιεργοτέρους καὶ τοὺς λόγους προβάλλεται. "By interrupting the meaning and wisdom set forth in this book and the hearing of it, he does not avoid suffering from pride. Succumbing to this he throws in countless digressions and sidetracks, proceeding as if he actually wants to interrupt the sequence of the main points that are being followed. For the author of the present work does not teach

things that are ill defined, but also throws in passages for those more inquisitive people who pose questions." This is Lauxtermann's scholion 3; "The Eugenian Recension," 104.

The fable originated with poets . . . books of myths: The reference, as Lauxtermann, "The Eugenian Recension," 102, points out, is to a passage in Aphthonios, *Progymnasmata,* ed. Michel Patillon, *Corpus Rhetoricum* (Paris, 2008), vol. 1, p. 112; English trans. George Alexander Kennedy, *Progymnasmata: Greek Textbooks of Prose Composition and Rhetoric* (Brill, 2003), 96. The translation here is influenced by that of Lauxtermann, "The Eugenian Recension," 69.

they think it unworthy to defile our language: Lauxtermann, "The Eugenian Recension," 85, takes this as referring to Eugenios being criticized for defiling his own tongue, rather than the Greek language.

secular and theological writings: The text more literally refers to Hellenic and theological writings.

But, in order to reap the benefit . . . what is harmful: Coupled with the reference in the subsequent paragraph to the bee, Lauxtermann, "The Eugenian Recension," 86, suggests this is probably an allusion to Basil the Great's *Address to Young Men on the Right Use of Greek Literature* 4, ed. Mario Naldini, *Discorso ai Giovani (Oratio ad adolescentes)* (Florence, 1984), 92–94. See also N. G. Wilson, *Saint Basil on the Value of Greek Literature* (London 1975), p. 23, lines 34–51 and, for commentary, p. 48.

But, while someone who prefers the flesh . . . taught by the Savior: As Lauxtermann suggests, this is a passage probably interpreting 1 Corinthians 15:42–54.

5 *roses grow in a bramble bush*: Lauxtermann, "The Eugenian Recension," 74, points to the problems in the Greek text here and suggests the original likely incorporated a well-known medieval saying that indicated good may come from bad. The line may thus have read κἂν γὰρ ἀκάνθαις καλὰ φύεται ῥόδα (for even a beautiful rose grows among thorns).

avoid the opposite like thorns: Following this verse, manuscripts LB and P insert a rubric to an illustration: Ἐλθόντος ἐνταῦθα

Περζουὲ ὁ βασιλεὺς συμβουλεύεται ὡς φιλοσόφῳ περὶ τῆς ἀποστολῆς τοῦ βιβλίου. "Here Perzoué has come, and the king is consulting him, as his philosopher, about the mission of the book." The bees are illustrated in manuscript B on fol. 5v, and this rubric may apply to the illustration on fol. 6r of the same manuscript. This is Lauxtermann's paratext 4, which, he suggests, was the caption to a frontispiece. It evidently depicted Perzoué talking to Chosroes and was perhaps intended as a tribute to Eugenios of Palermo and King Tancred of Sicily; see Lauxtermann, "The Eugenian Recension," 79.

6 *The Collared Dove*: A reference to the third chapter of *Stephanites and Ichnelates,* which, in the Arabic tradition but not in the Greek, starts with a fable about, specifically, a collared dove. See further, Lauxtermann, "The Eugenian Recension," 77.

Prologue A

1 *Chosroes . . . Kaïdad*: Chosroes is Khusrōy I, the Sasanian monarch who reigned from 531 to 579. Anasouranos is likely a corruption of Anōshagruwān or Anushirvan, "the immortal," an epithet by which he was also known. See François de Blois, *Burzoy's Voyage to India and the Origins of the Book of "Kalīlah wa Dimnah"* (London, 1990), p. 1. His father was Kavad I (r. 488–496, 498/9–531).

Kelilai and Dimnai: On this work, the *Kalīla wa-Dimna* in Arabic, see the Introduction. Note the differences in the Greek spelling of the title between here, where it appears as *Κηλίλαι καὶ Δίμναι,* below, Prol.A.12, where it is rendered instead as *Κιλίλε καὶ Δίμνε,* and Prol.C.19 and 1.1, where it is *Κυλίλε καὶ Δίμνε.*

2 *Just carry out my wishes*: After this phrase, a rubric was inserted in the text in manuscripts LB and P, which reads: Ἐκβολὴ τοῦ Περζουέ, καὶ διατριβὴ ἐν τοῖς Ἰνδικοῖς πρὸς τὰς τοῦ βασιλέως αὐλάς, μετὰ τῶν φιλοσόφων καὶ τῶν προσηκόντων τούτου. "Perzoué's departure, and time among the Indians at the king's palaces with his philosophers and retinue." This is Lauxtermann's rubric 1; "The Eugenian Recension," 104.

3 *told him why he had come*: As the story unfolds, it is clear this cannot be the "true" reason for Perzoué's visit, otherwise the "reveal" in the following paragraph would make no sense.

speaks to him alone: The following rubric appears after this phrase in manuscripts LB and P: Ἐνταῦθα ὁ Περζουὲ τῷ φίλῳ αὐτοῦ καταμόνας τὰ ἀνέκφορα φανερῶς πιστεύσας, ὡς φιλεῖται φιλῶν, καὶ ἀποσείεται τὸν αὐτοῦ δισταγμόν. Καὶ ὥσπερ τις γεωργὸς ὑπὲρ τοῦ τί τῶν ἀγρίων μεταφυτεῦσαι δένδρων βουλόμενος ἐντυγχάνει τινὶ χωρίῳ ἐπιτηδείῳ κατὰ τὸν τούτου σκοπόν· καὶ πρότερον μὲν ἐκριζοῖ πᾶν ὅ τι ἂν ἐκεῖσε ἐπιφύῃ ἢ ἀναφυὲν ἀκανθῶδες, εἶθ' οὕτως πονεῖ περὶ ὧν βούλεται μετακεντρίζειν, οὕτω δὴ καὶ ὁ Περζουὲ πᾶν ὅσον εἰς δειλίαν ἀποτιναξάμενος ἐκ τοῦ φιλεῖν καὶ φιλεῖσθαι καὶ θησαυρῷ ἀνελπίστῳ τῷ φίλῳ περιτυχὼν ἀνέλκει τὸν ποθούμενον θησαυρόν. "Then, Perzoué, when he is alone with his friend, openly entrusting his secret, friend to friend, shakes off his doubts. And in this matter he is just like a farmer who, when he wants to transplant some wild trees, finds a place suitable for his purpose. He first uproots everything that may have grown there or thorns which are flourishing there, and then he works hard on the trees he wants to transplant. Likewise, as a result of their mutual friendship, Perzoué has cast aside any timidity and, since he has come upon an unexpected treasure in his friend, reveals the treasure he desires." This is Lauxtermann's rubric 2; "The Eugenian Recension," 105.

4 *speaking through signs and riddles*: Another rubric appears after this phrase in manuscripts LB and P: Ἠθοποιεῖται τῷ φίλῳ ῥήμασιν ἠπίοις πρός τε φιλικὴν τοῖς ἀκούουσιν ἐντυχίαν καὶ πρὸς γνῶσιν συντείνουσι τοῦ προκειμένου σκοποῦ καὶ σαφήνειαν· ἐνδείκνυσι δὲ τὸν σκοπὸν διὰ τῶν ἐγκειμένων ἐνταῦθα ἀρετῶν, <καὶ> ὑπερνικῶντα πάντων (πασῶν all manuscripts) πραγμάτων τὸν κεκτημένον αὐτάς. "He expresses himself to his friend with soft words that suggest friendly conversation to those who hear them, but clear knowledge for the intended target; and he indicates his aim through the virtues implicit there, and the man who possesses these virtues is victorious in

all circumstances." This is Lauxtermann's rubric 3; "The Eugenian Recension," 105.

eight kinds of virtues: Another rubric appears after this phrase in manuscripts LB and P: Ἐνταῦθα δείκνυσιν ὁ φίλος τοῦ Περζουὲ πόσαι ἀρεταί εἰσιν ἃς ὀφείλει διατηρεῖν ὁ καλὸς ἄνθρωπος, αἵτινές εἰσιν αὗται· "Here Perzoué's friend shows how many virtues there are which the good man ought to observe, which are as follows." This is Lauxtermann's rubric 4; "The Eugenian Recension," 105.

5 *get what you are seeking*: Another brief rubric appears after this phrase in manuscripts LB and P: Τὸ φιλεῖν τετόλμηκε πολλάκις φθόνου. "Love has often endured jealousy." The Greek term φθόνος usually refers specifically to jealousy or envy, a meaning that seems appropriate to the general sentiment expressed in this aside, but it has at base a broader sense of ill will and malice; it is translated in that way in the following sentence. This is Lauxtermann's rubric 5; "The Eugenian Recension," 105.

6 *one of his truest brothers*: A verse rubric appears after this phrase in manuscripts LB and P: Προσσχὼν τέλος ἄριστον ἐνταῦθα, φίλε, / οἱ φιλοῦντες μάθετε φιλεῖν τοὺς φίλους. "If you want an excellent outcome here, my friend, those who love must learn how to love those who love them." This is Lauxtermann's rubric 6; "The Eugenian Recension," 105.

7 *I set many traps for you*: Another verse rubric appears after this phrase in manuscripts LB and P: Ὦ παγίδα ἄριστα τὰ τῇδε ξένε, / μὴ παγίδα νόει μοι, τὴν γνῶσιν ταύτην, / τὸ γὰρ φιλικὸν πρὸς φιλικὴν καρδίαν / σοφοῖ πρὸς αὐτὰ καὶ σκεδάννυσι δόλους. "The traps set here are the very best, stranger, but do not think this knowledge is a trap by me, for showing friendliness towards a friendly heart makes someone wise to such traps and scatters these tricks." This is Lauxtermann's rubric 7; "The Eugenian Recension," 105.

education that God had given you: Another verse rubric appears after this phrase in manuscripts LB and P, explaining what follows: Παραβολικῶς ἀποδεικνύει πάλιν / τὸν σοφὸν ὡς μά-

λιστα πρὸς πέτραν λέγων / τὴν οἰκίαν στήσαντα, ὥσπερ ἐχέφρων· / ἣν δ' ἀναγωγὴν τῆς παροιμίας ταύτης, / αὐτὸν Περζουὲ κατανόει, ὦ φίλε, / τὴν δὲ πέτραν ἄριστα τὸν τούτου φίλον / ᾧ (ὡς all manuscripts) ἂν νουνεχῶς προσερείσας τὴν γνῶσιν, / ἀκαμάντως ἔτυχε τοῦ ποθουμένου. "Through a parable again he presents the wise man who, as he says, has solidly constructed his house on a rock, being a sensible man. And the solution to this riddling mystery, you should understand, my friend, is Perzoué himself, and the rock is best understood as his friend, to whom he prudently entrusted his wish and gained what was desired without any trouble." This is Lauxtermann's rubric 8; "The Eugenian Recension," 106.

For the wise man . . . the winds that blow there: The phrasing here is very close to that of the parable in Matthew 24:7.

between two people . . . happens among three: It seems possible that the awkwardness of this passage has been caused by the incorporation into the text of a note ἴσως καὶ ἐν τρισίν, "perhaps among three," questioning the sense of the initial "between two."

punishes the least thing: Another verse rubric appears after this phrase in manuscripts LB and P: Ὦ φιλίας ἄριστον, φιλεῖν φιλεῖσθαι· / ὑπὲρ τοῦ φίλον (φίλον *AA*: φιλεῖν LBP) προδιδοῦναι πολλάκις / ἀνὴρ ἰσχυρός, ἰσχυρογνώμων μᾶλλον, / καὶ θανεῖν προκρίνοιτο ὑπὲρ τοῦ φίλου. / Εἰ δὲ παρ' Ἰνδεῖ, καὶ ταῦτα φυλῆς ἄλλης, / <. . .> καὶ πάντα καινὸν ὑπερβαίνει γὰρ λόγου. "The best thing about love is to love and be loved; often a strong or, rather, a strong-willed man would even prefer to die for his friend than betray him. And if this is so in India, and these things <are true> of an alien race <. . .> where everything is strange, for <love?> transcends reason." This is Lauxtermann's rubric 9; "The Eugenian Recension," 106.

10 *faithful servant*: Matthew 25:21 and 25:23.

All who heard were amazed: Almost a direct quotation from Luke 2:18.

11 *one cubit of the cloth from the land of Phouistan*: This is likely a reference to the Egyptian city of al-Fustat, which served as the cap-

ital of the country from the seventh century until its destruction in the twelfth century. Among other things, it was famous for its cotton manufacturing: the English term "fustian," which embraces a variety of types of thick cotton cloth, from jean to velveteen and corduroy, derives from the fabric traditionally made there; and the modern Greek φουστάνι (skirt) likely has the same derivation. A cubit is the measure taken from the tip of the middle finger to the elbow, so around eighteen inches. In other words, Perzoué makes a modest request.

live forever: Genesis 3:22.

12 *Kelilai and Dimnai*: As noted above, Prol.A.1, there is a slight variation here in the spelling of the title in the Greek: *Κιλίλε καὶ Δίμνε*.

Prologue B

5 *eleven thousand nomismata*: The Byzantine *nomisma* (plural *nomismata*), also known in Latin as the *solidus,* was a gold coin widely used in the Byzantine empire until the late eleventh century. Given an optimal weight of 4.5 grams for this coin, eleven thousand *nomismata* represent an enormous value.

that of the other story: It is unclear what "the other story" refers to, but it is possibly the one that follows.

6 *piece of yellow paper*: This probably refers to natural, yellow-brown (and therefore rough) paper as opposed to bleached (white) paper.

7 *About a careless man*: Manuscript B preserves a different heading here: Περὶ τοῦ οἰκοδεσπότου καὶ τοῦ κομπ[τ]ώματος τῶν κλεπτῶν. "About the householder and the deception of the thieves." It fits the story that follows.

8 *should both fall into a ditch*: Matthew 15:14.

13 *he who seeks, finds*: Matthew 7:8.

16 *we have placed these things . . . in Greek*: The wording here shows that the concluding sentence cannot have been part of the original Arabic prologue by Ibn al-Muqaffaʿ.

Prologue C

1 *translated by the teacher and philosopher, Symeon Seth*: Unless simply intended to refer to the tales, it would appear that this sentence must have been added to the Greek version at some point. If Sjöberg's view is accepted, Seth had nothing to do with translating the prologue.

into the Persian language: After this opening, manuscript P adds a note: Ἔλεγε δὲ τὰ περὶ ἑαυτοῦ, ἅπερ ποτὲ ἐκ νεότητος αὐτοῦ καὶ μαθήσεως ἔπραξεν ἀγαθουργήματα εἰς τὴν ἰατρικὴν τέχνην. "He spoke about himself, about the good deeds he used to do in the art of medicine, starting with his youth and learning."

provincial governors: Literally, "satraps."

3 *For if someone possesses something . . . remain with him*: Compare John 8:23, 17:14, 17:16.

an easily moveable wooden image: The Greek adjective πολυόρμητον, here translated as "easily moveable," is found only in lexicographical contexts, where it is used to explain the Homeric adjective πολυᾶϊξ, "much-rushing, impetuous, furious"; Erich Trapp, in the *LbG,* suggests "heftig ansturmend," that is, "violently assaulted." None of these meanings seems to fit the usage here. Richard Greenfield has suggested that a metaphor is being drawn to a shadow puppet, and the adjective is simply an intensification of ὁρμητόν, "set in motion," and thus "easily moveable."

10 *magi*: Possibly a remnant of the Persian version, since the magi were a priestly cast of the Zoroastrians. In this context, the Greek audience would probably understand the term as indicating "wise men" and think of the "magi" of the nativity story in Matthew 2:1–12.

11 *found the cistern covered*: The Greek μετηρμένον should imply that the cistern had somehow been moved or had disappeared. It is unclear from the text as it stands what exactly is thought to have happened.

13 *nomismata*: On the *nomisma,* see above Prol.B.5.

sistra: The sistrum was a musical instrument loosely related to the modern tambourine. In the ancient world it consisted of a handle to which was attached a metal frame supporting moveable crossbars from which hung small rings. When it was shaken, the rings produced a rattling or jangling sound.

14 *the ascetic, in his spiritual tranquility*: Further on the concept of spiritual tranquility, or *hesychia,* a key concept in Byzantine spirituality, see *ODB,* vol. 2, p. 924.

the dog with a piece of meat in its mouth . . . was left with nothing: The story of the dog that carried meat comes originally from Aesop. It is number 133 in Ben Edwin Perry's index, *Aesopica: A Series of Texts Relating to Aesop or Ascribed to Him or Closely Connected with the Literary Tradition that Bears His Name,* vol. 1, *Greek and Latin Texts* (Urbana, IL, 1952); compare *The Fables of Syntipas* 28, in Michael Andreopoulos, *The Byzantine Sinbad,* trans. Jeffrey Beneker and Craig A. Gibson (Cambridge, MA, 2021), 230–31.

15 *the bone smelling of meat . . . it damages itself instead*: Compare the fable of the weasel and the file in Aesop, number 59 in Perry's *Aesopica,* and the similar story of the cat and the file in *The Fables of Syntipas* 5, trans. Beneker and Gibson, *Byzantine Sinbad,* 206–7.

16 *four competing enemies*: The four enemies here describe the four humors of Greek medicine. Some Arabic manuscripts refer to them directly as humors; see de Blois, *Burzoy's Voyage,* 27.

17 *A human being is like a man . . . hung onto it*: This parable is a version of a well-known story originating in India and found in chapters 5–6 of book 11 of the *Mahabharata;* Kate Crosby, trans., *Mahabhárata,* book 11, *The Women,* Clay Sanskrit Library (New York, 2009), 200–207. It is also present in the Near Eastern version of the life of Buddha, which gave rise to the Greek work *Barlaam and Ioasaph.* Although attributed to John Damascene, the Greek text was likely a translation made from a Georgian original in the eleventh century. For the parable see *Barlaam and Ioasaph* 12, trans. G. R. Woodward and Harold

Mattingly, *Barlaam and Ioasaph,* Loeb Classical Library 34 (Cambridge, MA, 1914), 186–91. For more on its origins see de Blois, *Burzoy's Voyage,* 34.

18 *I likened the unicorn . . . from his salvation*: The text and the translation here follow manuscript P. Manuscripts BL and O, which omit initial mention of the unicorn, contain a somewhat different version of section 18: Εἶδον δὲ καὶ μονόκερων ζῷον ἀκολουθοῦντα τῷ ἀνθρώπῳ διὰ παντός, ὃ καὶ ὡμοίωσα τῷ θανάτῳ τῷ διὰ πάντα ἀκολουθοῦντι καὶ συμπαραμένοντι τῷ ἀνθρώπῳ, ὃν καὶ οὐ δύναταί τις ἐκφυγεῖν, εἰ καὶ ἐν τοῖς μείζοσι πέφυκεν· τὸν δὲ λάκκον ὡμοίωσα τῷ βίῳ τούτῳ τῷ πλήρει κακίας καὶ πονηρίας καὶ δεινῆς διατριβῆς καὶ ἀπωλείας ὑπάρχοντι· τοὺς δὲ τέσσαρας ὄφεις, τοῖς τέσσαρσι χυμοῖς τοῖς τῷ ἀνθρώπῳ συνοῦσι καὶ συνιστῶσι τὸ σῶμα διὰ τῶν φαρμάκων αὐτῶν, καὶ ὅταν τις τῶν τοιούτων χυμῶν ἐπαναστῇ τῷ ἑτέρῳ, ἔοικε τῷ δράκοντι τῷ θανατοῦντι διὰ τοῦ δήγματος τὸν ἄνθρωπον· τοὺς δὲ δύο κλάδους, τῇ προσκαίρῳ ζωῇ ταύτῃ· καὶ τοὺς δύο μύας, τόν τε λευκὸν καὶ τὸν μέλανα, τῇ ἡμέρᾳ τε καὶ τῇ νυκτί, αἵτινες πρὸς μικρὸν διαφθείρουσι τὴν ὠκύμορον ζωὴν τοῦ ἀνθρώπου· τὸν δὲ δράκοντα, τῷ θανάτῳ, ὃν οὐ δύναταί τις διαφυγεῖν κἂν εἰς οὐρανοὺς πετασθῇ· τὸ δ' ἄνωθεν τοῦ δένδρου διαρρέον μέλι, τὴν πικρὰν γλυκύτητα τοῦ βίου τούτου, τὴν πρὸς μικρὸν μὲν ἡδύνουσαν τὰς τοῦ ἀνθρώπου αἰσθήσεις, ἀηδῶς δὲ καὶ μετὰ πικρίας χωρίζουσαν αὐτὸν ἀπὸ τῆς σωτηρίας αὐτοῦ. "I also saw that there was a unicorn always following the man, and I likened this to death, which also always follows and remains with a man, and which no one can escape, even if he was born among the more powerful. I likened the pond to this life, which is full of wickedness and evil and terrible time wasting and depravity; and the four snakes to the four humors that are part of a man and maintain his body through their remedies; whenever one of these humors rises against another, it is like the serpent that inflicts death on a man through its bite. The two branches I likened to this transitory life, and the two mice, the white one and the black one, to the day and the night, which quickly destroy

man's brief existence. I likened the serpent to death, from which no one can escape, even if he is taken to heaven. The honey running from up in the tree is the bitter sweetness of this life, which delights a man's senses for a short time but then unpleasantly and bitterly separates him from his salvation."

19 *After I had considered . . . Stephanites and Ichnelates*: The text and the translation of section 19 again follow manuscript P. Manuscripts BL and O read more briefly: Καταμαθὼν δὲ ταῦτα πάντα, ἠράσθην τῆς ἐμαυτοῦ πολιτείας, καὶ μεγάλως ἠγωνίσθην τῆς ἀγαθοεργίας πρὸς τὴν ἐμαυτοῦ σωτηρίαν. Καὶ στέρξας ἐν τούτοις, ὑπέστρεψα εἰς τὴν ἐμὴν χώραν, μεταγράψας καὶ βιβλία ἱκανά· ἐξ ὧν δὴ καὶ τὸ τοιοῦτον βιβλίον ὑπάρχει ἕν, ὅπερ ὠνόμασται *Στεφανίτης καὶ Ἰχνηλάτης*. "After I had considered all these things, I loved my own way of life, and struggled mightily for my own salvation by doing good deeds. And although I was content with them, I returned to my own country after I had translated a lot of books, among which indeed is also this book, which is called *Stephanites and Ichnelates*."

which in Greek means Stephanites and Ichnelates: Once again, this anachronistic phrase, if not the whole sentence, must have been added to the Greek version.

Chapter 1

2 *abundant lifestyle*: See Hesiod, *Works and Days* 31; Pindar, *Nemea* 6.10.

5 *jackals*: The Greek has two terms here, paralleling the pairs already mentioned, but both θῶές and λυκοπάνθηρες refer to jackals.

10 *anyone who waits . . . quickly becomes a friend of the king*: An allusion to the parable of the rich man and Lazarus. See Luke 16:19–31.

11 *depicting things on a flat surface . . . receding*: Apparently, a reference to the use of perspective in painting.

12 *entrusting secrets to women*: This translation, which results from an emendation of the text, appears to make more sense in the context and matches the frequently misogynistic attitude of

the work. The reading of manuscript P, τοῦ τῶν γυναικῶν πιστεύειν μυστήρια, is possible, however, and would translate, "believing in the superstitions [or secrets] of women."

14 *for a small thing . . . something great*: Gregory of Nazianzos, *Carmina moralia* 30.19; PG 37:910A.

21 *So that night*: The Greek clearly says "one night," but "that night" makes better sense in the context.

22 *tentmaker*: The Greek term συσκιαστής is otherwise unknown, but the meaning may be conjectured from the verb συσκιάζω, "to shade over" or "obscure"; he is thus a maker of tents or awnings.

25–26 *When the wife . . . from punishment*: The text of manuscripts BL and O varies slightly in these two chapters from that of P, which is the basis for our text:

> Ἡ δὲ μαυλίστρια, ἣν ἔφθημεν εἰπεῖν, στερηθεῖσα τὴν μύτην αὐτῆς, ἀπελθοῦσα ἐν τῷ οἴκῳ αὐτῆς, ἐπανουργεύσατο τοῦ ἐκφυγεῖν τὴν αἰσχύνην ταύτην. Ὀρθρίσας δὲ ὁ ἀνὴρ αὐτῆς, λέγει αὐτῇ· "Ἐπίδος μοι τὰ τῆς τέχνης ἐργαλεῖα ὅπως ἀπέλθω ἐν τῷ ἐργαστηρίῳ μου," ἦν γὰρ οὗτος συσκιαστής. Ἡ δὲ λαβοῦσα τὸ ξυράφιον μόνον, δέδωκεν αὐτῷ. Ὁ δὲ λέγει αὐτῇ· "Πάντα μοι τὰ ἐργαλεῖα ἐπίδος." Καὶ ἀπελθοῦσα πάλιν, ἐδεδώκει αὐτῷ μόνον τὸ ξυράφιον. Καὶ ποιήσασα τοῦτο πολλάκις, ὀργισθεὶς ὁ ἀνὴρ αὐτῆς, ἔρριψε τὸ ξυράφιον μετὰ θυμοῦ πρὸς αὐτήν. Καὶ αὕτη ταῖς ἰδίαις χερσὶ δραξαμένη τὴν μύτην αὐτῆς, ἔκραξε μεγίστῃ φωνῇ· "Ἡ μύτη μου, ἡ μύτη μου."
>
> Καὶ συνδραμόντες, οἵ τε γείτονες καὶ οἱ ἴδιοι αὐτῆς, καὶ ἐπὶ τῷ γεγονότι θαυμάσαντες εἵλκυσαν αὐτὸν βιαίως πρὸς τὸν κριτήν. Ἔφη δὲ αὐτῷ μετ' ὀργῆς ὁ δικάζων· "Τίνος ἕνεκα τὸ τοιοῦτον τῇ γυναικί σου ἐποίησας;" Ὁ δὲ πρόφασιν μὴ ἐσχηκὼς εὔλογον ἀποδοῦναι, ἀπεφάνθη τοῦ κολασθῆναι αὐτόν. Ταῦτα πάντα ὁ μοναχὸς θεασάμενος, προσελθὼν ἔπεσε πρὸς τοῖς ποσὶ τοῦ δικαστοῦ καὶ λέγει αὐτῷ· "Μή σοι δοκείτω, ὦ δικαστά, παρὰ τοῦ κλέπτου ἀφαιρεθῆναι τὰ ὑφάσματα ἅπερ μοι ἐδόθησαν, ἢ οἱ κριοὶ ἀπέκτειναν τὴν

ἀλώπεκα, ἢ τὸ δηλητήριον τὴν πόρνην ἀπέκτεινε, ἢ οὗτος ὁ τιμωρούμενος ἀπέτεμε τὴν μύτην τῆς αὐτοῦ γυναικός," καὶ ἀνήγγειλεν αὐτῷ ἅπερ εἶδε καὶ ἤκουσε καὶ ἔπαθεν.

"As for the go-between, who, as we said, had gone off home deprived of her nose, she did her utmost to escape this shame. When her husband got up in the morning, he said to her, 'Give me my work tools so I can go to my workshop,' for he was a tentmaker. But she took just the razor and gave it to him. He said to her, 'Give me all the tools.' She went off again and gave him just the razor. After she had done this many times, her husband got angry and threw the knife at her in a rage. And she, clutching her nose in her hands, cried out in a very loud voice, 'My nose, my nose!'

"Her neighbors and relatives came running and, amazed at what had happened, dragged him off by force before the judge. The magistrate said angrily to him, 'What made you do such a thing to your wife?' As he had no reasonable excuse to give in reply, sentence was passed that he should be punished. The monk, who had witnessed all this, came forward, fell at the magistrate's feet, and said to him, 'Do not conclude, magistrate, that the clothes which were given to me were taken by the thief, or that the rams killed the vixen, or that the poison killed the prostitute, or that this one who is being punished cut off the nose of his own wife,' and he told him what he had seen and heard and experienced."

29 *live well or die well*: Sophocles, *Ajax* 479.

44 *sore throat*: The joke in Greek depends on understanding that the word κυνάγχη, here translated as "sore throat," may refer specifically to "dog quinsy" (peritonsillar abscess, in modern medicinal terms). The play is on wolf/dog.

45 *for a constantly falling drop hollows out solid rock*: This ancient saying is repeated in closely related versions, in a number of Byzantine writers: see, for example, John Chrysostom, *De poenitentia* 1.7, PG 60:695, line 43. Compare, from the late fifth century BCE, πέτρην κοιλαίνει ῥανὶς ὕδατος ἐνδελεχείῃ, "a drop of

water, by its persistence, hollows out a stone"; Choerilus of Samos, fragment 10, ed. Gottfried Kinkel, *Epicorum Graecorum Fragmenta* (Leipzig, 1877), vol. 1, p. 271.

sea nymph: The Greek term is νηρηΐς, "nereid." In ancient mythology, a nereid was conceived of as a female sea spirit that belonged to the broader category of nymphs. The context here, however, makes it clear that the story refers to an animal, rather than a spirit, but one with which the Greek translator was evidently not familiar, hence the supernatural interpretation. As we discuss below at 1.56, in relation to the parallel term νύμφη, "nymph," we are identifying this animal as a mongoose, but we retain "sea nymph" in the translation, since this is what the (perhaps puzzled) reader of the Greek original would have encountered.

46 *Don't you understand your own strength*: That is, how little strength you have.

52 *do not correct . . . hate you*: The original saying, Proverbs 9:8, speaks of "those who are evil," rather than "stupid."

53 *an insect that glowed*: A firefly, presumably.

54 *talents of gold*: The talent was an ancient measure of weight but one that varied considerably over time and in different places. A Roman talent was about seventy pounds, the biblical one, about sixty pounds. The point here is that this was a vast treasure.

56 *It belongs to a nymph*: The term in Greek here is νύμφη, "nymph," but, as in 1.45, above, the context makes clear that an animal is being described. The Greek translator was evidently unfamiliar with the creature in question and thus introduced a spiritual interpretation. Although Trapp suggests a translation of "weasel" (*LbG*, under νύμφη), the information provided here and in the stories at 6.4 and 8.2–4 below indicates that the creature is actually a mongoose, an animal well known for its ability to attack venomous snakes but whose habitat does not extend to the northern Mediterranean. Indeed, in the *Mahabharata,* the original version of the story at 8.2–4 clearly states that it is a mongoose.

57 *One must flee . . . close family*: Although this appears to be a quotation, we have been unable to find the source.

Chapter 2

3 *speak up . . . may know*: Homer, *Iliad* 1.363. In the original passage Achilles's mother, the nereid Thetis, is speaking with her son after he has lost his lover Briseis and quarreled with Agamemnon.

4 *monstrous behavior*: In Ancient and Byzantine Greek, τερατούργημα indicates a wonder or miracle, but here the sense is evidently that of Modern Greek, where it has a negative connotation of monstrosity or atrocity.

6 *the wide earth*: The phrase χθονὸς εὐρείας is found in a number of ancient authors, the earliest of whom is Pindar, *Hymn,* fragment 33c, line 3, ed. Herwig Maehler (after Bruno Snell), *Pindari carmina cum fragmentis,* 3rd ed. (Leipzig, 1964), vol. 2, p. 10.

tries hearts and minds: An almost direct quotation from Psalms 7:9(10).

has ten thousand souls: An almost direct quotation of a phrase frequently used by John Chrysostom, *In epistulam ad Philemonem* 2.4, PG 62:713.46.

7 *he took a scarf and painted it with her likeness*: The Greek word σινδών may refer to a wide range of garments and other items made of cloth. The story, as it unfolds in the following paragraph, appears to imply that the cloth in this case was used as a veil. It thus seems plausible that the reference is to some form of head scarf, like the traditional Arabian headdress, the *keffiyeh, ghutrah,* or *shemagh,* which may be arranged to cover the face.

10 *the minds of good people are easily swayed*: Homer, *Iliad* 15.203.

all . . . have turned aside, together they have gone wrong: Psalms 13(14):3 and 52:4(53:3); quoted in Romans 3:12.

14 *a laxative*: The translation has been derived from the context. The Greek term ἐντεριώνη refers specifically to "the inmost

part, the pith of plants," and it may be that the story once suggested the ignorant physician's error was in employing the wrong part of the plant. Maidenhair fern was well known in ancient medicine, where it was the fronds that were usually prescribed. On the medicinal properties of maidenhair fern, see Sahar Dehdari and Homa Hajimehdipoor, "Medicinal Properties of *Adiantum capillus-veneris* Linn. in Traditional Medicine and Modern Phytotherapy: A Review Article," *Iranian Journal of Public Health* 47, no. 2 (2018): 188–97.

15 *I can judge a man from his features*: The cook describes himself as a φυσιογνώμων, someone who was learned in the science or art of judging a person by their features. The concept was widely accepted in the ancient world, in India and China as well as Greece. A treatise on the subject, the *Physiognomonica,* was ascribed to Aristotle. See further, Sabine Vogt, trans., *Physiognomonica* (Berlin, 1999); Maria Fernanda Ferrini and Guido Giglione, eds., *Tra il visibile e l'invisibile: Testi di fisiognomica nella tradizione greco-latina e arabo-islamica* (Macerata, 2019).

the spiritual faculties . . . the body: The phrasing echoes the first sentence of Galen's work *Quod animi mores corporis temperamenta sequantur,* which reads: ταῖς τοῦ σώματος κράσεσιν ἕπεσθαι τὰς δυνάμεις τῆς ψυχῆς, "that the capacities of the soul follow the temperaments of the body"; see Galen, *On Temperaments; On Non-Uniform Distemperment; The Soul's Traits Depend on Bodily Temperament,* ed. and trans. Ian Johnston, Loeb Classical Library 546 (Cambridge, MA, 2020), 332–33.

not to notice the beam . . . your neighbor: A loose quotation of Matthew 7:3.

20 *fall into the pit which he has made*: See Proverbs 26:27.

Chapter 3

1 *There is nothing in existence that is a substitute for a faithful friend*: The opening words of Gregory of Nazianzos's *Orations* 11 *(Ad Gregorium Nyssenum);* ed. and trans. Marie-Ange Calvet-Sebasti,

Discours 6–12, Sources chrétiennes 405 (Paris, 1995), 328. The statement "There is no substitute for a faithful friend" is itself a direct quotation from Sirach 6:15.

2 *a crow, a mouse, a turtle, and a gazelle*: There is no mention here of a dove, although, in the Arabic tradition, this chapter is named after the dove (specifically, a collared dove) whose story begins the chapter. As this omission occurs in the Greek tradition as a whole, it probably dates to Symeon Seth's translation. See Lauxtermann, "The Eugenian Recension," 77.

3 *This "fisherman" is following us*: The use of the term ἁλιεὺς, "fisherman," here instead of θηρευτής, "hunter." likely lends a tone of derision to the dove's comment.

8 *those who are of the same shape . . . shape with you*: The repetition is present in the Greek. The mouse is emphasizing to the crow that the only thing that makes him different from all the other crows is attitude.

12 *nomismata*: On the *nomisma*, see note above on Prol.B.5.

not even a good conscience . . . gold: The point is perhaps that someone needs wealth in order to demonstrate their good conscience to others by spending or donating their wealth appropriately.

money is necessary . . . ought to be: Demosthenes, *Olynthiaca* 1.20.

someone fleeing poverty . . . precipitous rocks: See Theognis, *Elegiae* 1.174–75. The version here varies slightly from that of Theognis, in that the original Greek phrase βαθυκήτεα πόντον is replaced by the synonymous Homeric μεγακήτεα πόντον, "yawning depths" (see Homer, *Odyssey* 3.158), but thereby matches a version of the saying found in other classical authors; see, for example, Plutarch, *De communibus notitiis adversus Stoicos* 1069D, ed. Rolf Westman (after M. Pohlenz), *Plutarchi moralia,* 2nd ed. (Munich, 2001), vol. 6, part 2, p. 85, lines 8–9.

13 *it is better to depart life . . . your shame*: Aphthonios, *Progymnasmata* 8, ed. Hugo Rabe, *Aphthonii progymnasmata, Rhetores graeci* 10 (Leipzig, 1926), p. 8, line 22. In discussing the use of the maxim in rhetoric, Aphthonios (late fourth to early fifth century CE) takes as his example of an hortatory maxim the passage from

Theognis quoted in the previous paragraph. He then uses the present statement to illustrate a possible summary of its point. It thus seems likely that the author has Aphthonios's work directly in mind when composing this passage on poverty and its ills.

16 *things that are born . . . ebb and flow*: John Philoponus, *In Aristotelis analytica posteriora commentaria,* ed. Maximilianus Wallies, *Ioannis Philoponi in Aristotelis analytica posteriora commentaria cum anonymo in librum II, Commentaria in Aristotelem graeca* 13, part 3 (Berlin, 1909), p. 439, line 8.

20 *at a time of temptation*: Luke 8:13.

Chapter 4

4 *we will not be to blame . . . assault*: The sense of this statement is somewhat unclear, since it would be the owls who mounted the first assault, not the crows. Lars-Olof Sjöberg suggested emending the προσβολὴν of manuscript P to συμβουλὴν, which would translate: "we won't be to blame for following the first suggestion," that is, taking flight, as the first counselor suggested; Sjöberg, *Stephanites und Ichnelates: Überlieferungsgeschchte und Text* (Uppsala, 1962), 216.

6 *who sets himself against . . . his opponents*: The phrase echoes Hesiod, *Works and Days* 210–11, ed. and trans. Hugh G. Evelyn-White, *Theogony; Works and Days; Testimonia,* Loeb Classical Library 57 (Cambridge, MA, 1914), 17: ἄφρων δ' ὅς κ' ἐθέλῃ πρὸς κρείσσονας ἀντιφερίζειν· / νίκης τε στέρεται πρός τ' αἴσχεσιν ἄλγεα πάσχει. "He is a fool who tries to withstand the stronger, for he does not get the mastery and suffers pain besides his shame."

7 *for a man who has not received . . . enemy*: Hesiod, *Works and Days* 413. The saying is quite widely repeated and paraphrased in Ancient Greek and Byzantine literature.

8 *Secrets are broken . . . blame for the mishap*: As is the case in a number of other places, this segment appears to break the flow of the argument and has perhaps been inserted awkwardly dur-

ing the later development of the text. Compare the commentary on keeping secrets in Prol.A.4–8, above. It was perhaps prompted by the use of the Greek verb ἐκφαυλίζω, which is used at the end of the previous sentence for “scorning” advice, and here for “breaking” secrets.

10 *the great enmity*: That between the crows and the owls.

11 *The crow said to them . . . killed some of them*: Manuscripts BL and O here provide a rather different introduction to this story from that of manuscript P as presented in the text: Καὶ ὁ κόραξ ἔφη· “Λέγεται ὡς ἔν τινι χρόνῳ γέγονεν ἀνομβρία μεγίστη ὥστε ξηρανθῆναι καὶ τὰς πηγάς, καὶ τὰ φυτά, καὶ πανθ’ ὅσα ἦν ἐπὶ τὴν γῆν. Ἐστενοχωρήθησαν δὲ καὶ πάντα τὰ ζῷα, ἐπὶ πλεῖστον δὲ οἱ ἐλέφαντες, καὶ προσελθόντες ᾐτήσαντο τῷ προέχοντι αὐτῶν ἐλέφαντι μεταστῆναι αὐτούς, καὶ ἐπί τινα ὑδατώδη καὶ χλοηφόρον τόπον προσελθεῖν, καὶ μὴ ἀποθανεῖν αὐτοὺς ὑπό τε λιμοῦ καὶ τῆς δίψης. Ὁ δὲ ἐξέπεμψέν τινας ἐξ αὐτῶν ἐξετάσαι τόπον αὐτοῖς πρὸς ἀνάπαυσιν, καὶ ὑποστρέψαντες ἀνήγγειλαν τῷ βασιλεῖ αὐτῶν λέγοντες· ‘Καὶ ἔν τινι τόπῳ ἔστιν πηγὴ ὕδατος καὶ χλόη δαψιλής.’ Καὶ εὐθὺς μετανάσται γεγόνασι, καὶ κατέλυσαν ἐκεῖσε. Ἦσαν δὲ ἐν τῷ τόπῳ ἐκείνῳ ὀπαὶ καὶ καταδύσεις λαγωῶν, καὶ προσπελάσαντες ταῖς καταδύσεσιν οἱ ἐλέφαντες καὶ καταπατήσαντες τοὺς λαγωούς, ἀπέκτειναν αὐτούς.” “And the crow said, ‘It is said that, once upon a time, there was a drought so severe that even the springs dried up, and the plants, and everything that existed on the earth. All the animals, and especially the elephants, were hard-pressed, and they went to the elephant who was their leader and asked him to move them somewhere else and to go to a place where there was water and vegetation, so that they would not die from hunger and thirst. He sent some of them out to search for a place where they could settle, and when they had returned, they reported back to their king, saying, “There’s a place where there is a spring of water and plentiful vegetation.” They set off on their migration at once, and stayed there. In that place there were, however, holes and nests of hares, and the elephants, by coming close to the nests and trampling on the hares, killed them.’”

21 *a violent wind . . . that adapt themselves to it*: Compare the very similar example in 1.17, above. The phrase echoes the first version of fable 239 (Δένδρα καὶ κάλαμος, "The trees and the reed") of Aesop in August Hausrath and Herbert Hunger's edition, *Corpus fabularum Aesopicarum,* 2nd ed. (Leipzig, 1959), vol. 1, part 2, p. 59.

23 *do not break a reed . . . smoldering flax*: An adaptation of Isaiah 42:3 quoted in Matthew 12:20.

26 *Unless I see . . . I will not believe*: The reader would be reminded of the story of doubting Thomas, John 20:25, where the same words are used.

Chapter 5

5 *someone who shares a tent . . . creatures do*: The progression from tent dwellers to animals in a stable appears to be a disparaging comment on nomads. For Byzantine views of nomadic peoples see, for example, Hélène Ahrweiler, "Byzantine Concepts of the Foreigner: The Case of the Nomads," in Hélène Ahrweiler and Angeliki Laiou, eds., *Studies on the Internal Diaspora of the Byzantine Empire* (Washington, DC, 1998), 1–15.

11 *Why did you flee from the female donkey*: The fox pretends to the donkey that the lion was really the female donkey he had earlier promised him.

Chapter 6

3 *nomisma*: On the *nomisma,* see note above on Prol.B.5.

abundantly rich: Homer, *Odyssey* 15.426.

Pankalos: This name could be translated as "All-Good" or "Everything-Good."

4 *Then the man's wife had a baby*: A similar version of this story, but involving a maligned dog rather than a nymph, is found in Michael Andreopoulos, *The Book of Syntipas the Philosopher* 60–61, trans. Beneker and Gibson, *Byzantine Sinbad,* pp. 74–79.

a nymph jumped on it: In fact, a mongoose. See above, 1.45 and 1.56, and below, 8.2, for this identification.

Chapter 7

9 *laid down your lives for me*: Compare John 10:15; similar wording is used there of the good shepherd. The point here is that they were willing to sacrifice themselves for the king, rather than that they actually did so.

12 *an anxious mind is a worm eating away one's bones*: A direct quotation from Gregory of Nazianzos, *Carmina moralia* 32.101; PG 37:924A.

13 *For it is said that a male . . . expired from grief*: A similar version of this story is found in Michael Andreopoulos, *The Book of Syntipas the Philosopher* 75–76, trans. Beneker and Gibson, *Byzantine Sinbad,* pp. 94–97.

15 *last judgment*: Literally, "the last day."

16 *by her insatiable desires*: Or, possibly, "by his insatiable desires for her." The Greek is ambiguous.

Chapter 8

1 *the mouse and the weasel*: Somewhere in the progressive translation of this story from language to language, confusion has arisen over the identity of the latter animal. The original story in the *Mahabharata* 12.138 has a cat, a tradition followed by manuscripts LB and O of the present text.

2 *nymph*: See above, 1.45 and 1.56, on the identification of the Greek term νύμφη as a mongoose rather than a spiritual being. This identification is confirmed by the original *Mahabharata* version of the story, 12.138.

Chapter 9

Manuscripts BL and O contain a much abbreviated and somewhat different version of this chapter. In the main hand of L, this is the last (eighth) chapter; there, the preceding chapter (our chapter 8) and the two following this one (our chapters 10 and 11) are found as inserts in tiny writing and are not in the main hand. The BLO version of this chapter reads:

Ὁ δὲ βασιλεὺς ἔφη τῷ φιλοσόφῳ· "Ἀνάγγειλόν μοι πῶς δεῖ τὰς ἔχθρας εὐλαβεῖσθαι καὶ μνησικακίας παρατηρεῖν." Ὁ δὲ φιλόσοφος ὑπολαβὼν εἶπε·

Περὶ τῆς κίσσας καὶ τοῦ βασιλέως.

Λέγεταί ποτε ὡς βασιλεύς τις κίσσαν εἶχε πάνυ ὡραίαν καὶ λογικὴν ἔχουσαν στρουθόν, καὶ διῃτῶντο ἀμφότεροι περὶ τῇ τοῦ βασιλέως ὁμευνέτιδι. Ἔτυχε δὲ καί ποτε καιροῦ παιδίον τεκεῖν, ὃ δὴ καὶ συνέπαιζε τῷ τῆς κίσσης στρουθῷ. Καὶ ἡ κίσσα ὡς ἡμέραι ἀπεδήμει καὶ ἤνεγκε δύο ξένους καρπούς, τὸν μὲν ἕνα ἐδίδου τῷ τοῦ βασιλέως παιδί, τὸν δὲ ἕτερον τῷ ἑαυτῆς στρουθῷ, καὶ διὰ τοῦτο ἤγετο ἡ κίσσα διὰ πολλῆς καὶ μεγίστης τιμῆς τῷ βασιλεῖ. Συνέβη δὲ τὸν τοῦ βασιλέως παῖδά ποτε κατὰ τοῦ στρουθοῦ ὀργισθέντα τοῦτον κατὰ τοῦ ἐδάφους βαλεῖν καὶ ἀποκτεῖναι.

Ἐλθοῦσα δὲ ἡ κίσσα καὶ τὸν ἑαυτῆς στρουθὸν ἀνῃρημένον εὑροῦσα ἐφώνησε λέγουσα· "Οὐαὶ τοῖς συναναστρεφομένοις τοῖς βασιλεῦσιν ἀβεβαίοις οὖσιν καὶ τὴν γνώμην ἀσυστάτοις, οἵτινες οὐκ ἀντιποιοῦνται ἑτέρου, εἰ μὴ ὧν ἐπιδέονται. Καὶ μέχρι τούτου ἀντέχονται καὶ ἀντιλαμβάνονται, ἄχρις ὅτου ἐνδεεῖς τούτου καθεστήκασιν, οἵτινες τὰ μέγιστα πλημμελοῦντες οὐδὲν ἁμαρτάνειν λογίζονται. Εἶτα εἶπε πρὸς ἑαυτήν· "Ἀνταμείψομαι σήμερον καὶ ἀποτίσω τὸν ἀνελεήμονα τοῦτον καὶ σκληρότατον παῖδα." Καὶ ἐπεισπηδήσασα τῷ τοῦ παιδὸς προσώπῳ τοὺς ὀφθαλμοὺς αὐτοῦ ἐξεκέντησε, καὶ ἐπί τινα τόπον ὑψηλὸν ἀπέπτη καὶ ἄβατον.

Ὅπερ ἀκούσας ὁ βασιλεὺς καὶ θυμοῦ πλησθεὶς ὑπέλαβεν ἀπατῆσαι τὴν κίσσαν καὶ καταγαγεῖν, καὶ ἀπελθὼν πρὸς αὐτήν, ὀνομαστὶ προσεκαλέσατο. Ἡ δὲ εἶπεν· "Ὦ βασιλεῦ, μεγίστην ἔχει τιμωρίαν ἡ παρασπόνδησις, καὶ μὴ ἐν τῷ αἰῶνι τούτῳ γενήσεται, ἀλλ᾽ ἐν τῷ μέλλοντι τελεσθήσεται· διαβαίνει γὰρ ἄχρι καὶ παίδων καὶ προγόνων." Ὁ δὲ βασιλεύς ἔφη· "Ἀληθῶς εἶπας· παρασπονδησάμενός σε, σὺ δὲ εἰργάσω τὴν ἀντέκτισιν. Λοιπὸν οὔτε σὺ ὑπάρχεις ὑπόχρεος ἡμῖν, οὔτε ἡμεῖς σοί· ἐλθὲ οὖν πρὸς ἡμᾶς ἀνενδοιάστως."

Ἡ δὲ κίσσα εἶπε· "Μάτην με προσκαλεῖς. Οὐδεὶς γὰρ προσεγγίσαι τῷ ἐχθραινομένῳ αὐτοῦ τολμᾷ, οὐδὲ θαρρεῖν τοῖς τοῦ μνησικάκου κολακευτικοῖς λόγοις. Λυσιτελέστερον ὂν τὸ πόρρωθέν που τούτου ἀπεῖναι. Ὁ γὰρ νουνεχὴς φίλους μὲν ἡγεῖται τοὺς γονεῖς, τοὺς δὲ ἀδελφοὺς συντρόφους, συνήθεις δὲ τὰς γυναῖκας, τοὺς δὲ παῖδας μνημόσυνον, τὰς δὲ παιδίσκας ἐριδοποιάς, τοὺς δὲ συγγενεῖς δανειστὰς καὶ ἑαυτὸν μονότροπον. Κἀγὼ οὖν λαβοῦσα ἀνεξάλειπτον παρ' ὑμῶν λύπην ἄπειμι ἀνυποστρόφως ἐν ὄρεσι καὶ τόποις δυσβάτοις."

"The king again said to the philosopher, 'Tell me how one should be wary of one's enemies and watch out for grudges.' And the philosopher responded:

About the jay and the king.

"It is said that a king once owned an extremely beautiful and articulate jay, who had a chick, and they both lived with the king's wife. And, at some point, she gave birth to a child, who used to play with the jay's chick. The jay would fly off by day and bring back two strange fruits, one of which she would give to the king's child and the other to her chick, and because of this the jay was held in the greatest honor by the king. But on one occasion it happened that, after the king's child had become angry with the chick, he threw it on the ground and killed it.

"When the jay arrived back and found her chick dead, she cried out, saying, 'Alas for those who live with kings who are fickle and unreliable in their disposition, who do not do anything for anyone else unless they need it themselves, who make the biggest mistakes themselves but don't think they have done anything wrong, and who resist and attack someone until they are in need of him.' Then she said to herself, 'Today I will punish and pay back that merciless and most cruel child.' She leaped up at the child's face and pecked out his eyes and flew off to a high place that was out of reach.

"When the king heard about this he was filled with anger and tried to deceive the jay to make her come down, approaching her and calling her by name. But she said, 'My king, breaking faith carries the greatest punishment, and this will not take place in the present, but will be carried out in the future, for it passes down as far as one's children and one's children's children.' And the king said, 'You have spoken the truth: we broke faith with you, but you took your revenge. Now, you are neither indebted to us, nor we to you, so come to us without hesitating.'

"But the jay said, 'You're calling me in vain. No one would dare approach someone who has become his enemy, nor trust the flattering words of someone who bears a grudge. It is better to stay far from where that man is; for a sensible man considers his parents as friends, his brothers as companions, women as acquaintances, his sons as a memorial, young girls as troublemakers, his relatives as moneylenders, and himself as a solitary. And so I too, because I have suffered inconsolable grief at your hands, will leave for mountains and inaccessible places without looking back.'"

7 *it was my tongue that swore, not my mind*: Euripides, *Hippolytus* 612.

Chapter II

1 *men can meet men, but mountains are unable to meet*: A traditional saying, widely known in a variety of forms, particularly in the Near East, but also in Slavic and Gaelic languages. For the Arabic saying, see entry 167 in James R. Jewett, "Arabic Proverbs and Proverbial Phrases," *Journal of the American Oriental Society* 15 (1893): 28–120, at 84. Alexander Alexakis notes that there is a related modern Greek proverb, used as an exclamatory phrase when two people meet after long years of separation: μόνο βουνό με βουνό δεν σμίγει, "only mountains do not meet." The implication of the philosopher's words here is that a king can meet innumerable men worthy of his kindness and trust but should ignore the ungrateful ones, as they are incapable of forming a helpful relationship.

2 *Zantzour*: Possibly to be identified as Zarzur (or Zarzour) in northern Syria. The town is situated on the modern border with Turkey on the west bank of the Orontes; it is known to have been in existence since the Bronze Age.

Chapter 12

3 *nomismata*: See above, Prol.B.5.

4 *he came up last and did a deal . . . hundred thousand miliaresia*: The *miliaresion* was a Byzantine silver coin, in use primarily between the ninth and eleventh centuries. Its weight fluctuated over time but was somewhere between two and three grams. It is unclear from the story as it stands how the merchant's son made this money, and something appears to have been lost in translation into Greek. The Arabic version of this story makes more sense, for there the merchant's son buys up fish at the harbor on credit, creates a panic by telling the other traders he is going to take the fish to another city, and then sells it to them at a higher price, enabling him to both repay the fisherman and make a huge profit.

Chapter 13

1 *the last judgment*: See above, 7.15.

2 *by the measure you give, you will be measured*: Matthew 7:2; Mark 4:24.

what you sow, you will reap: See Galatians 6:7.

do not judge, so that you are not yourself judged: Matthew 7:2; Luke 6:37.

4 *you should do to people . . . to you*: A slight adaptation of the "golden rule" of Matthew 7:12.

Chapter 14

2 *Troglodytes*: "Troglodyte," that is, "cave dweller" or "hermit."

Tyrophagos: "Cheese eater."

Kreoboros: "Meat eater."

CHAPTER 14

Othonophagos: "Linen eater" or perhaps more generally in this context, "cloth eater."

the horde of creatures who were stronger than them: The Greek phrase, τὸ πλῆθος τῶν κρειττόνων, is vague. In the Arabic version the creatures are clearly identified as cats.

Bibliography

Editions

Husselmann, Elinor. *A Fragment of "Kalilah and Dimnah" from Ms. 397 in the Pierpoint Library.* London, 1938.

Lauxtermann, Marc. "The Eugenian Recension of *Stephanites and Ichnelates:* Prologue and Paratexts." *Νέα Ῥώμη* 15 (2018): 55–106.

Puntoni, Vittorio, ed. *Stephanites kai Ichnelates: Quattro recensioni della versione greca del "Kitab Kalila wa-Dimna."* Florence, 1889.

Sjöberg, Lars-Olof, ed. *Stephanites und Ichnelates: Überlieferungsgeschichte und Text.* Uppsala, 1962.

Stefou, Loukia. *Die neugriechische metaphrase von "Stephanites und Ichnelates" durch Theodosios Zygomalas.* Madrid, 2011.

Further Reading

Condylis-Bassoukos, Hélène. *"Stéphanitès kai Ichnélatès," traduction grecque (XIe siècle) du livre "Kalila wa-Dimna" d'Ibn al-Muquffaʿ (VIIIe siècle): Étude lexicologique et litteraire.* Louvain, 1997.

De Blois, François. *Burzoy's Voyage to India and the Origins of the Book of "Kalīlah wa Dimnah."* London, 1990.

Hernández de la Fuente, David. "Greek and Spanish Versions of *Kalila and Dimna,* with an Example of Fantastic Ornithology." *Literatura* 21, no. 1 (2019): 35–60.

Jamison, Evelyn. *Admiral Eugenius of Sicily.* London, 1957.

Krönung, Bettina. "The Wisdom of the Beasts: The Arabic *Book of Kalīla and Dimna* and the Byzantine *Book of Stephanites and Ichnelates.*" In *Fictional Storytelling in the Medieval Eastern Mediterranean and Beyond,* edited by Carolina Cupane and Bettina Krönung, 427–60. Leiden, 2016.

Metcalfe, Alex. *Muslims and Christians in Norman Sicily: Arabic-Speakers and the End of Islam.* London and New York, 2003.

Niehoff-Panagiotidis, Johannes. *Übersetzung und Rezeption: Die byzantinischen-neugriechischen und spanischen Adaptionen von "Kalila wa-Dimna."* Wiesbaden, 2003.

Von Falkenhausen, Vera. "Eugenio da Palermo." In *Dizionario biografico degli Italiani,* vol. 43, pp. 502–5. Rome, 1993.

Other Versions and Related Stories

Andreopoulos, Michael. *The Book of Syntipas the Philosopher.* In *The Byzantine Sinbad,* translated by Jeffrey Beneker and Craig A. Gibson. Dumbarton Oaks Medieval Library 67. Cambridge, MA, 2021.

Bowles, Adam, Alex Cherniak, Kate Crosby, Kathleen Garbutt, William J. Johnson, Justin Meiland, Vaughan Pilikian, Paul Wilmot, and Alexander Wynne, eds. and trans. *Mahabhárata.* Clay Sanskrit Library. New York, 2005–.

Cacho Blecua, Juan Manuel, and María Jesús Lacarra, eds. *Calila e Dimna: Edición, introducción y notas.* Madrid, 1984. Old Spanish text.

Cheikho, Louis, ed. *La version arabe de Kalilah et Dimnah ou les fables de Bidpai, traduit du persan par Abdallah Ibn al-Muqaffaʿ.* Beirut, 1905. Reprint, Amsterdam, 1981. Arabic text.

Derenbourg, Joseph, ed. *Deux versions hébraïques du livre de "Kalilah et Dimna."* Paris, 1881. Hebrew text.

———. *Joannis de Capua directorium vitae humanae, alias parabola antiquorum sapientum.* Paris, 1887–1889. Latin translation of Hebrew text.

Edgerton, Franklin, ed. and trans. *The "Panchatantra" Reconstructed.* Vol. 1, *Text and Critical Apparatus.* Vol. 2, *Introduction and Translation.* New Haven, CT, 1924. Sanskrit text and English translation.

Hilka, Alfons, ed. "Eine lateinische Übersetzung der griechischen Version des Kalilabuches." In *Beiträge zur lateinischen Erzählungsliteratur des Mittellalters II,* special issue, *Abhandlungen der Gesellschaft der Wissenschaften zu Göttingen philologisch-historische Klasse, neue Folge* 21, no. 3 (1928): 59–155. Latin text.

John Damascene [pseud.]. *Barlaam and Ioasaph.* Translated by G. R. Woodward and H. Mattingly. Loeb Classical Library 34. Cambridge, MA, 1967.

Keith-Falconer, I. G. N., trans. *Kalila and Dimnah or the Fables of Bidpai: Being an Account of Their Literary History, with an English Translation of the Same and Notes.* Cambridge, 1885. English translation from later Syriac.

Knatchbull, W., trans. *Kalila and Dimna or the Fables of Bidpai.* Oxford, 1819. English translation from Arabic.

Miquel, André, trans. *Le livre de Kalila et Dimna.* Paris, 1980. French translation from Arabic.

Olivelle, Patrick, ed. and trans. *The Five Discourses on Worldly Wisdom by Viṣṇuśarman.* New York, 2006. Sanskrit text and English translation.

Schulthess, Friedrich, ed. and trans. *Kalila und Dimna: Die altsyrische Version des indischen Fürstenspiegels ("Pantchatantra") oder Bidpai's Fabeln.* Berlin, 1911. Old Syriac text and translation.

Teza, Emilio, ed. *Del Governo de' Regni: Sotto morali esempi di animali ragionanti tra loro.* Bologna, 1872. Italian text.

Thackston, Wheeler, trans. *Kalila and Dimna.* By Nasrullah Munshi. Indianapolis, 2019. English translation from Persian.

Index